TRULY
tyler

TERRI LIBENSON

BALZER + BRAY

An Imprint of HarperCollins*Publishers*

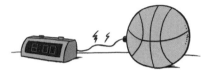

Balzer + Bray is an imprint of HarperCollins Publishers.

Truly Tyler
Copyright © 2021 by Terri Libenson
and reviews. For information address HarperCollins Children's Books, a division of
HarperCollins Publishers, 195 Broadway, New York, NY 10007.
www.harpercollinschildrens.com

Library of Congress Control Number: 2021931993
ISBN 978-0-06-289457-1 (trade)
ISBN 978-0-06-289456-4 (pbk.)
ISBN 978-0-06-311673-3 (special edition)
ISBN 978-0-06-311447-0 (special edition)
ISBN 978-0-06-311909-3 (special edition)
ISBN 978-0-06-309512-0 (special edition)
ISBN 978-0-06-311782-2 (special edition)

Typography by Terri Libenson and Laura Mock
21 22 23 24 25 PC/LSCC 10 9 8 7 6 5 4 3 2 1
❖
First Edition

To my mom, dad, and siblings Brad and Tina,
who were always cool with my love of comics.
(Brad, sorry for stealing your MAD Magazines.)

PROLOGUE

Sometimes I look around the cafeteria at lunch and wonder why everything is set up the way it is. Why the jocks sit near the front. And the Science Club kids sit in back. And the manga kids sit near the ice cream freezer. Why the volleyball team sits near the windows and the orchestra kids sit near the tray conveyor belt. Which, by the way, is kinda unfortunate.

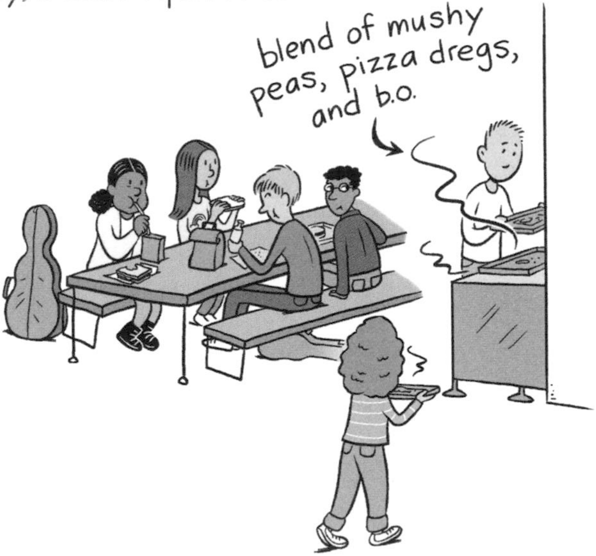
blend of mushy peas, pizza dregs, and b.o.

I guess I'm lucky I'm into sports. Otherwise I might end up here:

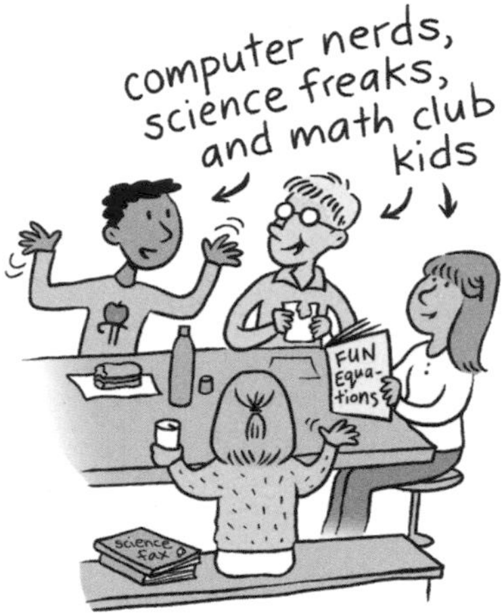
computer nerds, science freaks, and math club kids
FUN Equations
science fax

It's not that my friends aren't smart, too. Okay, maybe not **smart**-smart. But there are times I think . . .

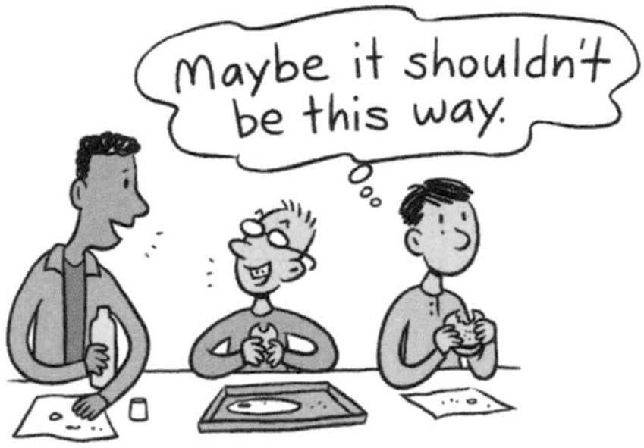
Maybe it shouldn't be this way.

I doubt anyone else in my group thinks about this stuff. They probably don't see the point of being friends with anyone else. Not sure if that's good or bad.

All I know is, more and more, I kinda like getting to know different kinds of people.

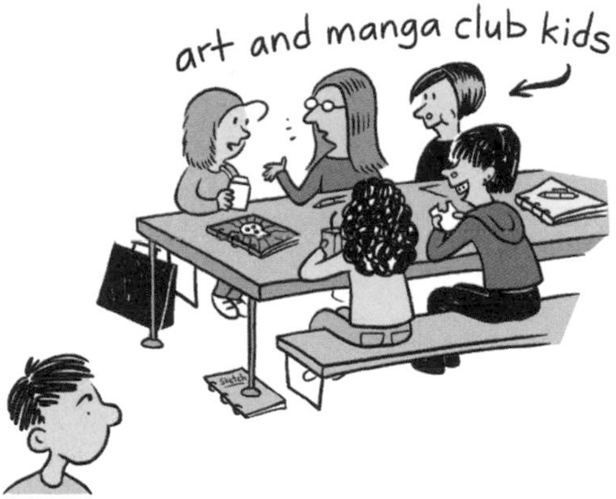
art and manga club kids

I just wish . . .

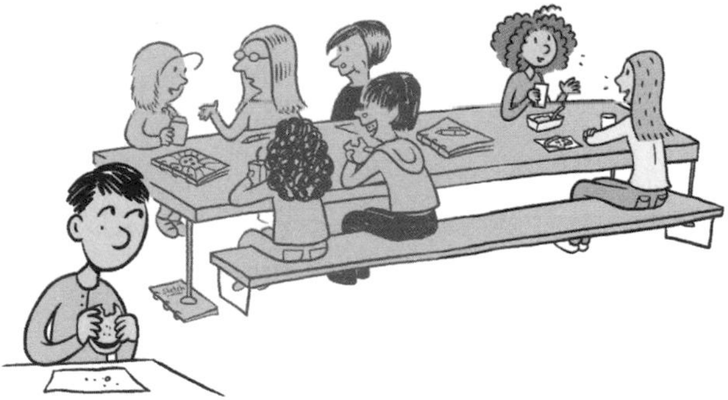

. . . we weren't so divided.

TYLER

I'm sure lots of kids are sad when winter break is over. Like the ones who get picked on at school. Or the kids who go away with their families to Florida and have to come back to the cold and snow. Even the ones who stay home during break and do regular stuff (playing video games, watching movies) probably hate it when they return to school.

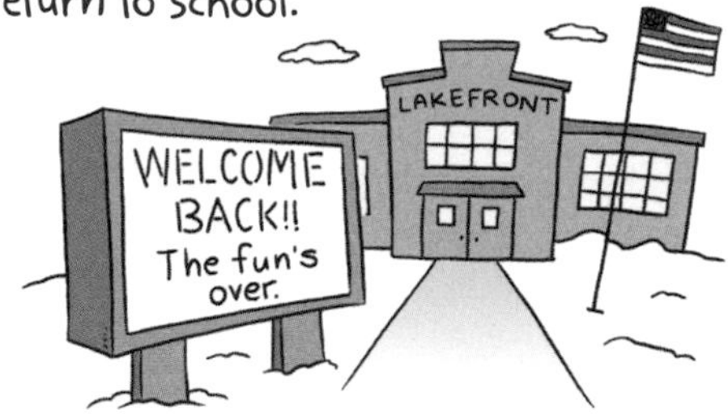
LAKEFRONT
WELCOME BACK!! The fun's over.

Me? I'm the opposite. I love going back. I know that sounds weird, but if you lived in my house, you'd understand. It's not exactly an amusement park.

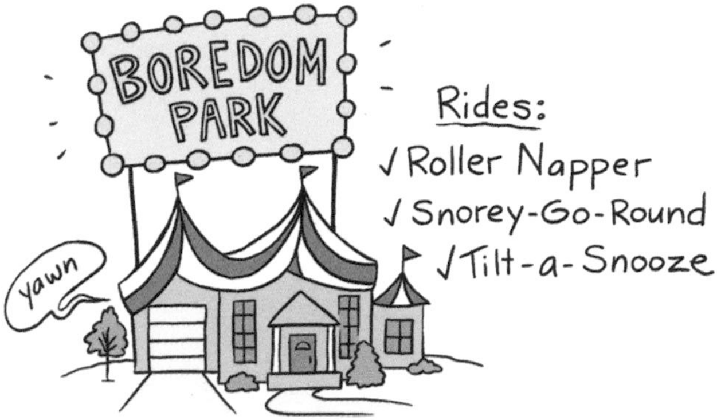
BOREDOM PARK
yawn
Rides:
√Roller Napper
√Snorey-Go-Round
√Tilt-a-Snooze

Things haven't been the same since Zach—that's my big brother—went to high school. Now he always goes out with friends or to practice or work. When he is home, he stays in his room and plays bass guitar or talks to his girlfriend. Zach stopped playing Fortnite with me a while ago.

And all my mom wants to do—when she's home—is play Scrabble.

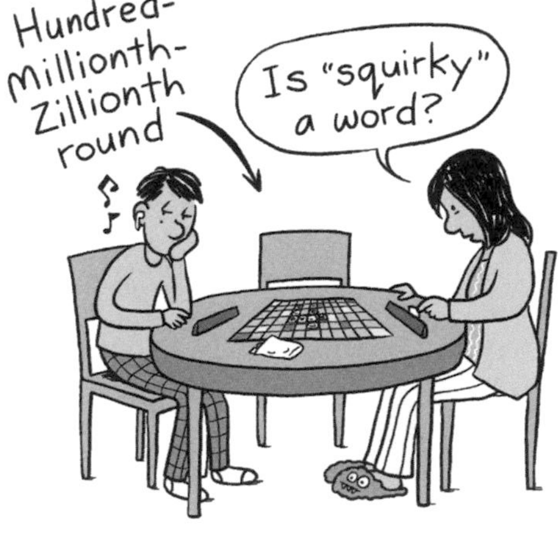
Hundred-Millionth-Zillionth round
Is "squirky" a word?

But I understand Zach. If I had a driver's license and my own car (bought with money from a tae kwon do assistant's job), I'd be gone, too. But that's not happening for:

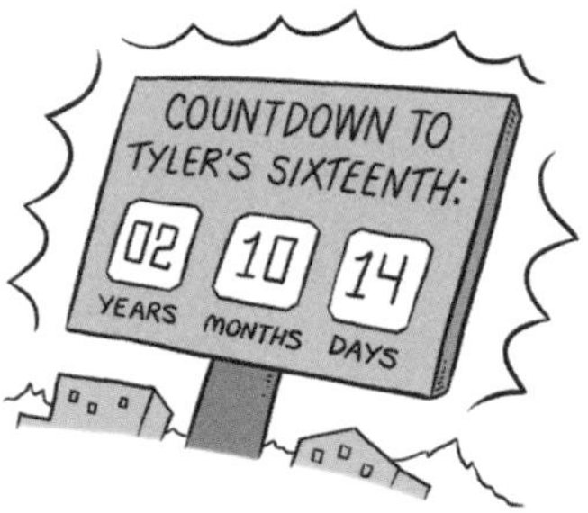
COUNTDOWN TO
TYLER'S SIXTEENTH:
02
10
14
YEARS
MONTHS
DAYS

I did try to make the most of being home. I played video games and pickup basketball at the Y with Anthony Randall and Joe Lungo the first week. But a huge blizzard kept us home the rest of break. All I did was practice my trumpet and draw.

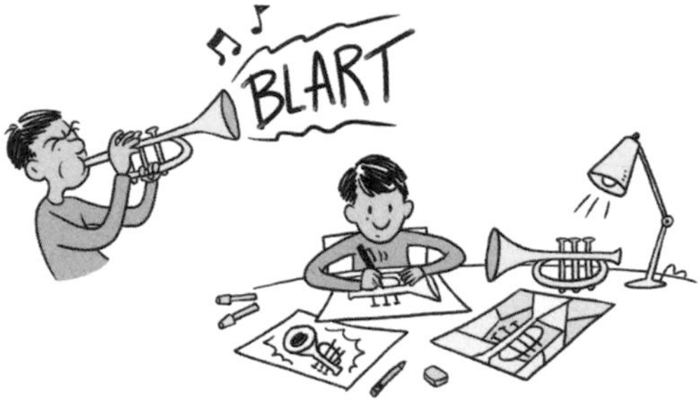
BLART

I did get special permission (think: begging), to go to Anthony's house for Christmas Eve. He's my best friend (don't tell Joe!).

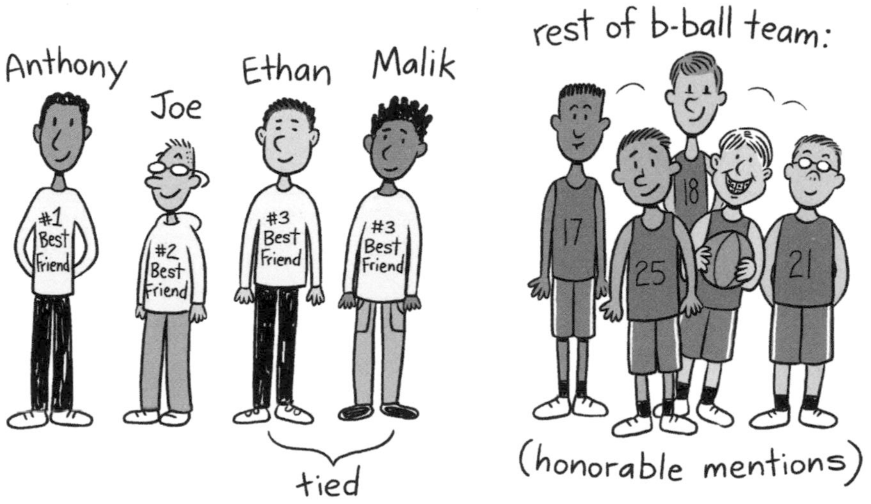
Anthony
Joe
Ethan
Malik
#1 Best Friend
#2 Best Friend
#3 Best Friend
#3 Best Friend
tied
rest of b-ball team:
17
18
25
21
(honorable mentions)

Anthony and I have known each other since preschool. I've only known Joe since last year when we came to Lakefront Middle from different elementary schools. We were put on the same team in sixth grade (our school is so big, they divide the classes into "teams"), and that's when we became friends.

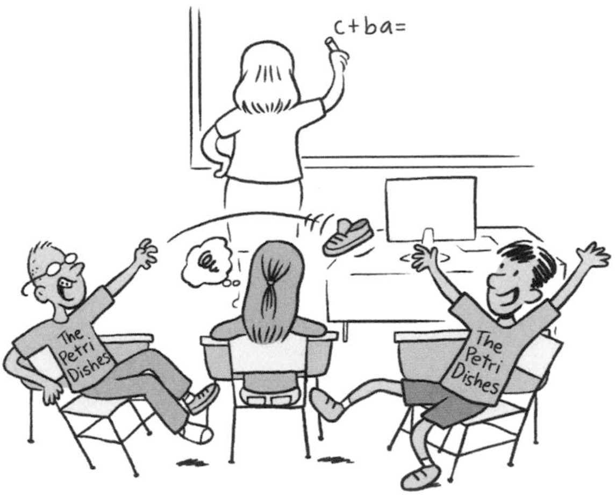
c+ba=
The Petri Dishes
The Petri Dishes

Anyway, back to Christmas Eve, which was awesome. Anthony's parents made this whole spread, and nothing was from a frozen bag. Anthony has two little two sisters who talked nonstop and fought over the butter rolls. His huge shaggy dog, Phineas, was under the table the whole time, taking turns licking crumbs and my big toe.

crumbs and sock-covered toe:
tied for deliciousness

His dad asked me lots of questions, which totally mortified Anthony but didn't bother me. My dad usually asks me the same two things on the phone when we talk:

How's school?

How's basketball?

Maybe he'd ask more, but he's always interrupted by Michelle.*

*more on her later

As you've probably guessed, my parents are divorced. Which is no big deal, I know. So are every other kid's. But my mom works a lot, and even though she's a good parent and involved and all that, she's pretty tired out by the end of the day.

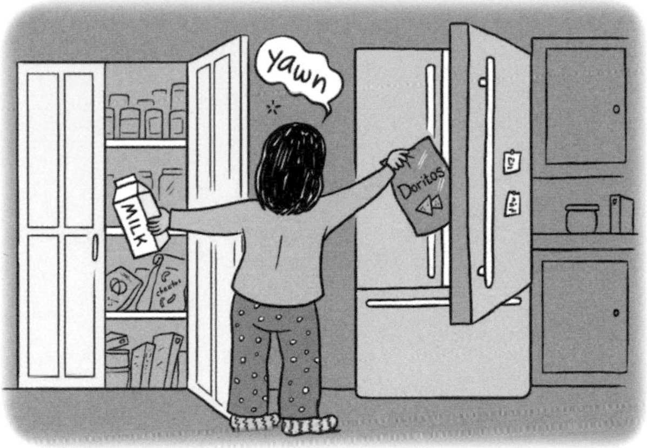
yawn
MILK
Doritos

And since she had to work most of break and only wanted a few low-key Scrabble nights, that just added to the boredom.

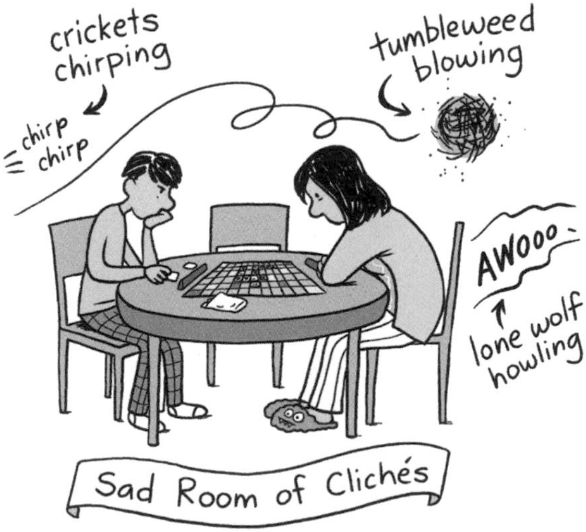
crickets chirping
chirp chirp
tumbleweed blowing
AWOOO
lone wolf howling
Sad Room of Clichés

I just got back to school. Guessing I'll be the only one happy to be here.

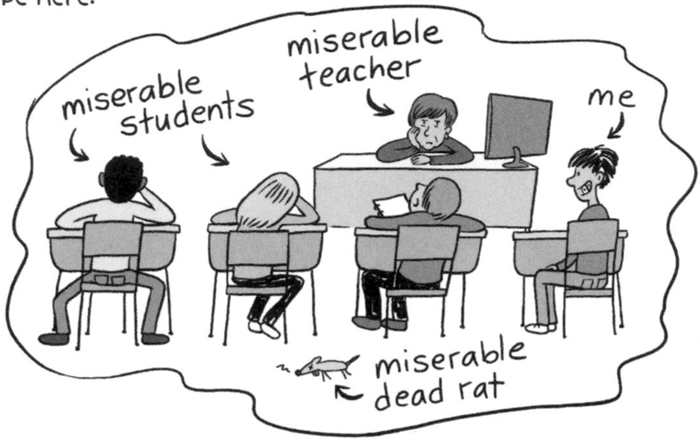
miserable students
miserable teacher
me
miserable dead rat

Definitely will be happy to be around my friends.

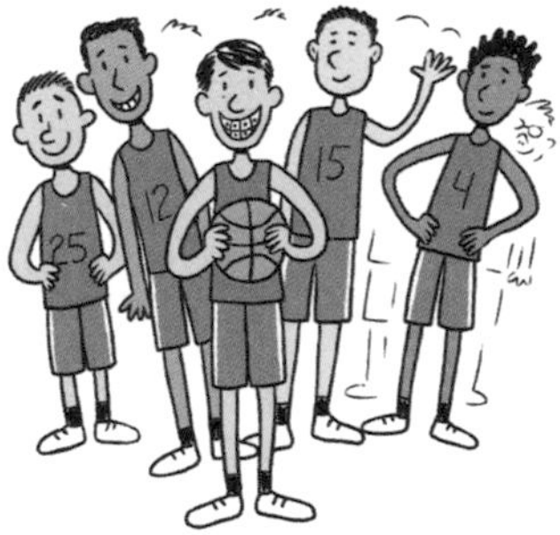

And pumped for my favorite classes, like PE and Ms. Laurie's art class. I started taking art this year, and I'm hooked. After our winter Zentangle project, I went home and made, like, five more Zentangle* drawings.

*a form of meditative doodling using structured patterns

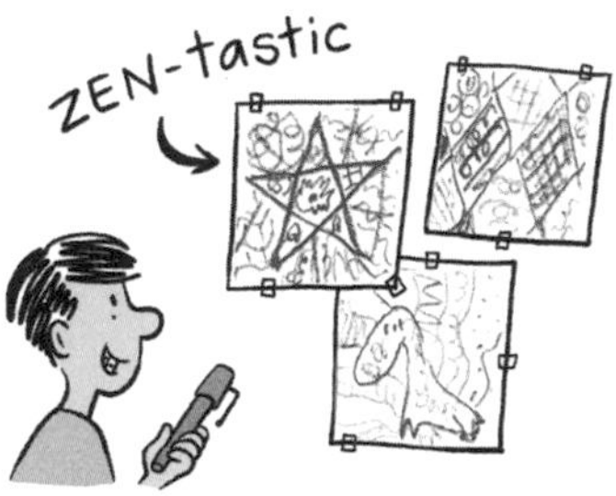
ZEN-tastic

I'm at my locker before homeroom. Anthony, in full winter gear, walks over. That's what I love about the guy—he never cares what anyone thinks.

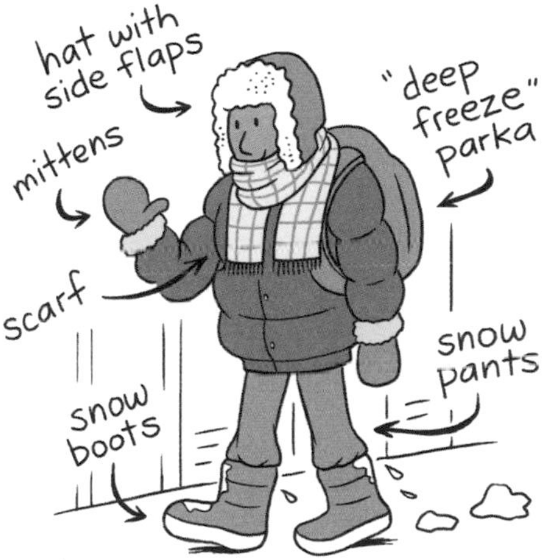
hat with side flaps
"deep freeze" parka
mittens
scarf
snow pants
snow boots

(probably keeps a bunch of quilts in locker)

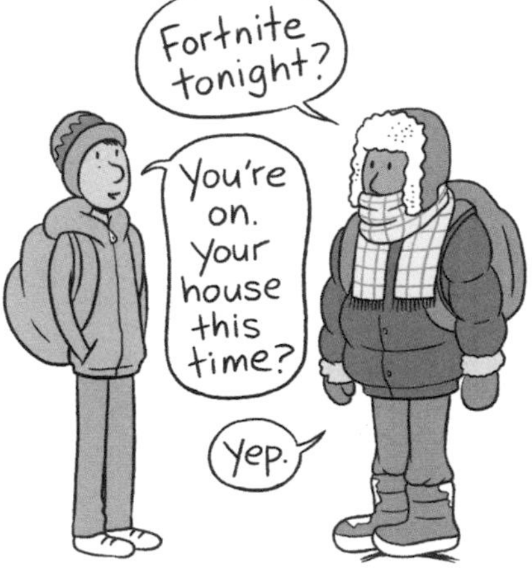
Fortnite tonight?
You're on. Your house this time?
Yep.

Technically, we can play apart and talk on our phones, but it's way more fun in person. I love playing at his house, mainly 'cause of my gaming partner:

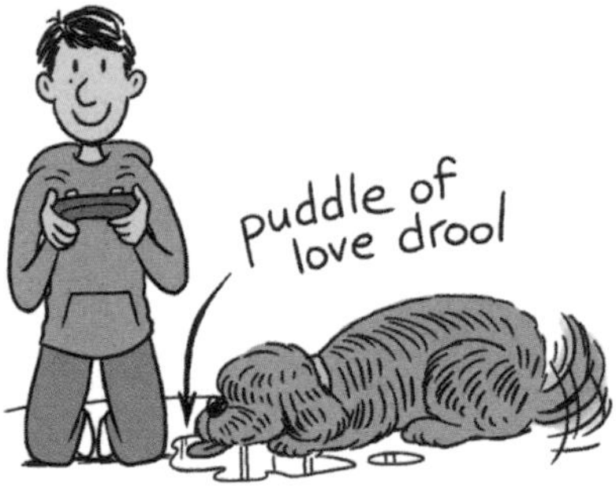
puddle of love drool

Anthony unloads about forty pounds of outerwear in his locker while I dump my slushy coat and hat in mine and grab my binder.

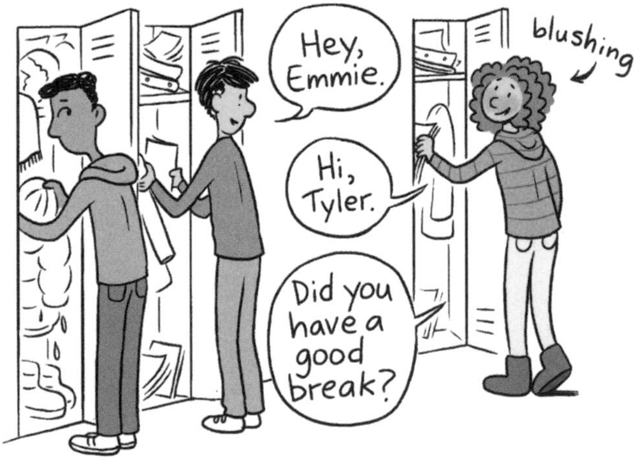
Hey, Emmie.
blushing
Hi, Tyler.
Did you have a good break?

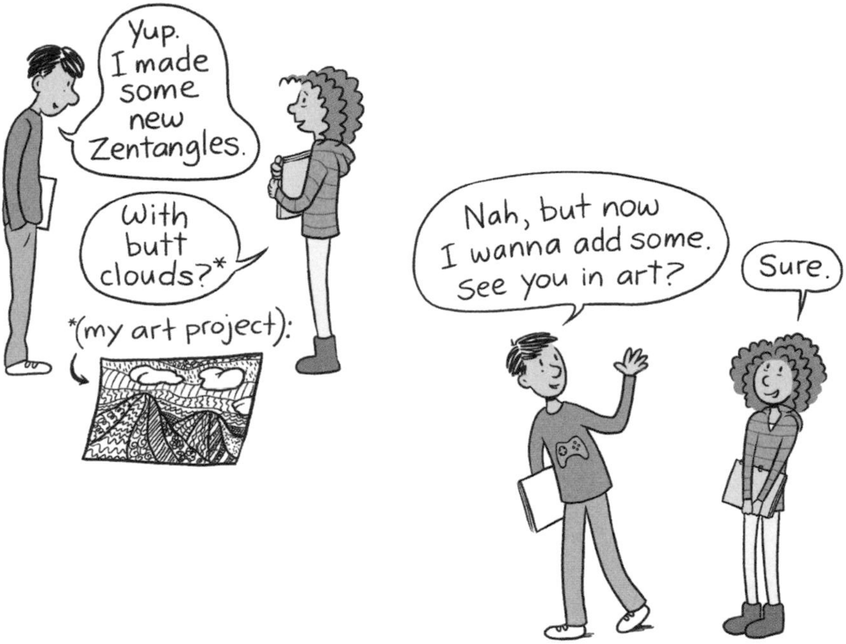
Yup. I made some new Zentangles.
With butt clouds?*
*(my art project):
Nah, but now I wanna add some. See you in art?
Sure.

Anthony and I make our way through the jungle—aka main hall—trying to dodge a couple of scary-looking eighth graders (fourteen-year-olds with beards just isn't right).

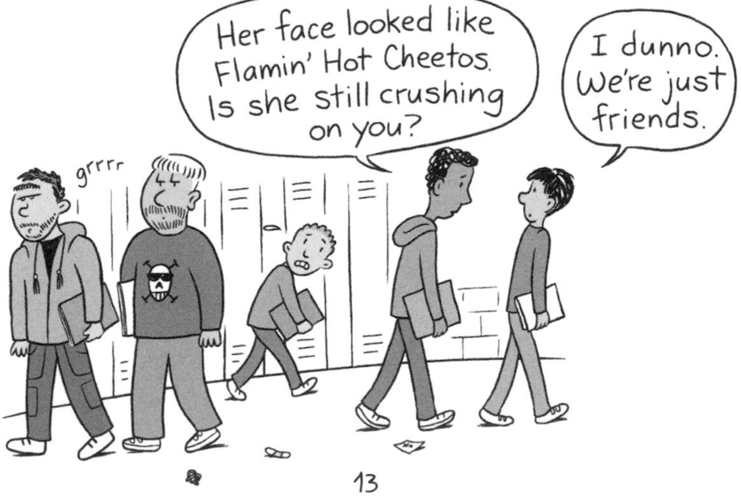
Her face looked like Flamin' Hot Cheetos. Is she still crushing on you?
I dunno. We're just friends.
grrrr

Before winter break, Emmie Douglass wrote me a really mushy love letter that I wasn't supposed to see. Joe found it and showed it to me (and half the school). I guess he thought it was funny, but it was totally uncool of him to do that.

Even though she said she wrote it as a joke, I felt really bad that she was embarrassed. So I started talking to her. And didn't mention the note again. Now we're kinda friends and hang out in art.

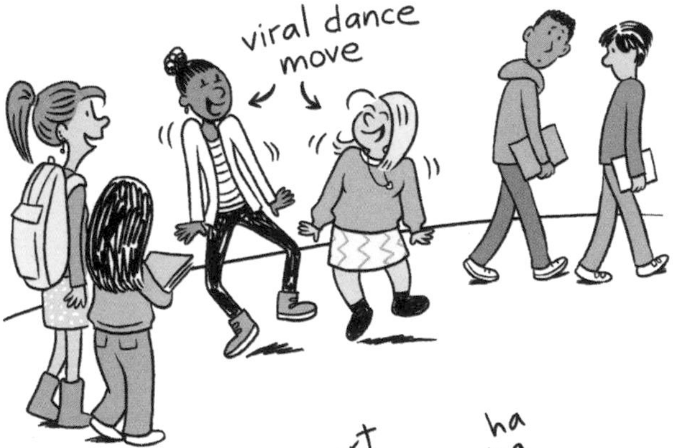
viral dance move

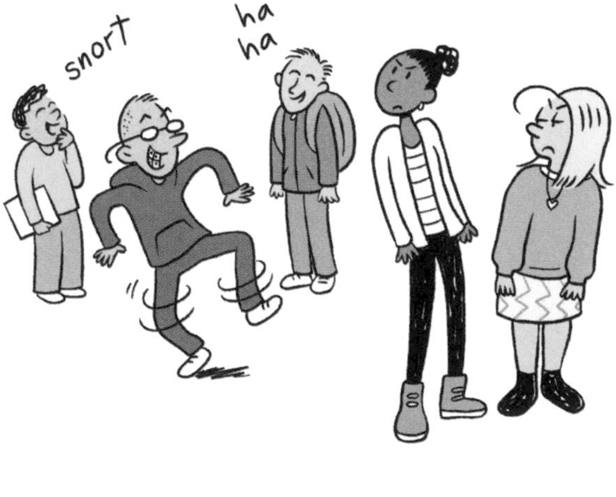
snort
ha ha

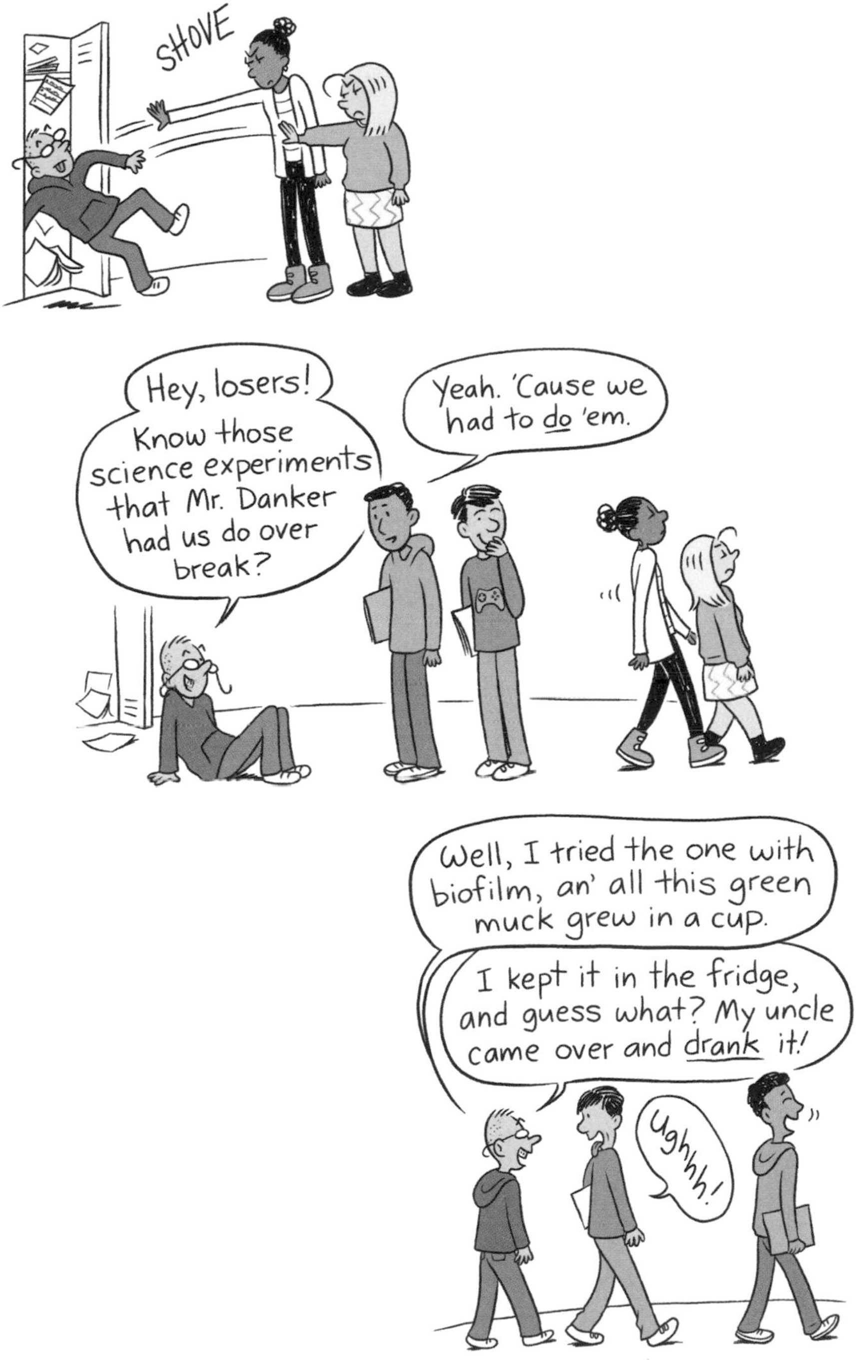
SHOVE
Hey, losers!
Know those science experiments that Mr. Danker had us do over break?
Yeah. 'Cause we had to do 'em.
Well, I tried the one with biofilm, an' all this green muck grew in a cup.
I kept it in the fridge, and guess what? My uncle came over and drank it!
Ughhh!

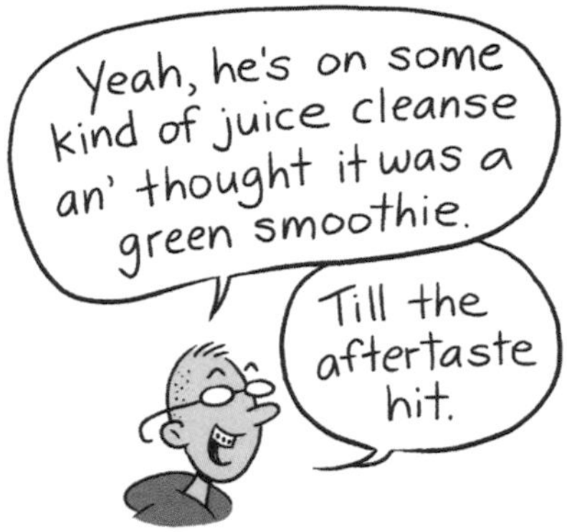
Yeah, he's on some kind of juice cleanse an' thought it was a green smoothie.
Till the aftertaste hit.

We all crack up. I pretend to vomit, and that's the exact moment Celia walks by with her girl posse.

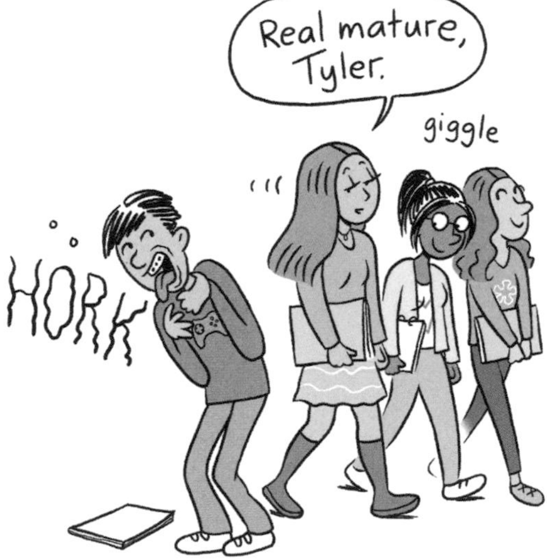
Real mature, Tyler.
giggle
HORK

Now it's my turn to go Flamin' Cheetos. Celia is the queen bee of our class. We dated for two weeks in the beginning of seventh grade. Two of the longest weeks of my life.

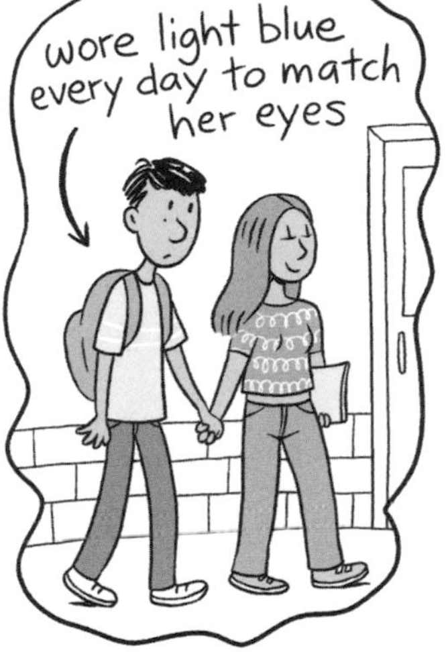
wore light blue every day to match her eyes

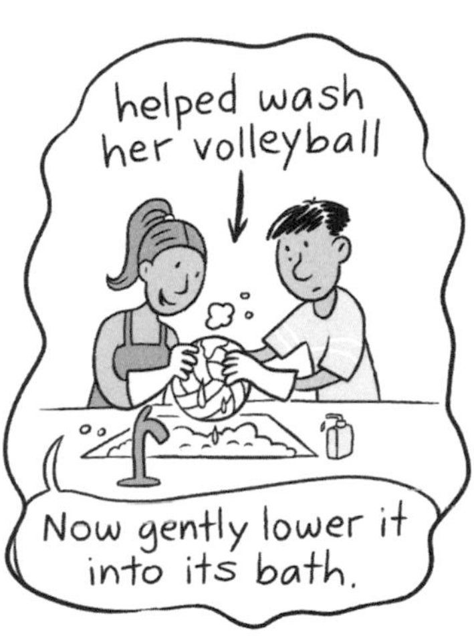
helped wash her volleyball
Now gently lower it into its bath.

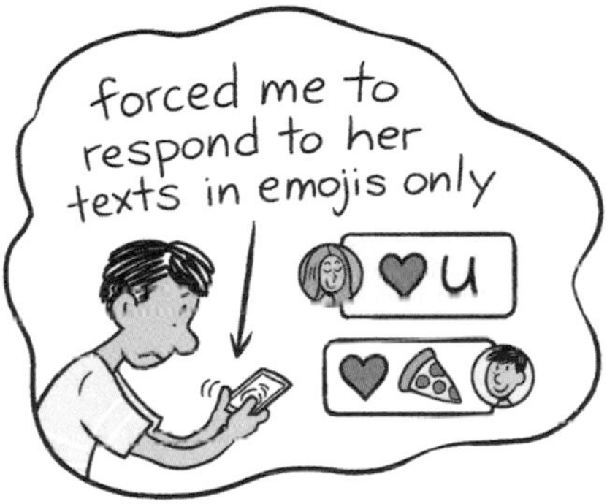
forced me to respond to her texts in emojis only

After that, I gave up on dating in middle school. Which, by the way, is just holding hands in the hallway and surrendering half your french fries.

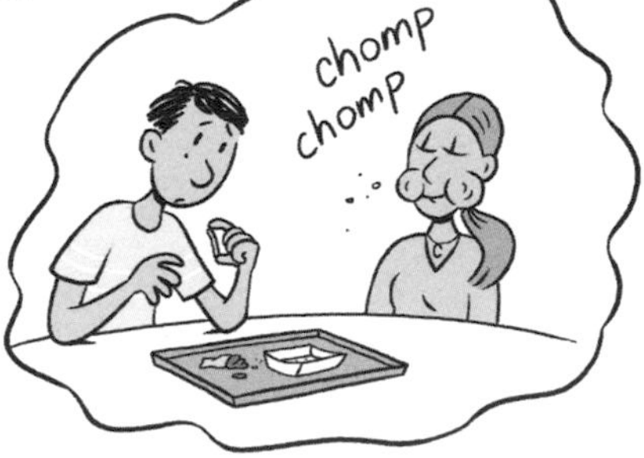
chomp chomp

The three of us head to our homerooms—Anthony and I in one direction, Joe in another.

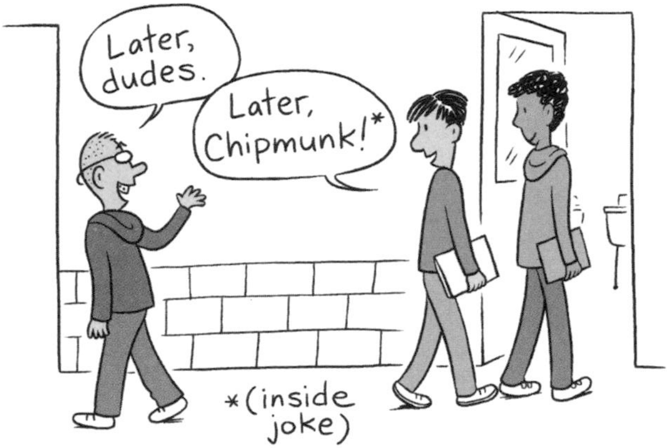
Later, dudes.
Later, Chipmunk!*
*(inside joke)

We walk in and see some guys from basketball. The season started last month, but we didn't have games or practice over break. We're so ready to get back to it, and we talk about our upcoming big game with Valley Bottom Middle. We've gotta beat them so we can go to the playoffs.

Mr. Fazekas blows in, red-faced from the cold, and takes roll.

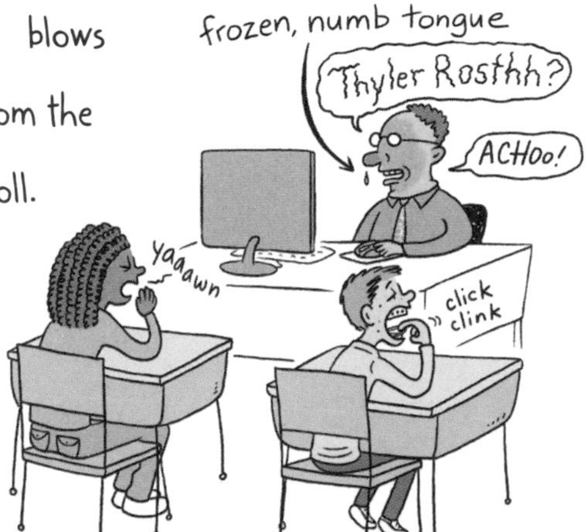
frozen, numb tongue
Thyler Rosthh?
ACHOo!
Yaaaawn
click clink

I sneak-text Joe a meme of an evil-looking chipmunk in a popcorn bowl and label it:

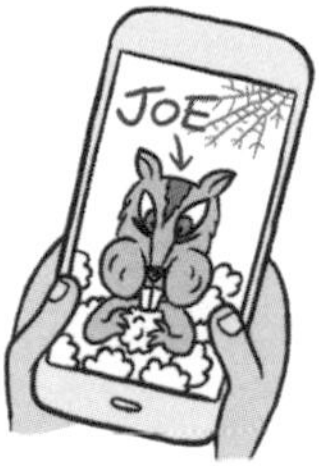
JOE

Joe sends me:

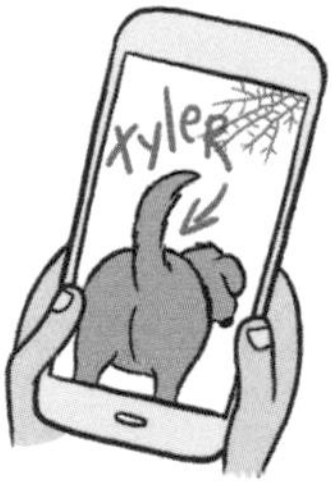
Xyler

I've missed these stupid sneaky school texts. I put my phone away and breathe in that familiar combo of textbooks, floor cleaner, and body spray.

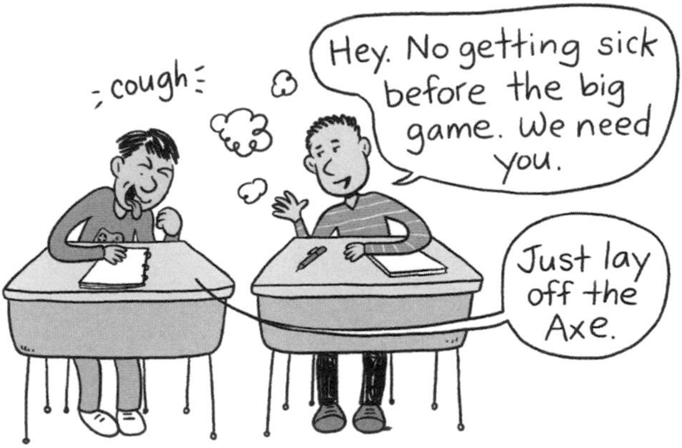
cough
Hey. No getting sick before the big game. We need you.
Just lay off the Axe.

I'm not worried about getting sick, and I'm excited about getting back into practice and stuff. But for some reason, Ethan's words give me a funny feeling.

The bell rings.

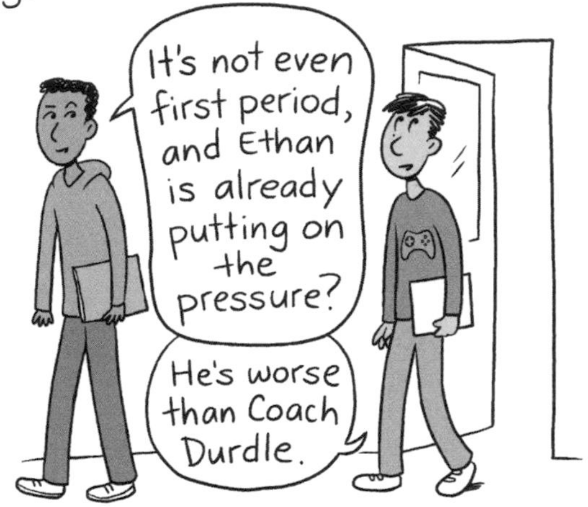
It's not even first period, and Ethan is already putting on the pressure?
He's worse than Coach Durdle.

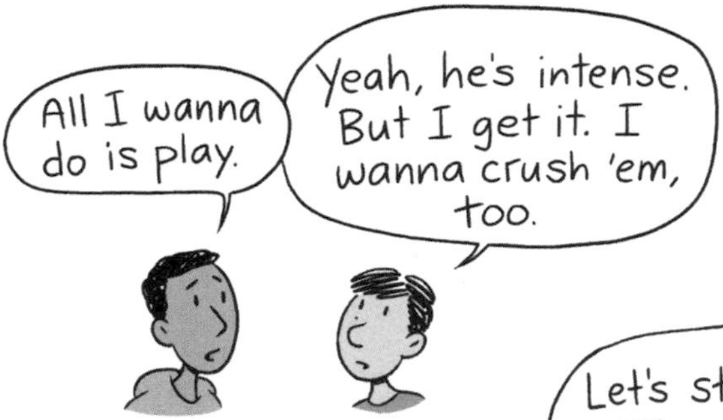
All I wanna do is play.
Yeah, he's intense. But I get it. I wanna crush 'em, too.

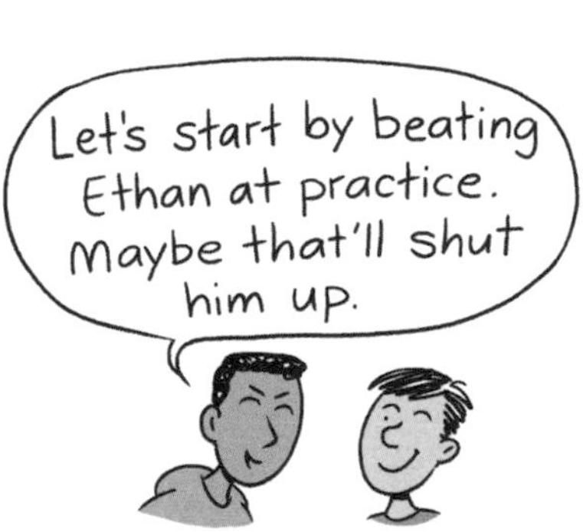
Let's start by beating Ethan at practice. Maybe that'll shut him up.

We laugh and walk into science. Yeah, it feels good to be back.

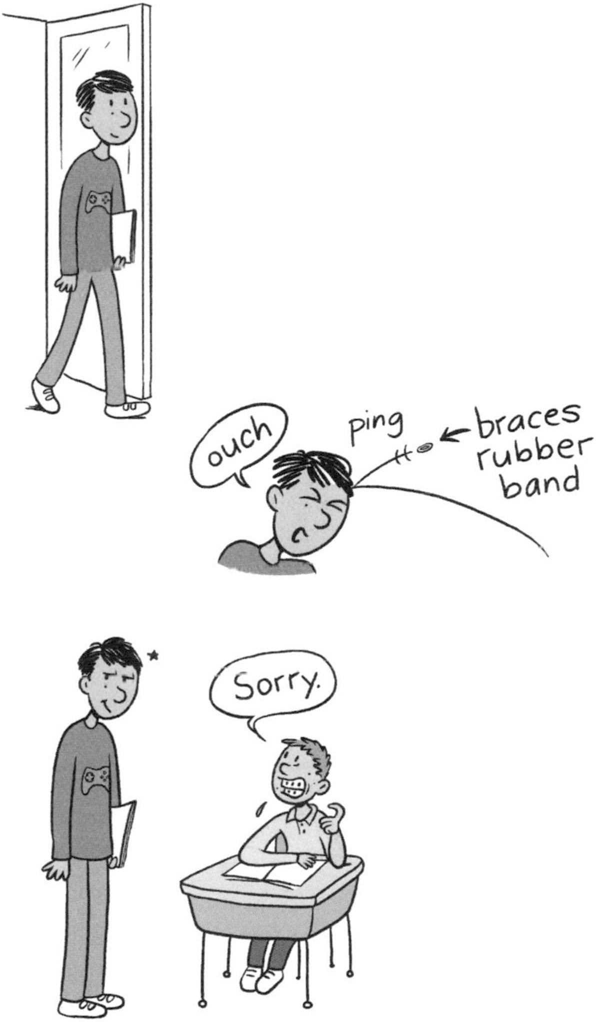
ouch
ping
braces rubber band
Sorry.

Emmie

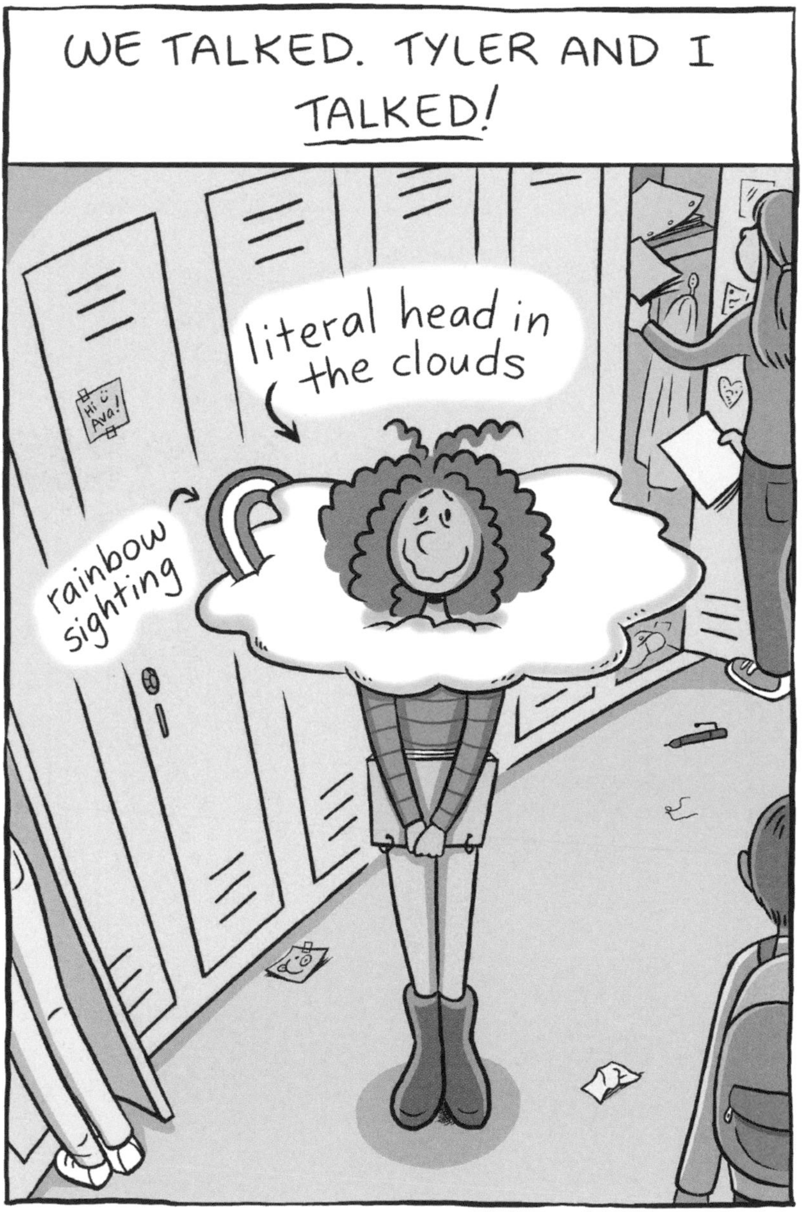
WE TALKED. TYLER AND I TALKED!
literal head in the clouds
rainbow sighting
Hi ü Ava!

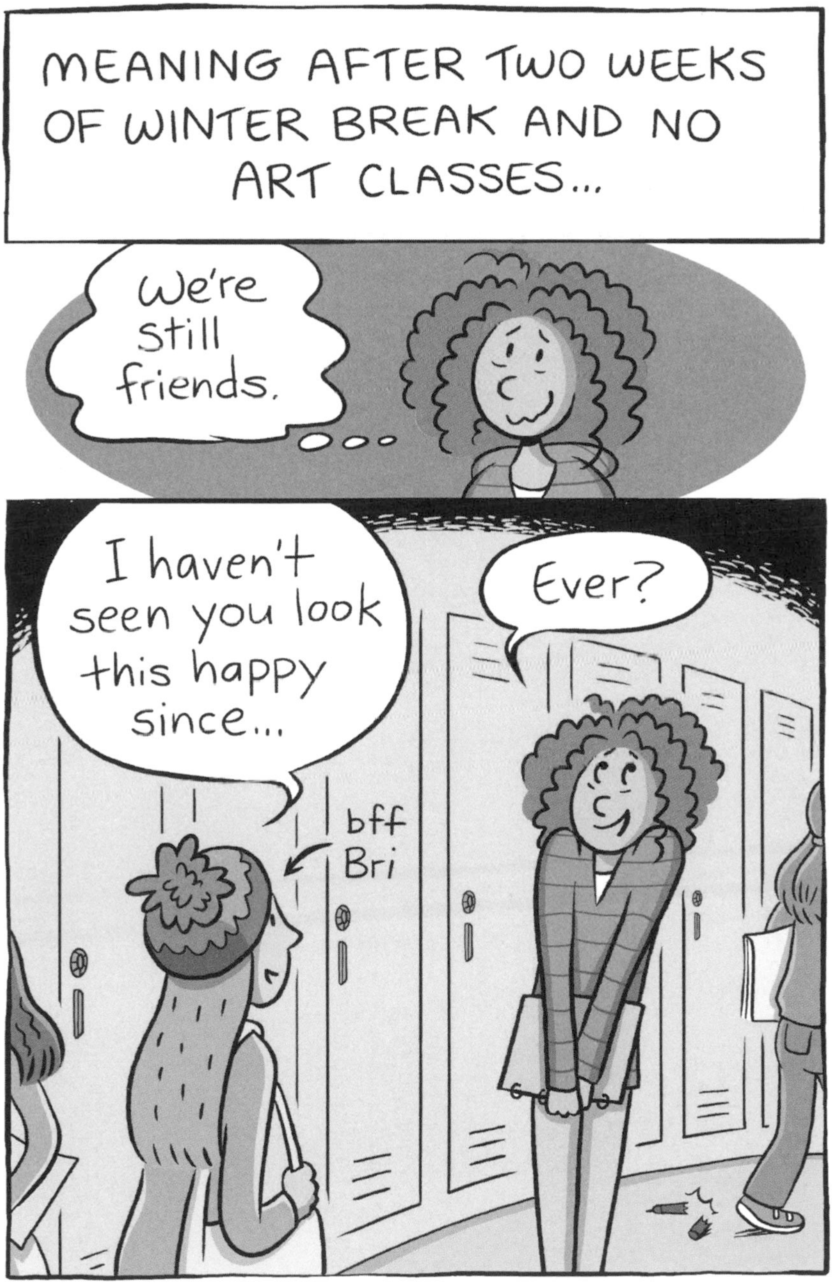
MEANING AFTER TWO WEEKS OF WINTER BREAK AND NO ART CLASSES...
We're still friends.
I haven't seen you look this happy since...
Ever?
bff Bri

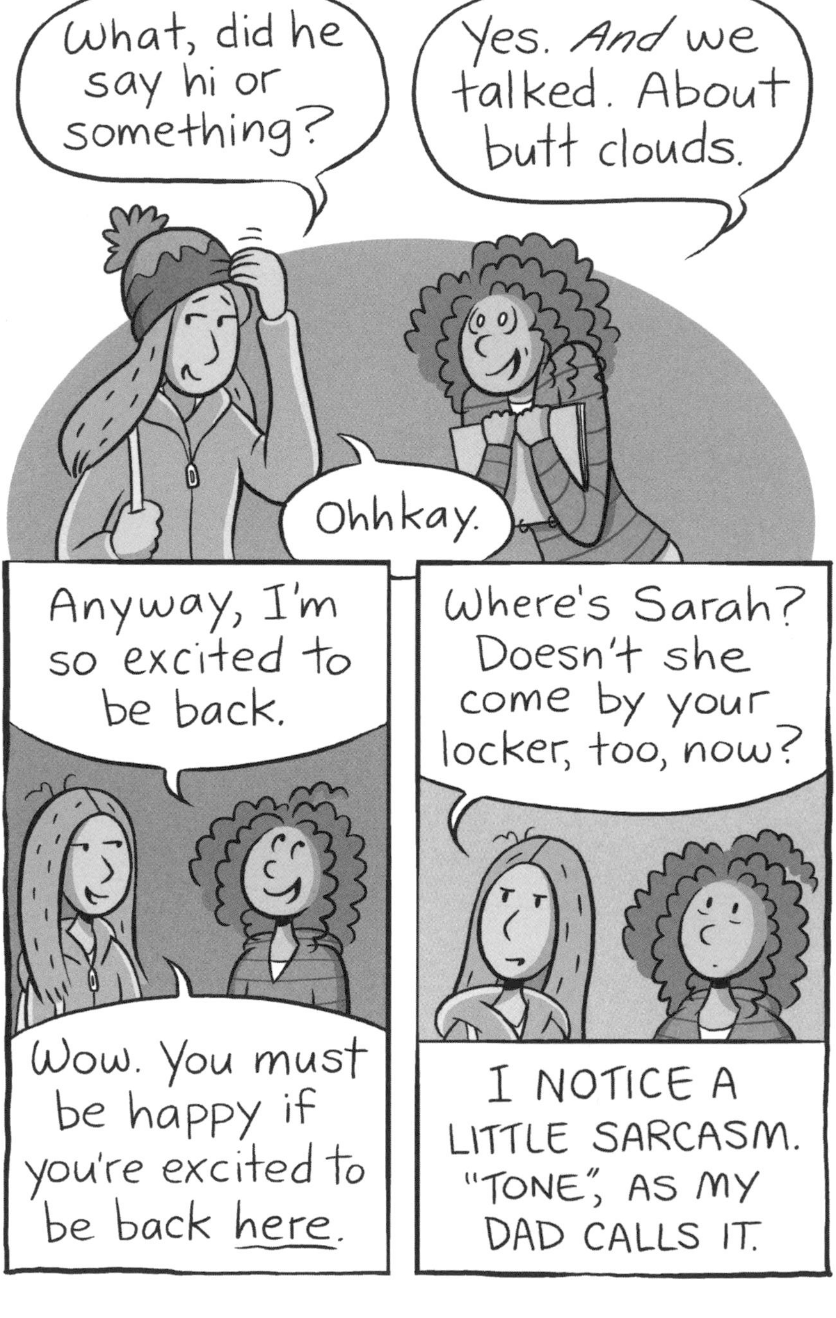
What, did he say hi or something?
Yes. *And* we talked. About butt clouds.
Ohhkay.
Anyway, I'm so excited to be back.
Wow. You must be happy if you're excited to be back here.
Where's Sarah? Doesn't she come by your locker, too, now?
I NOTICE A LITTLE SARCASM. "TONE", AS MY DAD CALLS IT.

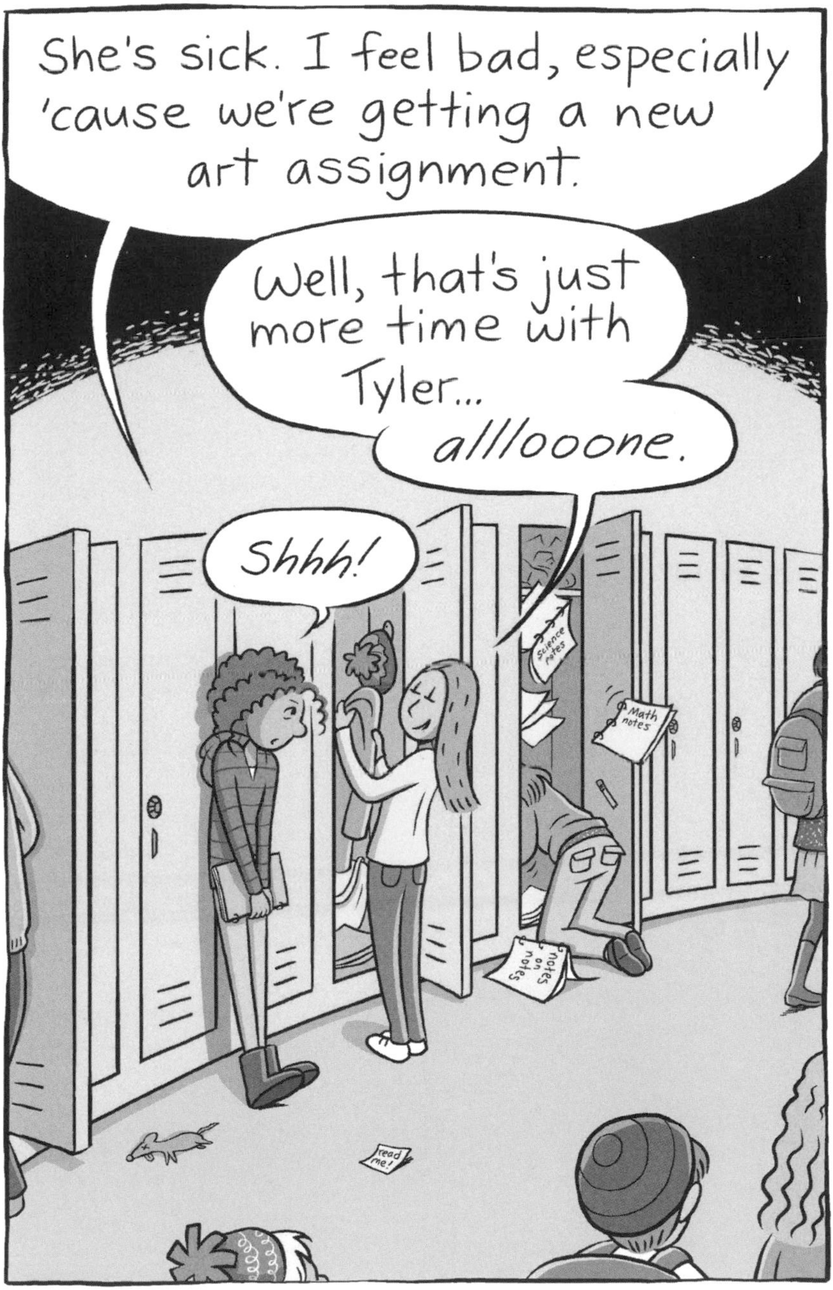
She's sick. I feel bad, especially 'cause we're getting a new art assignment.
Well, that's just more time with Tyler... alllooone.
Shhh!
Science notes
Math notes
notes on notes
read me!

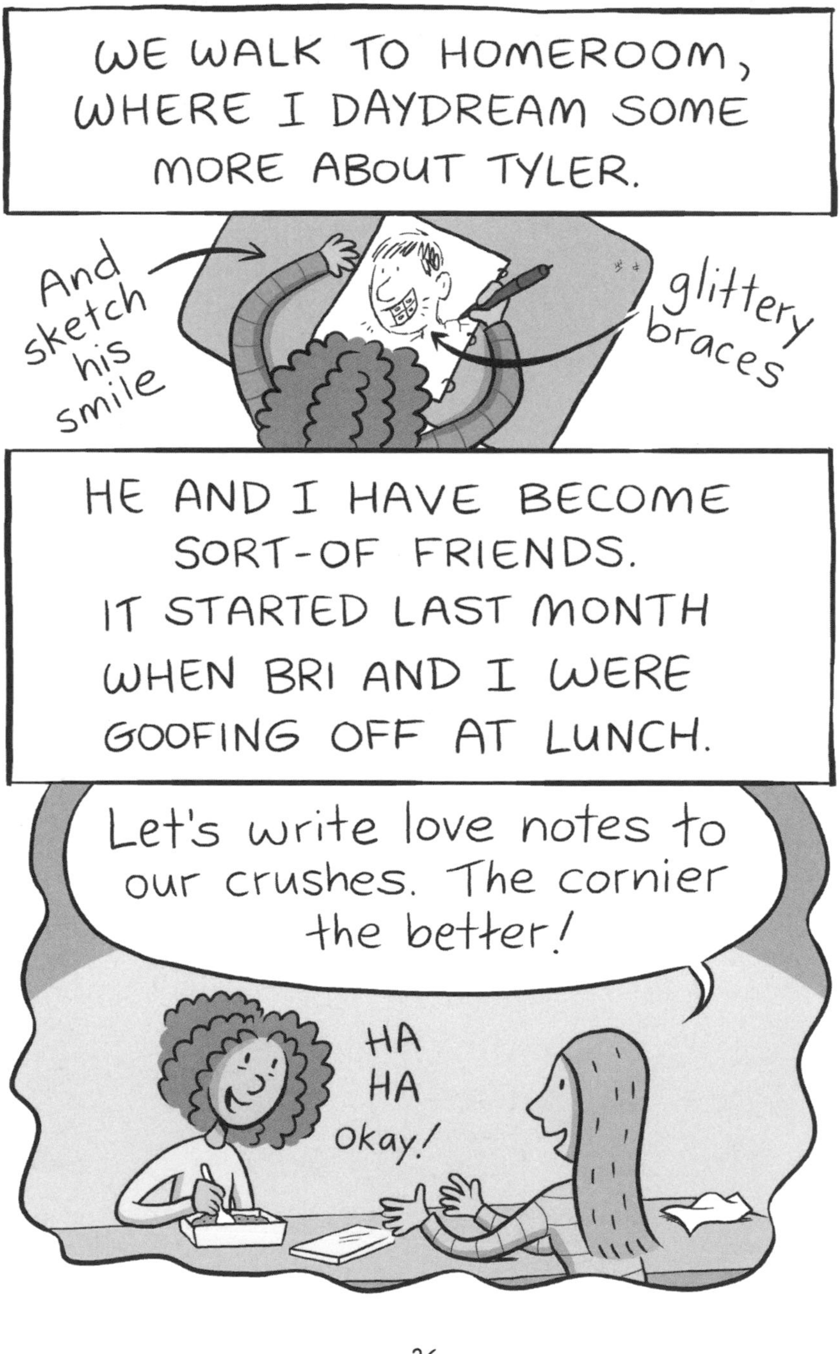
WE WALK TO HOMEROOM, WHERE I DAYDREAM SOME MORE ABOUT TYLER.
And sketch his smile
glittery braces
HE AND I HAVE BECOME SORT-OF FRIENDS. IT STARTED LAST MONTH WHEN BRI AND I WERE GOOFING OFF AT LUNCH.
Let's write love notes to our crushes. The cornier the better!
HA HA Okay!

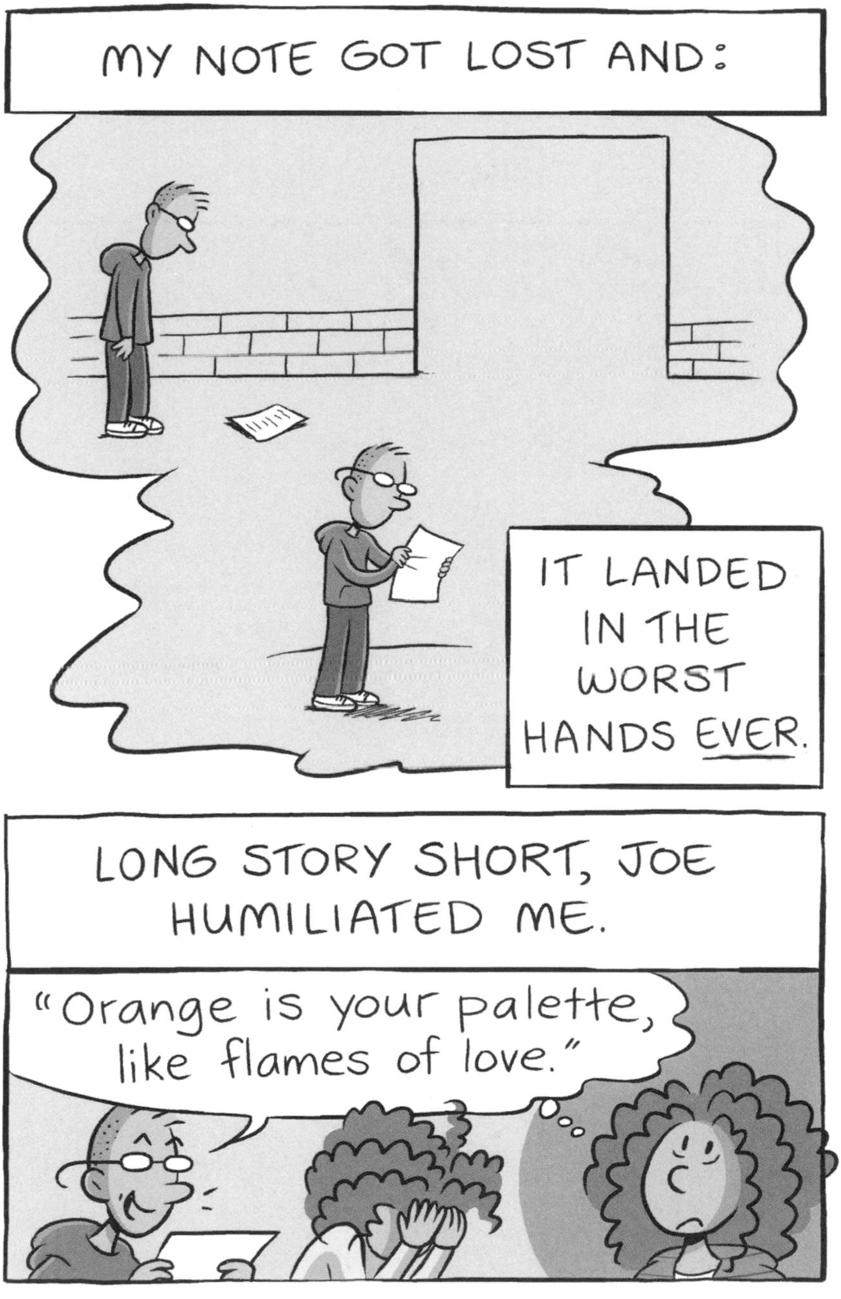
MY NOTE GOT LOST AND:
IT LANDED IN THE WORST HANDS EVER.
LONG STORY SHORT, JOE HUMILIATED ME.
"Orange is your palette, like flames of love."

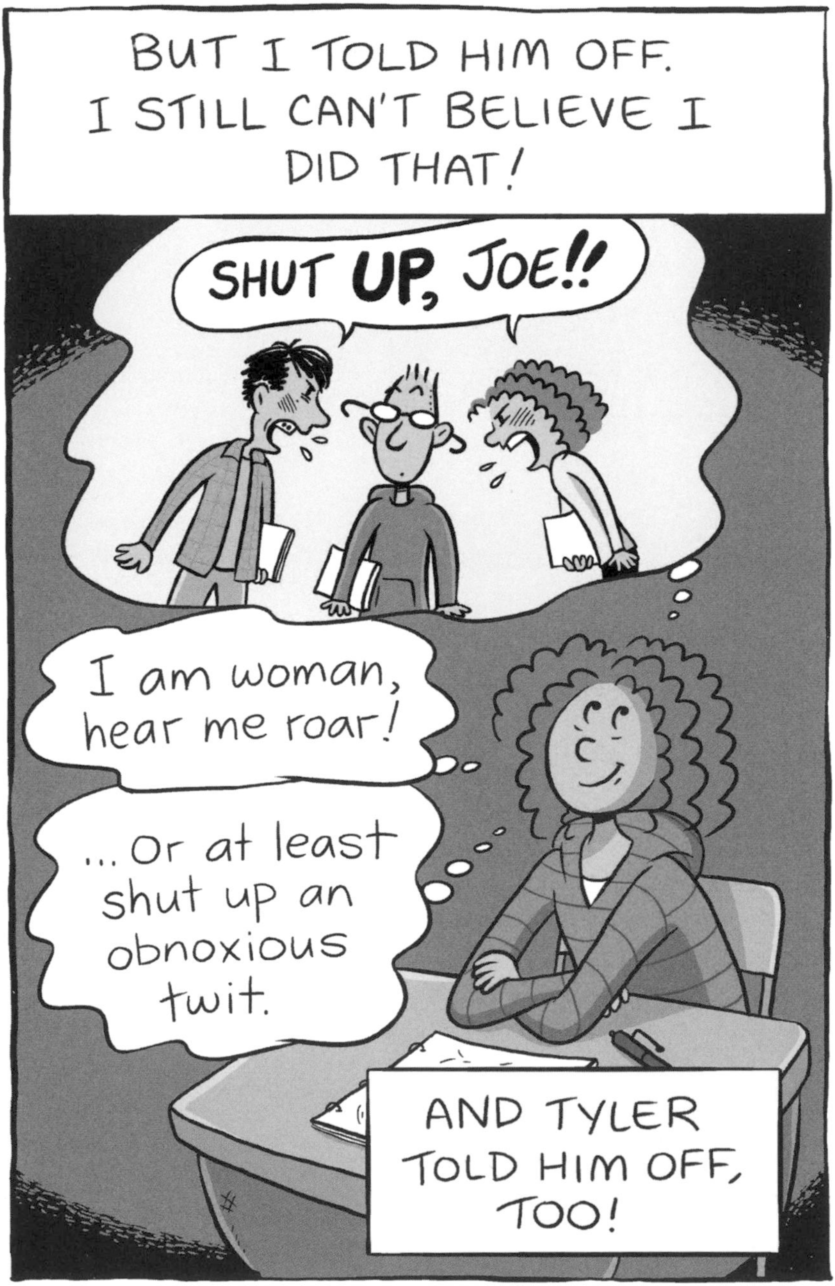
BUT I TOLD HIM OFF. I STILL CAN'T BELIEVE I DID THAT!
SHUT UP, JOE!!
I am woman, hear me roar!
...Or at least shut up an obnoxious twit.
AND TYLER TOLD HIM OFF, TOO!

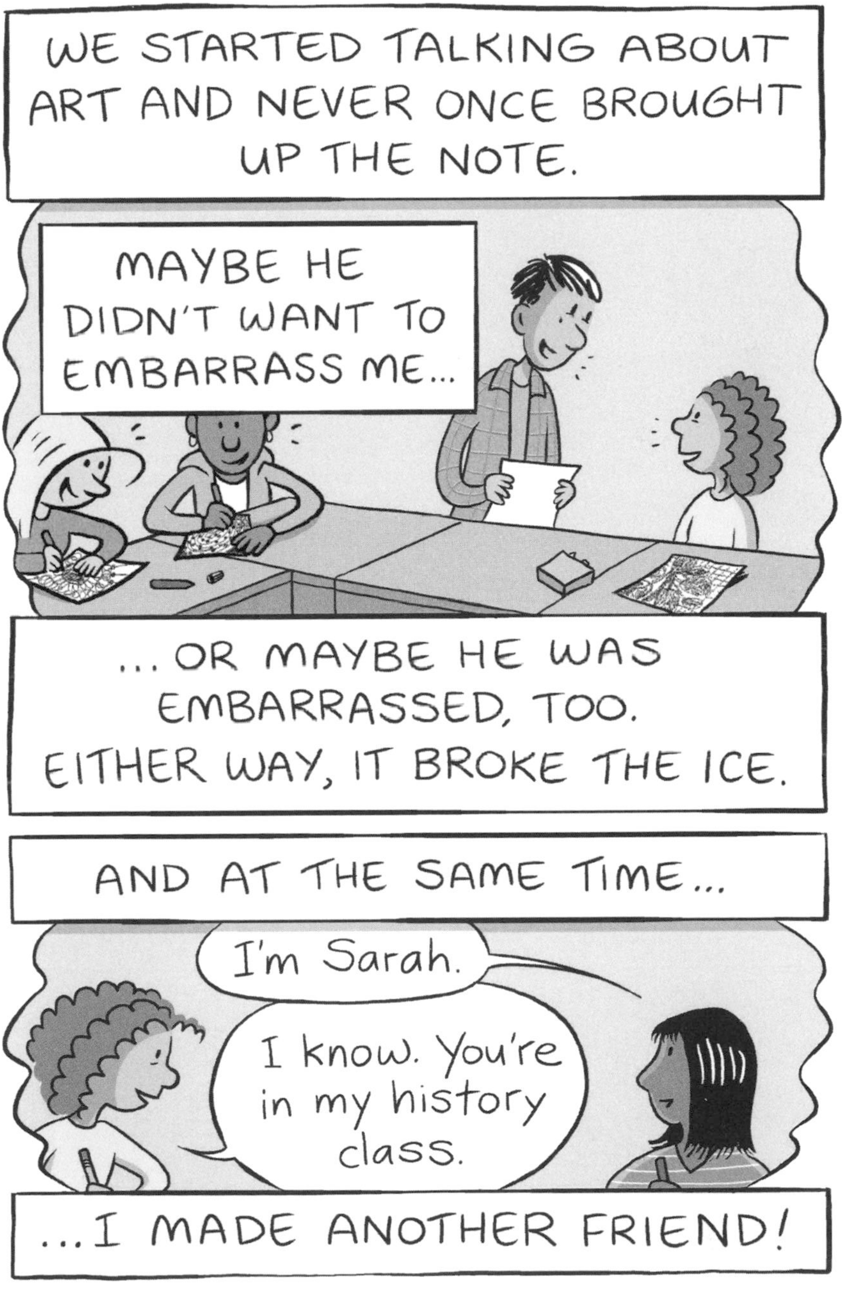
WE STARTED TALKING ABOUT ART AND NEVER ONCE BROUGHT UP THE NOTE.
MAYBE HE DIDN'T WANT TO EMBARRASS ME...
...OR MAYBE HE WAS EMBARRASSED, TOO. EITHER WAY, IT BROKE THE ICE.
AND AT THE SAME TIME...
I'm Sarah.
I know. You're in my history class.
...I MADE ANOTHER FRIEND!

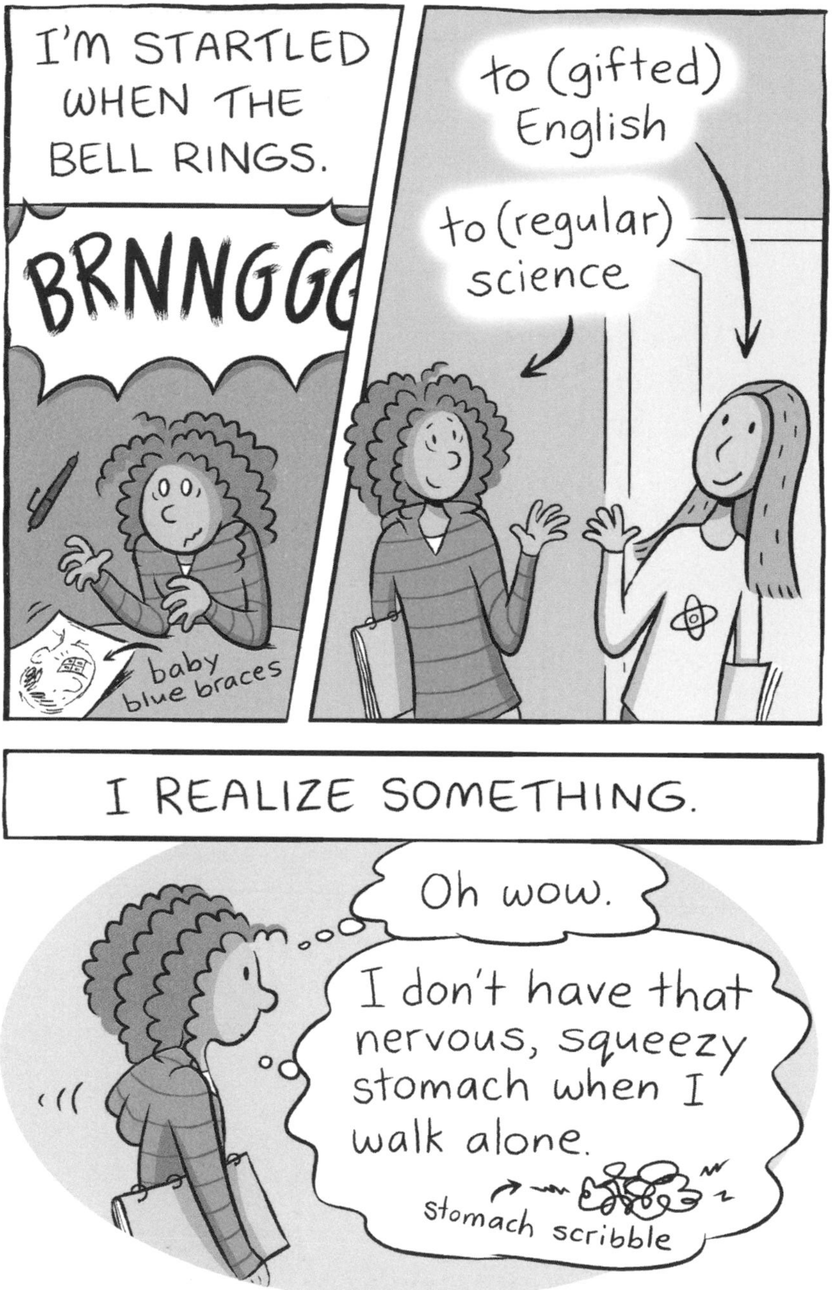
I'M STARTLED WHEN THE BELL RINGS.
BRNNGG
baby blue braces
to (gifted) English
to (regular) science
I REALIZE SOMETHING.
Oh wow.
I don't have that nervous, squeezy stomach when I walk alone.
stomach scribble

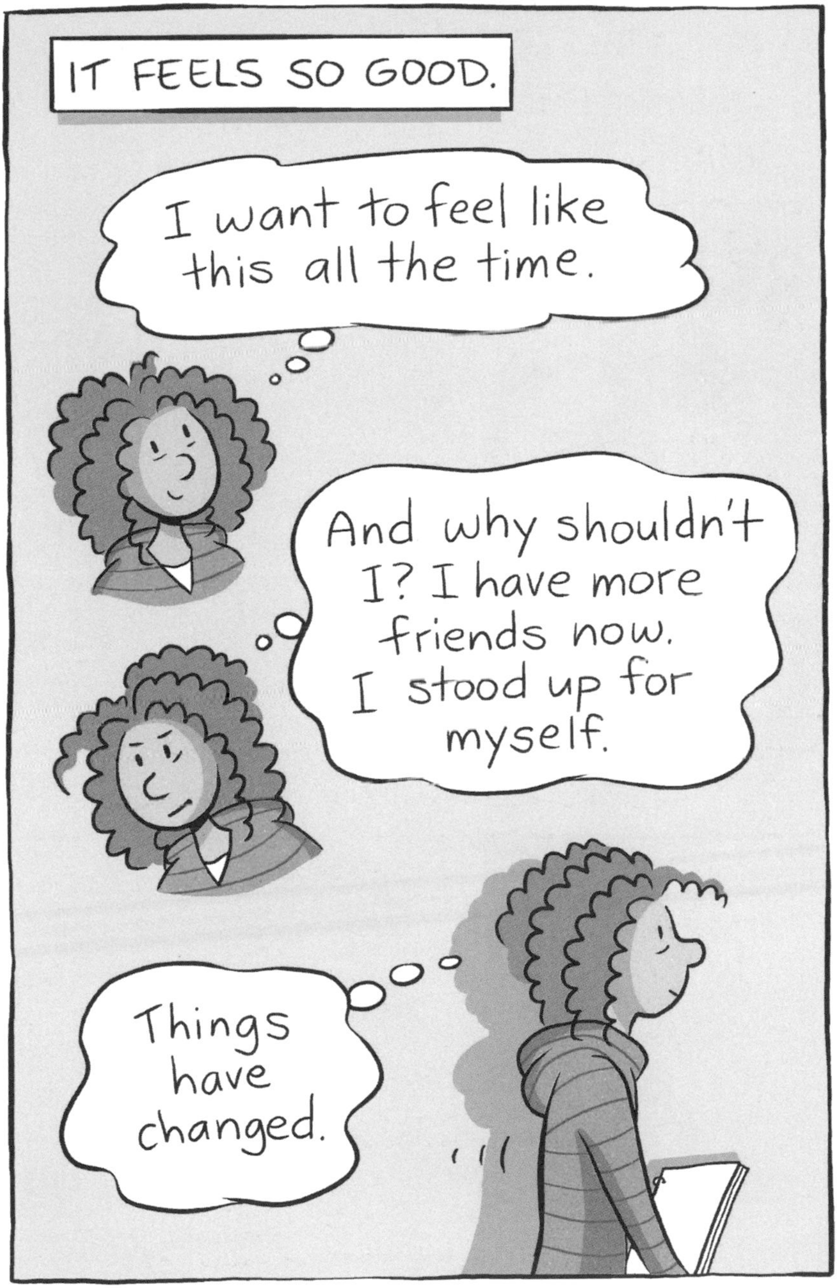
IT FEELS SO GOOD.
I want to feel like this all the time.
And why shouldn't I? I have more friends now. I stood up for myself.
Things have changed.

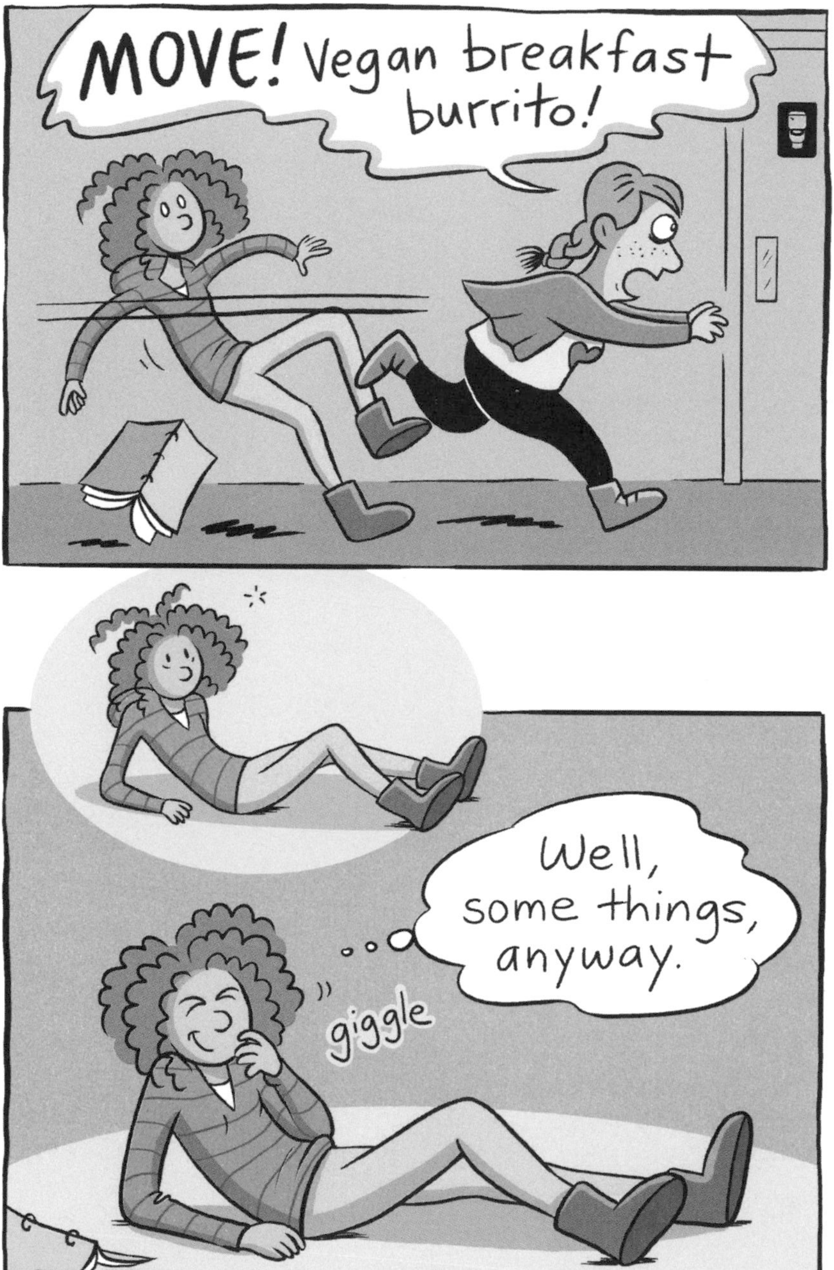
MOVE! Vegan breakfast burrito!
Well, some things, anyway.
giggle

TYLER

The day's going fast. I think it's because I'm not practicing my trumpet—or drawing it—to pass time during a blizzard.

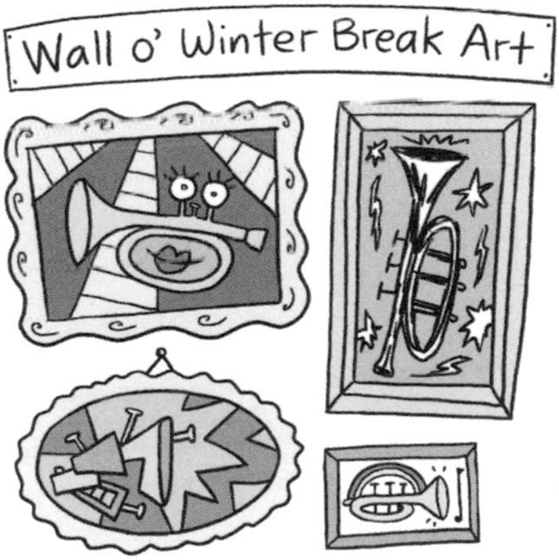
Wall o' Winter Break Art

Plus our teachers are just getting back into the routine, so they've mostly just talked about their breaks and haven't piled on the schoolwork . . . yet.

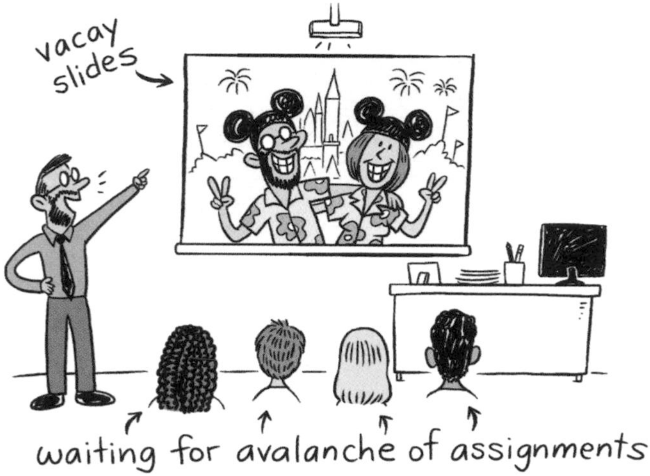
vacay slides
waiting for avalanche of assignments

Just getting to last period (aka the best one).

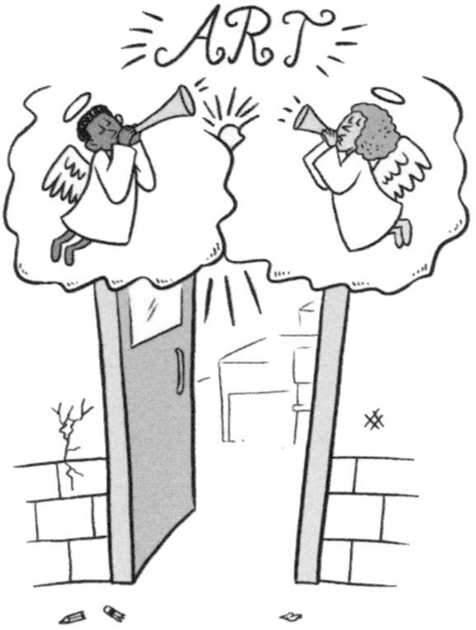
ART

At first, I feel like I'm walking into the wrong room. Instead of the desks put together to form a big square like they were before break, they're in regular rows.

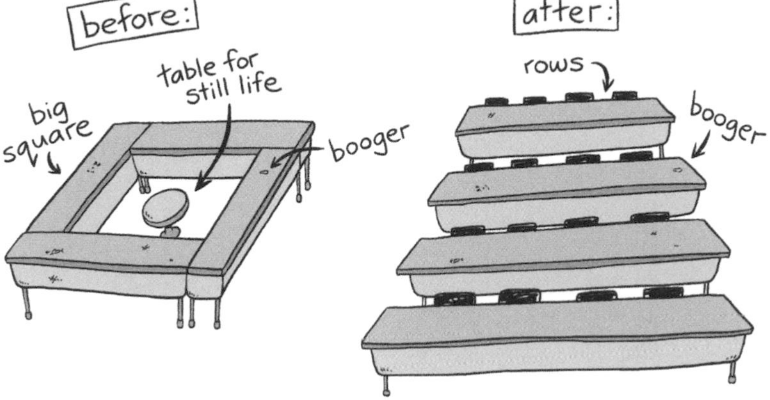
before:
table for still life
big square
booger
after:
rows
booger

Ms. Laurie sips smelly ginger tea in her usual mug:

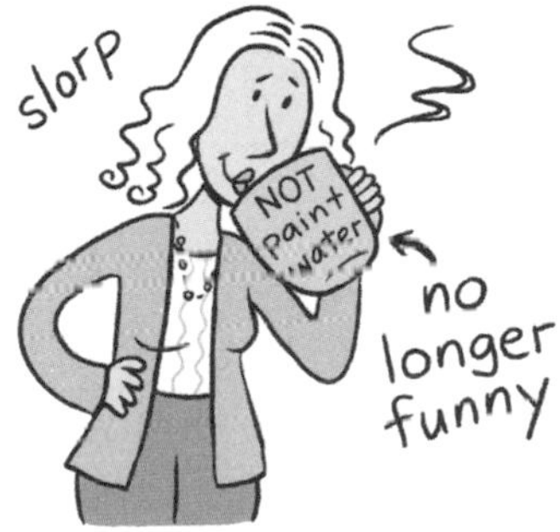
slorp
NOT paint water
no longer funny

She motions for us to sit anywhere. I pick a desk near the sink. Emmie walks in and—kinda cautiously—sits next to me.

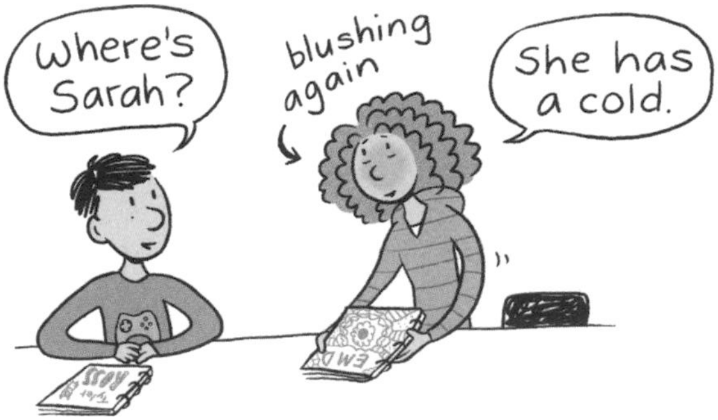
Where's Sarah?
blushing again
She has a cold.

We wait for the rest of the class to show up. Art is in the basement, so it can take a while to get here. Ms. Laurie knows this and usually doesn't give tardy slips if someone is a little late.

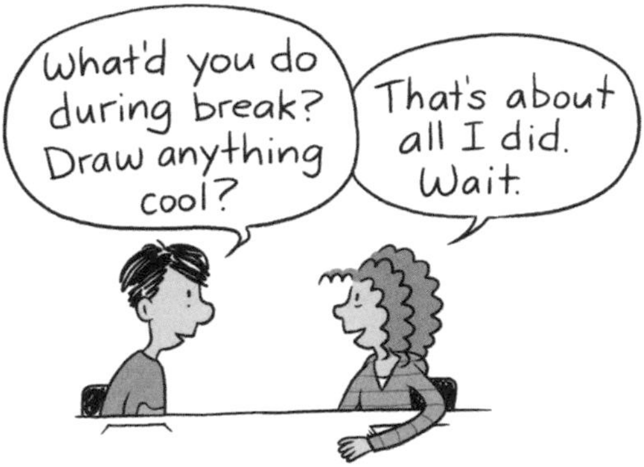
What'd you do during break? Draw anything cool?
That's about all I did. Wait.

She reaches in her pocket and pulls out a phone.

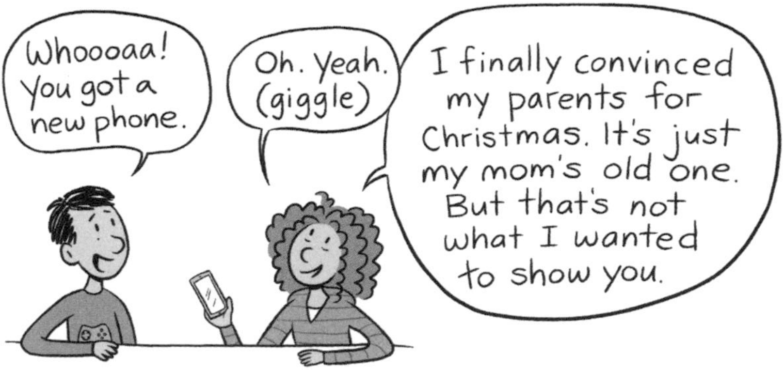
Whoooaa! You got a new phone.
Oh. Yeah. (giggle)
I finally convinced my parents for Christmas. It's just my mom's old one. But that's not what I wanted to show you.

She scrolls through her phone gallery. I can't help it, I admire the phone. Mine is really old (well, not **flip-phone** old like Emmie's last one) and I cracked the glass. The upper-right corner looks like a spiderweb and splits everything in twenty pieces.

She shows me a bunch of new sketches. Mainly hand studies, but there's a really good contour drawing (we did those in the fall) of her friend Brianna. And a colored-pencil still life of . . . I can't make it out.

What are those?

Oh. Um, my mom eats really healthy food. That's a pack of multi-seed crackers, goji berries, some kale chips, and... a kiwi. I think.

I fished it out of the bottom drawer of my fridge.

I stare at the picture, including the black dented kiwi. Then I look up at Emmie.

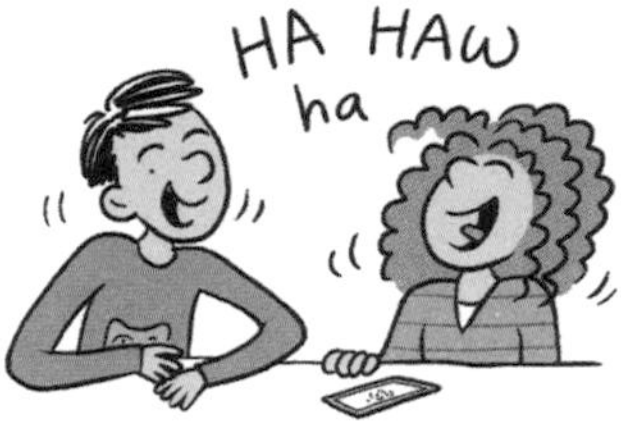
HA HAW
ha

Ms. Laurie begins class by clearing her throat. She does this a lot. Probably why she needs the ginger tea.

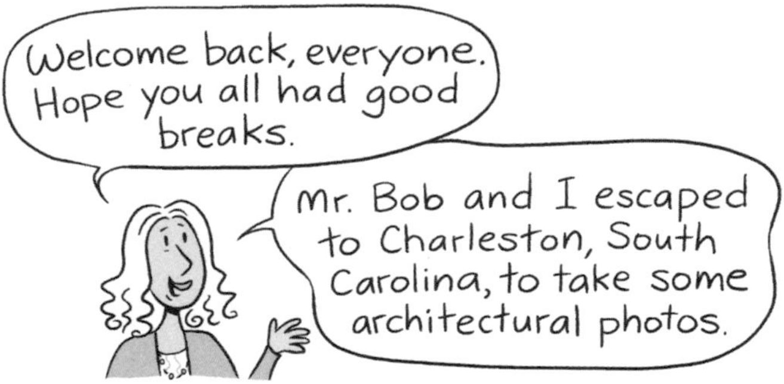
Welcome back, everyone. Hope you all had good breaks.
Mr. Bob and I escaped to Charleston, South Carolina, to take some architectural photos.

Ms. Laurie is the only adult in the building with a preschool teacher's name. She hates being formal (also, her last name is Squalwinskarski; enough said). Mr. Bob is her husband. They're both photographers. "Professional hobby," she calls it. Mr. Bob is a podiatrist or taxidermist or something by day.

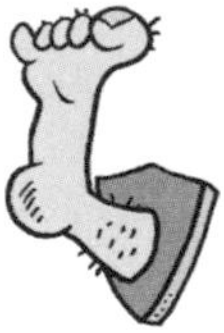

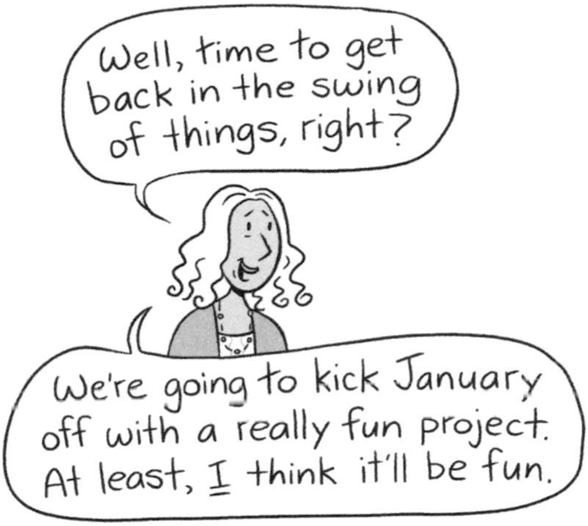
Well, time to get back in the swing of things, right?
We're going to kick January off with a really fun project. At least, I think it'll be fun.

She holds up a bunch of graphic novels, comic books, and manga magazines that are sitting on her desk.

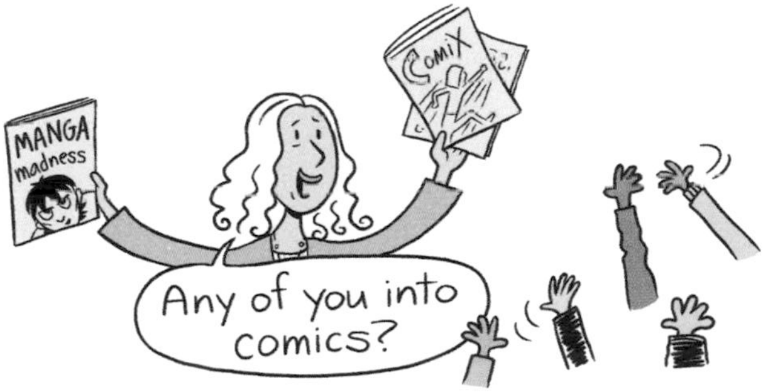
MANGA madness
COMIX
Any of you into comics?

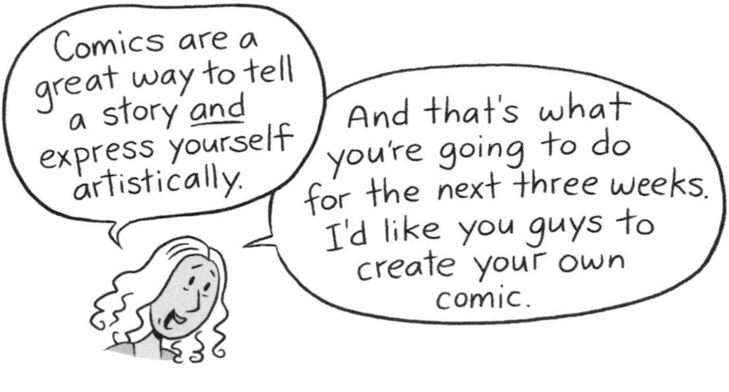
Comics are a great way to tell a story and express yourself artistically.
And that's what you're going to do for the next three weeks. I'd like you guys to create your own comic.

The room explodes with excitement.

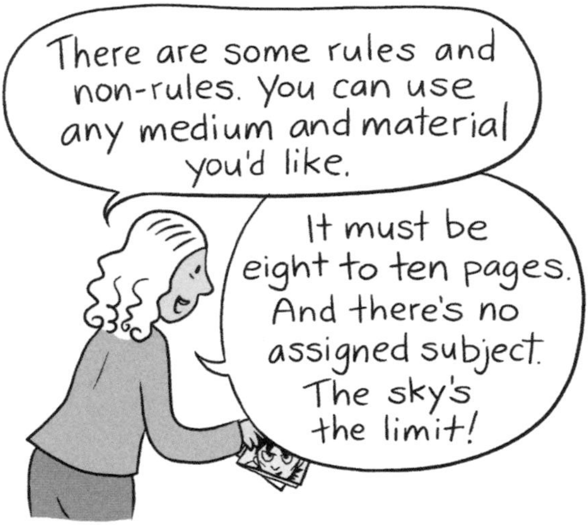
There are some rules and non-rules. You can use any medium and material you'd like.
It must be eight to ten pages. And there's no assigned subject. The sky's the limit!

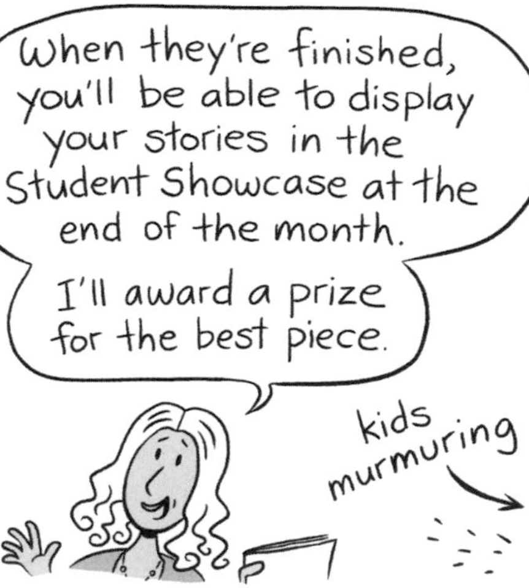
When they're finished, you'll be able to display your stories in the Student Showcase at the end of the month.
I'll award a prize for the best piece.
kids murmuring

This sounds seriously cool. First, we never get a chance to work on anything for that long. I always feel like I'm rushing to finish every project.

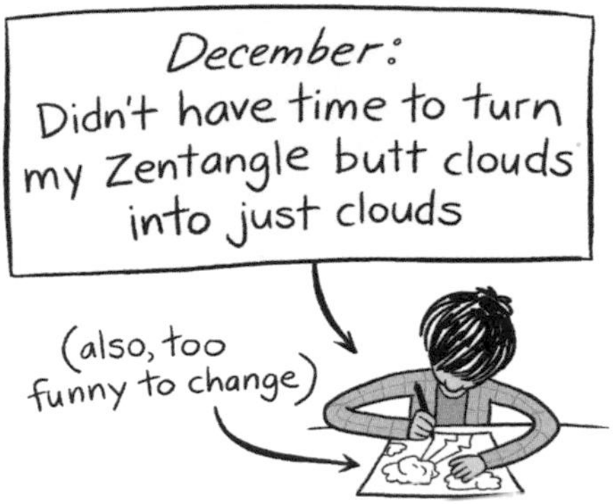
December:
Didn't have time to turn my Zentangle butt clouds into just clouds
(also, too funny to change)

Second, a PRIZE! I live for competition.

The Student Showcase is an actual event. It's held on a Friday night, and parents are invited. We get to see students' stuff on display, like science and history dioramas, art projects, poetry, and short stories. Basically, it's a whole big "school spirit" thing—but instead of sports, it's for academics and arts.

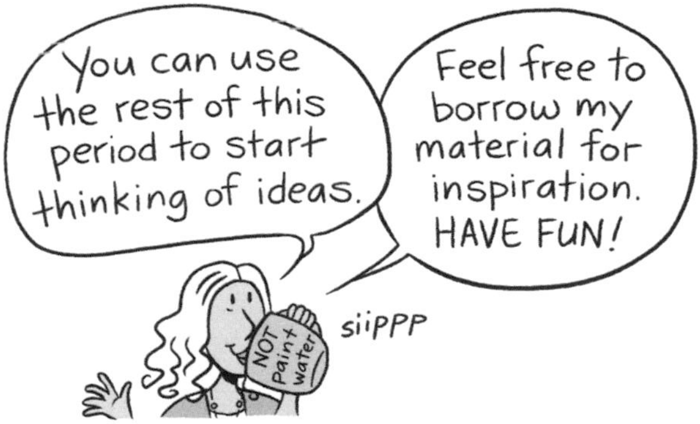
You can use the rest of this period to start thinking of ideas.
Feel free to borrow my material for inspiration. HAVE FUN!
siiPPP
NOT Paint water

As cool as this sounds, it suddenly hits me that I've never tried making my own comics.

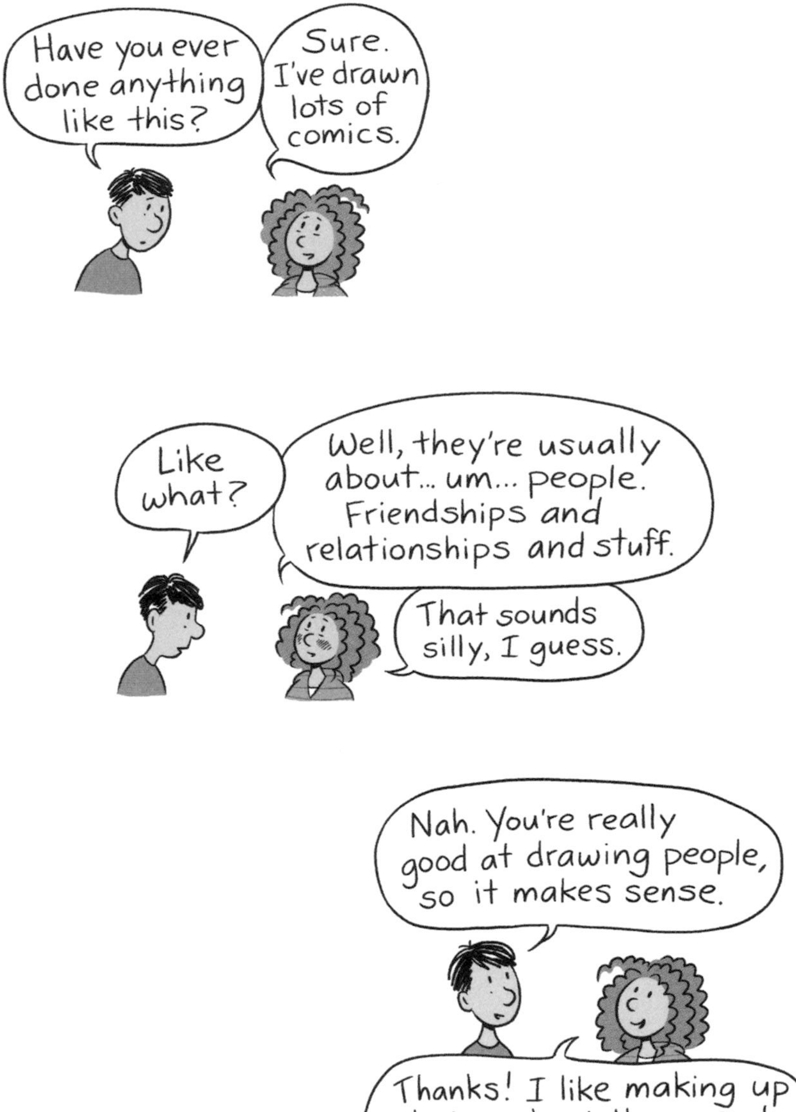
Have you ever done anything like this?
Sure. I've drawn lots of comics.
Like what?
Well, they're usually about... um... people. Friendships and relationships and stuff.
That sounds silly, I guess.
Nah. You're really good at drawing people, so it makes sense.
Thanks! I like making up stories about them. And adding dialogue and stuff.

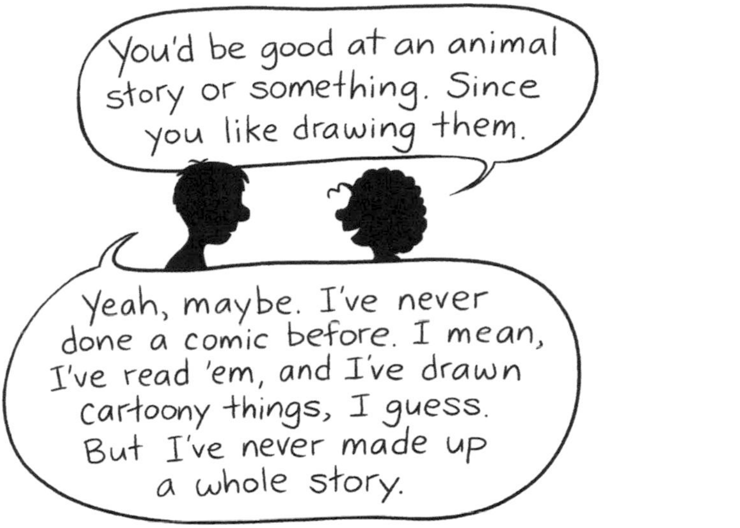
You'd be good at an animal story or something. Since you like drawing them.
Yeah, maybe. I've never done a comic before. I mean, I've read 'em, and I've drawn cartoony things, I guess. But I've never made up a whole story.

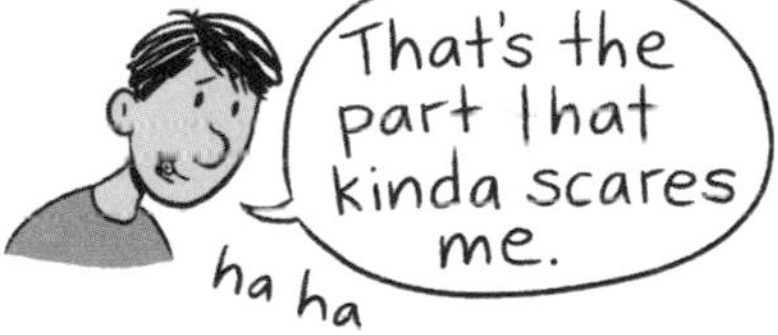
That's the part that kinda scares me.
ha ha

Emmie gets quiet for a moment.

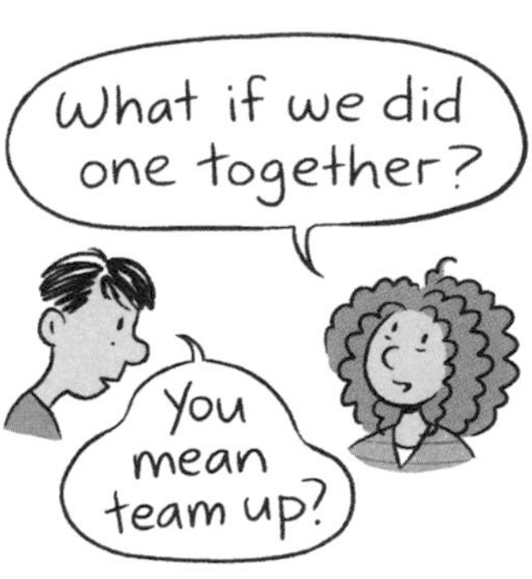
What if we did one together?
You mean team up?

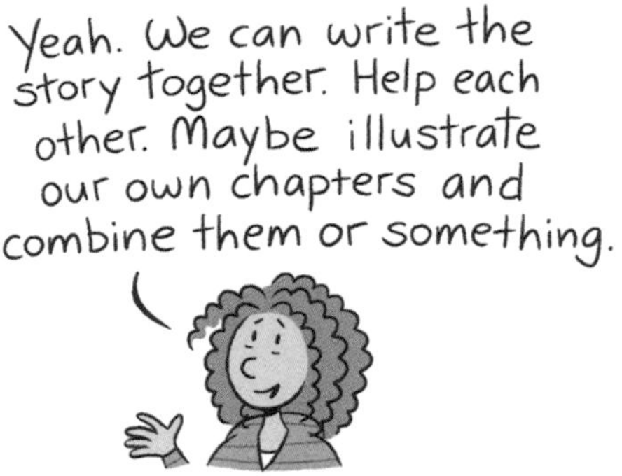
Yeah. We can write the story together. Help each other. Maybe illustrate our own chapters and combine them or something.

I think. I'd hate to drag her down in case I'm bad at this. But then again, how bad can I be? Emmie's a better artist, but I'm still pretty good. Plus it would be fun to brainstorm and bounce ideas off each other. That's the stuff I like to do. Teamwork.

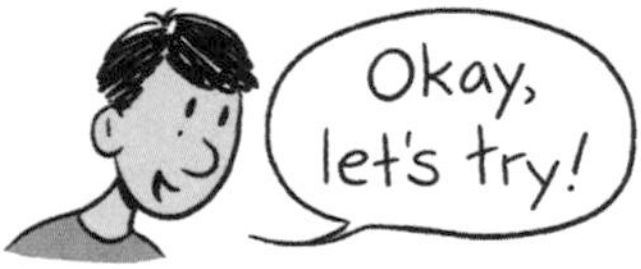
Okay, let's try!

We walk over to Ms. Laurie's desk. There are a gajillion art pens, markers, and knickknacks on it.

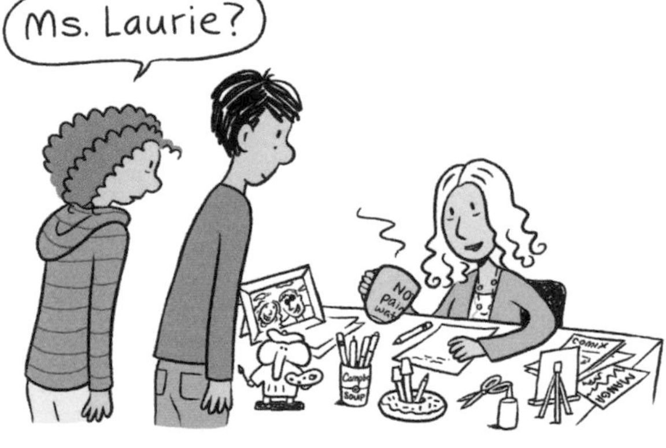
Ms. Laurie?

She looks up.

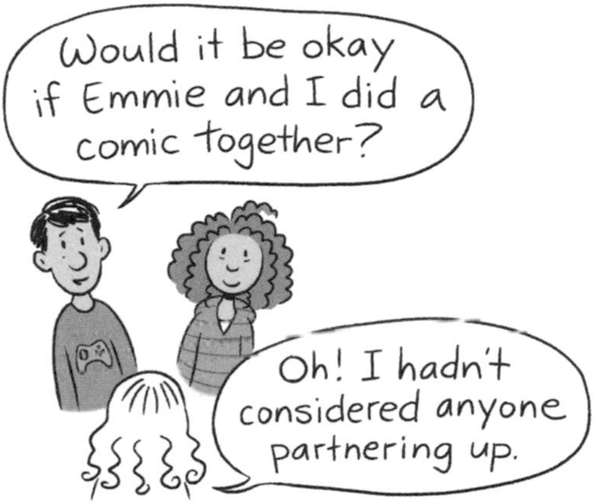
Would it be okay if Emmie and I did a comic together?
Oh! I hadn't considered anyone partnering up.

She thinks for a bit, concentrating on a elephant figurine wearing an artist's smock.

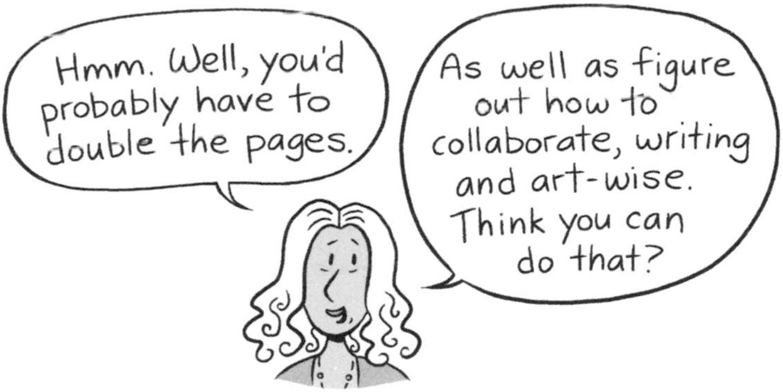
Hmm. Well, you'd probably have to double the pages.
As well as figure out how to collaborate, writing and art-wise. Think you can do that?

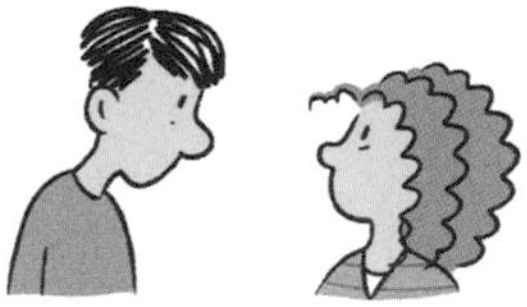

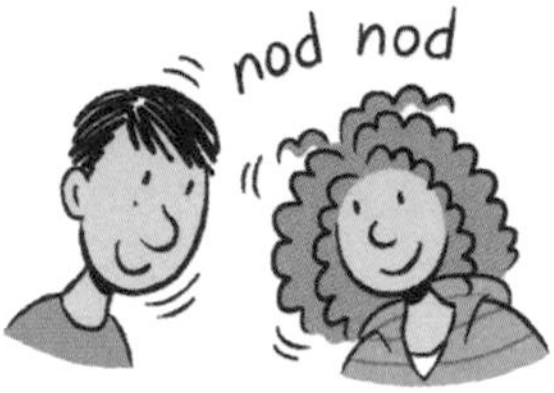
nod nod

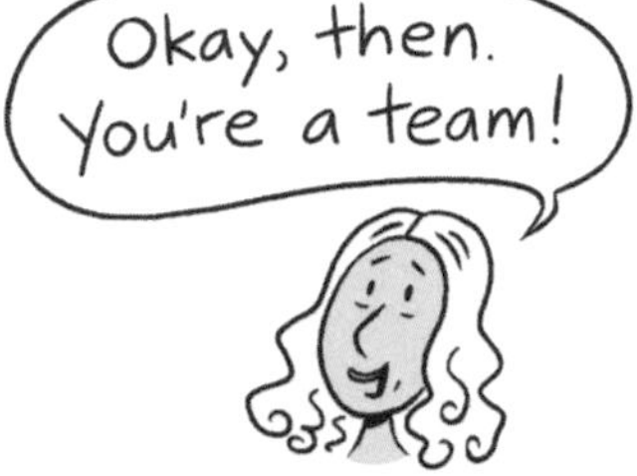
Okay, then.
You're a team!

I high-five Emmie. She just misses my hand.

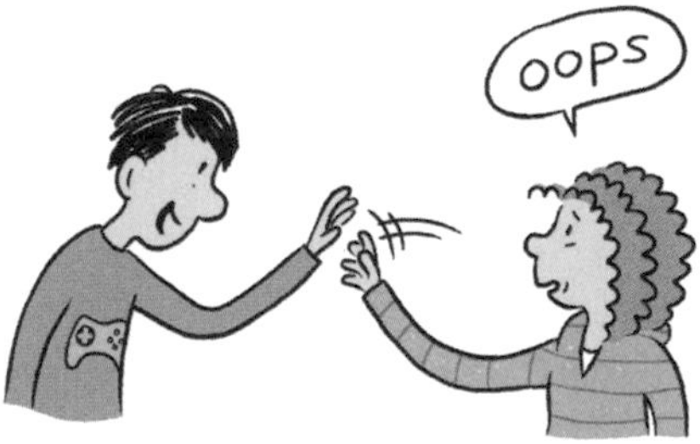
OOPS

I laugh and we head back to our desks.

I hope I did the right thing by partnering up. I don't always think stuff through.

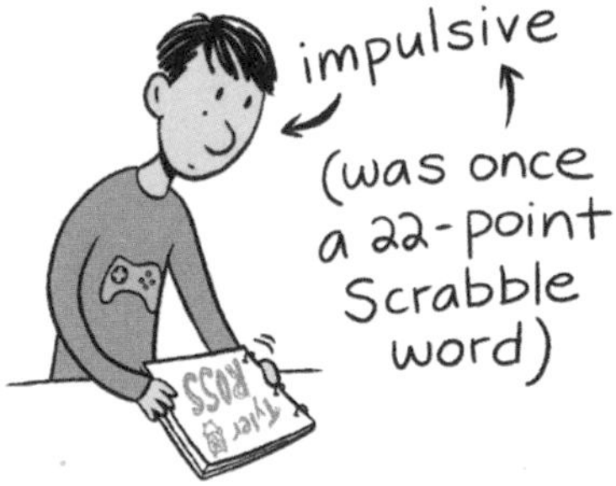
impulsive
(was once
a 22-point
Scrabble
word)
Tyler
ROSS

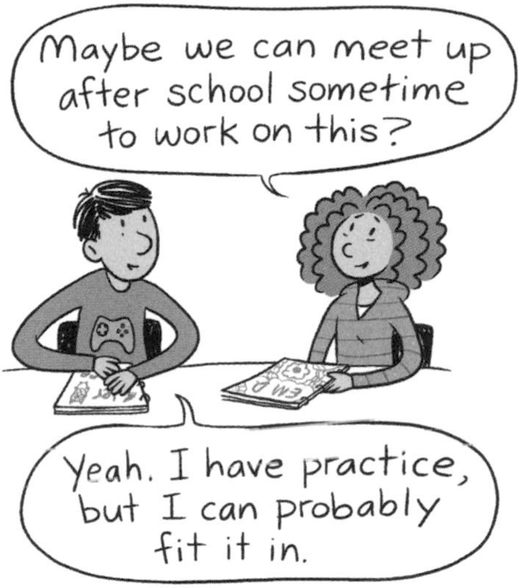
Maybe we can meet up after school sometime to work on this?
Yeah. I have practice, but I can probably fit it in.

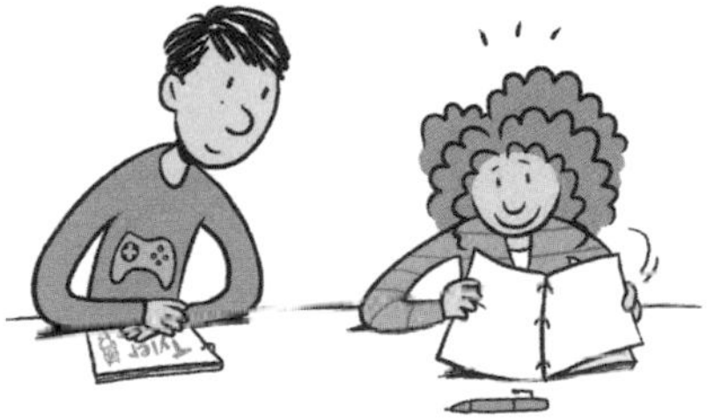

Her excitement is contagious.

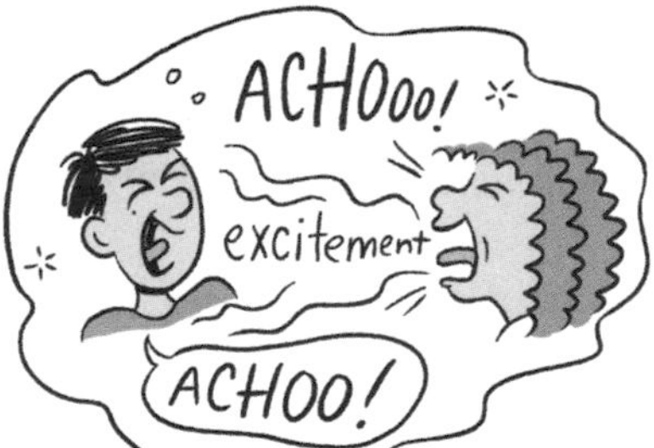
ACHOoo!
excitement
ACHOO!

Yeah, this can work.

In fact . . .

. . . this'll be fun!

Emmie

OMG. I'M PARTNERED WITH TYLER. OMG.

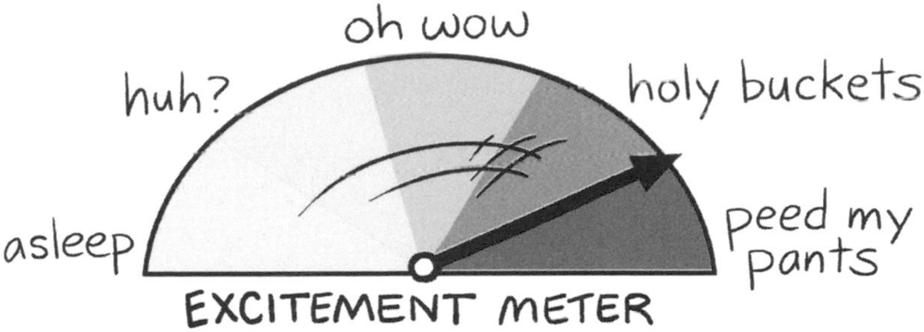

oh wow
huh?
holy buckets
asleep
peed my pants
EXCITEMENT METER

I WISH BRI WERE HERE SO I COULD SCREAM WITH HER.

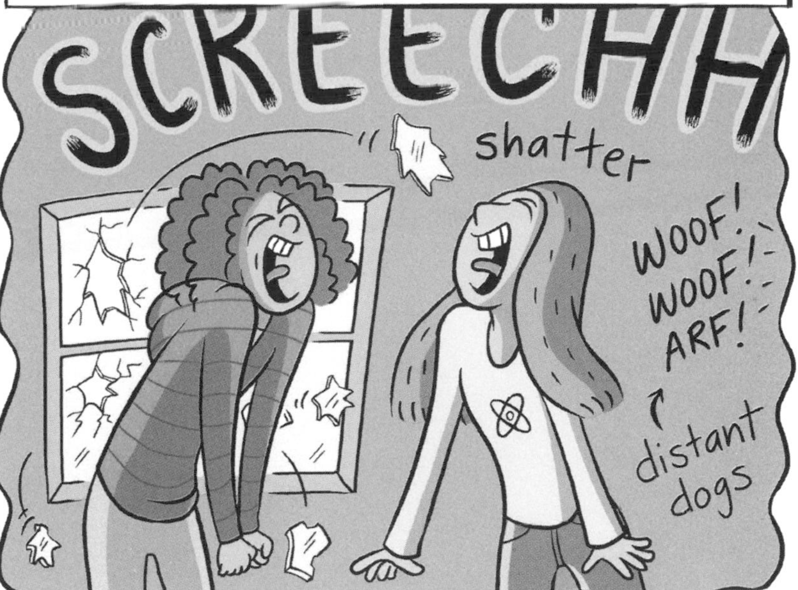

SCREECHH
shatter
WOOF! WOOF! ARF!
distant dogs

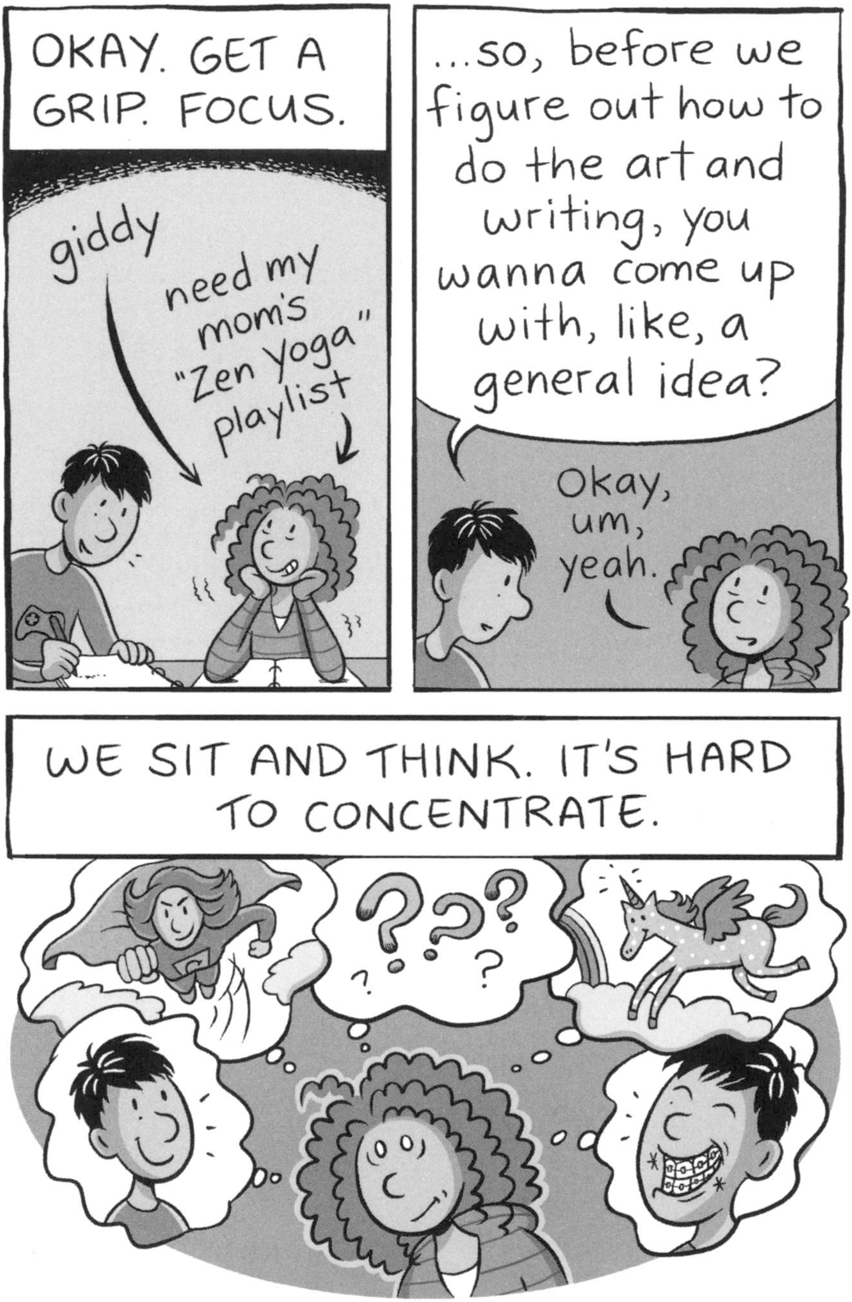
OKAY. GET A GRIP. FOCUS.
giddy
need my mom's "Zen Yoga" playlist
...so, before we figure out how to do the art and writing, you wanna come up with, like, a general idea?
Okay, um, yeah.
WE SIT AND THINK. IT'S HARD TO CONCENTRATE.
???
?
?

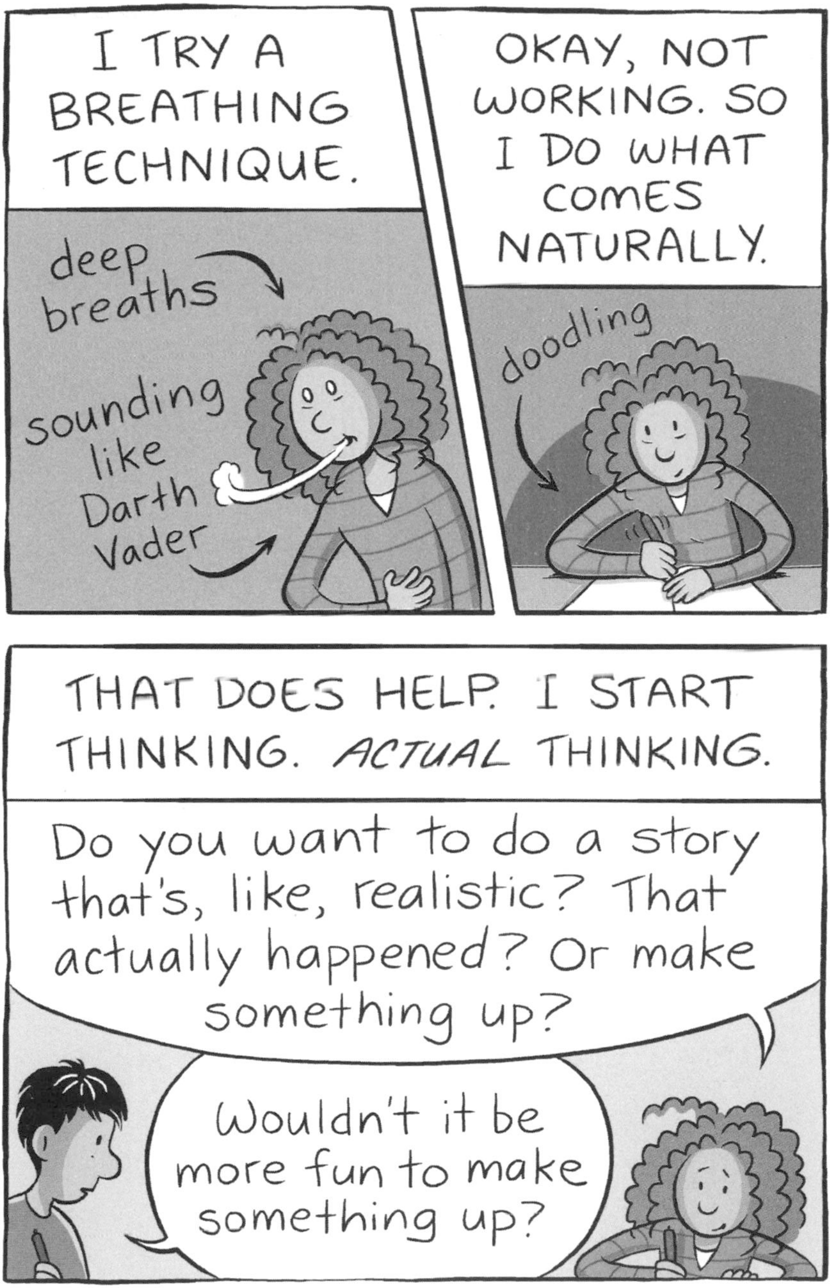
I TRY A BREATHING TECHNIQUE.
deep breaths
sounding like Darth Vader
OKAY, NOT WORKING. SO I DO WHAT COMES NATURALLY.
doodling
THAT DOES HELP. I START THINKING. *ACTUAL* THINKING.
Do you want to do a story that's, like, realistic? That actually happened? Or make something up?
Wouldn't it be more fun to make something up?

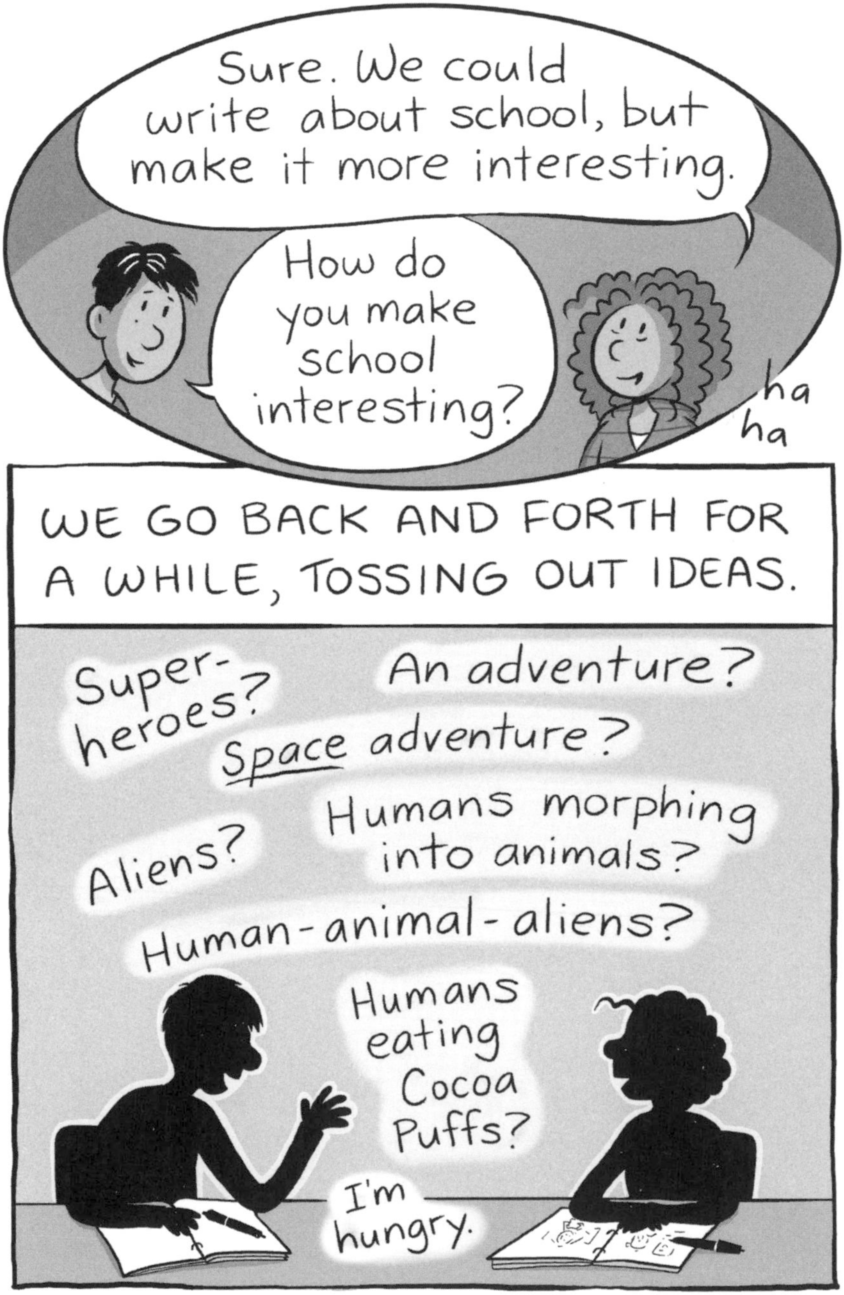

Sure. We could write about school, but make it more interesting.
How do you make school interesting?
ha ha
WE GO BACK AND FORTH FOR A WHILE, TOSSING OUT IDEAS.
Super-heroes?
An adventure?
Space adventure?
Aliens?
Humans morphing into animals?
Human-animal-aliens?
Humans eating Cocoa Puffs?
I'm hungry.

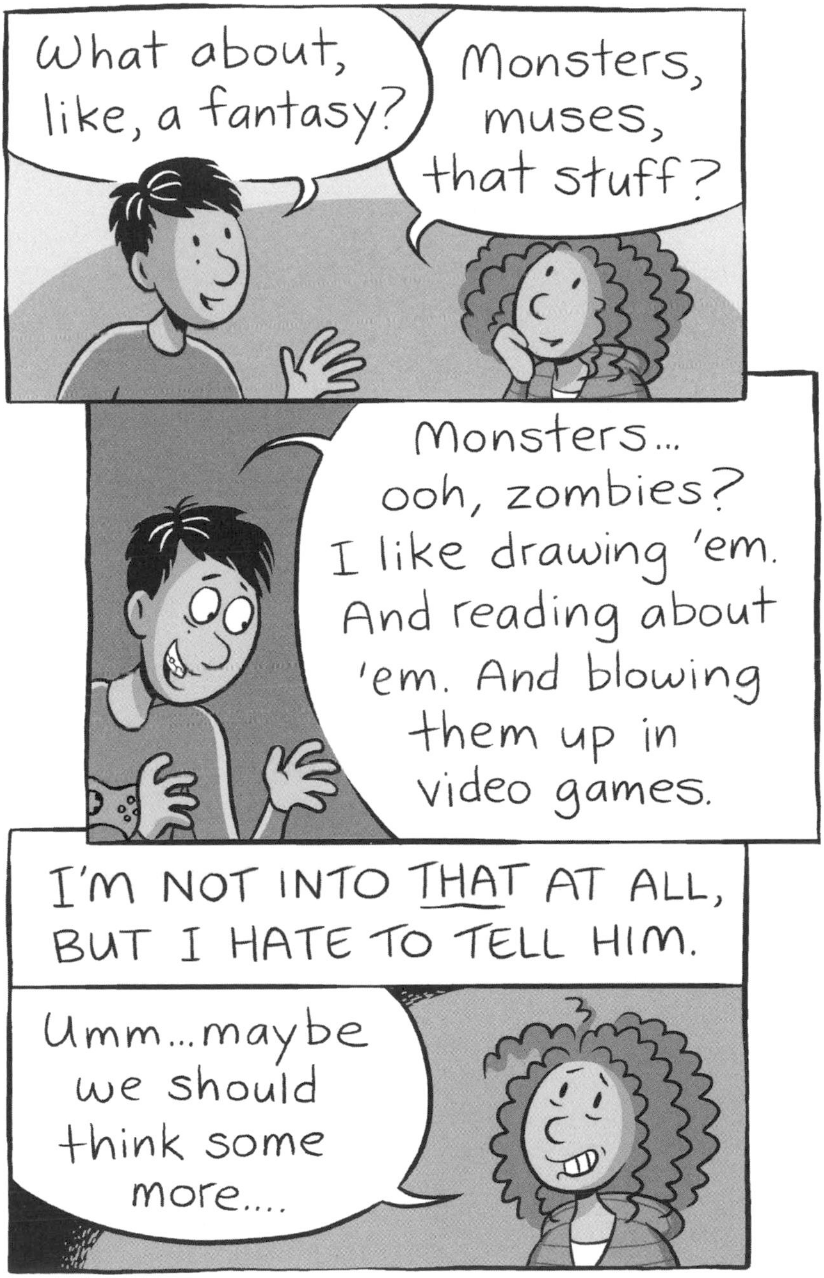
What about, like, a fantasy?
Monsters, muses, that stuff?
Monsters... ooh, zombies? I like drawing 'em. And reading about 'em. And blowing them up in video games.
I'M NOT INTO THAT AT ALL, BUT I HATE TO TELL HIM.
Umm...maybe we should think some more....

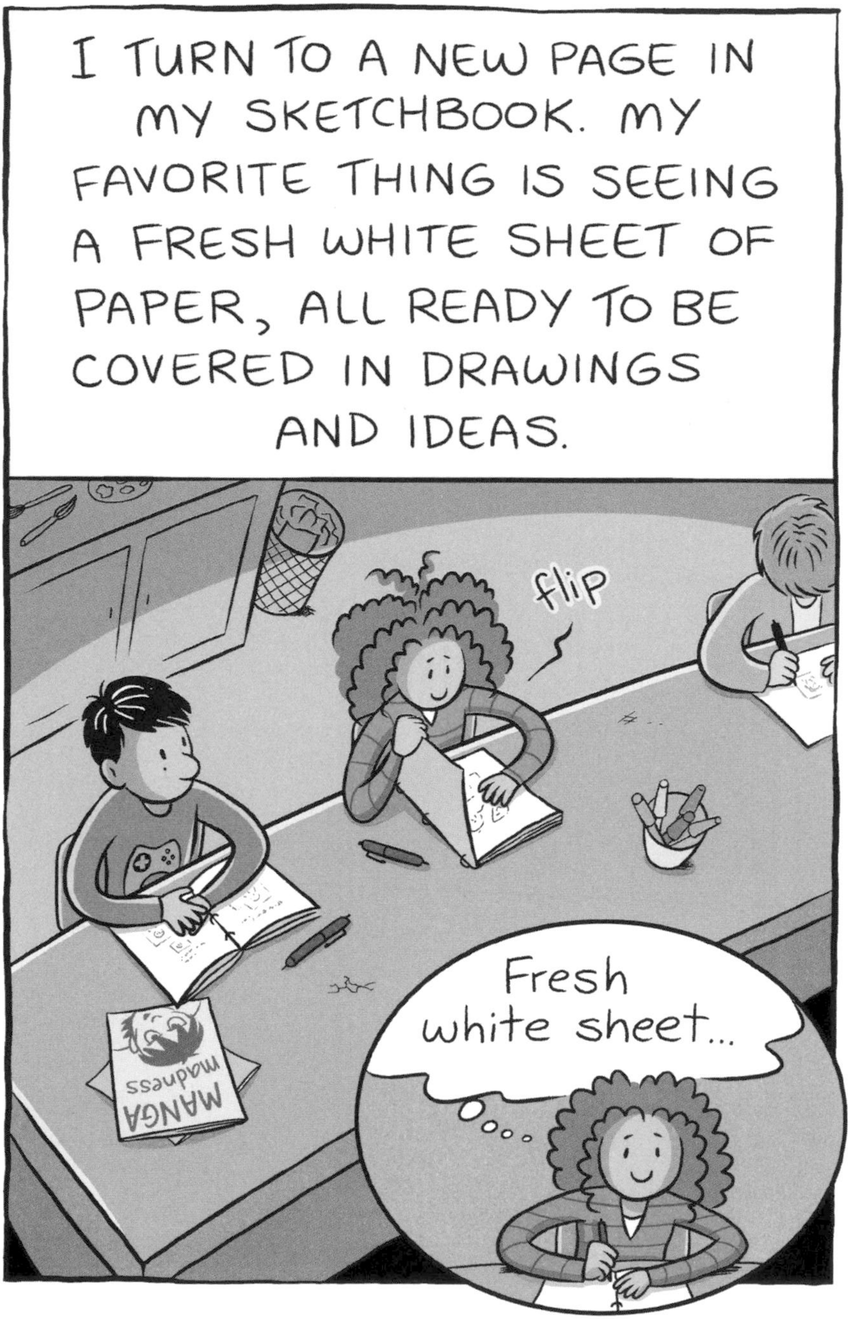

I TURN TO A NEW PAGE IN MY SKETCHBOOK. MY FAVORITE THING IS SEEING A FRESH WHITE SHEET OF PAPER, ALL READY TO BE COVERED IN DRAWINGS AND IDEAS.
flip
MANGA madness
Fresh white sheet...

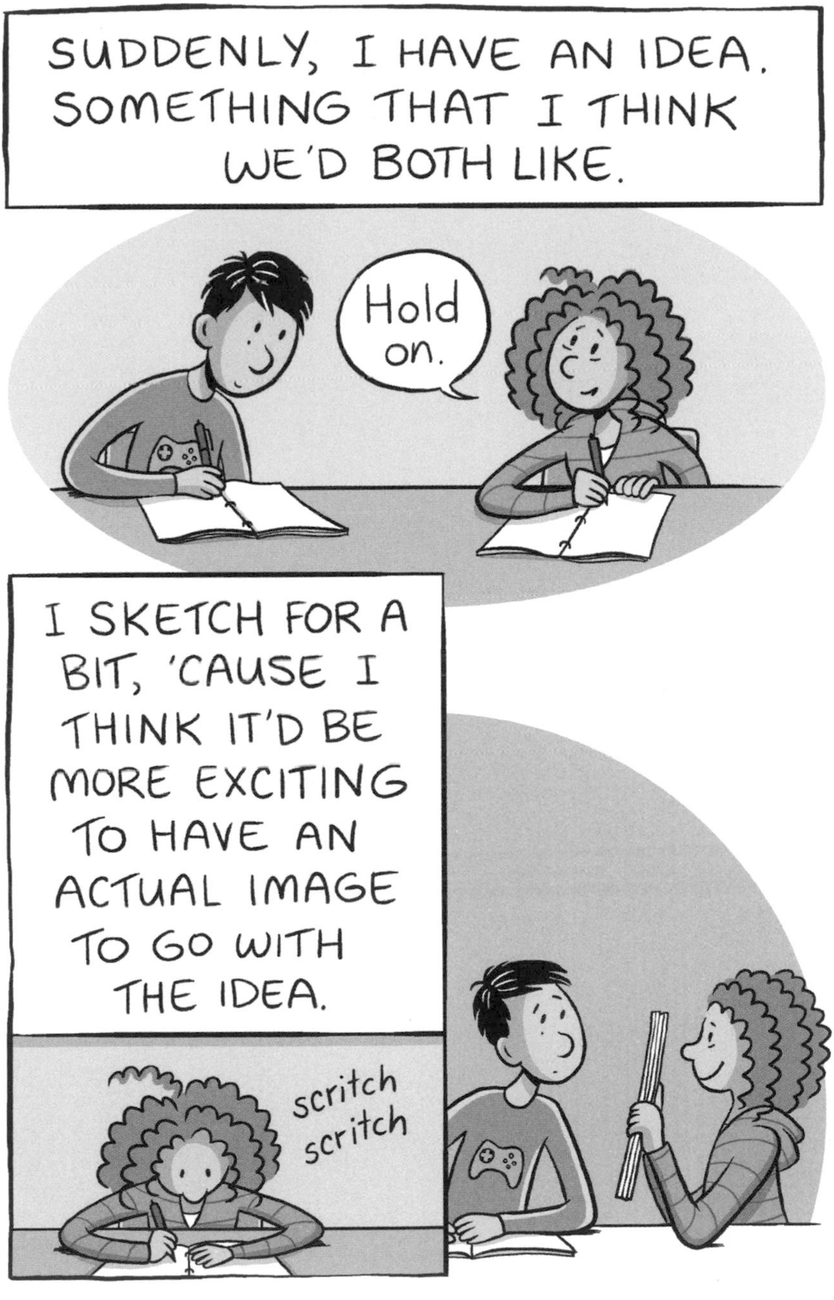
SUDDENLY, I HAVE AN IDEA. SOMETHING THAT I THINK WE'D BOTH LIKE.
Hold on.
I SKETCH FOR A BIT, 'CAUSE I THINK IT'D BE MORE EXCITING TO HAVE AN ACTUAL IMAGE TO GO WITH THE IDEA.
scritch scritch

HE LIKES MY IDEA!

erp

peed my pants

FOR THE SECOND TIME, WE HIGH-FIVE.

THIS TIME, I DON'T MISS.

TYLER

Lunch.

It's the day after the comics project announcement. I sit with Anthony, Joe, and a few other seventh graders from the basketball team. The volleyball girls sit near us.

Second Lunch Period (a handy blueprint):

ice cream freezer
doors
cashier (nice or mean, depending on day)
table
windows
bench
art club & manga kids
science clubs kids
orchestra & band kids
swim team; other cool kids
basketball team
volleyball team
tray shelf thing
lunch odors (good or bad, depending on day)
dirty tray conveyer belt
garbage
(stinky)
mystery place where trays land
recycling
windows

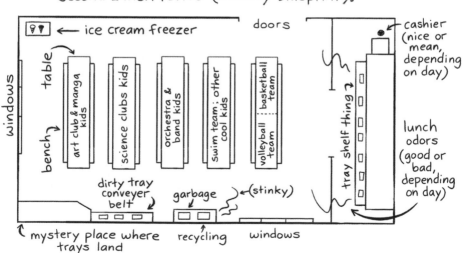

We're pretty close to the entrance, which lets us see who's walking in. In Celia's case, this is very important.

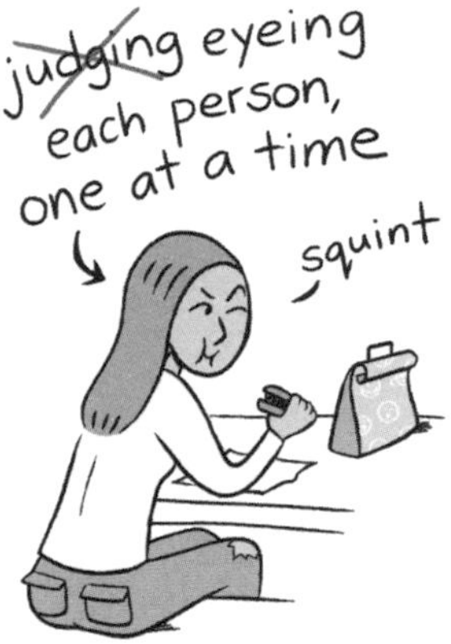
~~judging~~ eyeing each person, one at a time
squint

My older brother, Zach, used to sit at my table. He's kind of a legend.

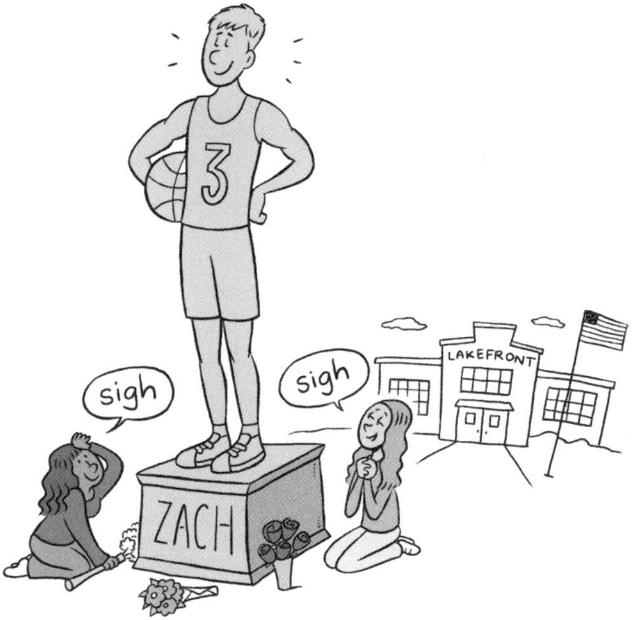
sigh
sigh
3
ZACH
LAKEFRONT

You'd think I'd have trouble filling his shoes, but being friendly and good at sports help. Or maybe the whole popularity thing is genetic.

parents

Or not.

Today is Pasta Day. That's just a fancy way of saying "spaghetti with red sauce and meatbombs."

mushy pasta

runny sauce

granite block

Luckily, I brought my lunch. Joe is eating spaghetti and talking while meatbomb shrapnel flies out of his mouth.

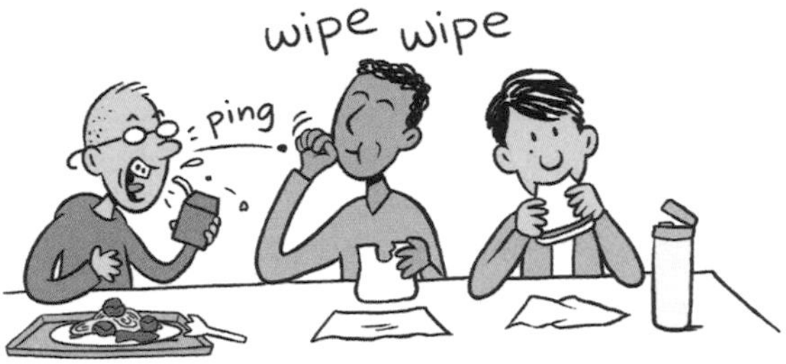
wipe wipe
ping

I spot Emmie and Brianna walking to their usual table.

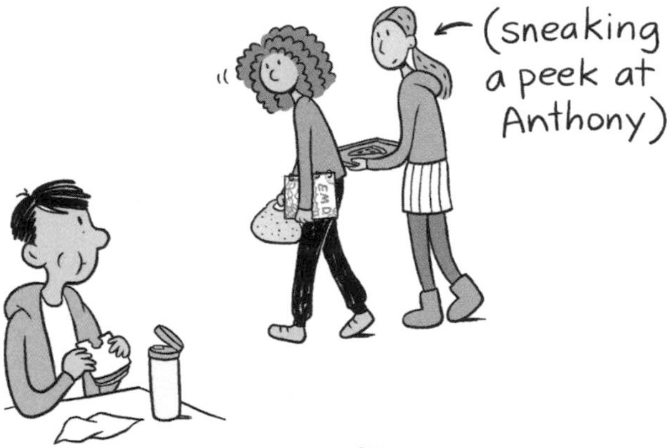
(sneaking a peek at Anthony)

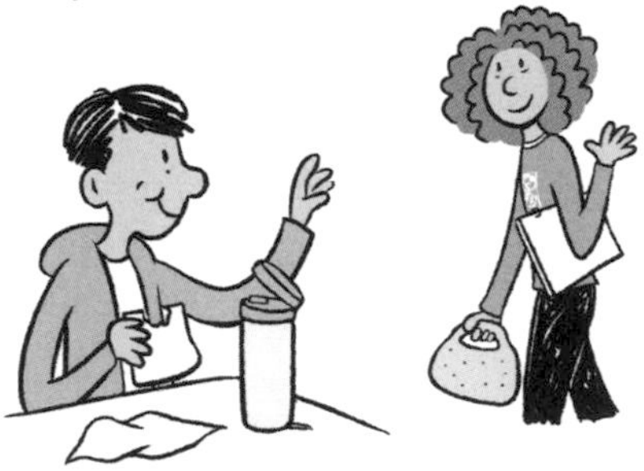

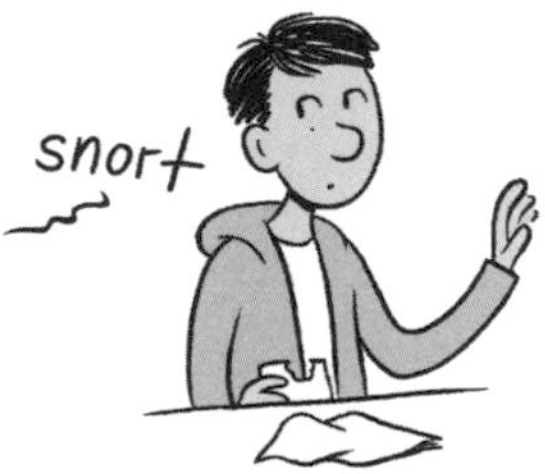
snort

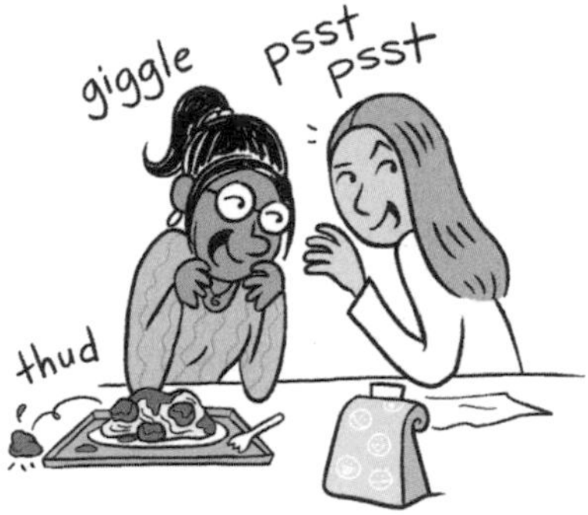
giggle
psst
psst
thud

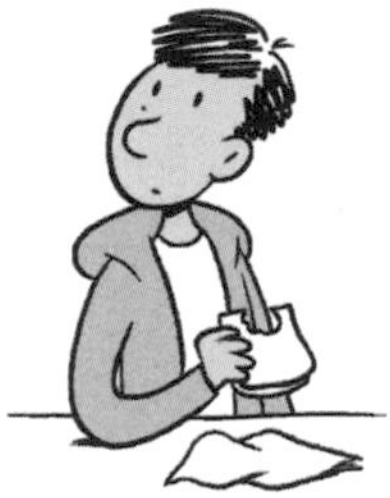

Great.

I turn back to my lunch, which I'm no longer hungry for. Usually I've got the appetite of someone three times my size.

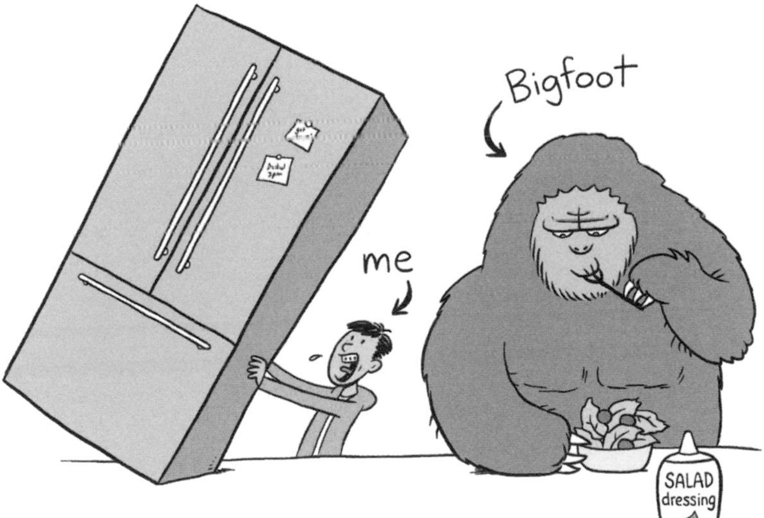
Bigfoot
me
SALAD
dressing

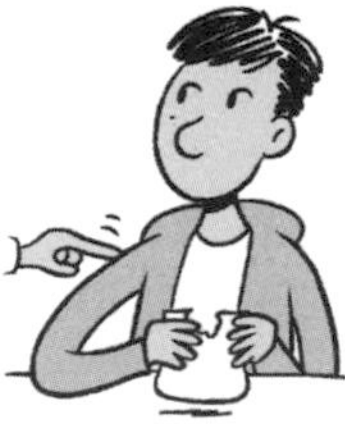

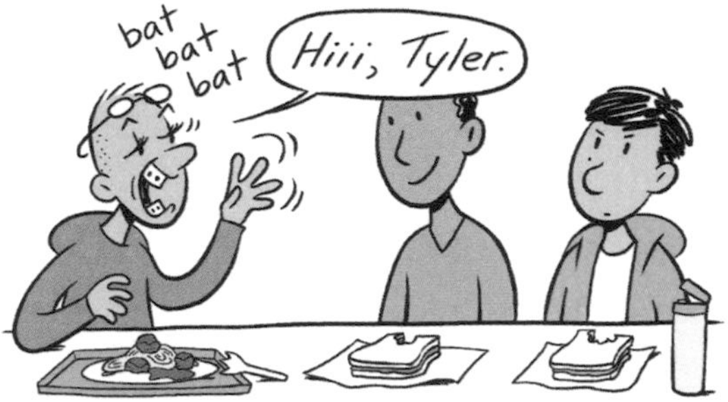
bat
bat
bat
Hiii, Tyler.

The other guys laugh.

Now I'm irritated **and** not hungry. I resort to a solid redirection strategy. I take a huge bite out of my PB and banana sandwich and open my mouth to show Joe. That starts a "see-food" war at the table.

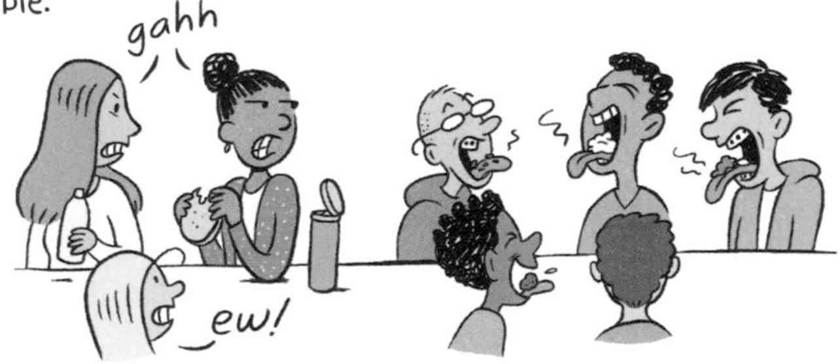
gahh
ew!

It worked. Once the lunch monitor threatens us with detention, we settle down.

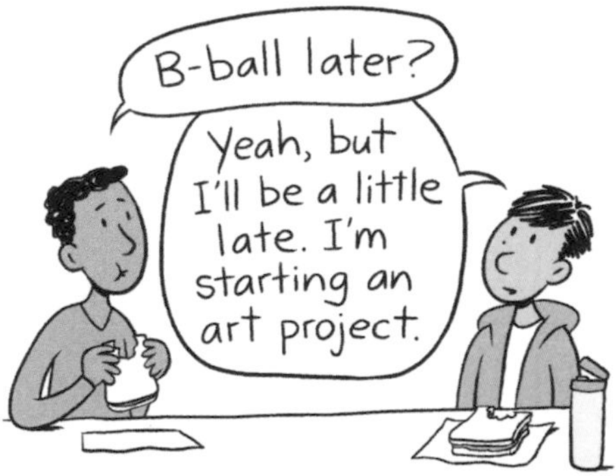
B-ball later?
Yeah, but I'll be a little late. I'm starting an art project.

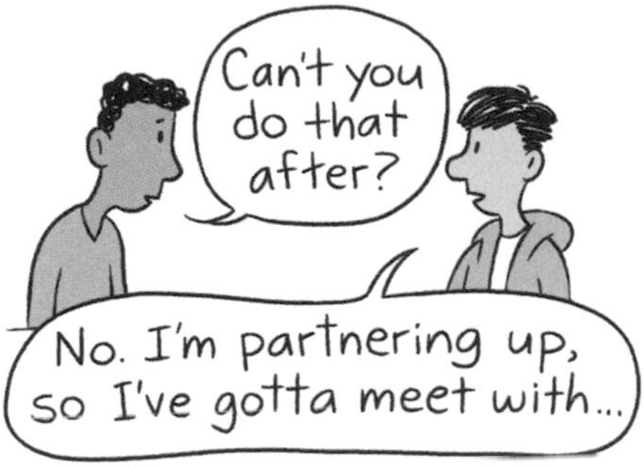
Can't you do that after?
No. I'm partnering up, so I've gotta meet with...

My voice trails off.

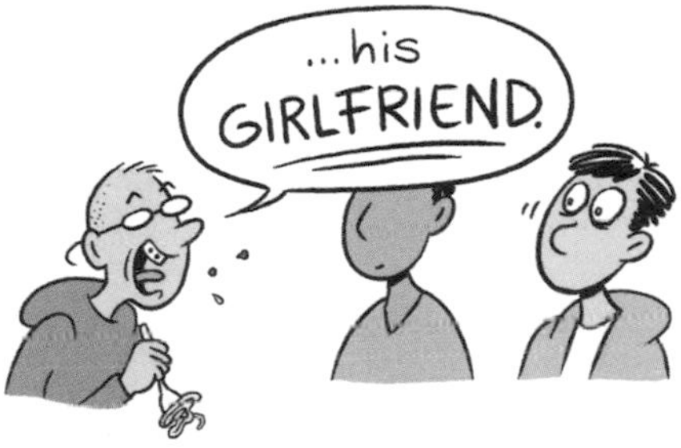
...his GIRLFRIEND.

He makes kissing noises as I clamp my hand over his mouth.

Oh crud, what if Emmie hears or worse . . . ?

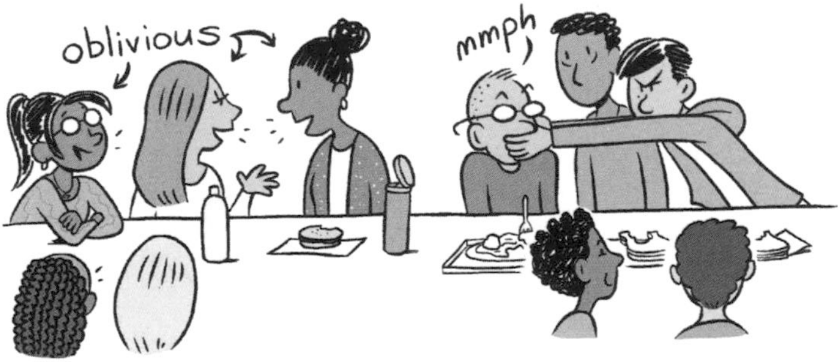
oblivious
mmph

Whew.

Quickly, I check to see if Emmie and Brianna were listening. Luckily, they're far enough away, and the cafeteria is really loud. Not to mention:

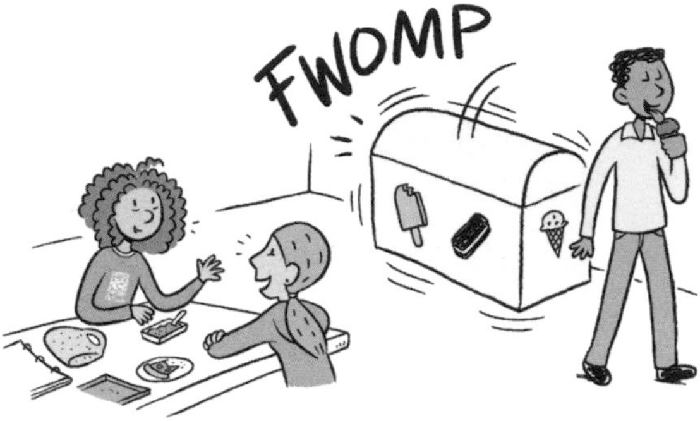
FWOMP

Not sure why I care, anyway. Celia always shoots her mouth off. And as for Joe, he cracks jokes—that's his thing. No big deal.

My appetite returns, and I scarf down my lunch while we talk about the Valley Bottom game.

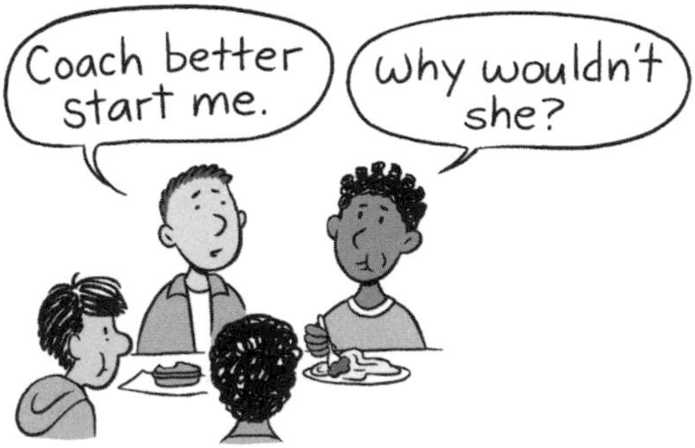
Coach better start me.
Why wouldn't she?

Remember? Last time I barely had a stupid cold, and she put Ryan Keiser in. He can't even dribble.

I could be *dead* and I'd still run circles around him.

Not starting is the worst. I'd rather grow a third arm and burst into blue zits than not be in the starting lineup. I couldn't face my friends.

It'd be stupid not to put you in.

Well, you can bet I'm not gonna miss any practice. No way am I gonna chance it.

I'm starting to feel weird about meeting with Emmie. Maybe Ethan's right. I shouldn't chance it, even if it's just for half an hour. The comics project is cool, but this game is way more important, and it's in two weeks.

The bell rings.

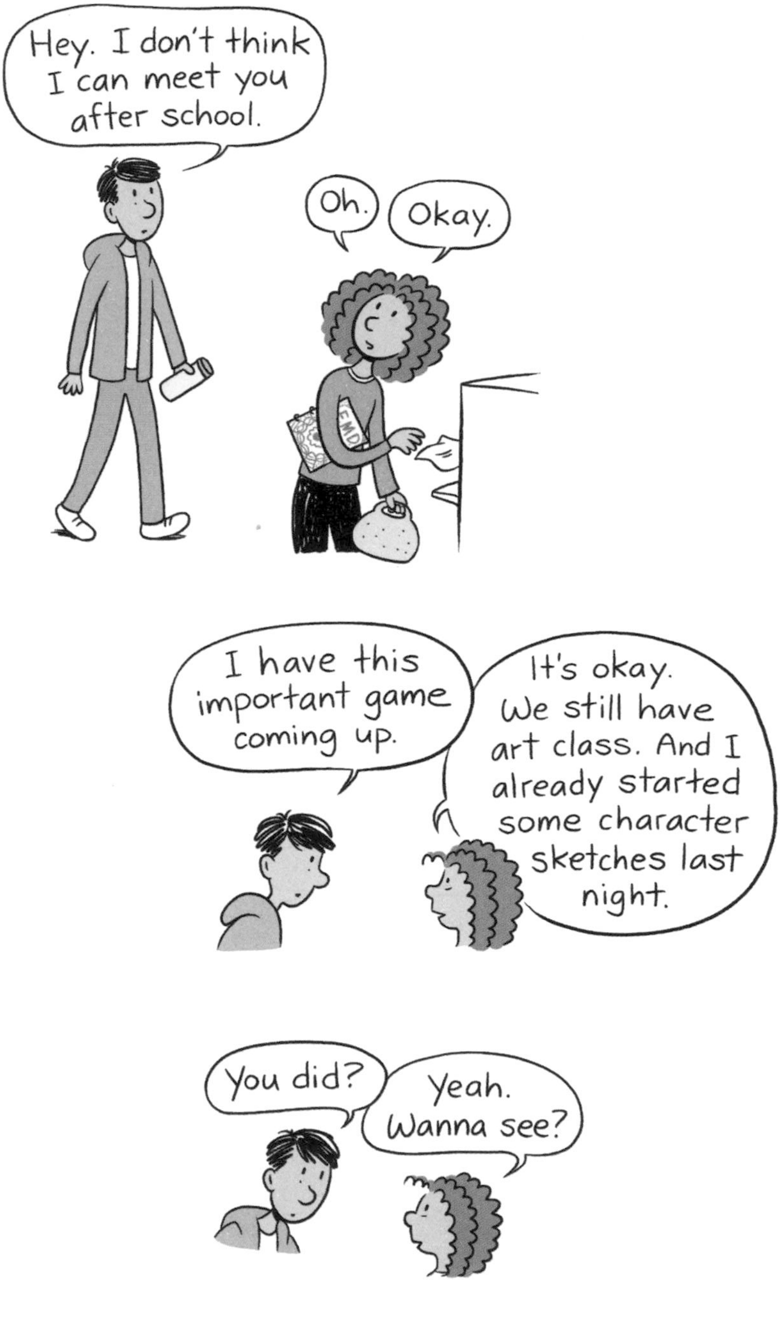
Hey. I don't think I can meet you after school.
Oh.
Okay.
I have this important game coming up.
It's okay. We still have art class. And I already started some character sketches last night.
You did?
Yeah. Wanna see?

She takes out her sketchbook (which she always has on her).

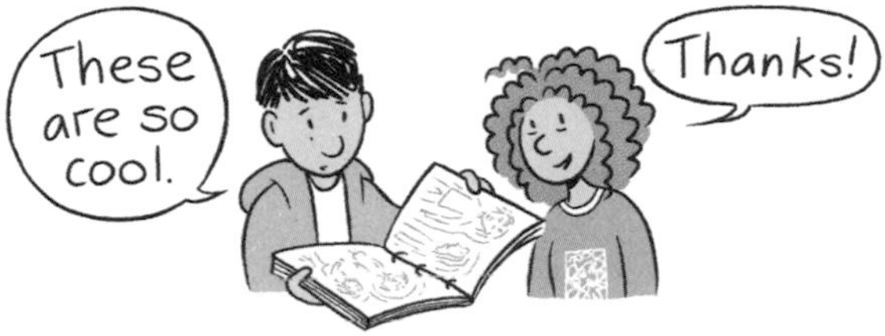
These are so cool.
Thanks!

I get a lump in my throat. Emmie's sketches are really good, and she's already farther along than me. There won't be enough time to draw **and** start writing our comic story in art.

Also, I just wanna work on this. Her drawings are totally motivating. We can win the art prize!

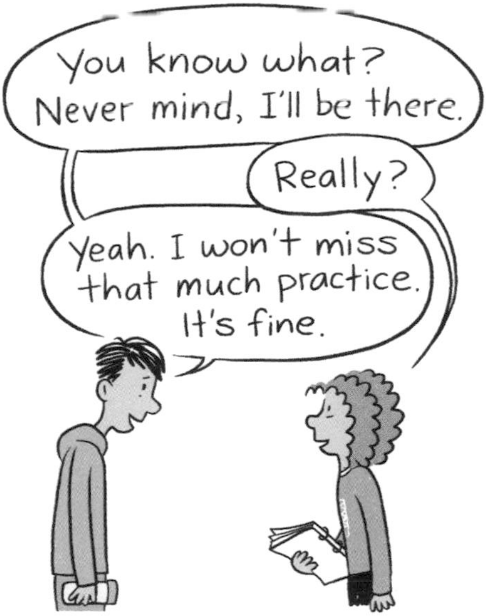
You know what? Never mind, I'll be there.
Really?
Yeah. I won't miss that much practice. It's fine.

She looks so happy.

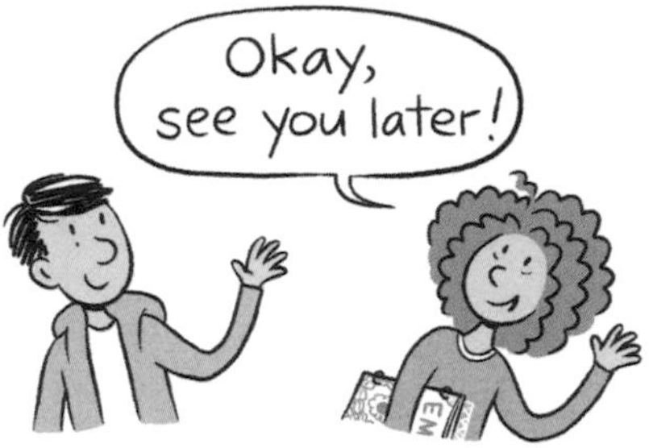
Okay, see you later!

We separate just as Joe and Anthony come up.

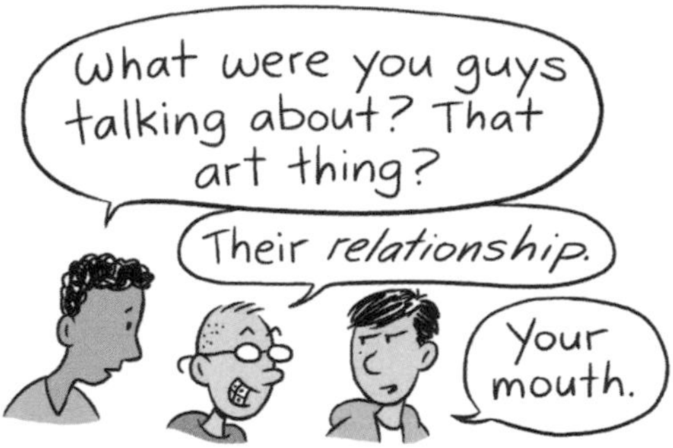
What were you guys talking about? That art thing?
Their *relationship.*
Your mouth.

We head out at the same time as Celia and her posse. Once again, she looks at me and then at Emmie. And grins wickedly.

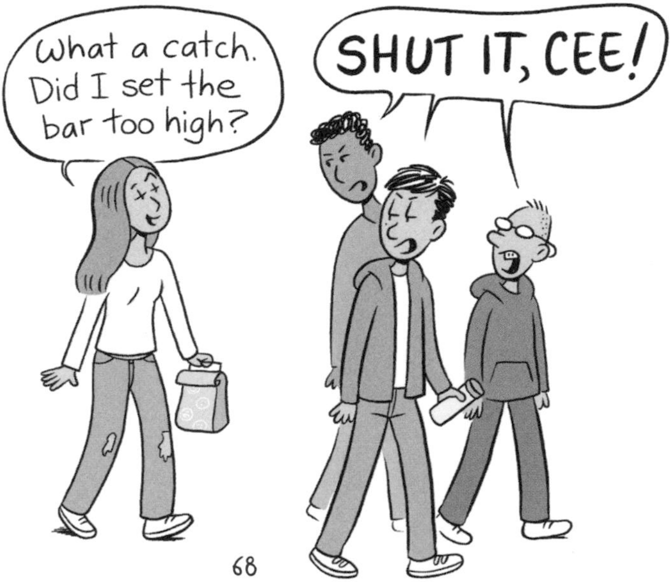
What a catch. Did I set the bar too high?
SHUT IT, CEE!

It's one thing for me to say stuff.

She gives us an epic eye roll and heads off with her giggling band of followers.

The second bell rings, which gets us moving. Joe and I are gonna be late for band. We both play trumpet (badly).

See ya at practice... a little late.

Ethan's right. Don't miss too much. Stakes are high.

I won't.

And I mean it.

Up in the ATTIC

by Emmie Douglass & Tyler Ross

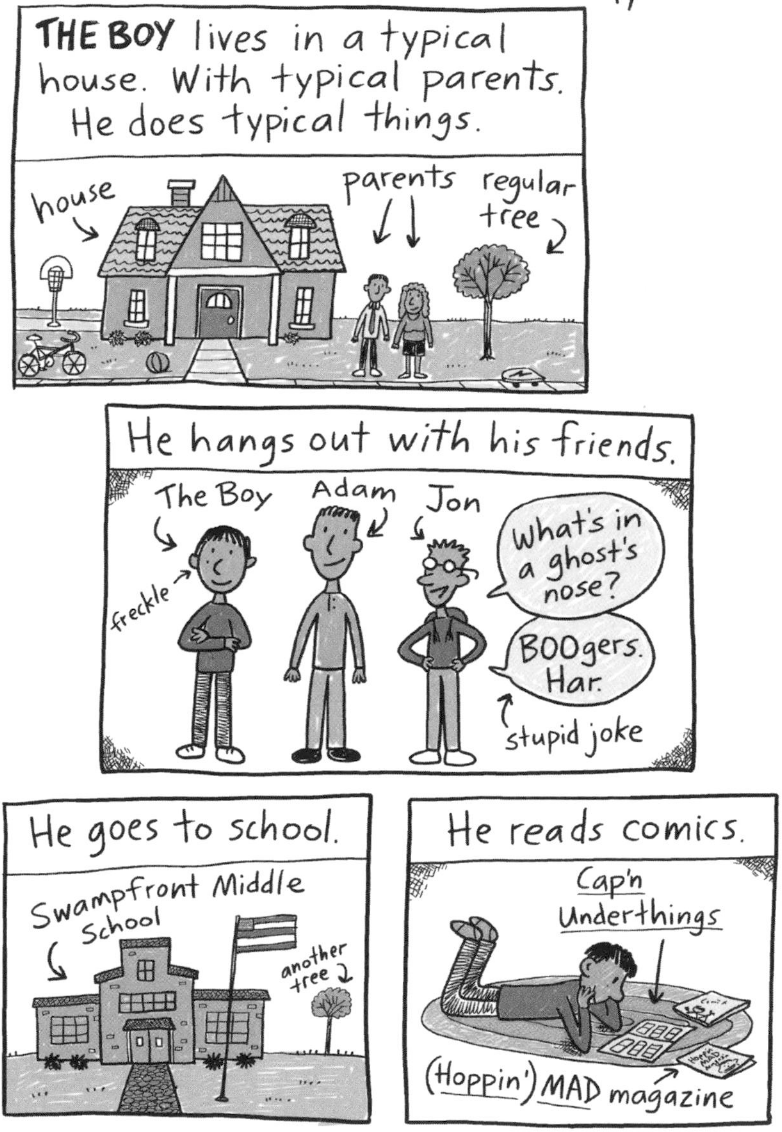
THE BOY lives in a typical house. With typical parents. He does typical things.
house
parents
regular tree
He hangs out with his friends.
The Boy
Adam
Jon
freckle
What's in a ghost's nose?
BOOgers. Har.
stupid joke
He goes to school.
Swampfront Middle School
another tree
He reads comics.
Cap'n Underthings
(Hoppin') MAD magazine

BUT...

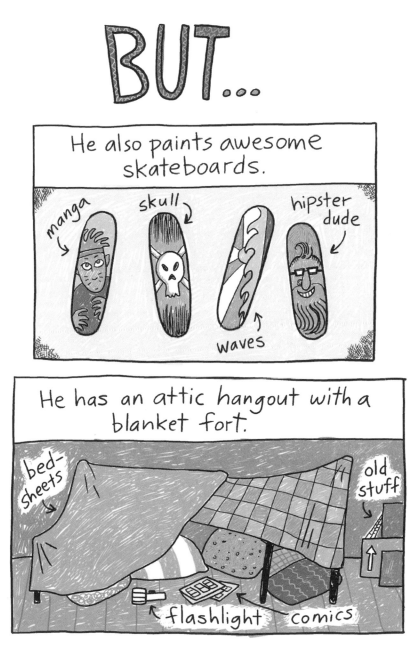

He also paints awesome skateboards.

manga

skull

hipster dude

waves

He has an attic hangout with a blanket fort.

bed-sheets

old stuff

flashlight

comics

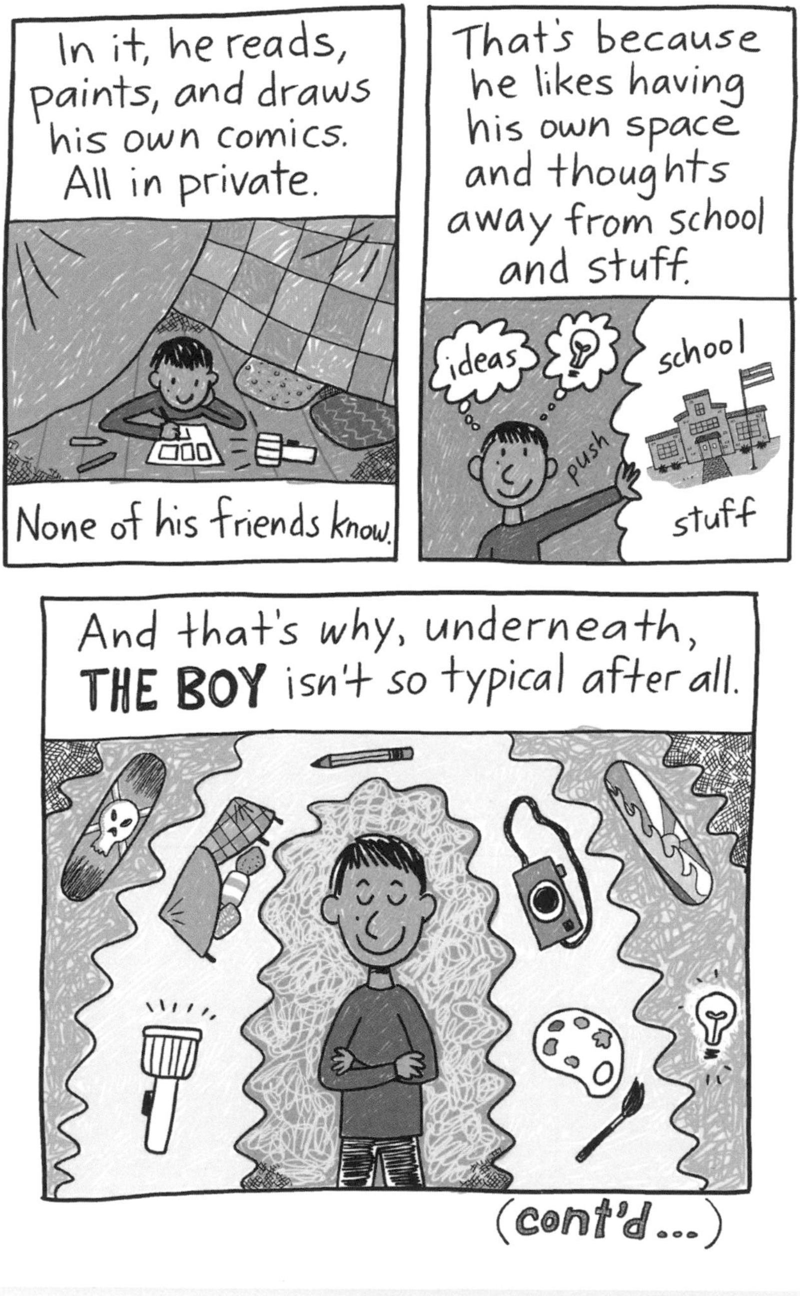
In it, he reads, paints, and draws his own comics. All in private.
None of his friends know.
That's because he likes having his own space and thoughts away from school and stuff.
ideas
school
push
stuff
And that's why, underneath, **THE BOY** isn't so typical after all.
(cont'd...)

Emmie

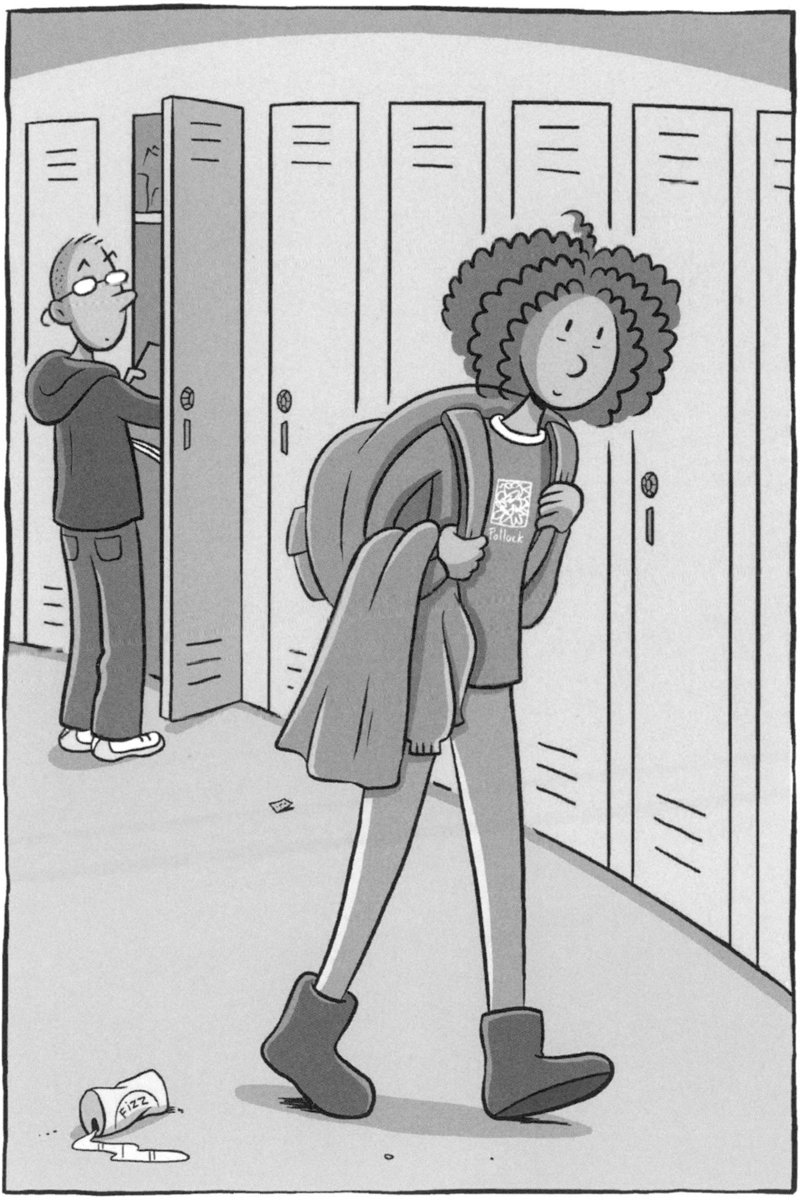
Pollock
Fizz

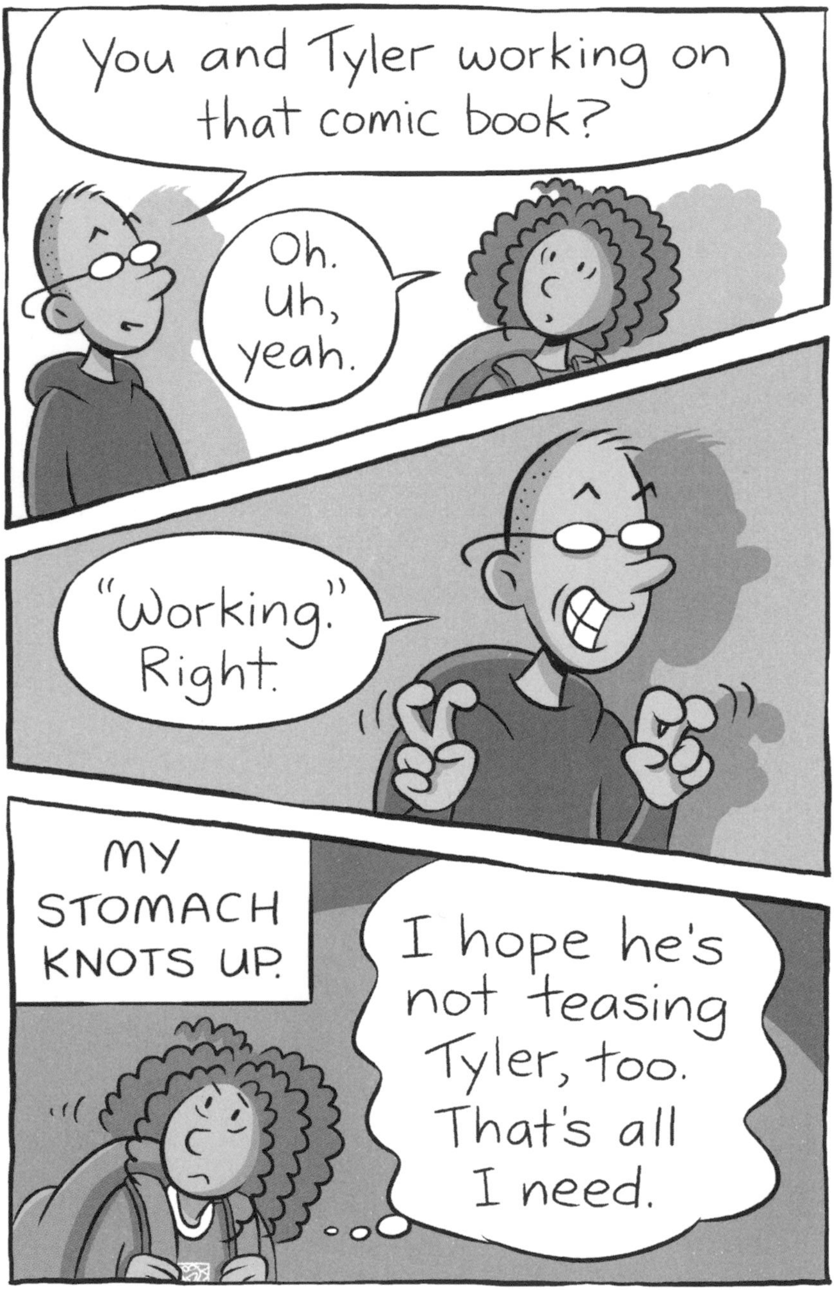
You and Tyler working on that comic book?
Oh. Uh, yeah.
"Working." Right.
MY STOMACH KNOTS UP.
I hope he's not teasing Tyler, too. That's all I need.

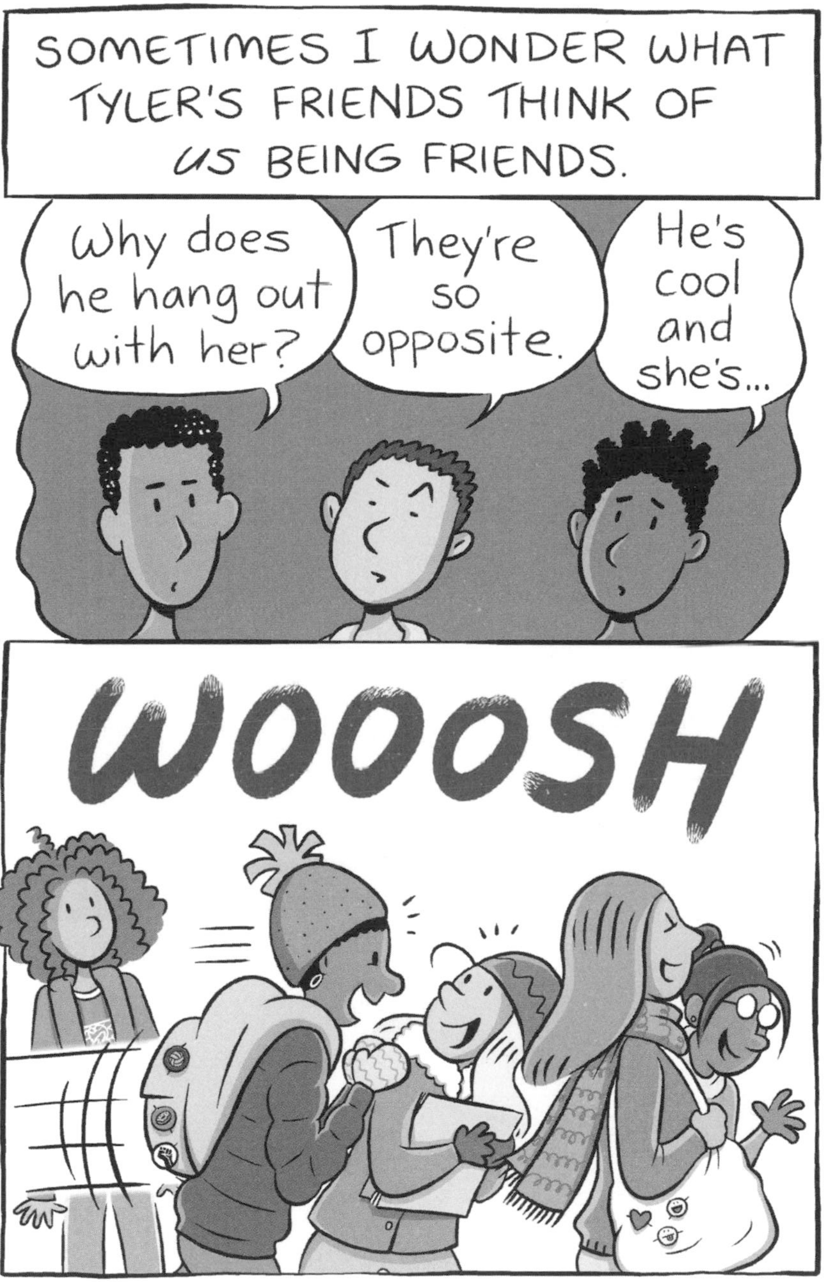
SOMETIMES I WONDER WHAT TYLER'S FRIENDS THINK OF *US* BEING FRIENDS.
Why does he hang out with her?
They're so opposite.
He's cool and she's...
WOOOSH

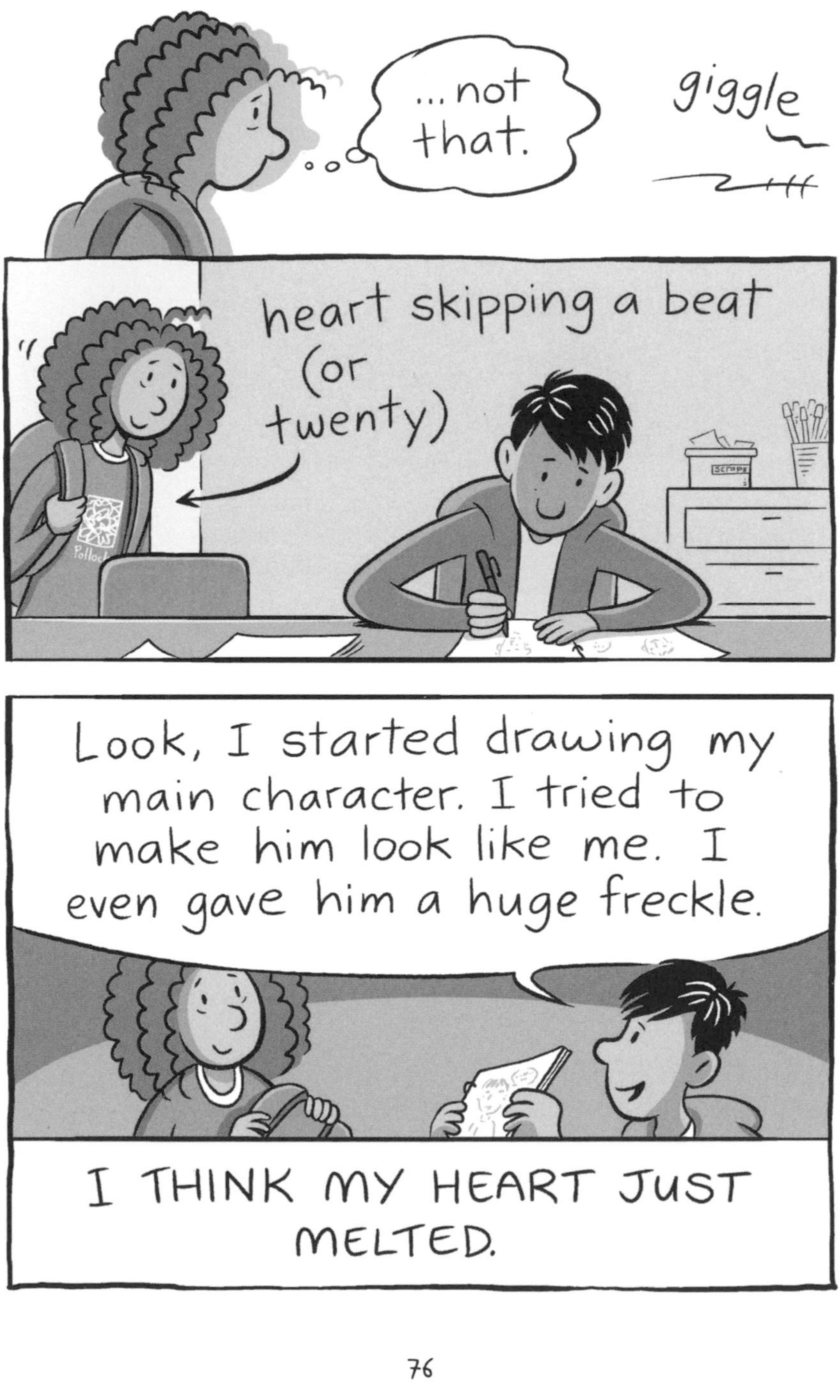
...not
that.
giggle
heart skipping a beat
(or
twenty)
Look, I started drawing my main character. I tried to make him look like me. I even gave him a huge freckle.
I THINK MY HEART JUST MELTED.

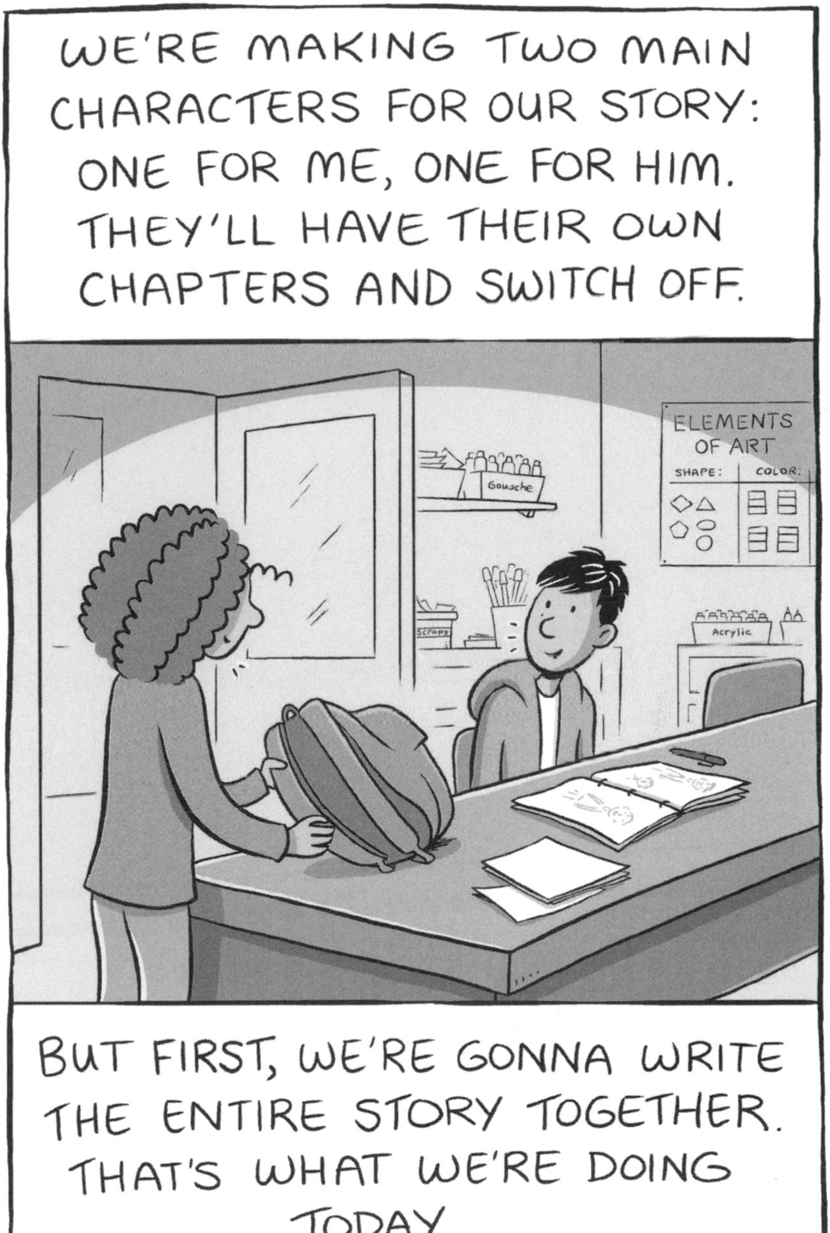
WE'RE MAKING TWO MAIN CHARACTERS FOR OUR STORY: ONE FOR ME, ONE FOR HIM. THEY'LL HAVE THEIR OWN CHAPTERS AND SWITCH OFF.
ELEMENTS OF ART
SHAPE:
COLOR:
Gouache
Scraps
Acrylic
BUT FIRST, WE'RE GONNA WRITE THE ENTIRE STORY TOGETHER. THAT'S WHAT WE'RE DOING TODAY.

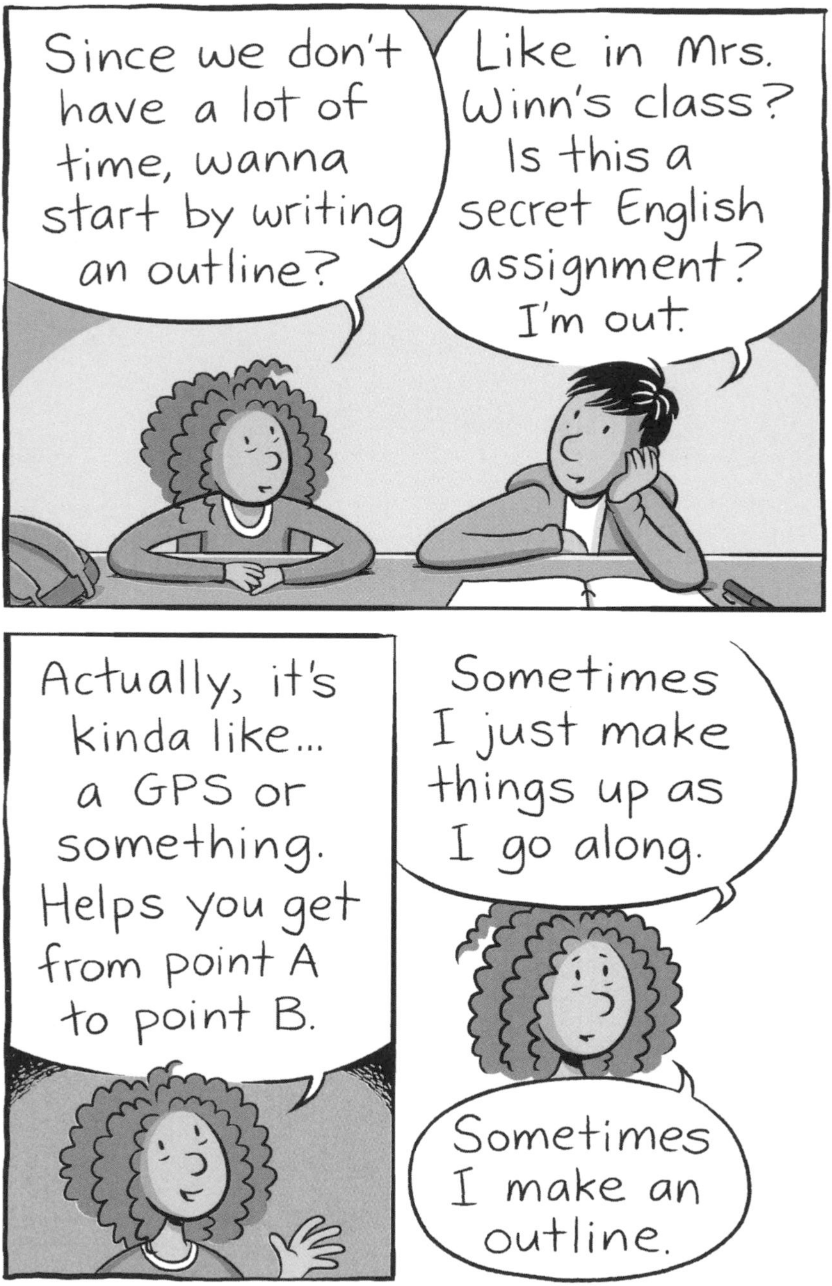
Since we don't have a lot of time, wanna start by writing an outline?
Like in Mrs. Winn's class? Is this a secret English assignment? I'm out.
Actually, it's kinda like... a GPS or something. Helps you get from point A to point B.
Sometimes I just make things up as I go along.
Sometimes I make an outline.

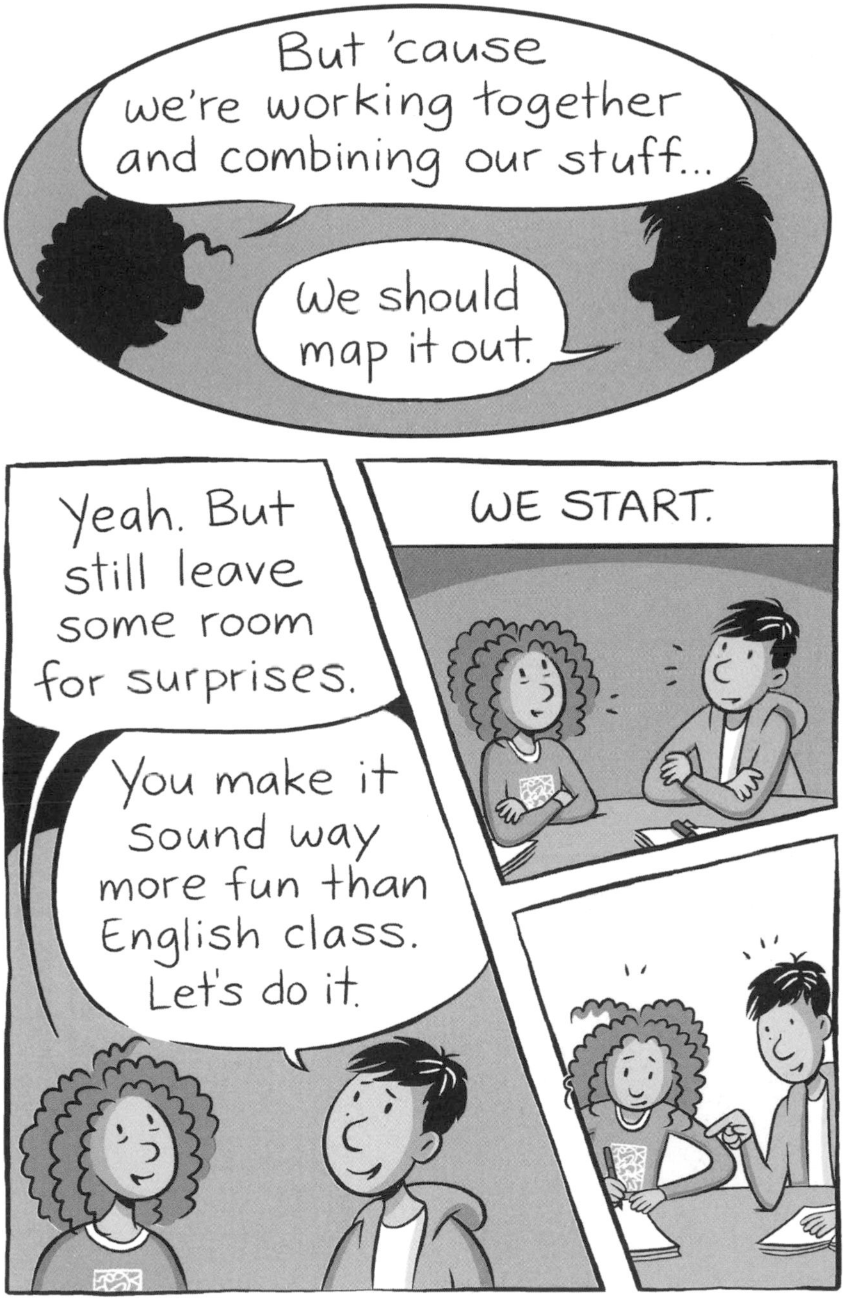
But 'cause we're working together and combining our stuff...
We should map it out.
Yeah. But still leave some room for surprises.
You make it sound way more fun than English class. Let's do it.
WE START.

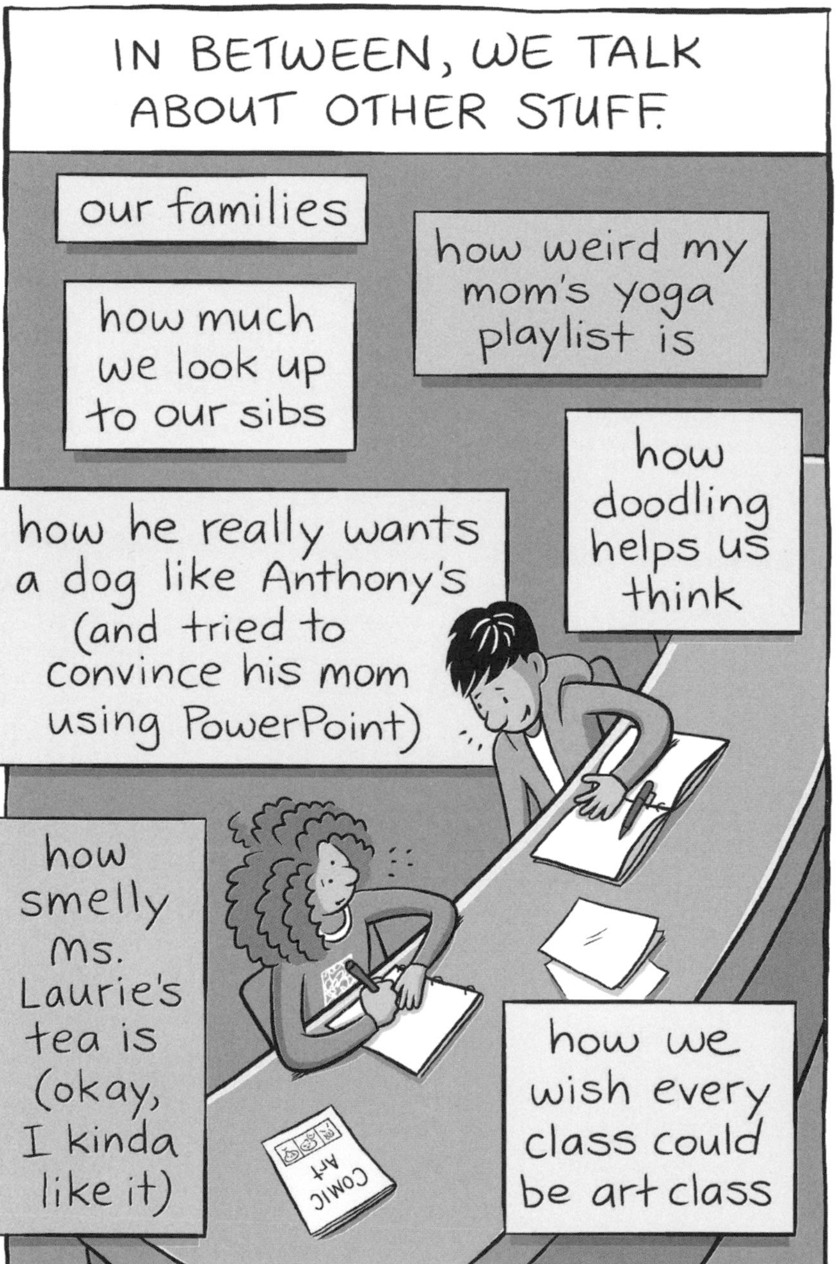
IN BETWEEN, WE TALK ABOUT OTHER STUFF.
our families
how weird my mom's yoga playlist is
how much we look up to our sibs
how doodling helps us think
how he really wants a dog like Anthony's (and tried to convince his mom using PowerPoint)
how smelly Ms. Laurie's tea is (okay, I kinda like it)
how we wish every class could be art class
COMIC Art

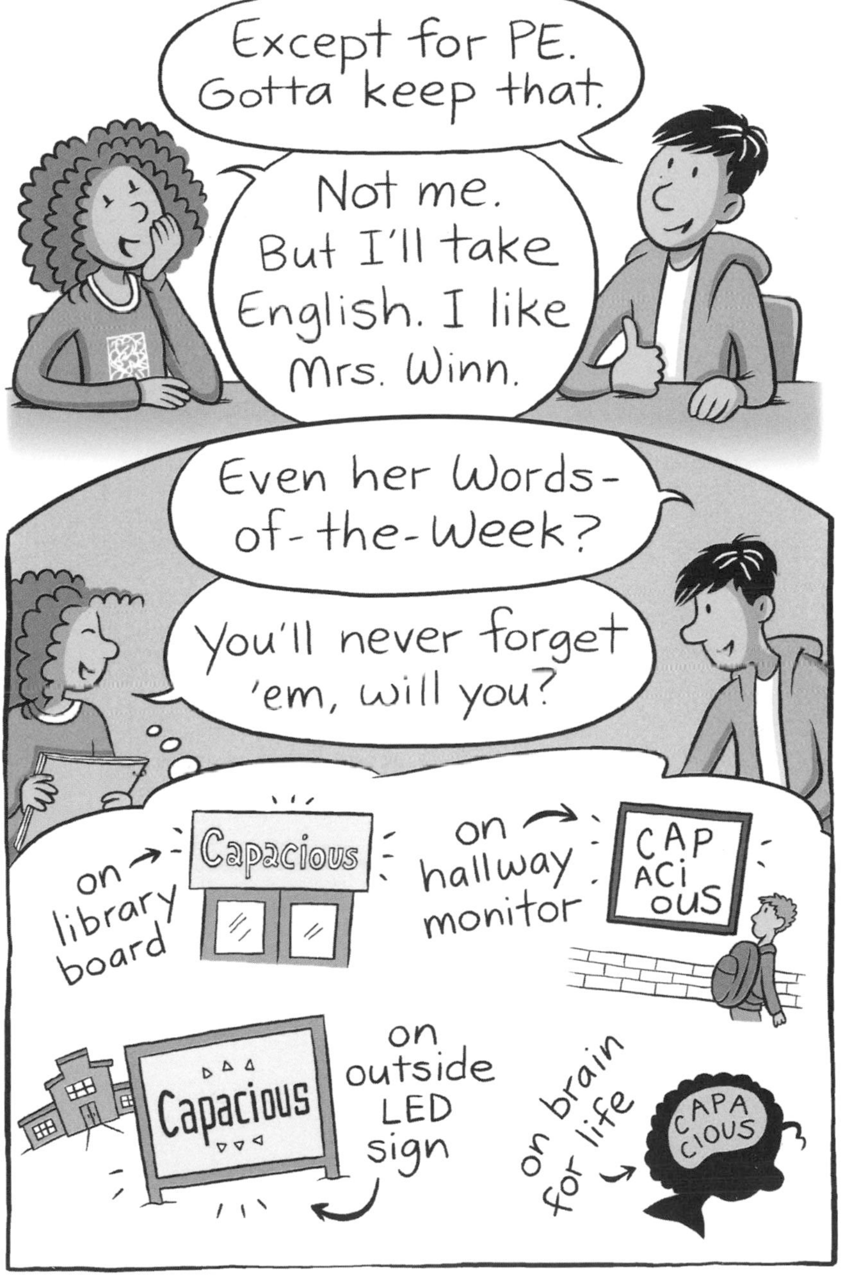

Except for PE. Gotta keep that.
Not me. But I'll take English. I like Mrs. Winn.
Even her Words-of-the-Week?
You'll never forget 'em, will you?
on library board
Capacious
on hallway monitor
CAP ACi OUS
Capacious
on outside LED sign
on brain for life
CAPA CIOUS

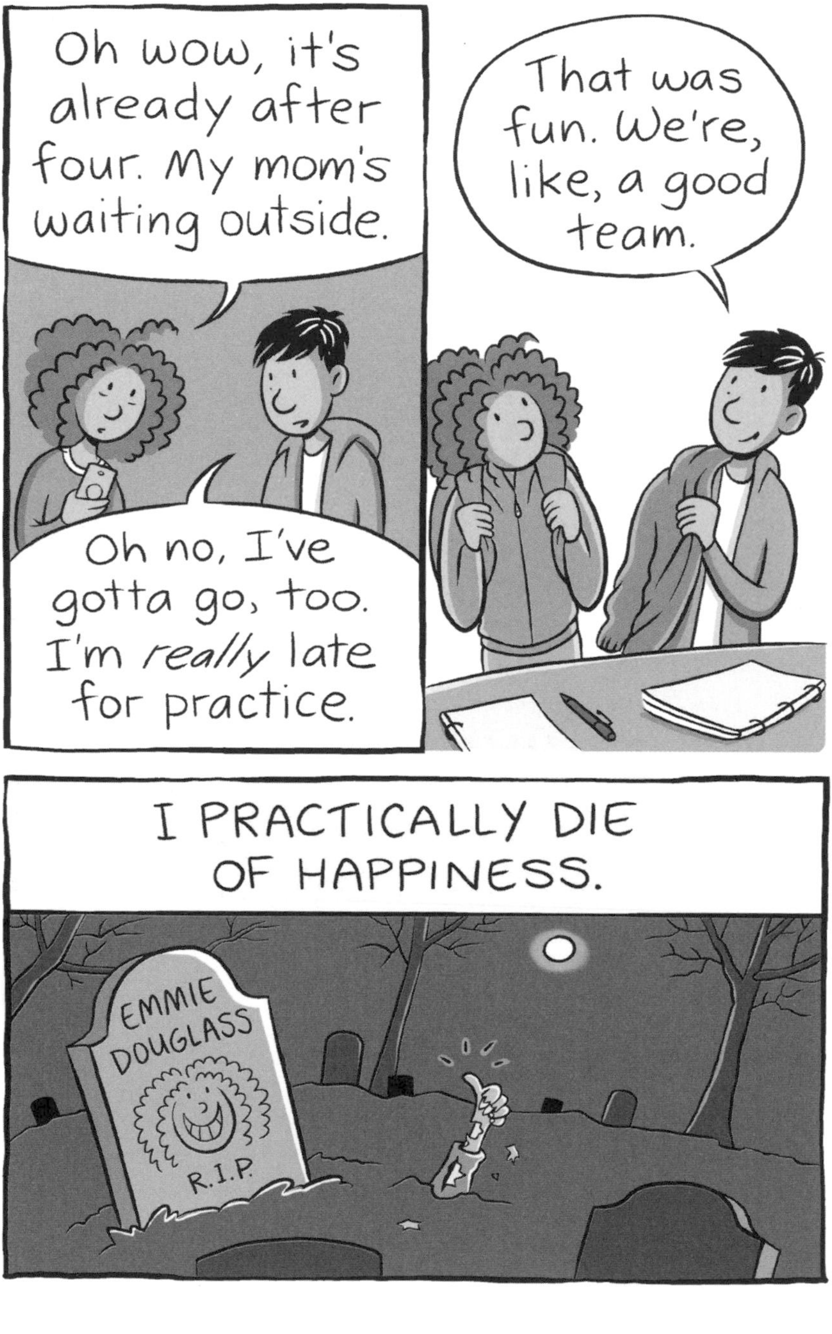
Oh wow, it's already after four. My mom's waiting outside.
Oh no, I've gotta go, too. I'm *really* late for practice.
That was fun. We're, like, a good team.
I PRACTICALLY DIE OF HAPPINESS.
EMMIE DOUGLASS
R.I.P.

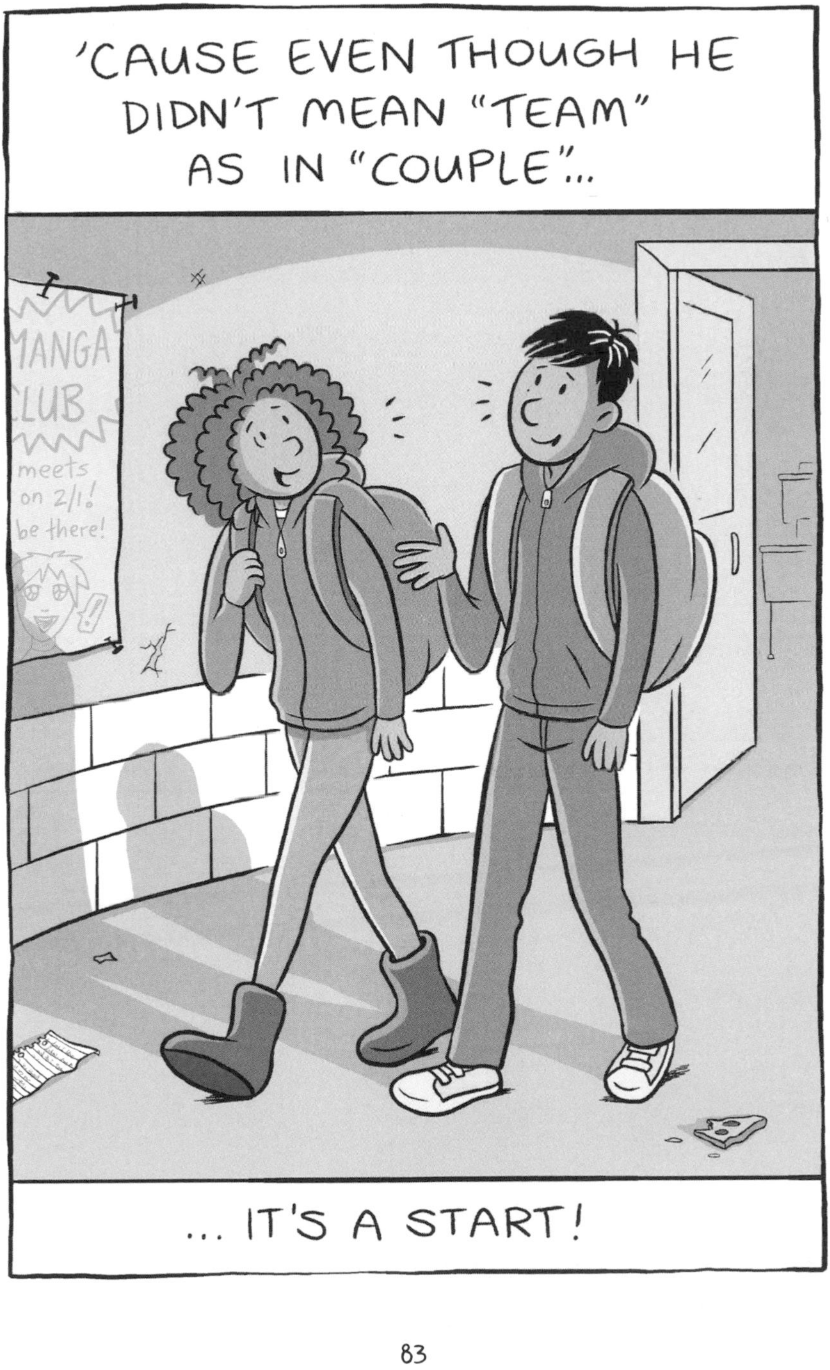
'CAUSE EVEN THOUGH HE DIDN'T MEAN "TEAM" AS IN "COUPLE"...
meets on 2/1! be there!
... IT'S A START!

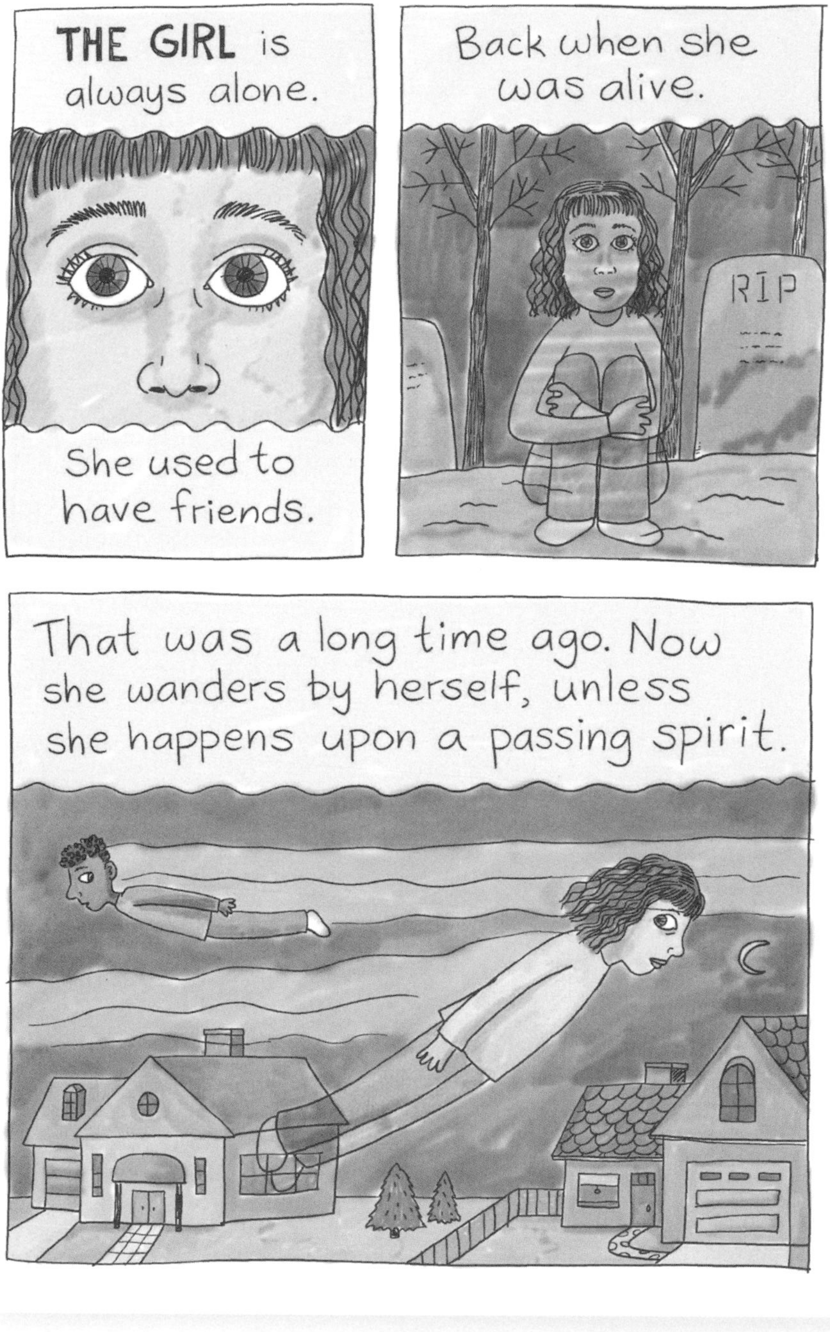
THE GIRL is always alone.
She used to have friends.
Back when she was alive.
RIP
That was a long time ago. Now she wanders by herself, unless she happens upon a passing spirit.

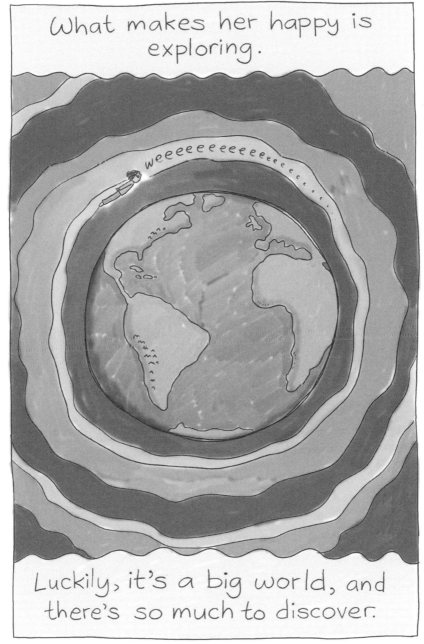

What makes her happy is exploring.

weeeeeeeeeeeeeeeeeeee

Luckily, it's a big world, and there's so much to discover.

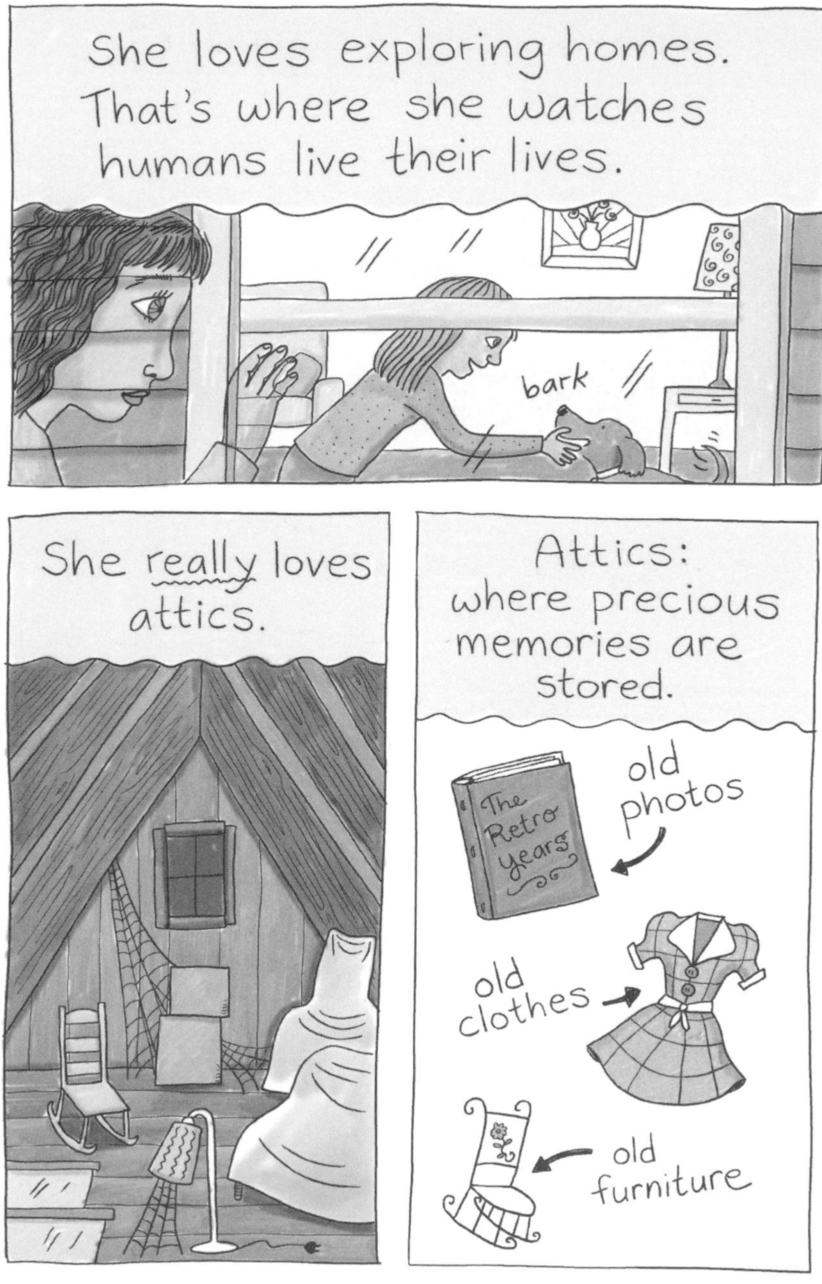
She loves exploring homes. That's where she watches humans live their lives.
bark
She really loves attics.
Attics: where precious memories are stored.
The Retro years
old photos
old clothes
old furniture

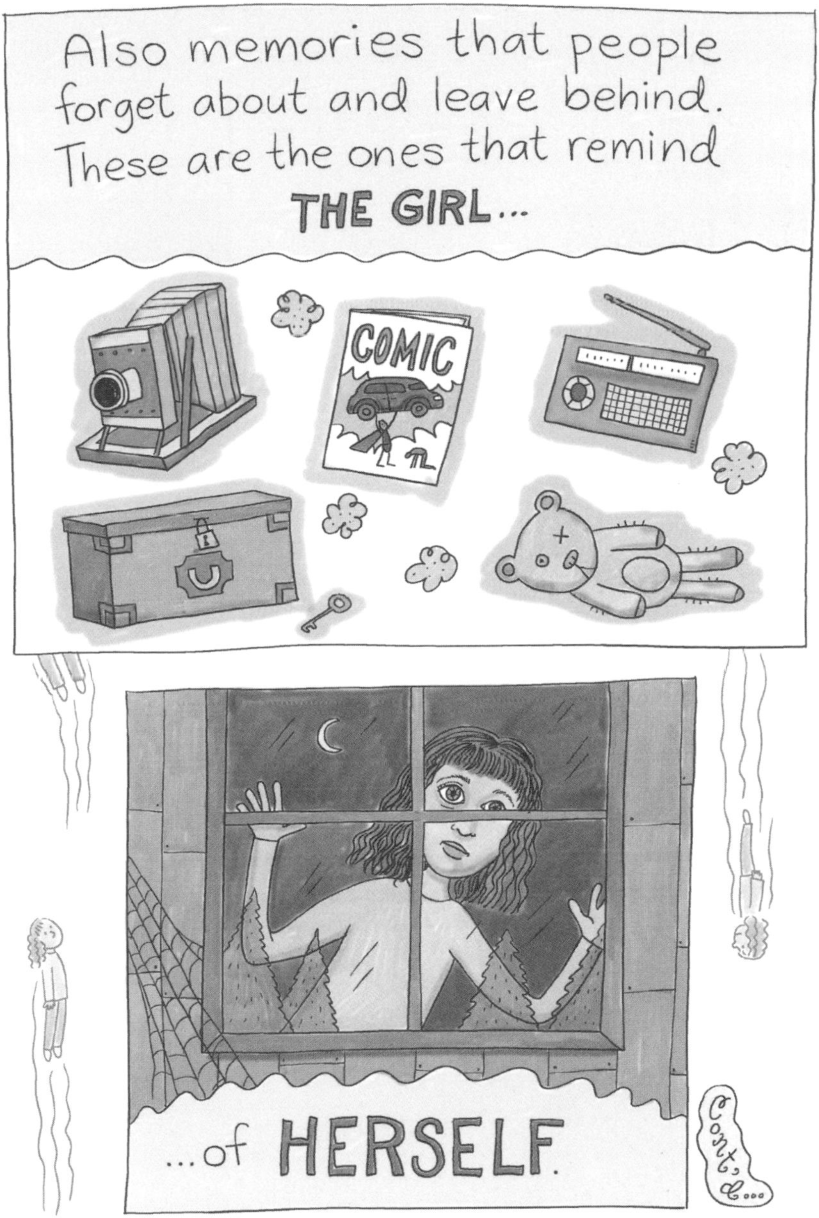

Also memories that people forget about and leave behind. These are the ones that remind THE GIRL...
COMIC
...of HERSELF.
Cont'd...

TYLER

I'm sitting on my bed, sketching out a comics page (and avoiding all my other homework), when my phone goes off.

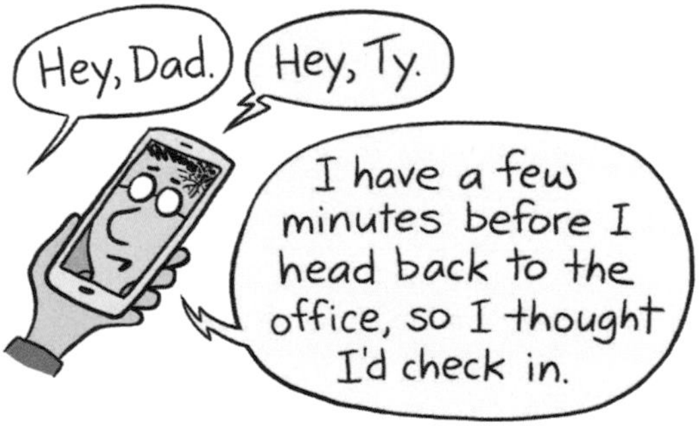
Hey, Dad.
Hey, Ty.
I have a few minutes before I head back to the office, so I thought I'd check in.

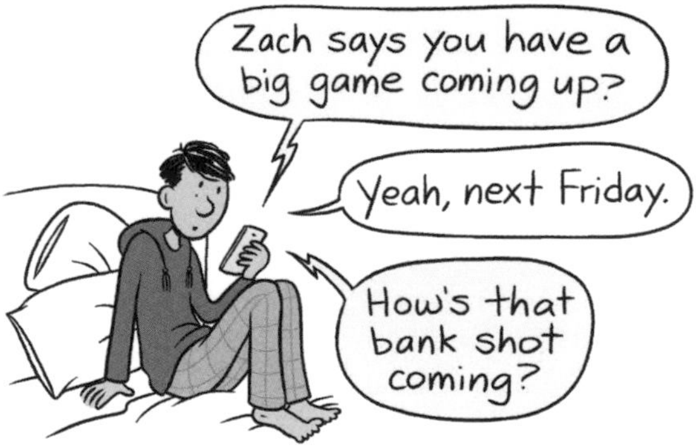
Zach says you have a big game coming up?
Yeah, next Friday.
How's that bank shot coming?

I can set my clock by this conversation. There's nothing more predictable.

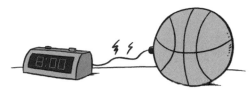

Still, I'm glad he called. He's pretty good about calling a lot, like a couple times a week. That's 'cause I don't get to see him much. Only during Thanksgiving and spring break. He lives far away, in Seattle. We used to visit during summers, but as we got older, Zach and I wanted to stay closer to home for sports camp and friends and stuff.

It's not like he has a lot of time for visits, anyway. My dad's a big-shot lawyer. He has a swanky condo downtown that he shares with his girlfriend, Michelle (another lawyer). She's okay, but it's obvious she's not that crazy about kids. Also, their place is really modern and not family friendly. The only decorations are some bizarre abstract paintings and expensive-looking, geometrical knickknacks. Crystal orbs and cubes.

yelled at me
for holding
orb

almost made me
drop it, ironically

Dad doesn't visit us much, either. He grew up in Seattle, and he barely has any ties left here. Just a few work friends and us.

The one thing he will do when we visit him is shoot hoops. He used to coach rec league—that's how Zach and I got hooked. Too bad Seattle isn't always the best place to play b-ball outside.

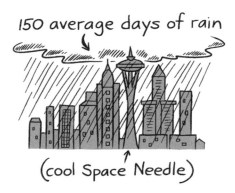

150 average days of rain

(cool Space Needle)

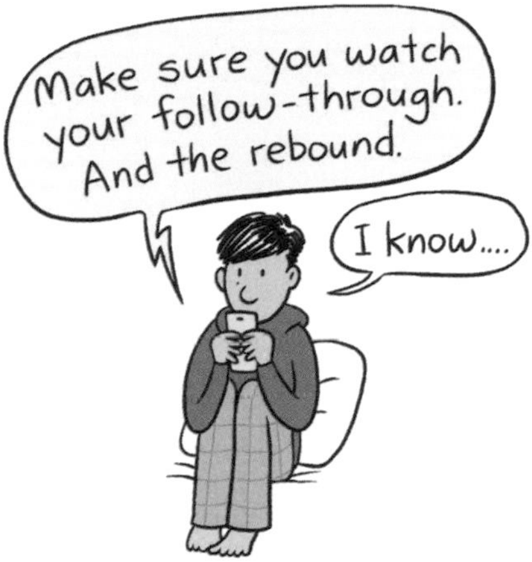
Make sure you watch your follow-through. And the rebound.
I know....

We talk a little more about the game, but I'm starting to get impatient. Which is a first. Usually I can talk hoops forever.

But I really wanna get back to drawing.

I'm about to make up an excuse when I hear Michelle in the background.

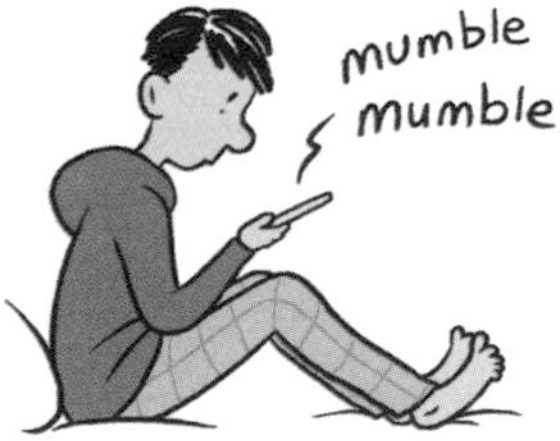
mumble mumble

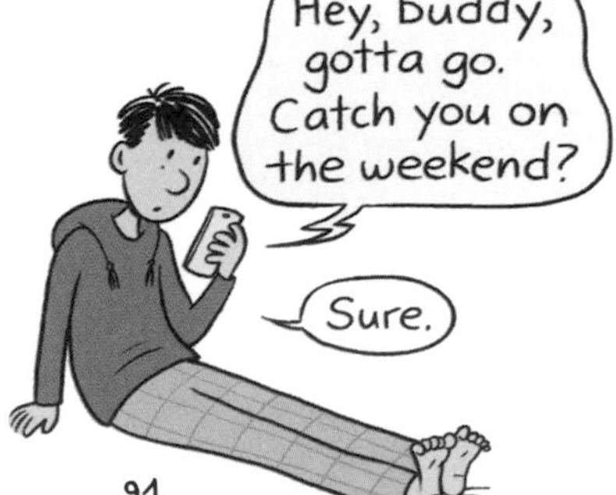
Hey, buddy, gotta go. Catch you on the weekend?
Sure.

Big surprise. I can't remember the last time Michelle didn't interrupt us. You'd think knowing how little my dad sees us, she'd be okay with our FaceTiming. I swear she butts into everything. Zach and I used to joke that she'd interrupt our weddings.

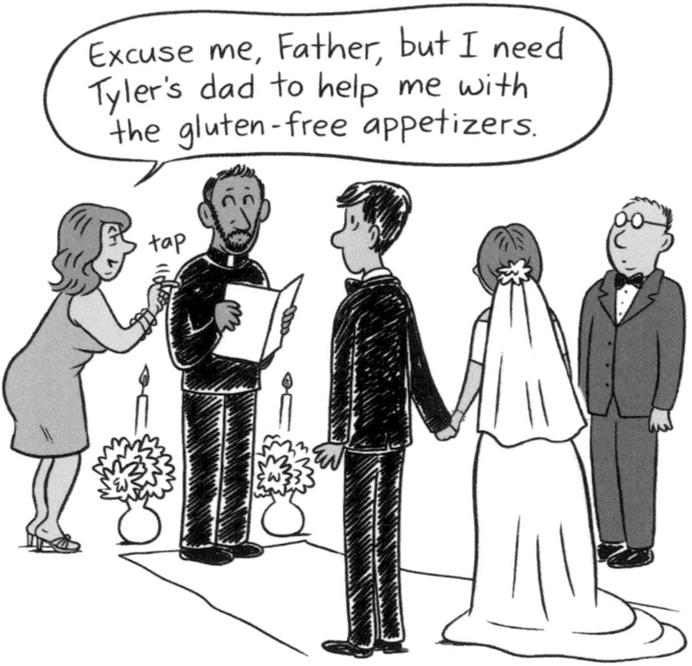
Excuse me, Father, but I need Tyler's dad to help me with the gluten-free appetizers.
tap

I shake it off. It could be worse. Michelle's not my favorite person, but (as my mom reminds us) she's no evil Disney stepmother.

Michelle and Disney stepmothers: a comparison

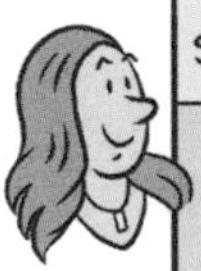

	MICHELLE	EVIL STEPMOM
cruel	✗	✓
wicked	✗	✓
dislikes kids	(ish)	✓
feeds kids poisoned apples	✗	✓
interrupts FaceTime	✓	✗

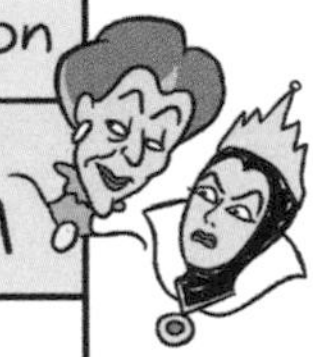

After I hang up, I reach for my sketchbook. That's when a huge rumbling almost makes me drop it. It's not an earthquake, though.

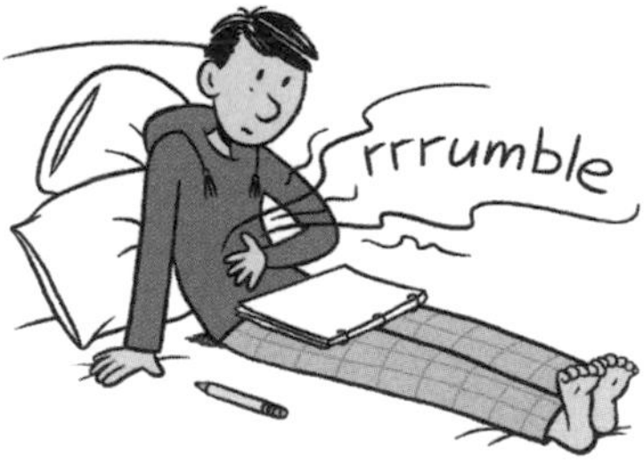
rrrumble

Time for my hundredth snack of the day. I head downstairs and make a beeline for the pantry. My mom is at the table, typing at her laptop and wearing her noise-canceling headphones.

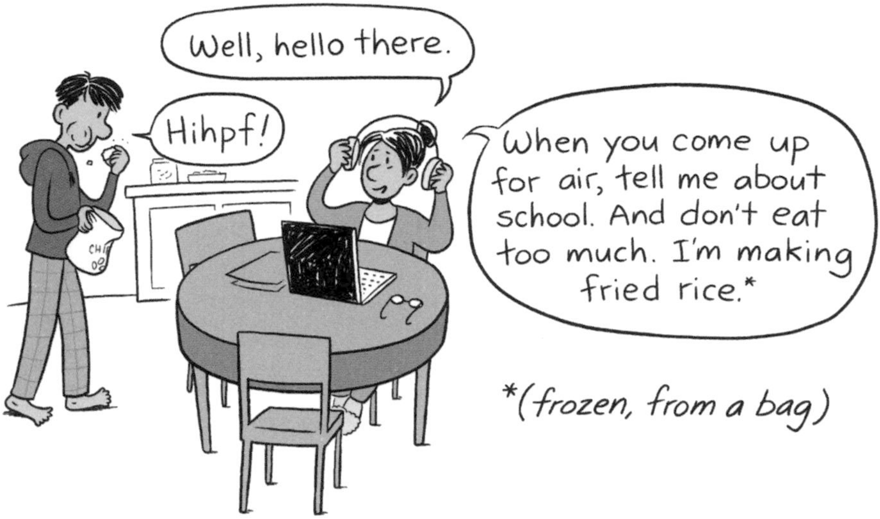
Well, hello there.
Hihpf!
When you come up for air, tell me about school. And don't eat too much. I'm making fried rice.*
*(frozen, from a bag)

I stop to take a breath. Ever since I turned thirteen, it feels like I can't get enough to eat. Like I need twenty bags of chips for every growing bone in my body.

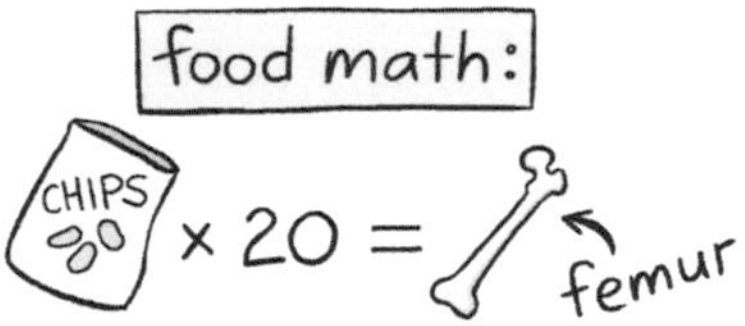
food math:
CHIPS
x 20 =
femur

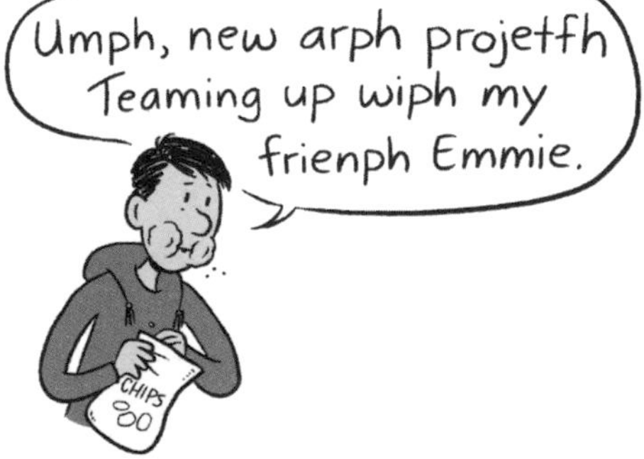
Umph, new arph projetfh Teaming up wiph my frienph Emmie.
CHIPS

Somehow, my mom has a knack for translating snack-speak.

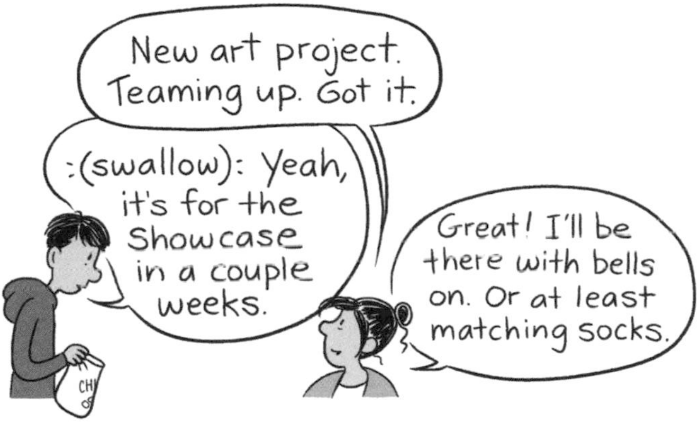
New art project. Teaming up. Got it.
:(swallow): Yeah, it's for the Showcase in a couple weeks.
Great! I'll be there with bells on. Or at least matching socks.

She jokes, but mismatched socks wouldn't be a surprise. My mom's a financial consultant. Outwardly, she's not very put-together (think: skirts and sneaks), but inwardly, she's really organized. She has to be. Even though she's busy and tired, she runs this house practically by herself.

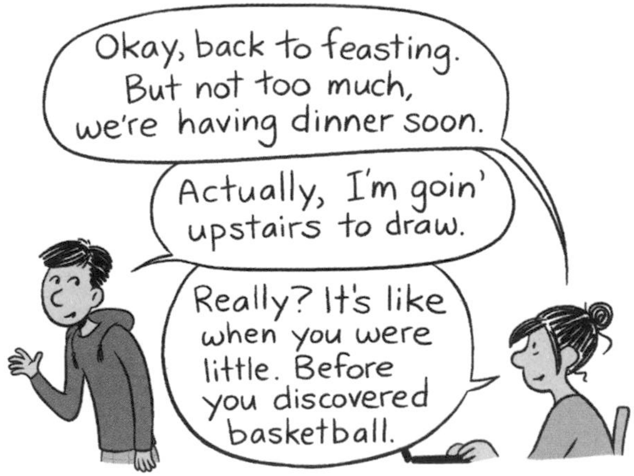
Okay, back to feasting. But not too much, we're having dinner soon.
Actually, I'm goin' upstairs to draw.
Really? It's like when you were little. Before you discovered basketball.

She's not wrong. As a little kid, all I did was draw. Just like Emmie. Getting back into it now, it feels like I never stopped.

Mom gives me a little Queen of England wave while I head upstairs. I can't help noticing she is wearing two different socks.

bass guitar wailing

chip crumbs

I consider knocking on Zach's door to say hi, but he'd probably throw his jar of picks at me. Zach doesn't like to be bothered when he's playing.

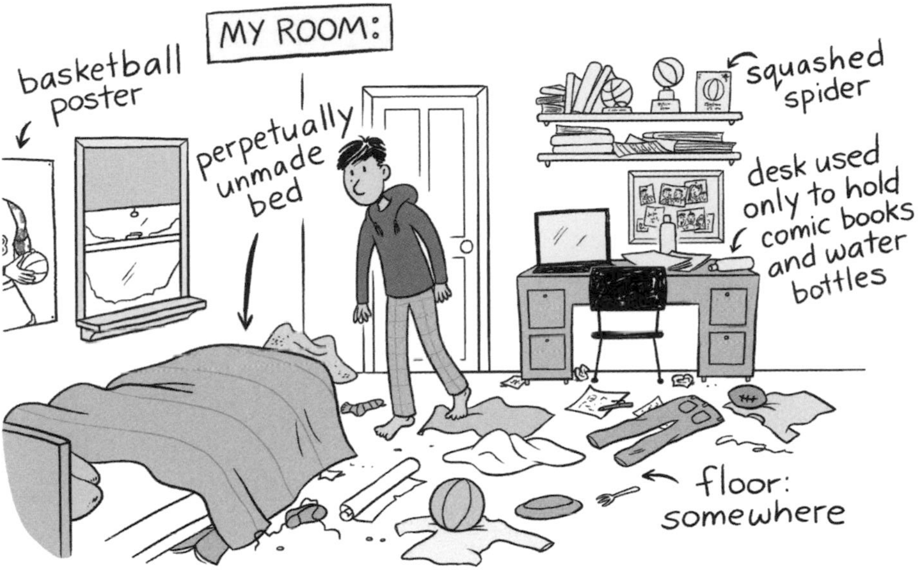
MY ROOM:
basketball poster
perpetually unmade bed
squashed spider
desk used only to hold comic books and water bottles
floor: somewhere

I take my sketchpad and plop on the bed. An eraser and some stray Skittles fly off. If my mom knew I had snacks up here, she'd kill me.

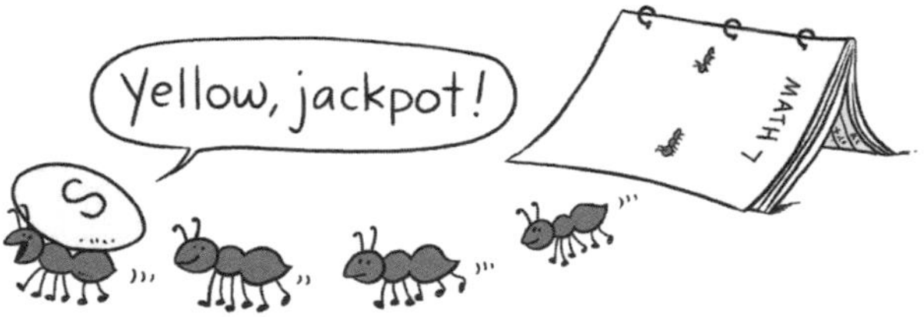
Yellow, jackpot!
S
MATH 7

I go back to sketching. I already have two-and-a-half pages done, which is something. I don't think I've ever been this hooked on a school project.

Too bad it's already caused me to be late to practice twice: once that first day after school with Emmie, and then again yesterday when I realized I left my sketchbook in the art room and needed (okay, wanted) to bring it home. I ended up thinking of a great idea right then and had to get it down before I forgot. Totally lost track of time.

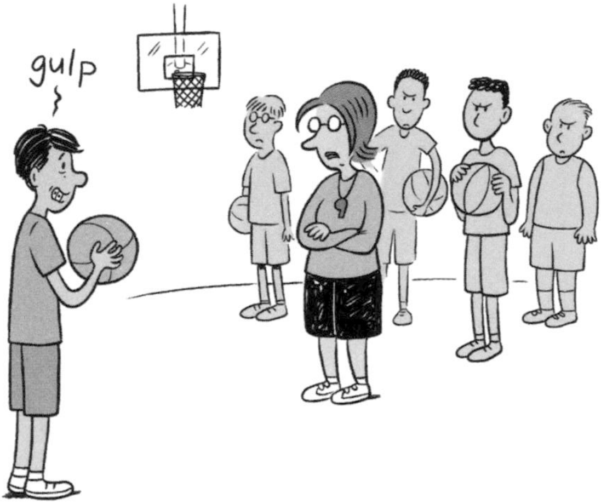
gulp

Anyway, I promised myself I wouldn't be late again. Ever. Especially if I wanna beat Valley Bottom. And make point guard in high school like a certain someone.

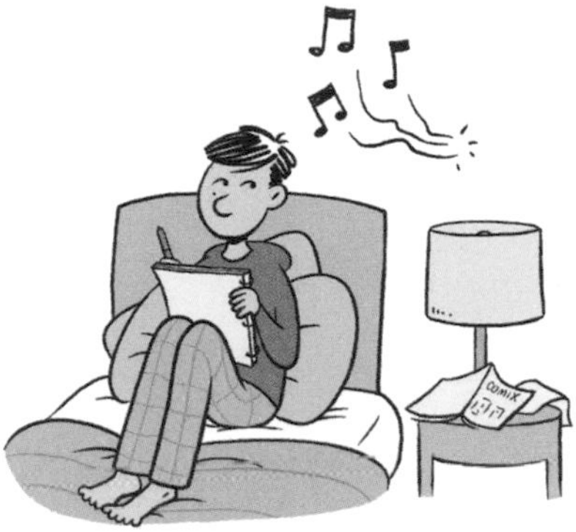
COMIX

Besides . . .

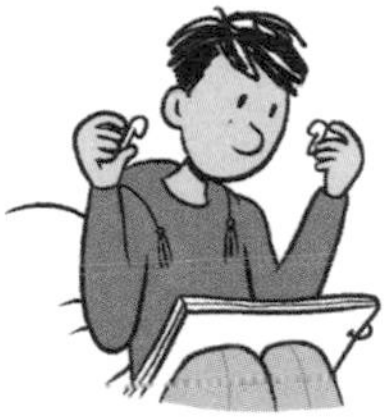

. . . it's not like this art project is gonna last forever.

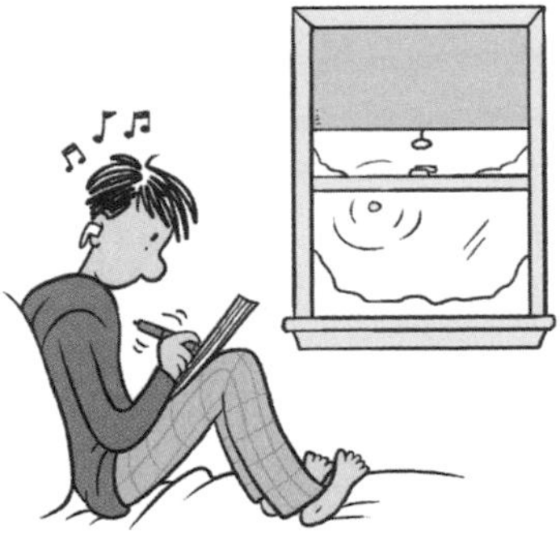

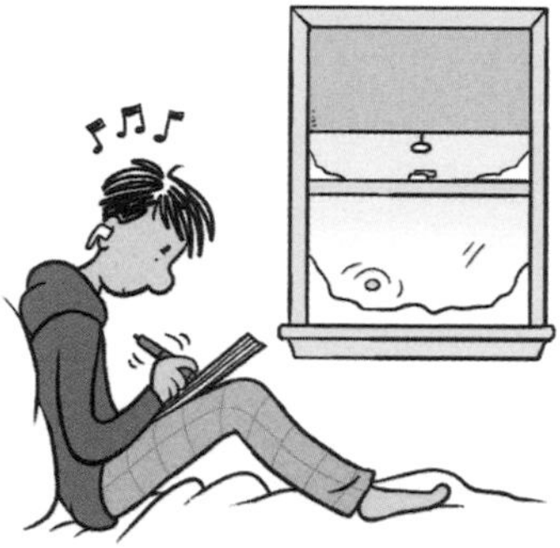

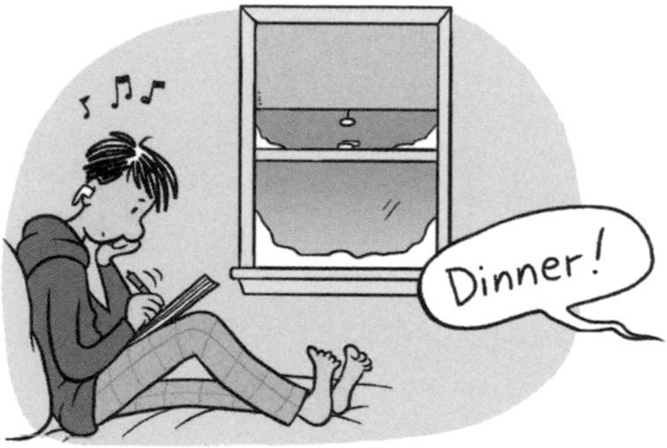
Dinner!

Emmie

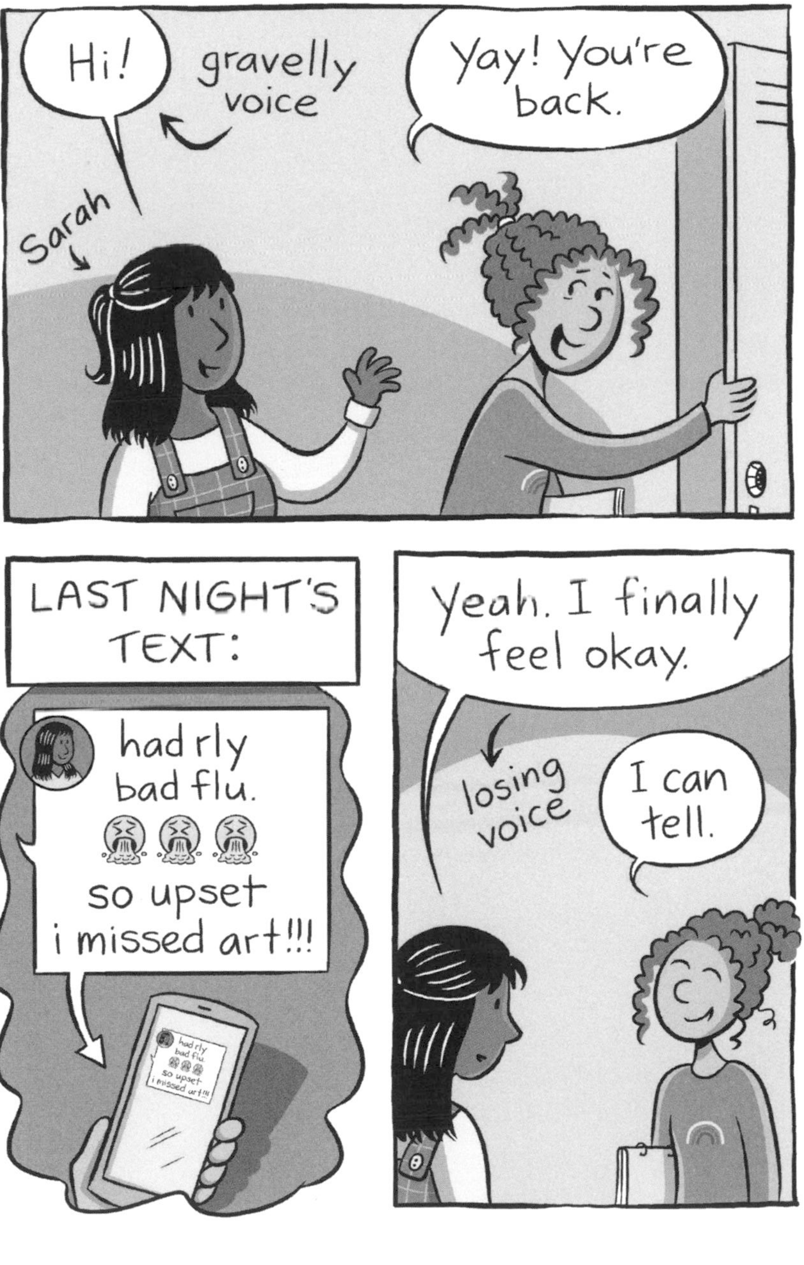
Hi!
gravelly voice
Sarah
Yay! You're back.
LAST NIGHT'S TEXT:
had rly bad flu.
so upset i missed art!!!
Yeah. I finally feel okay.
losing voice
I can tell.

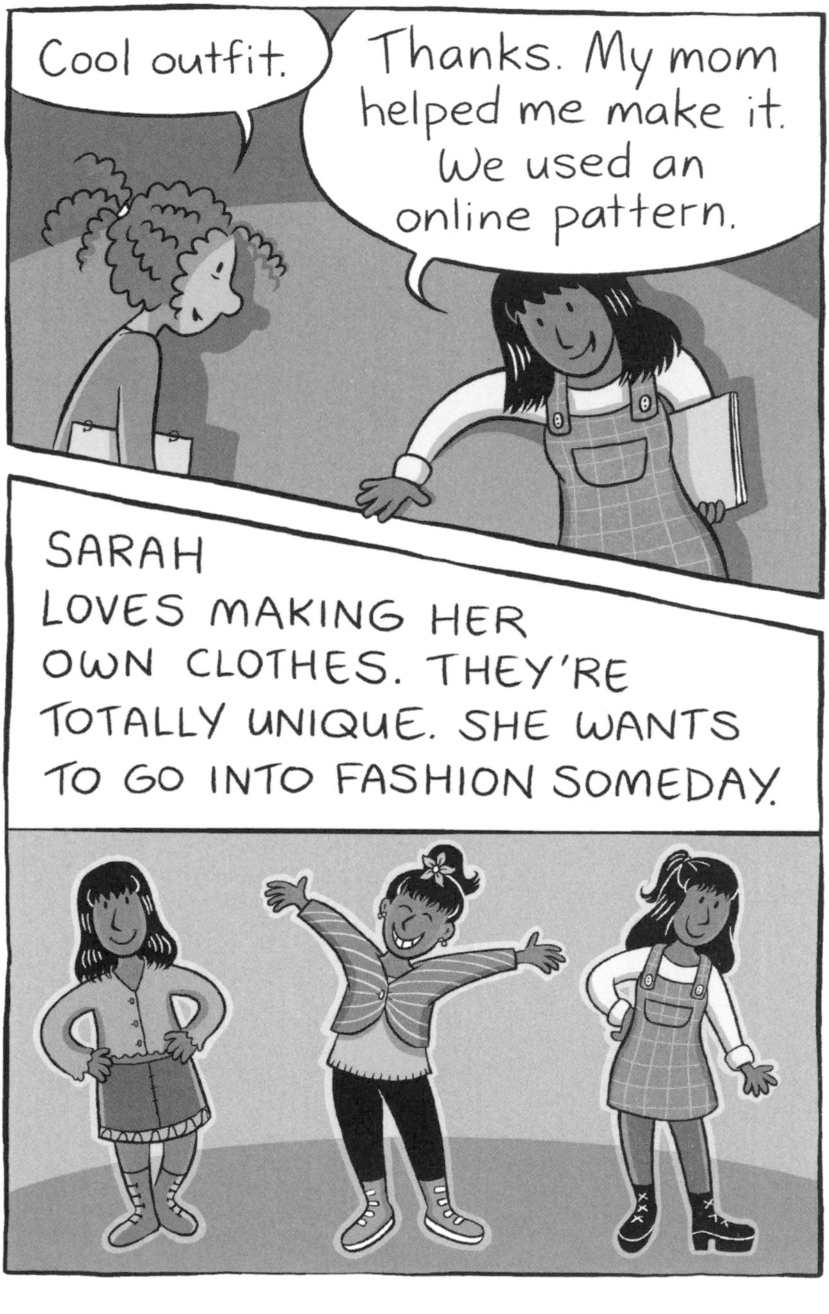
Cool outfit.
Thanks. My mom helped me make it. We used an online pattern.
SARAH
LOVES MAKING HER OWN CLOTHES. THEY'RE TOTALLY UNIQUE. SHE WANTS TO GO INTO FASHION SOMEDAY.

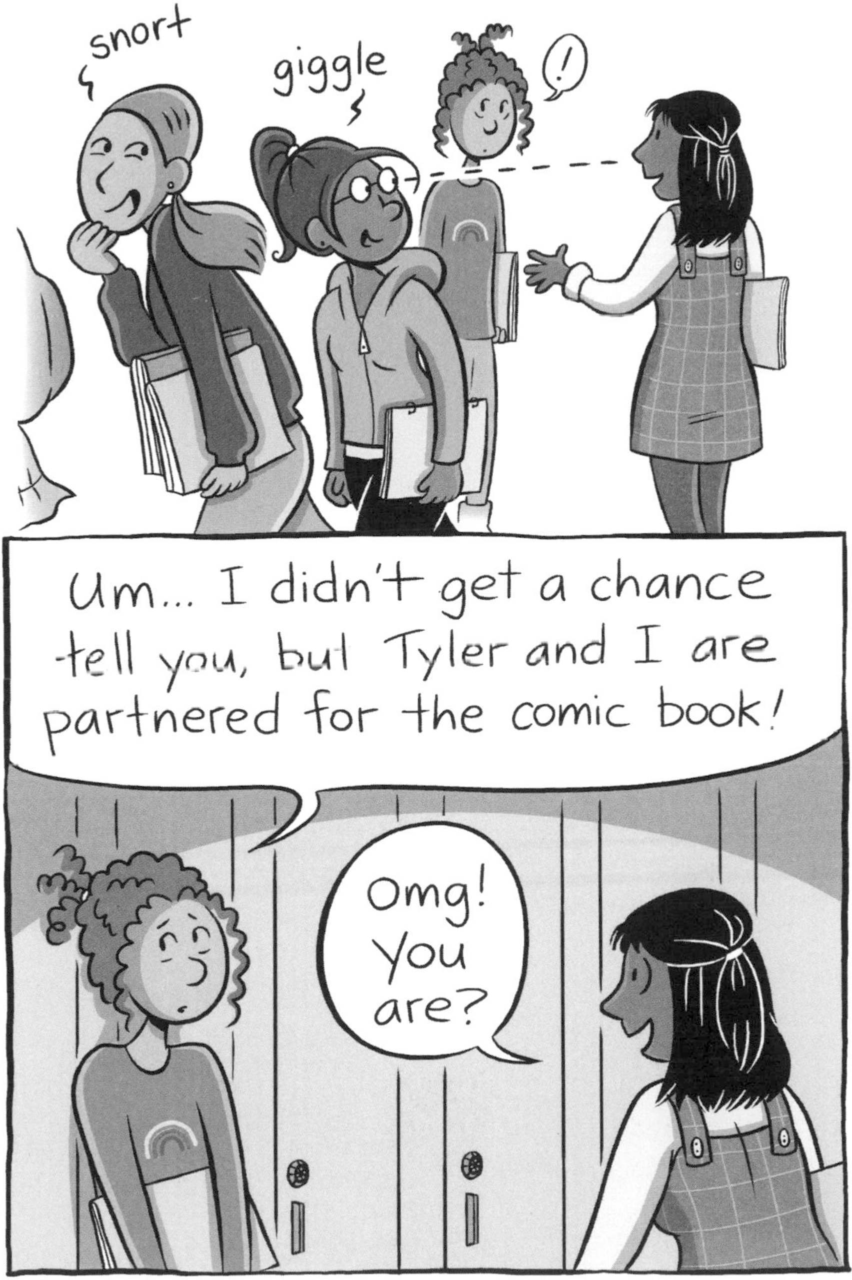
snort
giggle
!
Um... I didn't get a chance tell you, but Tyler and I are partnered for the comic book!
Omg! You are?

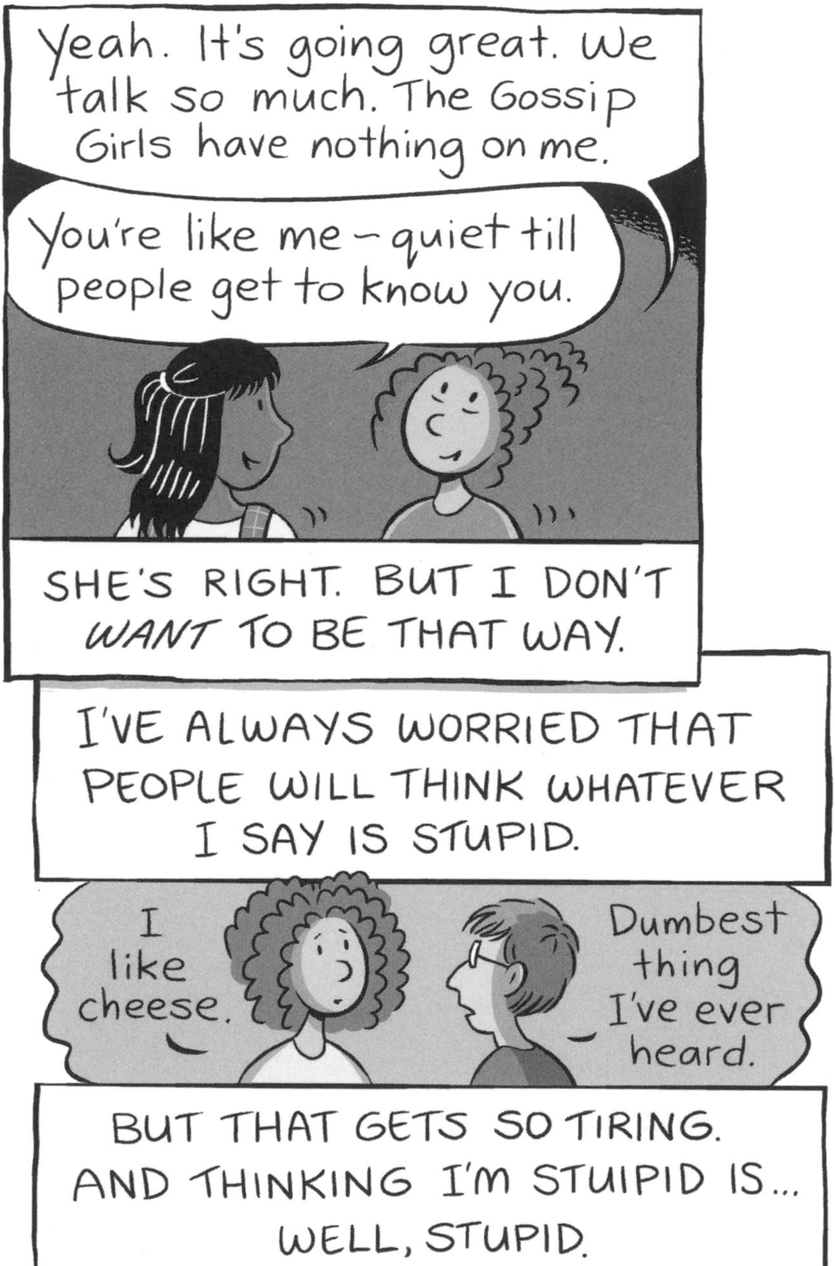
Yeah. It's going great. We talk so much. The Gossip Girls have nothing on me.
You're like me – quiet till people get to know you.
SHE'S RIGHT. BUT I DON'T *WANT* TO BE THAT WAY.
I'VE ALWAYS WORRIED THAT PEOPLE WILL THINK WHATEVER I SAY IS STUPID.
I like cheese.
Dumbest thing I've ever heard.
BUT THAT GETS SO TIRING. AND THINKING I'M STUIPID IS... WELL, STUPID.

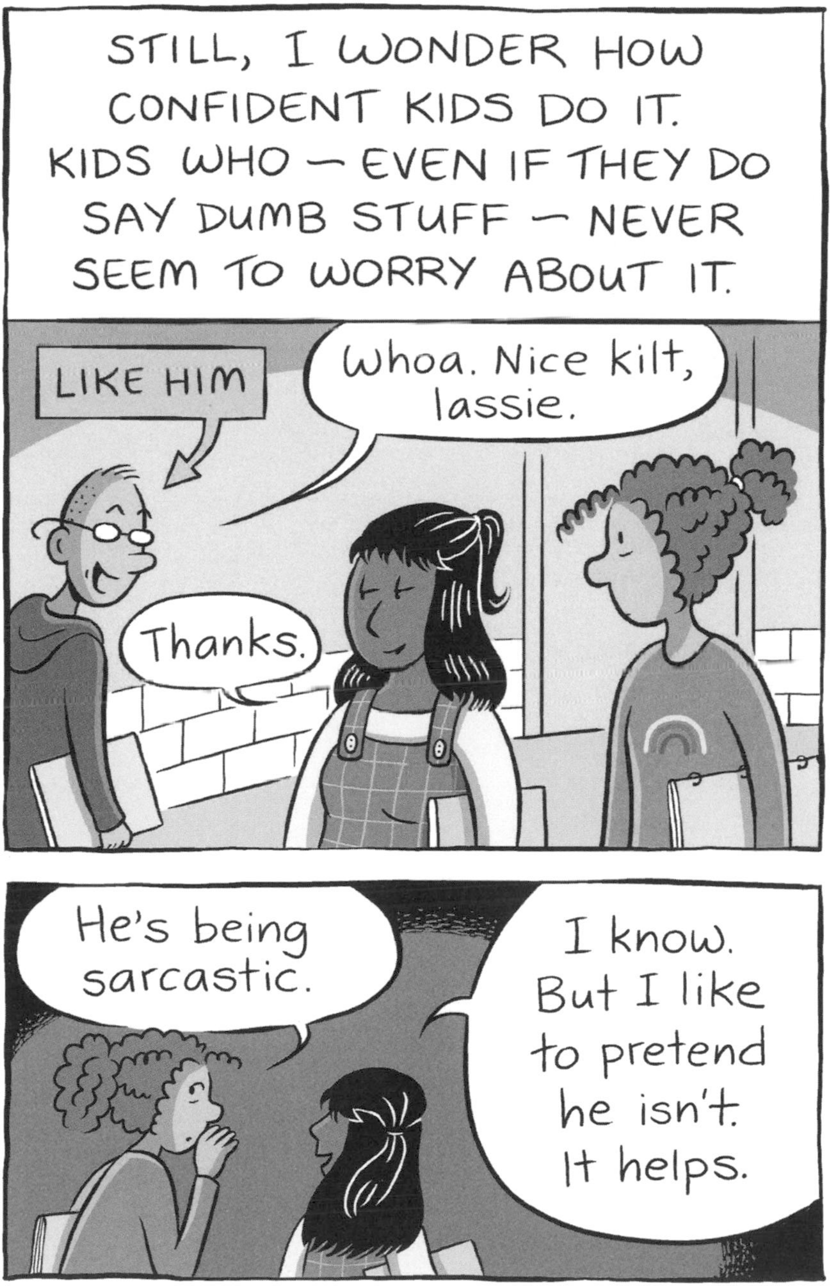
STILL, I WONDER HOW CONFIDENT KIDS DO IT. KIDS WHO — EVEN IF THEY DO SAY DUMB STUFF — NEVER SEEM TO WORRY ABOUT IT.
LIKE HIM
Whoa. Nice kilt, lassie.
Thanks.
He's being sarcastic.
I know. But I like to pretend he isn't. It helps.

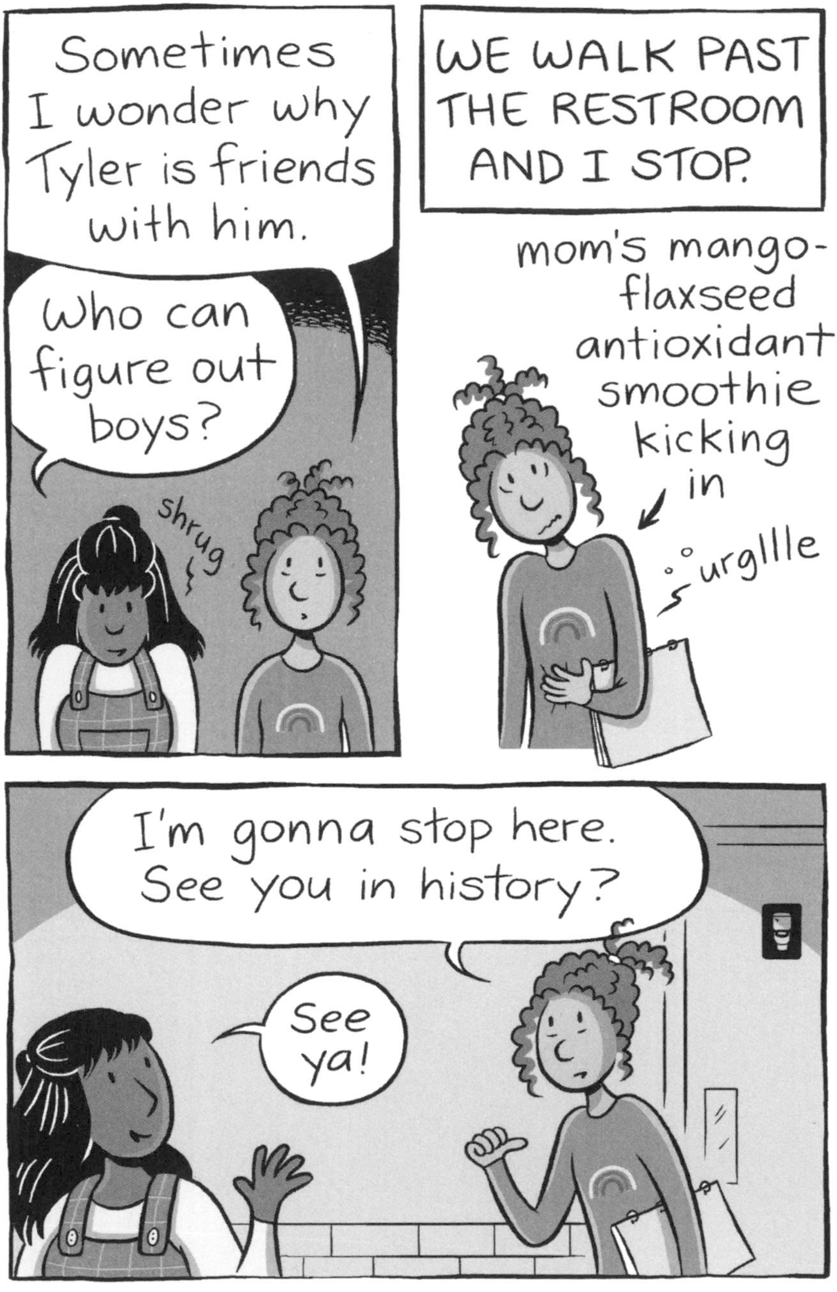
Sometimes I wonder why Tyler is friends with him.
Who can figure out boys?
shrug
WE WALK PAST THE RESTROOM AND I STOP.
mom's mango-flaxseed antioxidant smoothie kicking in
urgllle
I'm gonna stop here. See you in history?
See ya!

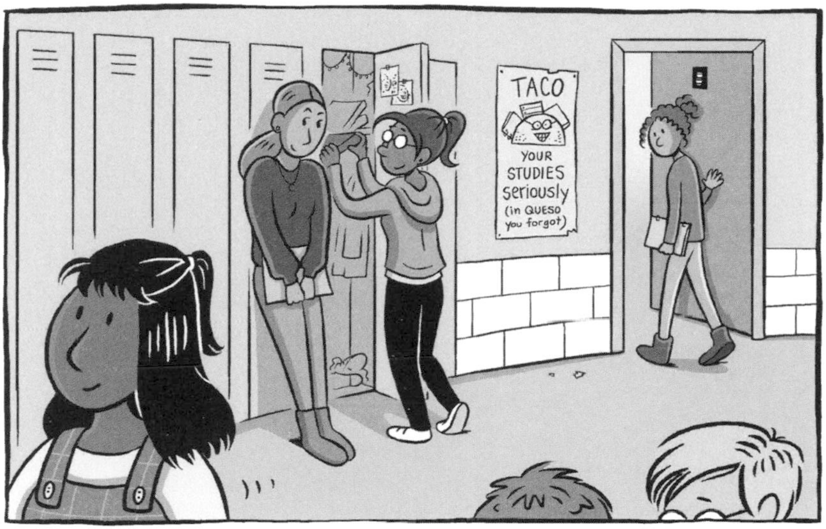
TACO
YOUR
STUDIES
seriously
(in QUESO
you forgot)

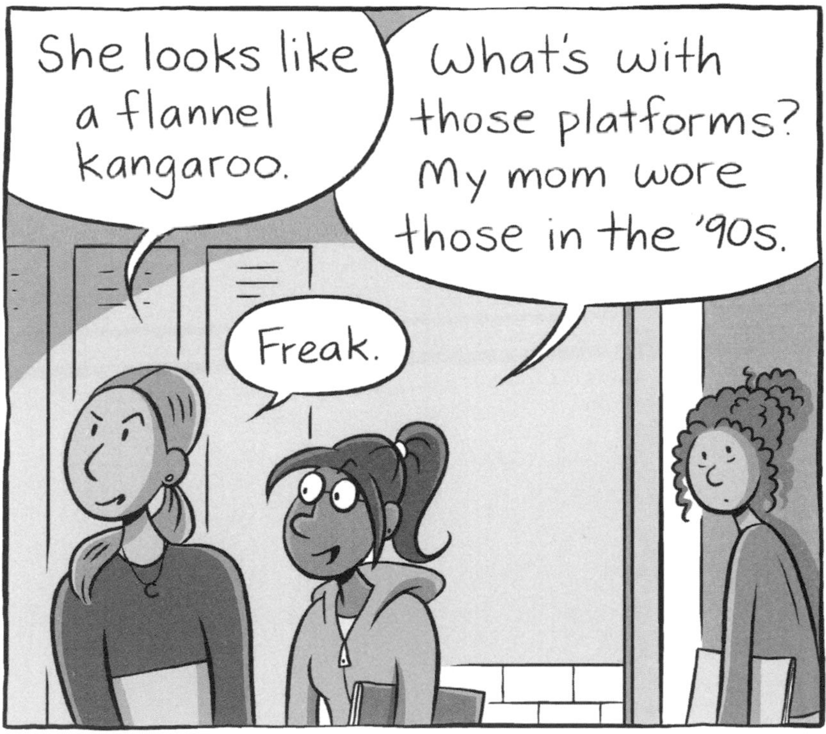
She looks like a flannel kangaroo.
What's with those platforms? My mom wore those in the '90s.
Freak.

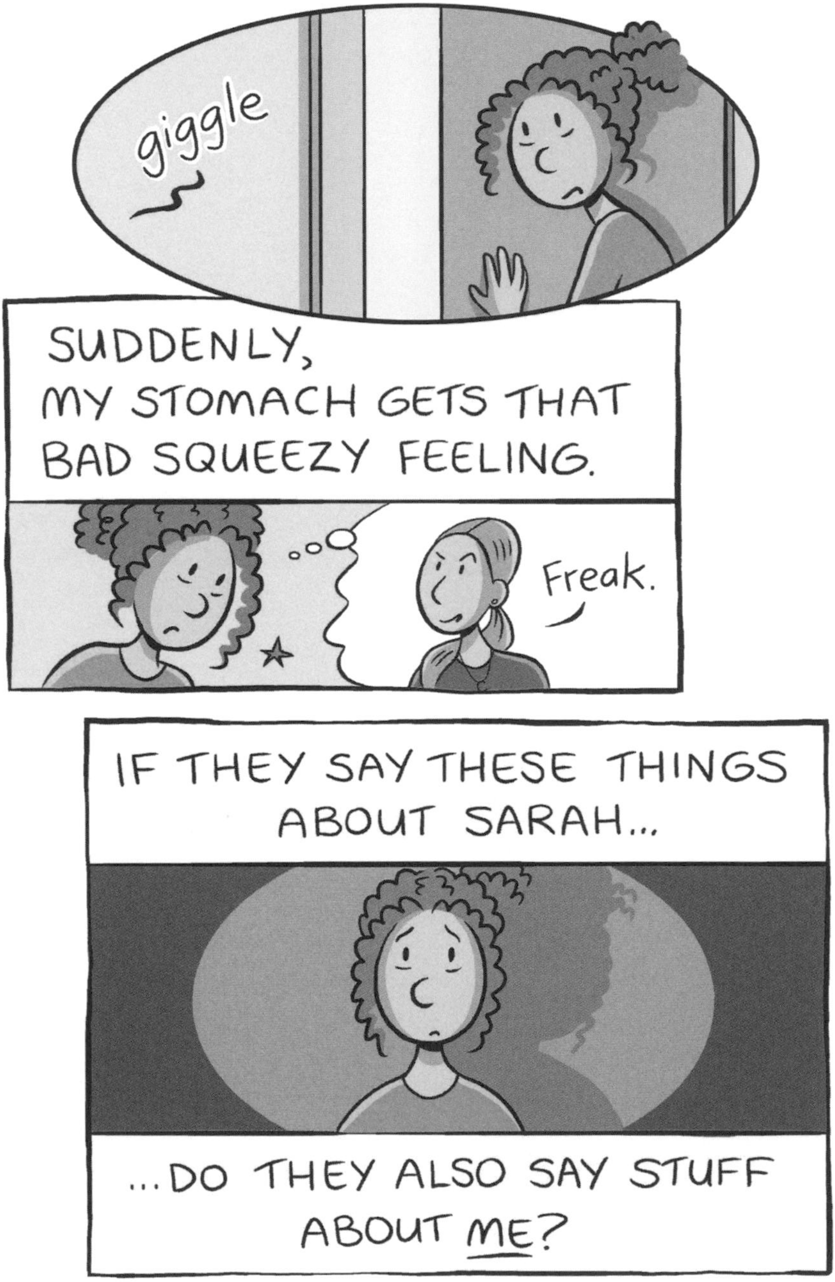
giggle
SUDDENLY, MY STOMACH GETS THAT BAD SQUEEZY FEELING.
Freak.
IF THEY SAY THESE THINGS ABOUT SARAH...
...DO THEY ALSO SAY STUFF ABOUT ME?

TYLER

Basketball practice. I'm trying not to miss as much. I did skip a couple days ago when Emmie and I had to brainstorm some stuff for the last pages (told Coach I had an orthodontist appointment. Yeah, I know, not proud). Luckily, we got a lot done in class today. We're almost halfway through. And we would've done more if we hadn't kept getting sidetracked.

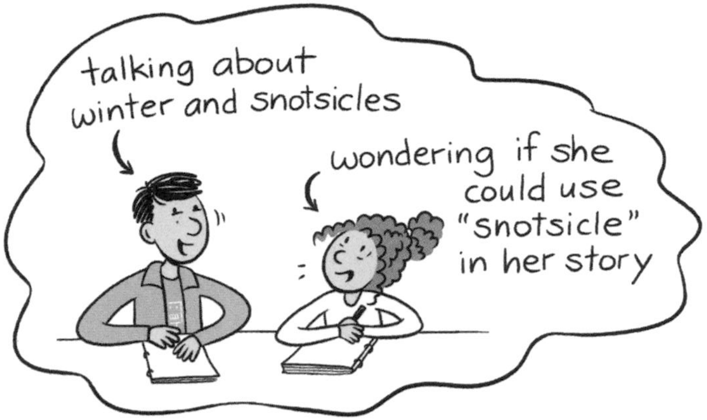
talking about winter and snotsicles
wondering if she could use "snotsicle" in her story

The more we worked, the more we talked, and the more annoyed Ms. Laurie got.

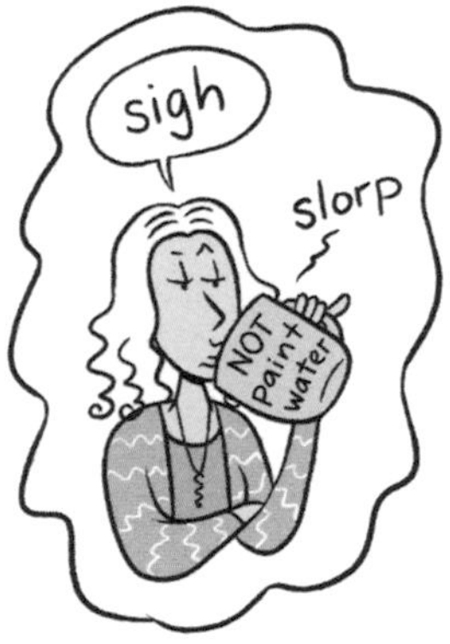
sigh
slorp
NOT paint water

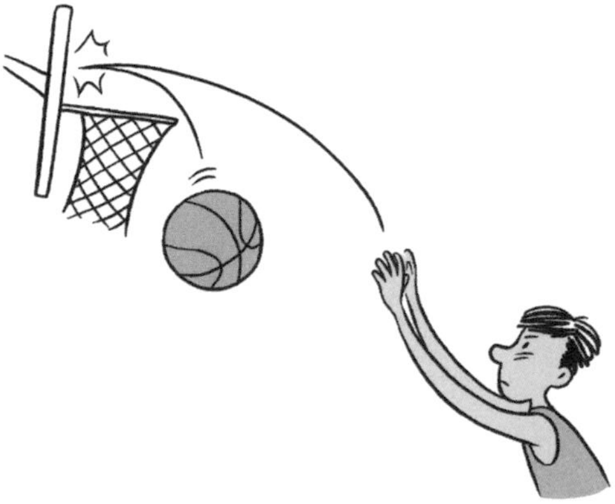

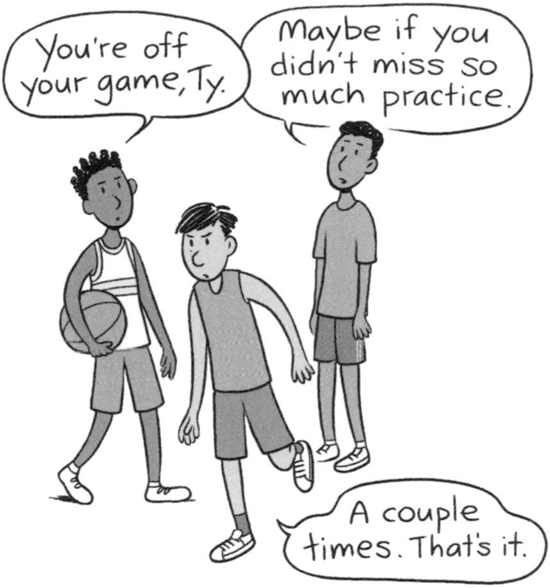
You're off your game, Ty.
Maybe if you didn't miss so much practice.
A couple times. That's it.

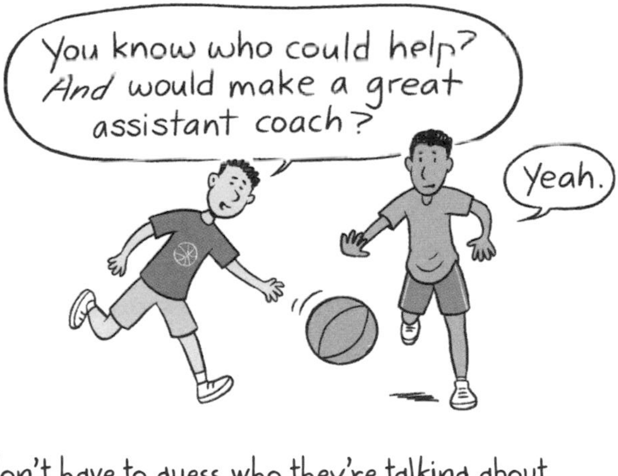
You know who could help? *And* would make a great assistant coach?
Yeah.

I don't have to guess who they're talking about.

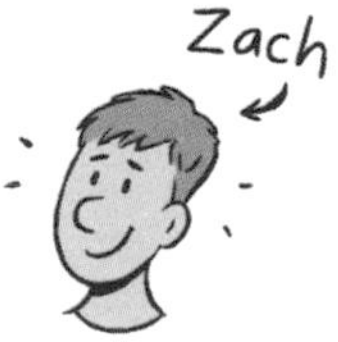
Zach

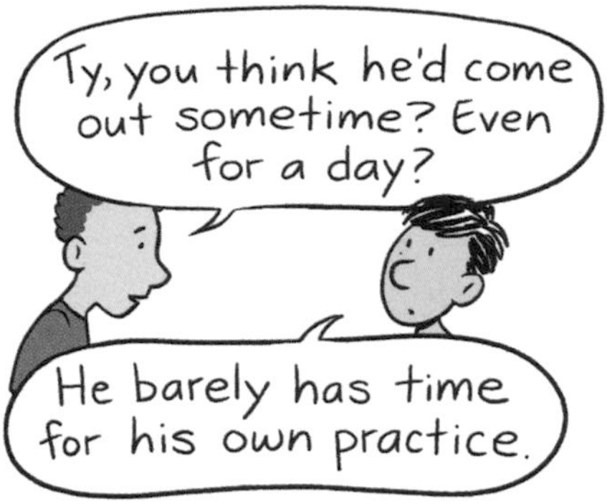
Ty, you think he'd come out sometime? Even for a day?
He barely has time for his own practice.

I shoot again. This time I make it.

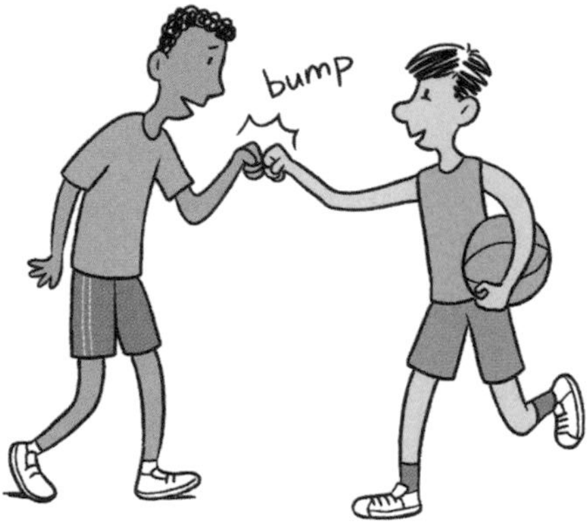
bump

Everyone on our team worships Zach. Especially the eighth graders who remember him when they were sixth-grade peons waiting to get off the bench.

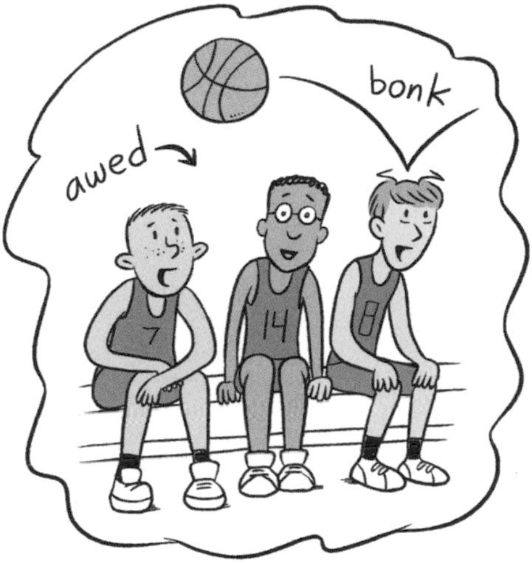
bonk
awed
7
14
8

Truth is, I'm almost as good. Zach used to play pickup with me at home and taught me a lot of techniques.

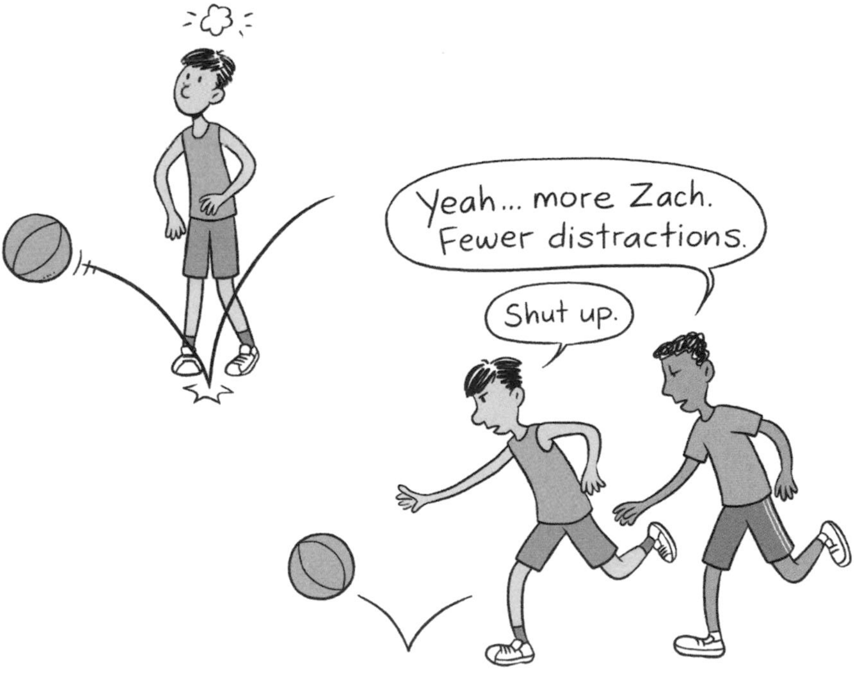
Yeah... more Zach. Fewer distractions.
Shut up.

I can tell Anthony and the other guys are a little miffed at me. They don't think I'm taking the game seriously enough, which is flat-out untrue.

It's not that I'm not committed, it's just . . .

. . . maybe I'm not as . . .

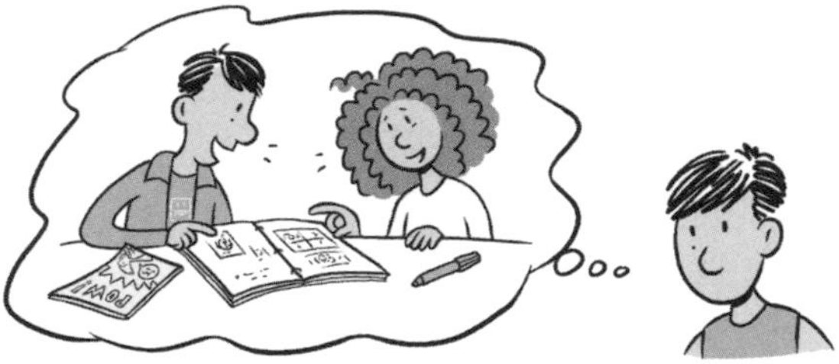

. . . obsessed about it?

Malik passes me the ball and I (barely) score.

Anthony high-fives me but not enthusiastically. He doesn't get peeved often. He's easygoing, like me, and keeps a lot of stuff inside (also like me).

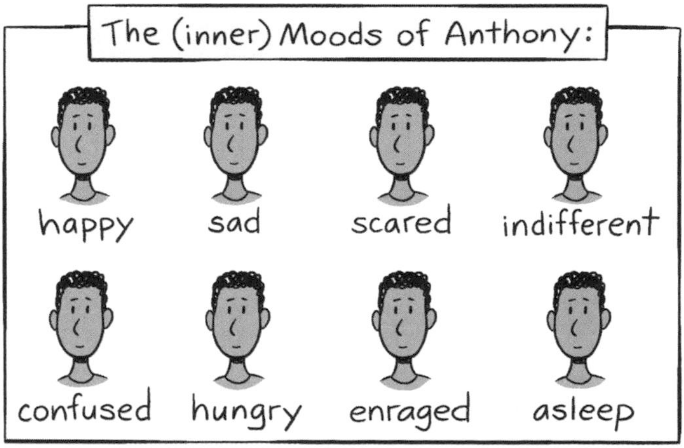
The (inner) Moods of Anthony:
happy
sad
scared
indifferent
confused
hungry
enraged
asleep

We've both been into basketball ever since I can remember. That's what unites us.

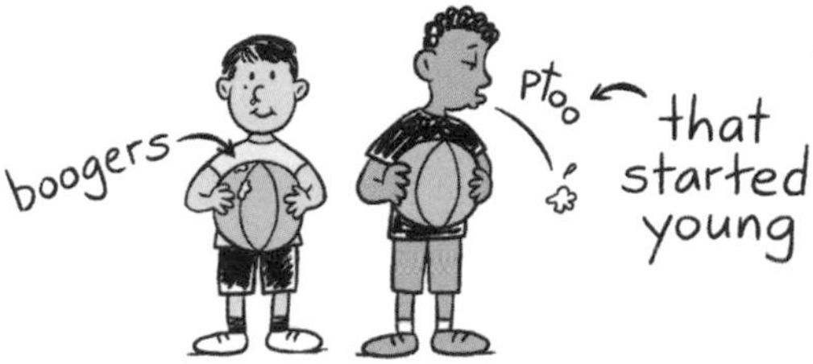
boogers
Ptoo
that started young

Also, we've always gone to each other's homes after school for pickup. Once we hit sixth grade, we added Joe to our mix, although he's terrible. But he's a great supporter. He comes to all our games and cracks jokes to cheer us up if we play lousy.

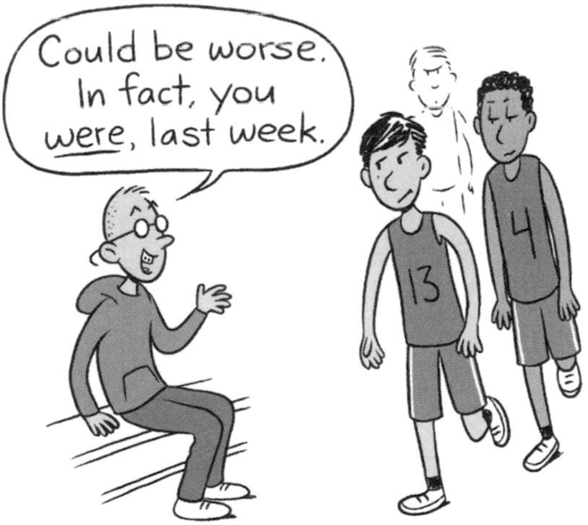
Could be worse. In fact, you were, last week.
13
4

When we played at my house, Zach (before he got busy) used to join us and teach us stuff, including his famous hook shot. That one's still hit or miss, but I'm determined to perfect it by high school.

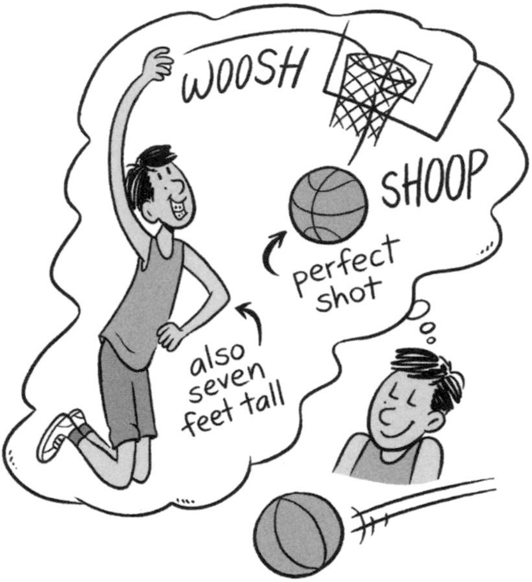
WOOSH
SHOOP
perfect shot
also seven feet tall

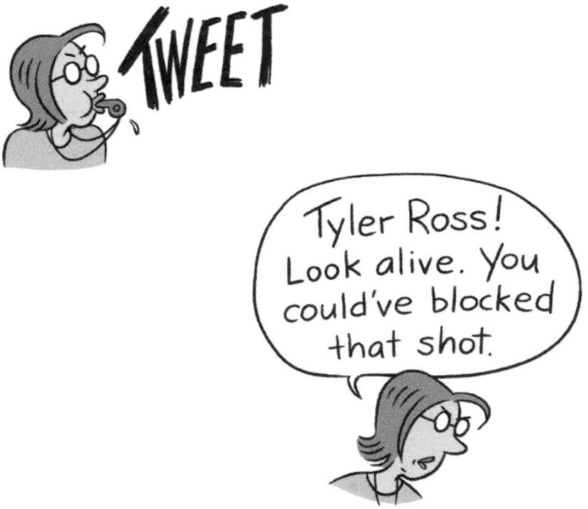
TWEET
Tyler Ross! Look alive. You could've blocked that shot.

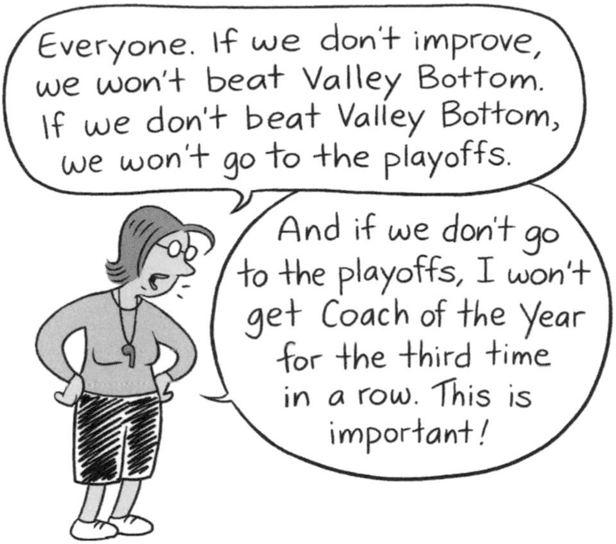
Everyone. If we don't improve, we won't beat Valley Bottom. If we don't beat Valley Bottom, we won't go to the playoffs.
And if we don't go to the playoffs, I won't get Coach of the Year for the third time in a row. This is important!

We fall back into scrimmage.

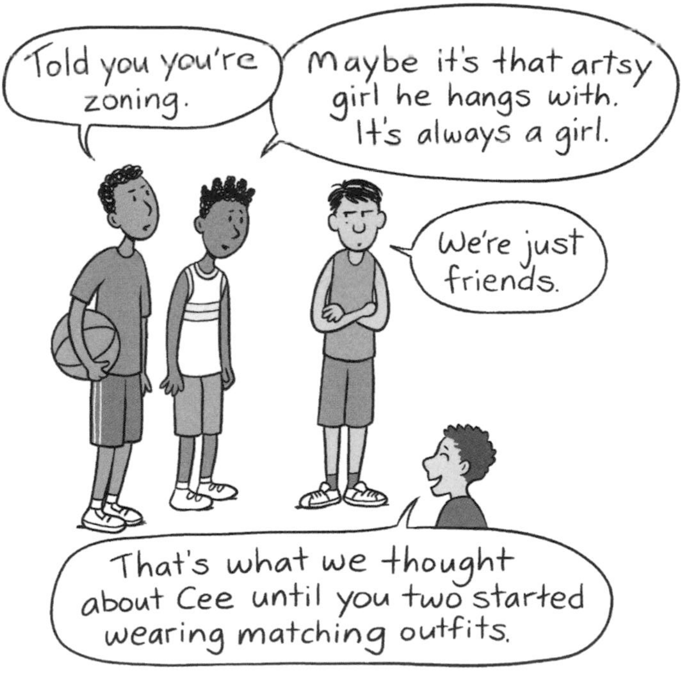
Told you you're zoning.
Maybe it's that artsy girl he hangs with. It's always a girl.
We're just friends.
That's what we thought about Cee until you two started wearing matching outfits.

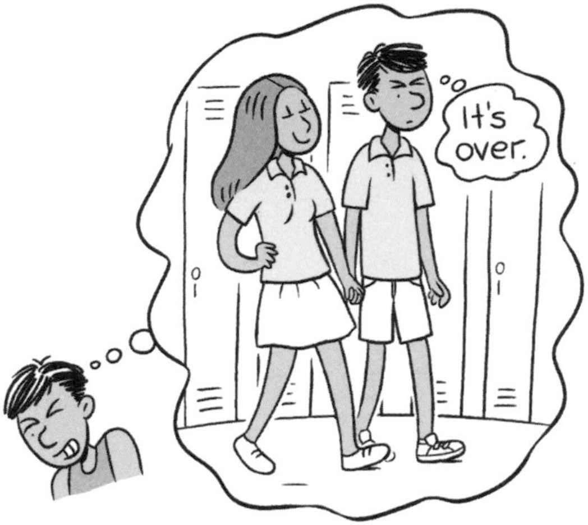
It's over.

They all laugh. I start to get mad. Why do I feel like the butt of everyone's jokes? Good thing Joe isn't here.

And how do I convince them that I **do** take the game seriously and that I'm **not** distracted by a girl?

My anger fuels me. I grab the ball from Anthony's hands, run to the three-point-line, and . . .

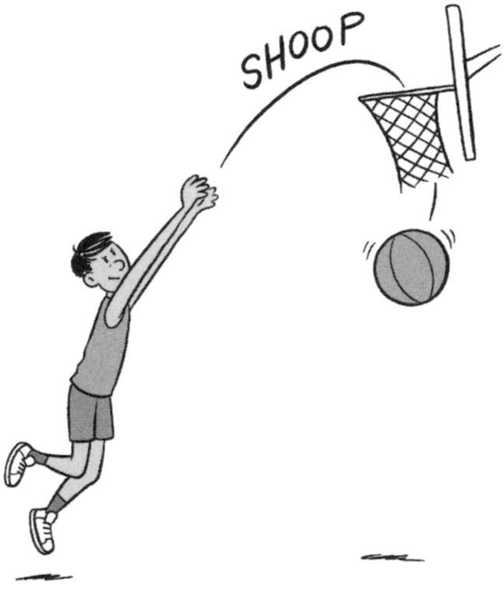
SHOOP

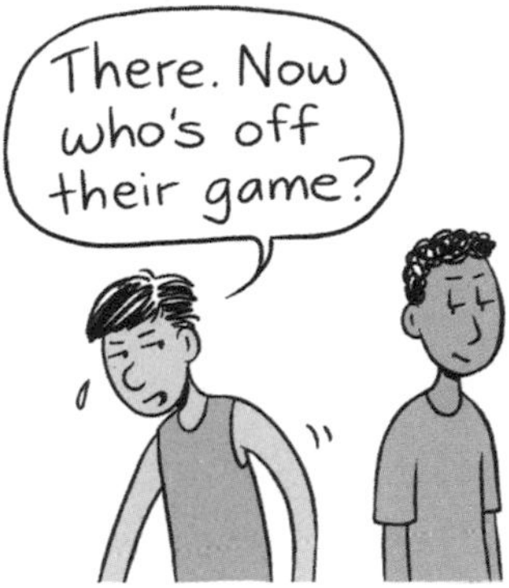
There. Now who's off their game?

Anthony gives me a half smile.

But he doesn't look convinced.

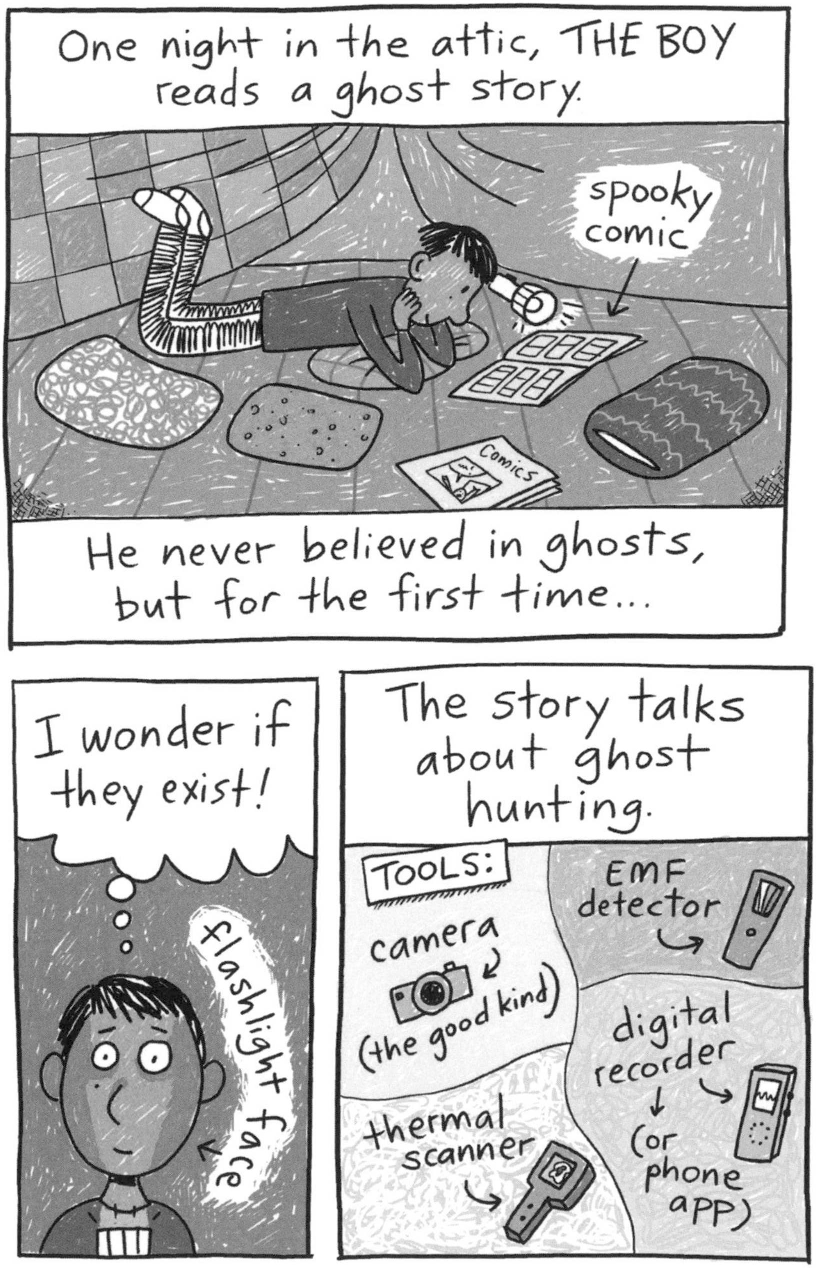
One night in the attic, THE BOY reads a ghost story.
spooky comic
Comics
He never believed in ghosts, but for the first time...
I wonder if they exist!
flashlight face
The story talks about ghost hunting.
TOOLS:
camera
(the good kind)
EMF detector
digital recorder
(or phone app)
thermal scanner

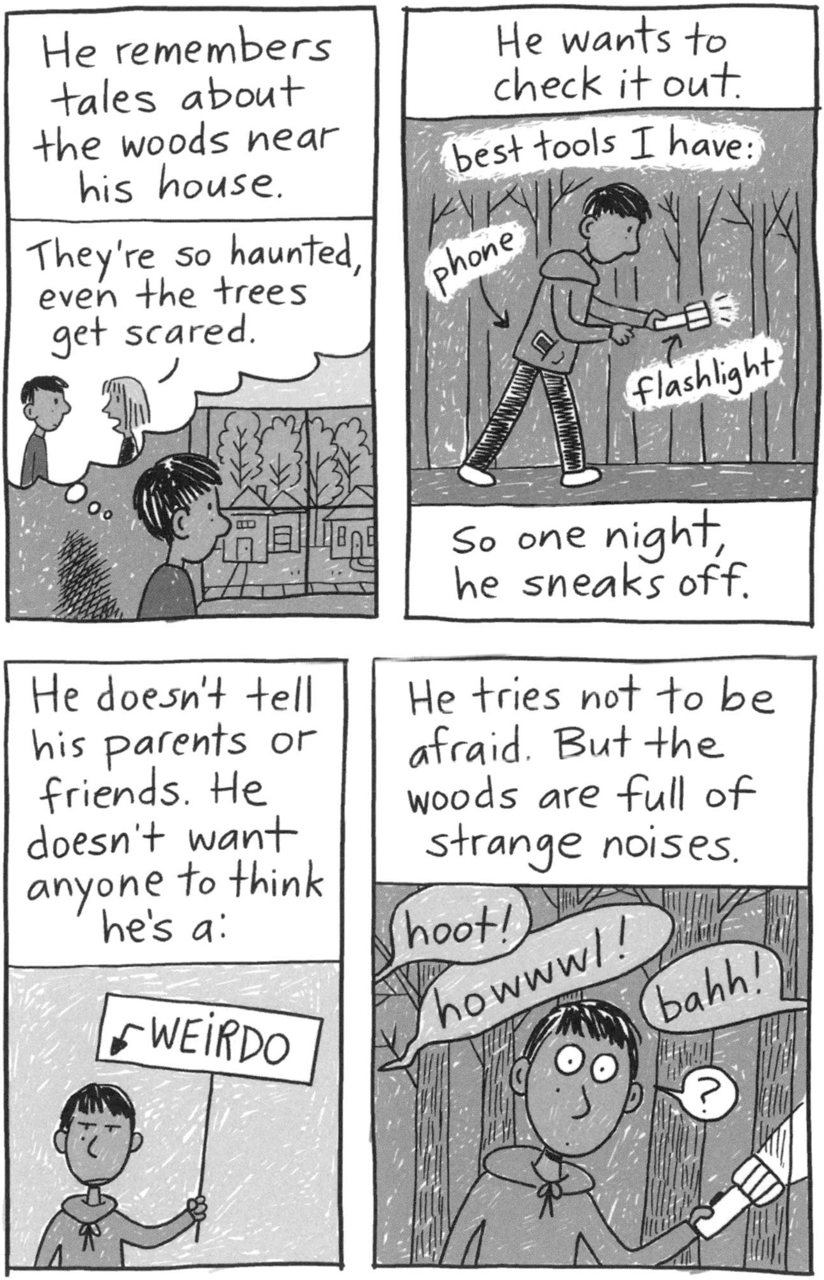
He remembers tales about the woods near his house.
They're so haunted, even the trees get scared.
He wants to check it out.
best tools I have:
phone
flashlight
So one night, he sneaks off.
He doesn't tell his parents or friends. He doesn't want anyone to think he's a:
WEIRDO
He tries not to be afraid. But the woods are full of strange noises.
hoot!
howwwl!
bahh!
?

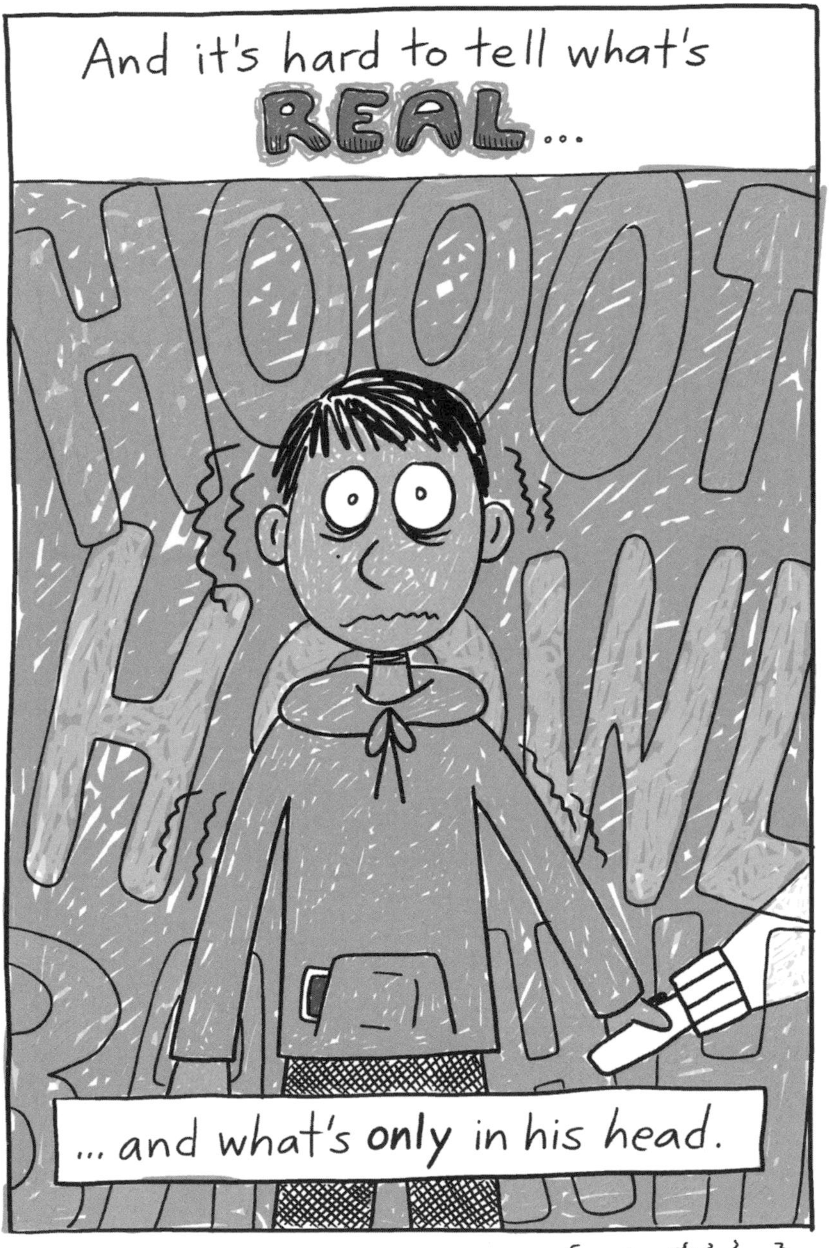
And it's hard to tell what's
REAL...
HOOT
... and what's only in his head.

(cont'd...)

Emmie

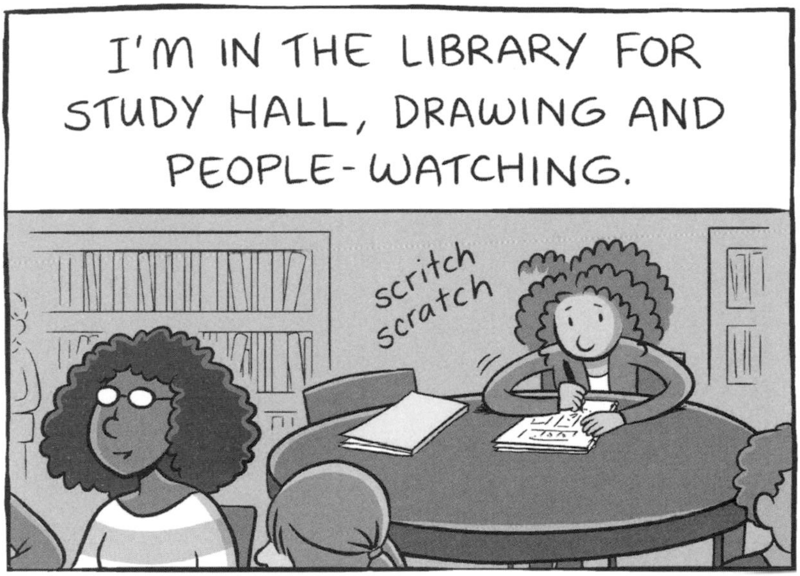
I'M IN THE LIBRARY FOR STUDY HALL, DRAWING AND PEOPLE-WATCHING.
scritch scratch

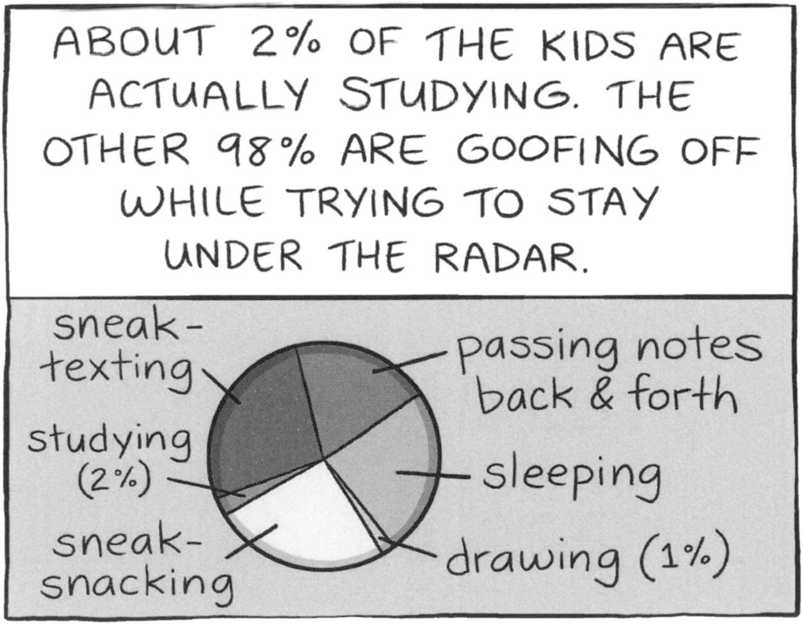
ABOUT 2% OF THE KIDS ARE ACTUALLY STUDYING. THE OTHER 98% ARE GOOFING OFF WHILE TRYING TO STAY UNDER THE RADAR.
sneak-texting
passing notes back & forth
studying (2%)
sleeping
sneak-snacking
drawing (1%)

ONE OF THE GOSSIP GIRLS TAKES IT A STEP FURTHER AND SENDS HER GOSSIP TWIN A SELFIE.

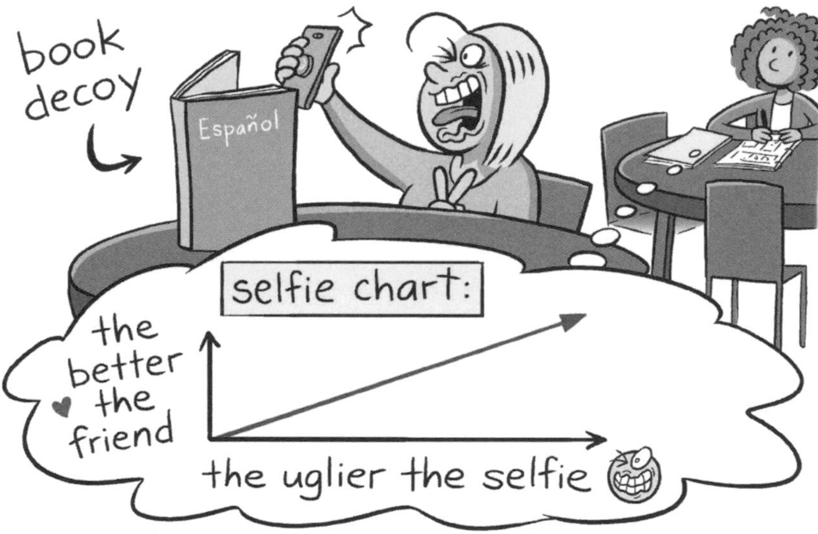
book decoy
Español
selfie chart:
the better the friend
the uglier the selfie

BRI WALKS IN TO RETURN A BOOK.

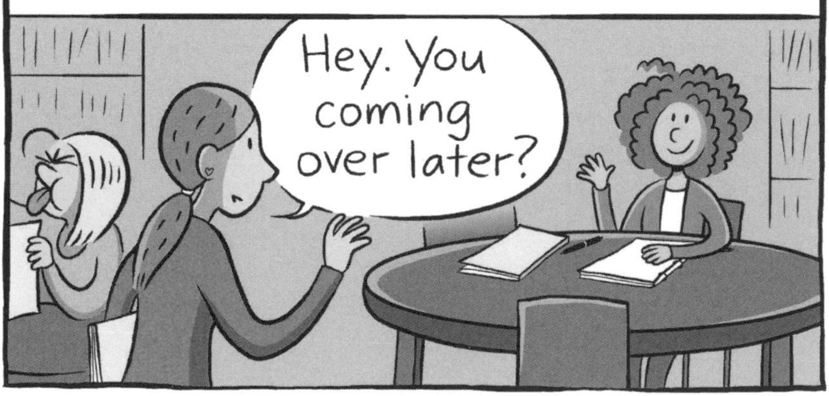
Hey. You coming over later?

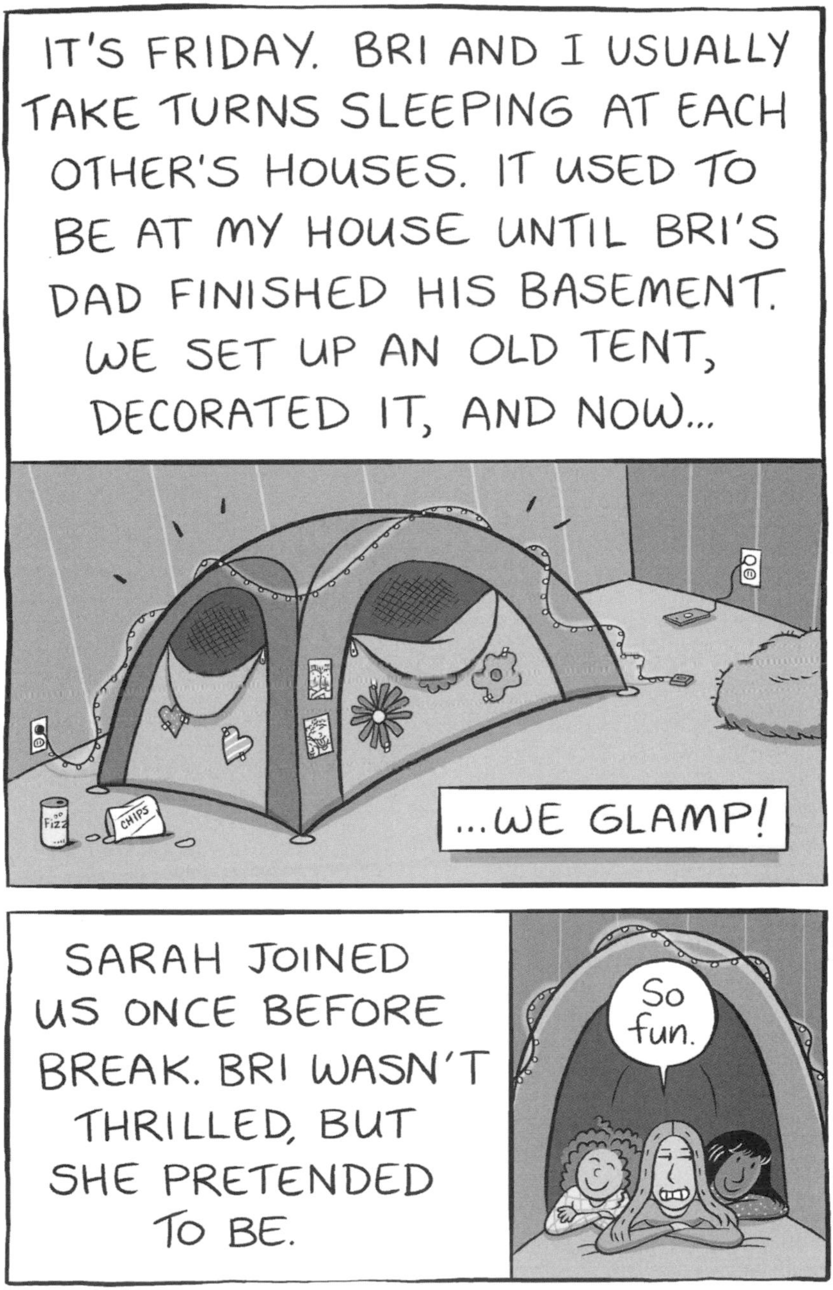
IT'S FRIDAY. BRI AND I USUALLY TAKE TURNS SLEEPING AT EACH OTHER'S HOUSES. IT USED TO BE AT MY HOUSE UNTIL BRI'S DAD FINISHED HIS BASEMENT. WE SET UP AN OLD TENT, DECORATED IT, AND NOW...
Fizz
CHIPS
...WE GLAMP!
SARAH JOINED US ONCE BEFORE BREAK. BRI WASN'T THRILLED, BUT SHE PRETENDED TO BE.
So fun.

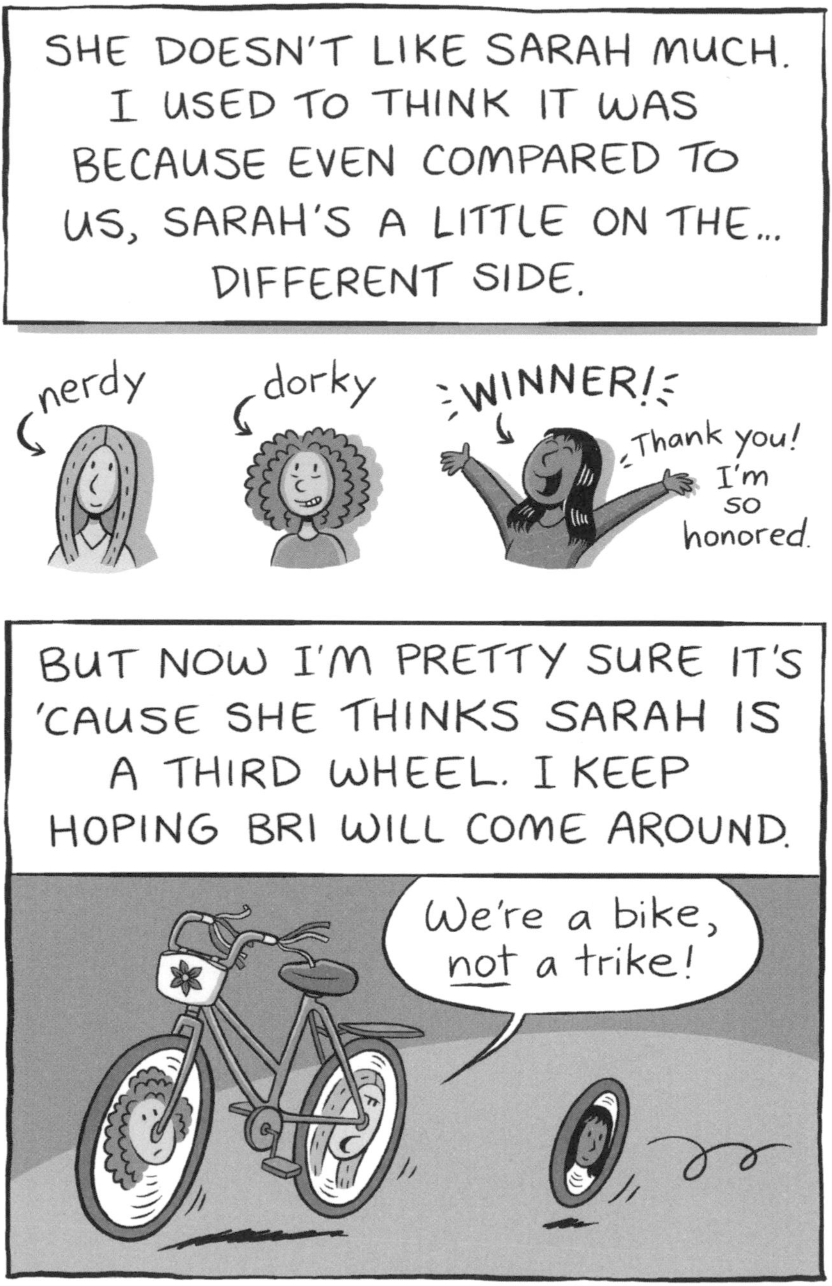
SHE DOESN'T LIKE SARAH MUCH. I USED TO THINK IT WAS BECAUSE EVEN COMPARED TO US, SARAH'S A LITTLE ON THE... DIFFERENT SIDE.
nerdy
dorky
WINNER!
Thank you! I'm so honored.
BUT NOW I'M PRETTY SURE IT'S 'CAUSE SHE THINKS SARAH IS A THIRD WHEEL. I KEEP HOPING BRI WILL COME AROUND.
We're a bike, not a trike!

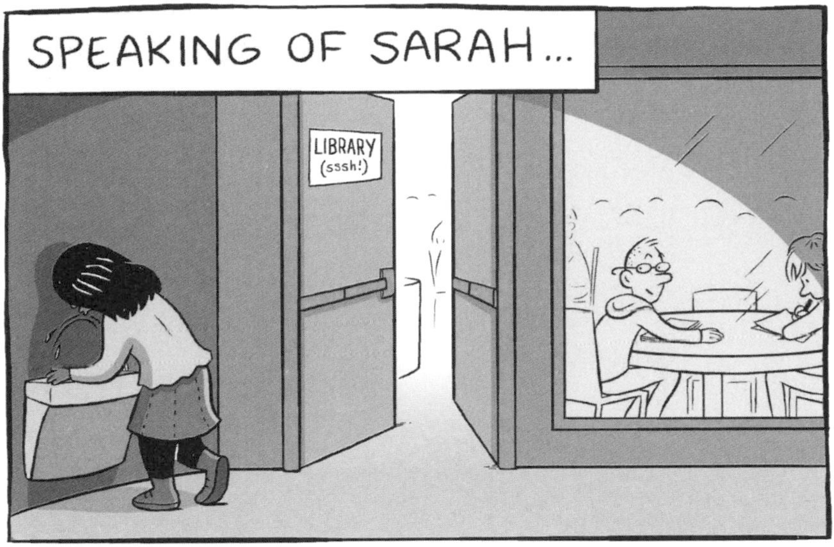
SPEAKING OF SARAH...
LIBRARY
(sssh!)

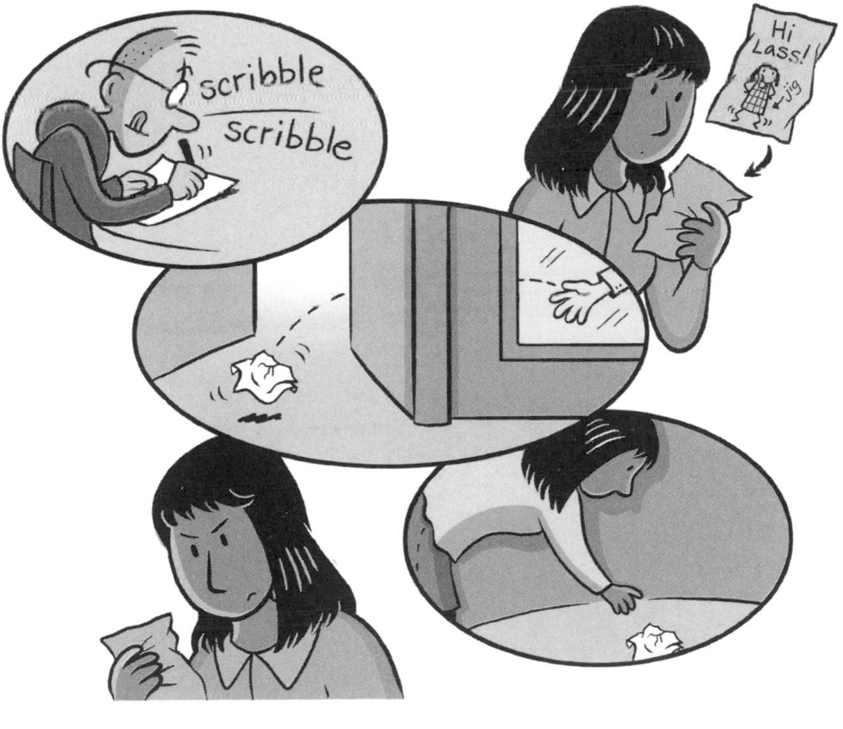
scribble
scribble
Hi
Lass!
jig

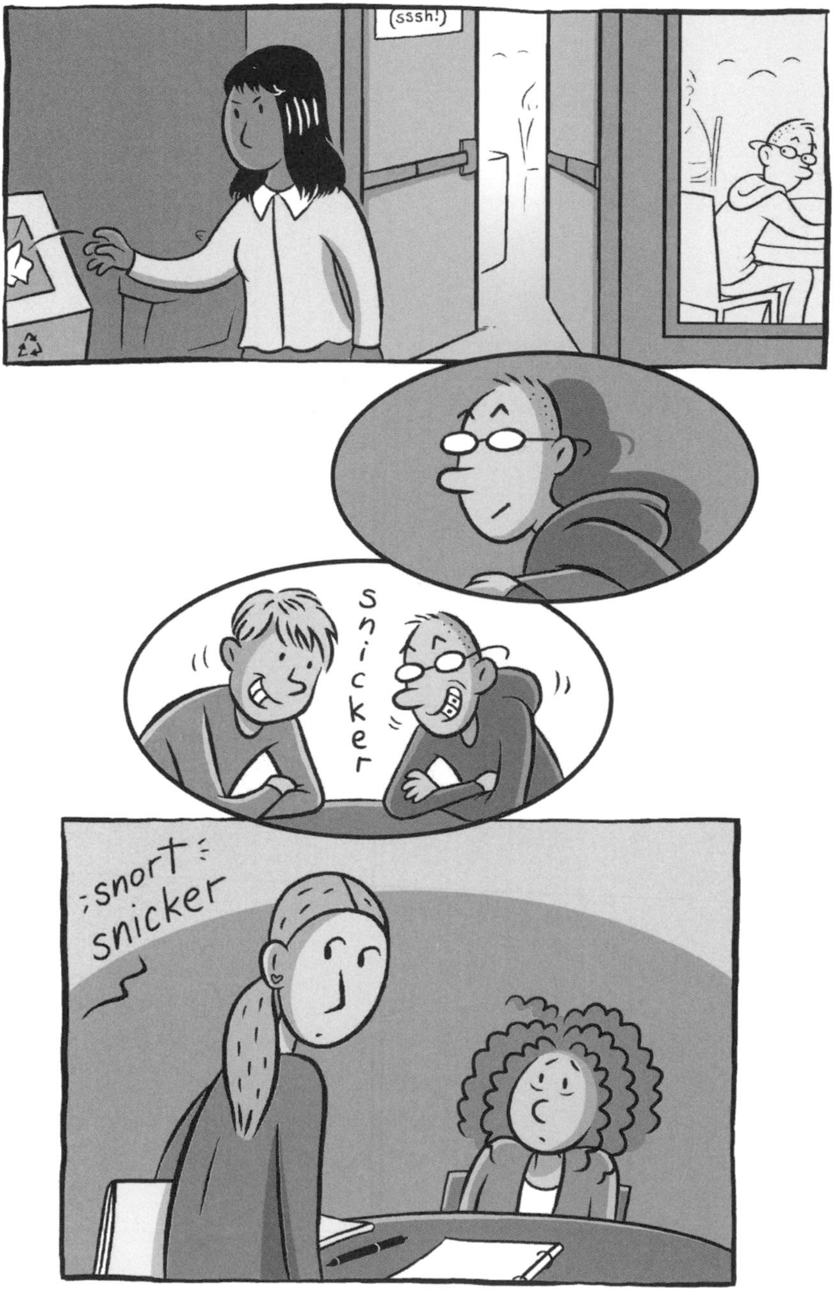
(sssh!)
snicker
snort
snicker

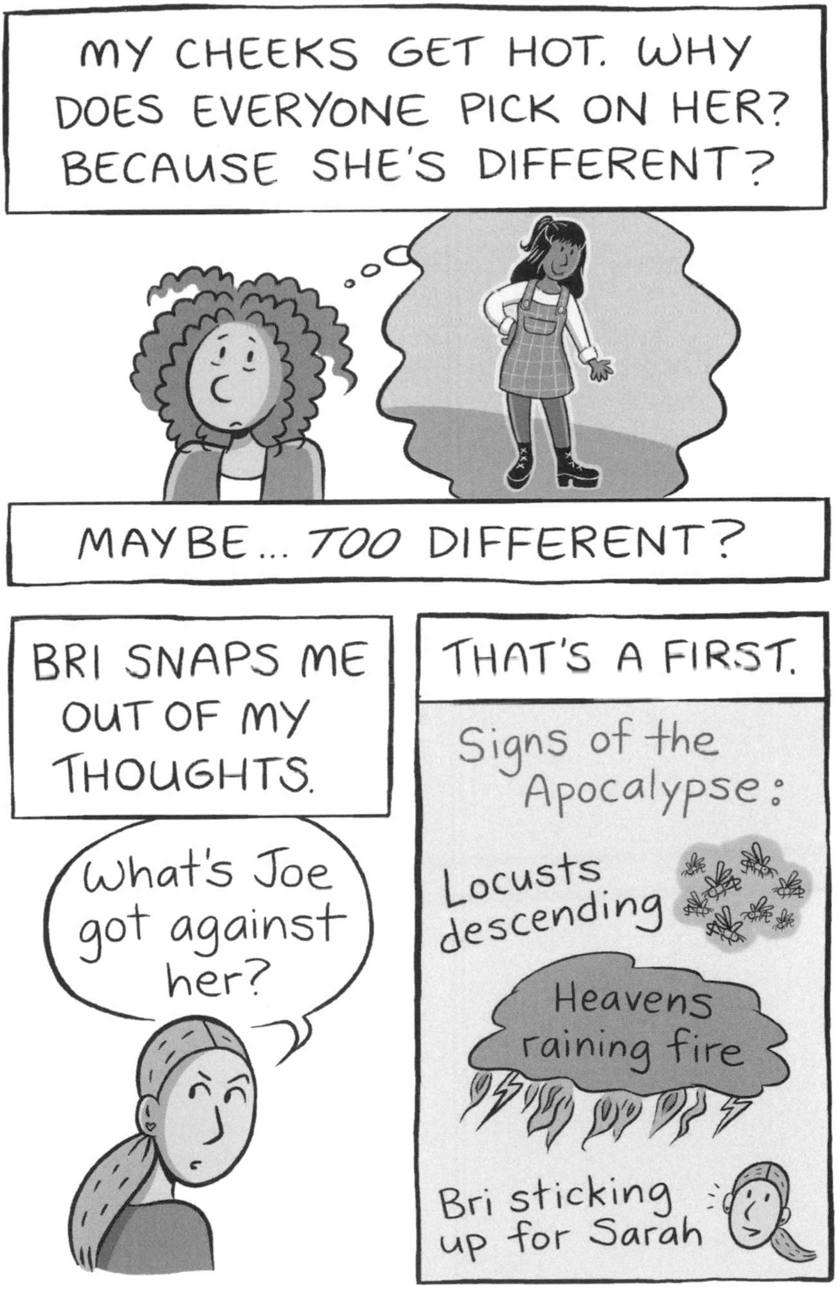
MY CHEEKS GET HOT. WHY DOES EVERYONE PICK ON HER? BECAUSE SHE'S DIFFERENT?
MAYBE... *TOO* DIFFERENT?
BRI SNAPS ME OUT OF MY THOUGHTS.
What's Joe got against her?
THAT'S A FIRST.
Signs of the Apocalypse:
Locusts descending
Heavens raining fire
Bri sticking up for Sarah

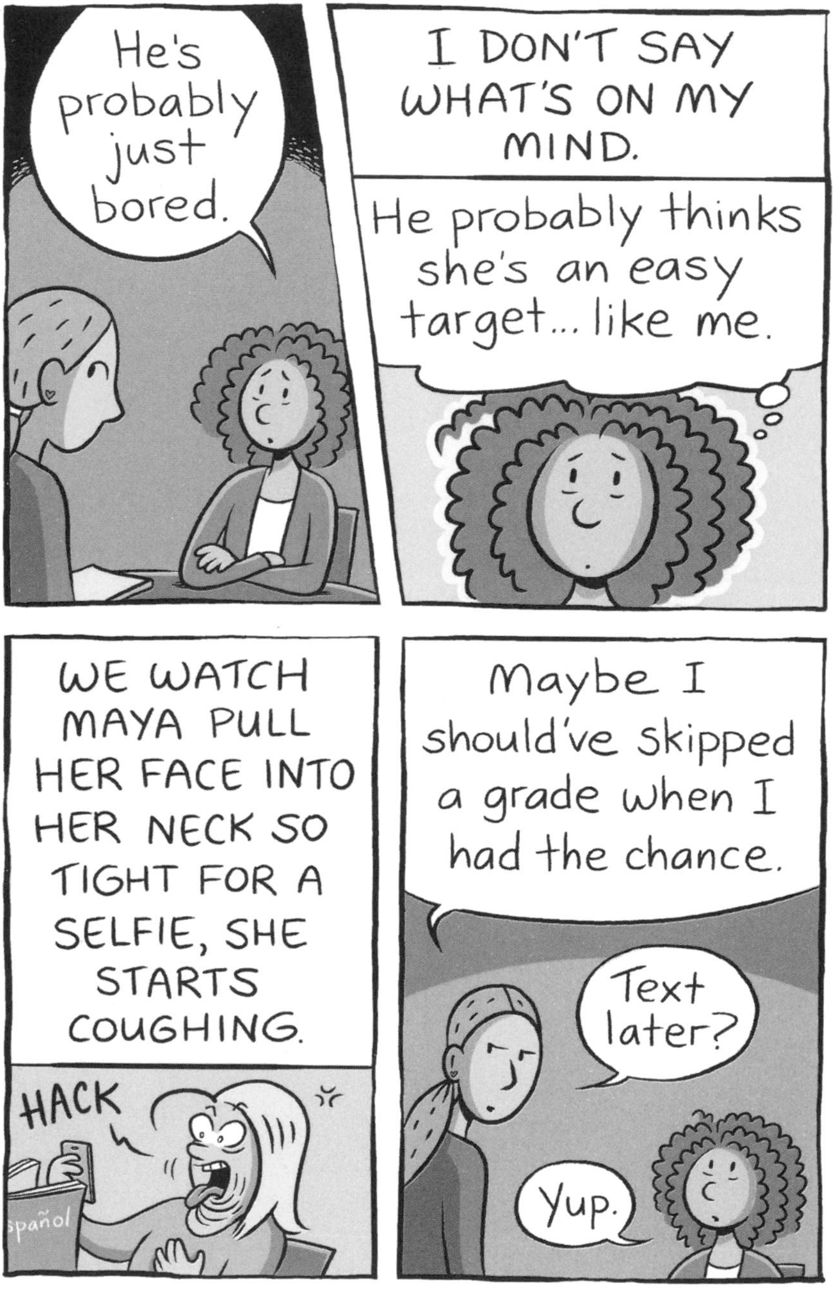
He's probably just bored.
I DON'T SAY WHAT'S ON MY MIND.
He probably thinks she's an easy target... like me.
WE WATCH MAYA PULL HER FACE INTO HER NECK SO TIGHT FOR A SELFIE, SHE STARTS COUGHING.
HACK
spañol
Maybe I should've skipped a grade when I had the chance.
Text later?
Yup.

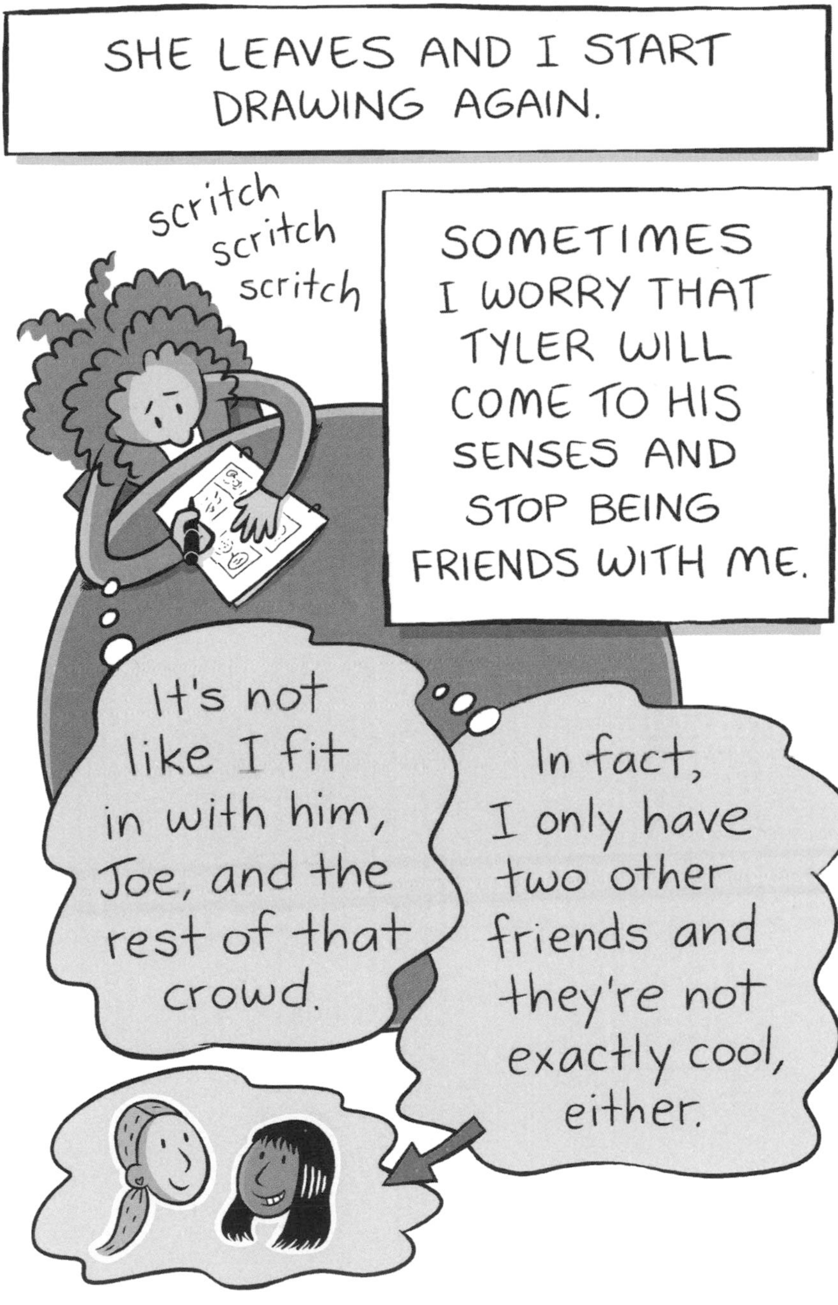
SHE LEAVES AND I START DRAWING AGAIN.
scritch scritch scritch
SOMETIMES I WORRY THAT TYLER WILL COME TO HIS SENSES AND STOP BEING FRIENDS WITH ME.
It's not like I fit in with him, Joe, and the rest of that crowd.
In fact, I only have two other friends and they're not exactly cool, either.

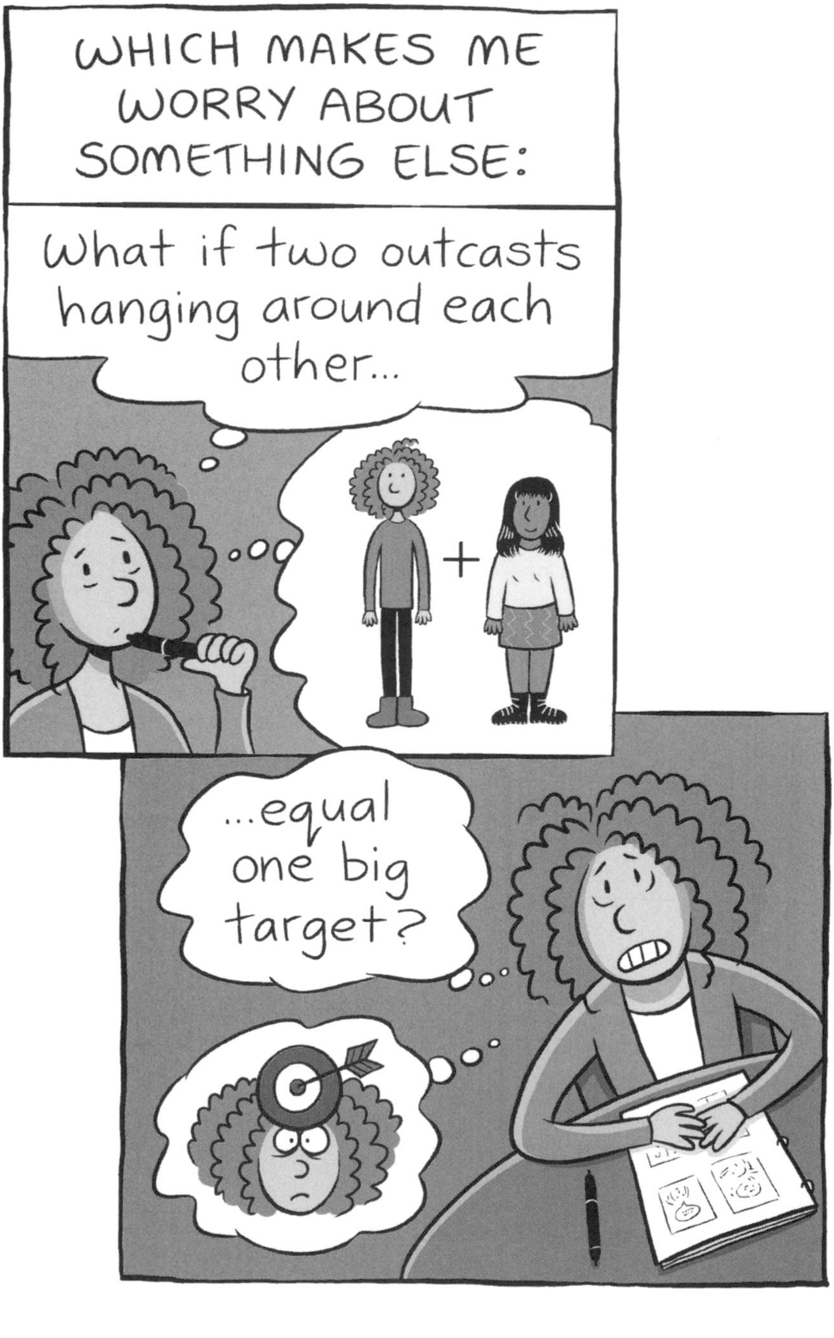
WHICH MAKES ME WORRY ABOUT SOMETHING ELSE:
What if two outcasts hanging around each other...
+
...equal one big target?

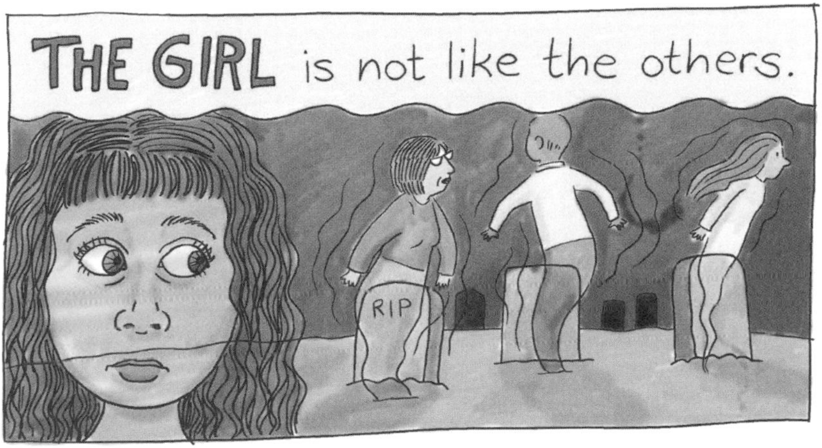
THE GIRL is not like the others.
RIP

She thinks humans are...

...well...

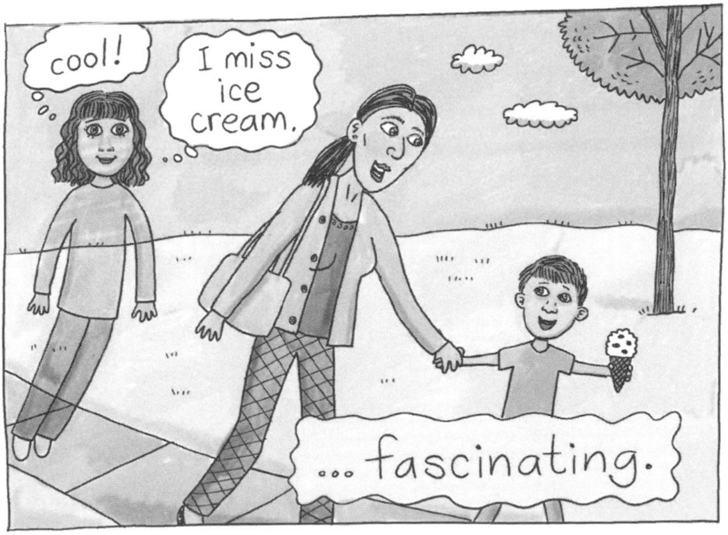
cool!
I miss ice cream.
...fascinating.

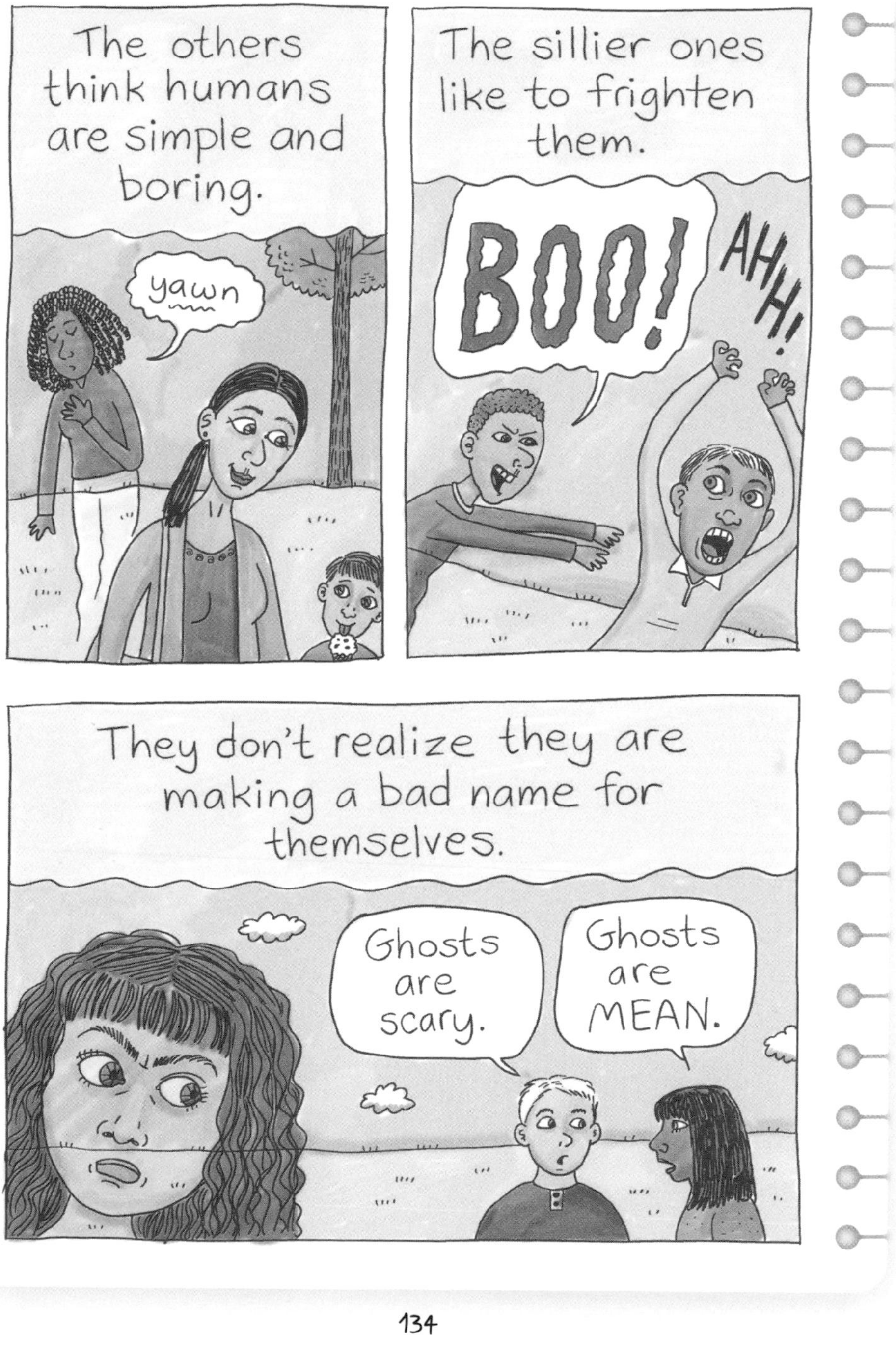
The others think humans are simple and boring.
yawn
The sillier ones like to frighten them.
BOO!
AHH!
They don't realize they are making a bad name for themselves.
Ghosts are scary.
Ghosts are MEAN.

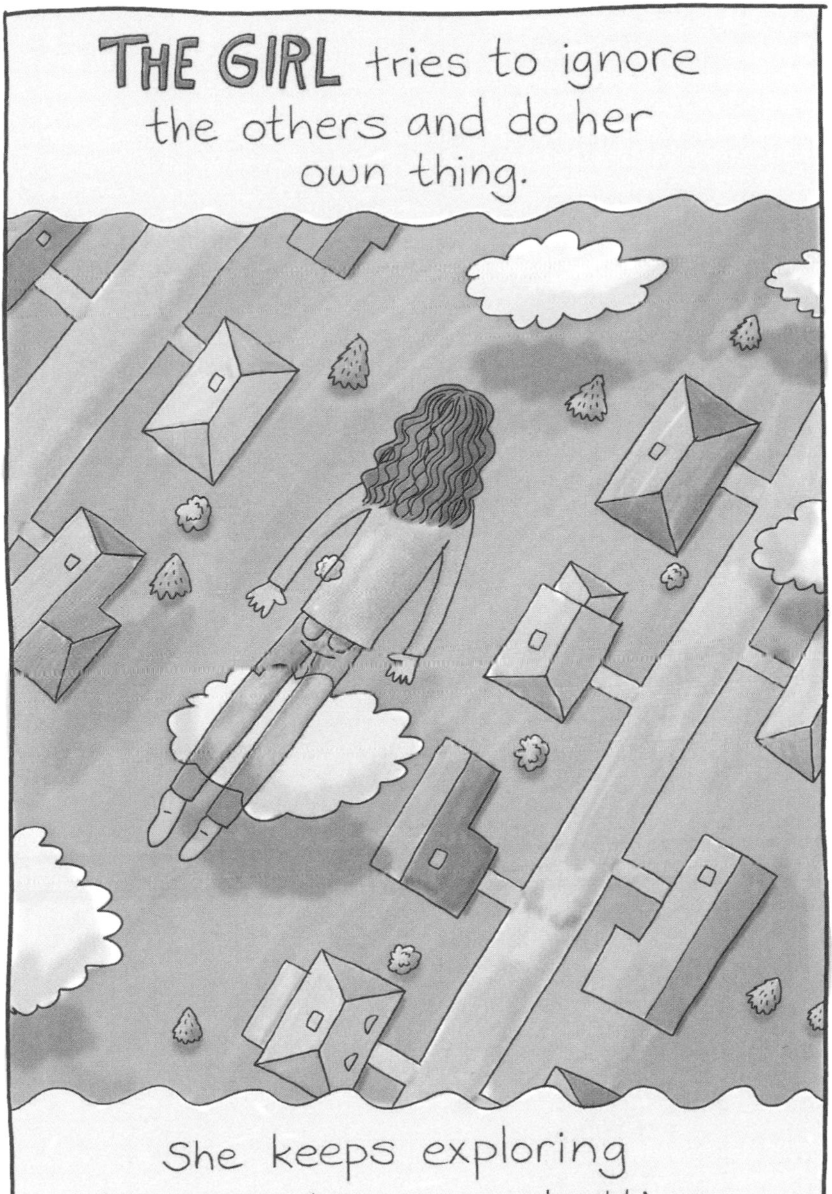
THE GIRL tries to ignore the others and do her own thing.
She keeps exploring humans' homes and attics.

Until one night, when something interesting catches her eye.
So she investigates.
WOOOSH
And discovers someone else investigating, too.
Cont'd...

TYLER

I come home to a familiar sound.

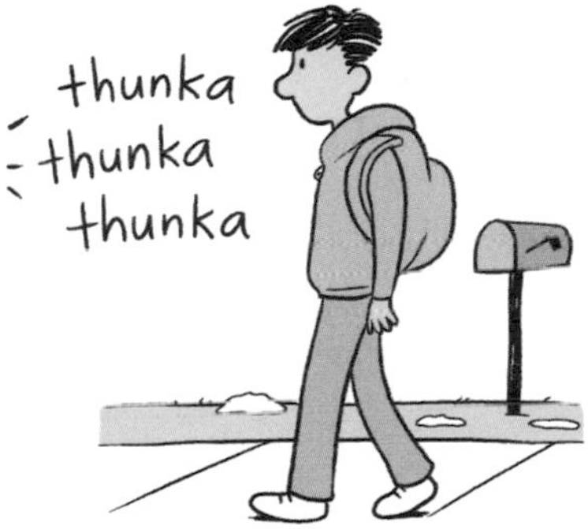
thunka
thunka
thunka

It's, like, unusually warm out. Almost fifty degrees. I only know that 'cause our science teacher, Mr. Danker, gives us updates every twenty minutes.

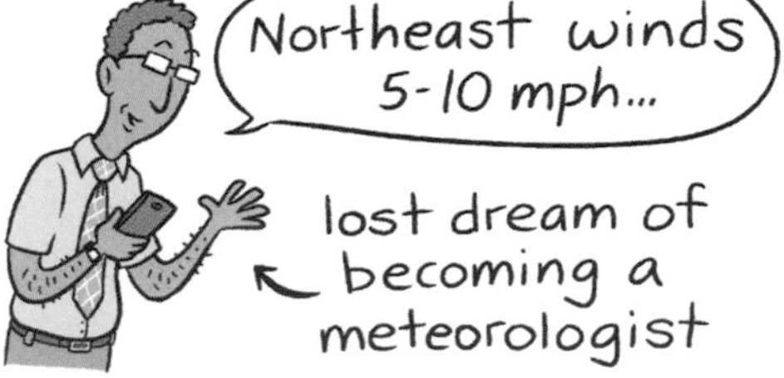
Northeast winds 5-10 mph...
lost dream of becoming a meteorologist

Even though it's the second week of January, all the snow has melted and the sun's out. That's one way to be fooled into thinking it's spring.

The other:

Guys in shorts

pale legs skinny legs overly hairy legs

No practice today, so I stayed at school a little late to work on the comic book. Emmie had a dentist appointment, so it was just me, Emo Girl, and two kids from Manga Club.

sticking out like a

On my way out, I almost bumped into Celia, who just had volleyball practice.

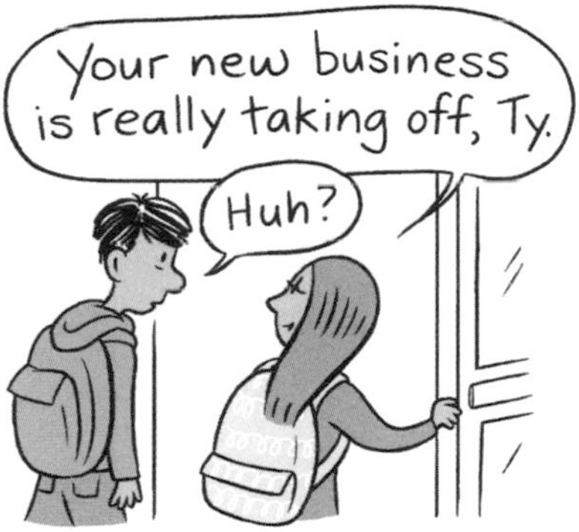
Your new business is really taking off, Ty.
Huh?

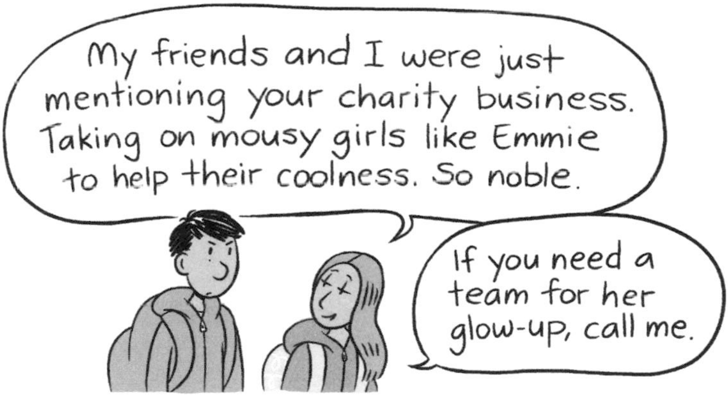
My friends and I were just mentioning your charity business. Taking on mousy girls like Emmie to help their coolness. So noble.
If you need a team for her glow-up, call me.

I didn't say anything. I was too mad. I just shoved past her and knew the perfect comeback would probably hit me in the middle of the night.

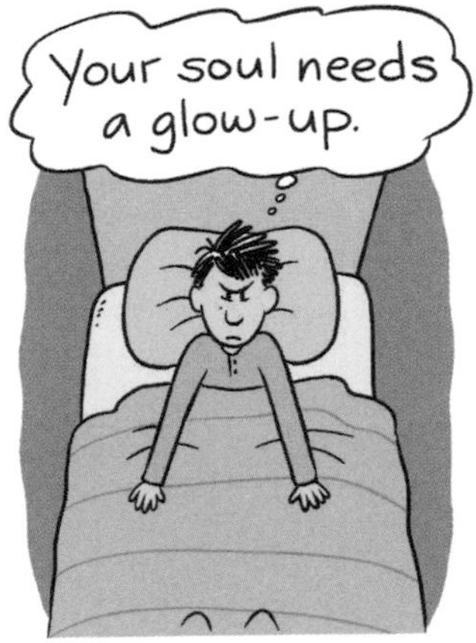
Your soul needs a glow-up.

Stuff like this has been going on ever since Emmie and I teamed up for the comic book. It's making me really . . . well . . .

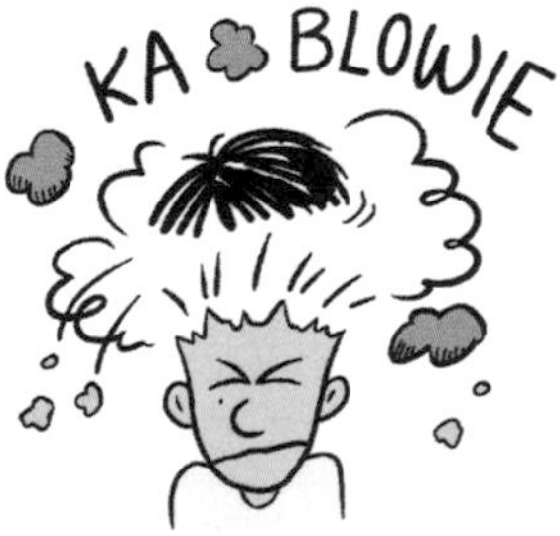
KA BLOWIE

Zach and his two best friends, Jonathan and Eli, are playing pickup in our driveway. I wish I could join them to blow off some steam, but I have homework to do. Also, they probably don't want a seventh grader invading their turf. They're cool guys, though. Eli reminds me of Anthony, super chill. Jonathan is all high energy. He's a small forward at Lakefront High. Eli is a shooting guard, and Zach, of course, is a point guard . . . an unofficial leader. Even as a sophomore, he earned it.

That's **my** goal for high school, too. Malik is our point guard now but not for long.

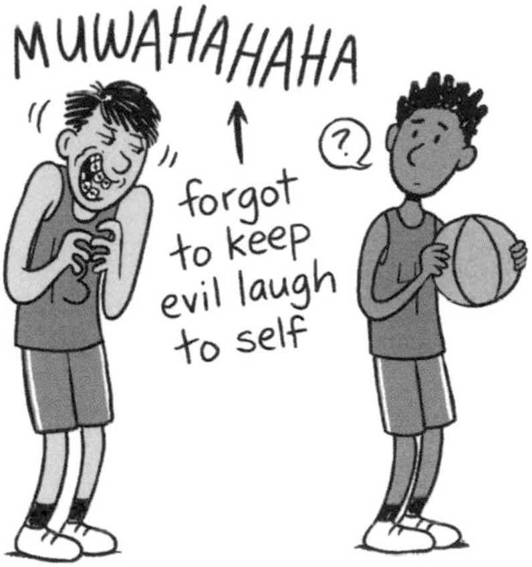
MUWAHAHAHA
?
forgot to keep evil laugh to self

Also, I promised myself to step it up. After today, I'm gonna give it my all at practice, get back to the Y this weekend, and beat Valley Bottom!

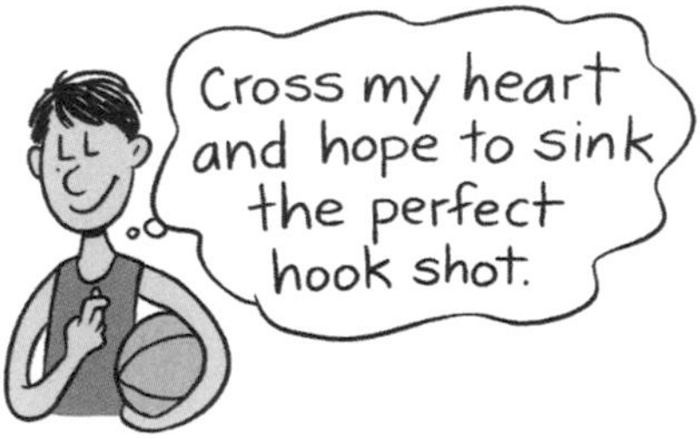
Cross my heart and hope to sink the perfect hook shot.

The guys take a break as I approach.

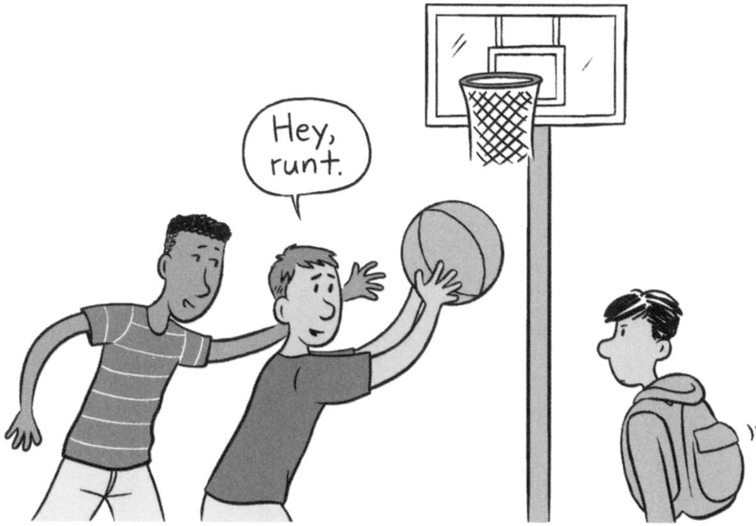
Hey,
runt.

He's just joking about the nickname, but I cringe, anyway. Being popular in middle school means nothing to high schoolers. I'll always just be the little baby brother.

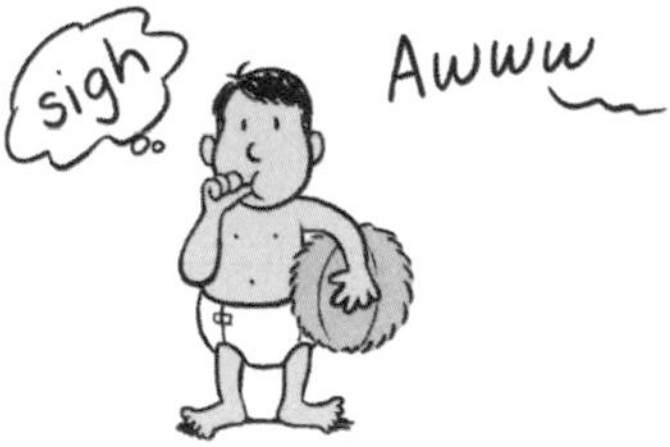
sigh
Awww

Jonathan wipes his forehead with the hem of his T-shirt, and Zach chugs Gatorade, which my mom calls "sugar soup."

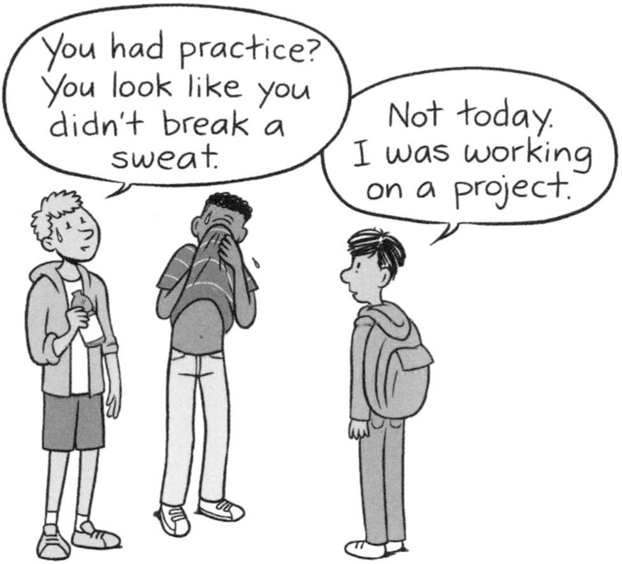
You had practice? You look like you didn't break a sweat.
Not today. I was working on a project.

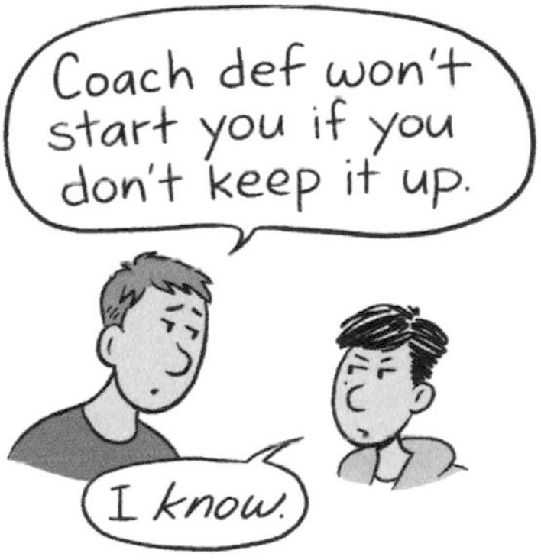
Coach def won't start you if you don't keep it up.
I *know*.

I'm a little testy when I say that. Zach knows my b-ball goals.

It would be nice if he actually **helped** me with 'em.

Maybe Jonathan's thinking the same thing.

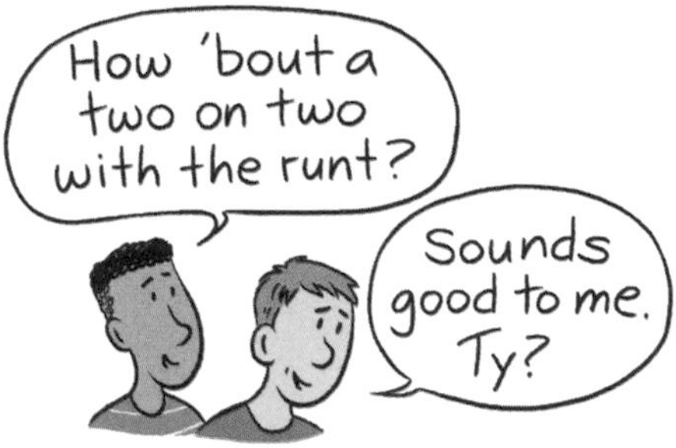
How 'bout a two on two with the runt?
Sounds good to me. Ty?

I have so much homework, and I should do it now so I can finally play Fortnite with Anthony later, but I can't resist. Playing with (good) high schoolers is next-level awesome.

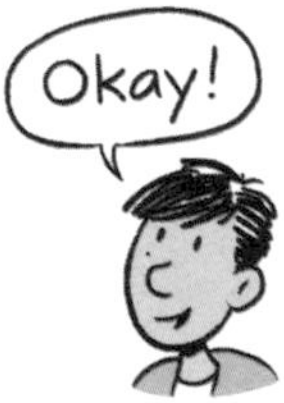
Okay!

I team up with Zach—who's the best player—so it's even.

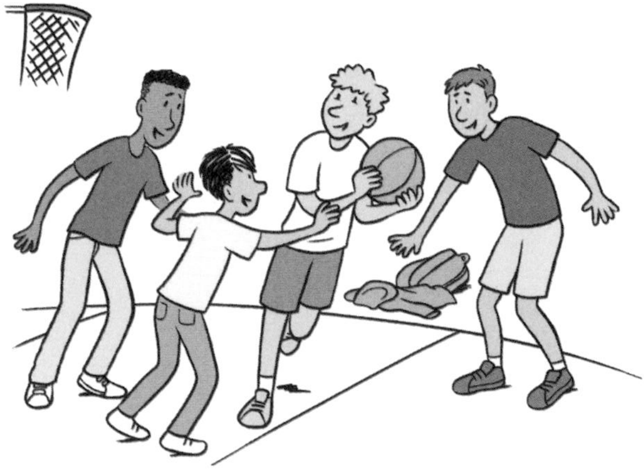

We play for about fifteen minutes when . . .

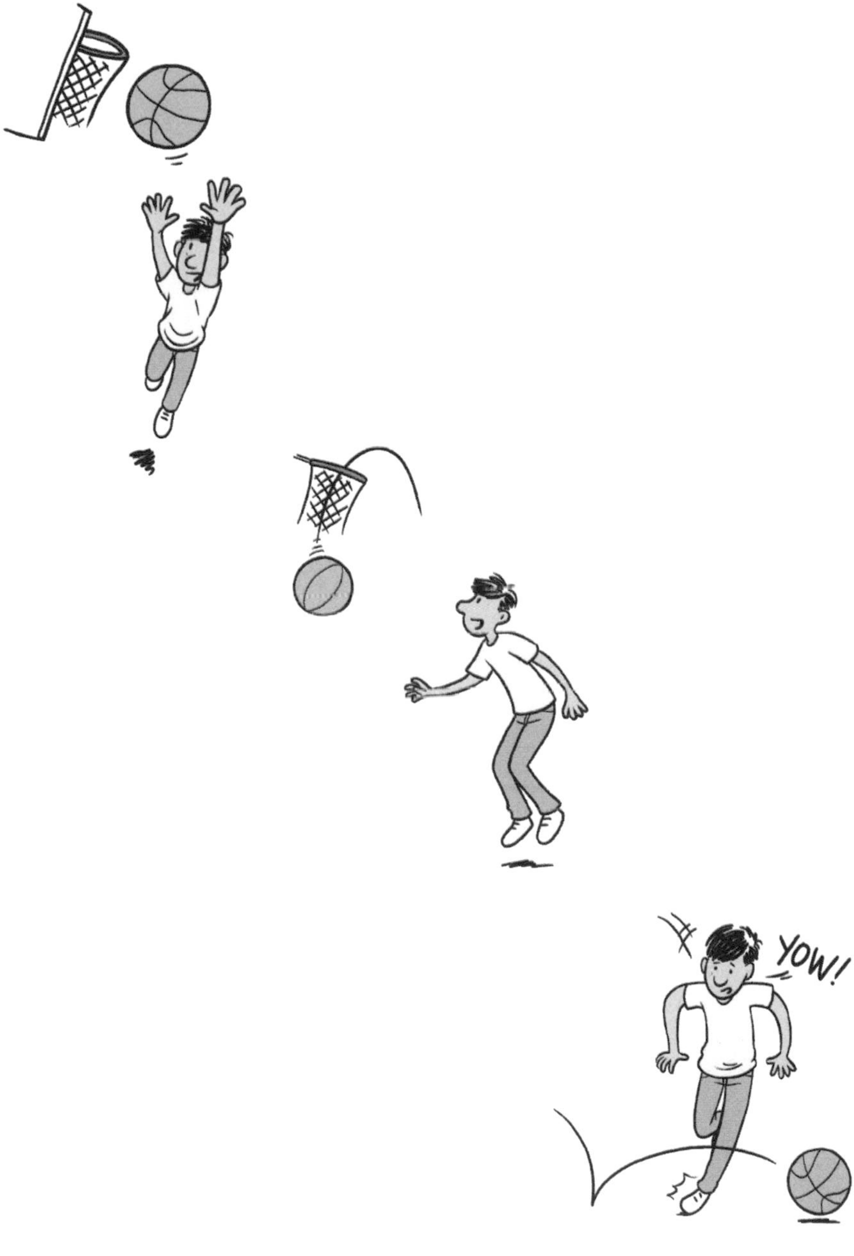
YOW!

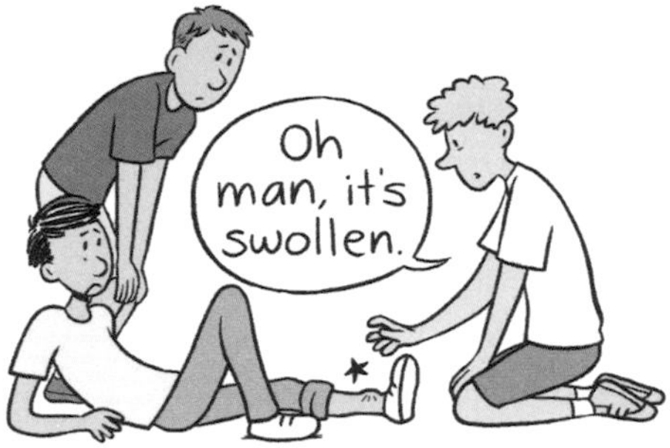
Oh man, it's swollen.

Zach runs inside to get some ice while I sit on the cement and think the worst.

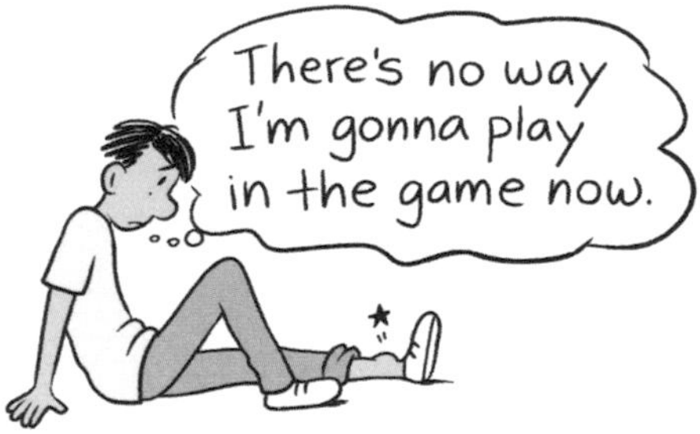
There's no way I'm gonna play in the game now.

Zach comes back with the ice and I keep it on my ankle. The guys give me a pep talk, saying they've done the same kind of stuff, but I'm miserable. I can't believe I hurt myself!

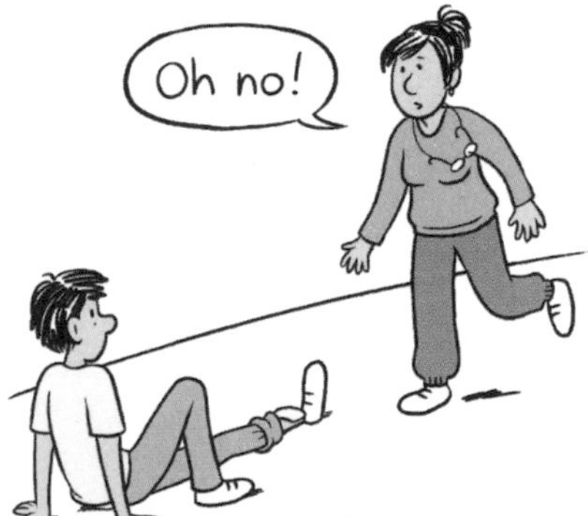
Oh no!

I tell Mom what happened, and she and Zach walk me inside. I sit on the couch, depressed.

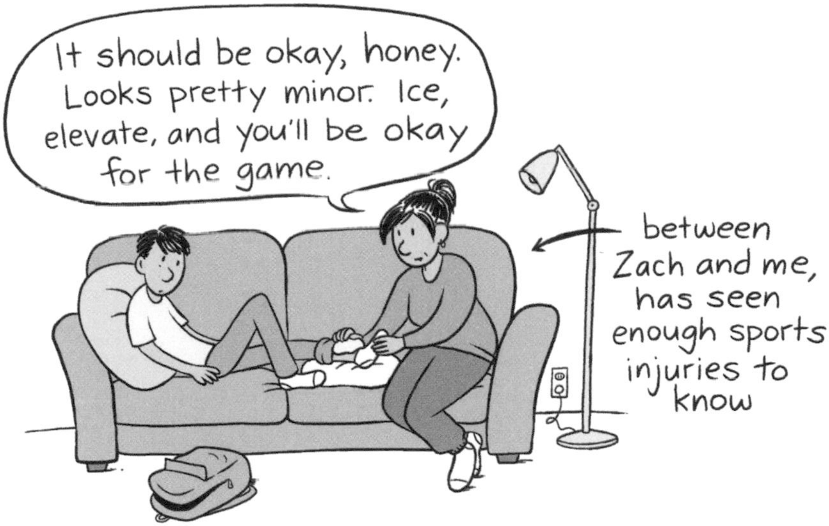
It should be okay, honey. Looks pretty minor. Ice, elevate, and you'll be okay for the game.
between Zach and me, has seen enough sports injuries to know

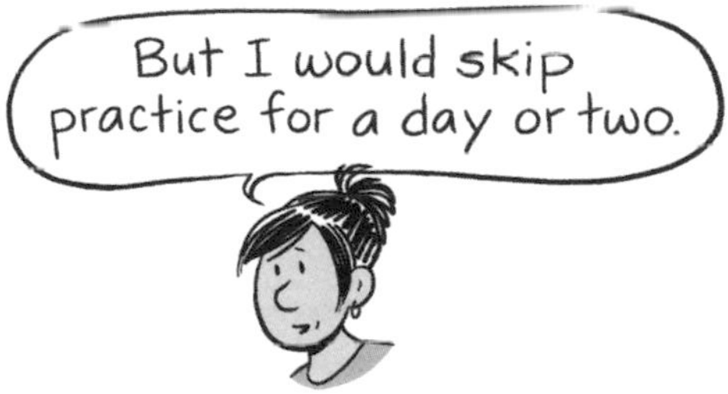
But I would skip practice for a day or two.

I groan. Coach will not be happy.

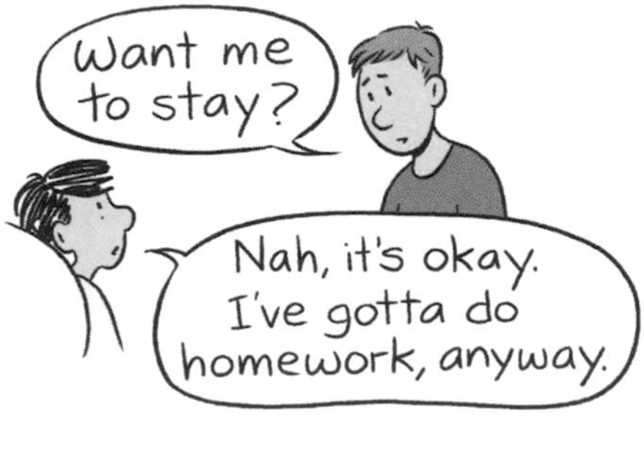
Want me to stay?
Nah, it's okay. I've gotta do homework, anyway.

He musses my hair and heads back out. He's being extra nice. Maybe I should injure myself more often.

My mom hovers for a while, concerned. But my ankle is starting to feel better.

It's okay, you can go. I'm fine.

You sure, honey? I can make you something. I was thinking about some comfort food tonight. Lasagna?

The only thing scarier than my mom making boxed or bagged dinners is her attempt to make meals from scratch.

flashback to the green soup incident

was supposed to be chicken noodle

here you go, Ty

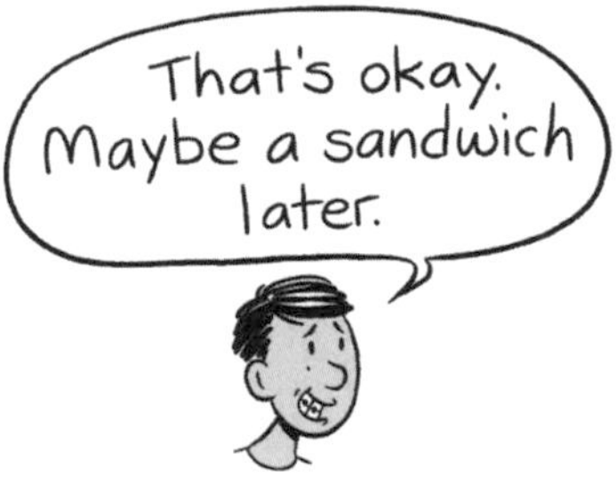
That's okay. Maybe a sandwich later.

Zach and I got used to making our own meals whenever she worked late. Zach makes the world's best panini, and I nailed Spaghetti à la Ty.

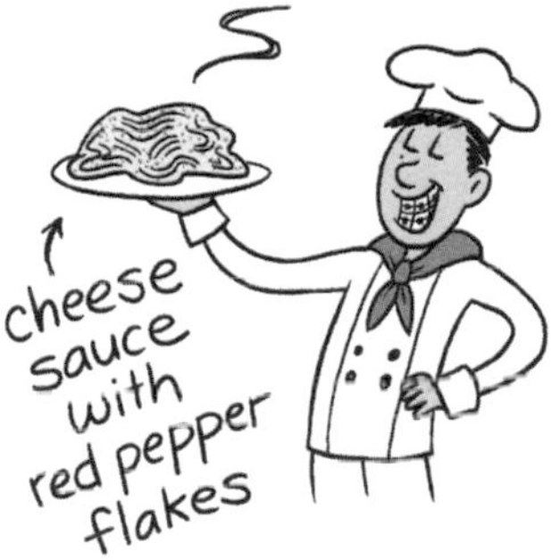
cheese sauce with red pepper flakes

The window faces the front yard. I hear Zach and his friends playing again.

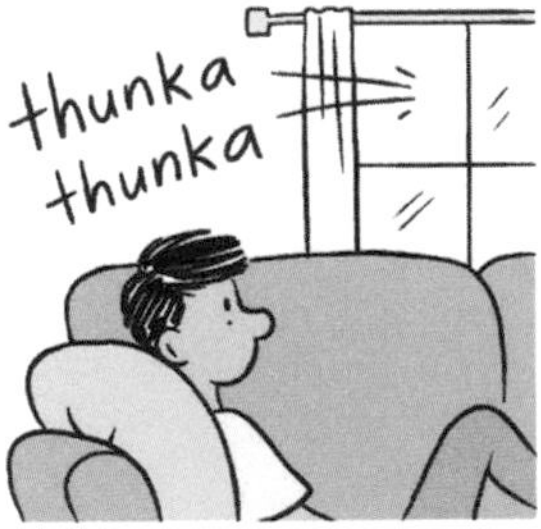
thunka
thunka

They're sophomores and don't go to prom or anything, but they have dances and stuff. Zach, Eli, and Jonathan were all part of the "Sweet Six," which is the tenth-grade version of a homecoming court. Six guys and six girls. The name is gag-worthy, but it's a such huge deal that the guys don't mind.

(...or they put up with it)

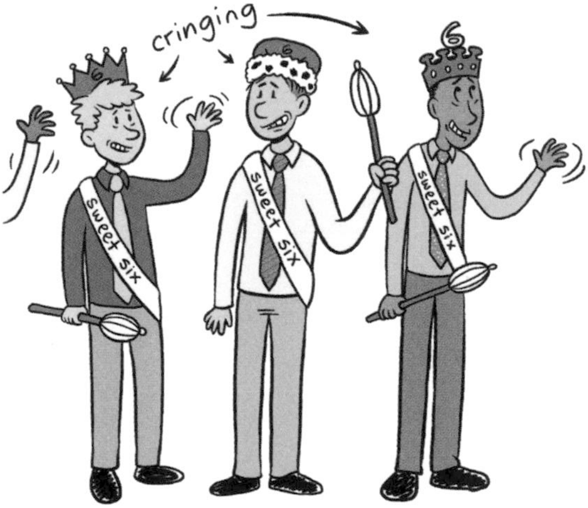
cringing
Sweet Six
Sweet Six
Sweet Six

Reminds me of what I could be. Me and my friends. All of us, with our dorky crowns, waving from the stage.

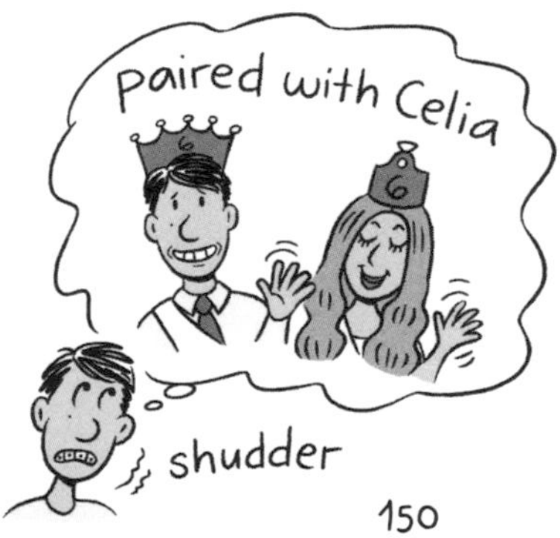
paired with Celia
shudder

Sometimes it's hard being related to Zach. It feels like there's a lot to live up to. Especially when your older brother is . . . well . . .

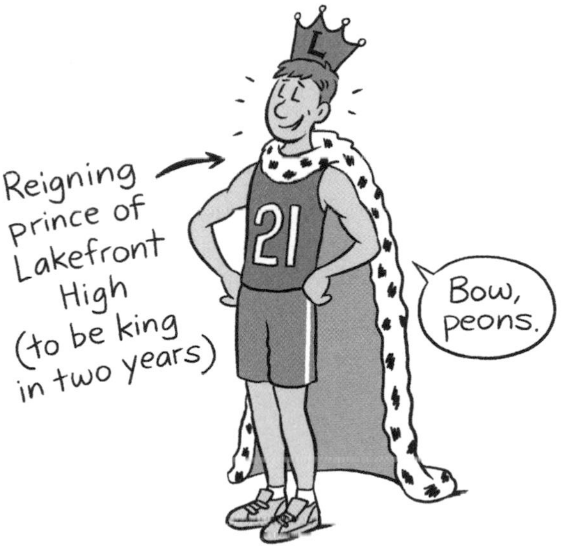
L
21
Reigning prince of Lakefront High (to be king in two years)
Bow, peons.

My phone goes off.

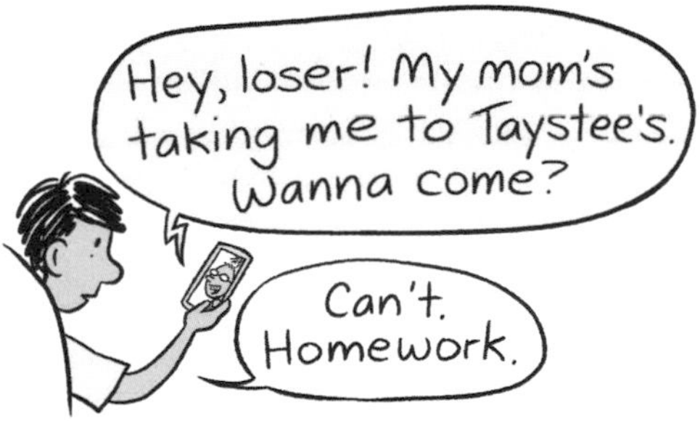
Hey, loser! My mom's taking me to Taystee's. Wanna come?
Can't. Homework.

I don't tell Joe about my ankle. For some reason, I don't want it to get back to Anthony.

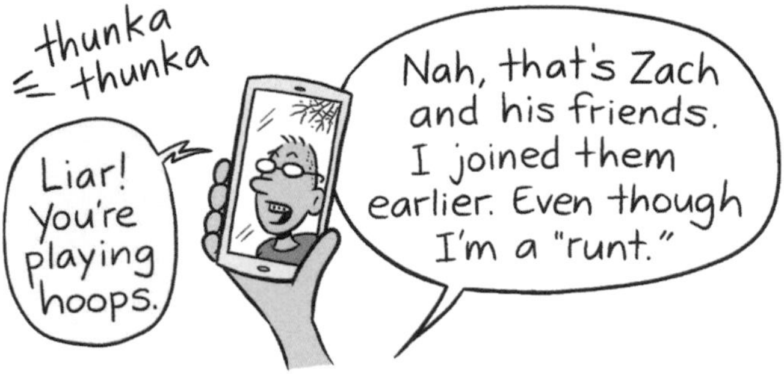
thunka thunka
Liar! You're playing hoops.
Nah, that's Zach and his friends. I joined them earlier. Even though I'm a "runt."

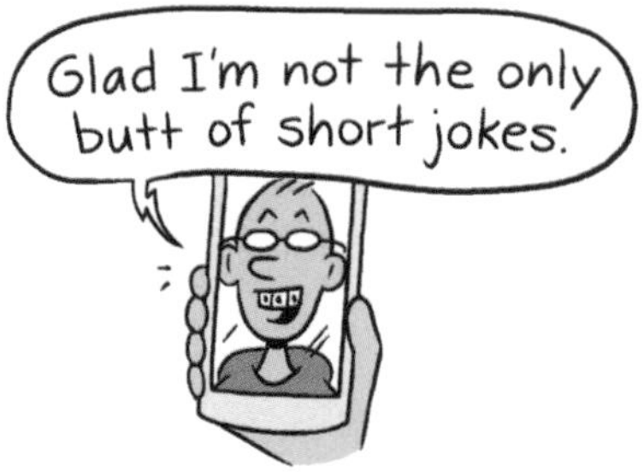
Glad I'm not the only butt of short jokes.

Actually, Joe's a lot shorter than me. He used to get picked on for being so little. But back in elementary school, he started deflecting with jokes. You know, making fun of himself before anyone else could.

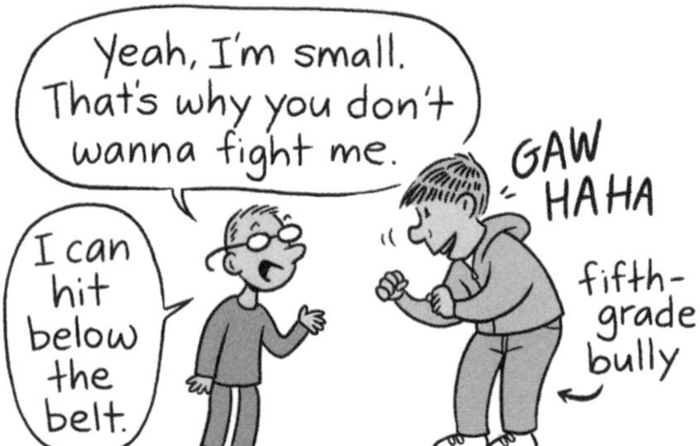
Yeah, I'm small. That's why you don't wanna fight me.
I can hit below the belt.
GAW HAHA
fifth-grade bully

Then he started deflecting by making fun of others.

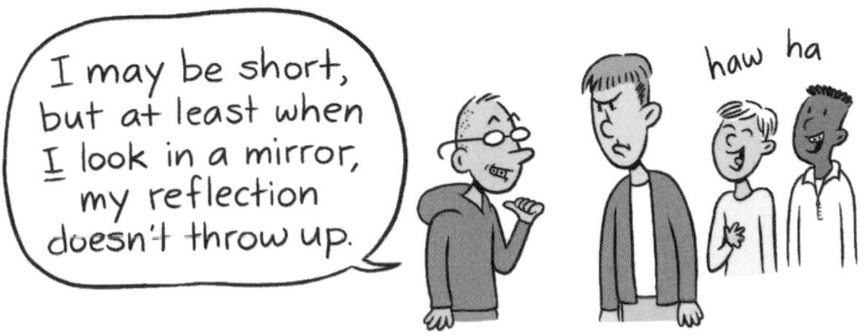
I may be short, but at least when I look in a mirror, my reflection doesn't throw up.
haw ha

Not the most mature thing to do, but it was one way to get kids to stop picking on him. He also got a reputation for being a clown, which won him some friends, like us. And predictably, some enemies.

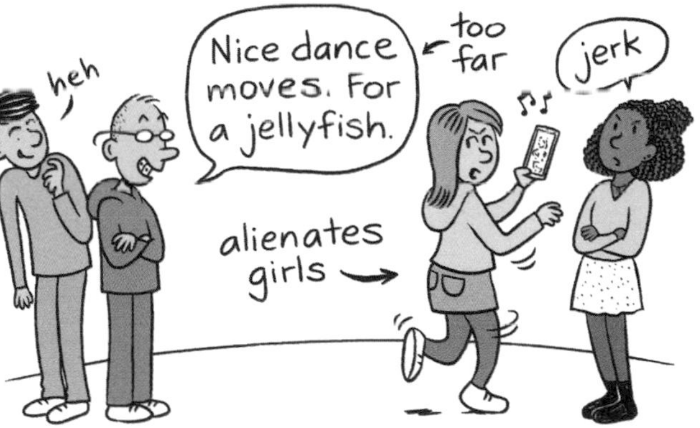
heh
Nice dance moves. For a jellyfish.
too far
jerk
alienates girls

Joe can be kinda polarizing, but if there's one thing he is, it's loyal. Proven by an incident at the beginning of sixth grade.

There was this mangy cat that used to roam around the field behind our school. She liked to hunt and leave behind dead rodents and birds.

dead pigeon →

could smell it from the science room →

One day, Joe, Anthony, and I decided it would be funny if we left one of her "presents" at our most hated teacher's desk: Mr. Dromacelli. He was awful—gave us mean nicknames (mine was "Fang" for my snaggletooth before braces), and made us **stand up** if he called on us in class.

uh...er...

imaginary spotlight on fang

Anyway, he was not amused by the rotting chipmunk we left in a shoebox on his desk chair—which he almost sat on. He was sure it was us 'cause, well, we weren't exactly angels. First, he made Joe go to the principal. Anthony and I knew we were next.

But Joe took the heat.

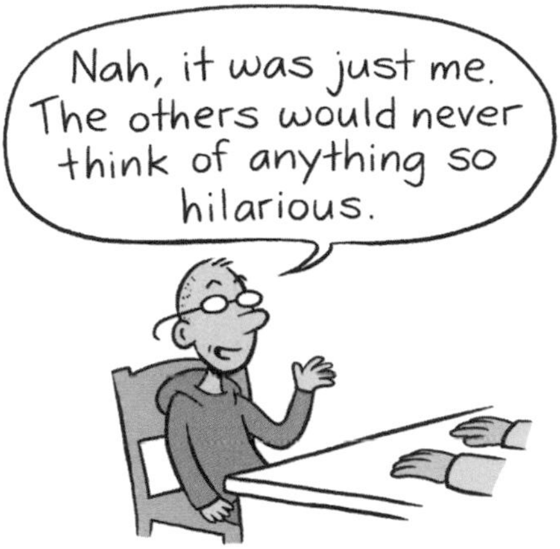
Nah, it was just me. The others would never think of anything so hilarious.

Anthony and I were so impressed (and relieved!), we made up for it by bringing Joe treats for detention. He especially loved my mom's rainbow Jell-O squares.

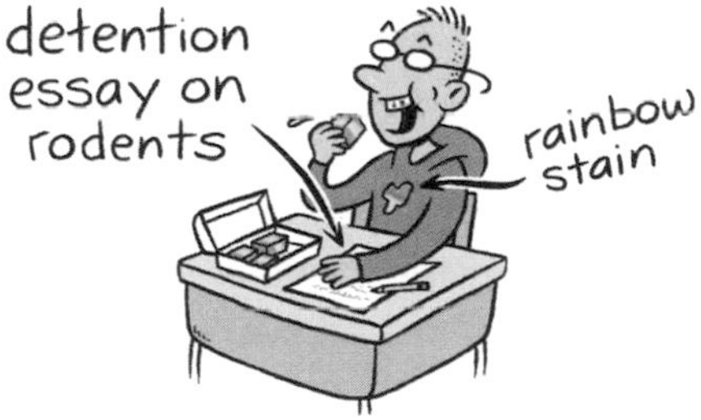
detention essay on rodents
rainbow stain

So that's why we hang out with Joe despite his big mouth. He'd stick with us through thick, thin . . . and dead rodents.

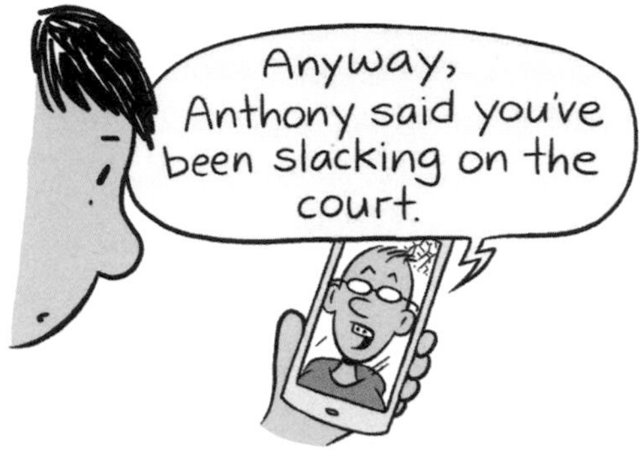
Anyway, Anthony said you've been slacking on the court.

At that, my temper flares.

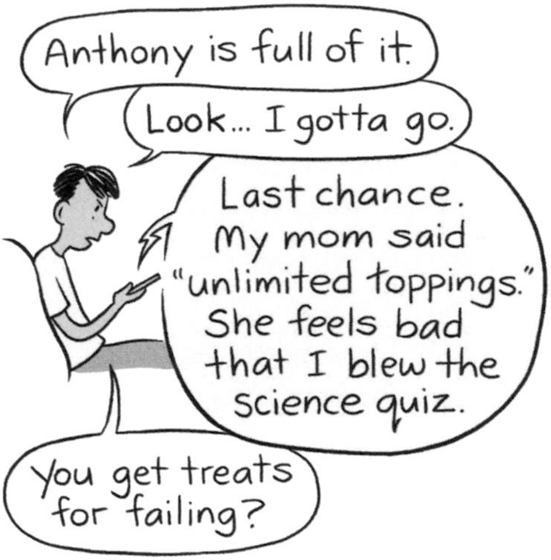
Anthony is full of it.
Look... I gotta go.
Last chance. My mom said "unlimited toppings." She feels bad that I blew the science quiz.
You get treats for failing?

Sometimes I think Joe gets away with everything. Even after the rodent thing, he joked his way out of an extra week of detention.

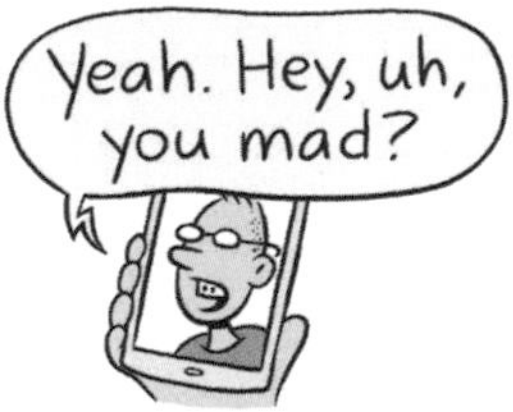
Yeah. Hey, uh, you mad?

I am, but not at him.

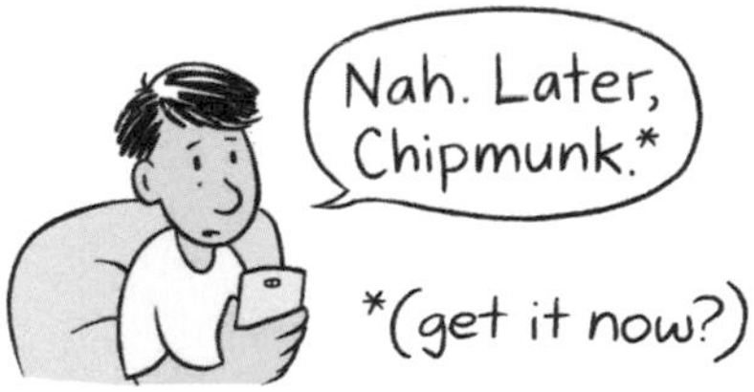
Nah. Later, Chipmunk.*
*(get it now?)

I hang up and fume.

It's one thing for Anthony to get in my face, but now he's saying things behind my back? I grab my phone again.

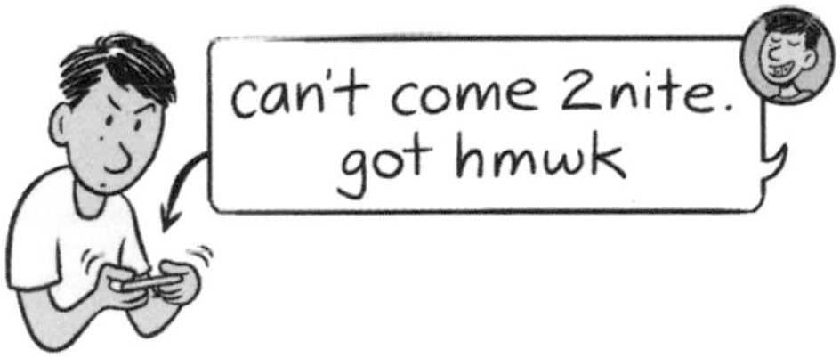
can't come 2nite. got hmwk

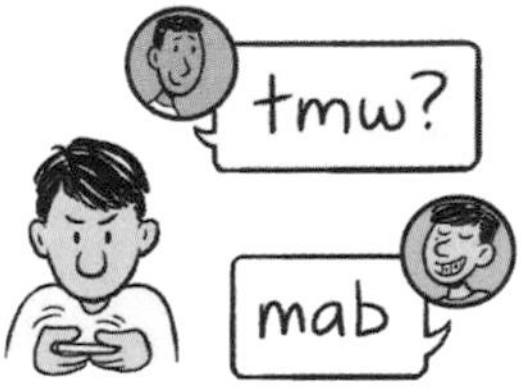
tmw?
mab

I put my phone down. I'm so mad, I can't even do homework.

Instead, I reach into my backpack and pull out my sketchbook. I pick up where I left off in my story. I don't even glance at the outline or anything. I have most of it memorized, anyway.

I draw and draw until I lose track of time. I even forget about my ankle.

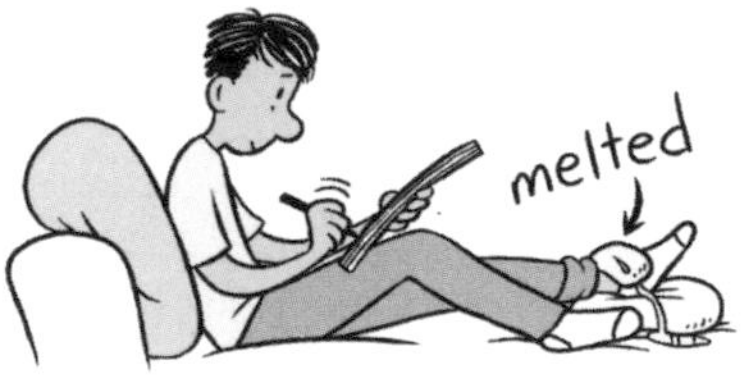
melted

And I realize . . .

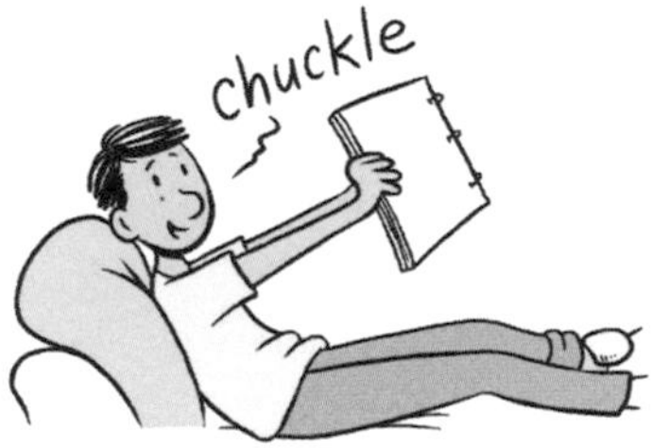
chuckle

. . . this is the only thing that makes me feel better.

Emmie

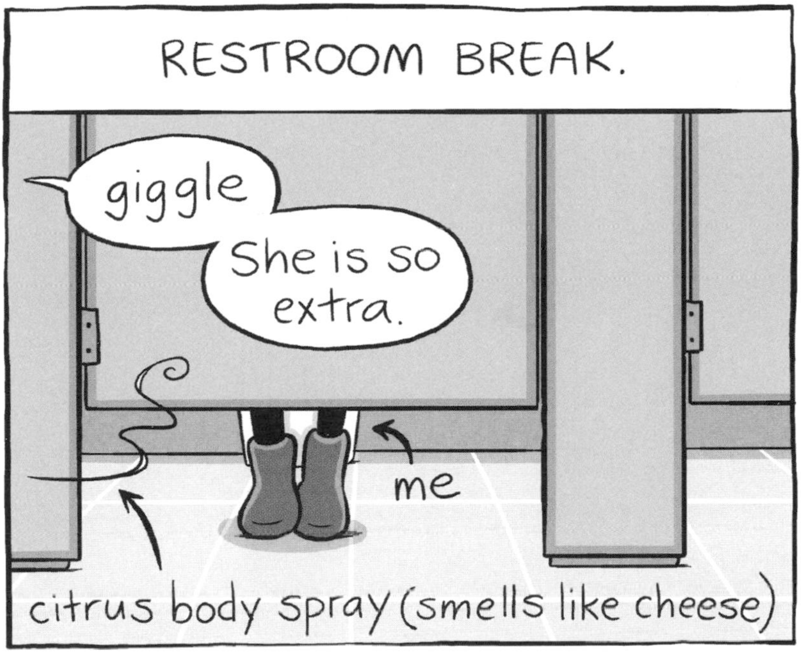
RESTROOM BREAK.
giggle
She is so extra.
me
citrus body spray (smells like cheese)

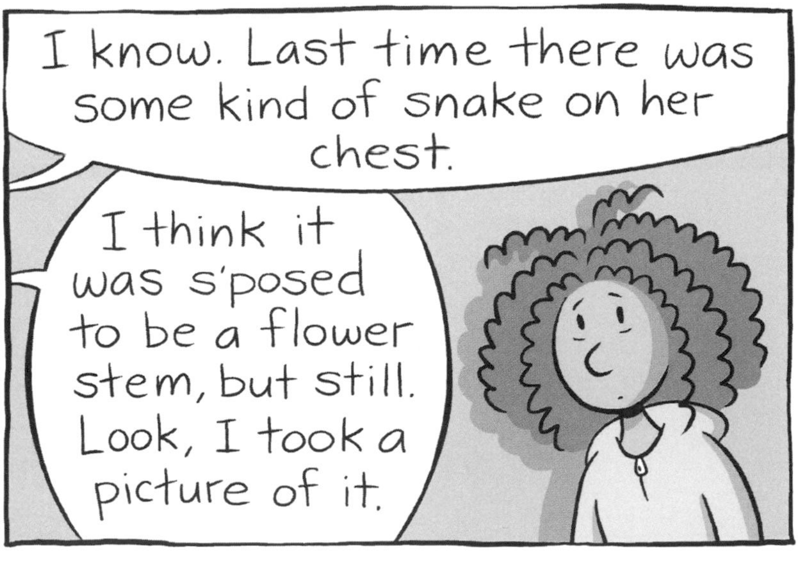
I know. Last time there was some kind of snake on her chest.
I think it was s'posed to be a flower stem, but still. Look, I took a picture of it.

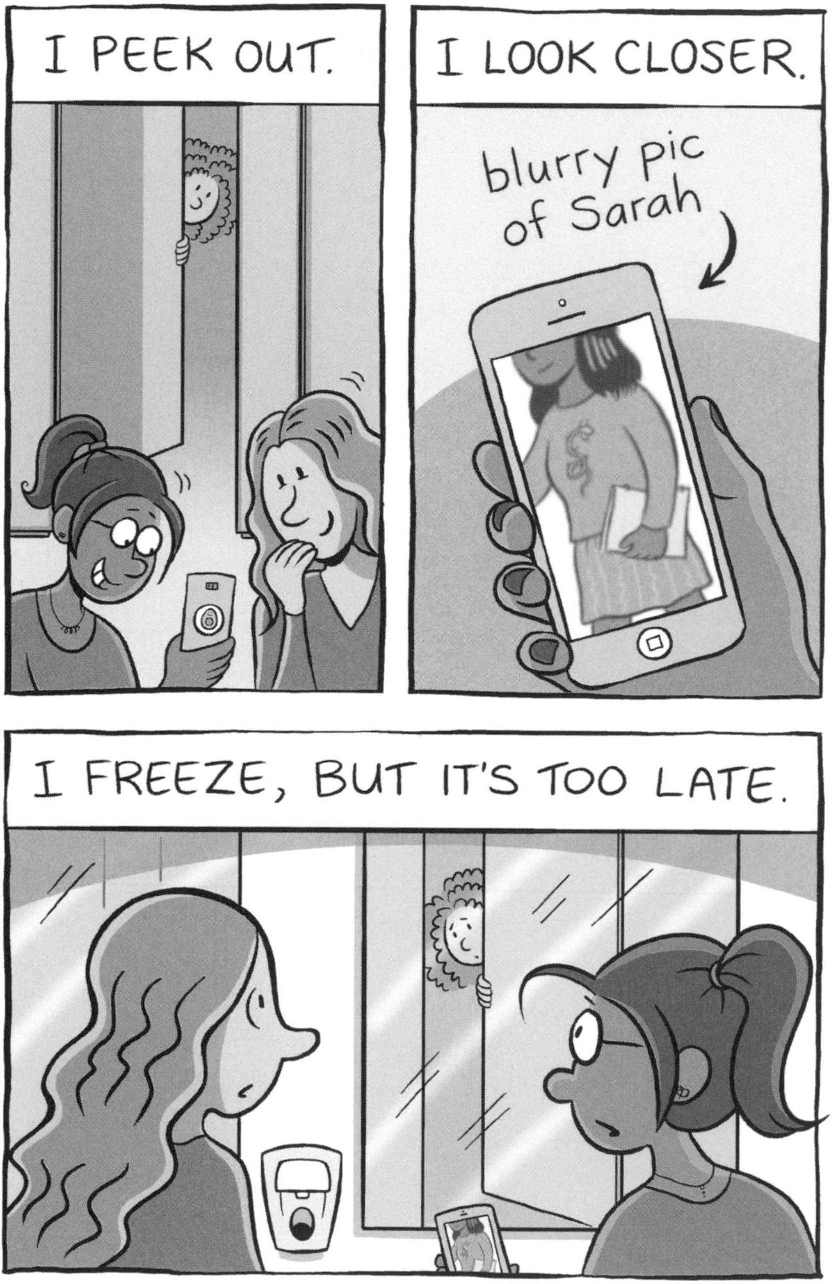
I PEEK OUT.
I LOOK CLOSER.
blurry pic of Sarah
I FREEZE, BUT IT'S TOO LATE.

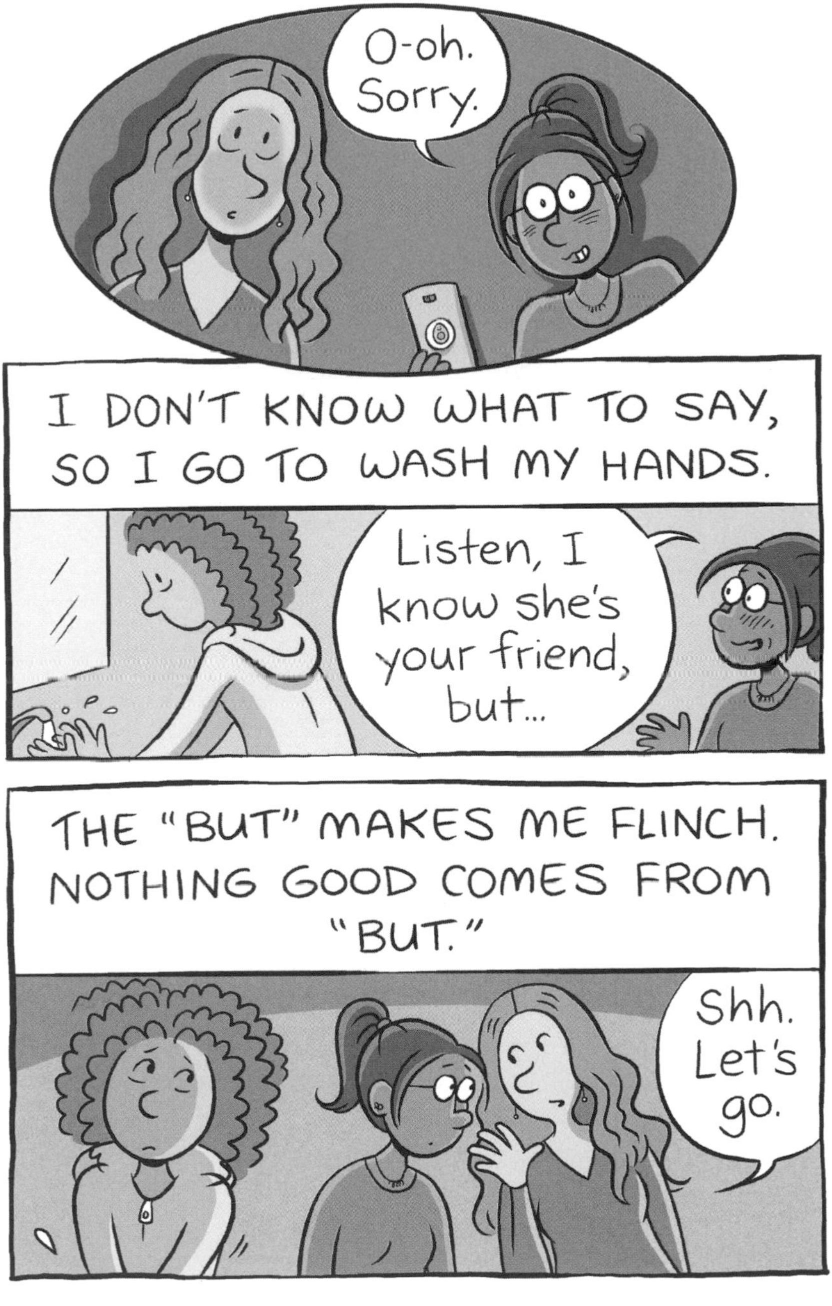
O-oh. Sorry.
I DON'T KNOW WHAT TO SAY, SO I GO TO WASH MY HANDS.
Listen, I know she's your friend, but...
THE "BUT" MAKES ME FLINCH. NOTHING GOOD COMES FROM "BUT."
Shh. Let's go.

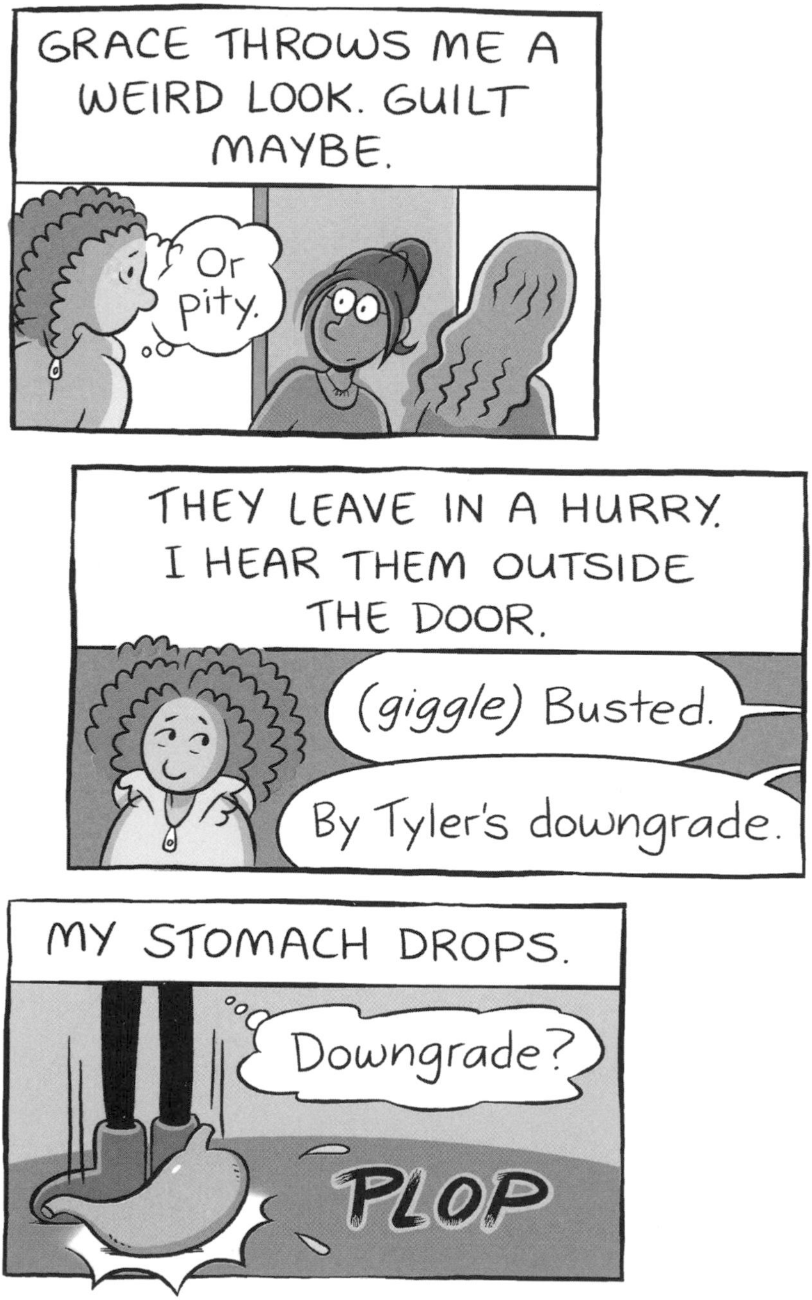
GRACE THROWS ME A WEIRD LOOK. GUILT MAYBE.
Or pity.
THEY LEAVE IN A HURRY. I HEAR THEM OUTSIDE THE DOOR.
(giggle) Busted.
By Tyler's downgrade.
MY STOMACH DROPS.
Downgrade?
PLOP

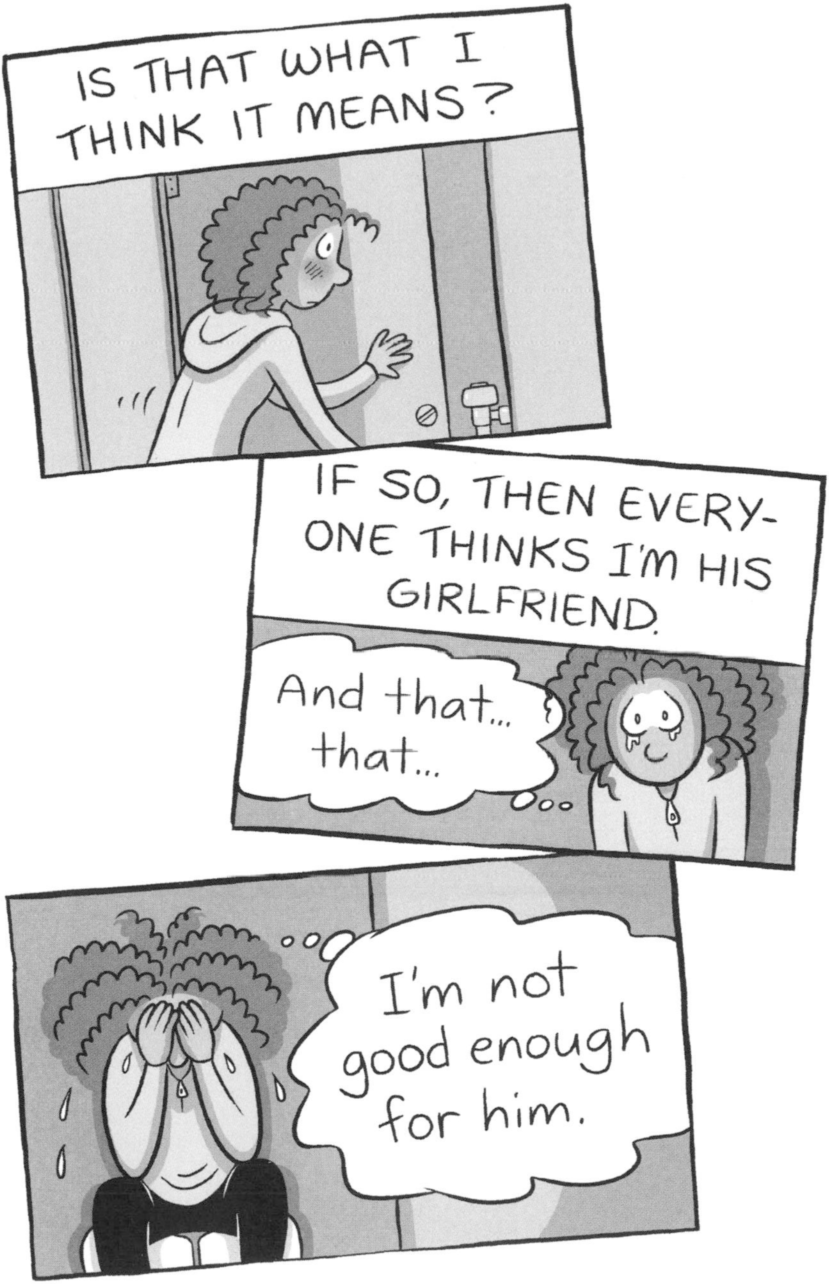
IS THAT WHAT I THINK IT MEANS?
IF SO, THEN EVERY-ONE THINKS I'M HIS GIRLFRIEND.
And that... that...
I'm not good enough for him.

TYLER

It's been three days since I twisted my ankle. My mom was right: it feels fine now. I was lucky. But I had to miss practice the last two days. Coach wasn't pleased, but she understood.

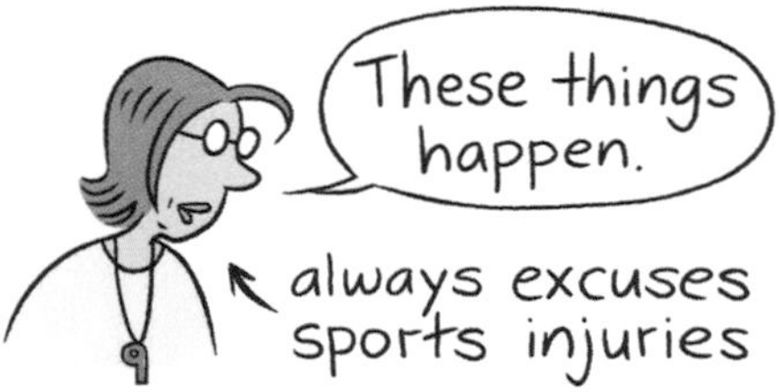
These things happen.
always excuses sports injuries

I'm in art class. Emmie's acting kinda weird. She's hiding her face and is super quiet, even for her. Then again, I've been pretty quiet, too.

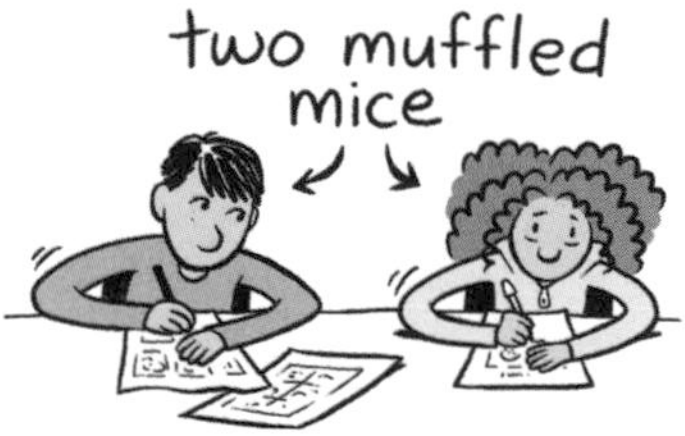
two muffled mice

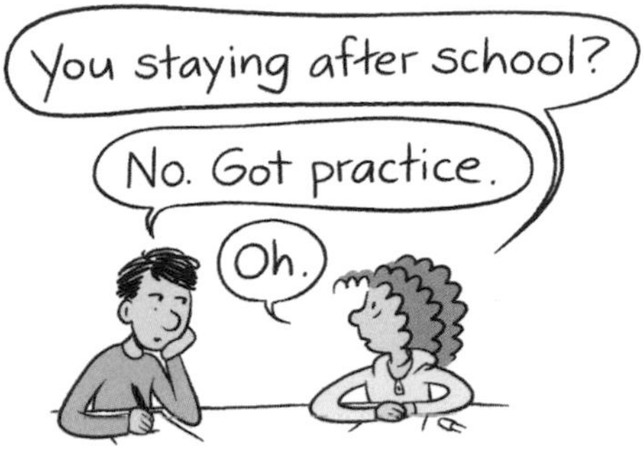
You staying after school?
No. Got practice.
Oh.

Silence again while we get back to the book. We're each working a little differently. Emmie's sketching all her pages first, then inking them, then adding color. I'm doing all the sketching, inking, and coloring as I go. We're both doing a pretty good job of sticking to the "script," although sometimes we'll ask each other if we can make small changes here and there. It's a good system.

It reminds me of basketball. You have to work as a team; otherwise it falls apart. Strategies are mapped out, and if we follow 'em, it usually goes our way. If we deviate, it can go either way.

Today I'm deviating. I'm kinda rushing this page.

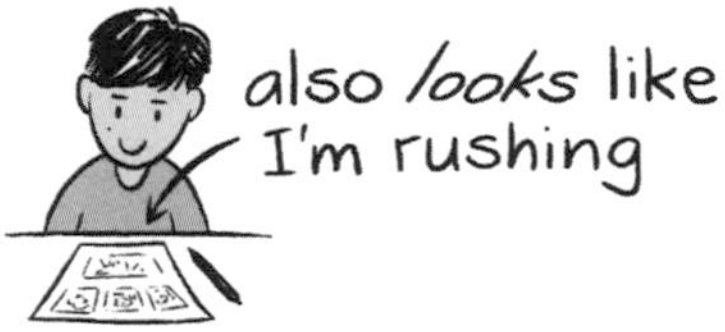
also *looks* like I'm rushing

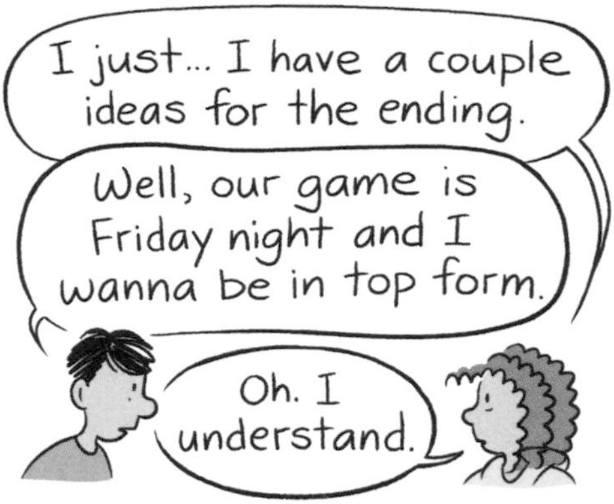
I just... I have a couple ideas for the ending.
Well, our game is Friday night and I wanna be in top form.
Oh. I understand.

I feel bad. It's not Emmie's fault I injured myself and got behind.

After laying off my ankle, I had to get back at it. The weather stayed warm-ish, and I was able to play in the driveway yesterday. Luckily, I was sinking more balls than missing. Zach even joined me once.

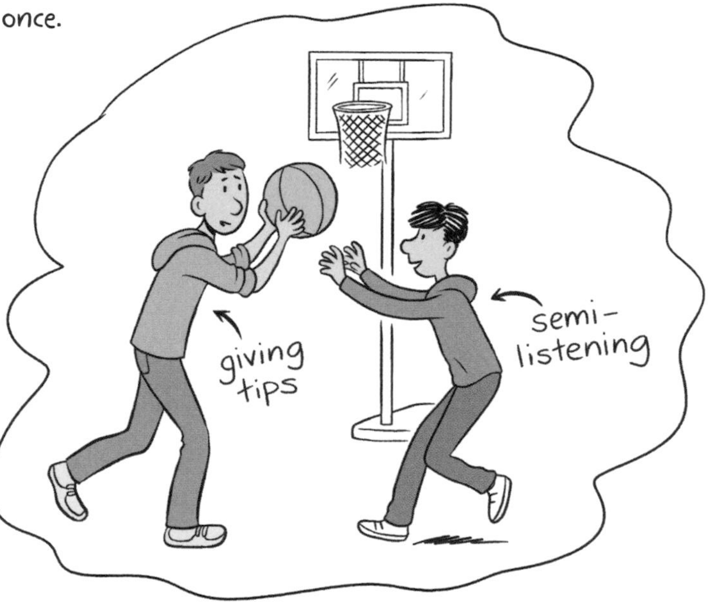
giving tips
semi-listening

It didn't last long, though.

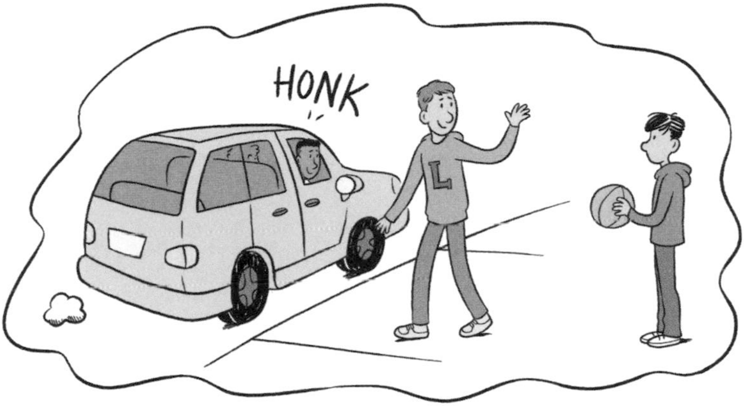
HONK

I look down at my paper.

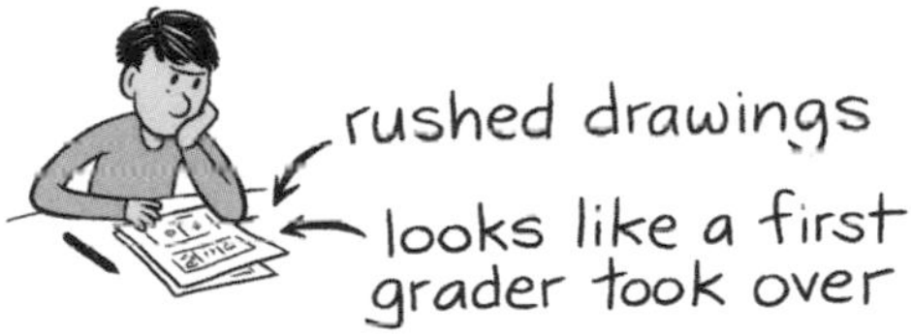
rushed drawings
looks like a first grader took over

I growl, crumple the page, and toss it in the trash.

Ms. Laurie comes over.

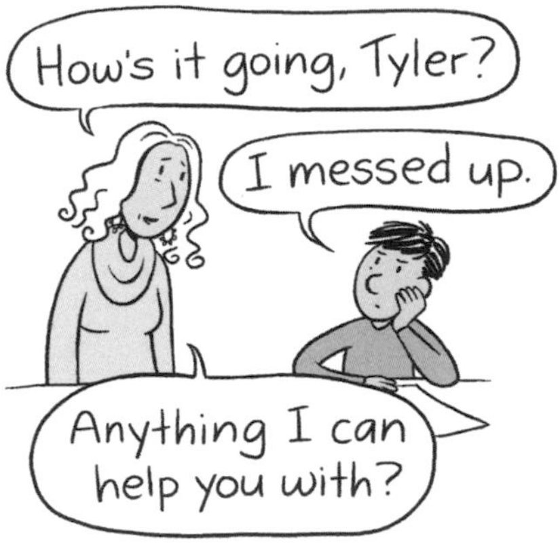
How's it going, Tyler?
I messed up.
Anything I can help you with?

Ms. Laurie has been checking our work as we go.

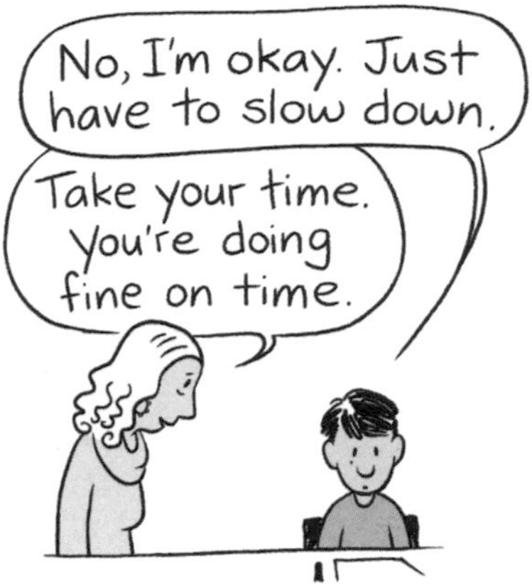
No, I'm okay. Just have to slow down.
Take your time. You're doing fine on time.

I am, but I'm trying to keep up with Emmie. I know I should slow down. I work a lot better when I do. Some kids are fast and good. I'm slow and good. And I like lots of detail.

And I really, really like working on this. I guess I'm just upset about missing practice. I wanna win the game, **and** I want to win that art prize.

Without realizing I'm doing it, I put my head in my hands and:

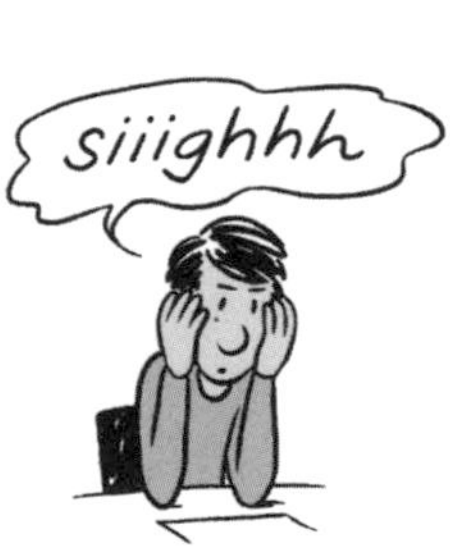
siiighhh

I look up and find Emmie looking right back at me curiously.

But I'm not in the mood to be watched.

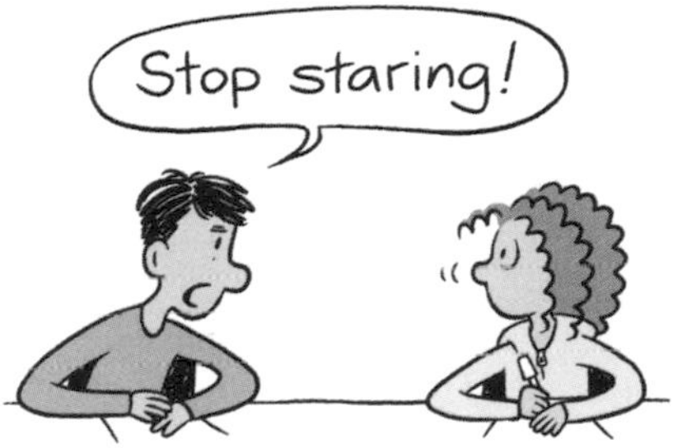
Stop staring!

She immediately turns away, but I can see she's getting red and tears are forming.

Argh! I hate it when girls cry.

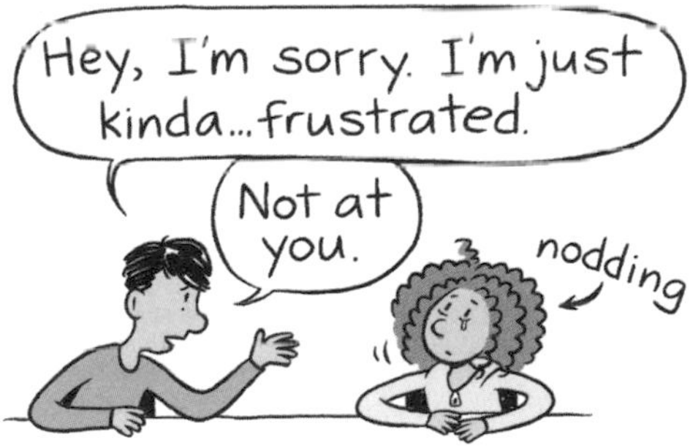
Hey, I'm sorry. I'm just kinda... frustrated.
Not at you.
nodding

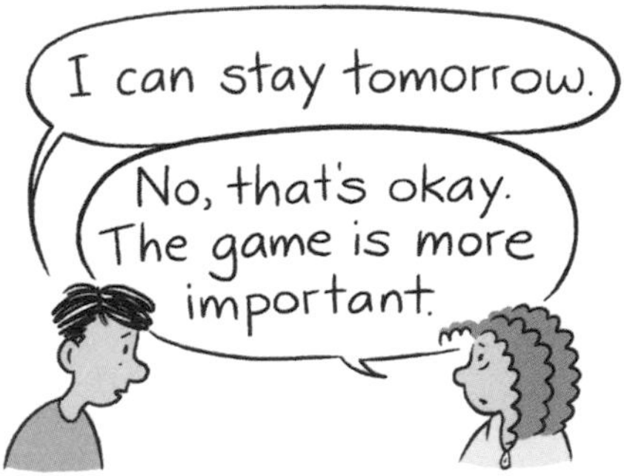
I can stay tomorrow.
No, that's okay. The game is more important.

I think for a moment.

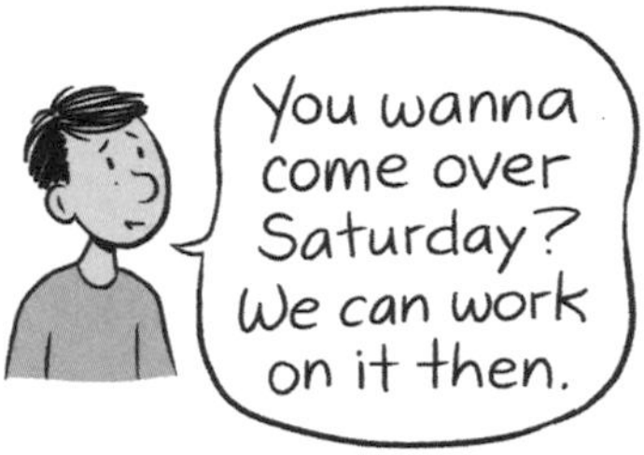
You wanna come over Saturday? We can work on it then.

Her eyes get really wide—happy wide—like I just offered her Phineas.

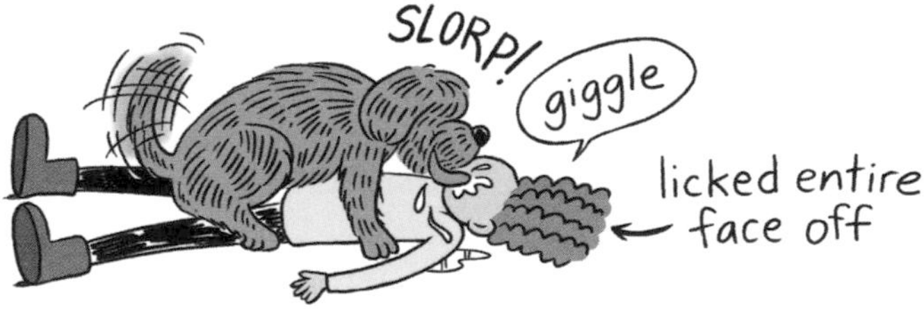
SLORP!
giggle
licked entire face off

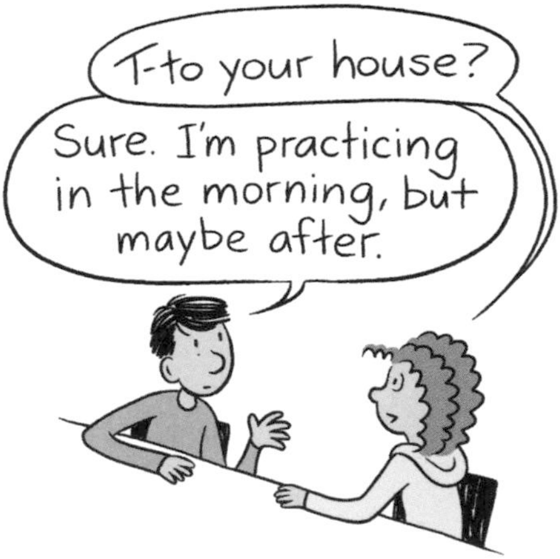
T-to your house?
Sure. I'm practicing in the morning, but maybe after.

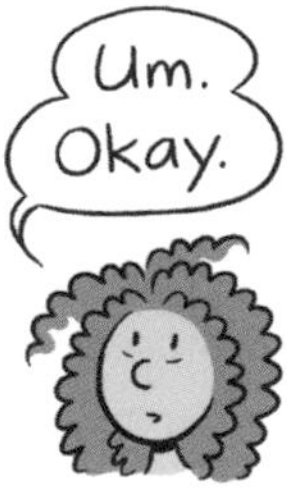
Um. Okay.

I hold up my palm and she high-fives it.

Good. Doing this at my house means getting more done. In private. Away from other people. People who make comments.

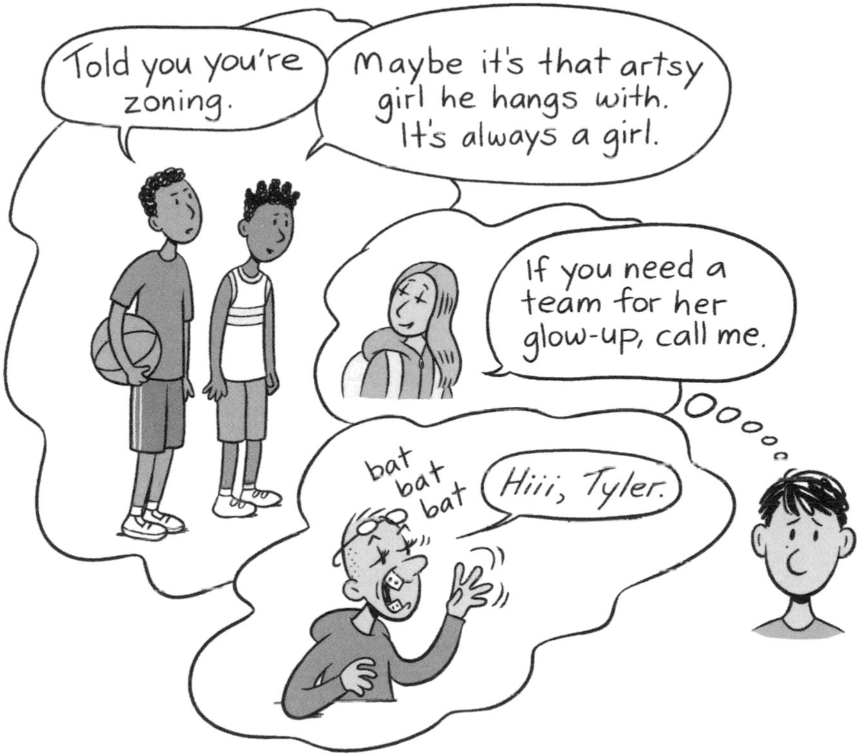
Told you you're zoning.
Maybe it's that artsy girl he hangs with. It's always a girl.
If you need a team for her glow-up, call me.
bat bat bat
Hiii, Tyler.

Yeah, privacy is what we need.

The thought of it makes me feel better already.

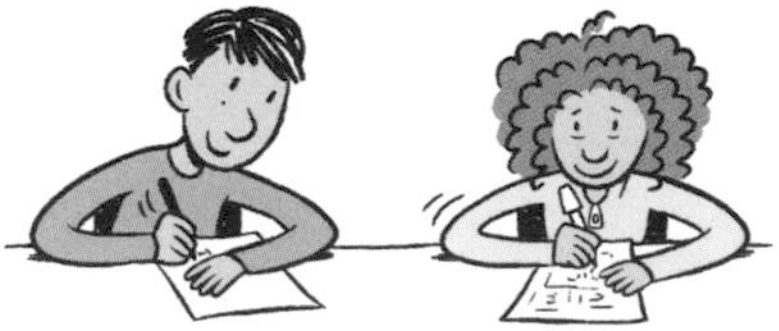

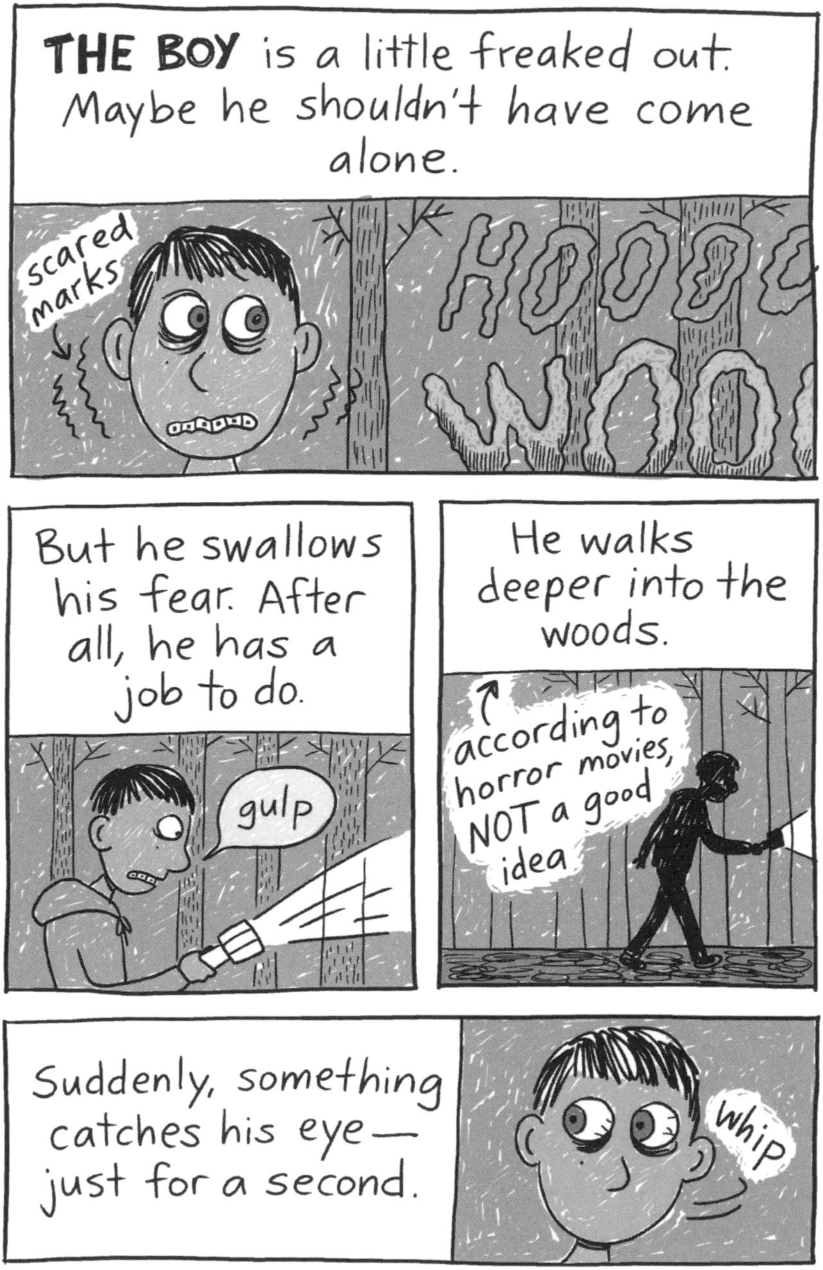
THE BOY is a little freaked out. Maybe he shouldn't have come alone.
scared marks
HOOOO
WOOO
But he swallows his fear. After all, he has a job to do.
gulp
He walks deeper into the woods.
according to horror movies, NOT a good idea
Suddenly, something catches his eye— just for a second.
whip

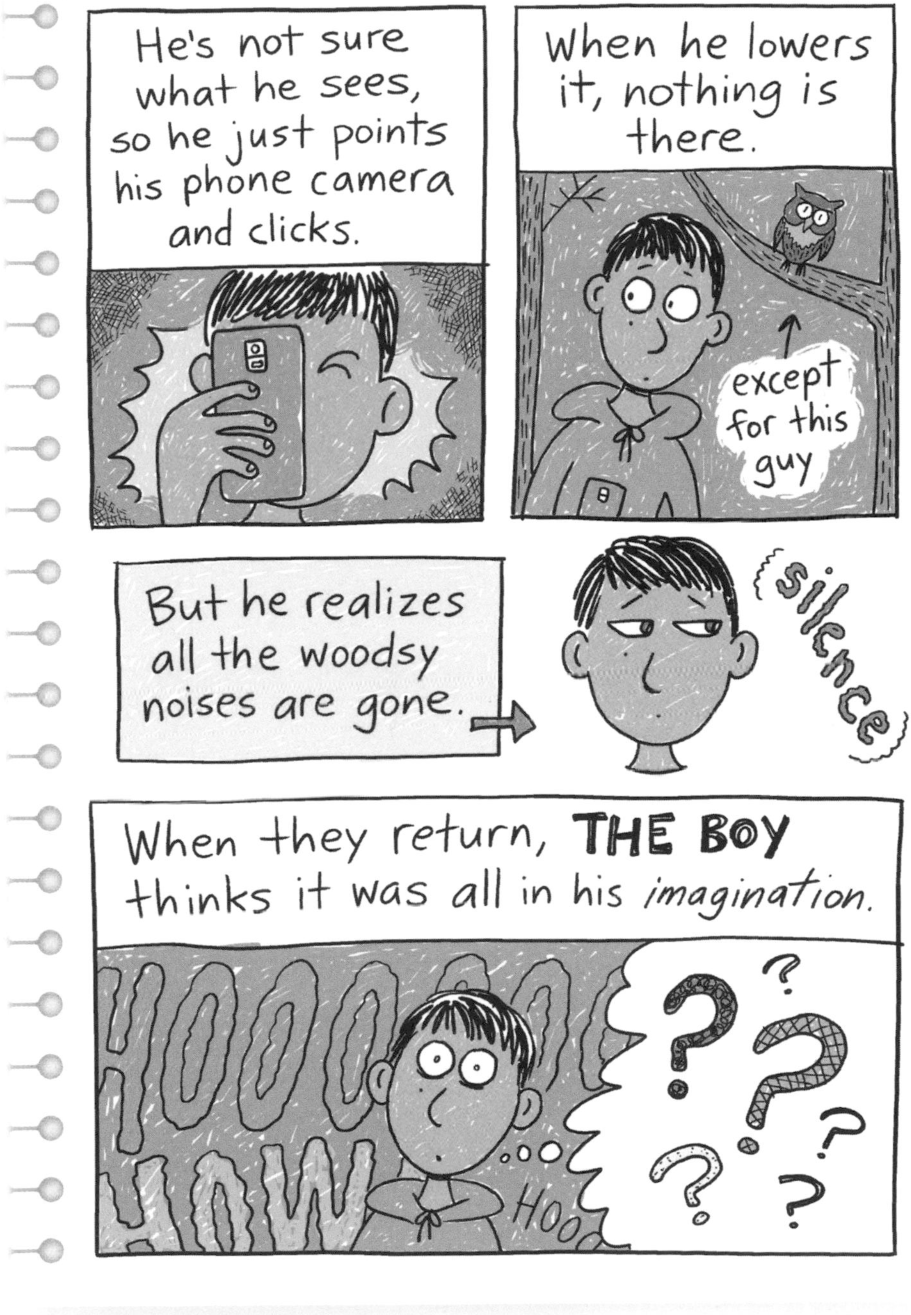
He's not sure what he sees, so he just points his phone camera and clicks.
When he lowers it, nothing is there.
except for this guy
But he realizes all the woodsy noises are gone.
(silence)
When they return, THE BOY thinks it was all in his imagination.
HOO

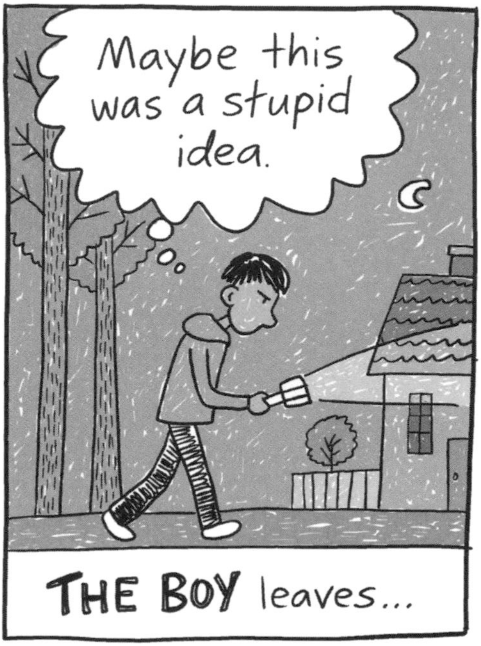
Maybe this was a stupid idea.
THE BOY leaves...

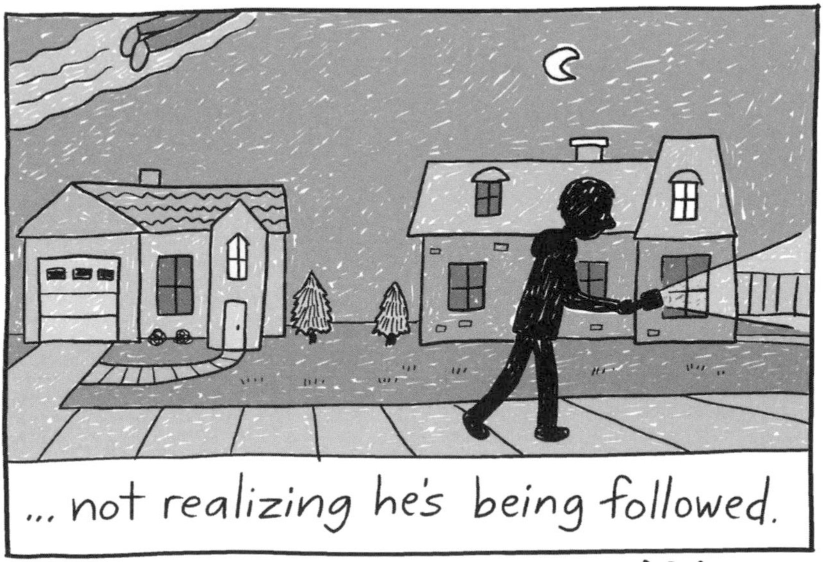
... not realizing he's being followed.

cont'd

Emmie

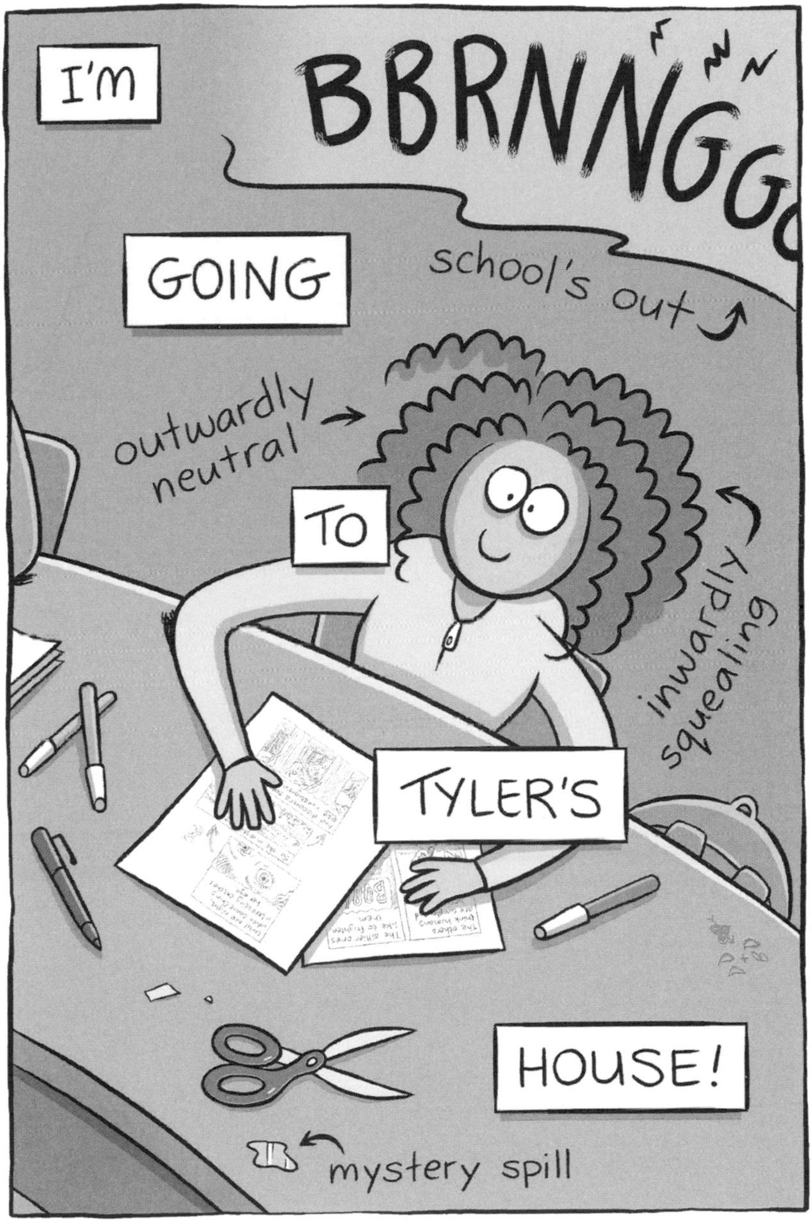
I'M
BBRNNGGG
GOING
school's out
outwardly neutral
TO
inwardly squealing
TYLER'S
HOUSE!
mystery spill

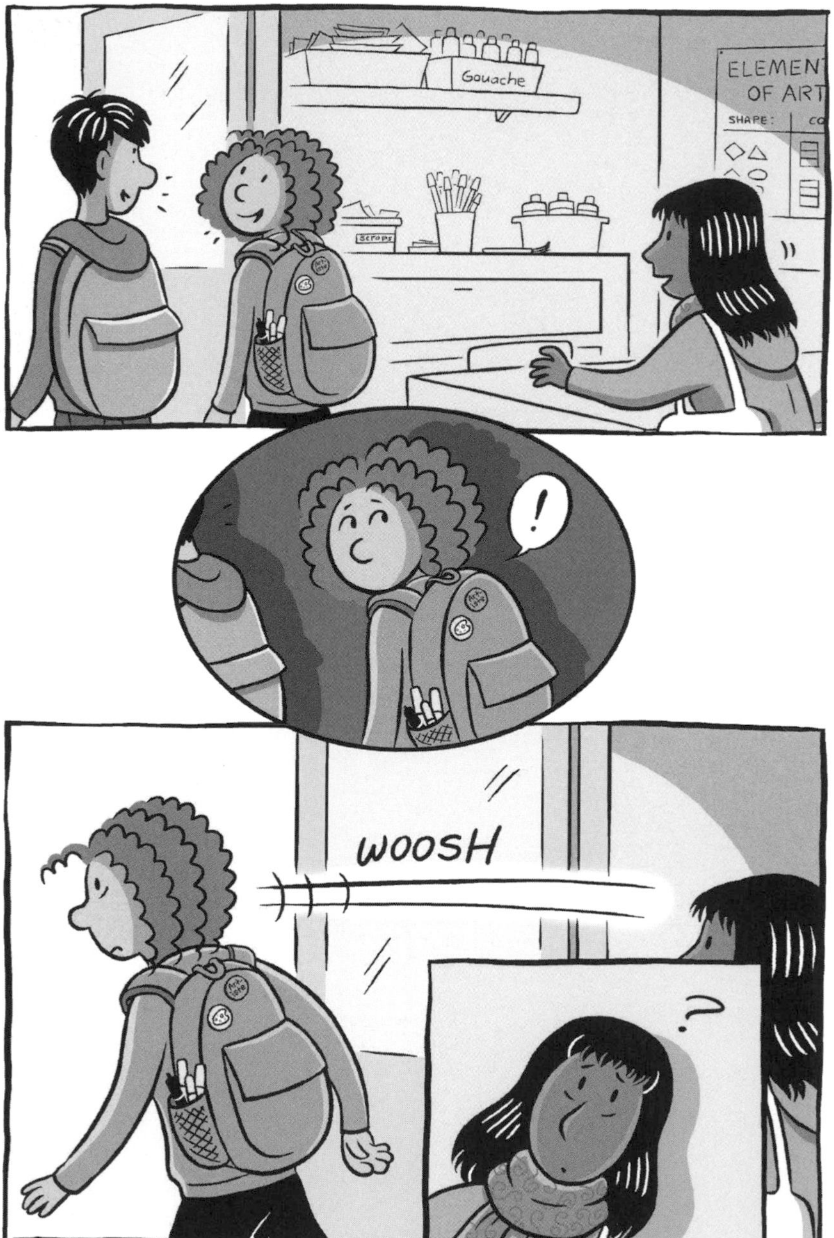
Gouache
ELEMENT
OF ART
SHAPE:
Scraps
!
WOOSH
?

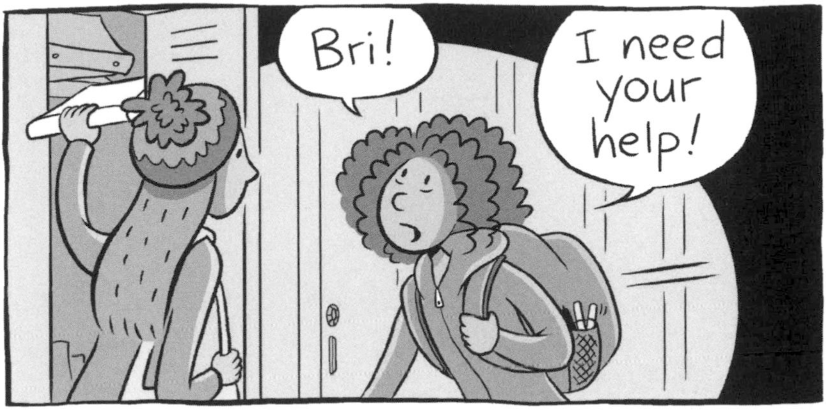
Bri!
I need your help!

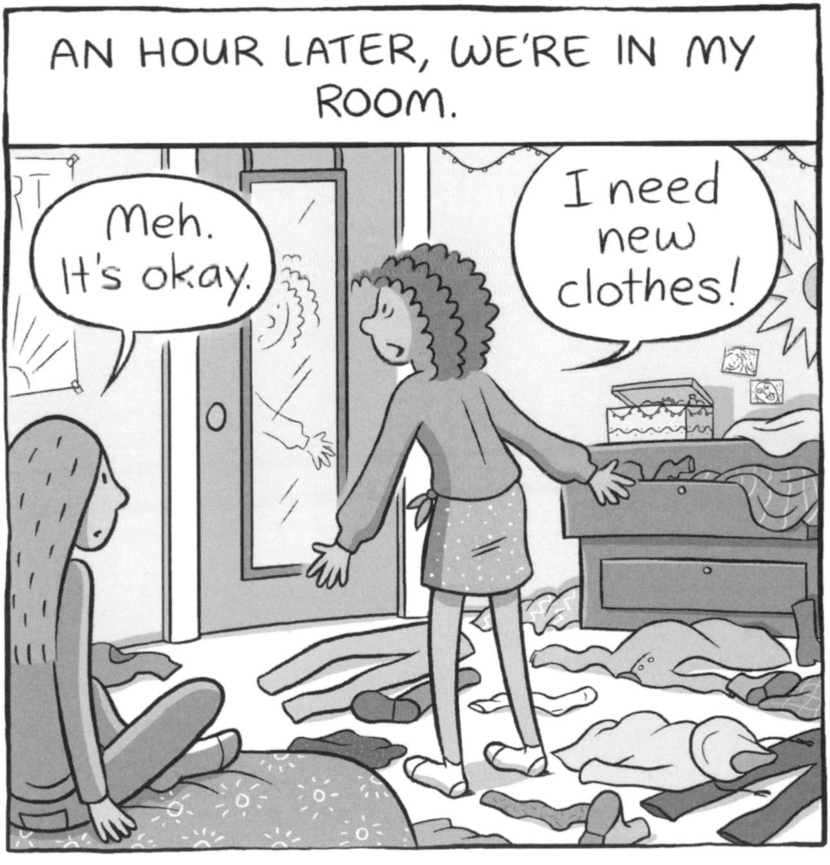
AN HOUR LATER, WE'RE IN MY ROOM.
I need new clothes!
Meh. It's okay.

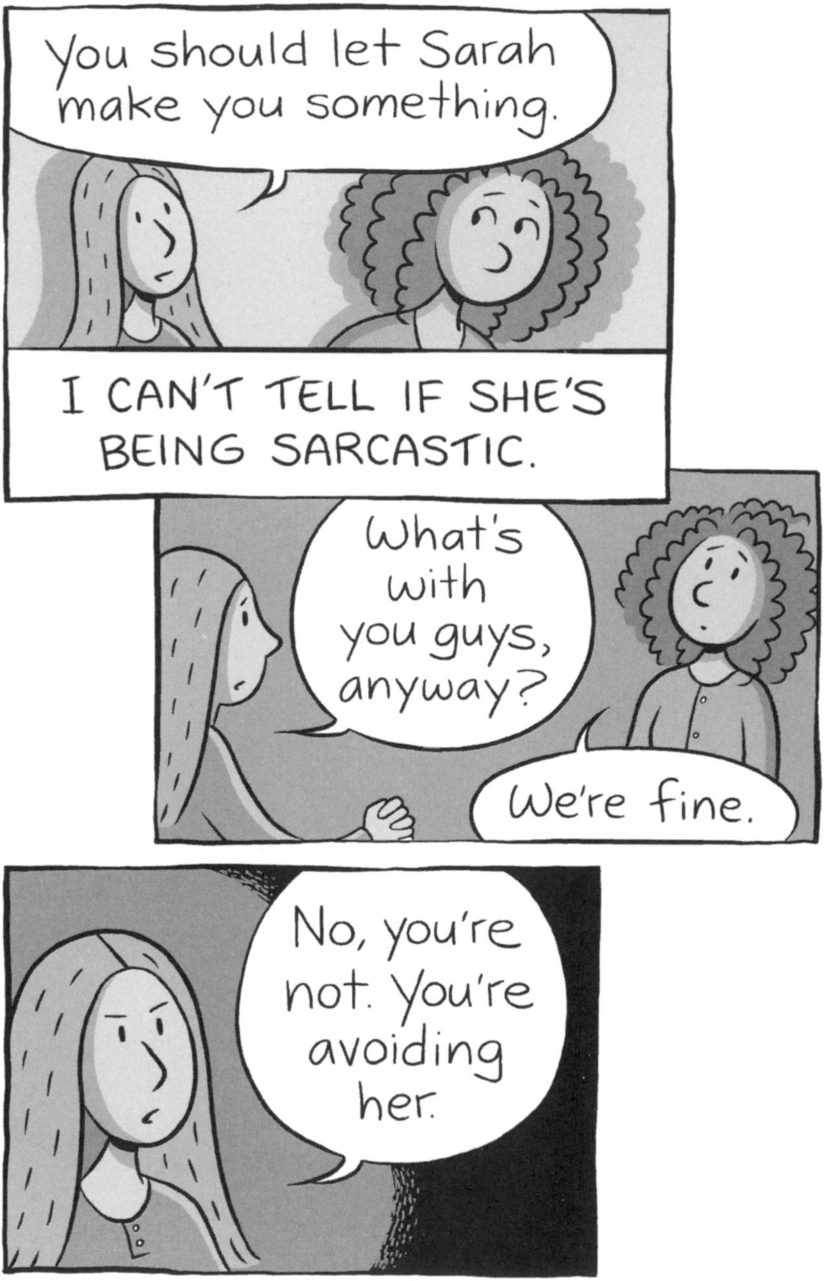
you should let Sarah make you something.
I CAN'T TELL IF SHE'S BEING SARCASTIC.
What's with you guys, anyway?
We're fine.
No, you're not. You're avoiding her.

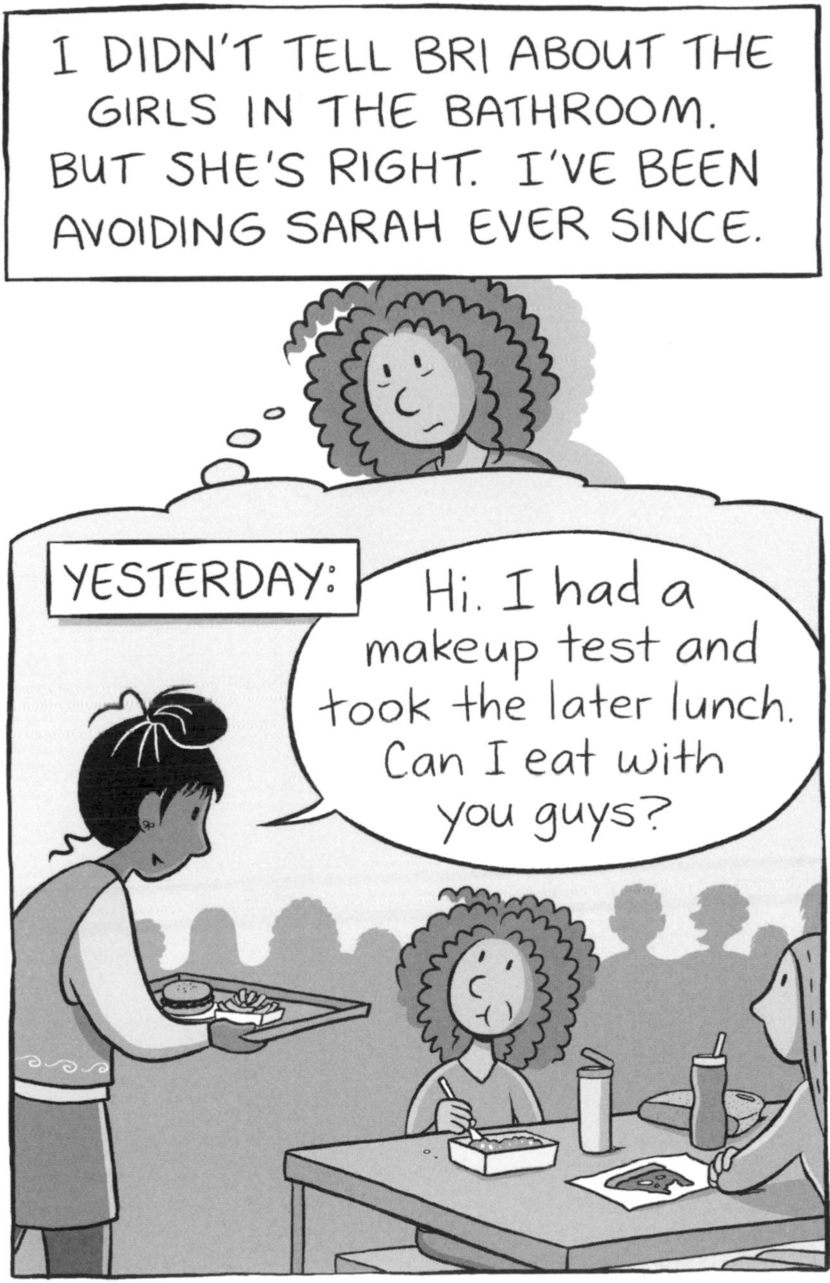
I DIDN'T TELL BRI ABOUT THE GIRLS IN THE BATHROOM. BUT SHE'S RIGHT. I'VE BEEN AVOIDING SARAH EVER SINCE.
YESTERDAY:
Hi. I had a makeup test and took the later lunch. Can I eat with you guys?

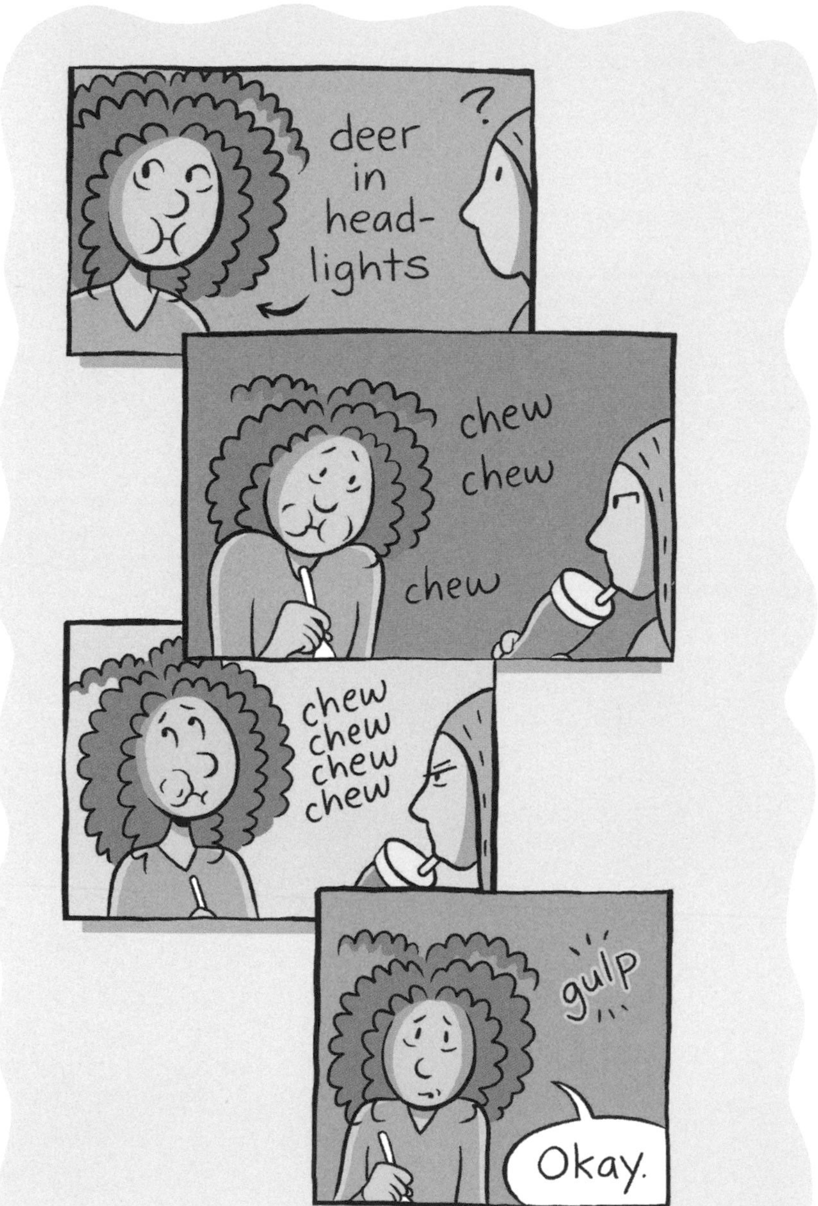
?
deer in head-lights
chew
chew
chew
chew
chew
chew
chew
gulp
Okay.

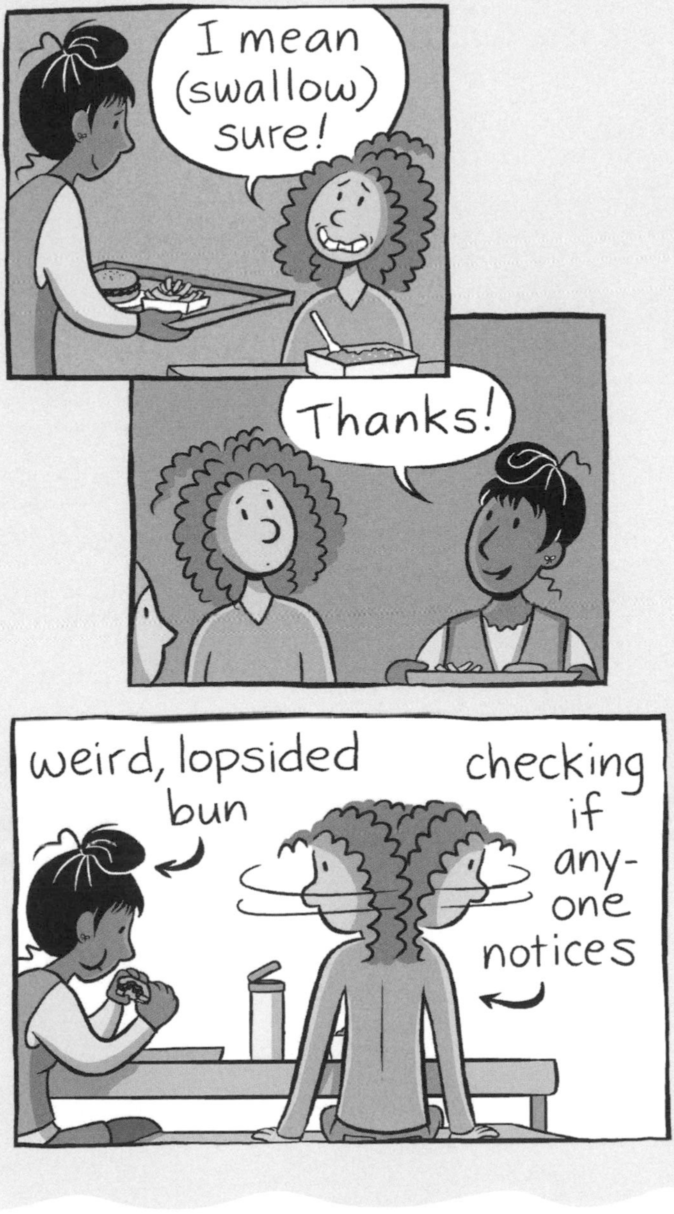
I mean
(swallow)
sure!
Thanks!
weird, lopsided
bun
checking
if
any-
one
notices

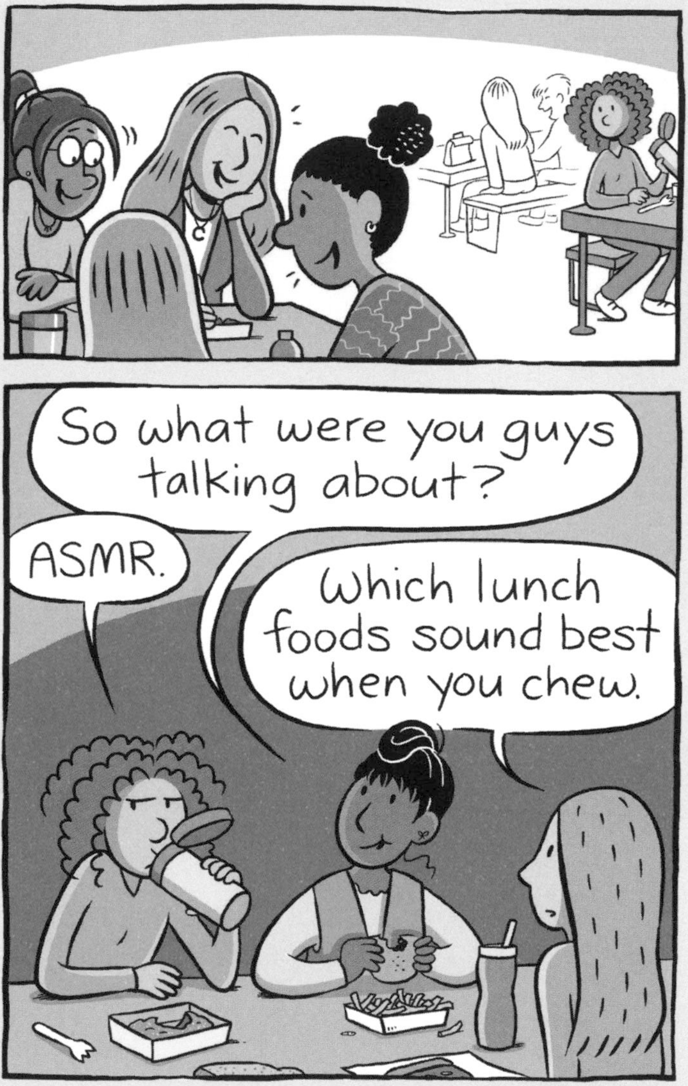
So what were you guys talking about?
ASMR.
Which lunch foods sound best when you chew.

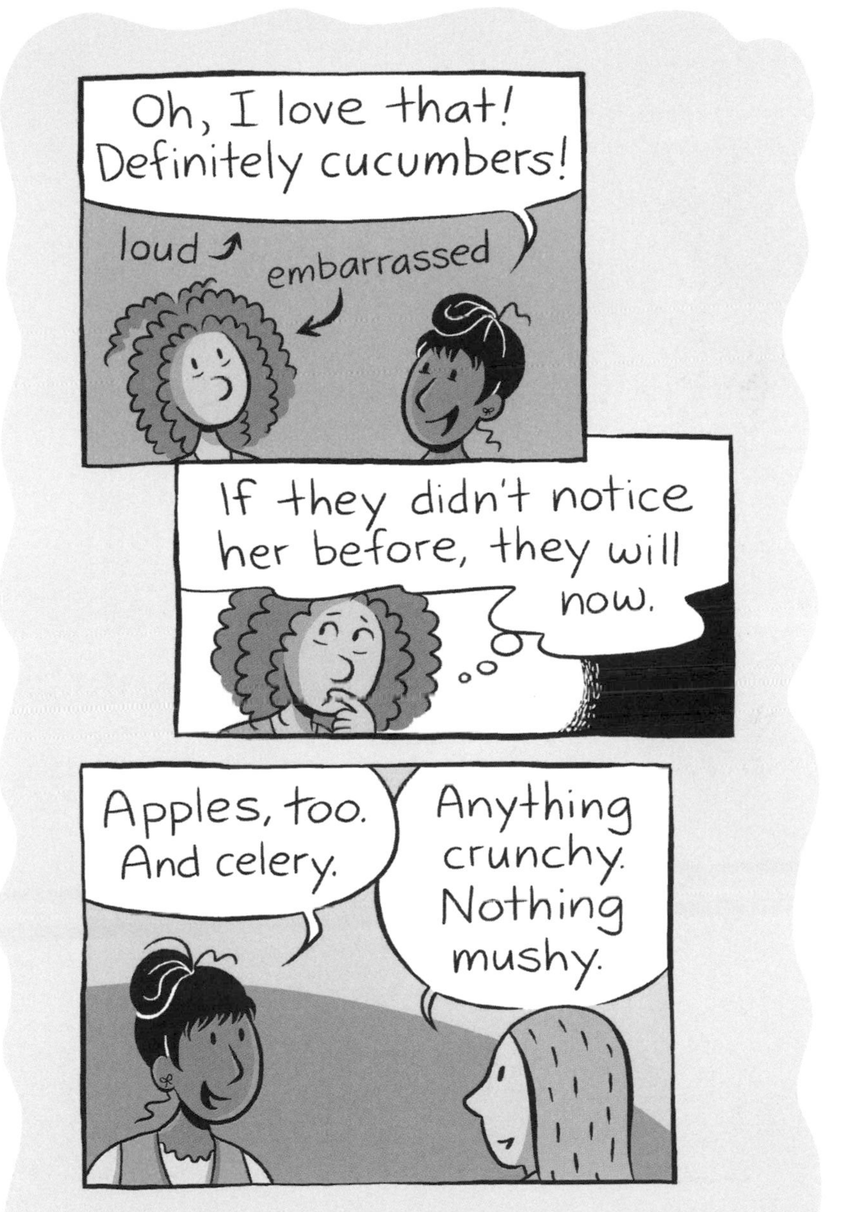
Oh, I love that! Definitely cucumbers!
loud
embarrassed
If they didn't notice her before, they will now.
Apples, too. And celery.
Anything crunchy. Nothing mushy.

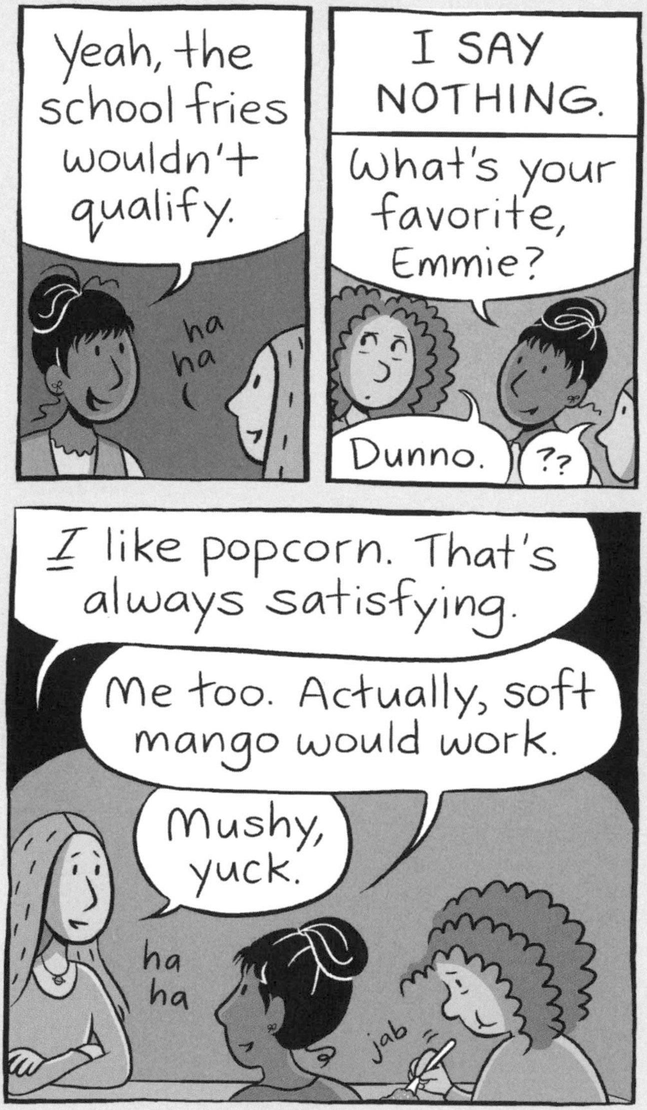
Yeah, the school fries wouldn't qualify.
ha ha
I SAY NOTHING.
What's your favorite, Emmie?
Dunno.
??
I like popcorn. That's always satisfying.
Me too. Actually, soft mango would work.
Mushy, yuck.
ha ha
jab

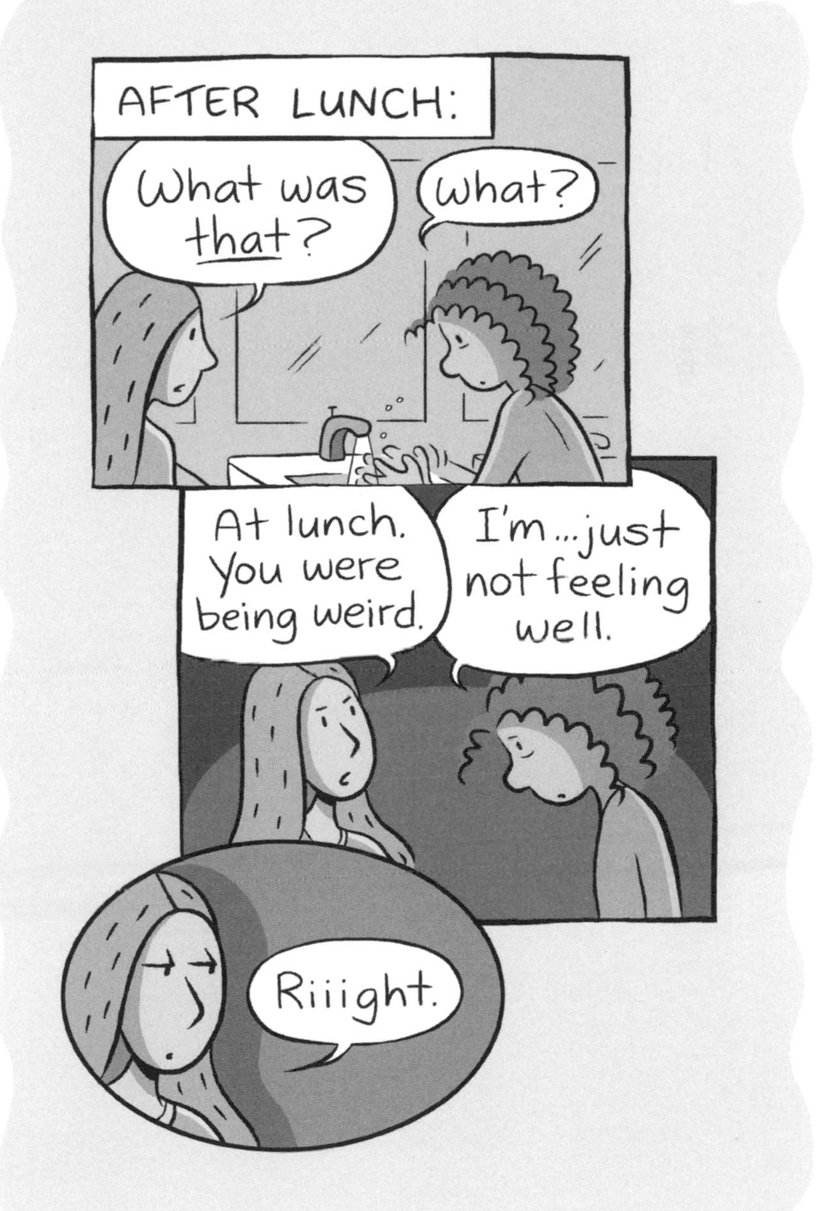
AFTER LUNCH:
What was that?
What?
At lunch. You were being weird.
I'm...just not feeling well.
Riiight.

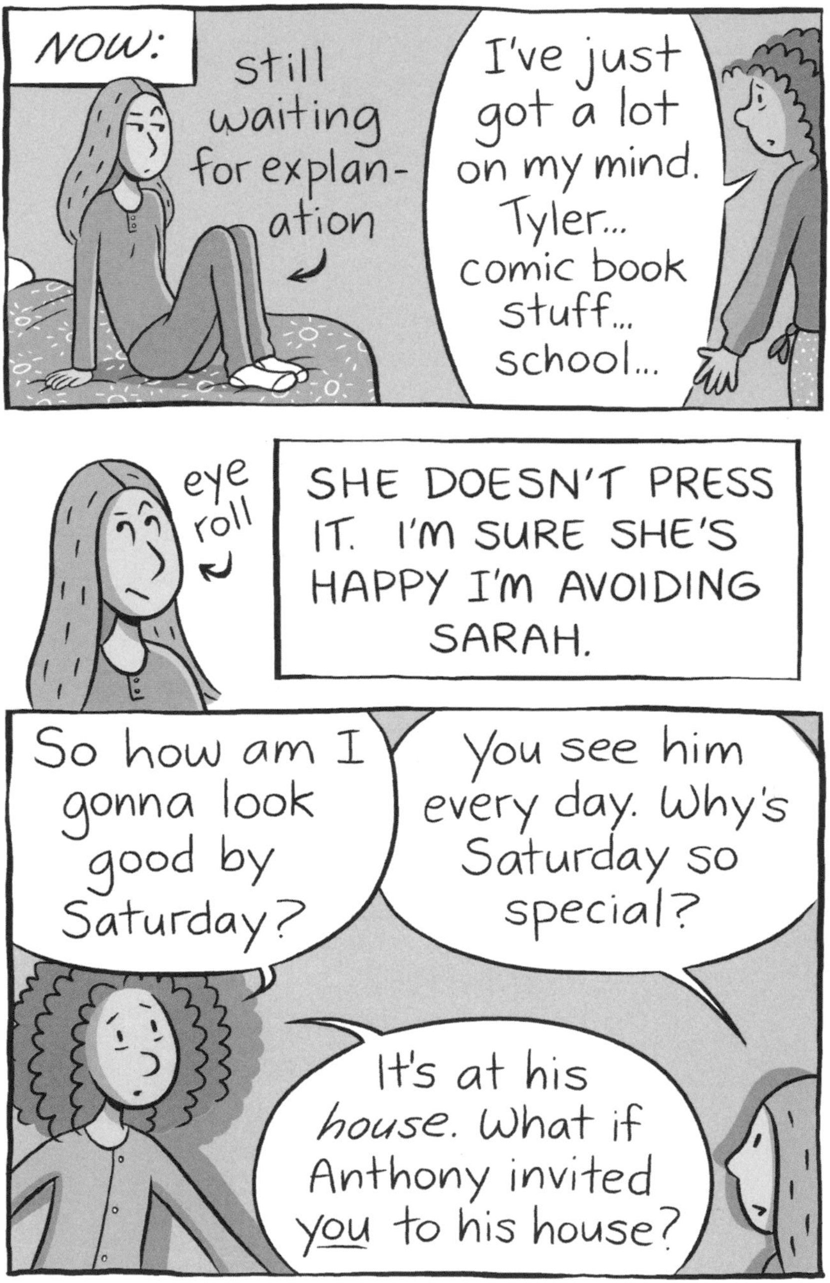
NOW:
still waiting for explan-ation
I've just got a lot on my mind. Tyler... comic book stuff... school...
eye roll
SHE DOESN'T PRESS IT. I'M SURE SHE'S HAPPY I'M AVOIDING SARAH.
So how am I gonna look good by Saturday?
You see him every day. Why's Saturday so special?
It's at his *house*. What if Anthony invited you to his house?

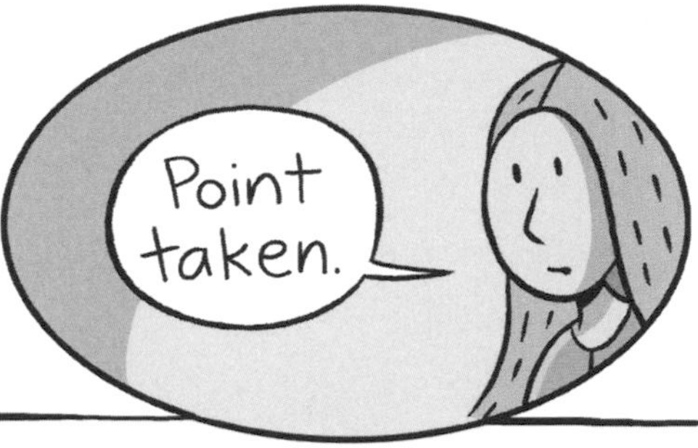
Point taken.

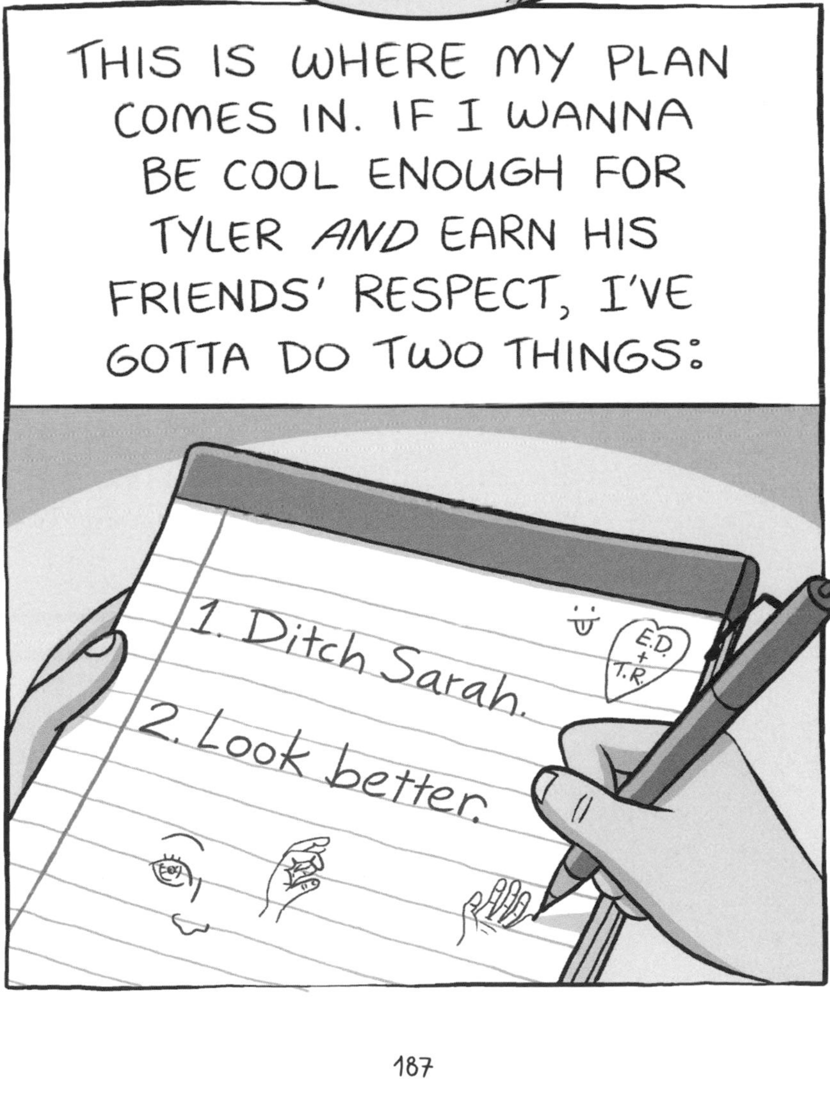
THIS IS WHERE MY PLAN COMES IN. IF I WANNA BE COOL ENOUGH FOR TYLER *AND* EARN HIS FRIENDS' RESPECT, I'VE GOTTA DO TWO THINGS:
1. Ditch Sarah.
2. Look better.
E.D. + T.R.

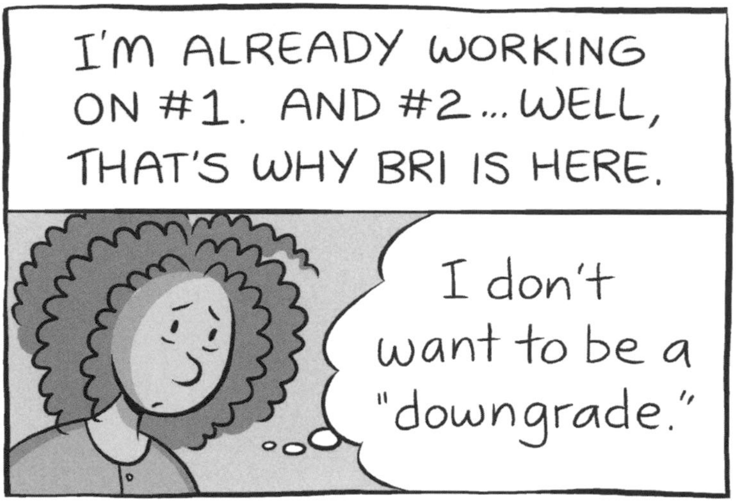
I'M ALREADY WORKING ON #1. AND #2...WELL, THAT'S WHY BRI IS HERE.
I don't want to be a "downgrade."

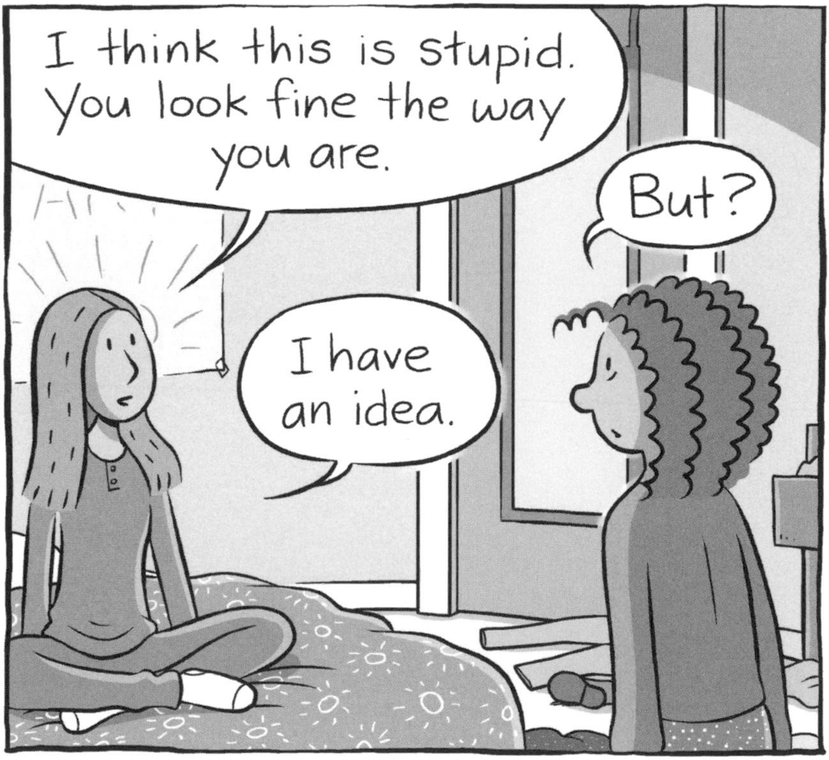
I think this is stupid. You look fine the way you are.
But?
I have an idea.

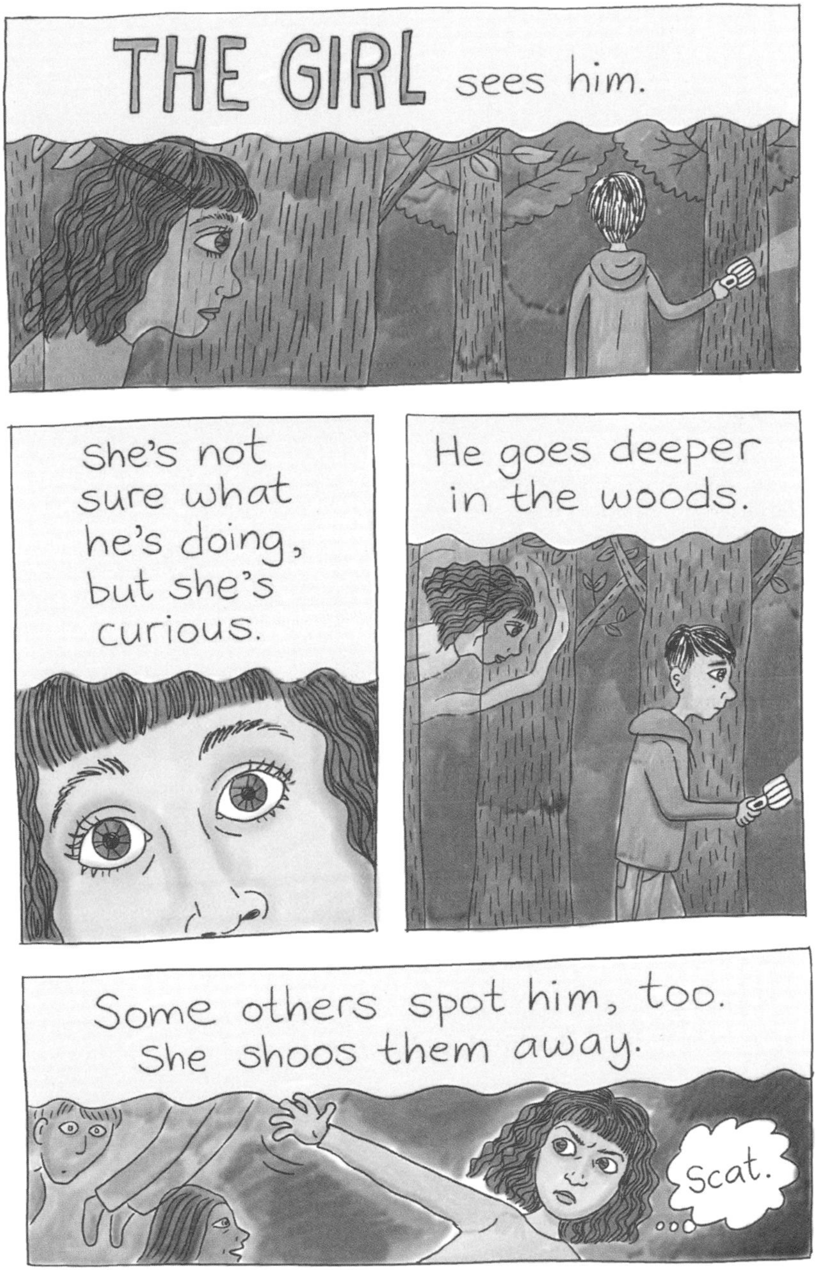
THE GIRL sees him.
She's not sure what he's doing, but she's curious.
He goes deeper in the woods.
Some others spot him, too. She shoos them away.
Scat.

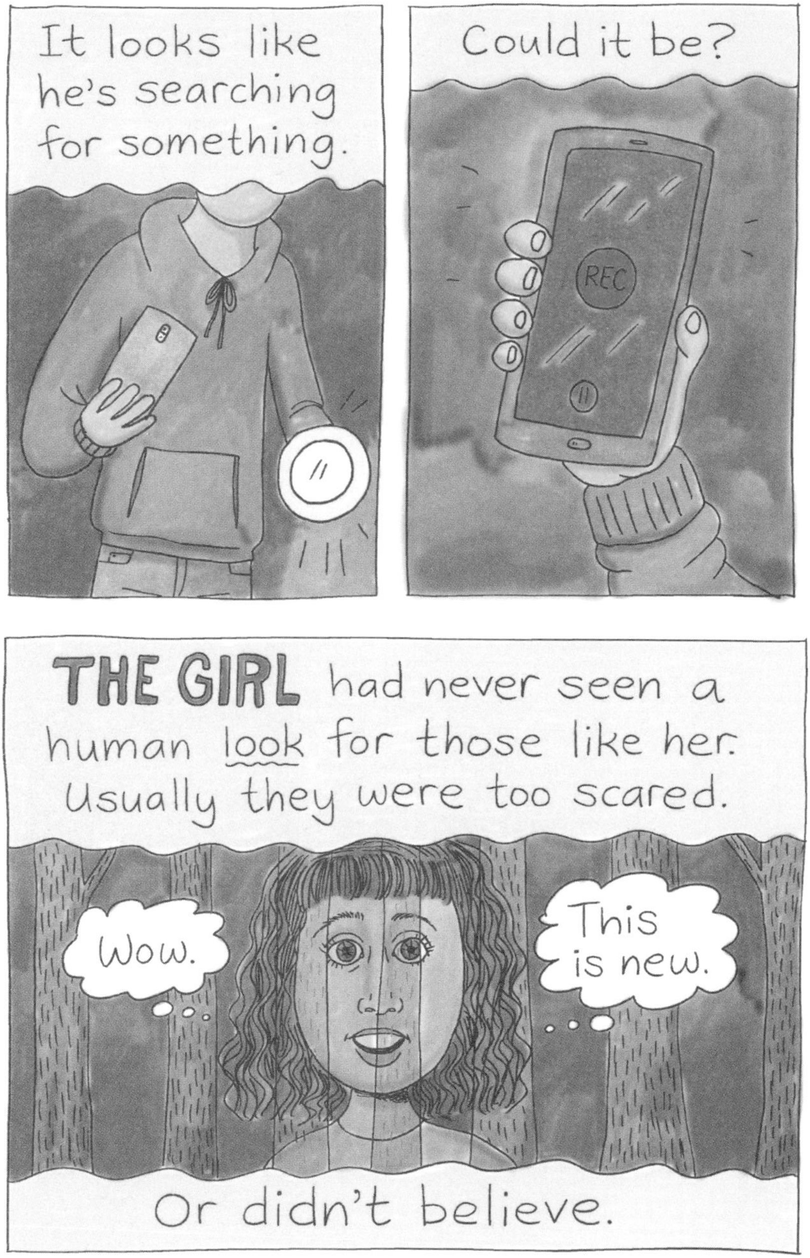
It looks like he's searching for something.
Could it be?
REC
THE GIRL had never seen a human look for those like her. Usually they were too scared.
Wow.
This is new.
Or didn't believe.

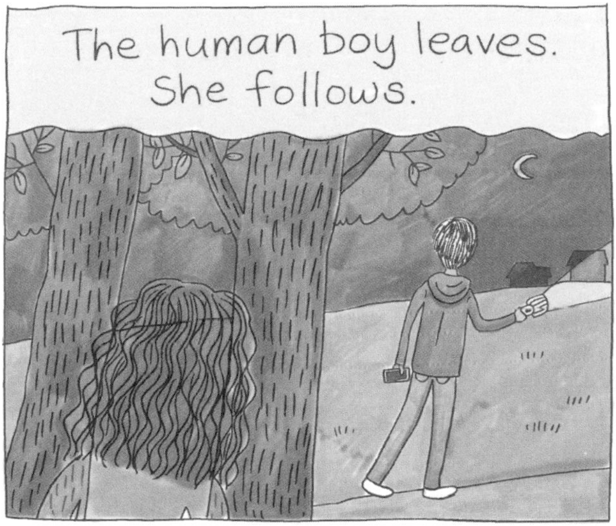
The human boy leaves.
She follows.

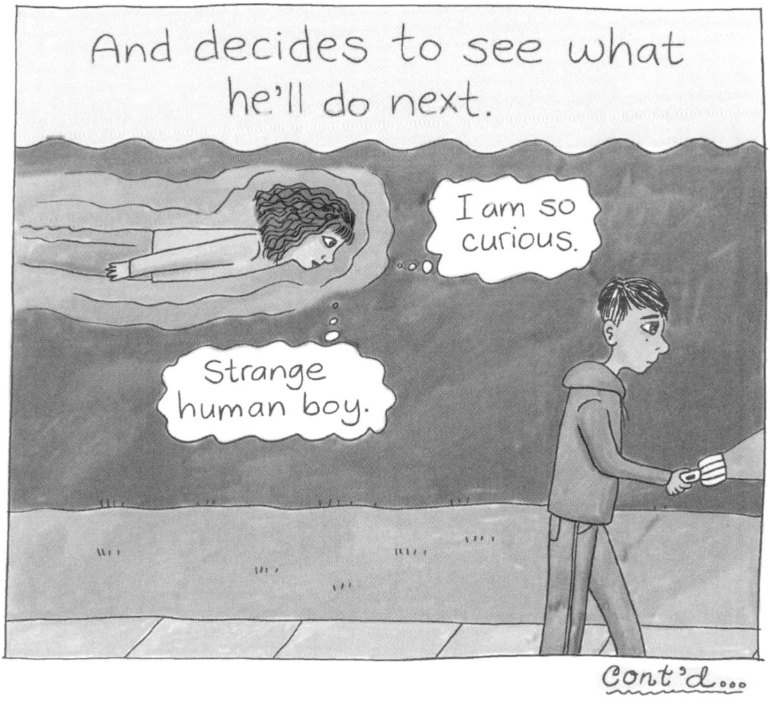
And decides to see what
he'll do next.
I am so
curious.
Strange
human boy.

Cont'd...

TYLER

Having the usual post-dinner FaceTime call with my dad.

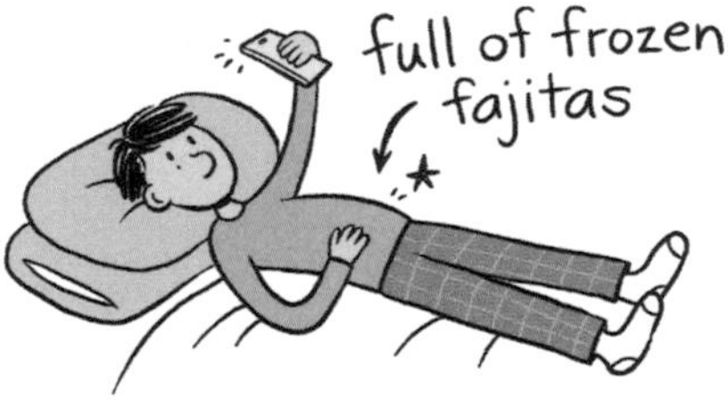
full of frozen fajitas

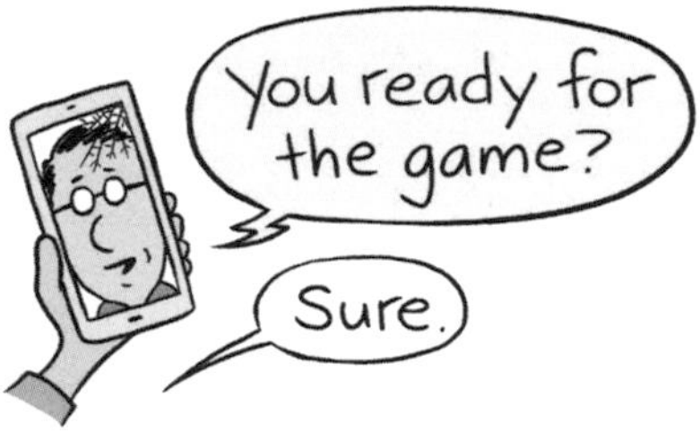
You ready for the game?
Sure.

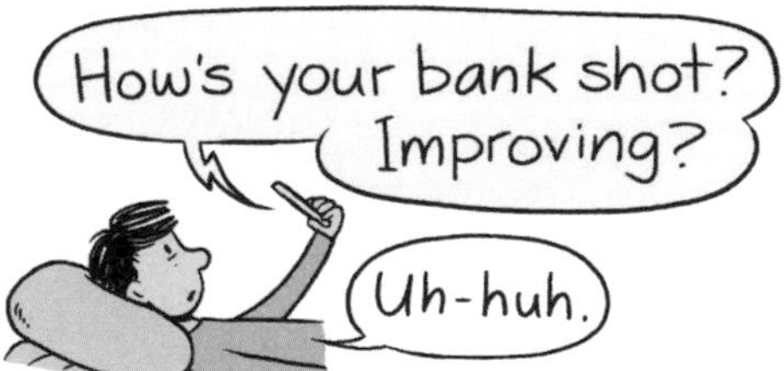
How's your bank shot? Improving?
Uh-huh.

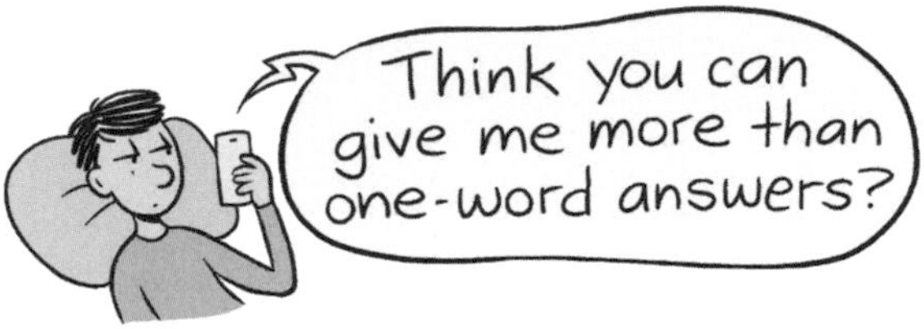
Think you can give me more than one-word answers?

He's trying to keep it light, but I'm not in the mood.

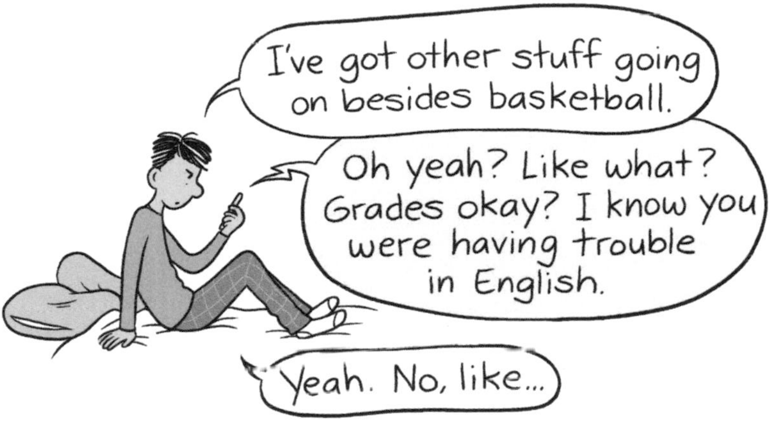
I've got other stuff going on besides basketball.
Oh yeah? Like what? Grades okay? I know you were having trouble in English.
Yeah. No, like...

Why am I bothering? All he cares about are sports and grades. He never says anything about art, and he knows I'm into that, too.

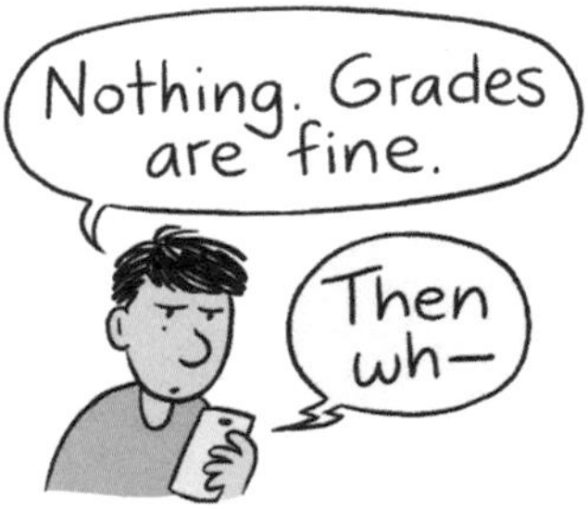
Nothing. Grades are fine.
Then wh—

Michelle pokes her head into the screen. Right where the cracks are.

multiple Michelles ↓

Hi, Ty! Sorry to bother, but I need your dad! Somebody's gotta walk Petey* and I have to cook!

*a cat. They walk a cat.

Michelle is one of those people who speaks entirely in exclamation points. Doesn't matter if she's happy, angry, or confused.

Okay, gotta go. Bye, son.

Click. Record time. Six minutes until she nabbed him.

Barely a second later, I get another FaceTime call.

Dude! Come over. Fortnite marathon.

Joe needs you to watch me KICK BOTH YOUR BUTTS.

(About the Anthony thing: I'm trying to let it go)

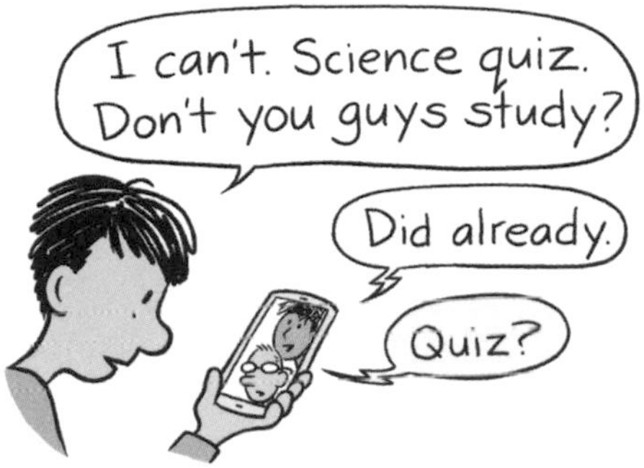
I can't. Science quiz. Don't you guys study?
Did already.
Quiz?

I laugh and am about to hang up when:

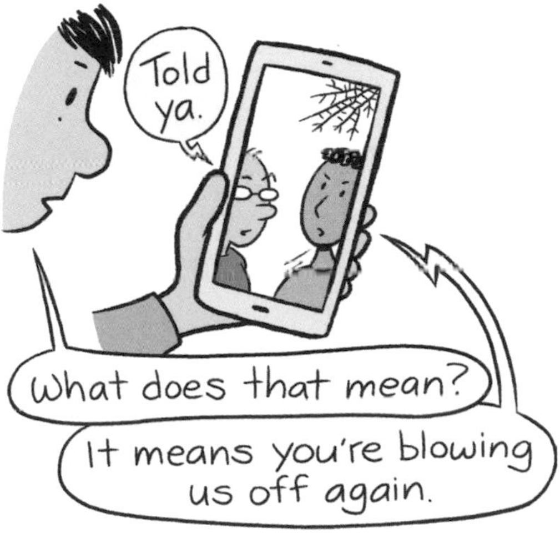
Told ya.
What does that mean?
It means you're blowing us off again.

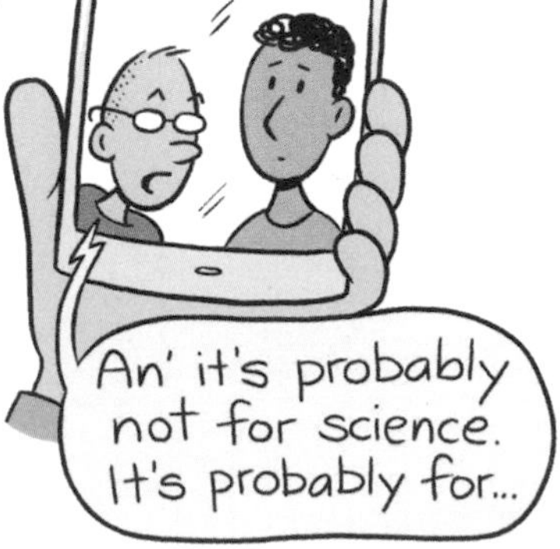
An' it's probably not for science. It's probably for...

mmm
kiss
kiss
smooch

Stop it, man. I really have to study.
With Quiet Girl?
Is she really your girlfriend, Ty? Are you just not telling us?
NO!

Well, she might as well be. You're with her all the time.
Actually, I haven't met her after school in a while. I've been at practice.
pointing to Anthony
With **HIM**.

I don't tell them she's coming over Saturday.

Whatever.
Go study, nerd. The only thing I wanna pass is this next level.

With that, Phineas sticks his face in front of the camera and licks it, his giant tongue taking up the screen.

SLORP

They hang up, and I flop on my back and stare at my ceiling. Definitely not in the mood to study now.

textured ceiling
seeing basketballs

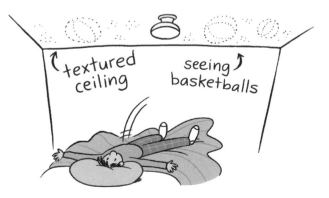

So my friends think I'm blowing them off. And losing my edge. I'm not!

Am I?

eyeing my sketchbook comics

And they think Emmie's my girlfriend! Come on.

Can't I be friends with a girl? What's wrong with that? Anthony is tight with Jaime.

YAP YAP YAP

(everyone <u>just</u> stopped thinking they were a couple)

'Course, they've been friends forever. Emmie's only been my friend for a couple months. Also, she's not . . . well . . . like Jaime or the others.

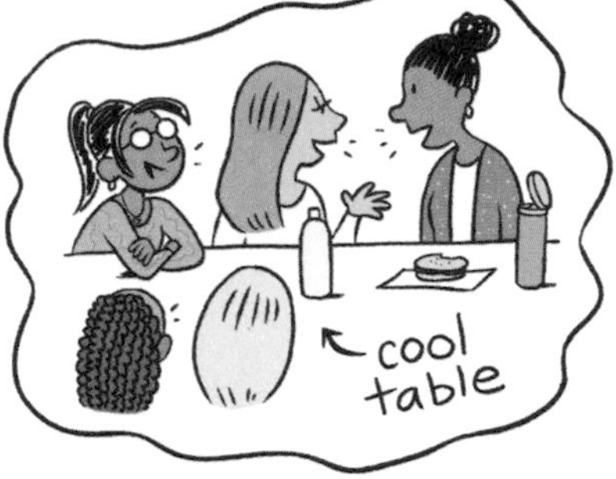
cool table

Sometimes I wish that Emmie wasn't so . . . different or something. Quiet. Artsy. Then maybe people wouldn't make such a big deal of us hanging out.

I know it's not her fault. But I can't help feeling . . .

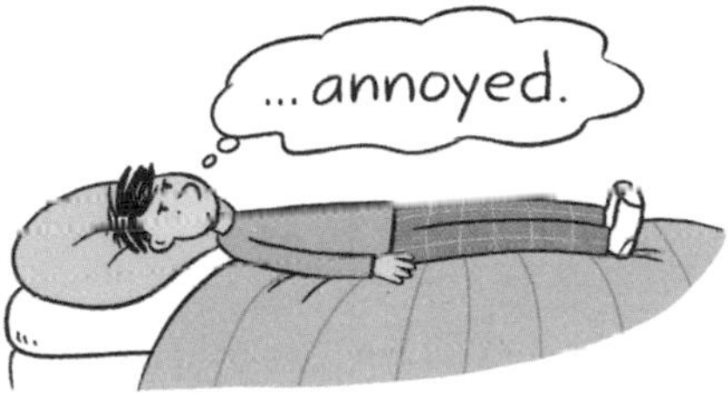
. . . annoyed.

Enough. I sit up. Gonna forget all this and get a snack. I heave myself off the bed, making more secret Skittles fly off.

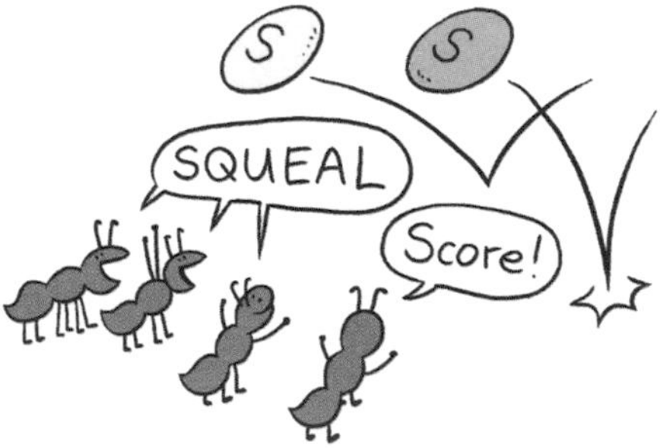
S
S
SQUEAL
Score!

I almost bump into Zach coming out of his room.

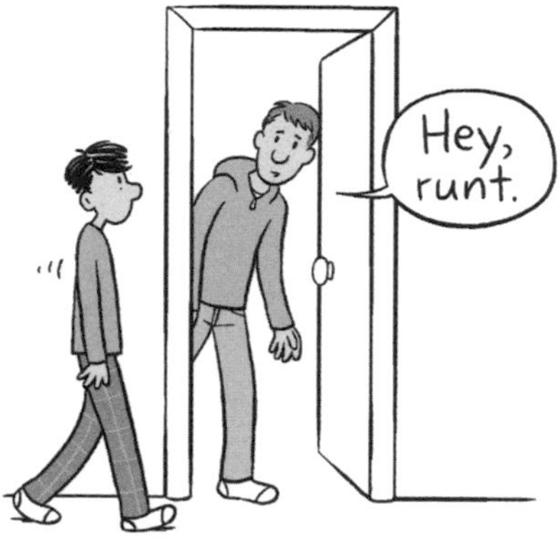
Hey, runt.

I groan. Not that again.

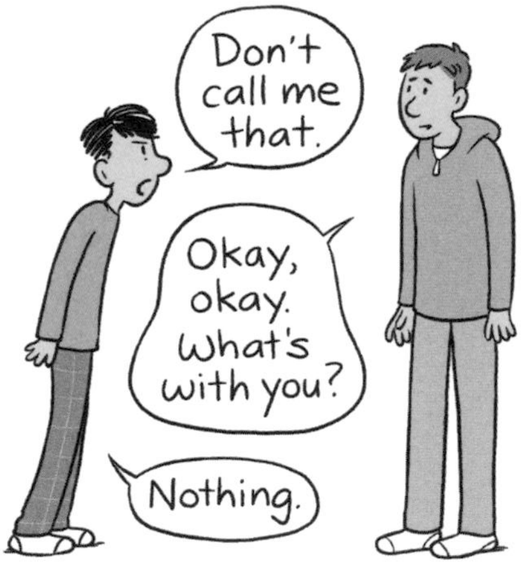
Don't call me that.
Okay, okay. What's with you?
Nothing.

Zach shrugs and starts heading downstairs.

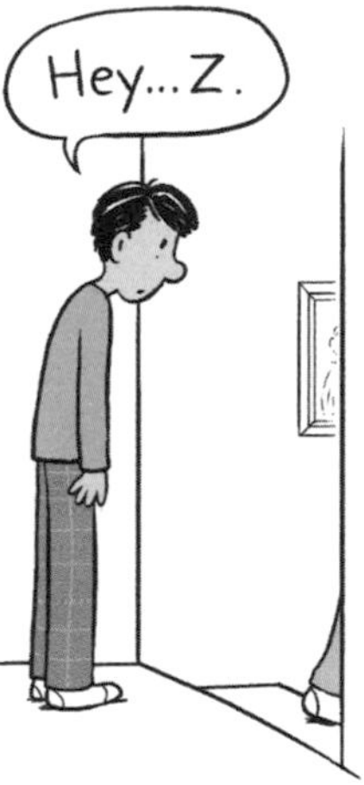
Hey...Z.

He looks up.

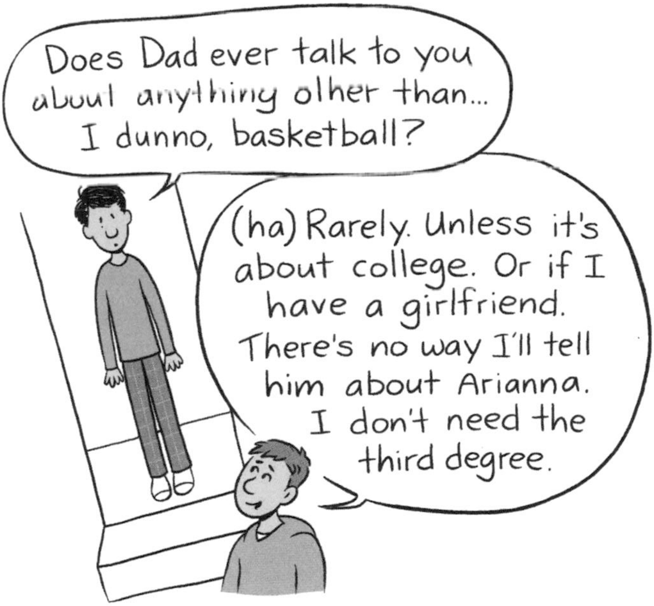
Does Dad ever talk to you about anything other than... I dunno, basketball?
(ha) Rarely. Unless it's about college. Or if I have a girlfriend. There's no way I'll tell him about Arianna. I don't need the third degree.

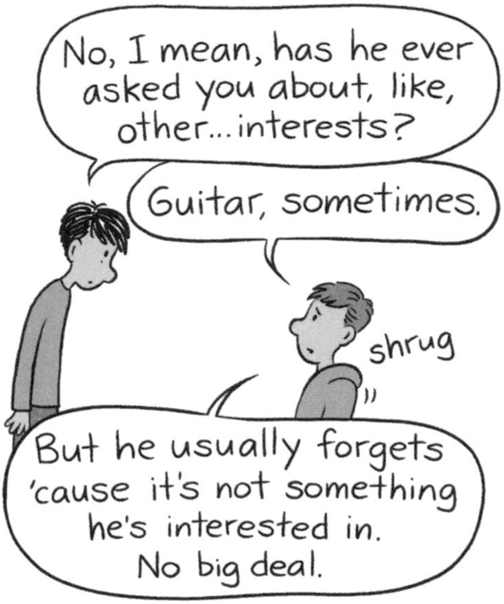
No, I mean, has he ever asked you about, like, other...interests?
Guitar, sometimes.
shrug
But he usually forgets 'cause it's not something he's interested in. No big deal.

I nod.

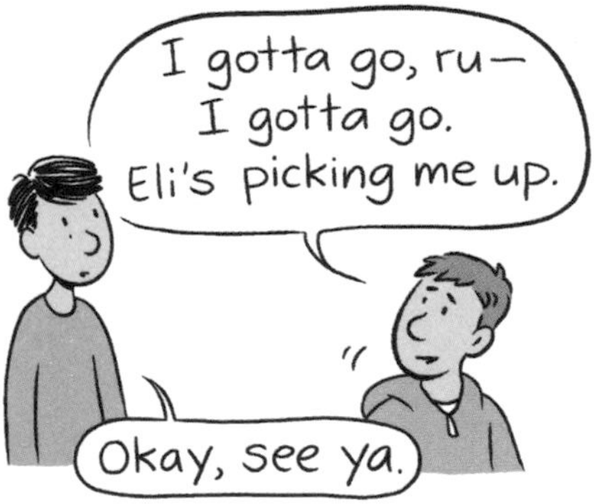
I gotta go, ru— I gotta go. Eli's picking me up.
Okay, see ya.

I change my mind about the snack.

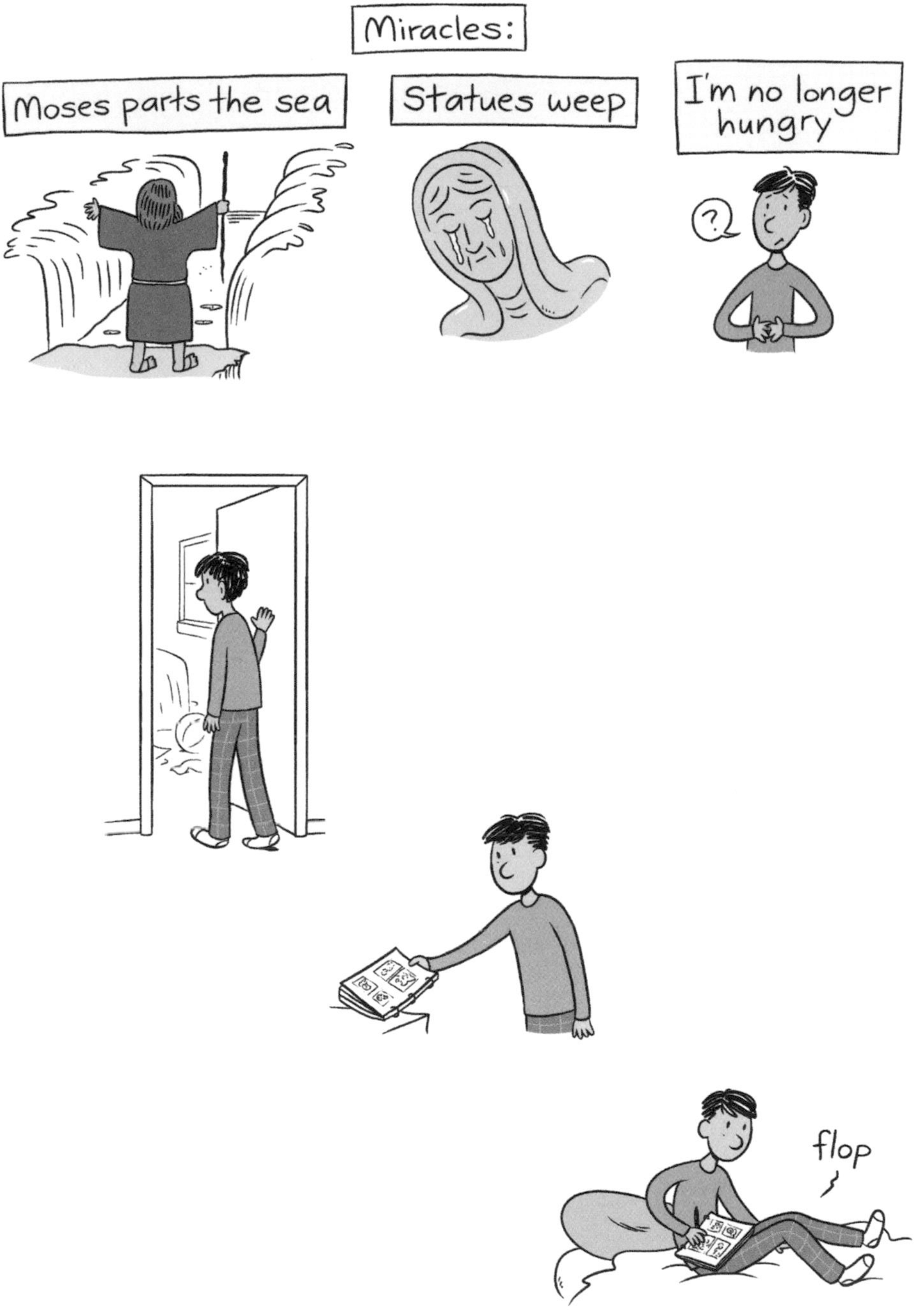
Miracles:
Moses parts the sea
Statues weep
I'm no longer hungry
?
flop

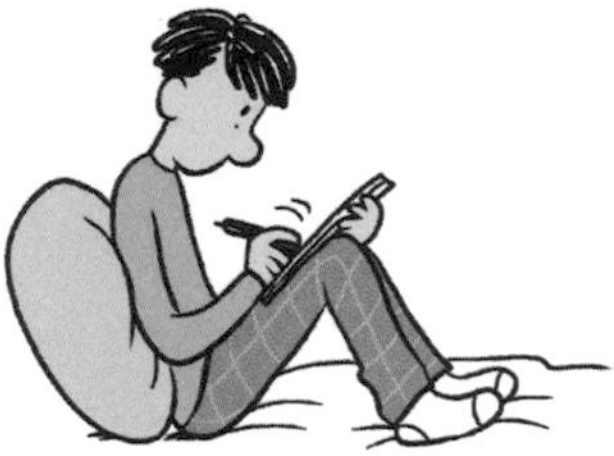

Here's one more miracle:

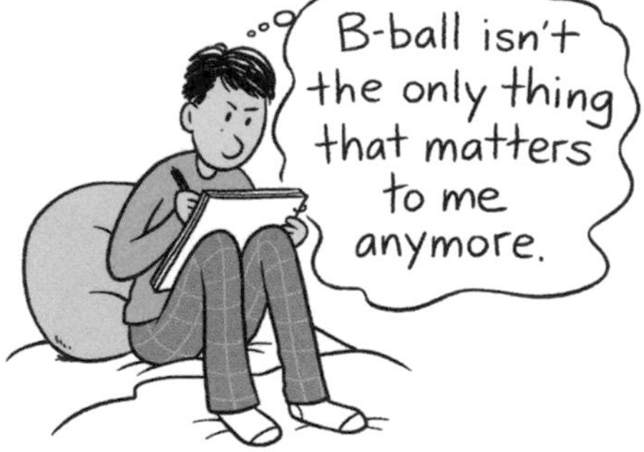
B-ball isn't the only thing that matters to me anymore.

Emmie

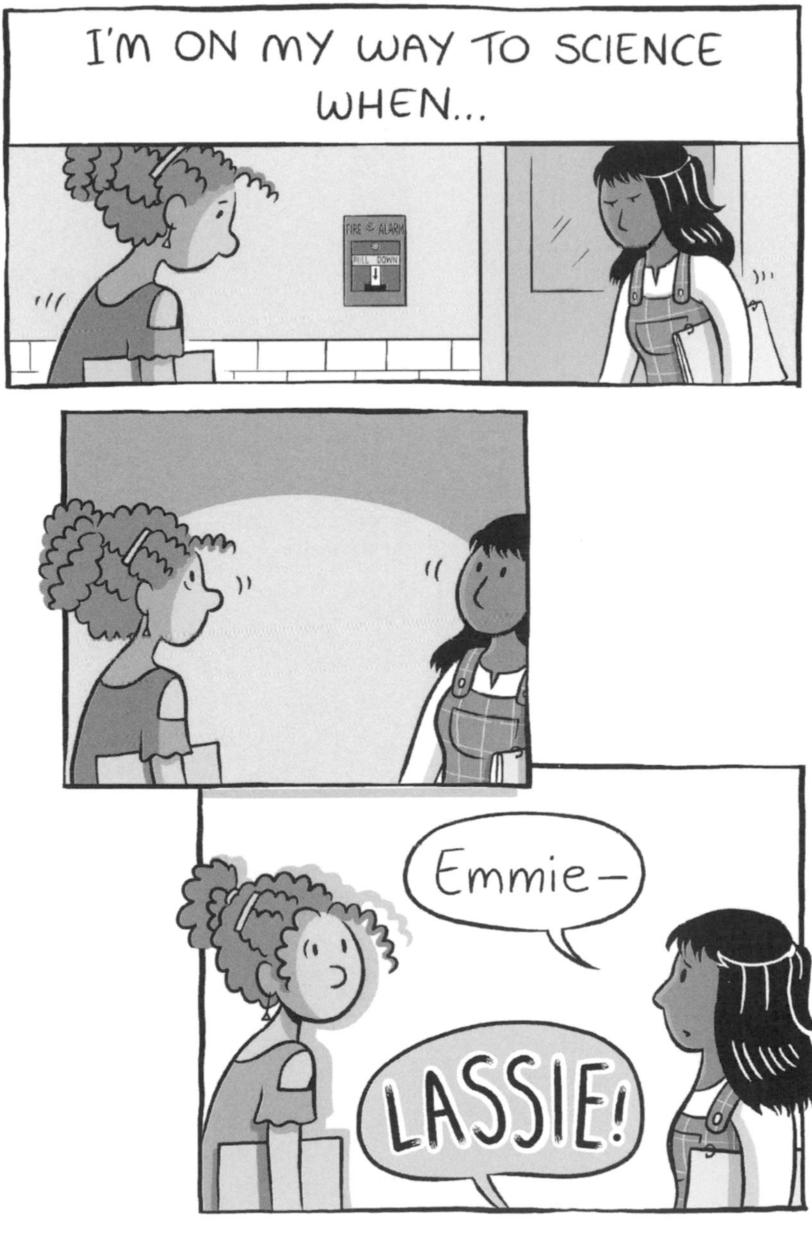
I'M ON MY WAY TO SCIENCE WHEN...
FIRE ALARM
PULL DOWN
Emmie–
LASSIE!

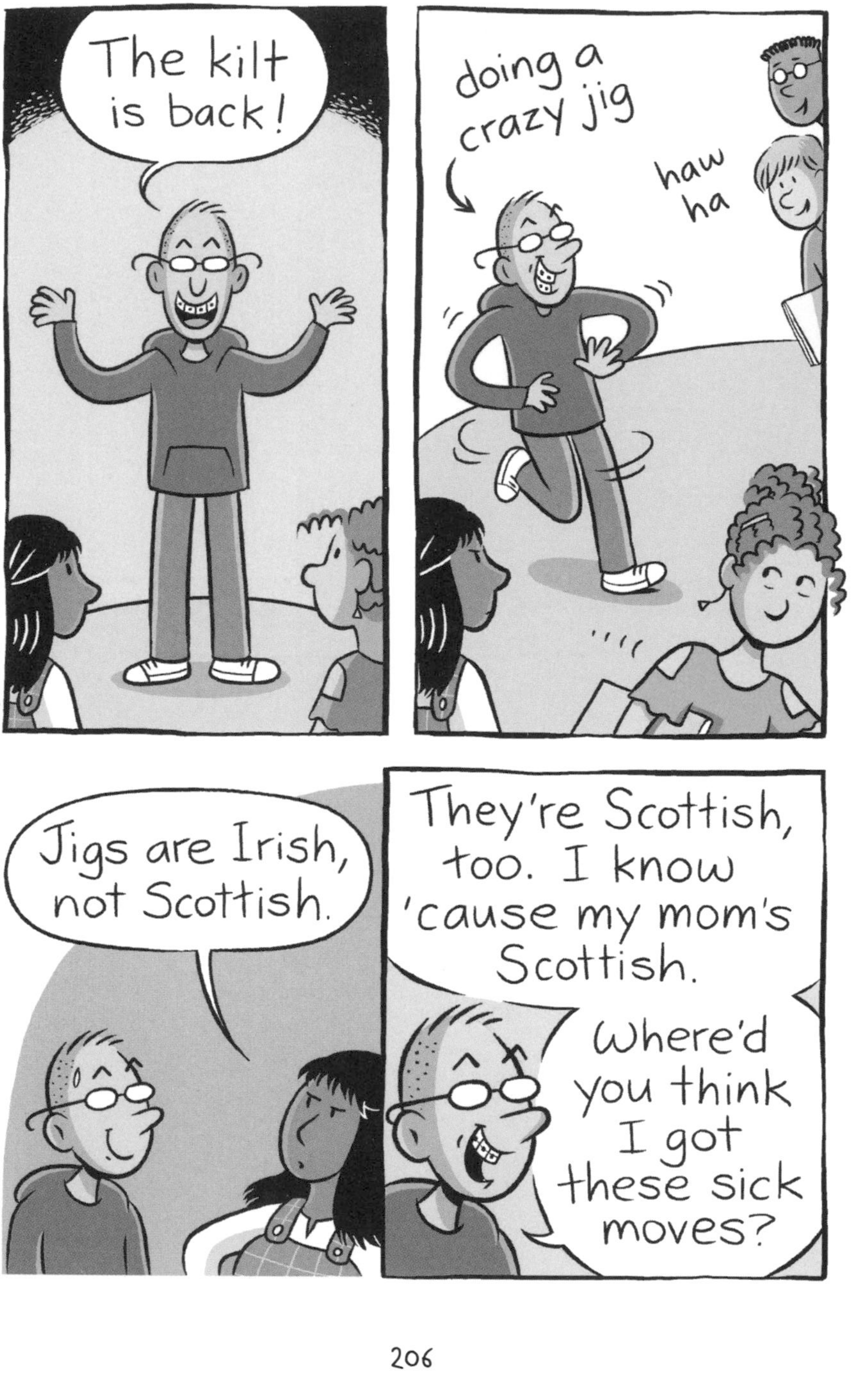
The kilt is back!
doing a crazy jig
haw ha
Jigs are Irish, not Scottish.
They're Scottish, too. I know 'cause my mom's Scottish.
Where'd you think I got these sick moves?

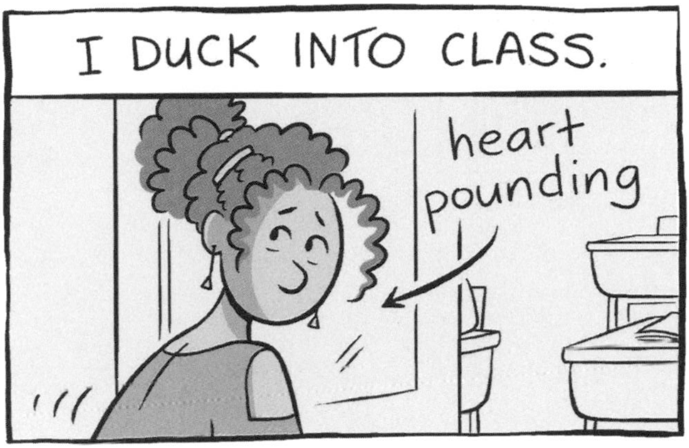
I DUCK INTO CLASS.
heart pounding

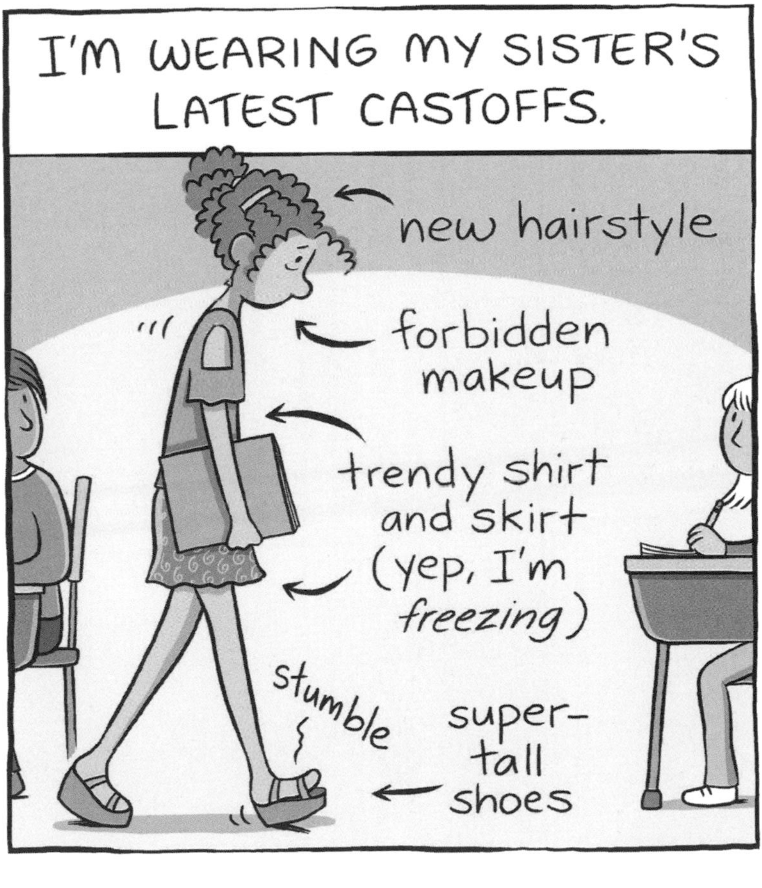
I'M WEARING MY SISTER'S LATEST CASTOFFS.
new hairstyle
forbidden makeup
trendy shirt and skirt (yep, I'm *freezing*)
stumble
super-tall shoes

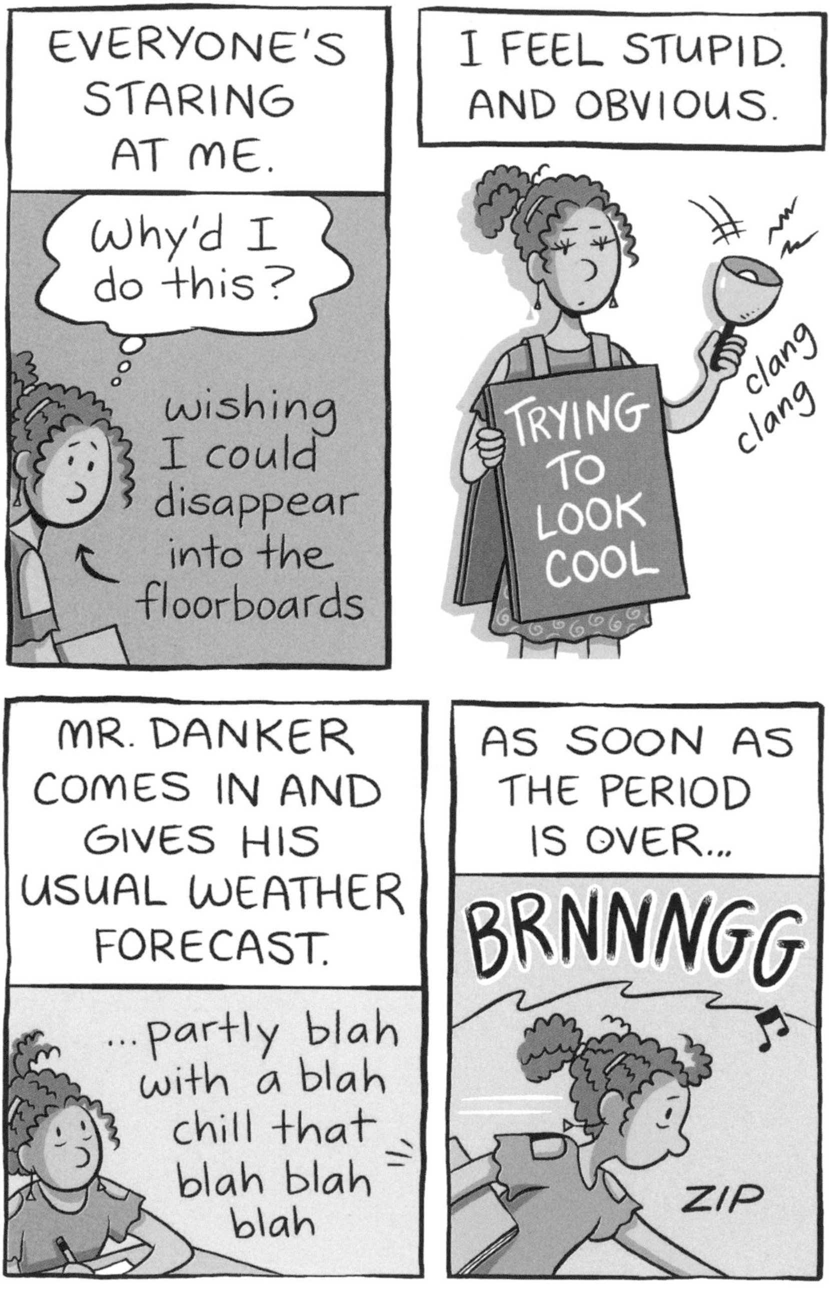
EVERYONE'S STARING AT ME.
Why'd I do this?
wishing I could disappear into the floorboards
I FEEL STUPID. AND OBVIOUS.
TRYING TO LOOK COOL
clang clang
MR. DANKER COMES IN AND GIVES HIS USUAL WEATHER FORECAST.
...partly blah with a blah chill that blah blah blah
AS SOON AS THE PERIOD IS OVER...
BRNNNGG
ZIP

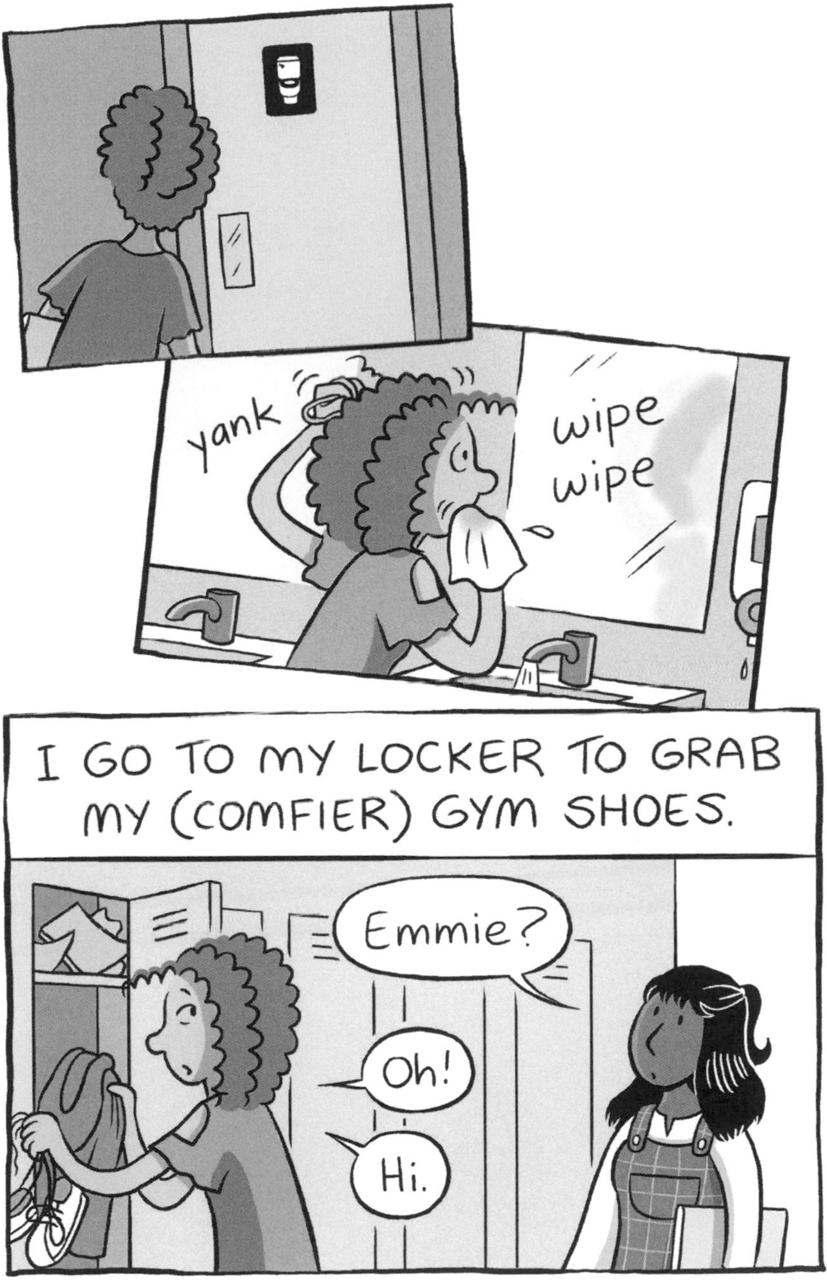
yank
wipe wipe
I GO TO MY LOCKER TO GRAB MY (COMFIER) GYM SHOES.
Emmie?
Oh!
Hi.

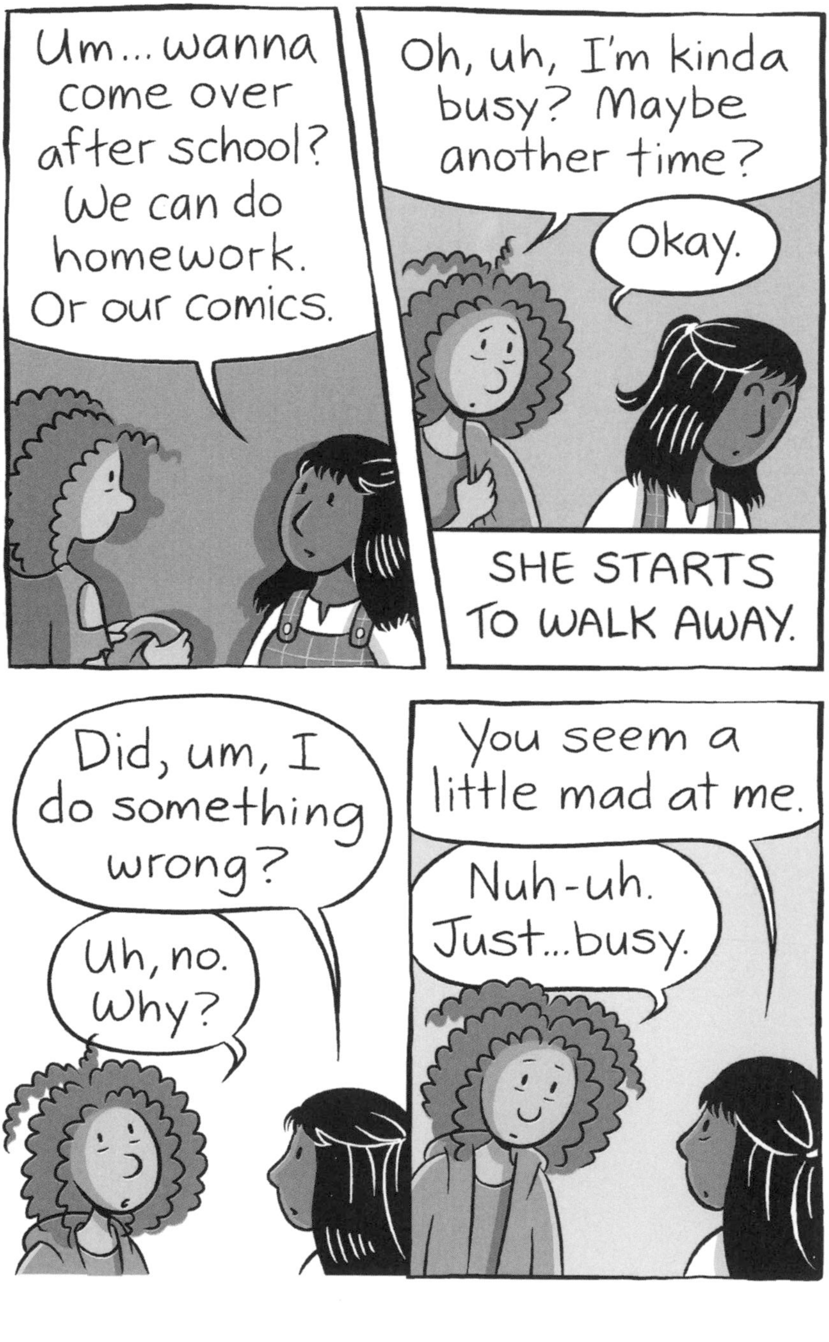
Um...wanna come over after school? We can do homework. Or our comics.
Oh, uh, I'm kinda busy? Maybe another time?
Okay.
SHE STARTS TO WALK AWAY.
Did, um, I do something wrong?
Uh, no. Why?
You seem a little mad at me.
Nuh-uh. Just...busy.

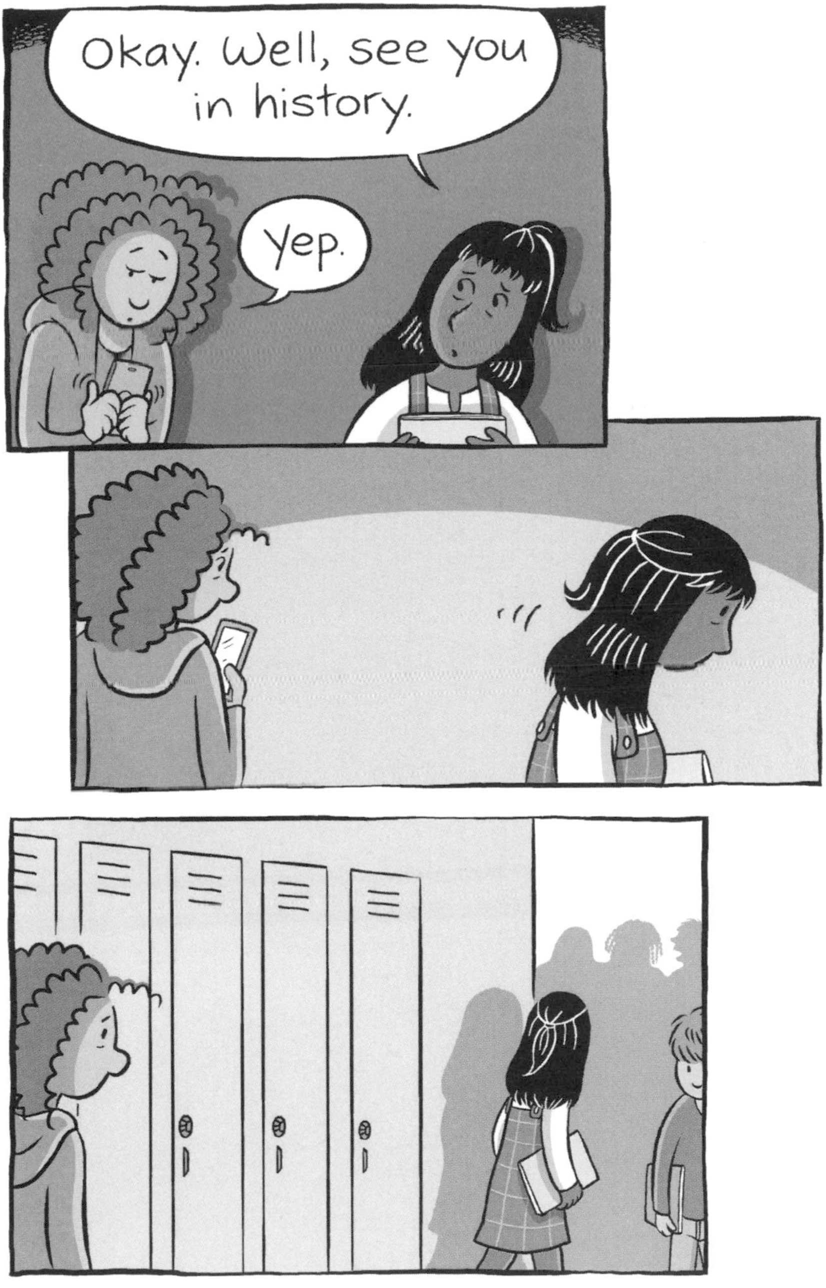
Okay. Well, see you in history.
Yep.

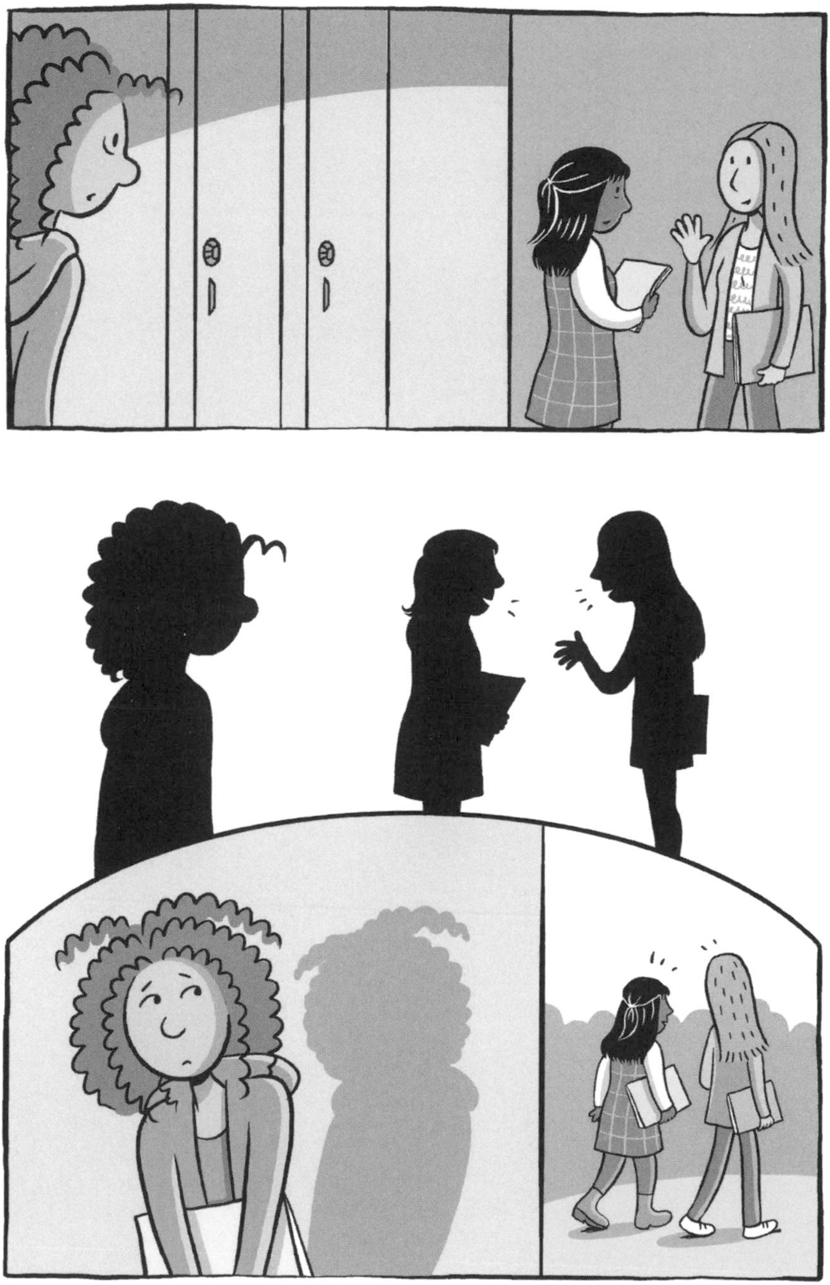

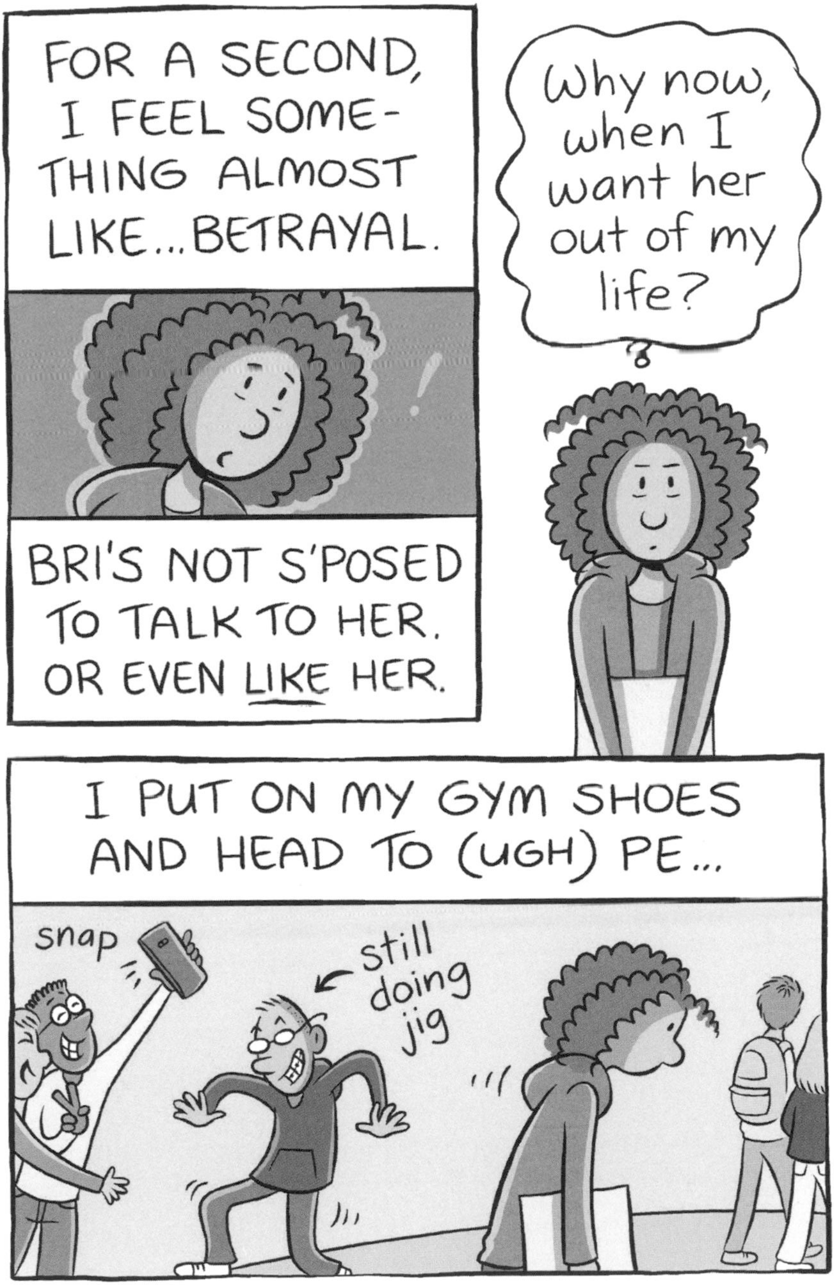
FOR A SECOND, I FEEL SOME- THING ALMOST LIKE...BETRAYAL.
Why now, when I want her out of my life?
!
BRI'S NOT S'POSED TO TALK TO HER. OR EVEN LIKE HER.
I PUT ON MY GYM SHOES AND HEAD TO (UGH) PE...
snap
still doing jig

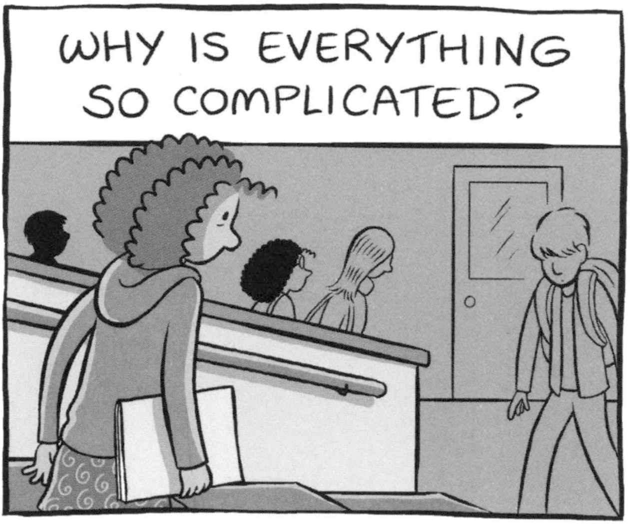
WHY IS EVERYTHING SO COMPLICATED?

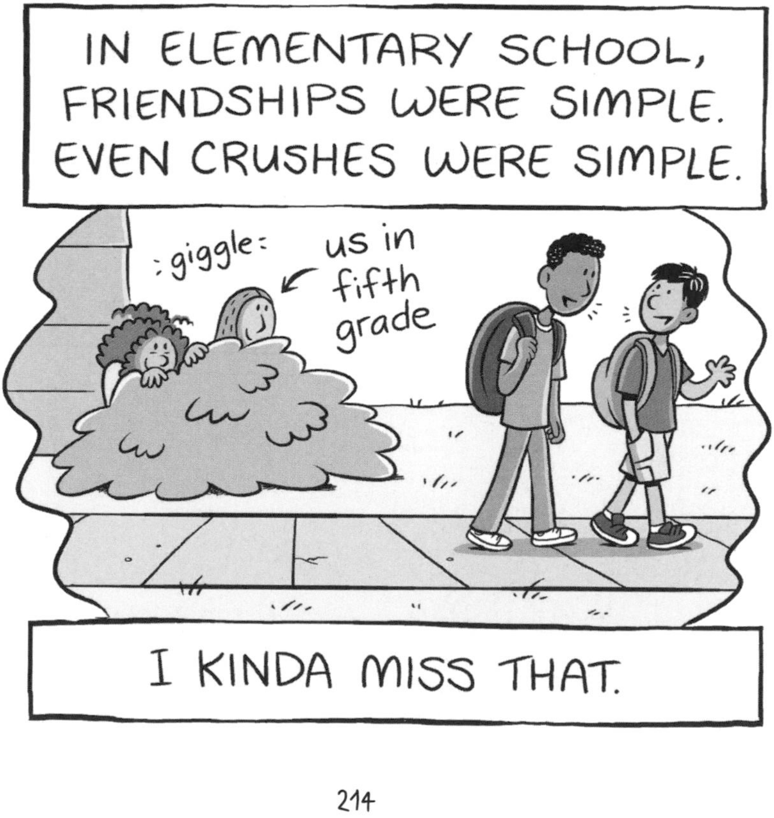
IN ELEMENTARY SCHOOL, FRIENDSHIPS WERE SIMPLE. EVEN CRUSHES WERE SIMPLE.
:giggle:
us in fifth grade
I KINDA MISS THAT.

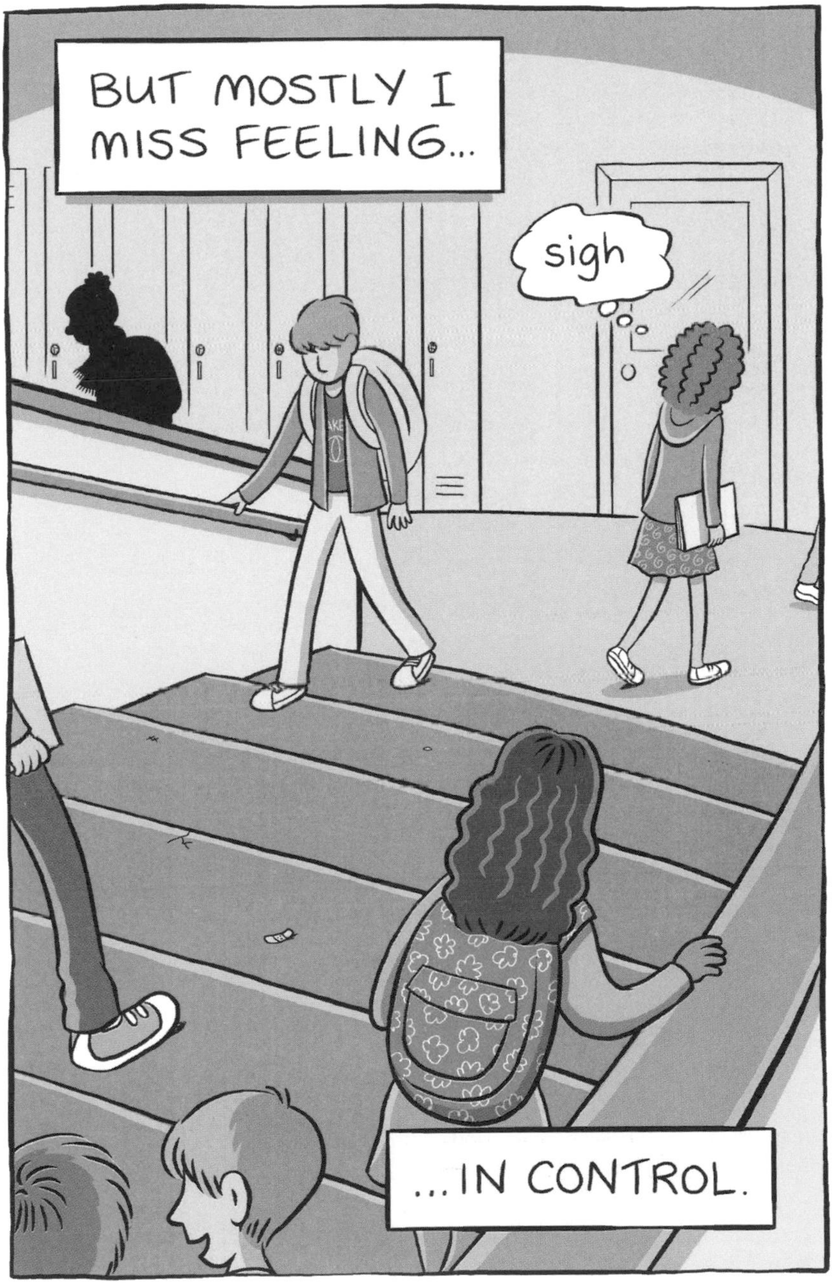
BUT MOSTLY I MISS FEELING...
sigh
...IN CONTROL.

TYLER

History class.

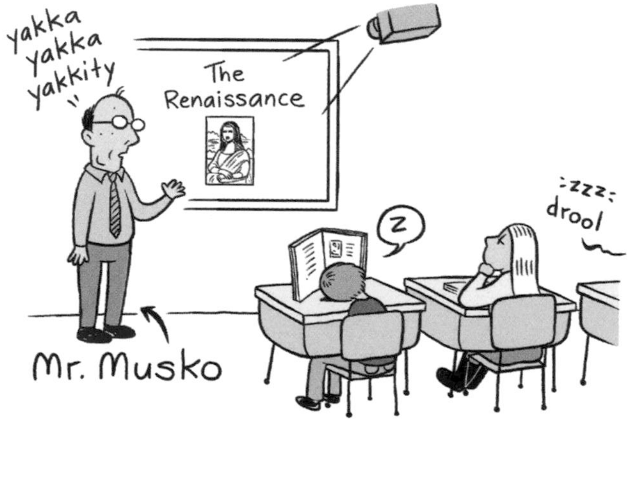
yakka
yakka
yakkity
The
Renaissance
zzz
drool
z
Mr. Musko

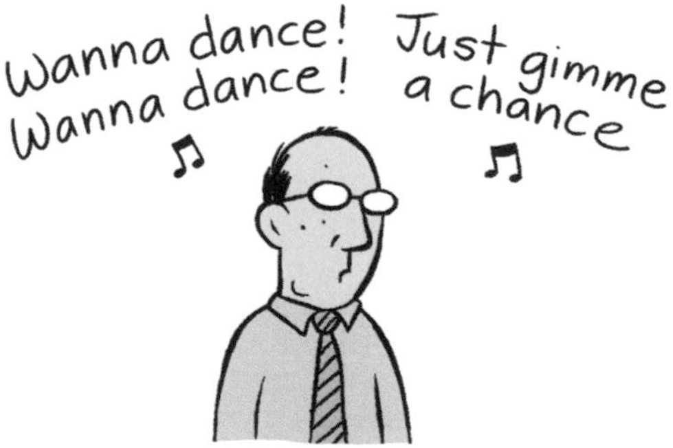
Wanna dance! Wanna dance!
Just gimme a chance

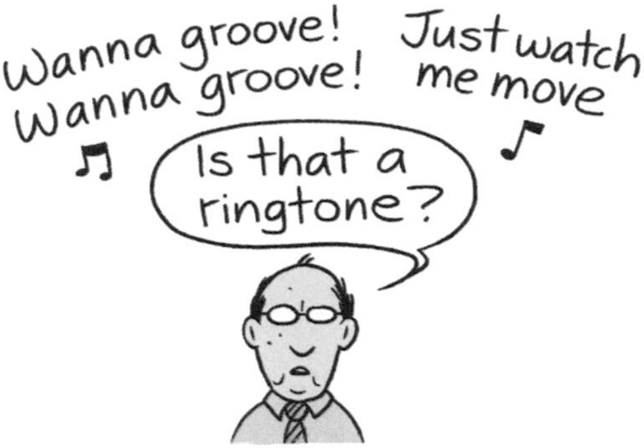
Wanna groove! Wanna groove! Just watch me move
Is that a ringtone?

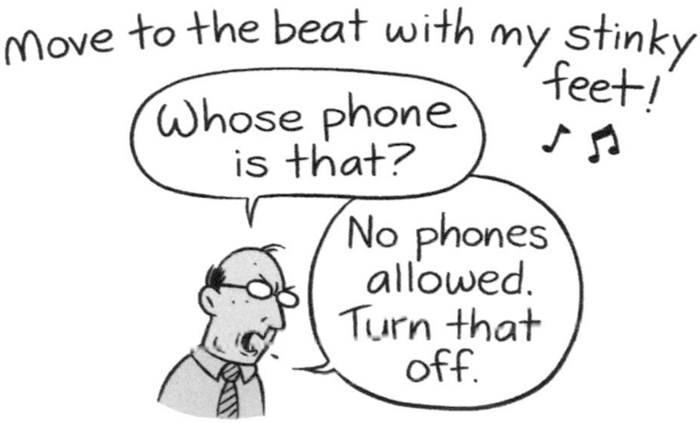
Move to the beat with my stinky feet!
Whose phone is that?
No phones allowed. Turn that off.

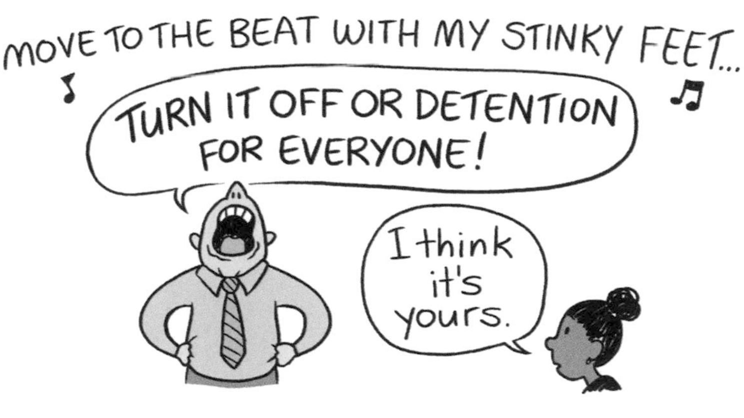
MOVE TO THE BEAT WITH MY STINKY FEET...
TURN IT OFF OR DETENTION FOR EVERYONE!
I think it's yours.

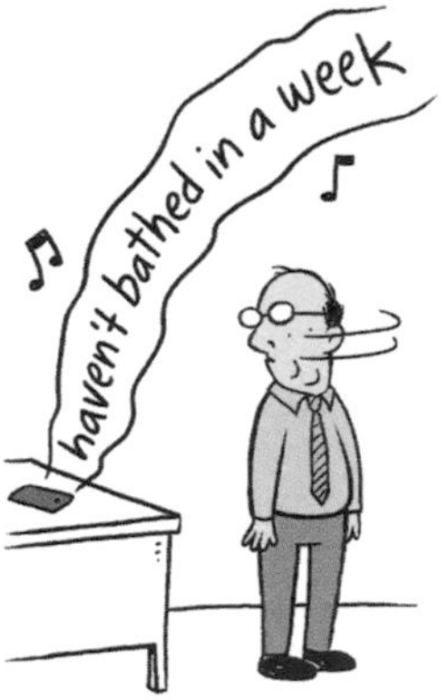
haven't bathed in a week

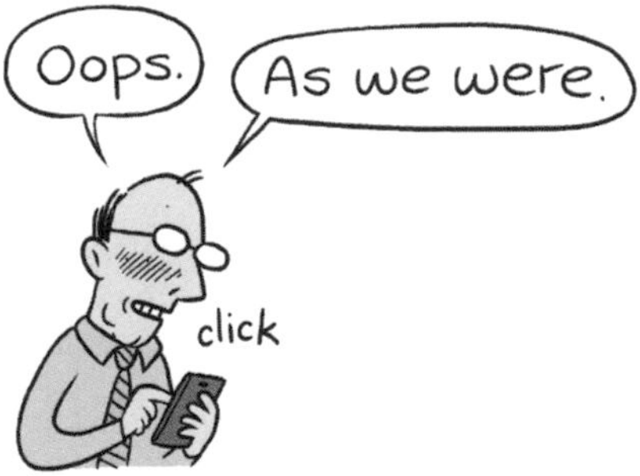
Oops.
As we were.
click

Everyone laughs. First time Mr. Musko ever broke out of his monotone.

The bell rings.

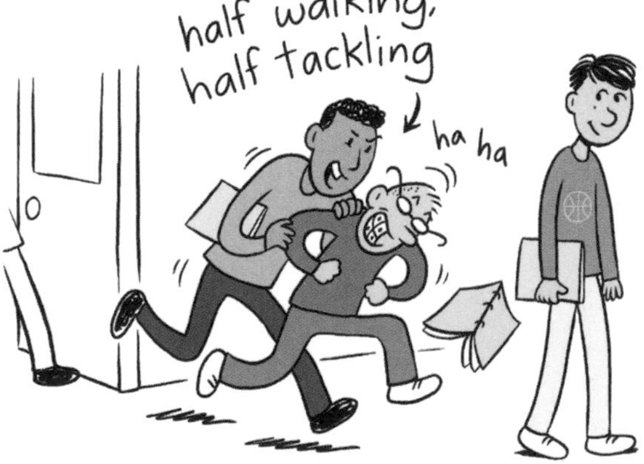
half walking, half tackling
ha ha

Soon they get enough dirty looks (and one hall monitor's glare) to straighten up and attempt to walk like regular human beings.

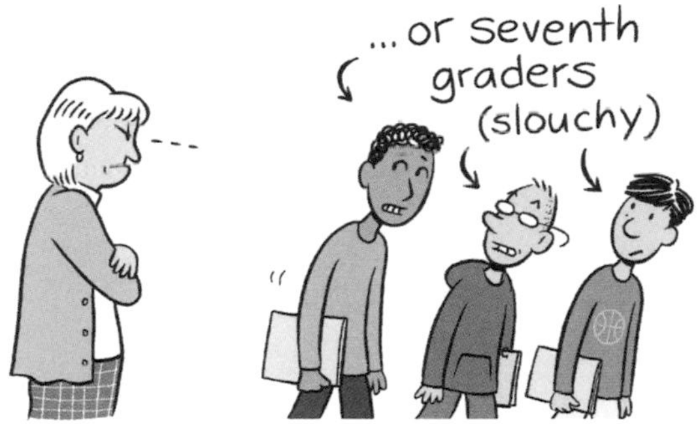
...or seventh graders
(slouchy)

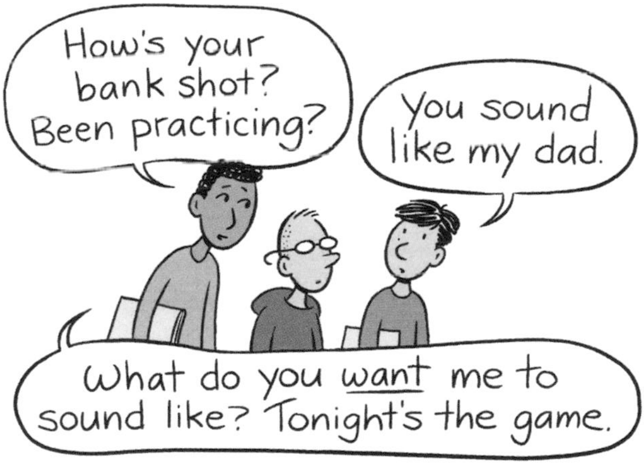
How's your bank shot? Been practicing?
You sound like my dad.
What do you want me to sound like? Tonight's the game.

I try to stay . . . What's that word? That word Emmie says her mom uses a lot.

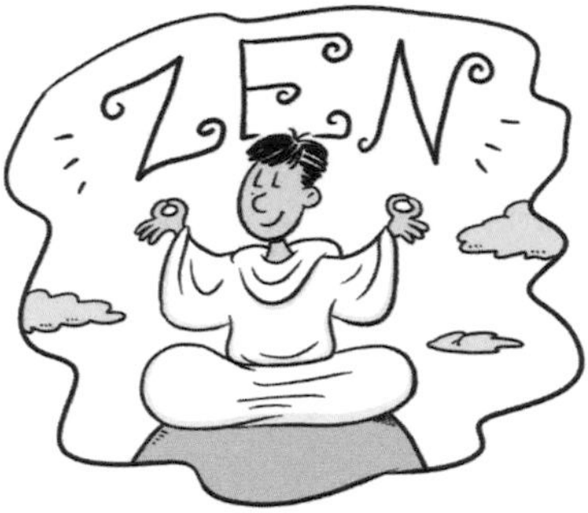
ZEN

Yeah, been trying to hold my zen for a while now.

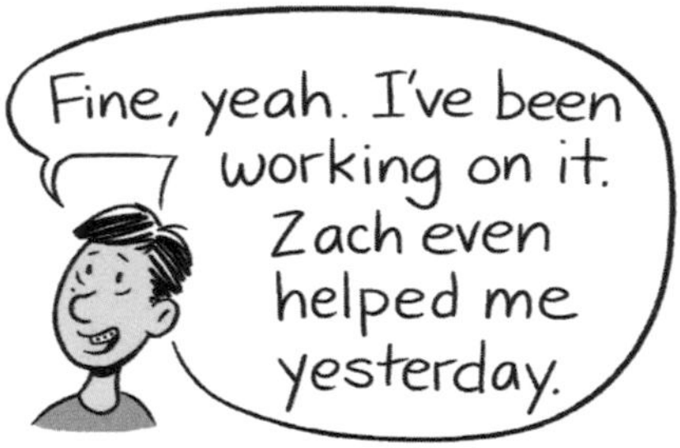
Fine, yeah. I've been working on it. Zach even helped me yesterday.

That's a lie.

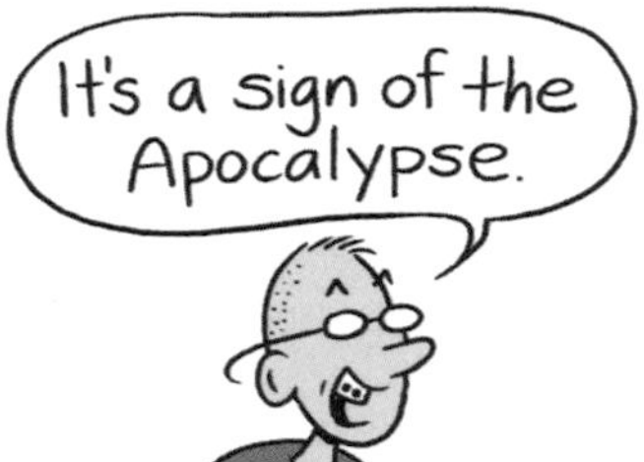
It's a sign of the Apocalypse.

That makes me laugh, in a depressing way.

Truth is, I'm kinda nervous for tonight. And Anthony harping

about the game isn't helping. Normally when I'm nervous for a game, it's a good kind of nervous.

brain buzzing with excitement
stomach wiggling with butterflies
13
heart racing with...
... too much Gatorade?

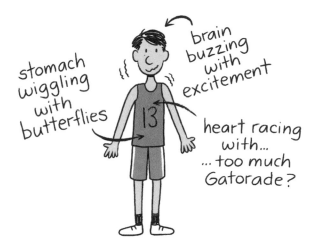

But today, it feels like there are worms crawling around in my gut.

weeee!

Ms. Laurie appears in the hall, on her way to the teachers' lounge.

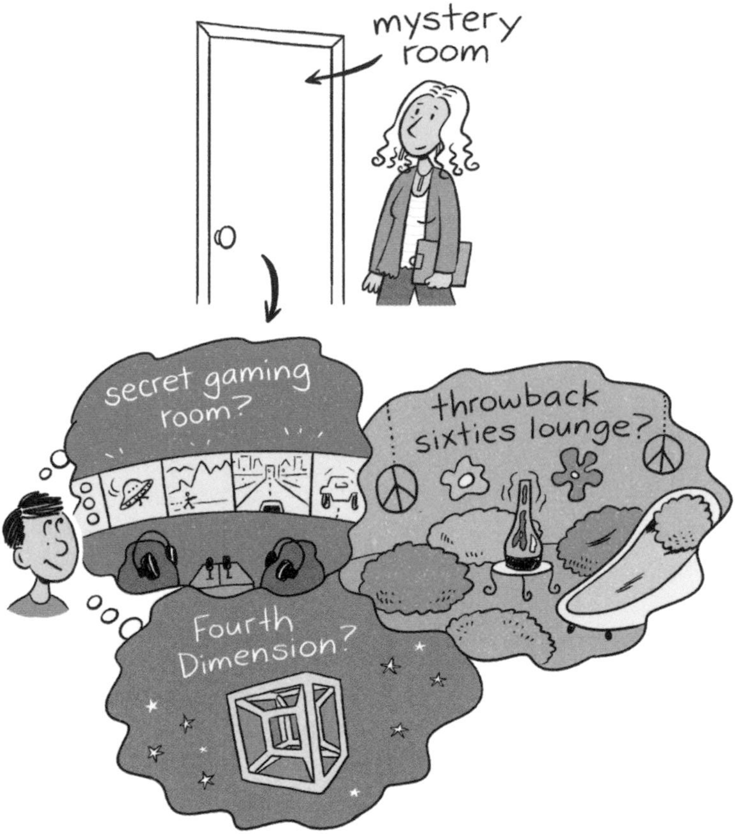
mystery room
secret gaming room?
throwback sixties lounge?
Fourth Dimension?

It's always weird seeing teachers out of their rooms. Even weirder to see them in the wild.

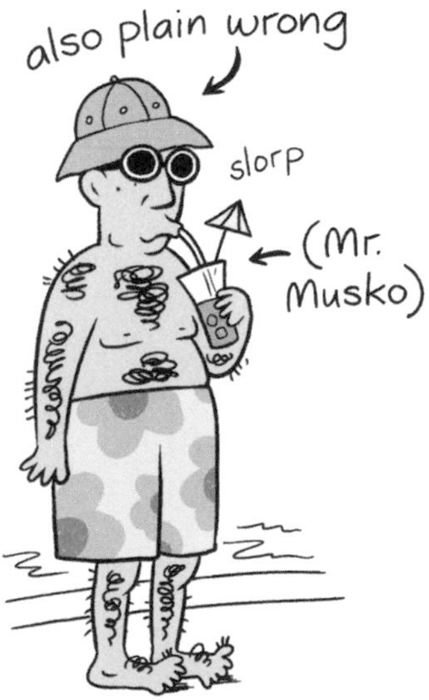
also plain wrong
slorp
(Mr. Musko)

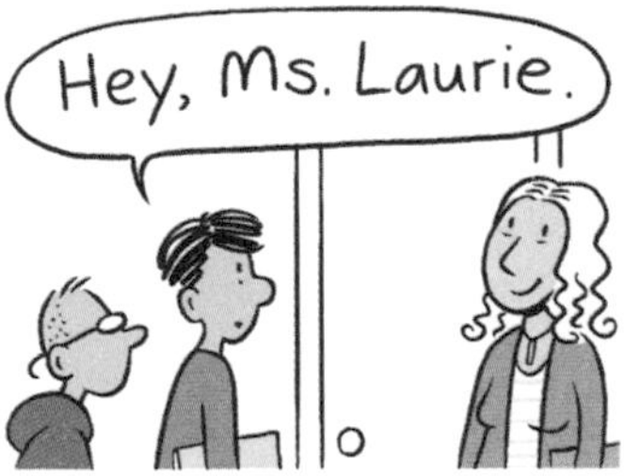
Hey, Ms. Laurie.

Joe and Anthony snicker at her preschool name. I shove them.

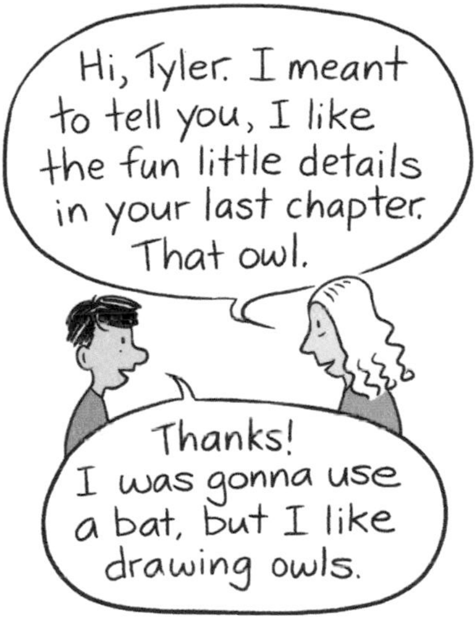
Hi, Tyler. I meant to tell you, I like the fun little details in your last chapter. That owl.
Thanks! I was gonna use a bat, but I like drawing owls.

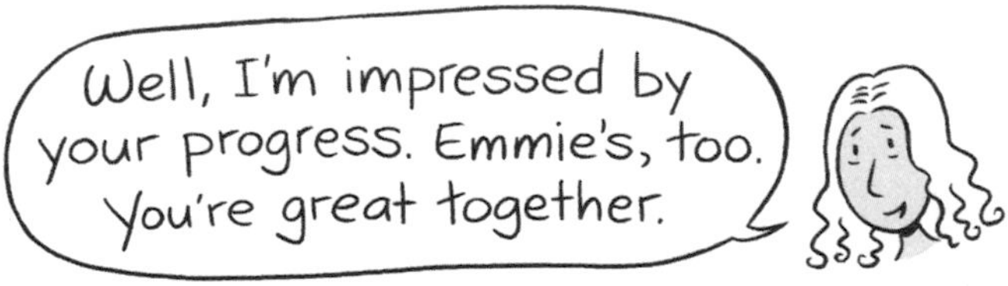
Well, I'm impressed by your progress. Emmie's, too. You're great together.

Joe and Anthony snort.

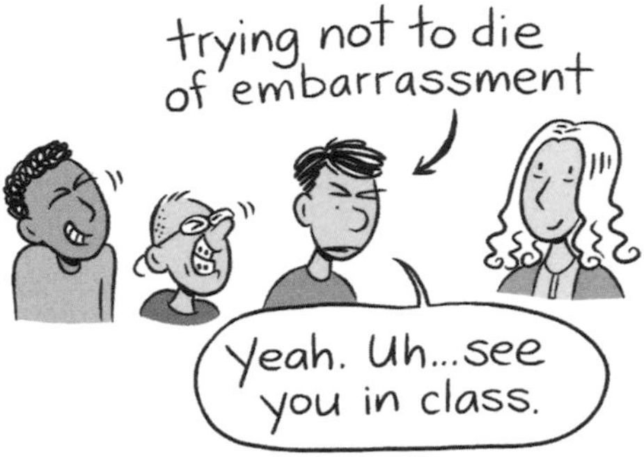
trying not to die of embarrassment
Yeah. Uh...see you in class.

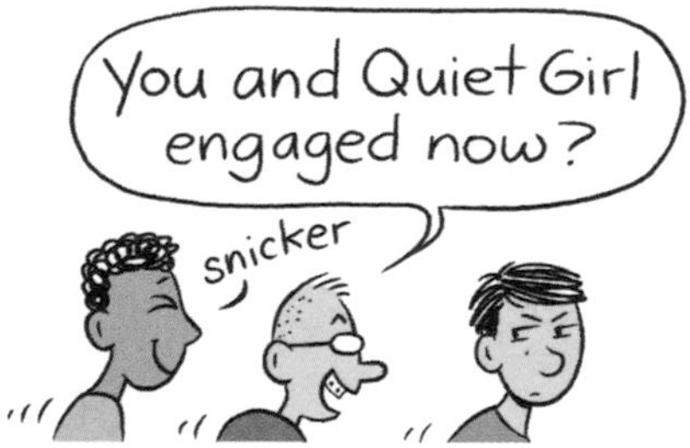
You and Quiet Girl engaged now?
snicker

I shove him again.

And, of course, right at that moment:

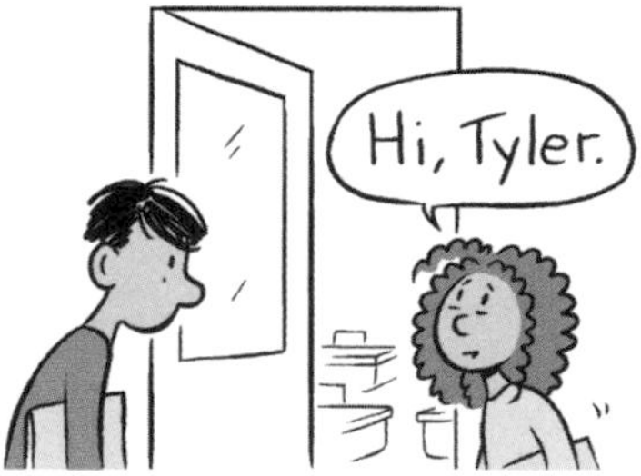
Hi, Tyler.

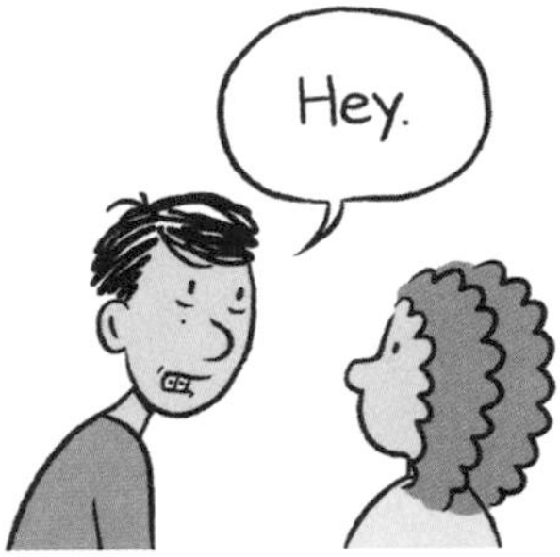
Hey.

Joe and Anthony burst into laughter. Emmie gets all red and looks confused. She ducks into math so fast, you'd think she actually liked the class.

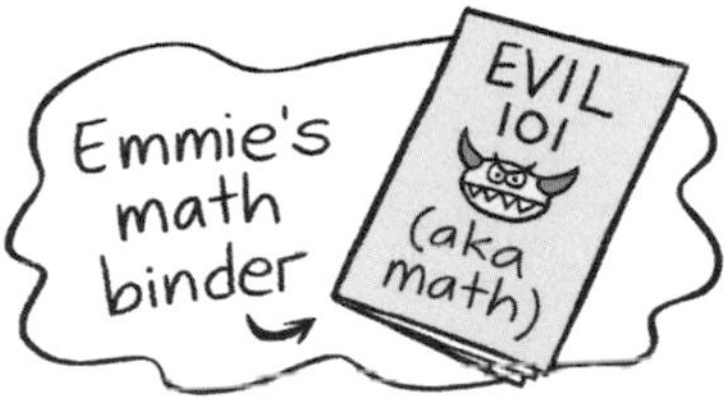
Emmie's math binder
EVIL 101
(aka math)

Coach Durdle walks by. She sees me and stops.

And hesitates.

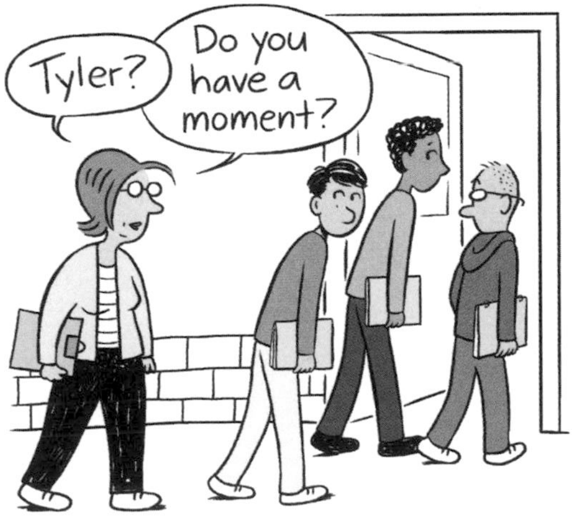
Tyler?
Do you have a moment?

I have a couple minutes before class starts. The guys give me a questioning look and walk into the room. Coach and I stand in the hallway a little farther from the door. I feel a weird sense of dread.

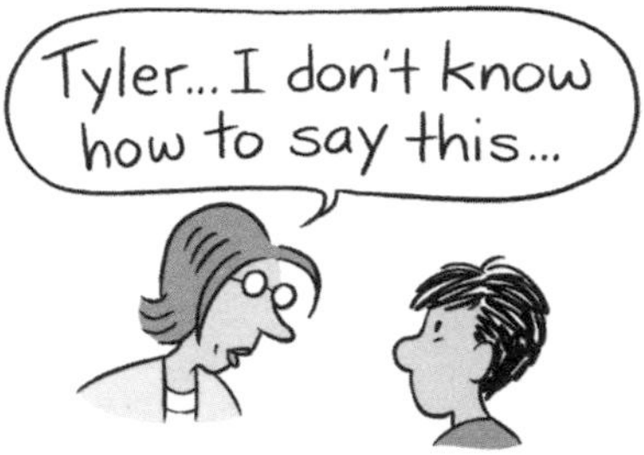
Tyler... I don't know how to say this...

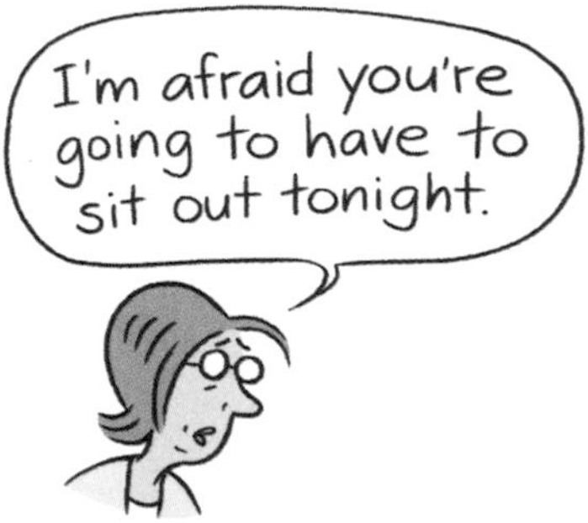
I'm afraid you're going to have to sit out tonight.

At first, this doesn't register.

Then it hits.

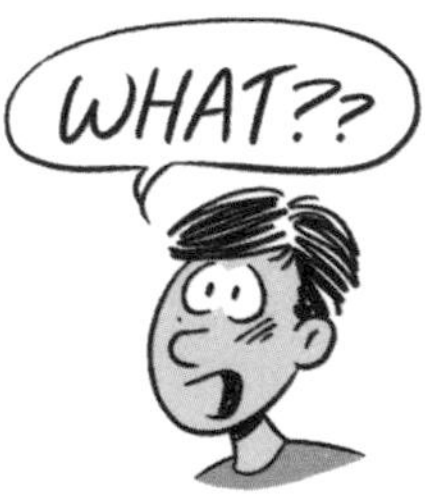
WHAT??

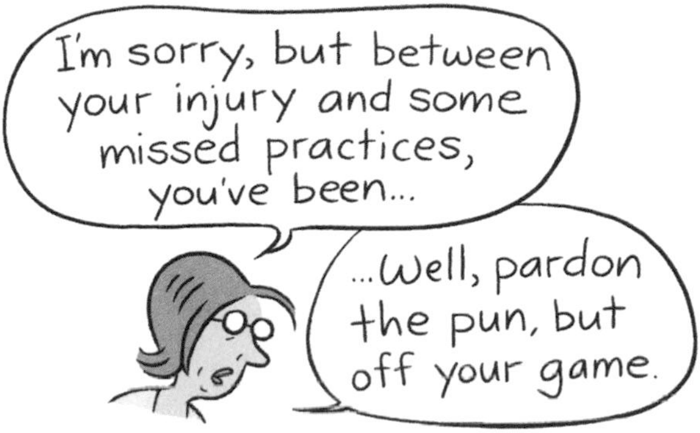
I'm sorry, but between your injury and some missed practices, you've been...
...Well, pardon the pun, but off your game.

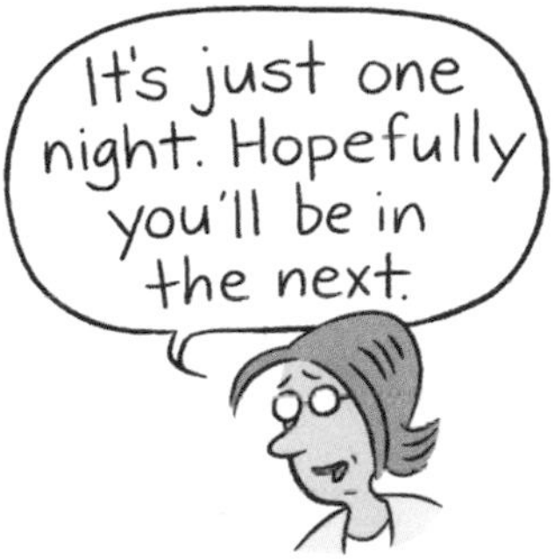
It's just one night. Hopefully you'll be in the next.

Hopefully? No, no, no. I have to play! I can't miss the most important game before playoffs!

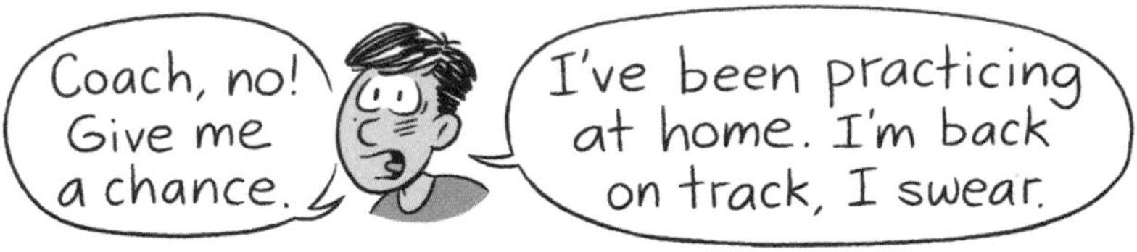
Coach, no! Give me a chance.
I've been practicing at home. I'm back on track, I swear.

She doesn't say anything. But I can see she's thinking it over.

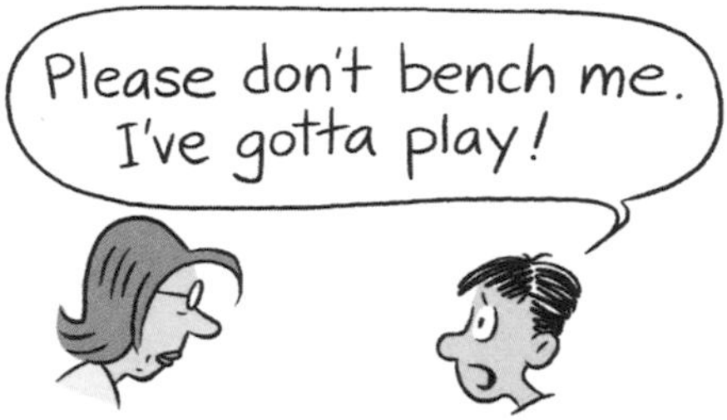
Please don't bench me. I've gotta play!

I give her the saddest, most pleading look that I save for my mom whenever I mess up at home.

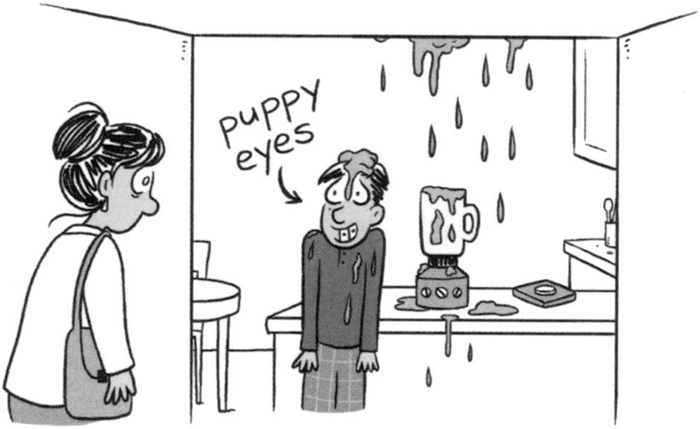
puppy eyes

Coach fires back her sternest look.

But then her eyes get all soft.

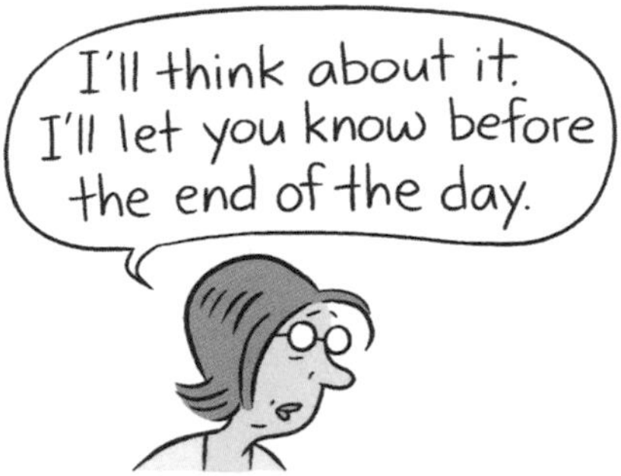
I'll think about it.
I'll let you know before
the end of the day.

I walk into class and sit down, feeling like my brain ran a marathon.

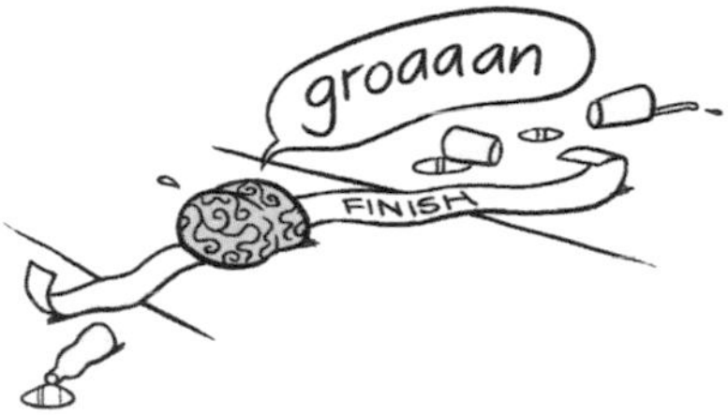
groaaan
FINISH

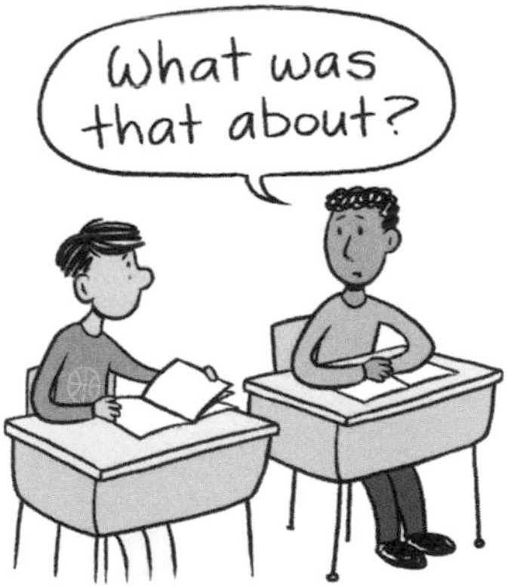
What was
that about?

I can't tell him. I just can't.

Nothing...
just a pep talk.

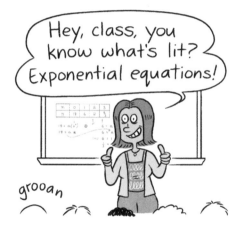

Mrs. Dietrich arrives at that moment. We get started.

Hey, class, you know what's lit? Exponential equations!
grooan

Ethan

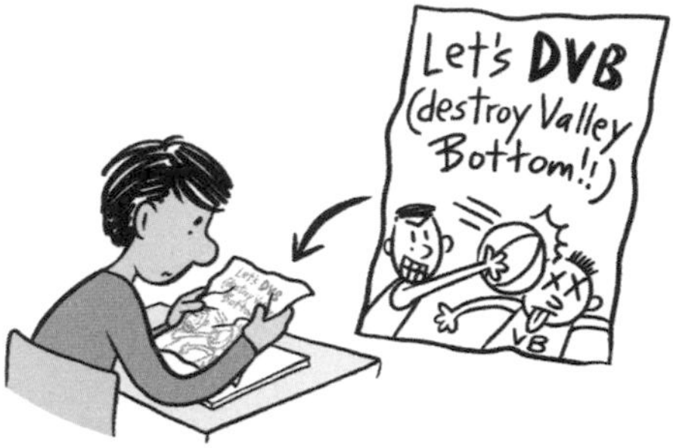
Let's DVB
(destroy Valley
Bottom!!)
VB

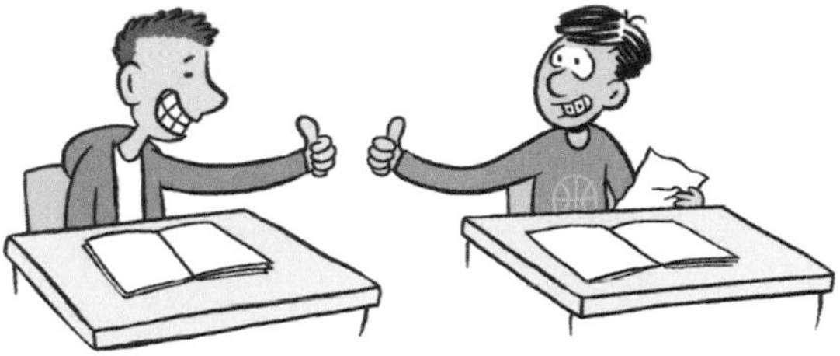

My wormy gut lurches. This day is turning into a roller coaster.

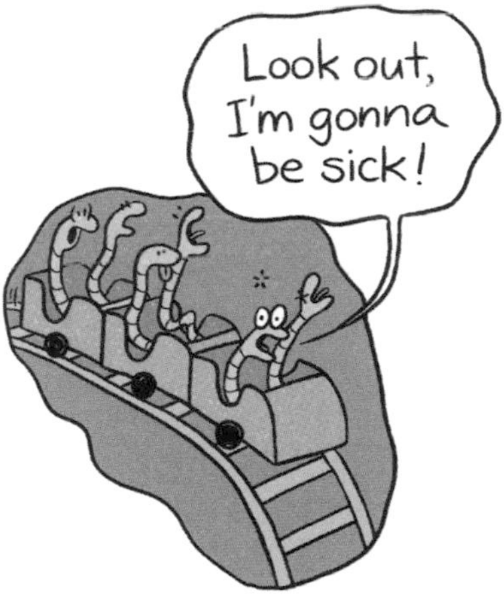
Look out,
I'm gonna
be sick!

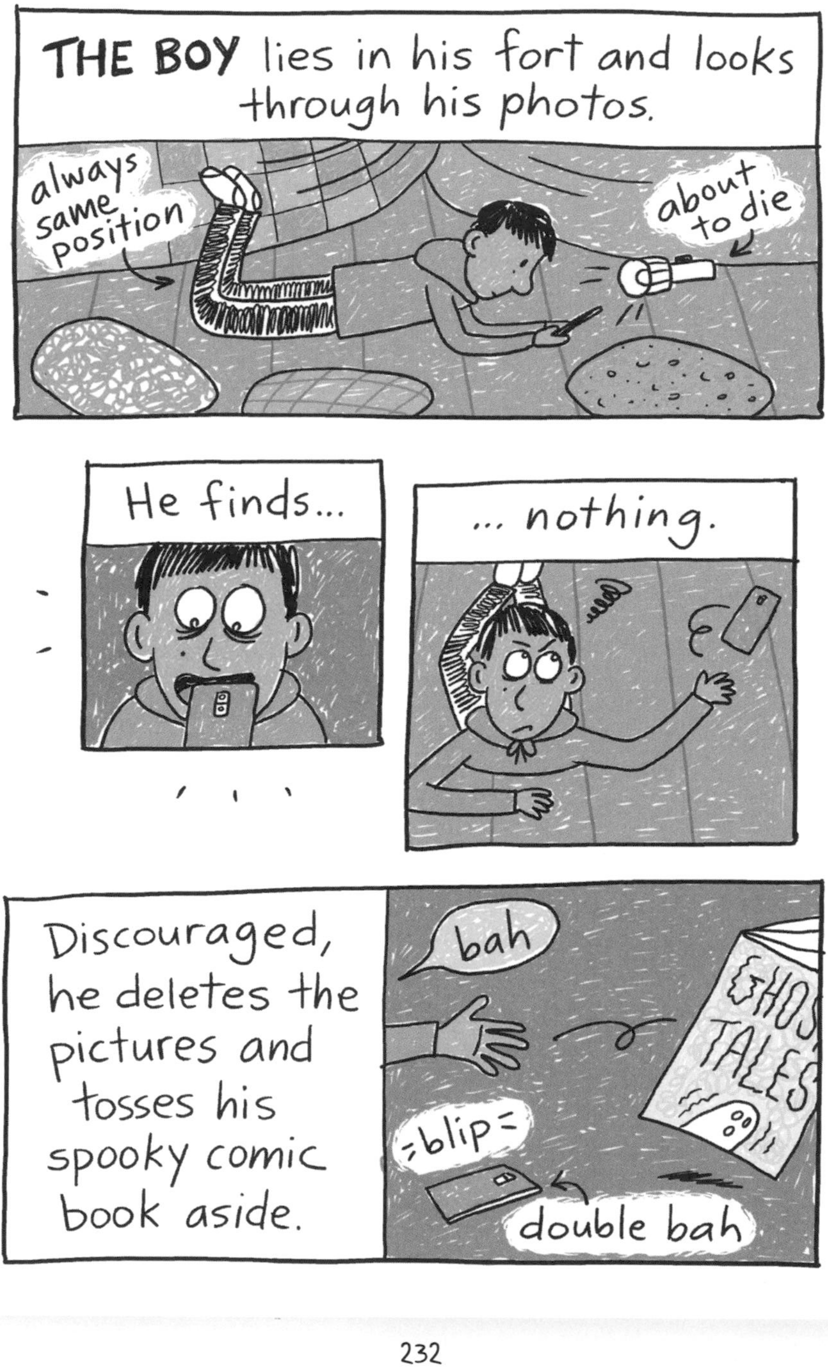
THE BOY lies in his fort and looks through his photos.
always same position
about to die
He finds...
... nothing.
Discouraged, he deletes the pictures and tosses his spooky comic book aside.
bah
GHOS TALES
blip
double bah

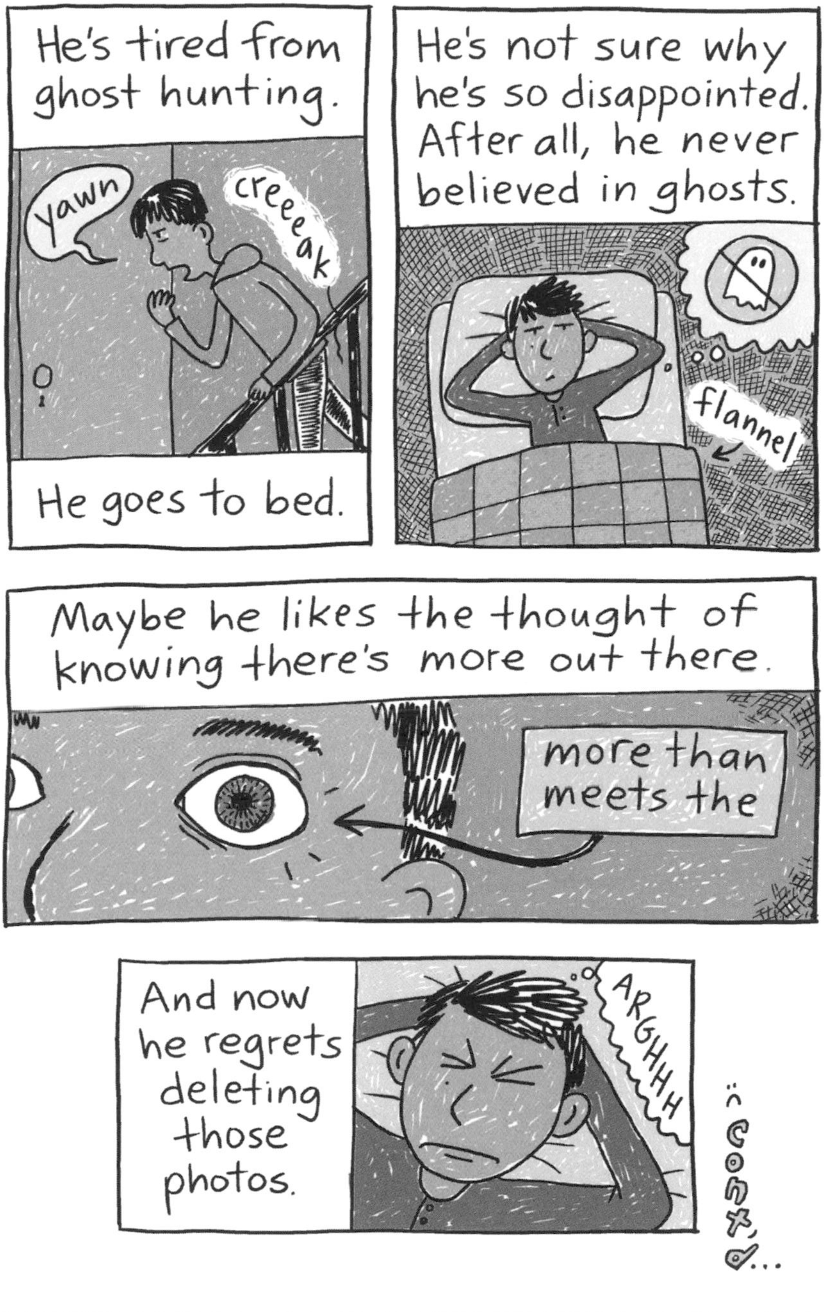
He's tired from ghost hunting.
yawn
creeeeak
He goes to bed.
He's not sure why he's so disappointed. After all, he never believed in ghosts.
flannel
Maybe he likes the thought of knowing there's more out there.
more than meets the
And now he regrets deleting those photos.
ARGHHHH
cont'd...

Emmie

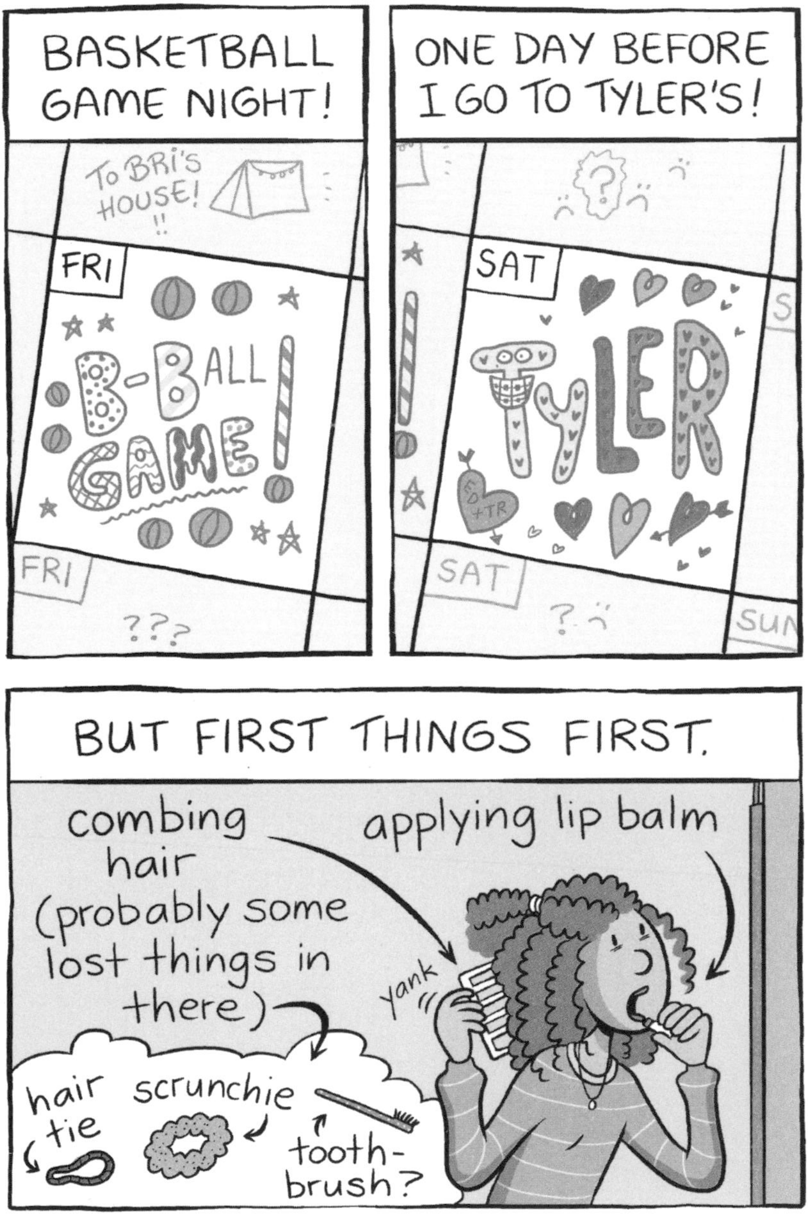
BASKETBALL GAME NIGHT!
To BRI'S HOUSE! !!
FRI
B-BALL GAME!
FRI
???
ONE DAY BEFORE I GO TO TYLER'S!
SAT
TYLER
ED +TR
SAT
SUN
BUT FIRST THINGS FIRST.
combing hair
applying lip balm
(probably some lost things in there)
yank
hair tie
scrunchie
tooth-brush?

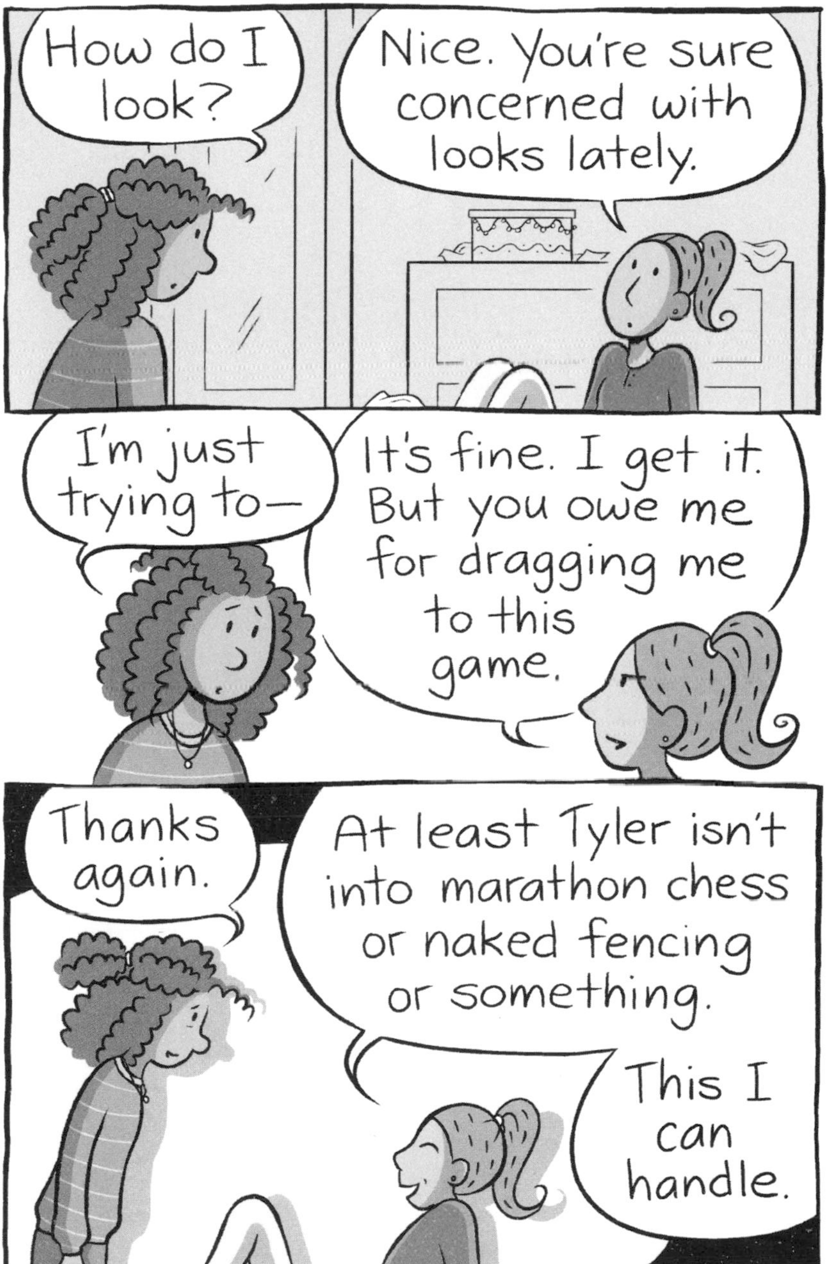
How do I look?
Nice. You're sure concerned with looks lately.
I'm just trying to—
It's fine. I get it. But you owe me for dragging me to this game.
Thanks again.
At least Tyler isn't into marathon chess or naked fencing or something.
This I can handle.

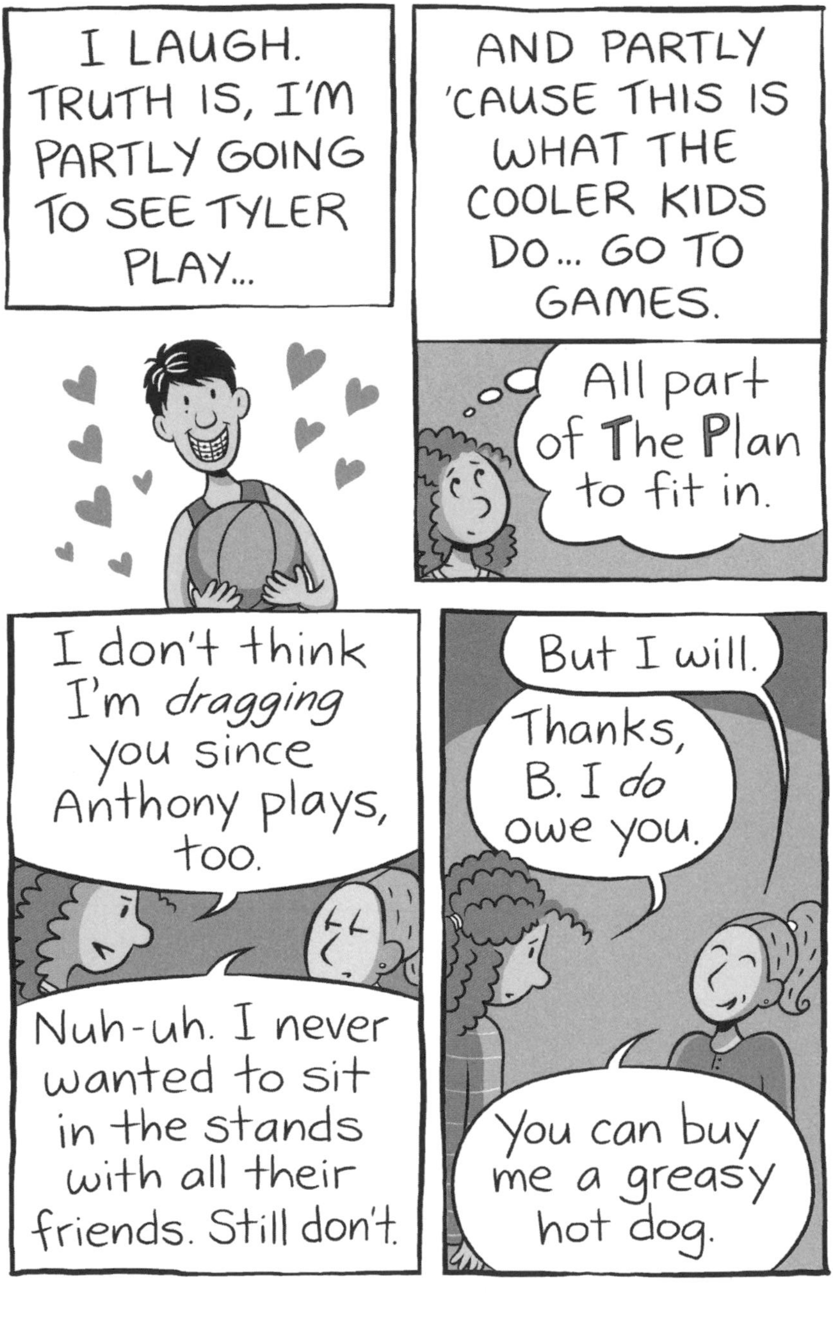
I LAUGH. TRUTH IS, I'M PARTLY GOING TO SEE TYLER PLAY...
AND PARTLY 'CAUSE THIS IS WHAT THE COOLER KIDS DO... GO TO GAMES.
All part of The Plan to fit in.
I don't think I'm *dragging* you since Anthony plays, too.
Nuh-uh. I never wanted to sit in the stands with all their friends. Still don't.
But I will.
Thanks, B. I *do* owe you.
You can buy me a greasy hot dog.

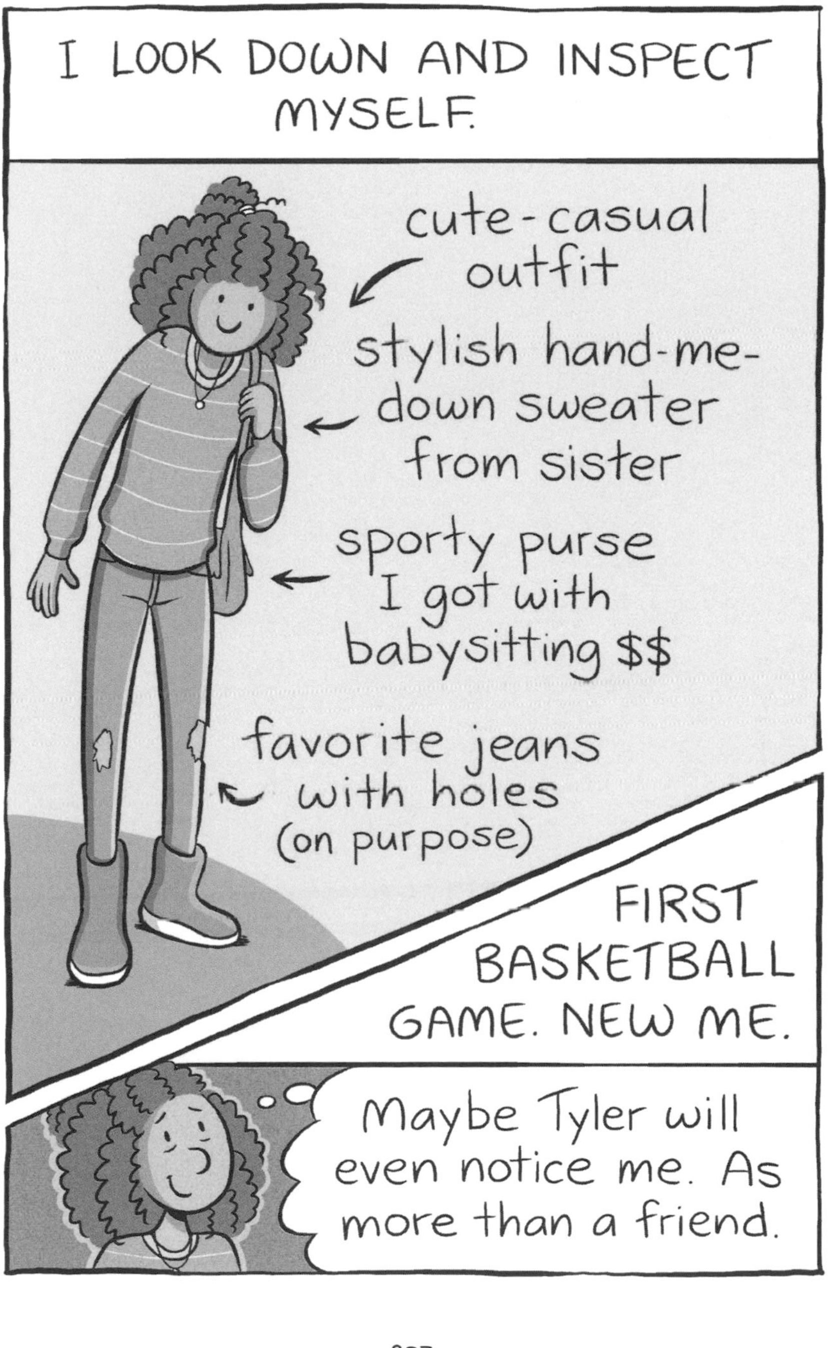
I LOOK DOWN AND INSPECT MYSELF.
cute-casual outfit
stylish hand-me-down sweater from sister
sporty purse I got with babysitting $$
favorite jeans with holes (on purpose)
FIRST BASKETBALL GAME. NEW ME.
Maybe Tyler will even notice me. As more than a friend.

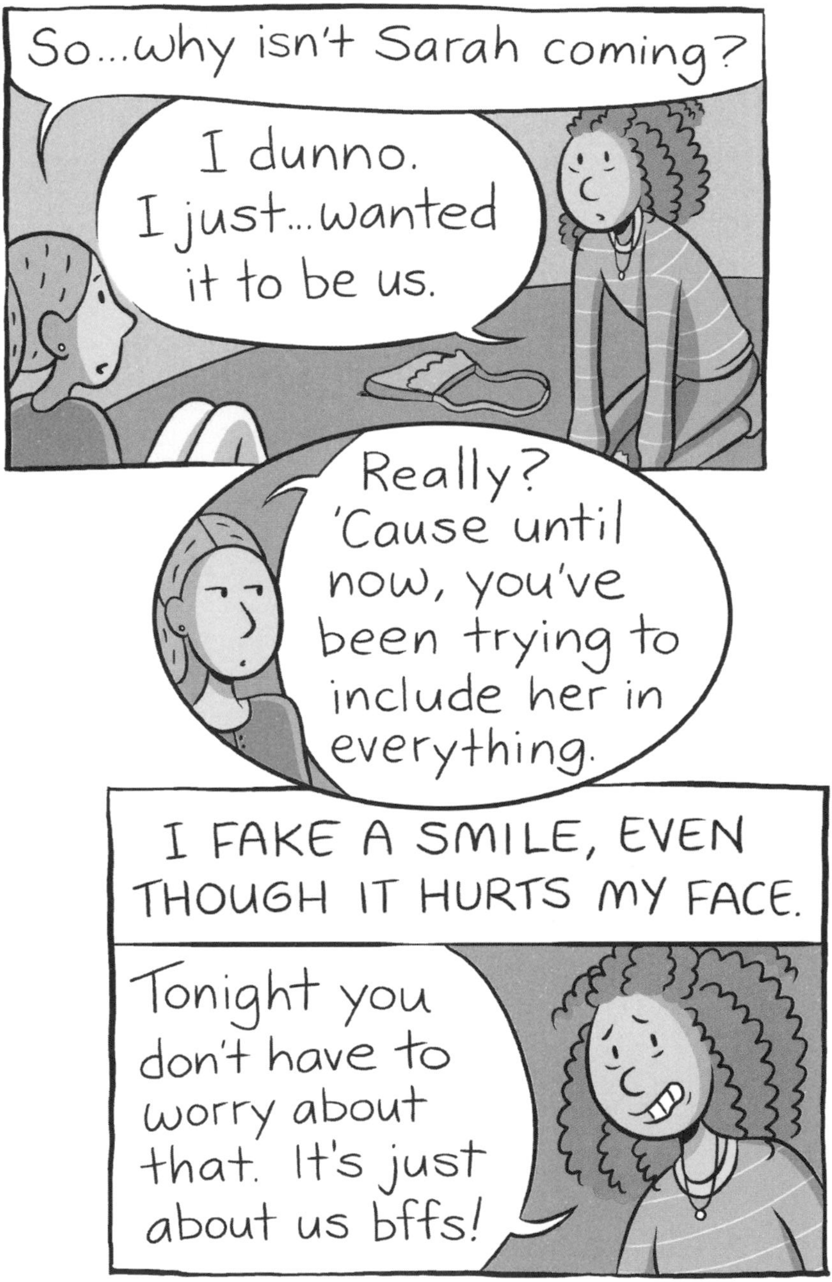
So...why isn't Sarah coming?
I dunno. I just...wanted it to be us.
Really? 'Cause until now, you've been trying to include her in everything.
I FAKE A SMILE, EVEN THOUGH IT HURTS MY FACE.
Tonight you don't have to worry about that. It's just about us bffs!

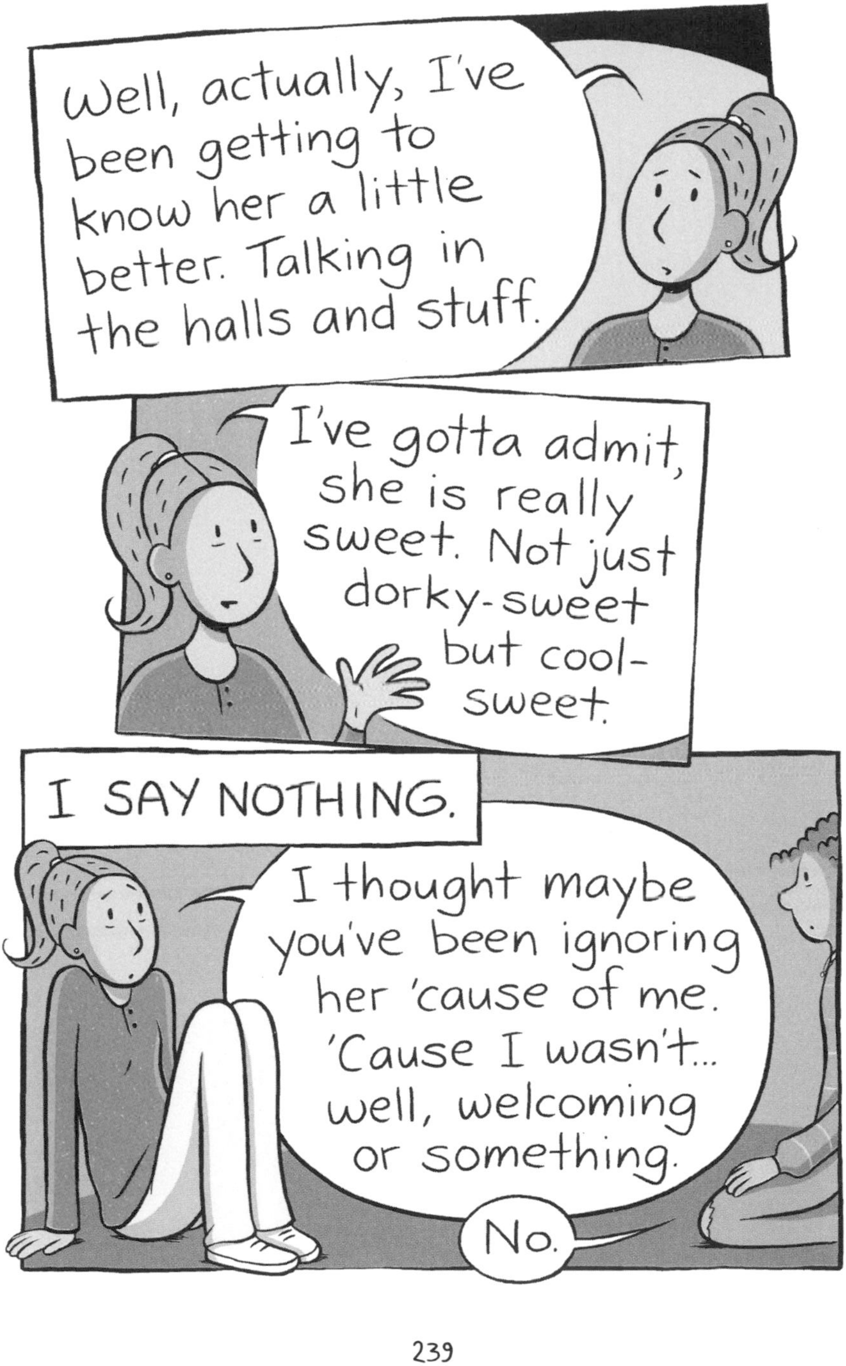
Well, actually, I've been getting to know her a little better. Talking in the halls and stuff.
I've gotta admit, she is really sweet. Not just dorky-sweet but cool-sweet.
I SAY NOTHING.
I thought maybe you've been ignoring her 'cause of me. 'Cause I wasn't... well, welcoming or something.
No.

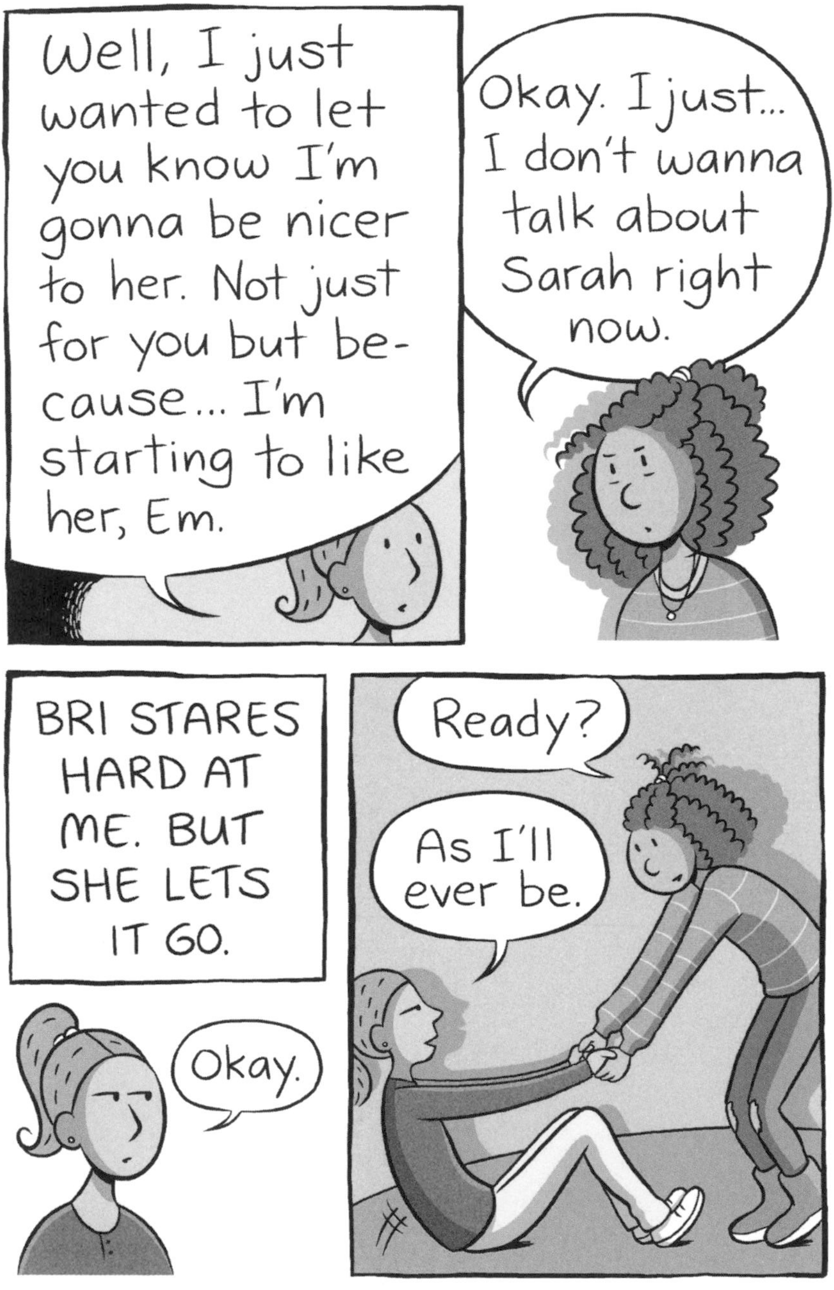
Well, I just wanted to let you know I'm gonna be nicer to her. Not just for you but be-cause... I'm starting to like her, Em.
Okay. I just... I don't wanna talk about Sarah right now.
BRI STARES HARD AT ME. BUT SHE LETS IT GO.
Okay.
Ready?
As I'll ever be.

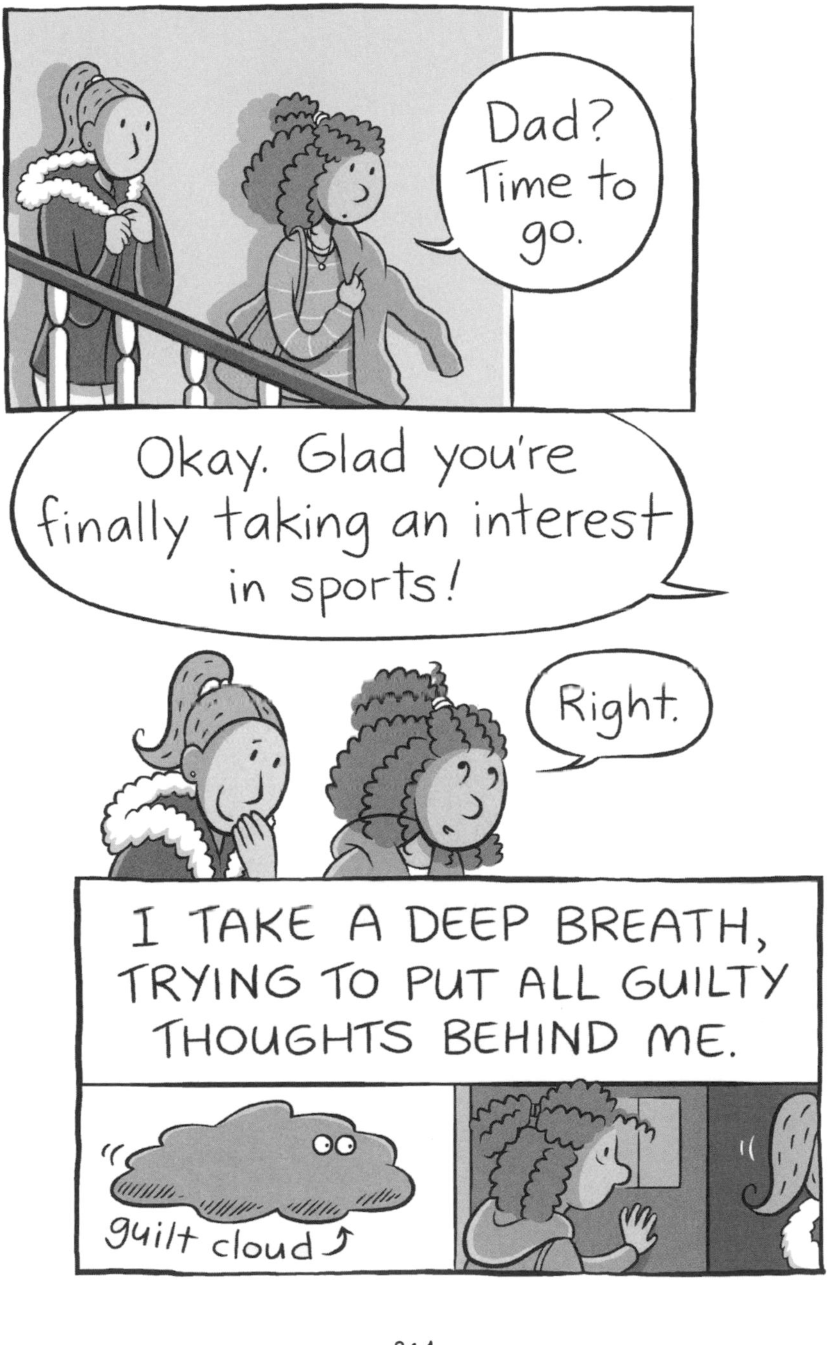
Dad? Time to go.
Okay. Glad you're finally taking an interest in sports!
Right.
I TAKE A DEEP BREATH, TRYING TO PUT ALL GUILTY THOUGHTS BEHIND ME.
guilt cloud

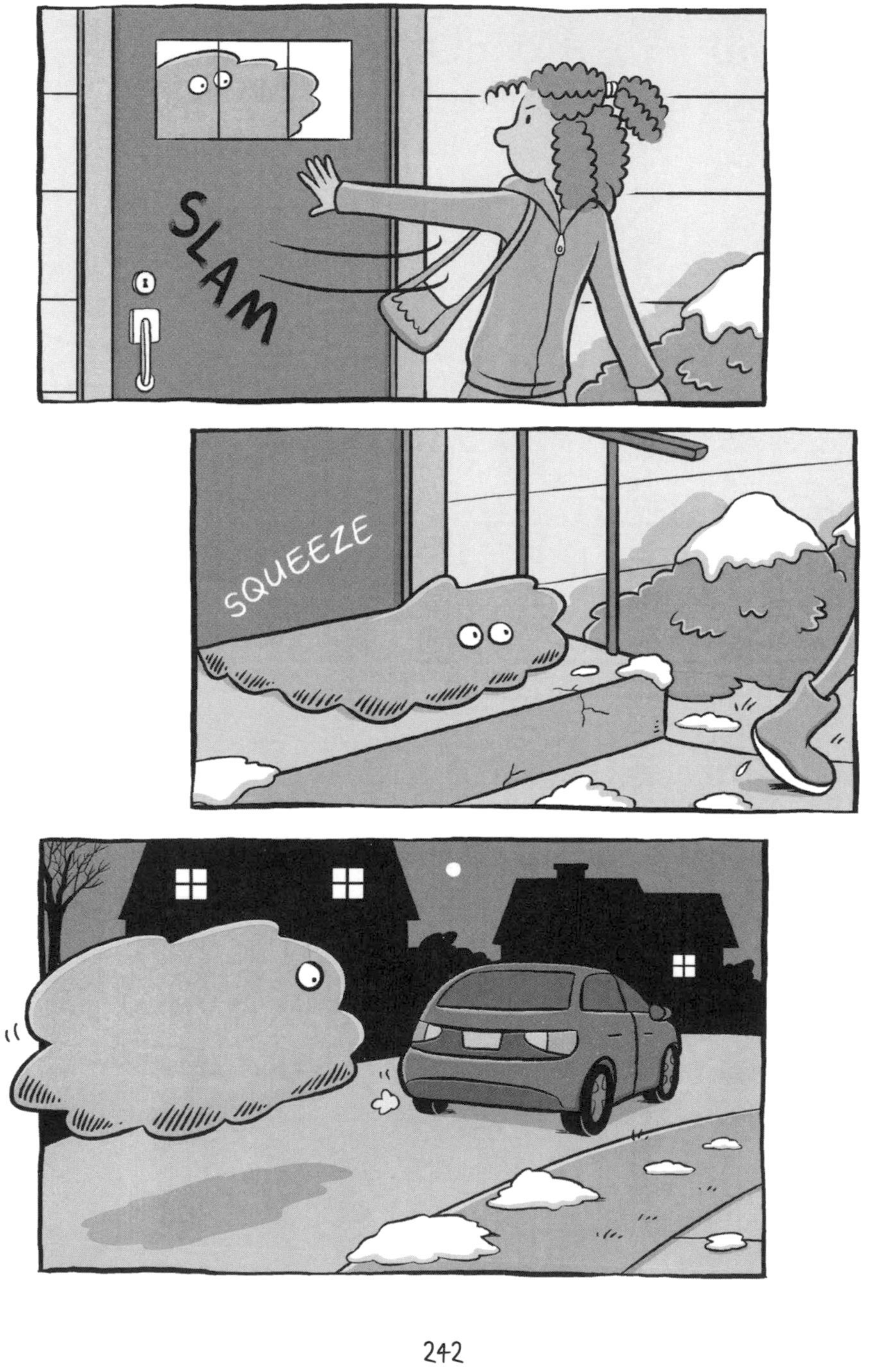
SLAM
SQUEEZE

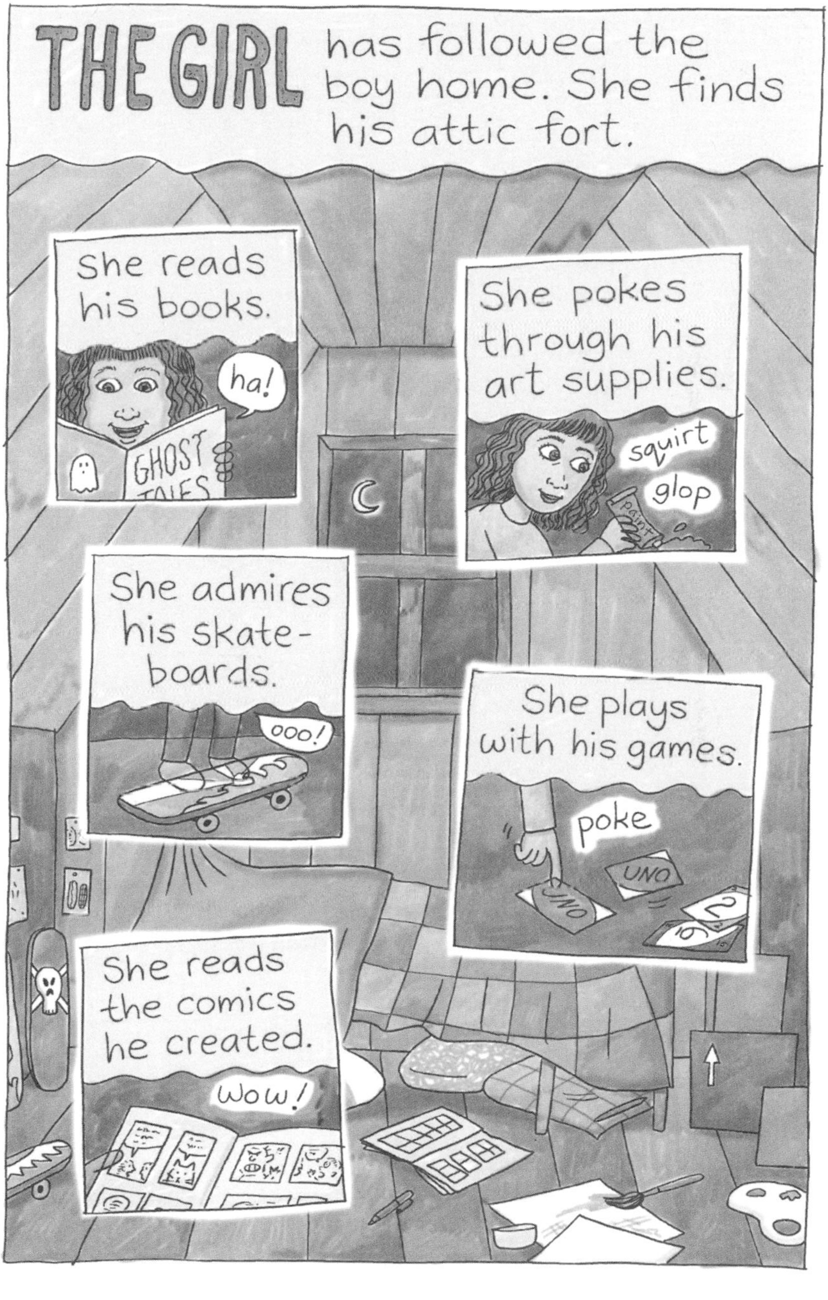
THE GIRL has followed the boy home. She finds his attic fort.
She reads his books.
ha!
GHOST TALES
She pokes through his art supplies.
squirt
glop
paint
She admires his skate-boards.
ooo!
She plays with his games.
poke
UNO
She reads the comics he created.
wow!

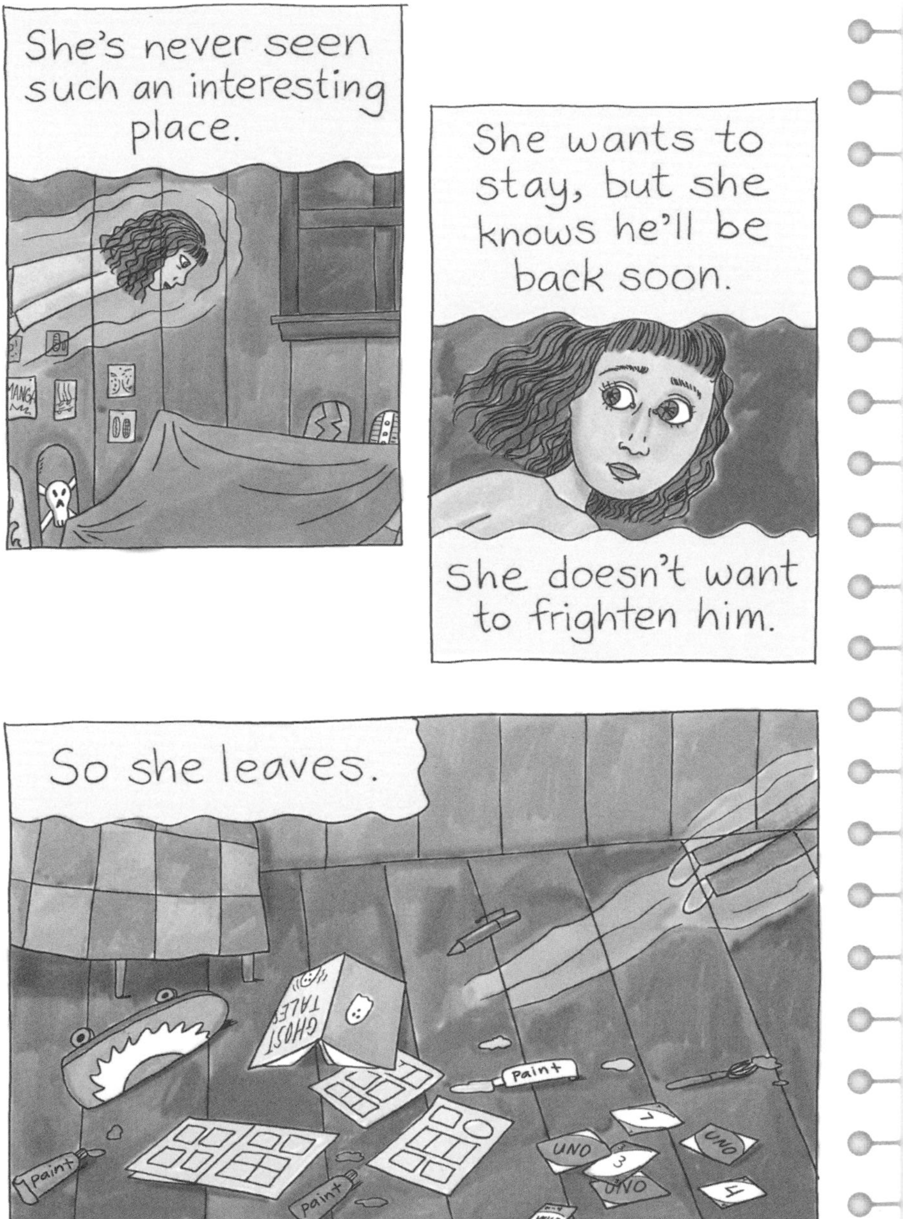
She's never seen such an interesting place.
MANGA
She wants to stay, but she knows he'll be back soon.
She doesn't want to frighten him.
So she leaves.
GHOST TALES
Paint
paint
paint
UNO
UNO
UNO
WILD
(cont'd...)

TYLER

All eyes are on me.

But I'm not nervous anymore. And even though I just missed the last free throw, I'm super focused. I can make this one.

Ready.

Aim.

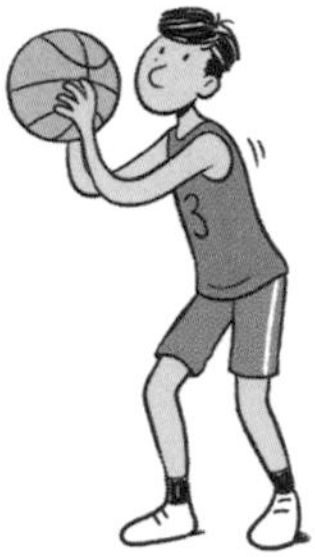

Shoot.

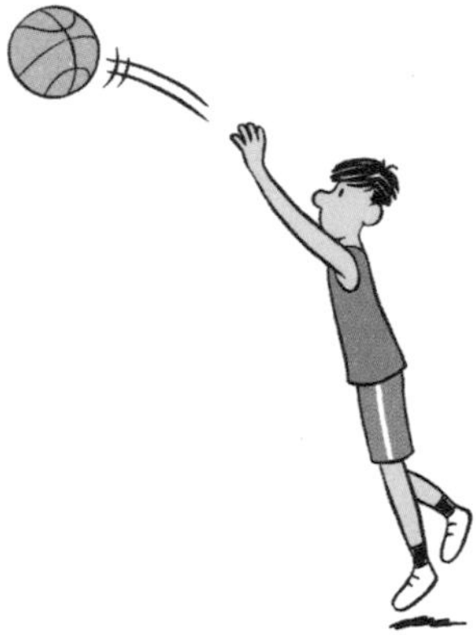

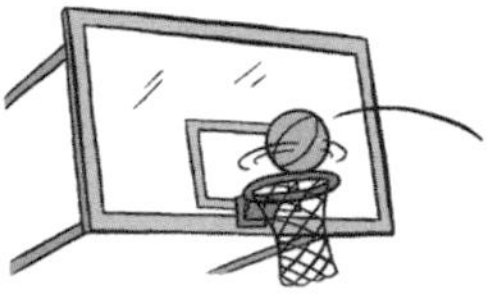

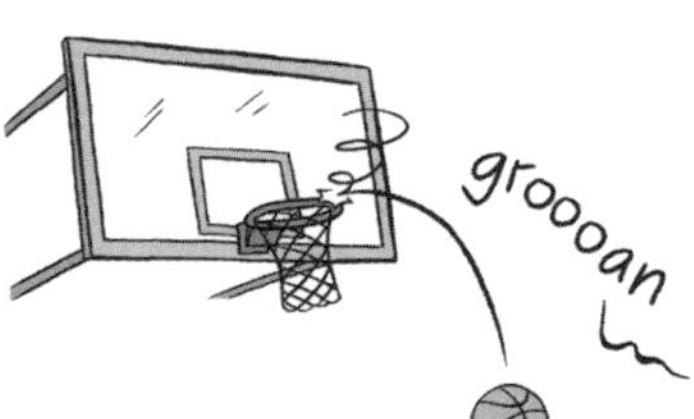
groooan

I hear the groans and boos. Malik gives me a reassuring pat on the back as we settle into our positions.

I'm so upset, I can't see straight. We're behind by two. Freaking. Points.

Two points I could've won back.

And it's not just those I missed. All night, my shooting's been erratic.

↰ "Winn Word"

I look at Coach Durdle. She nods grimly at me. She took a huge chance when she finally agreed to let me play.

Okay, Tyler, you're in.

I've gotta make it up to her.

Luckily, in the last quarter we catch up. Ethan and Anthony score six points. Valley Bottom also gets six. And finally . . .

YES!!

Ross the Boss is *baaack!*

Twenty seconds later, the buzzer sounds. We won. Barely.

Everyone's excited by the last-minute win. Coach Durdle even lets out a:

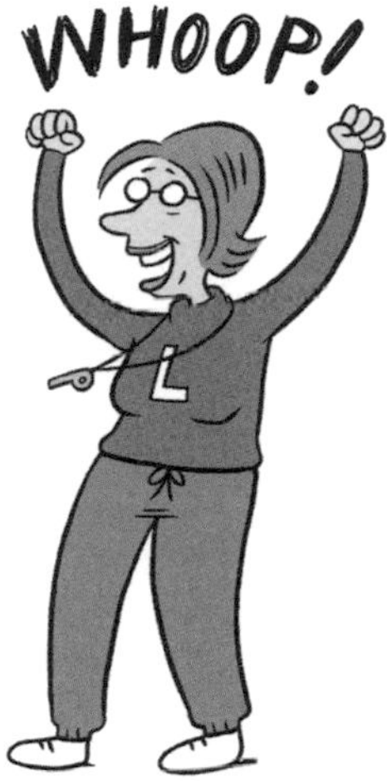
WHOOP!

So does my mom, who's sitting in the first row of bleachers.

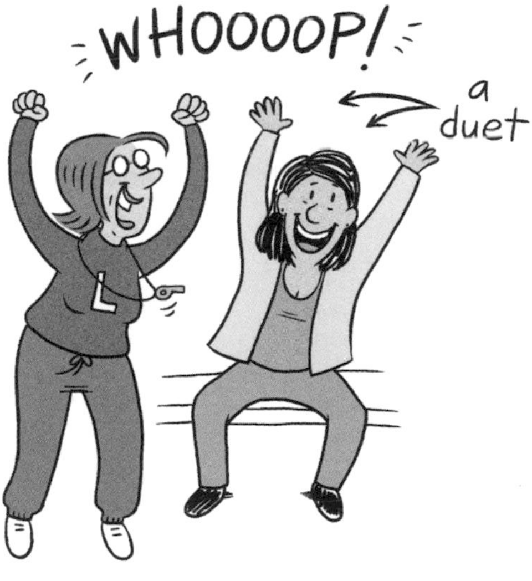
WHOOOOP!
a duet

But I'm shook. If this all-over-the-place playing keeps up, I'm never gonna make point guard. I'll be lucky if Coach keeps starting me the rest of the season. If Zach were here, he'd be shaking his head. I'm glad he's not. He has late practice at the high school.

I try to look on the bright side. We **did** win. And I made the winning shot! At least it was exciting. And now we get to go to the playoffs!

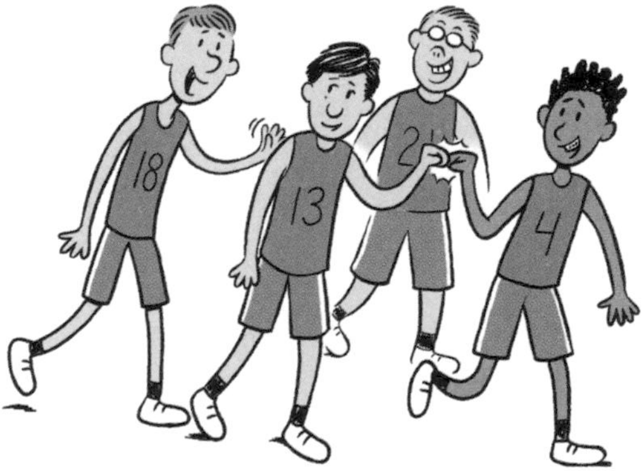
18
13
21
4

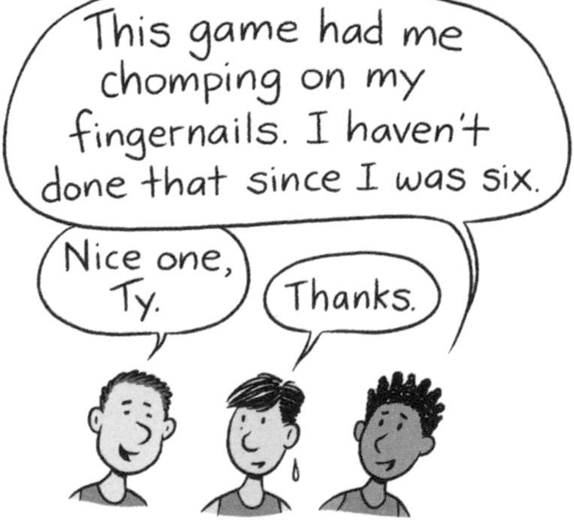
This game had me chomping on my fingernails. I haven't done that since I was six.
Nice one, Ty.
Thanks.

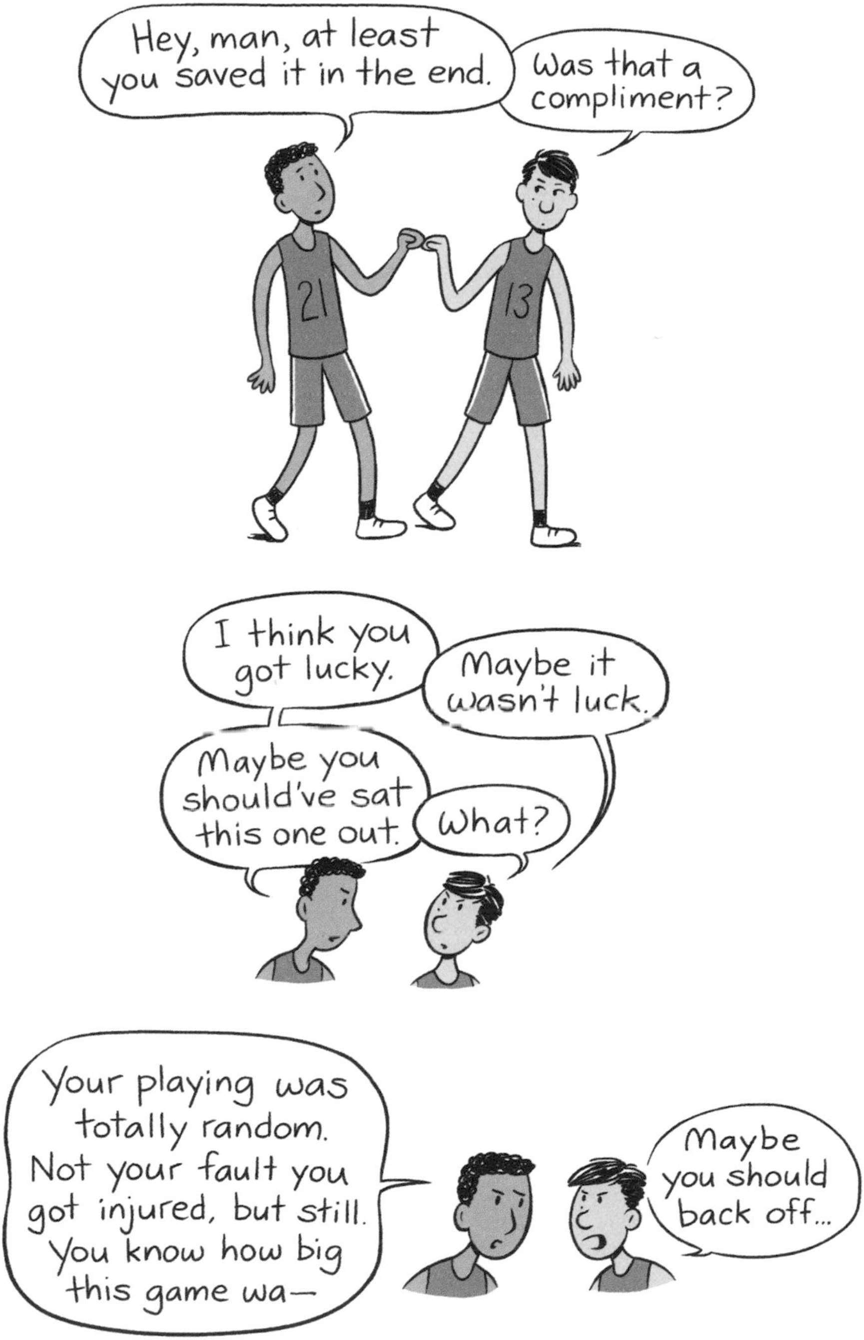
Hey, man, at least you saved it in the end.
Was that a compliment?
21
13
I think you got lucky.
Maybe it wasn't luck.
Maybe you should've sat this one out.
What?
Your playing was totally random. Not your fault you got injured, but still. You know how big this game wa—
Maybe you should back off...

We glare at each other, and I feel this close to popping him, but I see Coach Durdle eyeing us to go shake hands with the other team. So we separate, Anthony and I giving each other the stink eye.

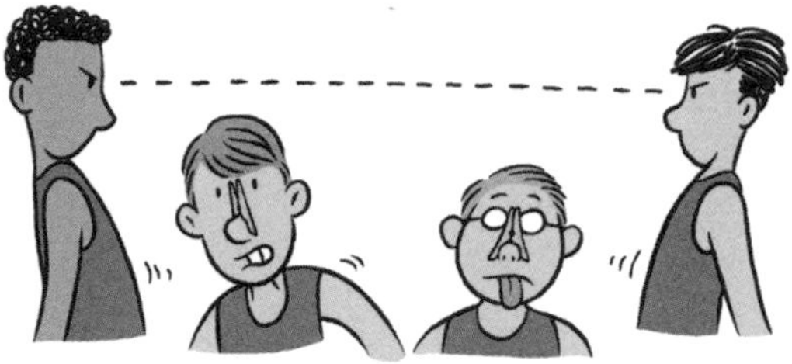

I don't believe this. Anthony and I haven't argued since fifth grade when he copied my science worksheet, including all the wrong answers and one specific one where we had to name a star after us. We both got in trouble.

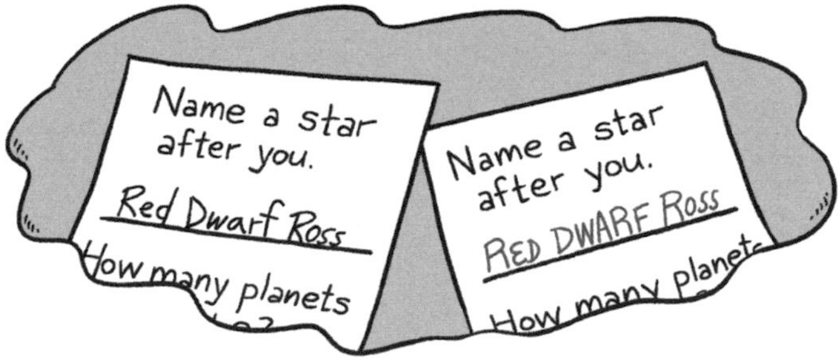
Name a star after you.
Red Dwarf Ross
How many planets
Name a star after you.
RED DWARF ROSS
How many planet

I try to find my inner zen (again). We shake the other team's hands and head toward the locker room near the stands. That's when I see Emmie and Brianna, a few benches up. It's not hard to spot them; middle school games are always half full at best.

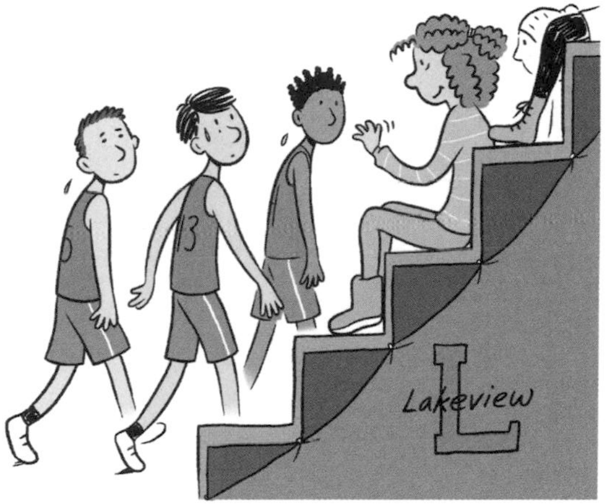
Lakeview

Uh-oh.

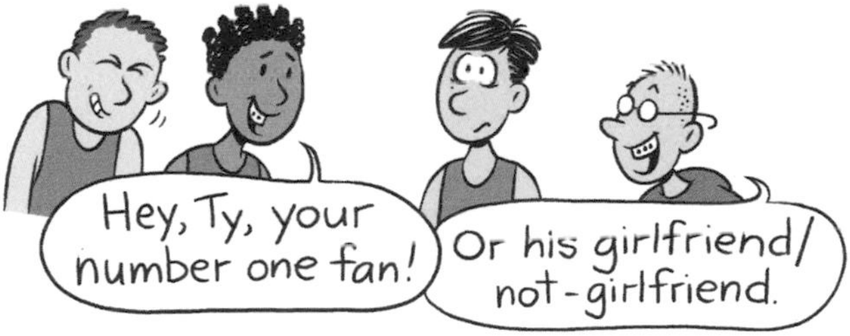
Hey, Ty, your number one fan!
Or his girlfriend/not-girlfriend.

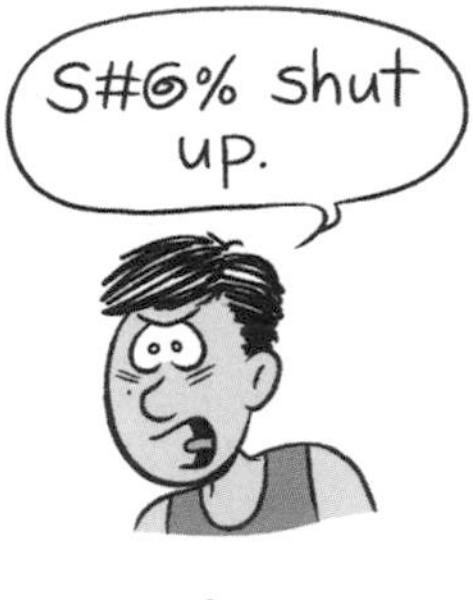
S#@% shut up.

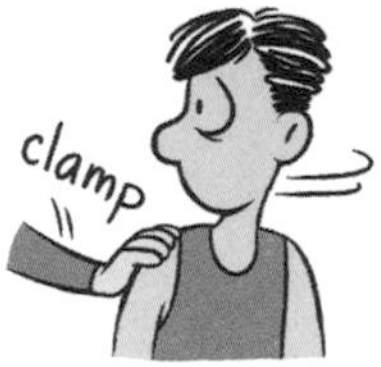
clamp

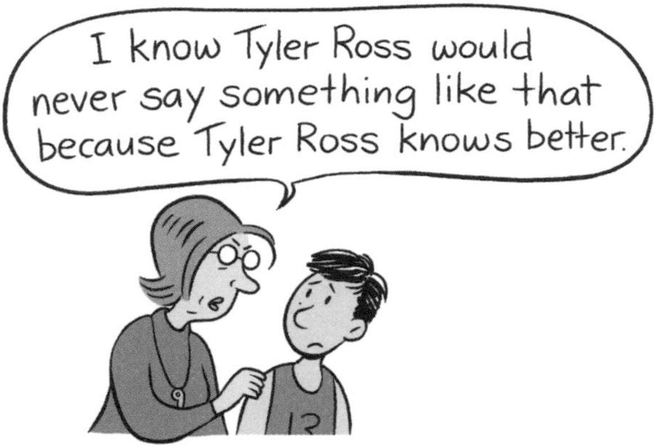
I know Tyler Ross would never say something like that because Tyler Ross knows better.

Great. On top of everything, I got in trouble. And third-personed.

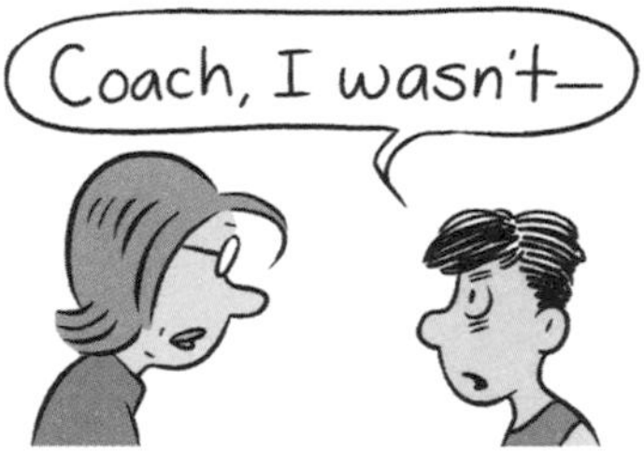
Coach, I wasn't—

I stop. There's no way I'm gonna rat my friends out.

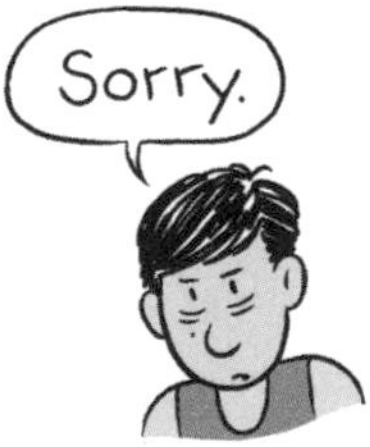
Sorry.

She nods and goes to talk to the other coach while we walk to the locker room. Some of the guys are smirking at me while checking out Emmie.

Who is looking at them and me, confused. Or embarrassed. Or both.

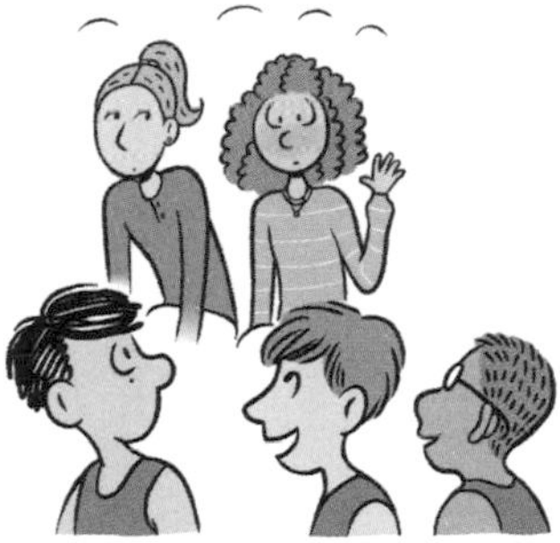

But I don't care. I'm so tired of all the teasing and trash talk. Even if it's just joking. It's no longer funny.

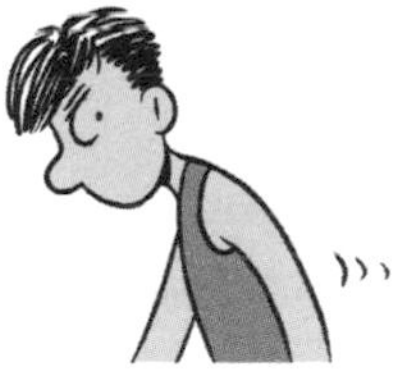

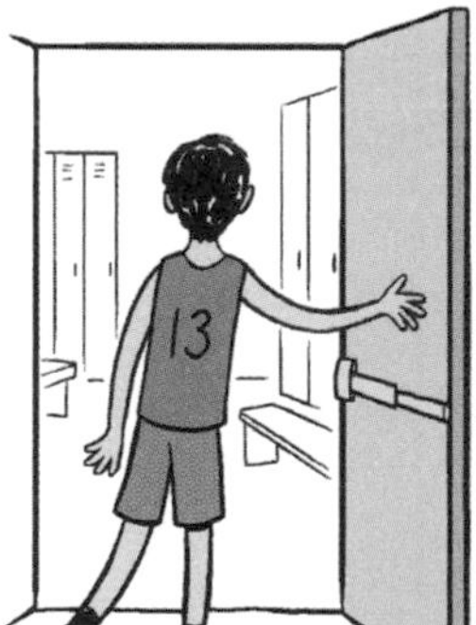

13

I don't wave back.

Emmie

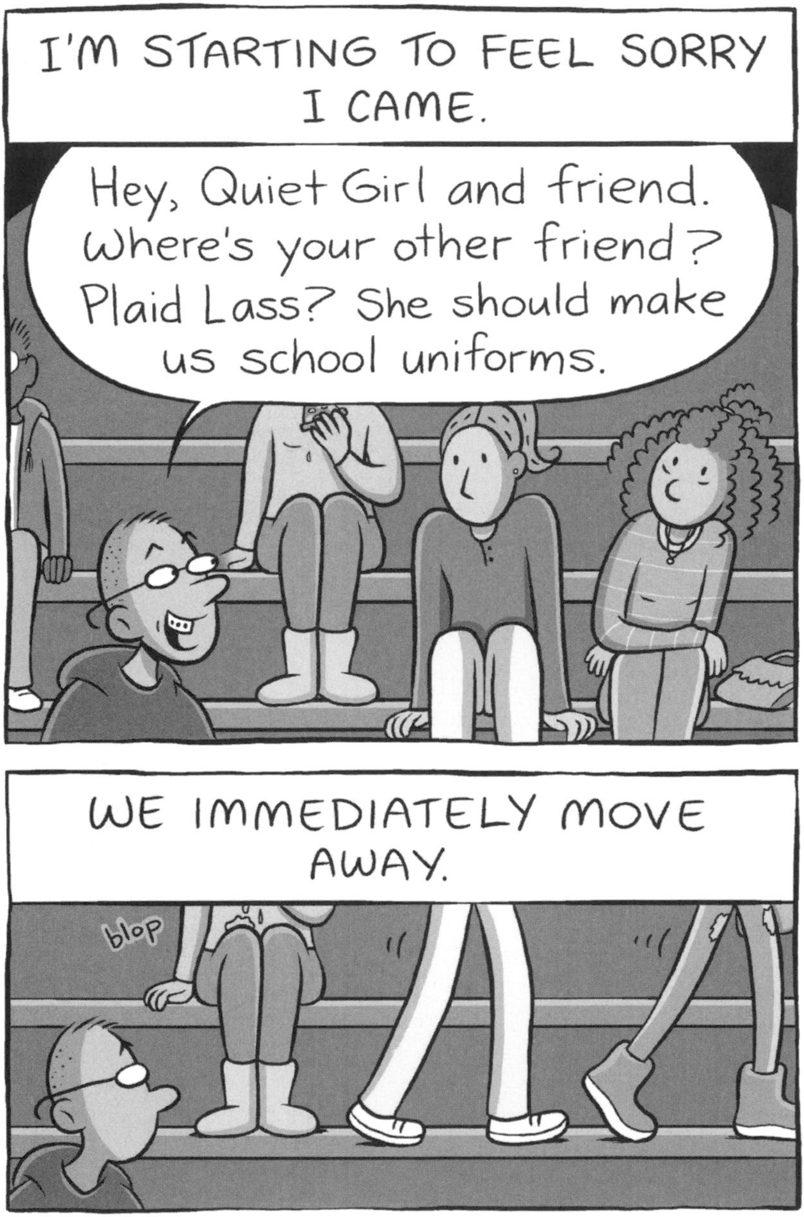
I'M STARTING TO FEEL SORRY I CAME.
Hey, Quiet Girl and friend. Where's your other friend? Plaid Lass? She should make us school uniforms.
WE IMMEDIATELY MOVE AWAY.
blop

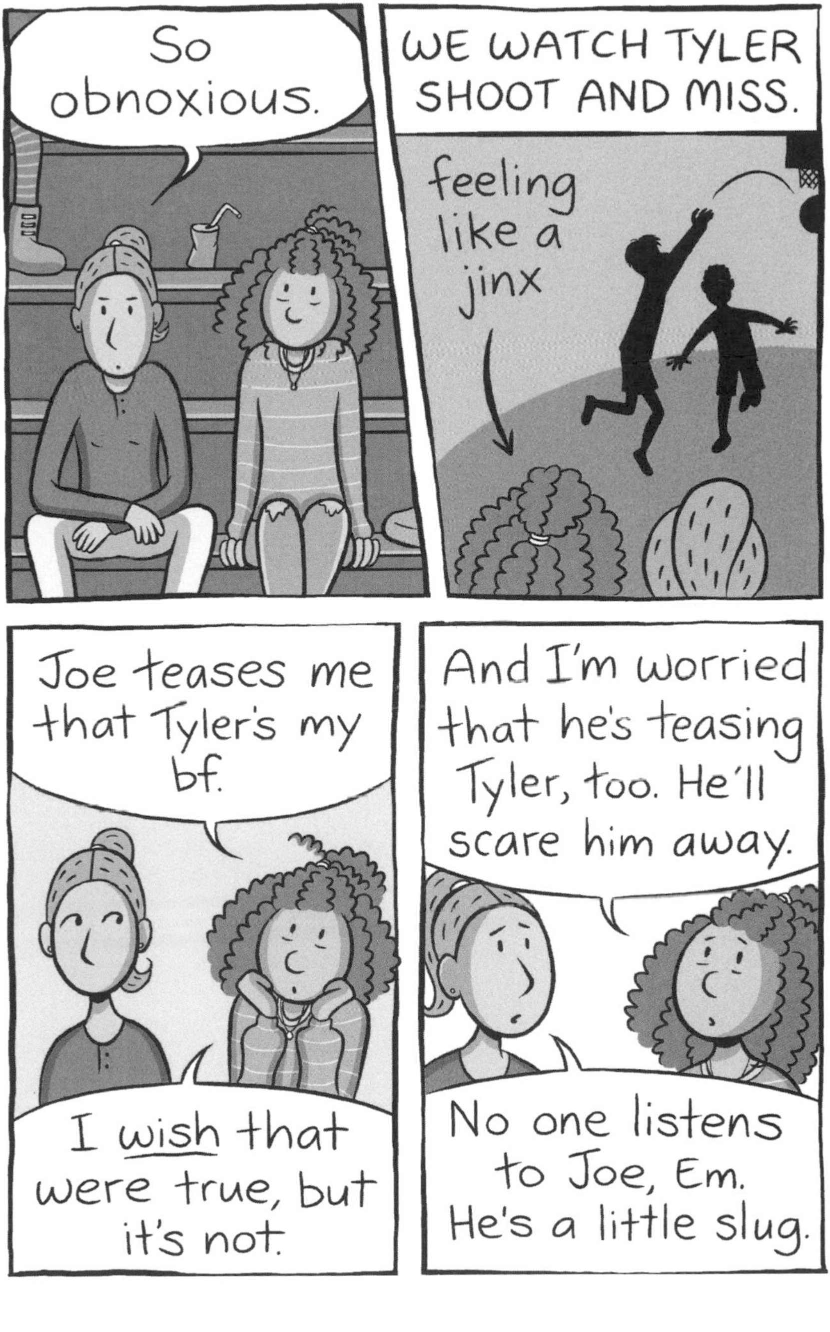
So obnoxious.
WE WATCH TYLER SHOOT AND MISS.
feeling like a jinx
Joe teases me that Tyler's my bf.
I wish that were true, but it's not.
And I'm worried that he's teasing Tyler, too. He'll scare him away.
No one listens to Joe, Em. He's a little slug.

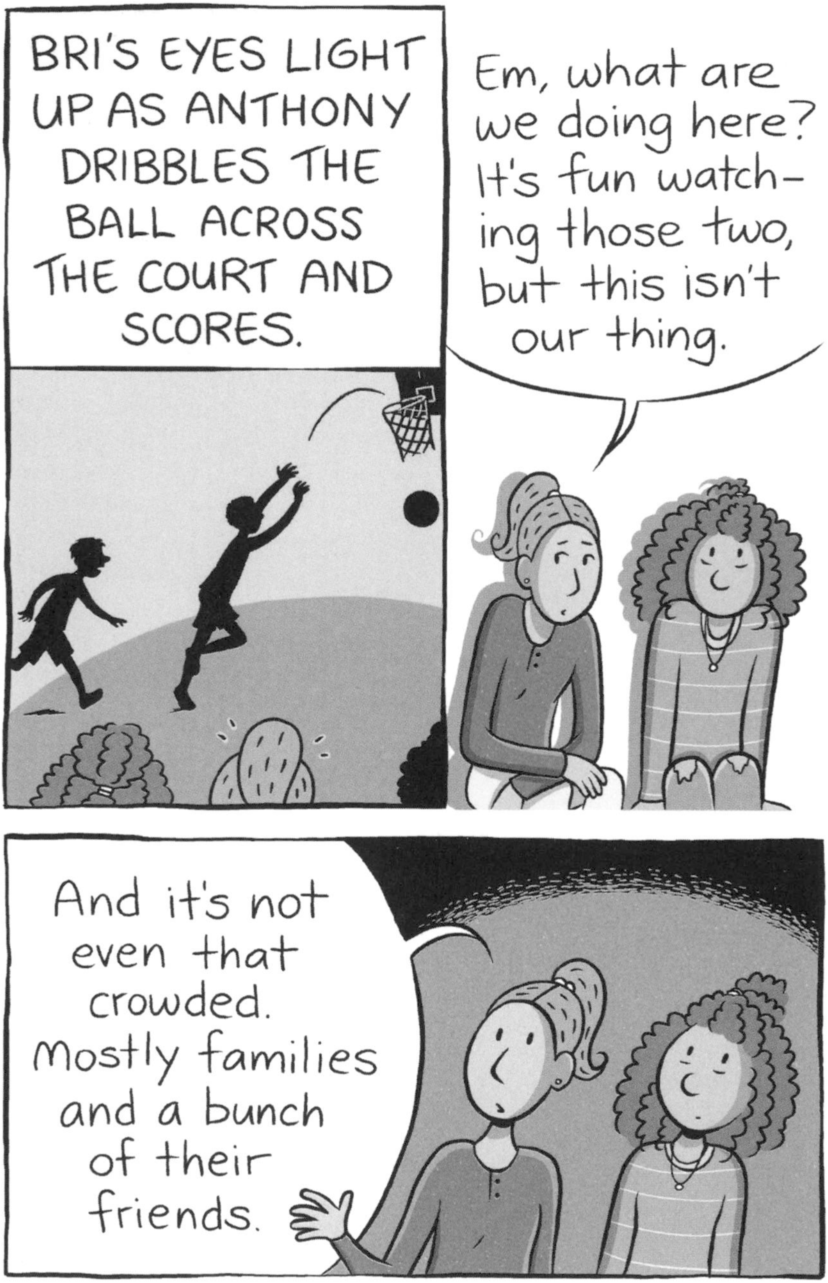
BRI'S EYES LIGHT UP AS ANTHONY DRIBBLES THE BALL ACROSS THE COURT AND SCORES.
Em, what are we doing here? It's fun watch-ing those two, but this isn't our thing.
And it's not even that crowded. Mostly families and a bunch of their friends.

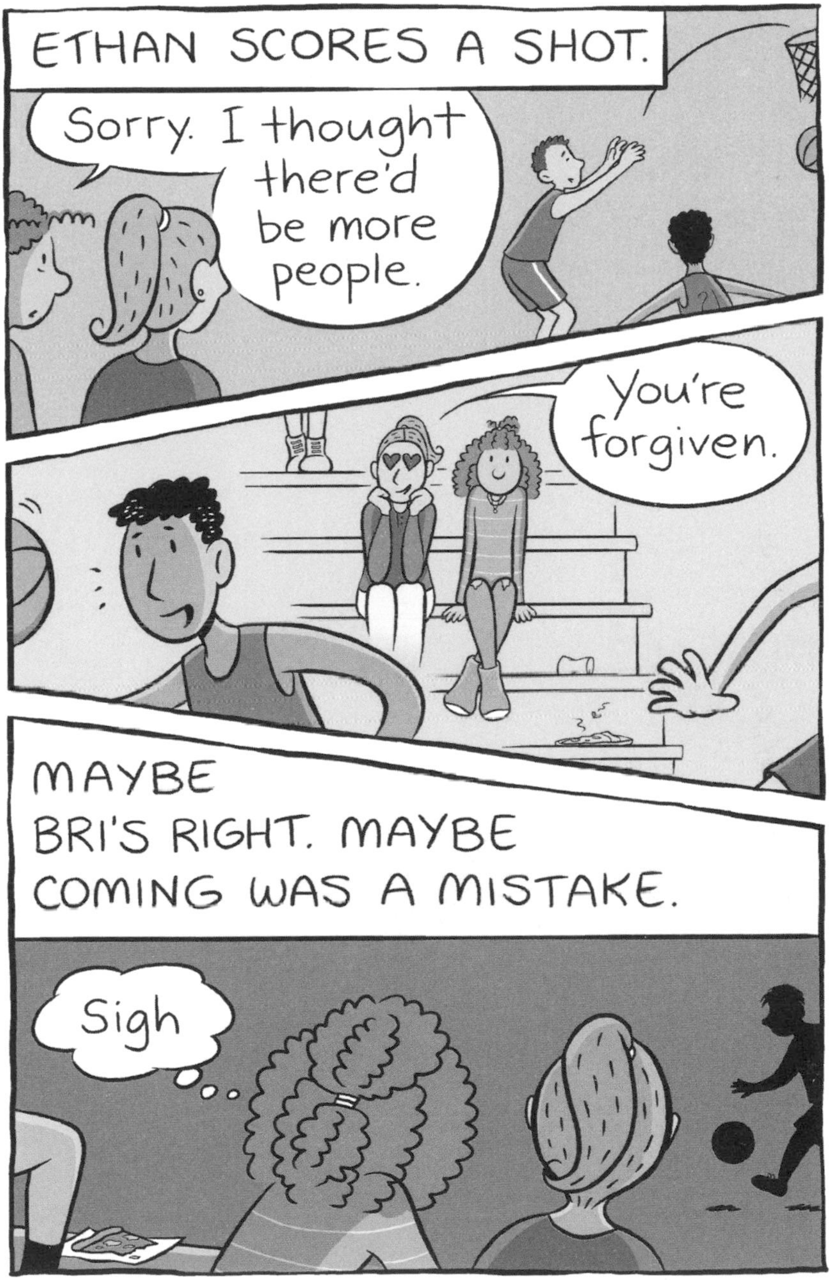
ETHAN SCORES A SHOT.
Sorry. I thought there'd be more people.
You're forgiven.
MAYBE BRI'S RIGHT. MAYBE COMING WAS A MISTAKE.
Sigh

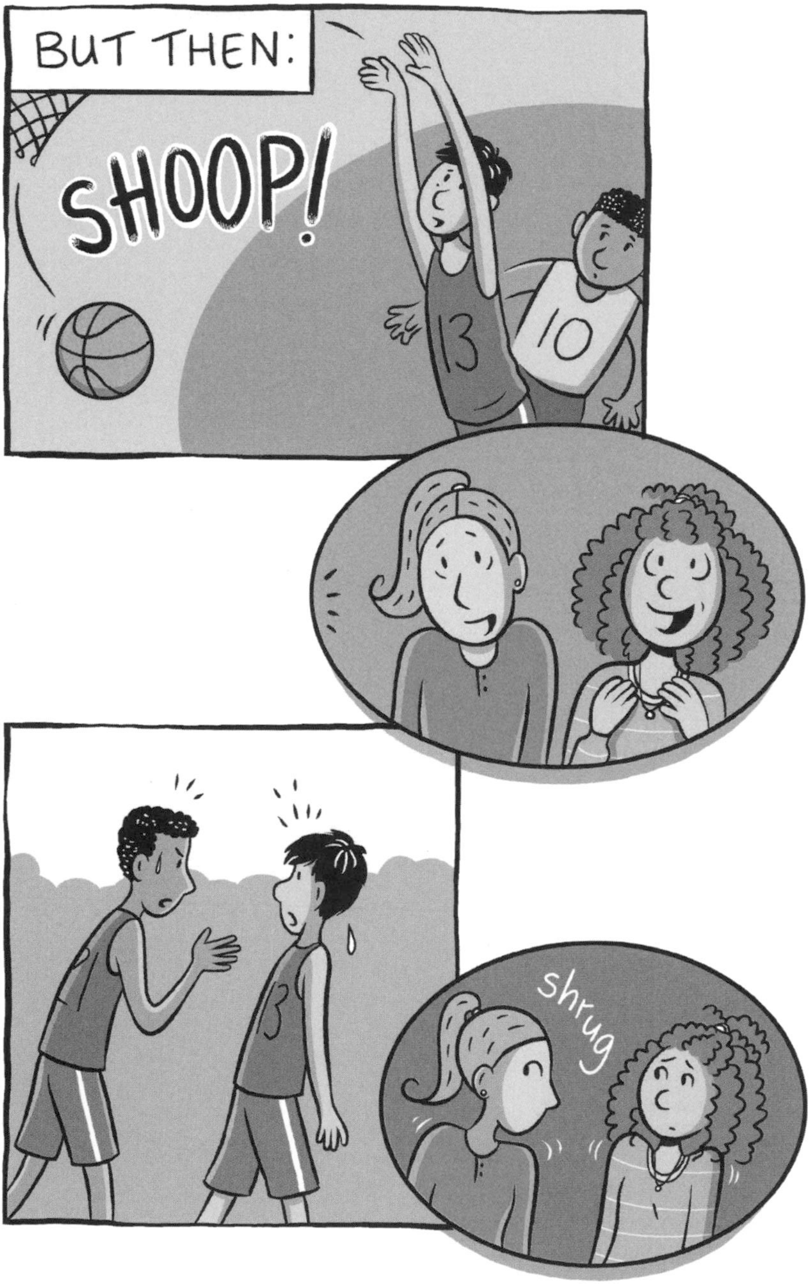
BUT THEN:
SHOOP!
13
10
shrug

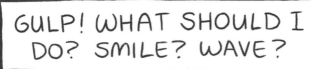

GULP! WHAT SHOULD I DO? SMILE? WAVE?

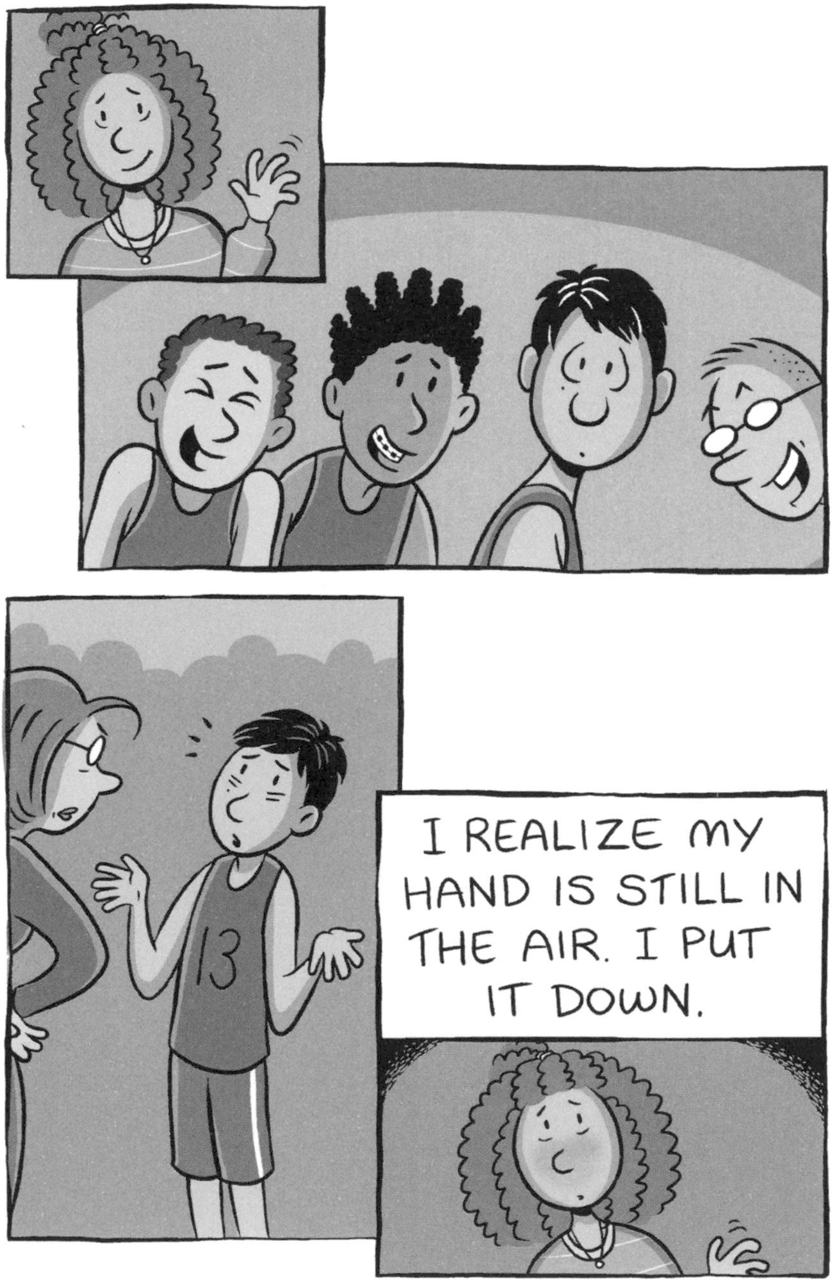
I REALIZE MY HAND IS STILL IN THE AIR. I PUT IT DOWN.

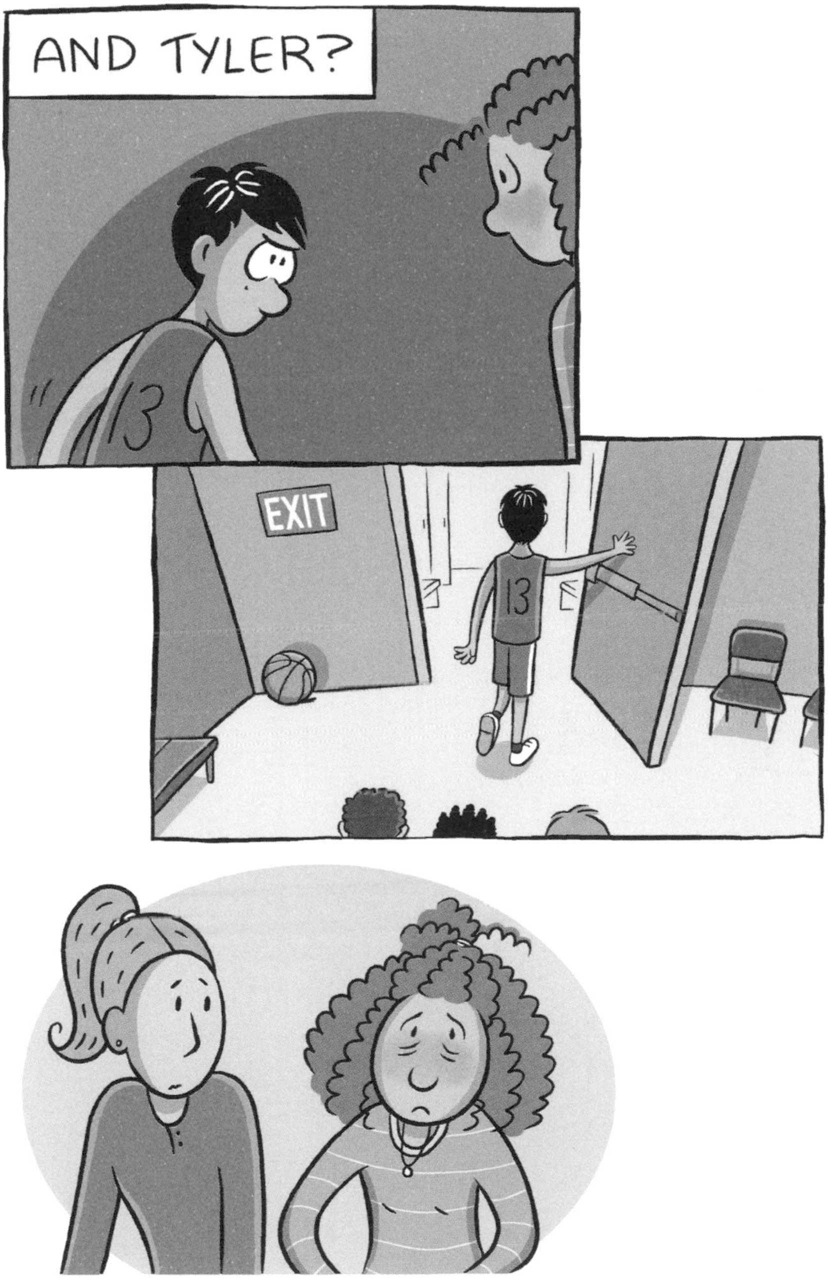
AND TYLER?
EXIT

TYLER

Just got home from the game. Usually I'd go to Taystee's for hot chocolate afterward (always after a win), but I wasn't in the mood. Instead, I'm curled up under my mom's favorite old Sherpa blanket, watching TV.

Comfort stuff:
✓ thick blanket
✓ squishy couch
✓ cheese curls
✓ cartoon rerun
✓ big fluffy dog
    (I wish!)

My phone goes off.

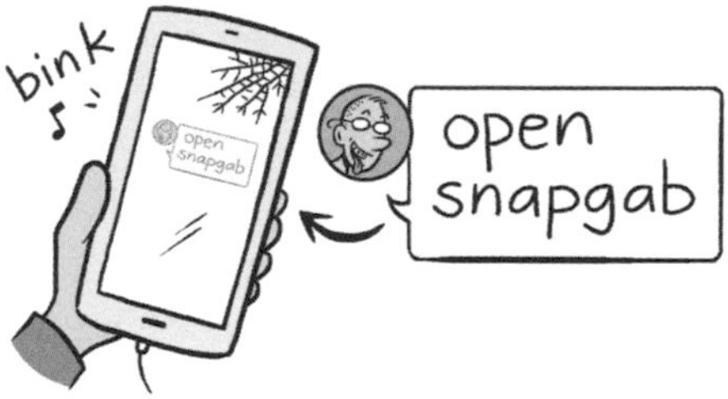
bink
open snapgab
open snapgab

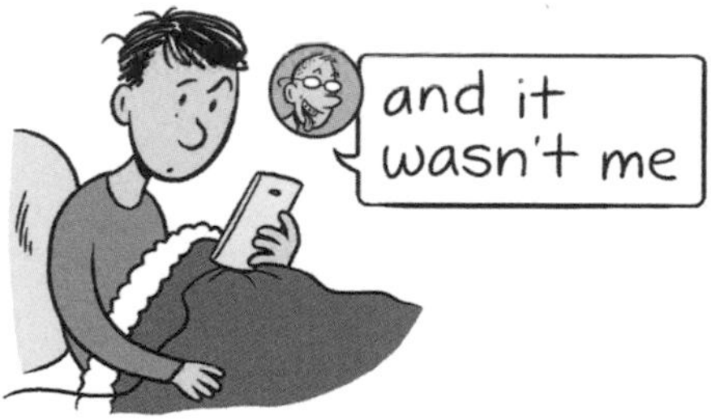
and it wasn't me

I open the app. I barely have to scroll to see that a dozen kids posted the same meme.

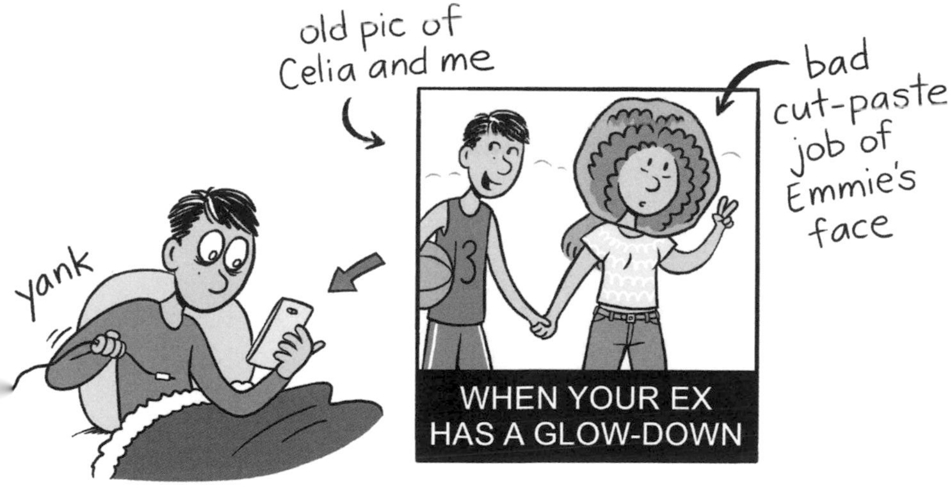
old pic of Celia and me
bad cut-paste job of Emmie's face
yank
13
WHEN YOUR EX HAS A GLOW-DOWN

I go cold.

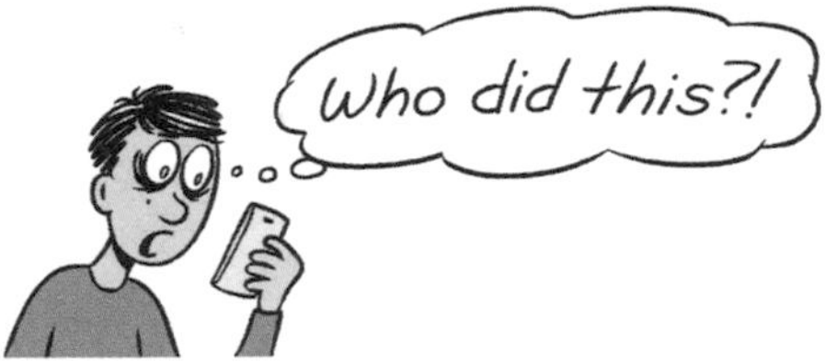
Who did this?!

I text that to Joe.

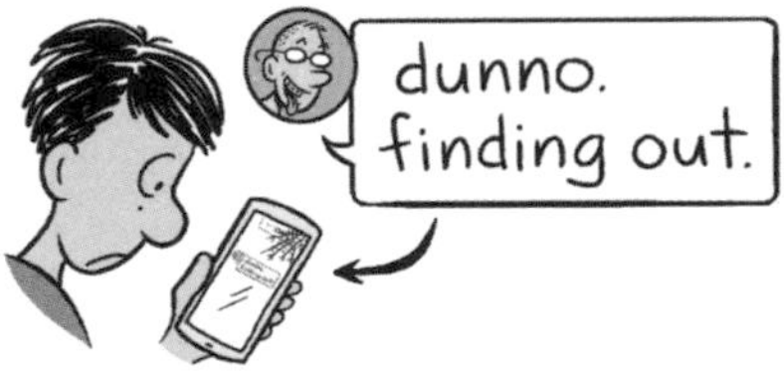
dunno.
finding out.

This isn't happening. This has to be Celia and her friends. No one else I know would do this.

I wait for about two years until Joe texts back. I use all my willpower not to open SnapGab.

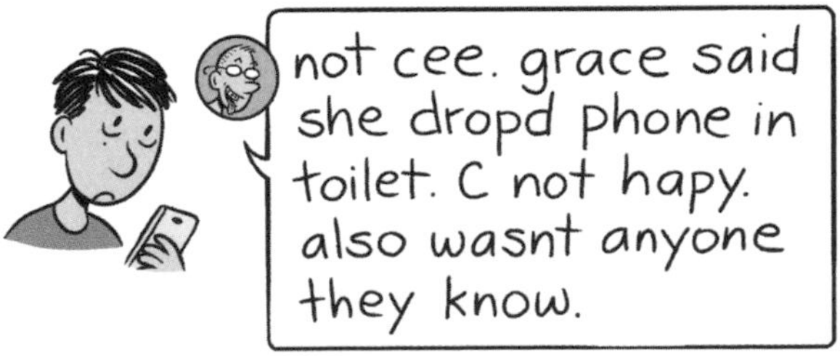
not cee. grace said she dropd phone in toilet. C not hapy. also wasnt anyone they know.

Not sure if I believe that. I just hope Emmie didn't see it.

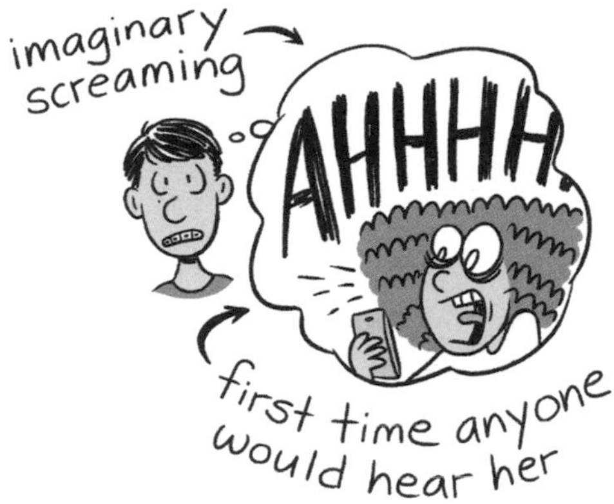
imaginary screaming
AHHHH!
first time anyone would hear her

My phone vibrates.

I check my texts, expecting to see something from Joe or Anthony (who I'm still mad at).

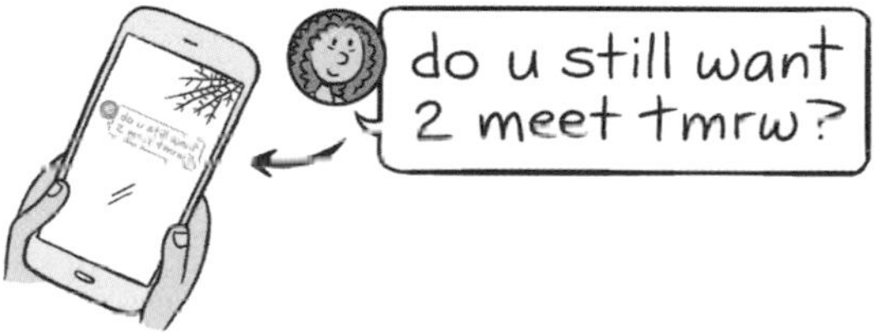
do u still want 2 meet tmrw?

I freeze. Does she know?

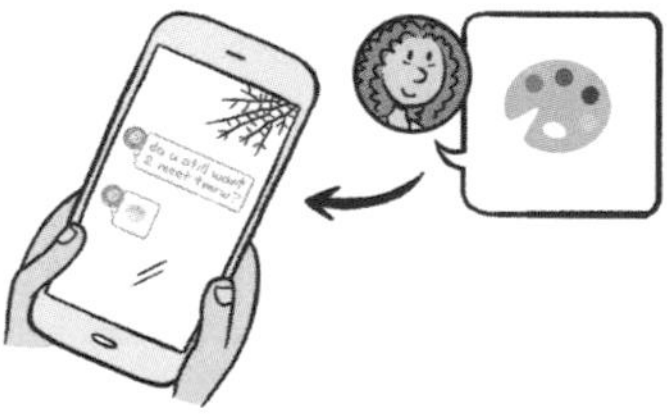

Guess not.

I don't respond. My mind is all jumbled up, and I can't think about tomorrow or anything else until I find out who posted that meme.

Except . . .

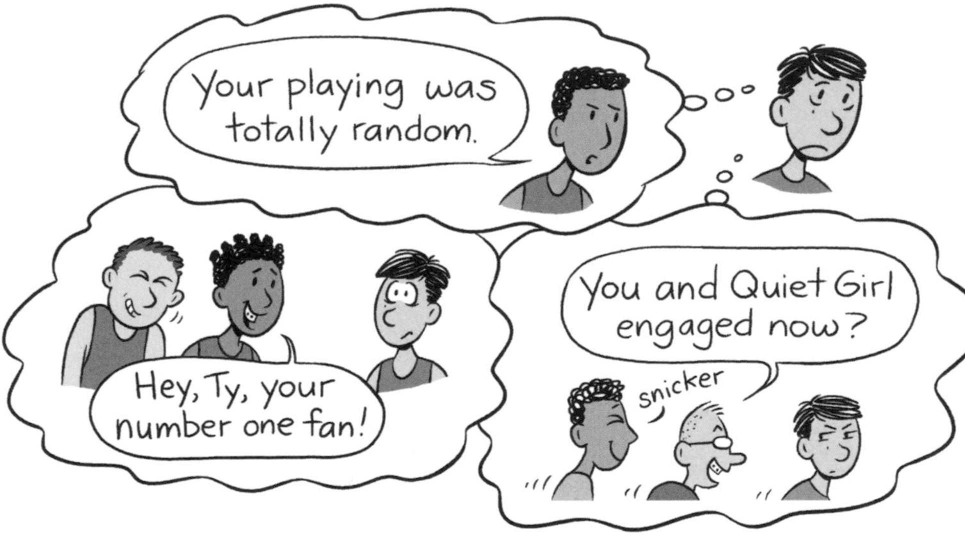
Your playing was totally random.
Hey, Ty, your number one fan!
You and Quiet Girl engaged now?
snicker

My face gets all hot again.

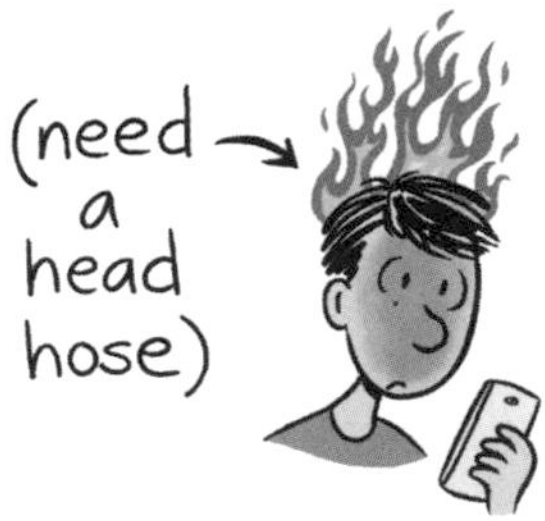
(need a head hose)

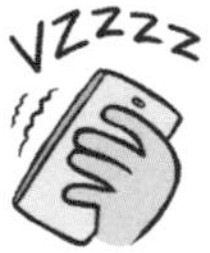
VZZZZ

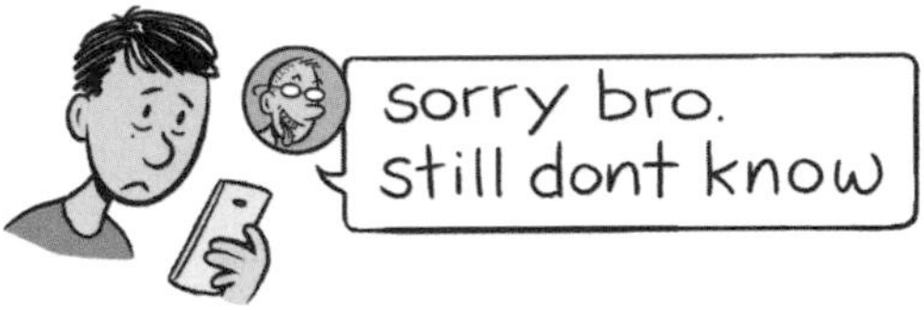
sorry bro.
still dont know

I can't think. That stupid meme!

The worst part is . . .

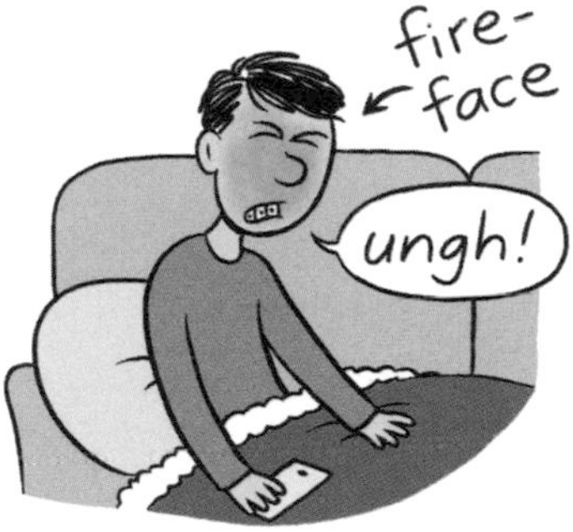
fire-
face
ungh!

. . . after seeing it, I don't know if I can even look at Emmie again.

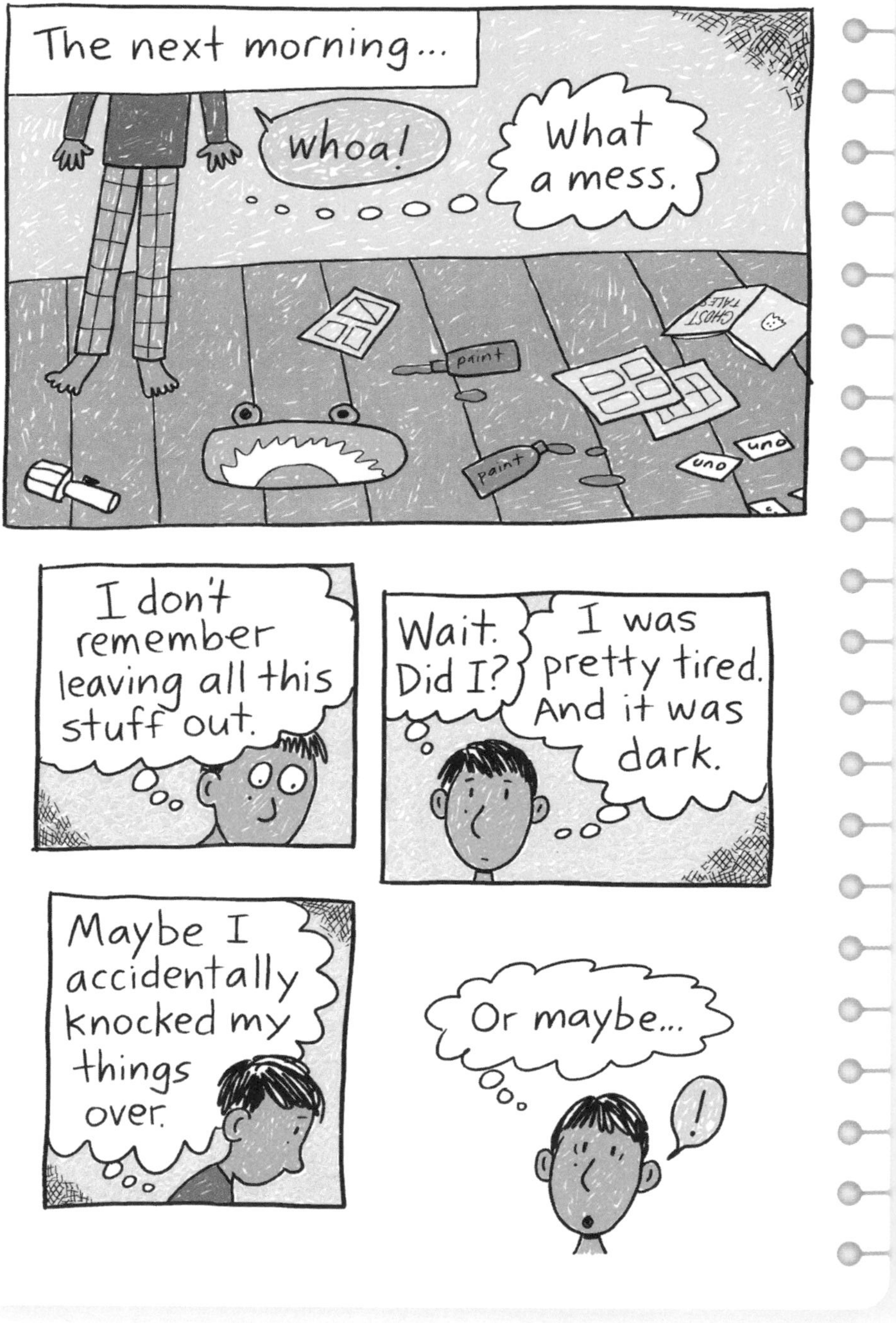

The next morning...
whoa!
What a mess.
GHOST TALES
paint
paint
uno
uno
I don't remember leaving all this stuff out.
Wait. Did I?
I was pretty tired. And it was dark.
Maybe I accidentally knocked my things over.
Or maybe...
!

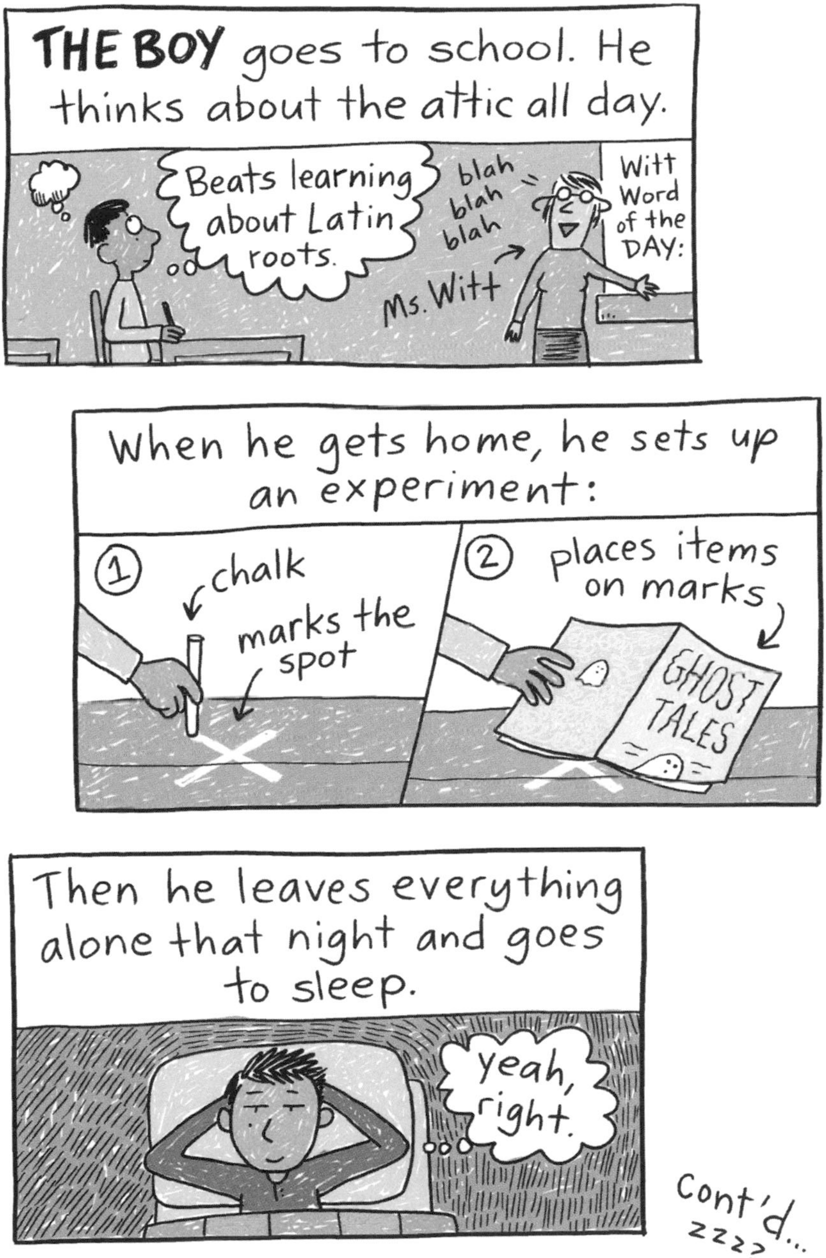
THE BOY goes to school. He thinks about the attic all day.
Beats learning about Latin roots.
blah blah blah
Ms. Witt
Witt Word of the DAY:
When he gets home, he sets up an experiment:
① chalk
marks the spot
② places items on marks
GHOST TALES
Then he leaves everything alone that night and goes to sleep.
yeah, right.
Cont'd...
zzz?

Emmie

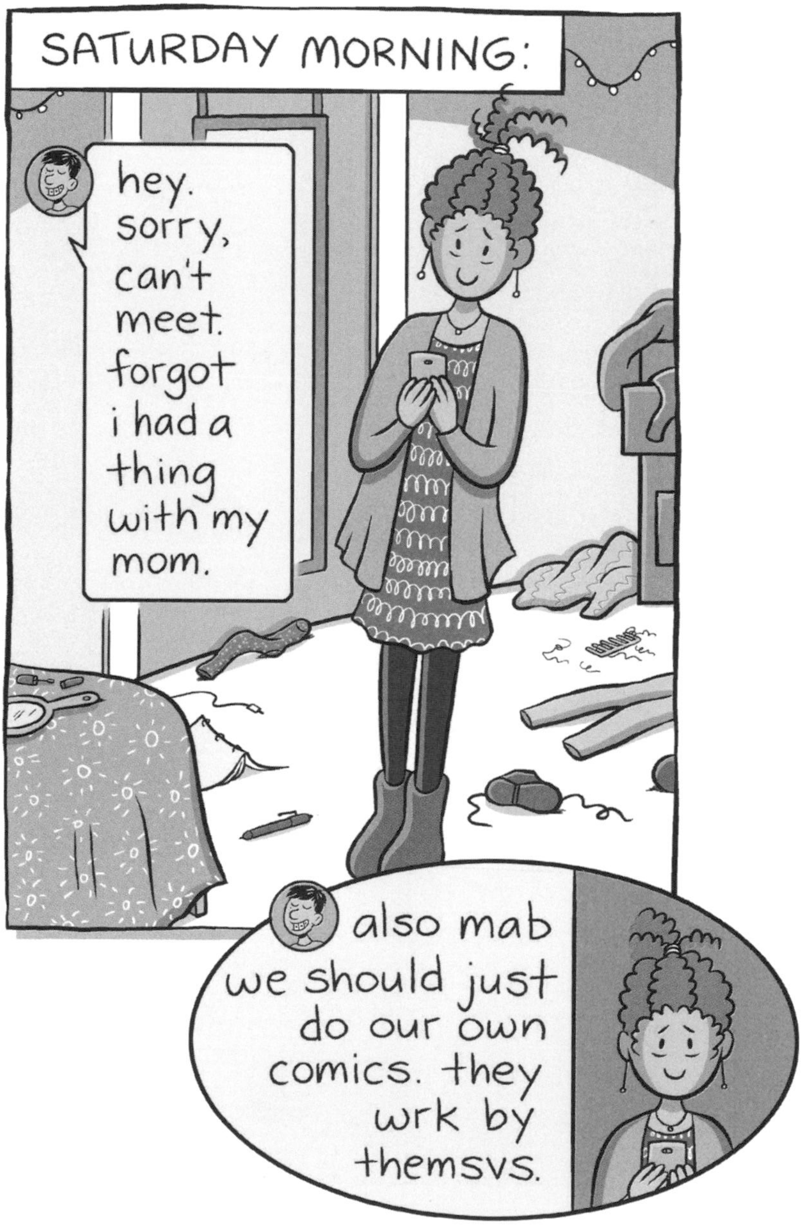
SATURDAY MORNING:
hey. sorry, can't meet. forgot i had a thing with my mom.
also mab we should just do our own comics. they wrk by themsvs.

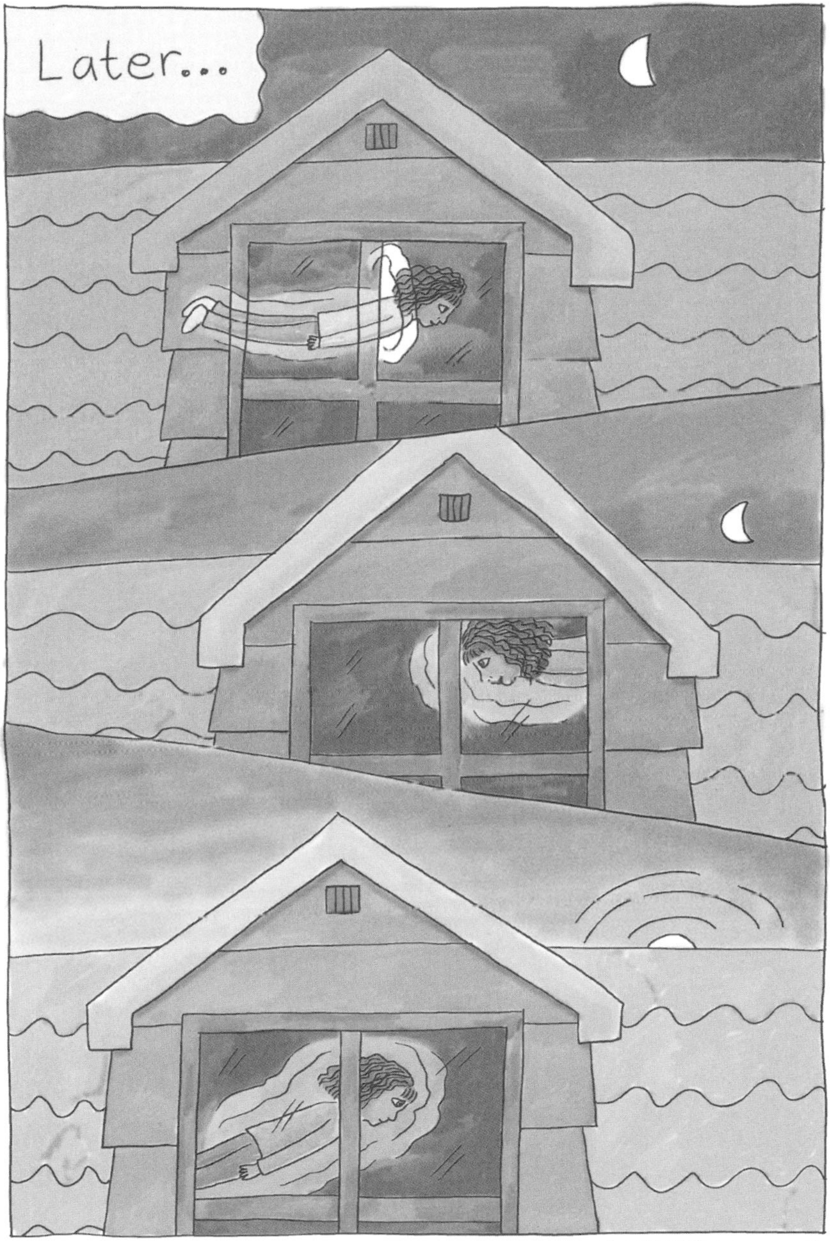
Later...

(Cont'd.......)

TYLER

It was Ethan and Malik.

Being dumb. Playing a stupid joke. They weren't trying to be malicious.*

But they **were**:

stupid

hurtful

more damaging than the fire Kyle Duncan set in the chemistry lab last year

foosh!

WHEN YOUR EX HAS A GLOW-DOWN

Joe got it out of them. They apologized and deleted the meme, but not before half the school saw it or shared it.

*Winn Word

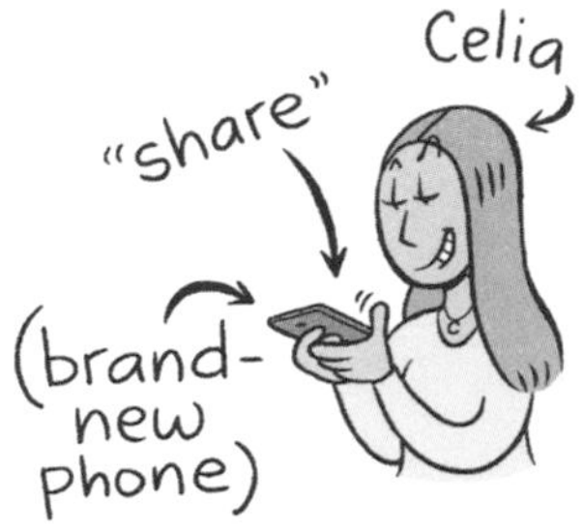
Celia
"share"
(brand-new phone)

I don't know if Emmie saw it. I really, really hope not. I feel bad about blowing her off in those texts, but there's no way I can face her.

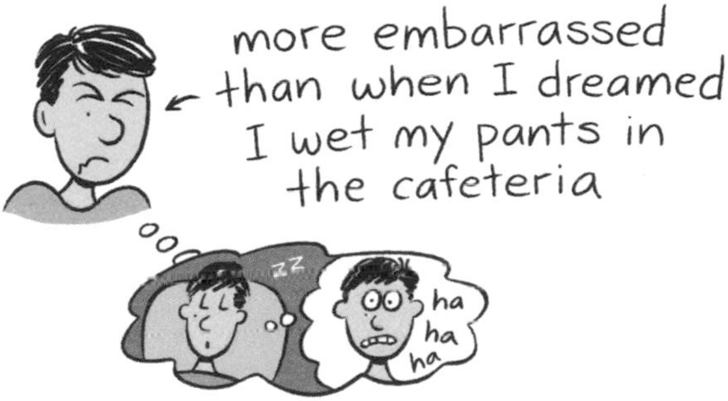
more embarrassed than when I dreamed I wet my pants in the cafeteria
zz
ha
ha
ha

Still, I guess I could've handled it better.

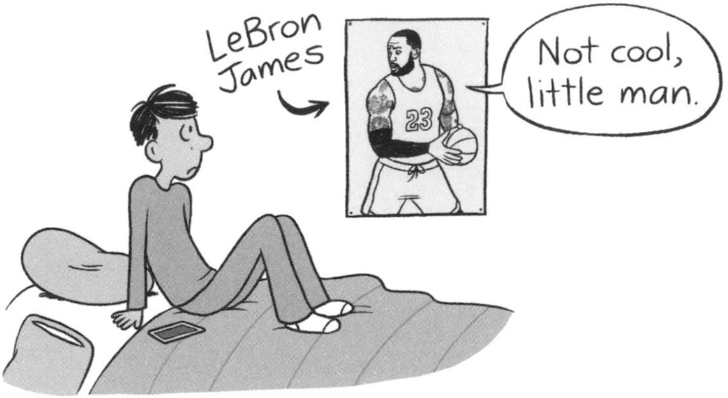
LeBron James
Not cool, little man.

I think about doing something distracting: homework, drawing my comic, playing Fortnite, practicing my trumpet, getting a snack (or five), listening to music, or going on SnabGab.

I do nothing.

I just sit here and feel bad.

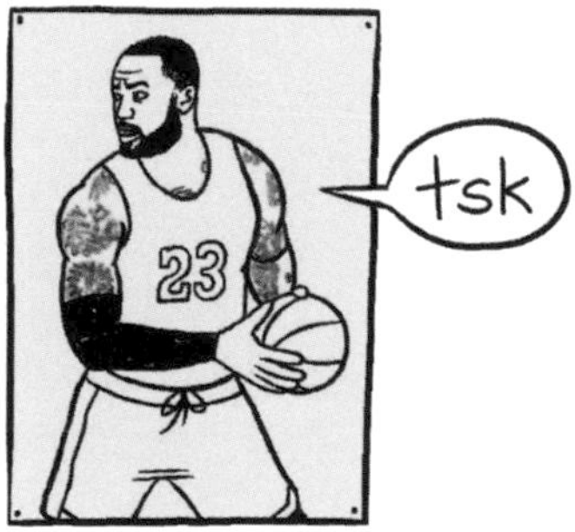
23
tsk

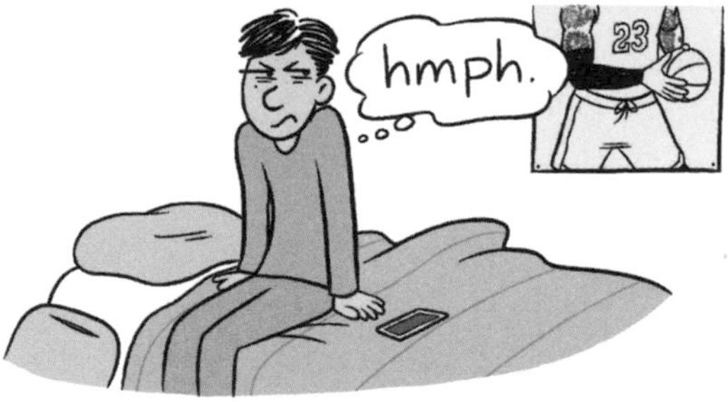
hmph.
23

I finally decide to go down to the kitchen.

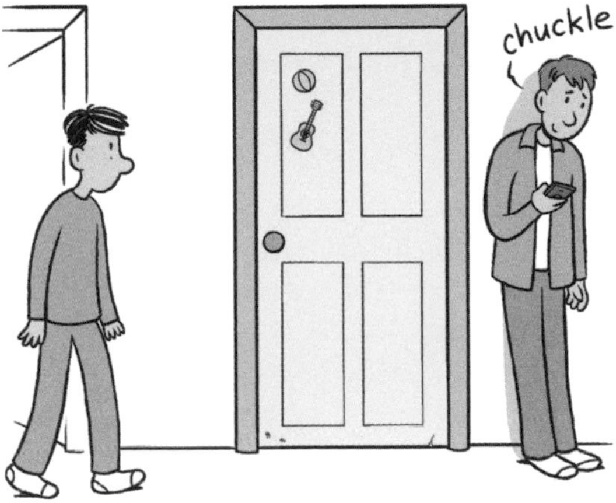
chuckle

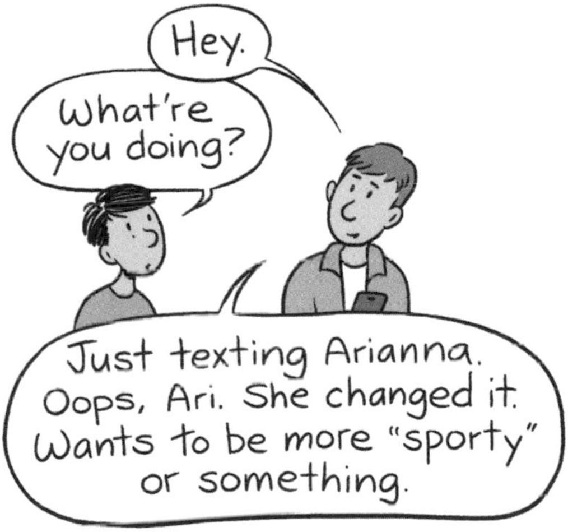
Hey.
What're you doing?
Just texting Arianna. Oops, Ari. She changed it. Wants to be more "sporty" or something.

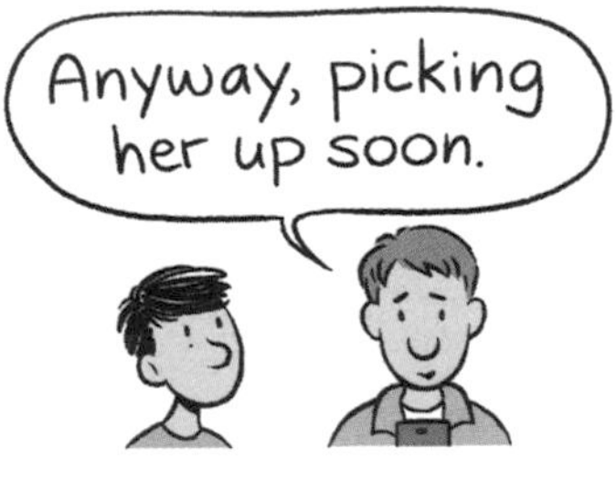
Anyway, picking her up soon.

This is one of the few times in months that Zach's said more than a couple words to me.

Well, later.

So much for that.

He begins heading downstairs. But I suddenly have something to ask. And he's in a good mood, so . . .

Hey, Z? You have a minute?

Just a few. What's up?

I think about how to phrase this.

Say you have this friend. And she's nice and all, but she's not really...cool, you know?

Okay.

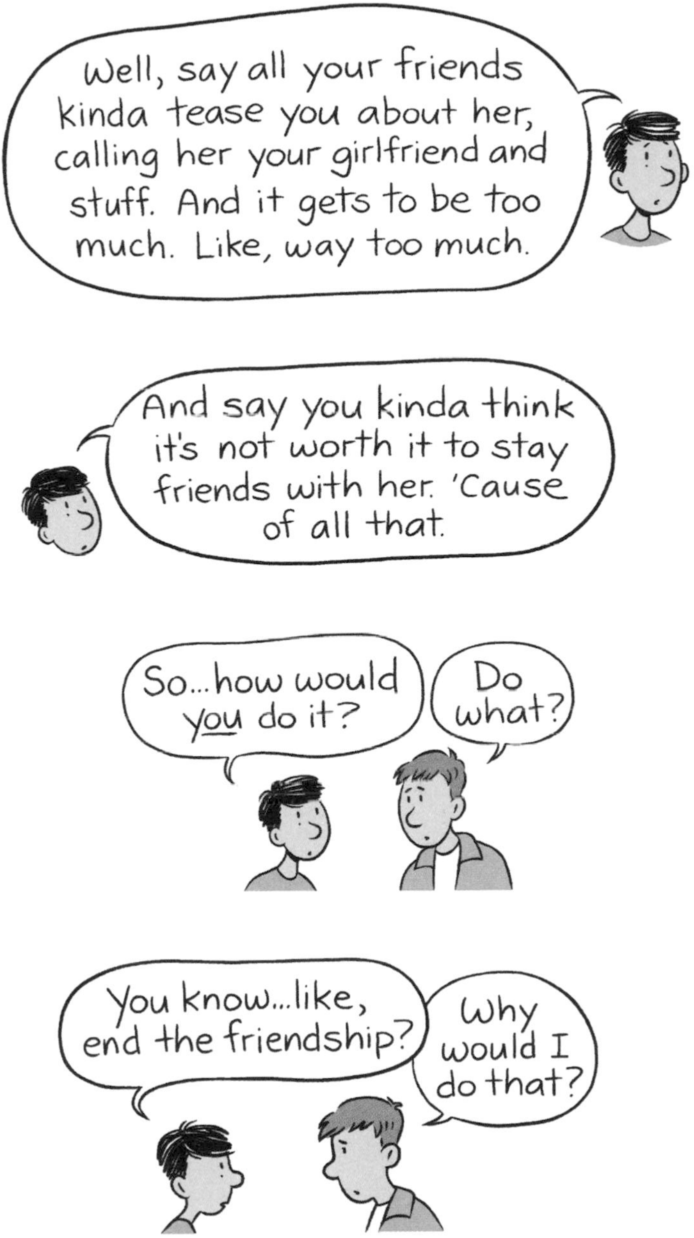
Well, say all your friends kinda tease you about her, calling her your girlfriend and stuff. And it gets to be too much. Like, way too much.
And say you kinda think it's not worth it to stay friends with her. 'Cause of all that.
So...how would you do it?
Do what?
You know...like, end the friendship?
Why would I do that?

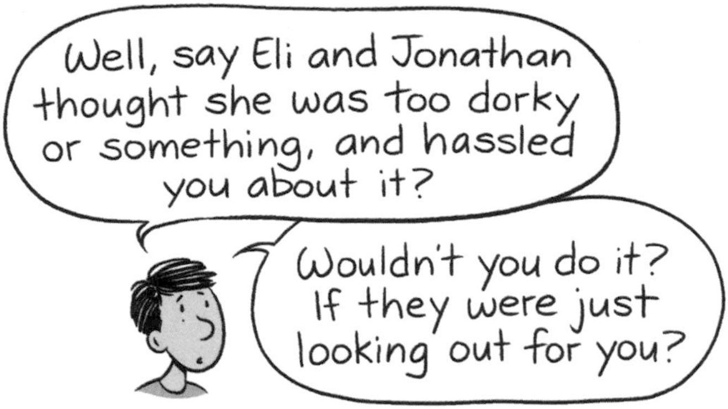
Well, say Eli and Jonathan thought she was too dorky or something, and hassled you about it?
Wouldn't you do it? If they were just looking out for you?

Zach just stares at me.

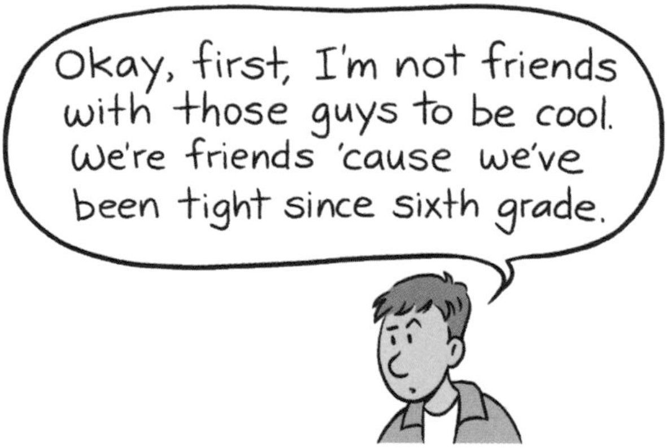
Okay, first, I'm not friends with those guys to be cool. We're friends 'cause we've been tight since sixth grade.

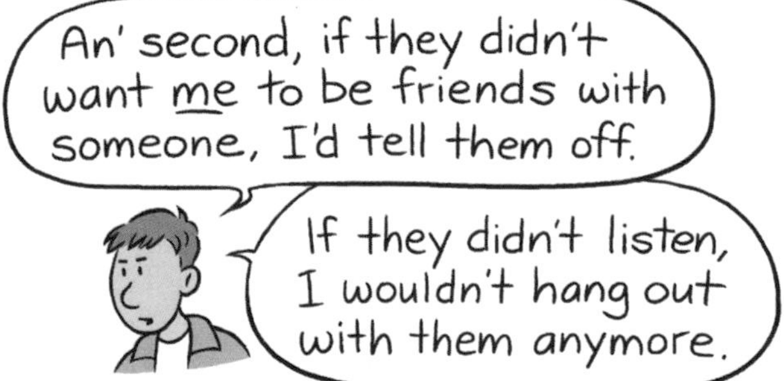
An' second, if they didn't want me to be friends with someone, I'd tell them off.
If they didn't listen, I wouldn't hang out with them anymore.

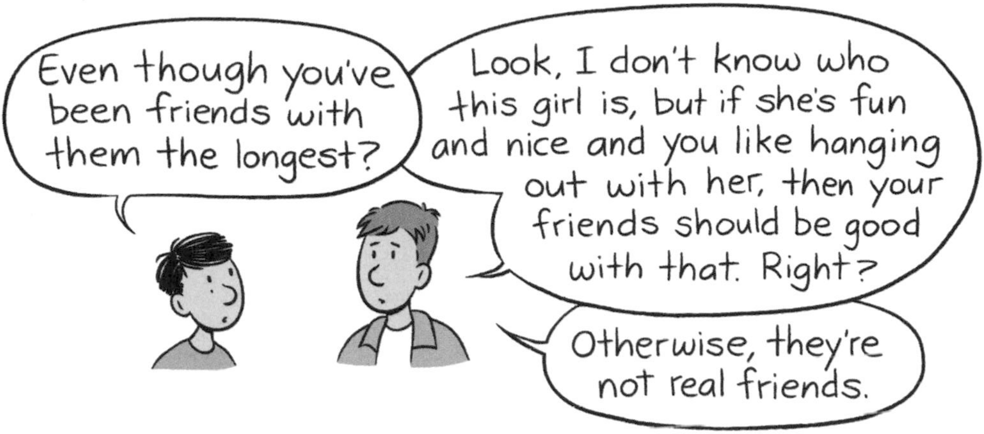
Even though you've been friends with them the longest?
Look, I don't know who this girl is, but if she's fun and nice and you like hanging out with her, then your friends should be good with that. Right?
Otherwise, they're not real friends.

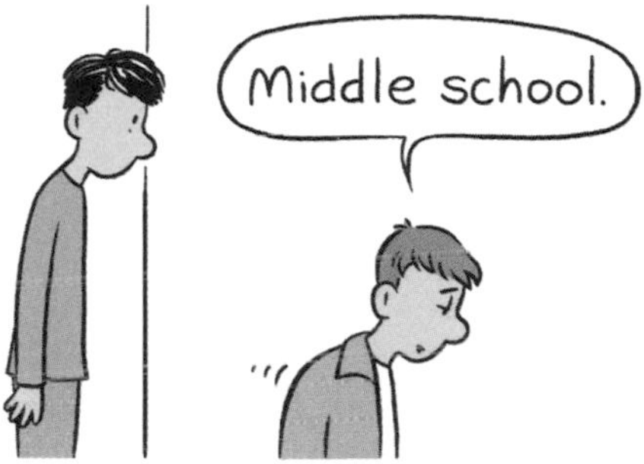
Middle school.

He starts to leave but stops.

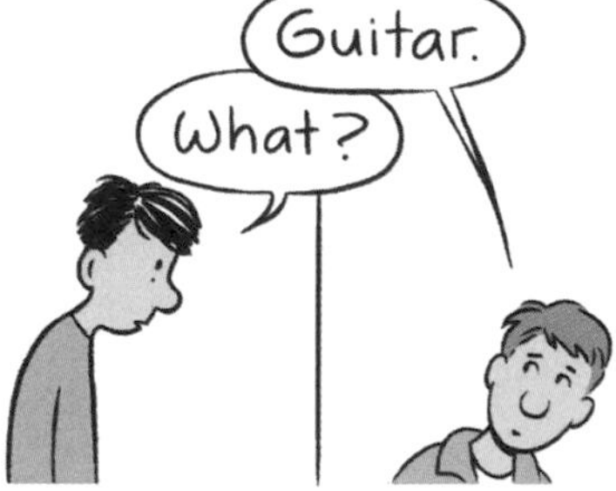
Guitar.
What?

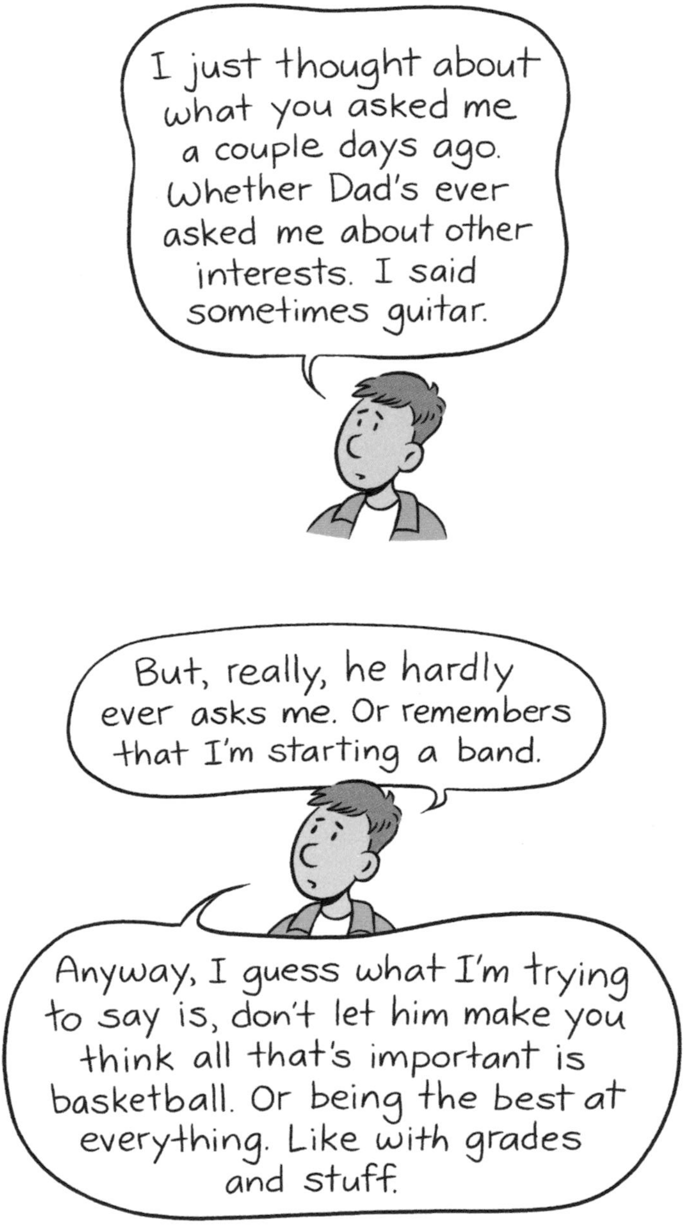
I just thought about what you asked me a couple days ago. Whether Dad's ever asked me about other interests. I said sometimes guitar.
But, really, he hardly ever asks me. Or remembers that I'm starting a band.
Anyway, I guess what I'm trying to say is, don't let him make you think all that's important is basketball. Or being the best at everything. Like with grades and stuff.

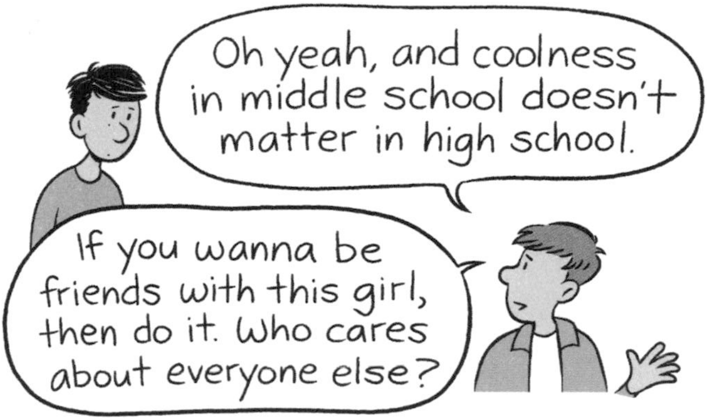
Oh yeah, and coolness in middle school doesn't matter in high school.
If you wanna be friends with this girl, then do it. Who cares about everyone else?

He heads downstairs.

And I'm left staring after him.

It's the first time I realize that Zach's popularity isn't 'cause of "status."

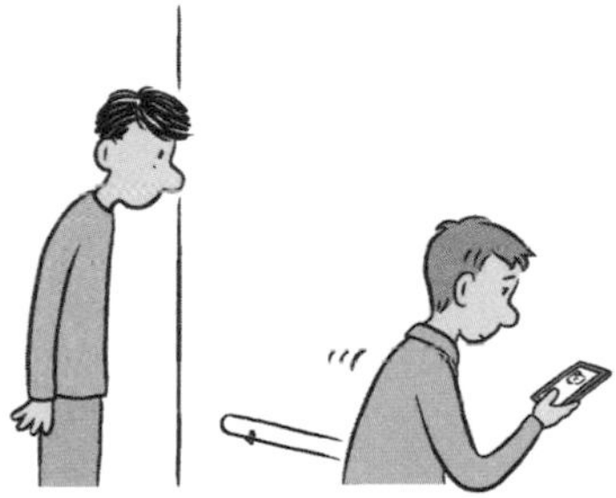

It's 'cause he has something that I've kinda lost . . .

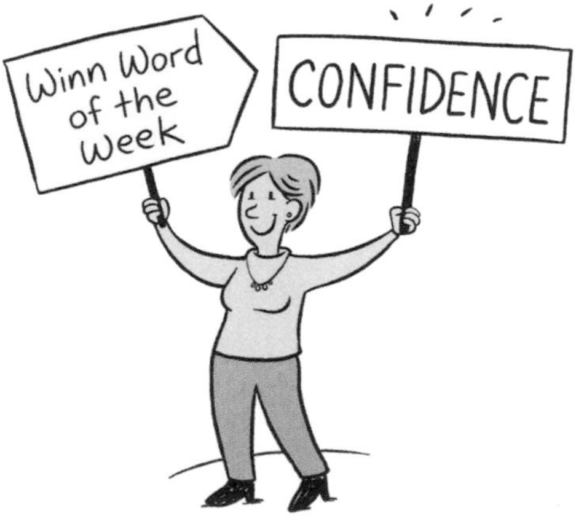
Winn Word of the Week
CONFIDENCE

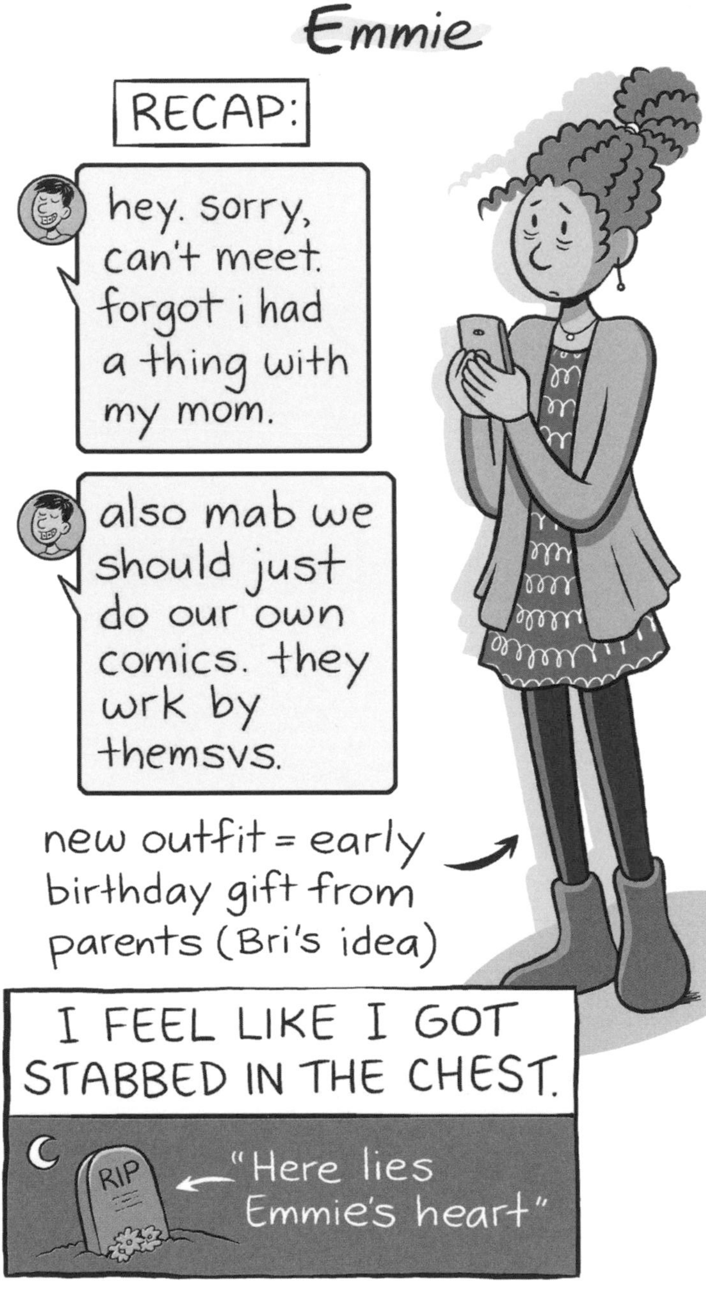
Emmie
RECAP:
hey. sorry, can't meet. forgot i had a thing with my mom.
also mab we should just do our own comics. they wrk by themsvs.
new outfit = early birthday gift from parents (Bri's idea)
I FEEL LIKE I GOT STABBED IN THE CHEST.
RIP
"Here lies Emmie's heart"

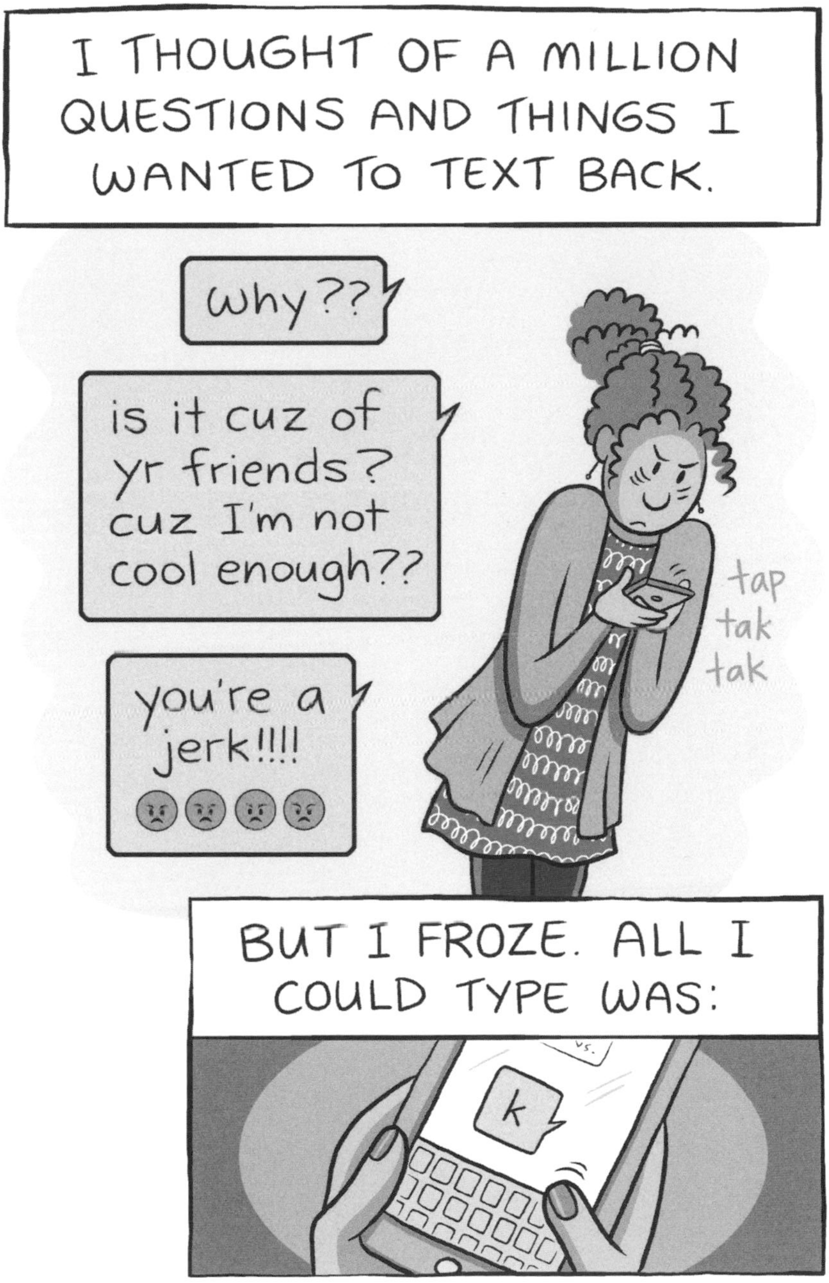
I THOUGHT OF A MILLION QUESTIONS AND THINGS I WANTED TO TEXT BACK.
why??
is it cuz of yr friends? cuz I'm not cool enough??
you're a jerk!!!!
tap tak tak
BUT I FROZE. ALL I COULD TYPE WAS:
k

I'M SO STUPID. I SHOULD'VE KNOWN. ESPECIALLY AFTER WHAT HAPPENED AT THE GAME.

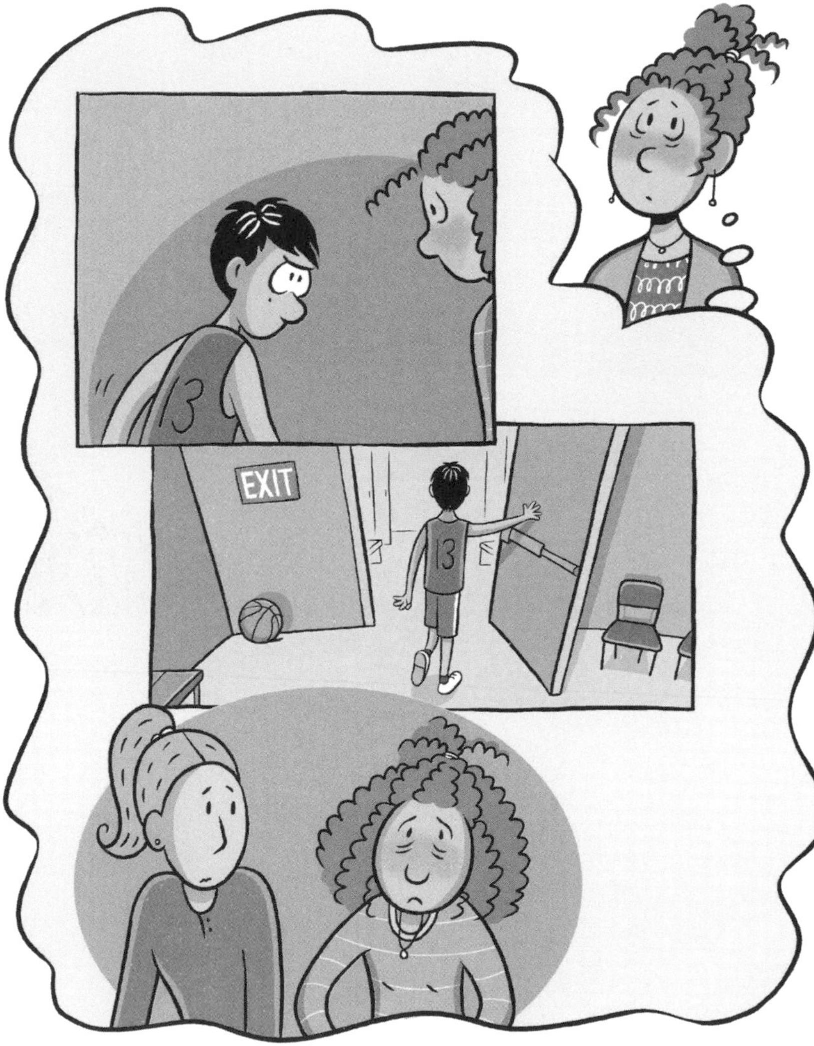

EXIT

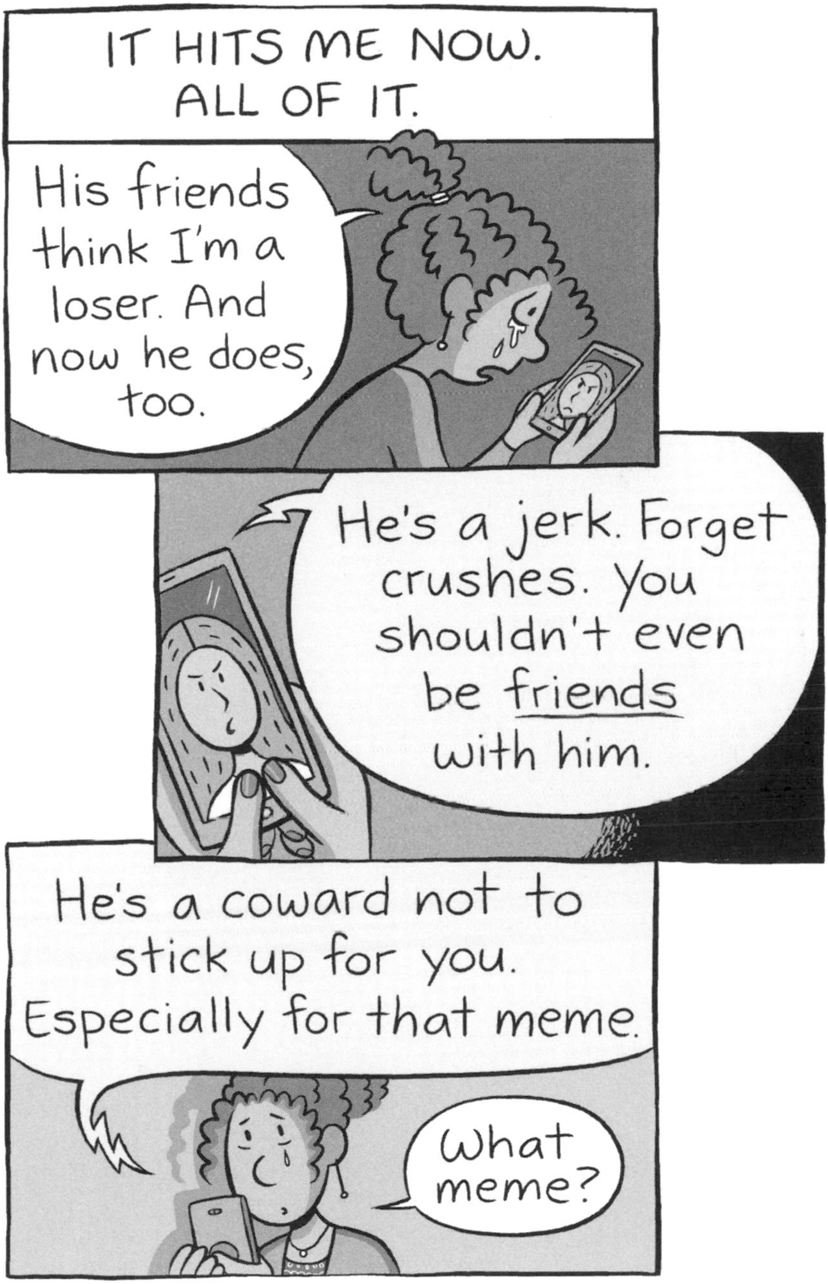
IT HITS ME NOW. ALL OF IT.
His friends think I'm a loser. And now he does, too.
He's a jerk. Forget crushes. You shouldn't even be friends with him.
He's a coward not to stick up for you. Especially for that meme.
What meme?

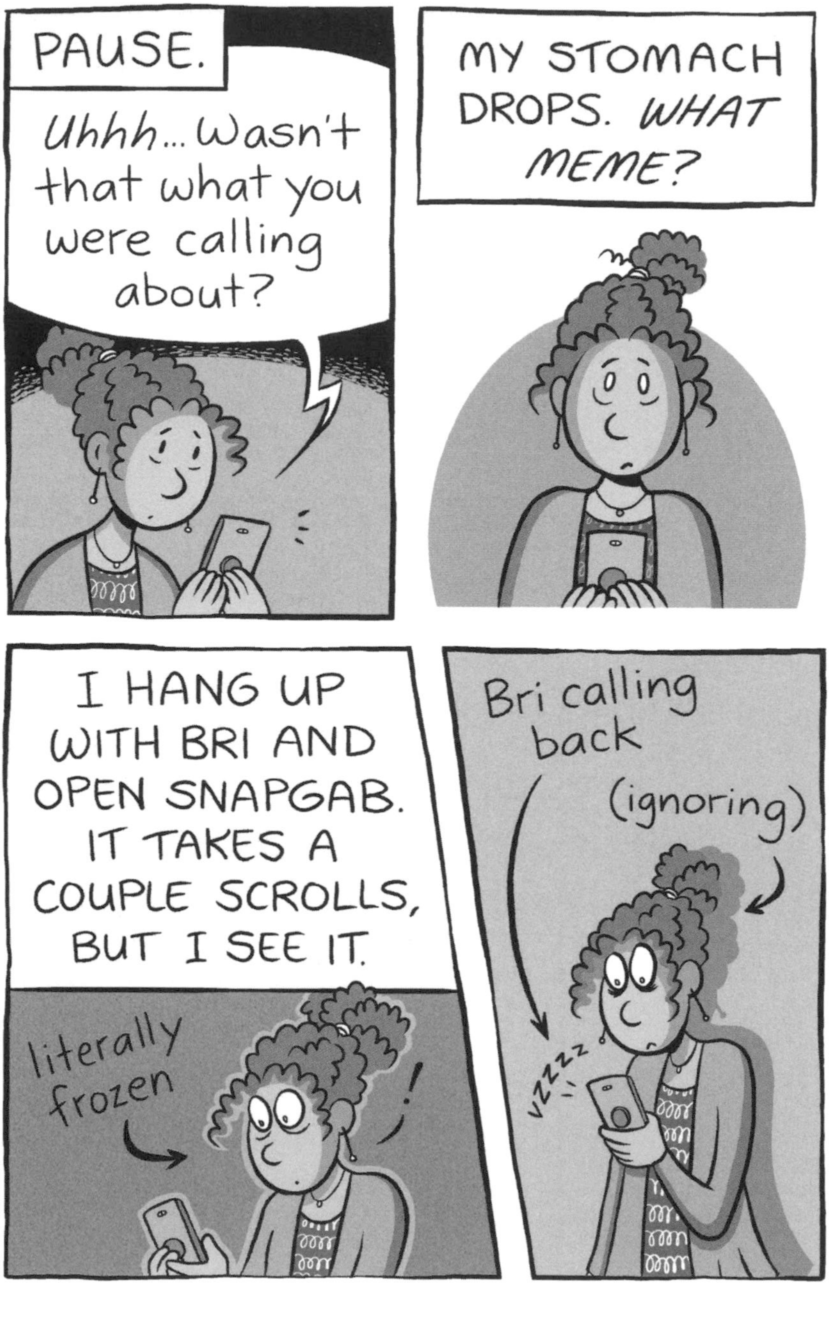
PAUSE.
Uhhh... Wasn't that what you were calling about?
MY STOMACH DROPS. WHAT MEME?
I HANG UP WITH BRI AND OPEN SNAPGAB. IT TAKES A COUPLE SCROLLS, BUT I SEE IT.
literally frozen
!
Bri calling back
(ignoring)
VZZZZ

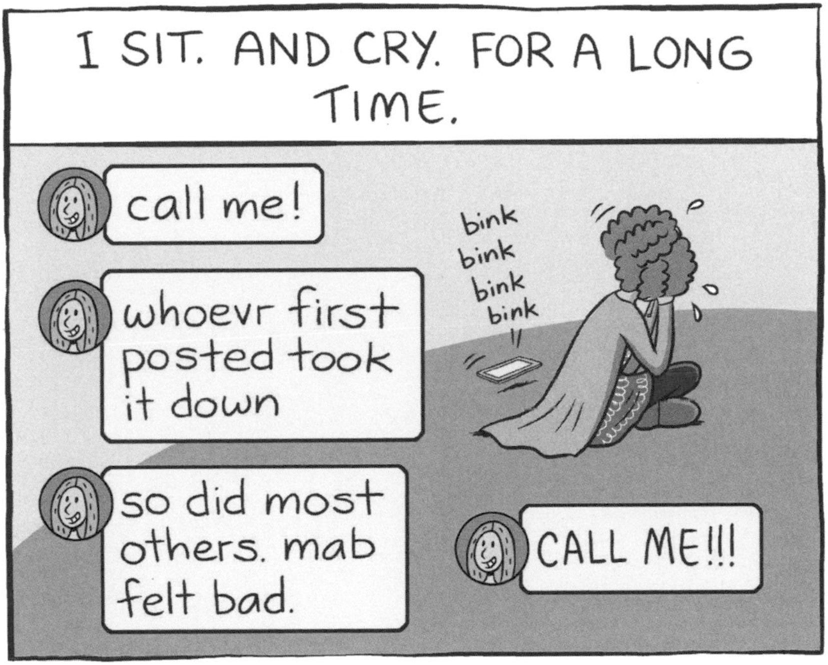
I SIT. AND CRY. FOR A LONG TIME.
call me!
whoevr first posted took it down
bink
bink
bink
bink
so did most others. mab felt bad.
CALL ME!!!

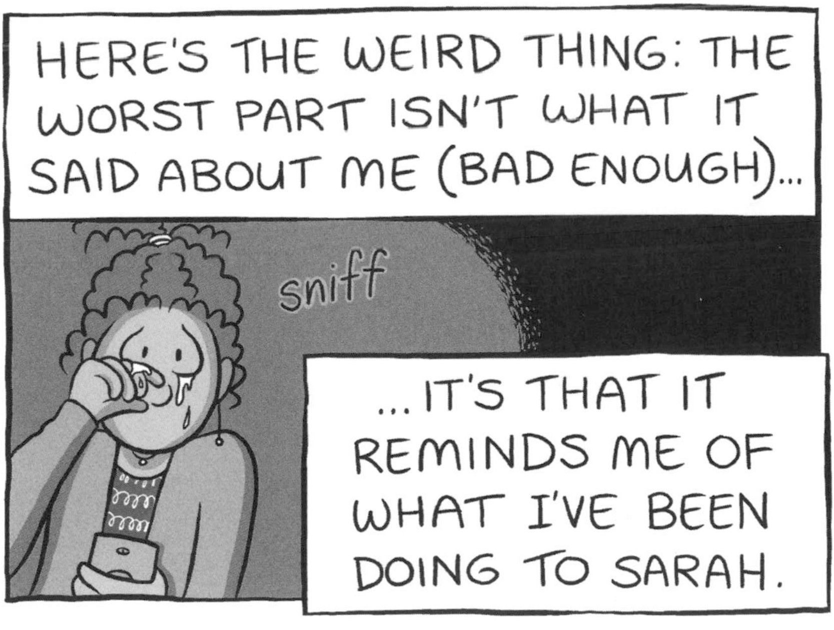
HERE'S THE WEIRD THING: THE WORST PART ISN'T WHAT IT SAID ABOUT ME (BAD ENOUGH)...
sniff
...IT'S THAT IT REMINDS ME OF WHAT I'VE BEEN DOING TO SARAH.

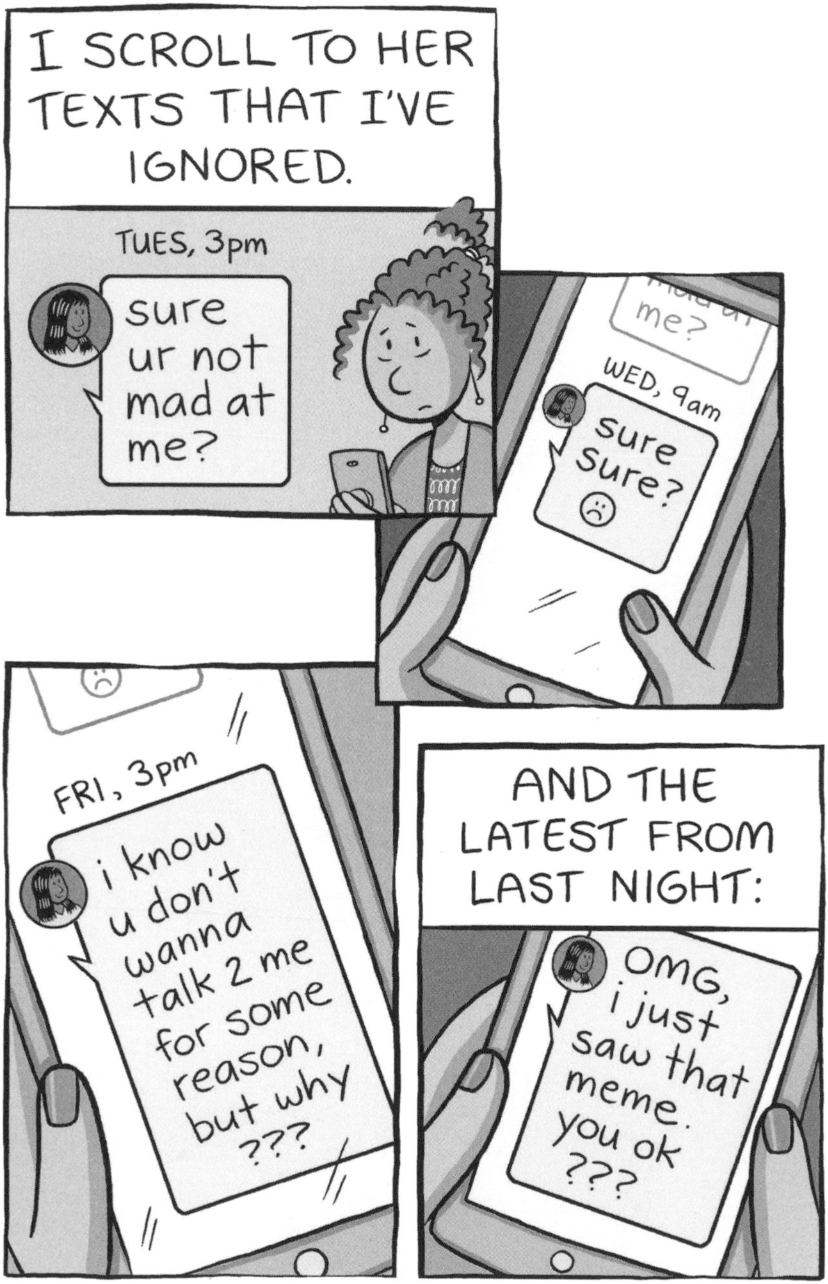
I SCROLL TO HER TEXTS THAT I'VE IGNORED.
TUES, 3pm
sure ur not mad at me?
me?
WED, 9am
sure sure? ☹
FRI, 3pm
i know u don't wanna talk 2 me for some reason, but why ???
AND THE LATEST FROM LAST NIGHT:
OMG, i just saw that meme. you ok ???

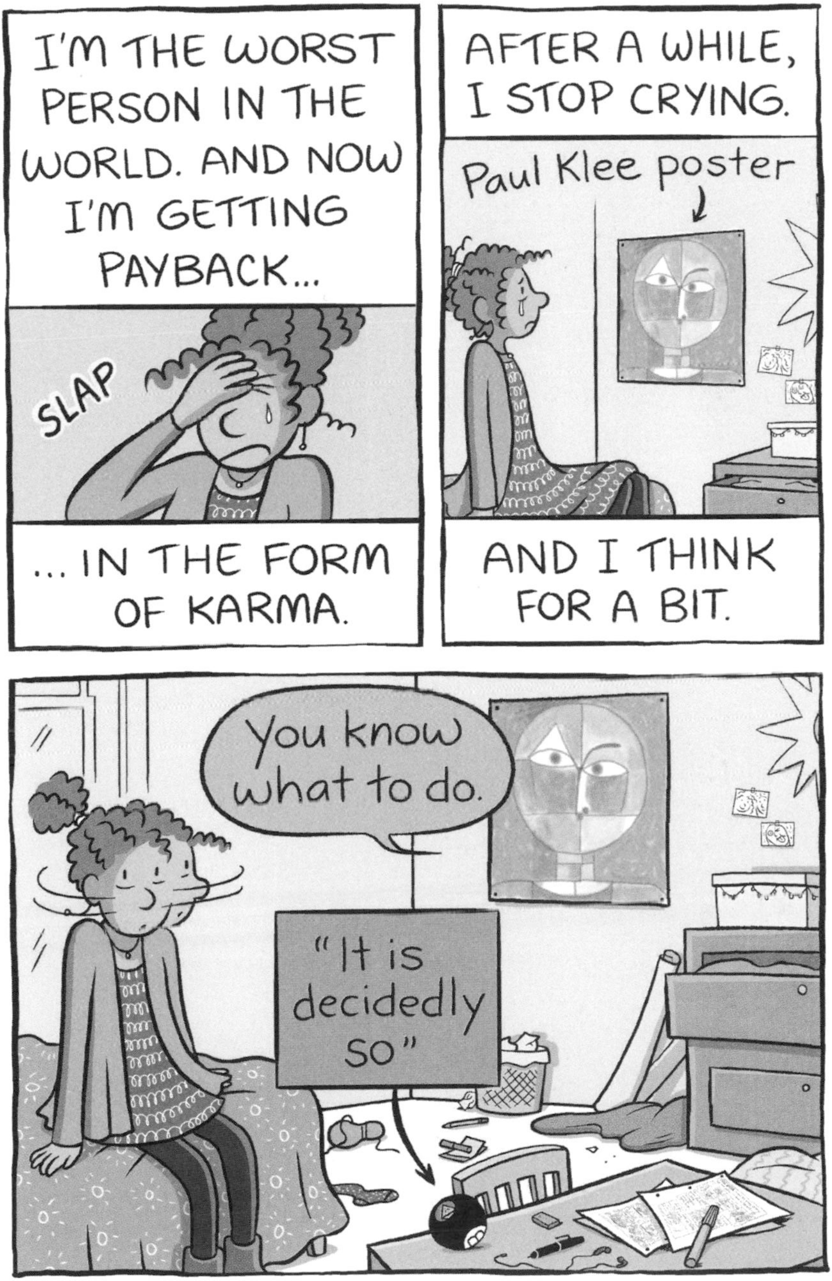
I'M THE WORST PERSON IN THE WORLD. AND NOW I'M GETTING PAYBACK...
SLAP
... IN THE FORM OF KARMA.
AFTER A WHILE, I STOP CRYING.
Paul Klee poster
AND I THINK FOR A BIT.
You know what to do.
"It is decidedly so"

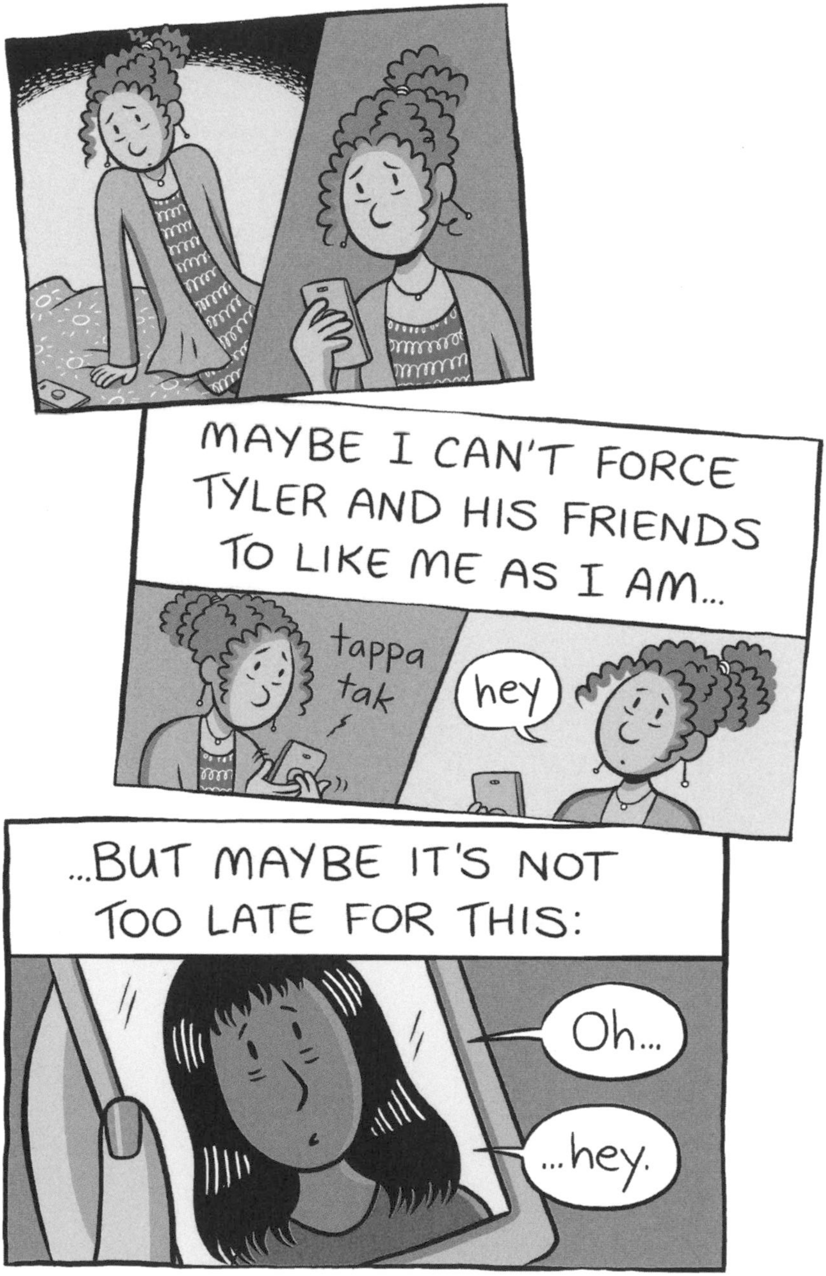
MAYBE I CAN'T FORCE TYLER AND HIS FRIENDS TO LIKE ME AS I AM...
tappa tak
hey
...BUT MAYBE IT'S NOT TOO LATE FOR THIS:
Oh...
...hey.

TYLER

Monday morning.

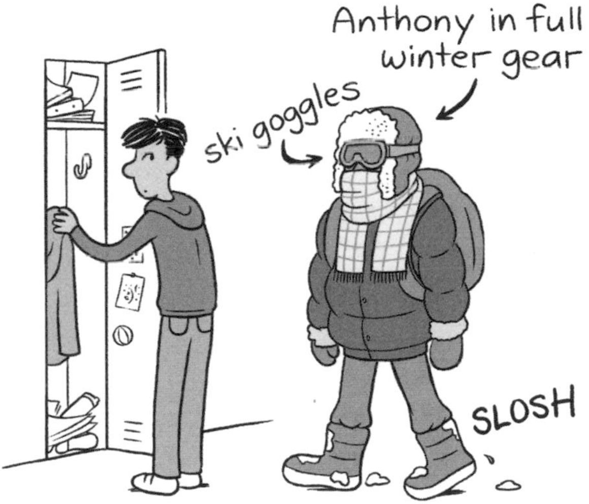

Anthony in full winter gear
ski goggles
SLOSH

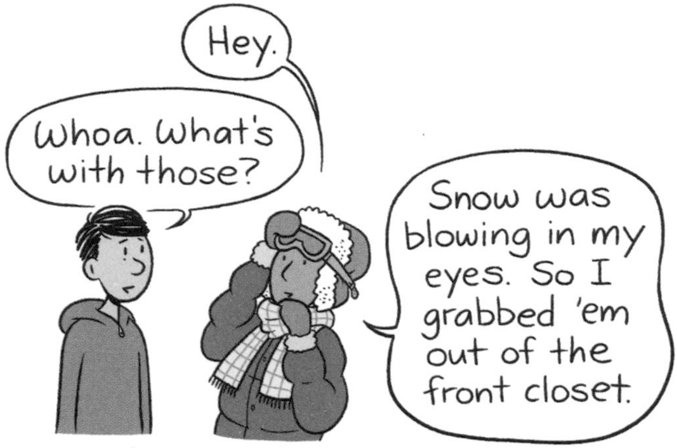
Hey.
Whoa. What's with those?
Snow was blowing in my eyes. So I grabbed 'em out of the front closet.

I laugh, even though I feel like garbage.

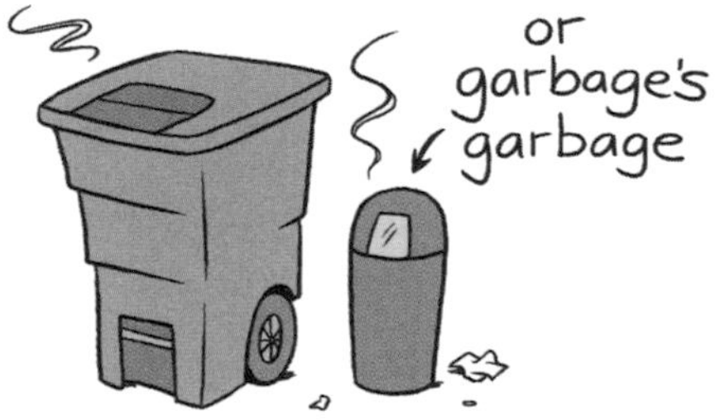
or garbage's garbage

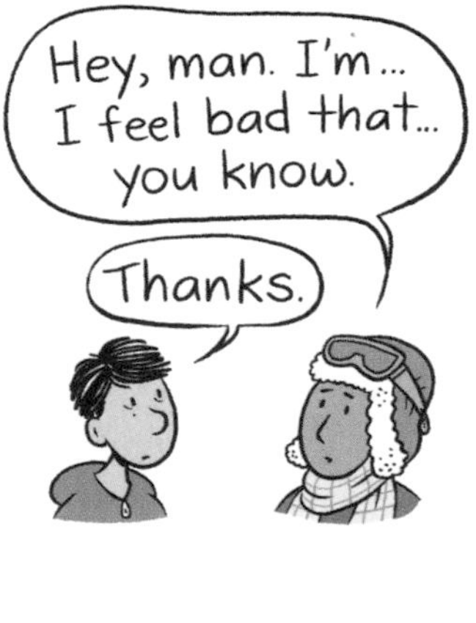
Hey, man. I'm... I feel bad that... you know.
Thanks.

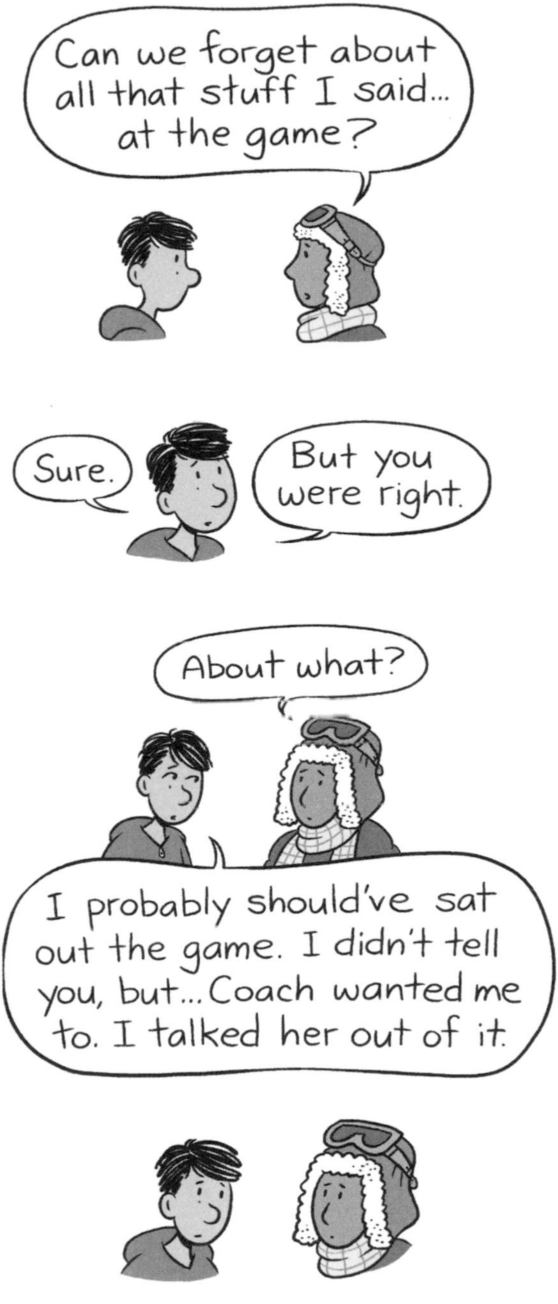
Can we forget about all that stuff I said... at the game?
Sure.
But you were right.
About what?
I probably should've sat out the game. I didn't tell you, but... Coach wanted me to. I talked her out of it.

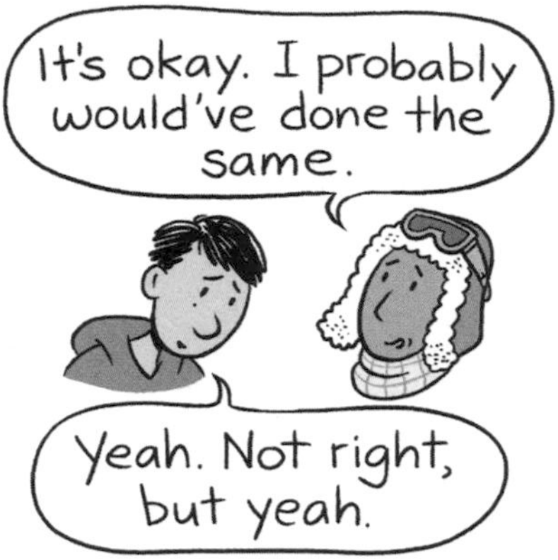
It's okay. I probably would've done the same.
Yeah. Not right, but yeah.

We leave it at that. One good thing about both Anthony and me: we don't hold grudges. Ever.

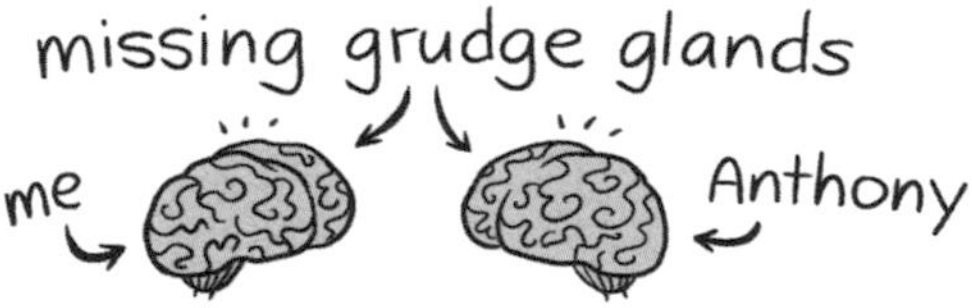
missing grudge glands
me
Anthony

I see Emmie walking to the restroom and I look away.

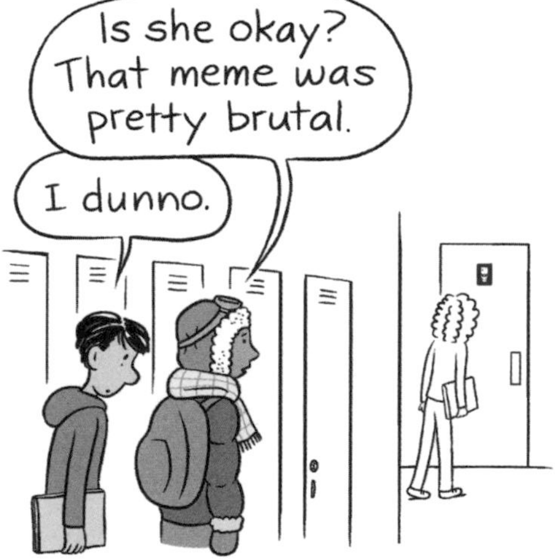
Is she okay? That meme was pretty brutal.
I dunno.

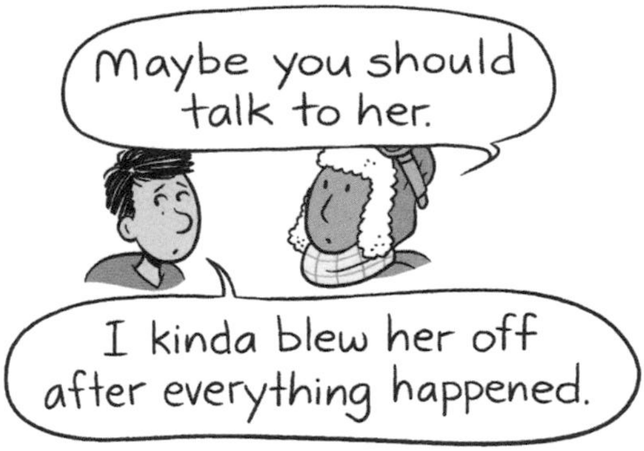
Maybe you should talk to her.
I kinda blew her off after everything happened.

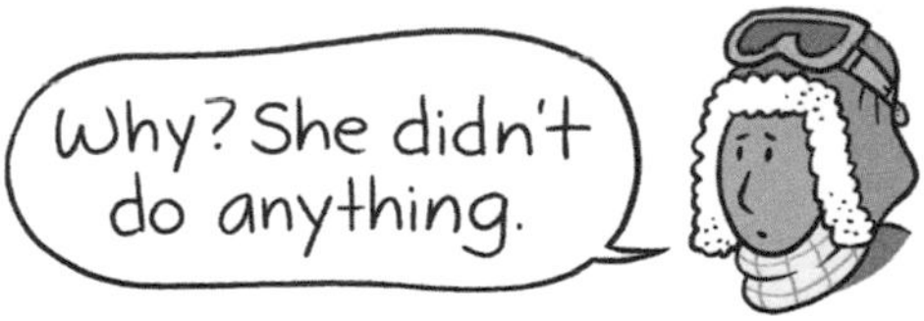
Why? She didn't do anything.

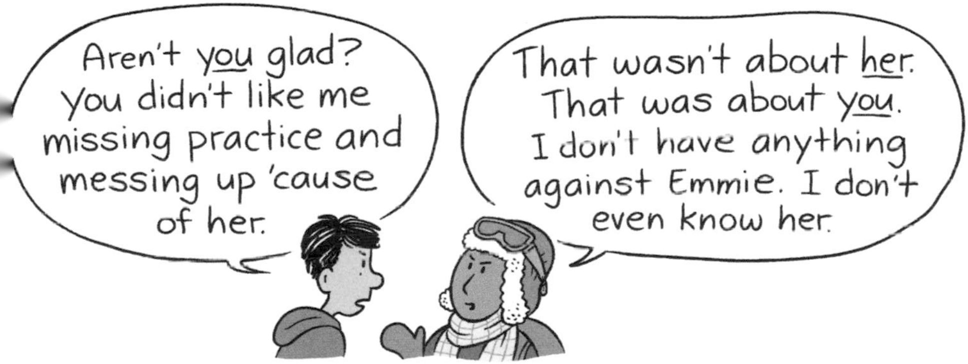
Aren't you glad? You didn't like me missing practice and messing up 'cause of her.
That wasn't about her. That was about you. I don't have anything against Emmie. I don't even know her.

I stop. It's true. Anthony never said anything bad about her.

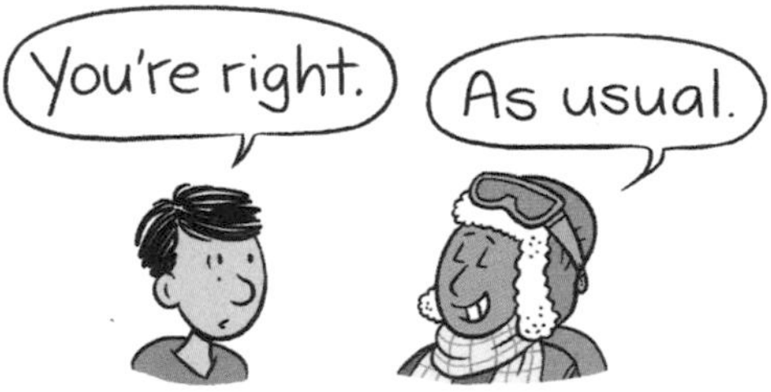
You're right.
As usual.

I sock him on the arm jokingly. It feels good that we're okay again. But . . . it isn't enough.

I know what I need to do.

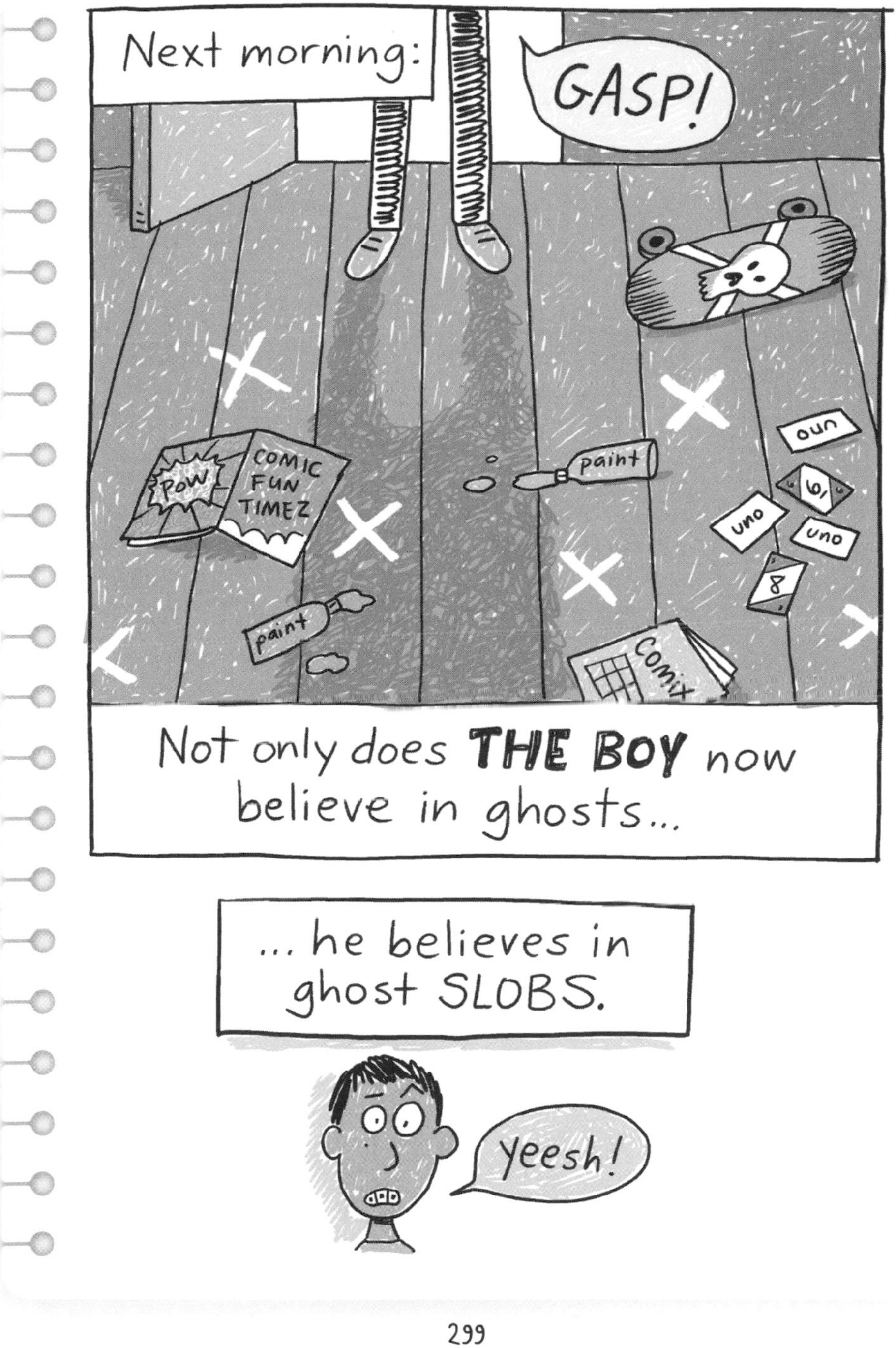
Next morning:
GASP!
COMIC FUN TIMEZ
POW
paint
uno
uno
uno
uno
paint
COMIX
Not only does **THE BOY** now believe in ghosts...
... he believes in ghost SLOBS.
yeesh!

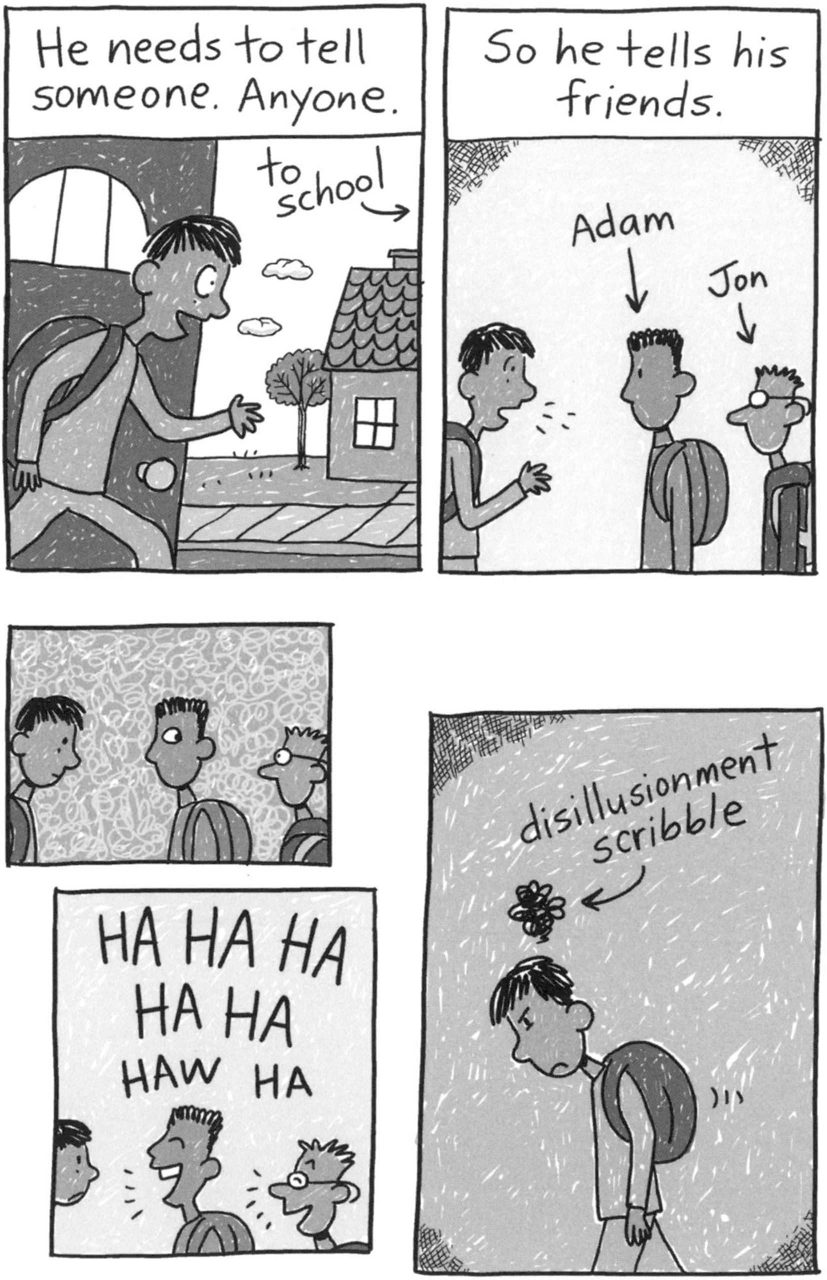
He needs to tell someone. Anyone.
to school
So he tells his friends.
Adam
Jon
HA HA HA
HA HA
HAW HA
disillusionment scribble

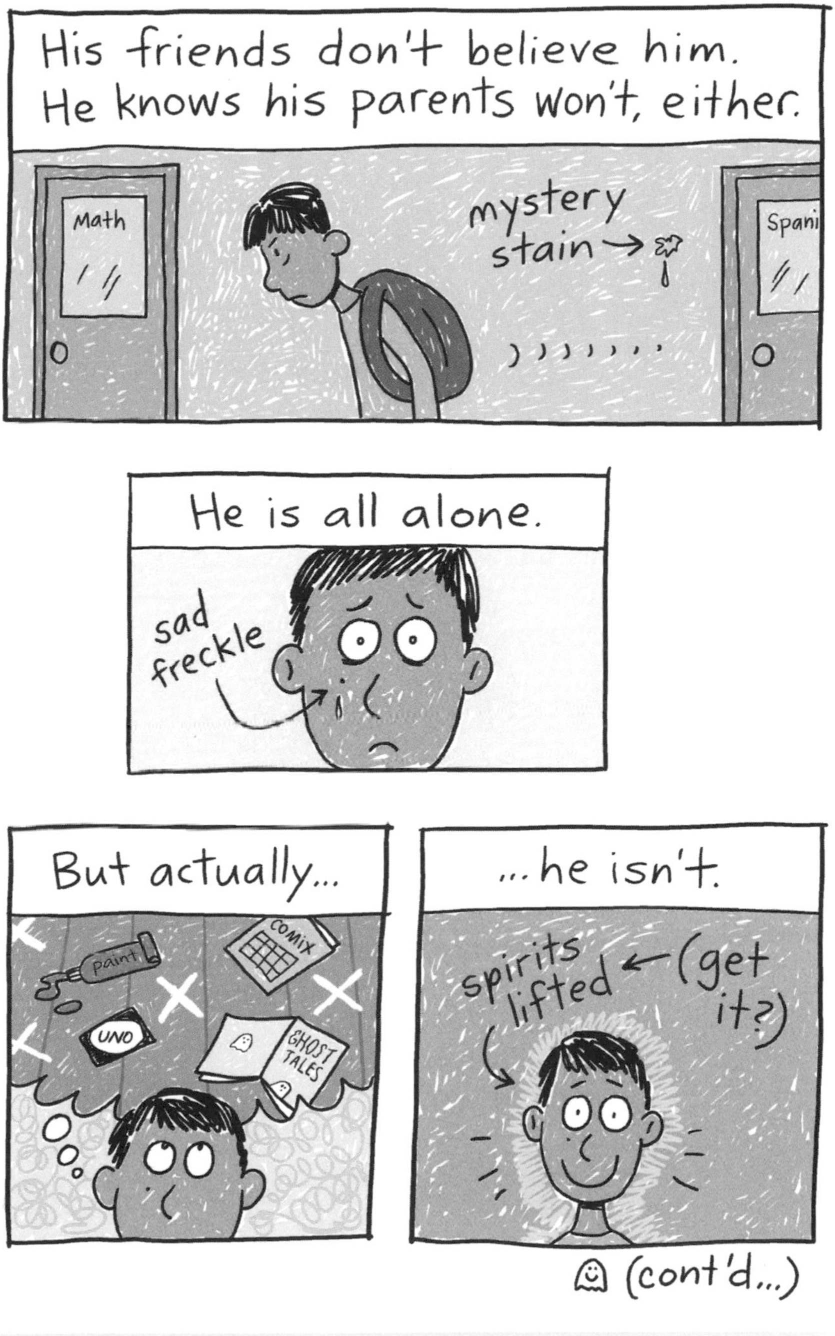
His friends don't believe him.
He knows his parents won't, either.
Math
mystery
stain
He is all alone.
sad
freckle
But actually...
paint
COMIX
UNO
GHOST
TALES
...he isn't.
spirits
lifted
(get
it?)
(cont'd...)

Emmie

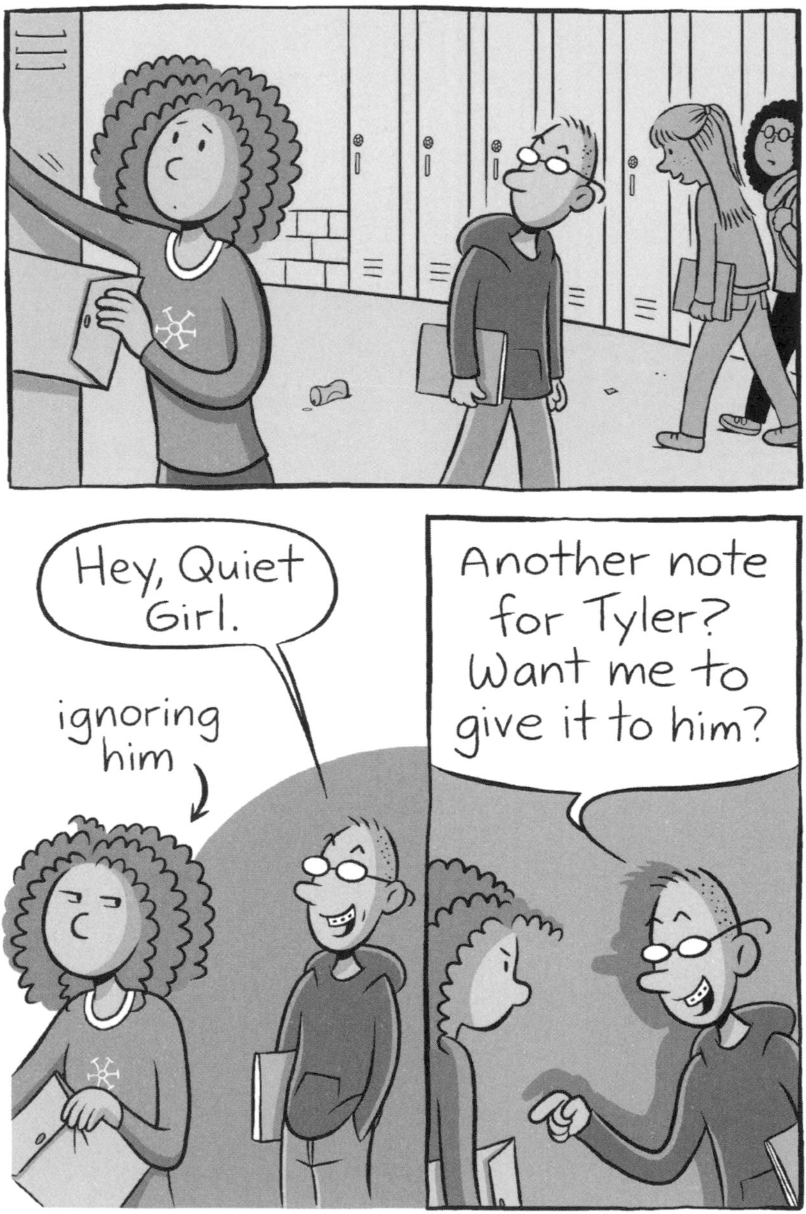
Hey, Quiet Girl.
ignoring him
Another note for Tyler? Want me to give it to him?

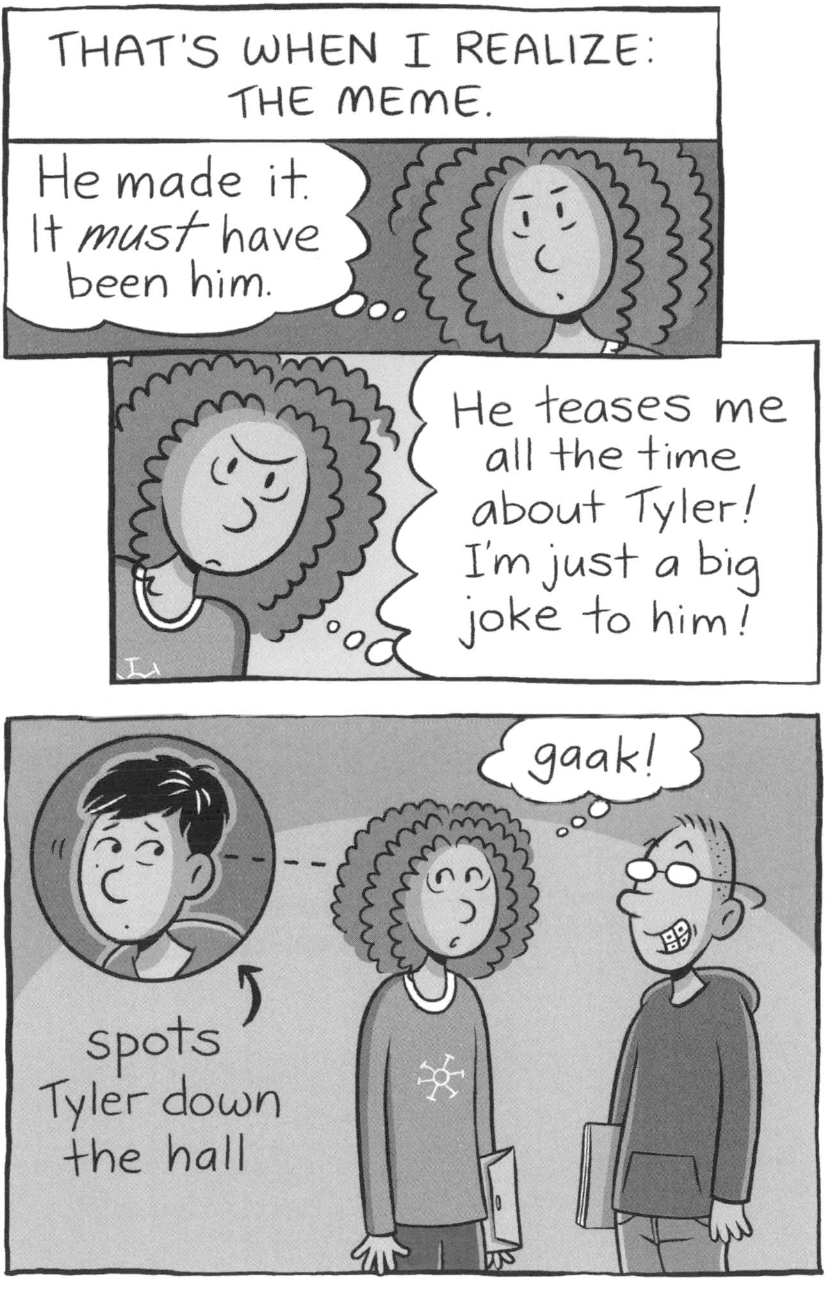
THAT'S WHEN I REALIZE:
THE MEME.
He made it. It *must* have been him.
He teases me all the time about Tyler! I'm just a big joke to him!
gaak!
spots Tyler down the hall

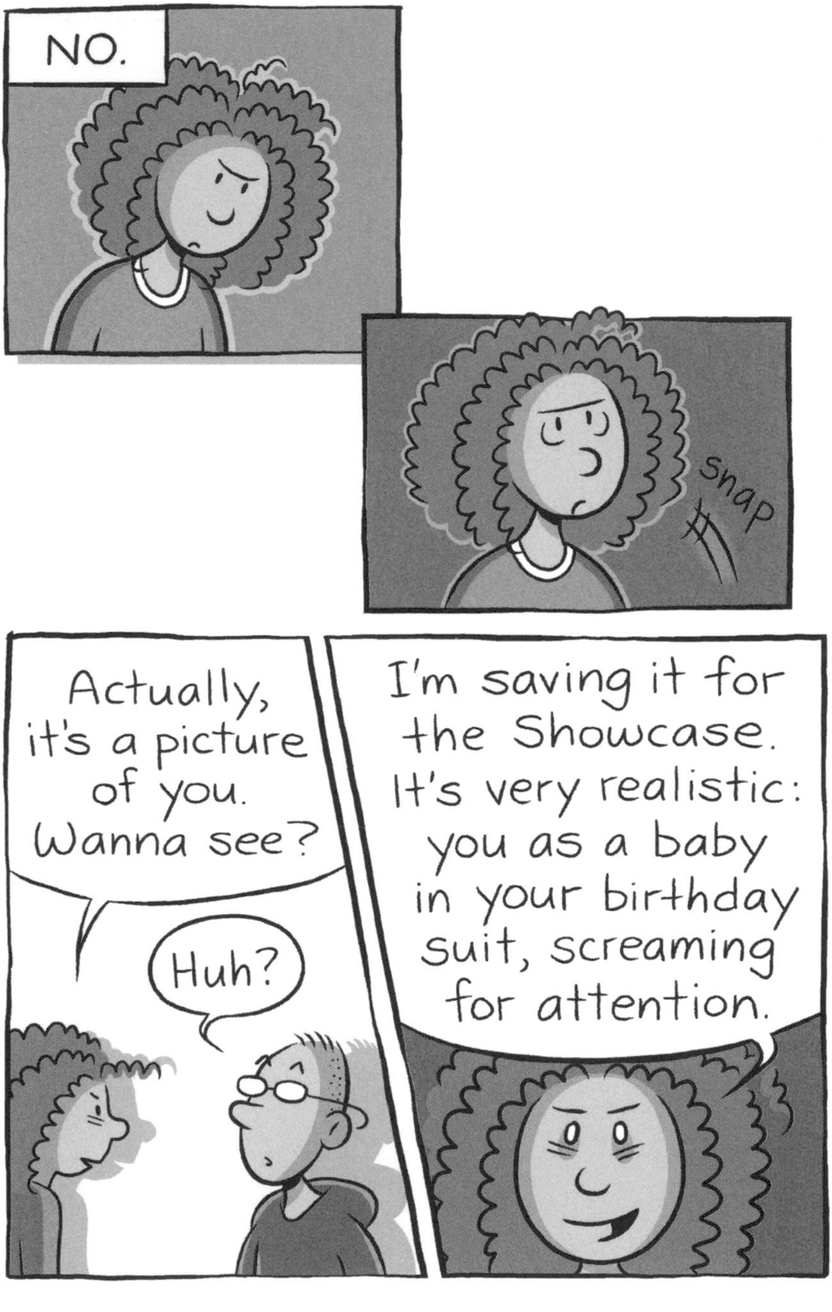
NO.
snap
Actually, it's a picture of you. Wanna see?
Huh?
I'm saving it for the Showcase. It's very realistic: you as a baby in your birthday suit, screaming for attention.

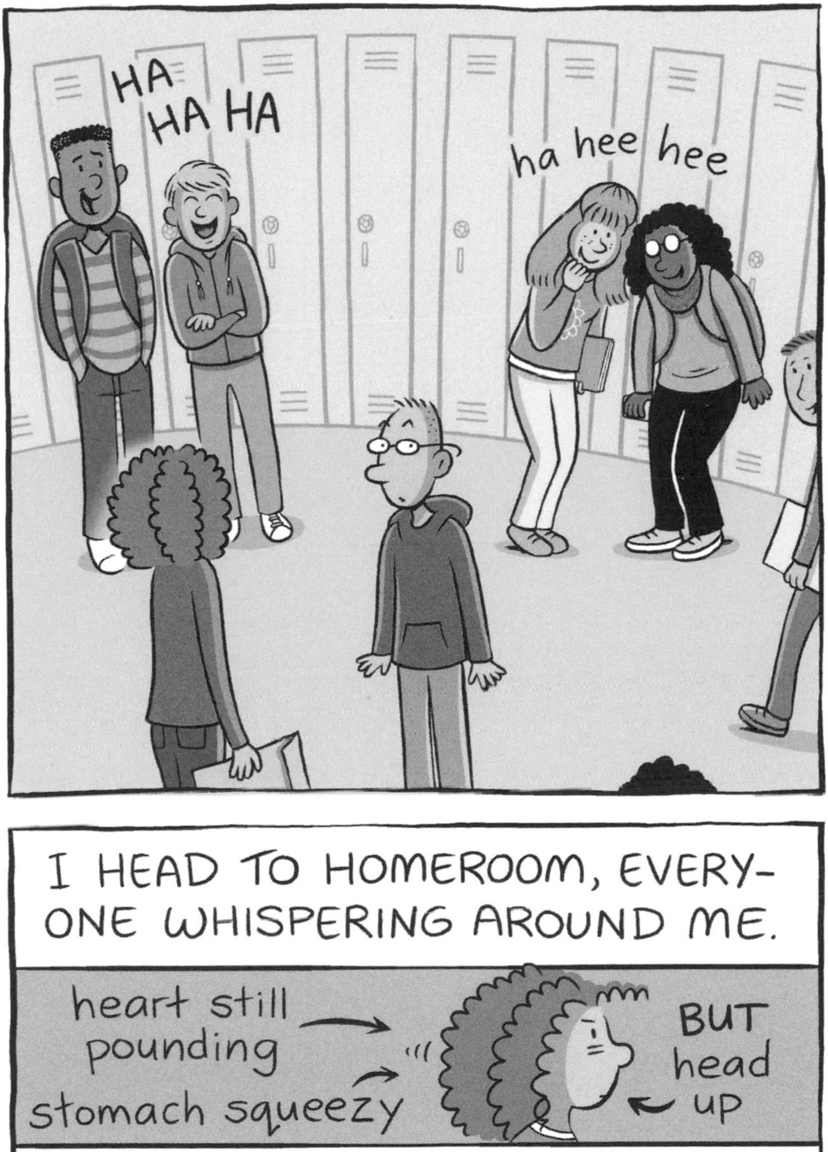
HA
HA HA
ha hee hee
I HEAD TO HOMEROOM, EVERY-
ONE WHISPERING AROUND ME.
heart still pounding
stomach squeezy
BUT head up
I DON'T CARE.
I DON'T EVEN LOOK FOR TYLER.

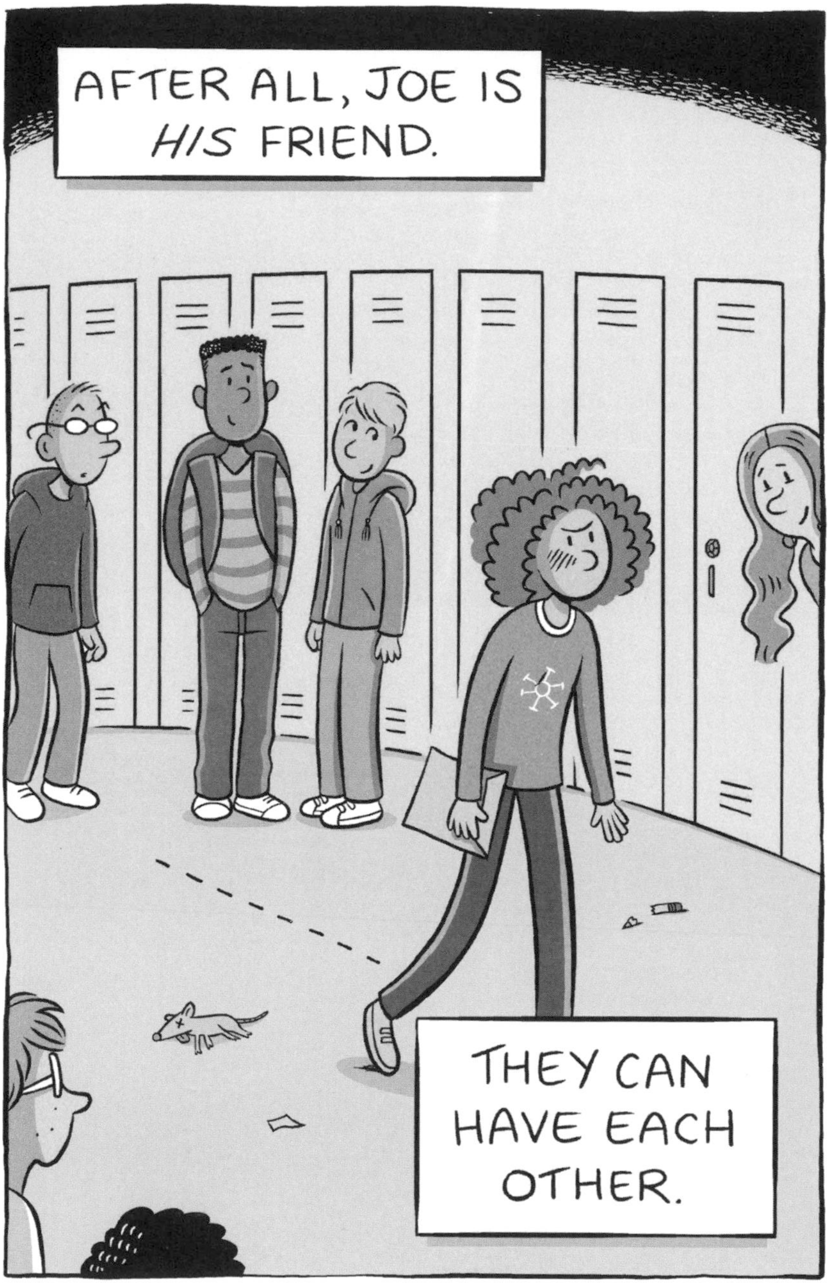
AFTER ALL, JOE IS *HIS* FRIEND.
THEY CAN HAVE EACH OTHER.

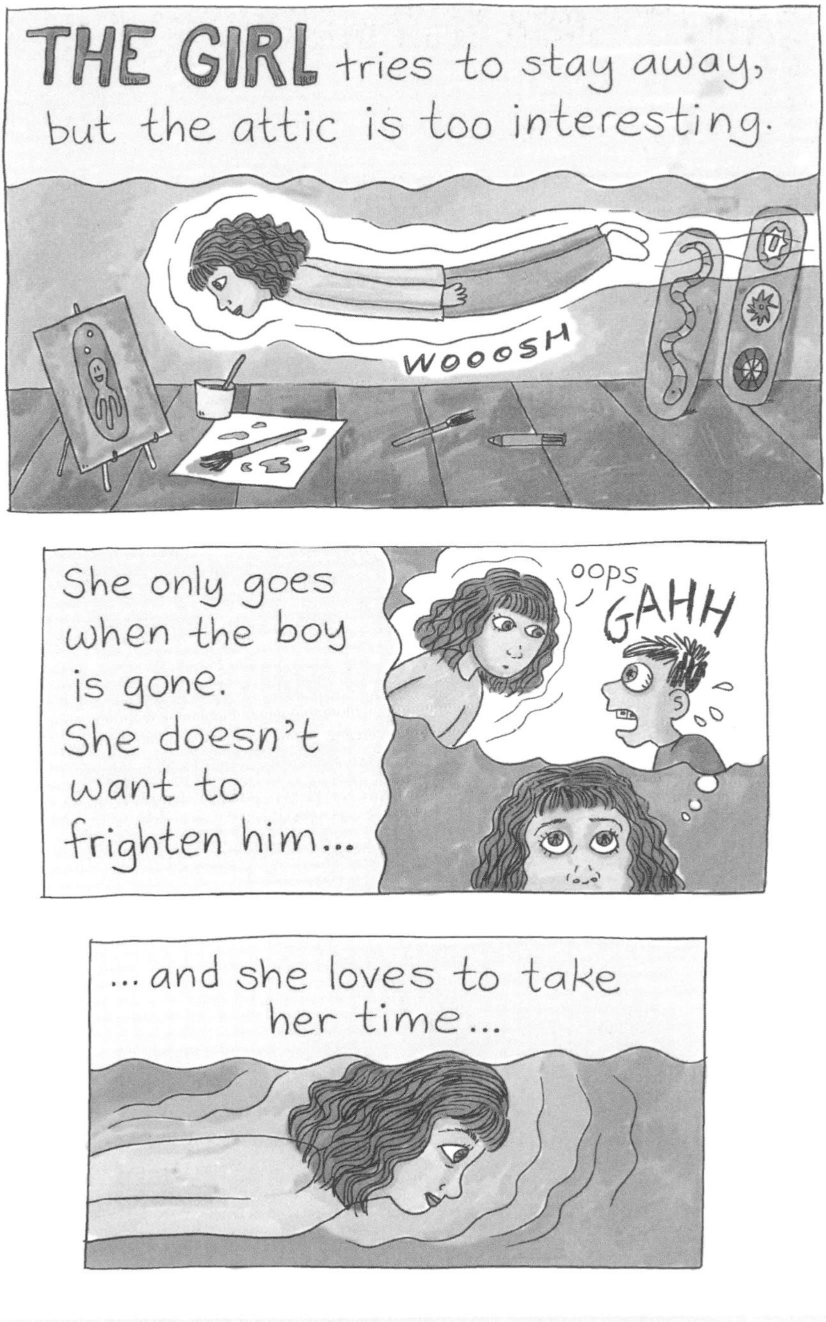
THE GIRL tries to stay away, but the attic is too interesting.
WOOOSH
She only goes when the boy is gone. She doesn't want to frighten him...
oops
GAHH
... and she loves to take her time...

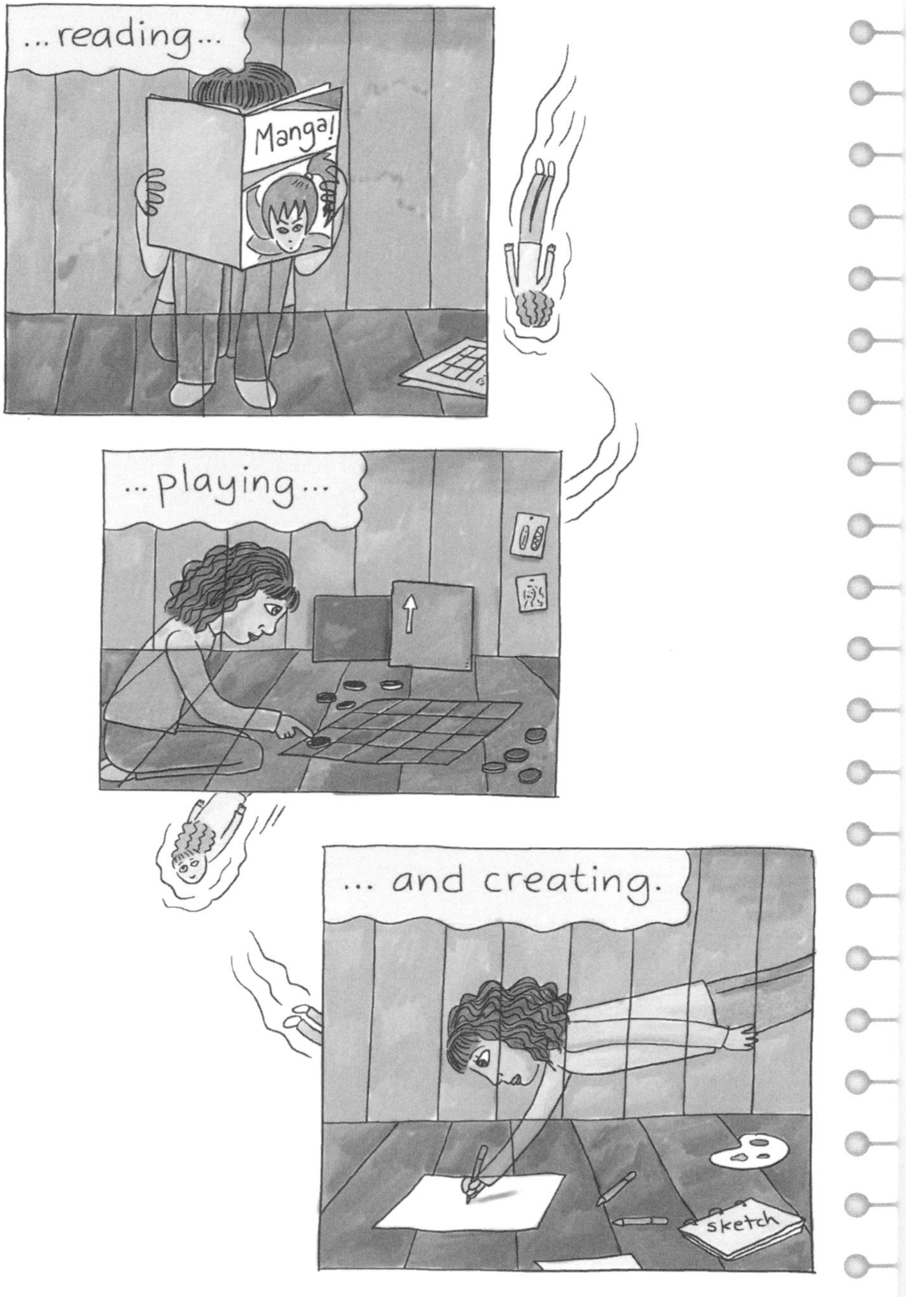
...reading...
Manga!
...playing...
... and creating.
sketch

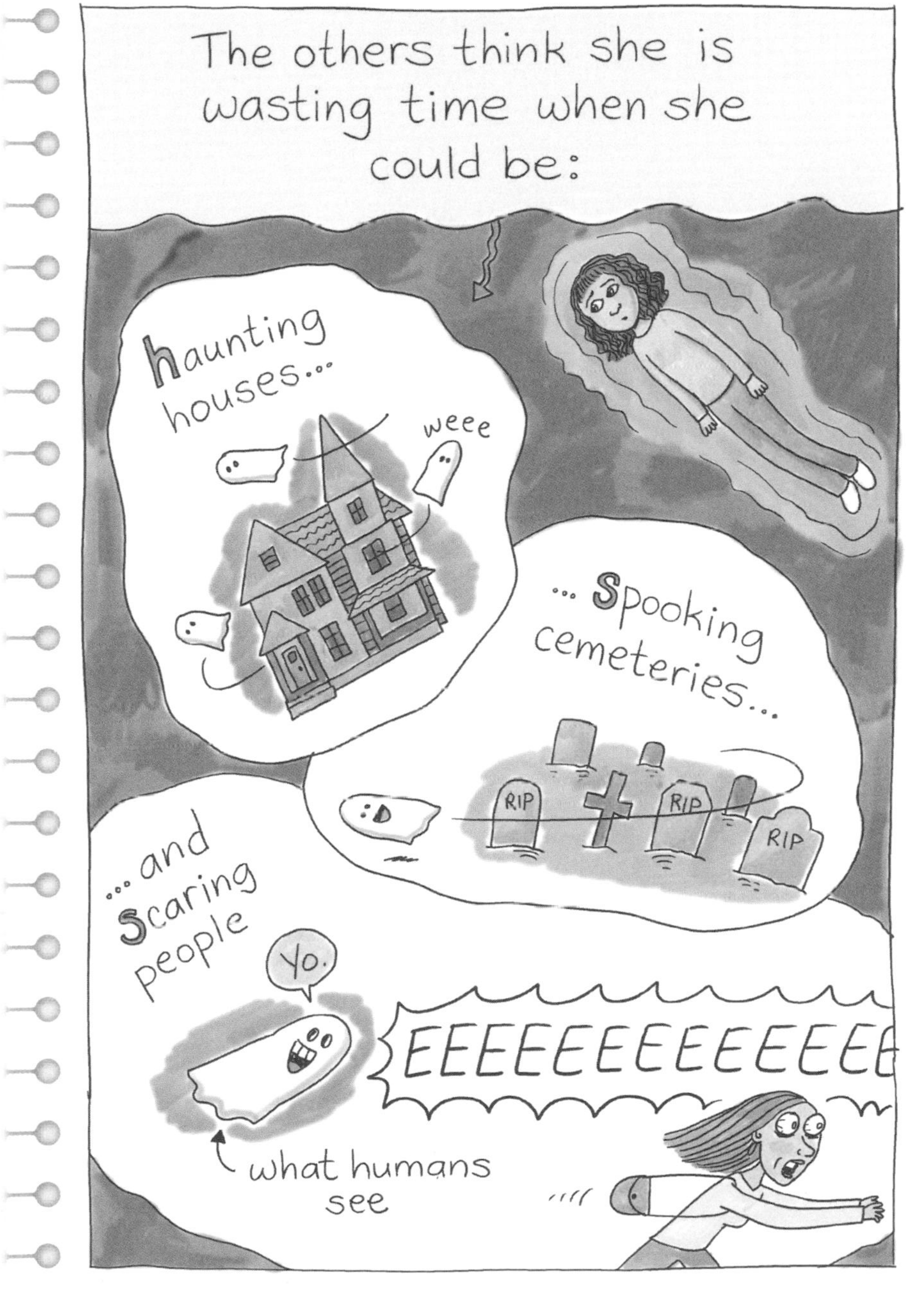
The others think she is wasting time when she could be:
haunting houses...
weee
... spooking cemeteries...
RIP
RIP
RIP
...and scaring people
Yo.
EEEEEEEEEEEEEEE
what humans see

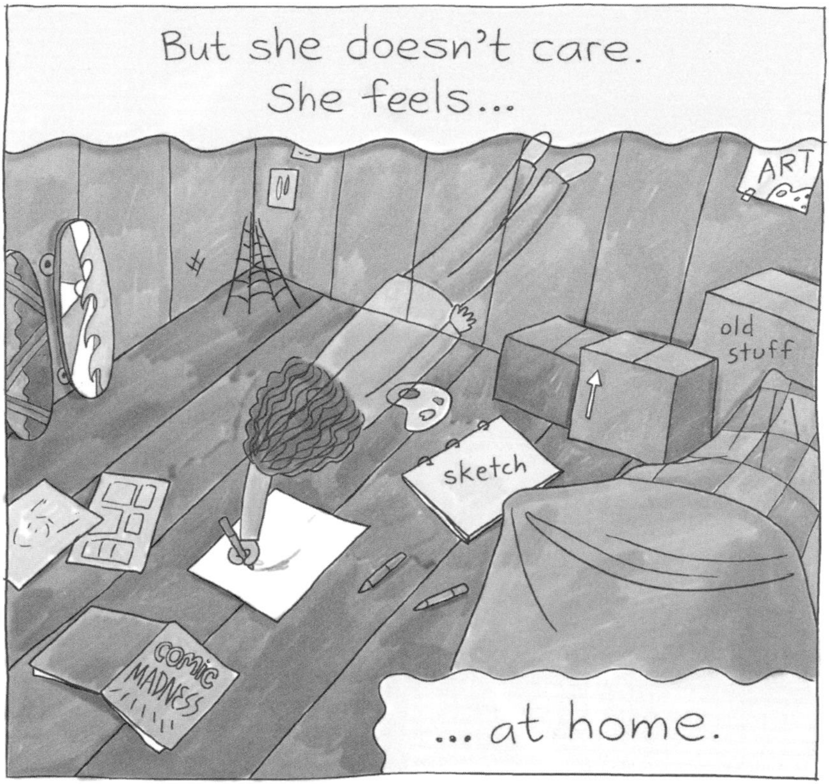
But she doesn't care.
She feels...
ART
old
stuff
sketch
COMIC
MADNESS
... at home.

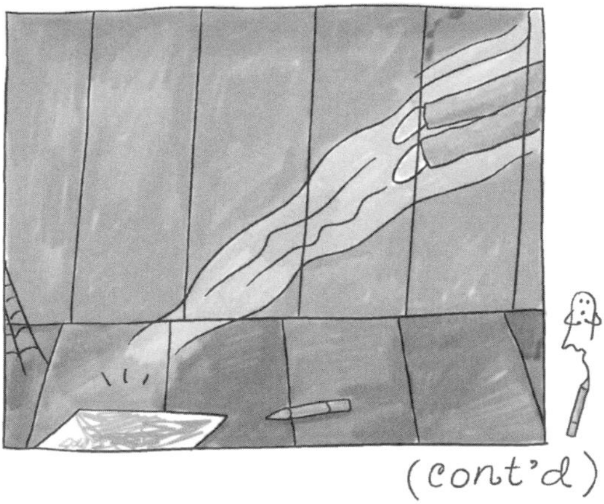
(cont'd)

TYLER

Whoa. Emmie did something really . . .

. . . un-Emmie-like.

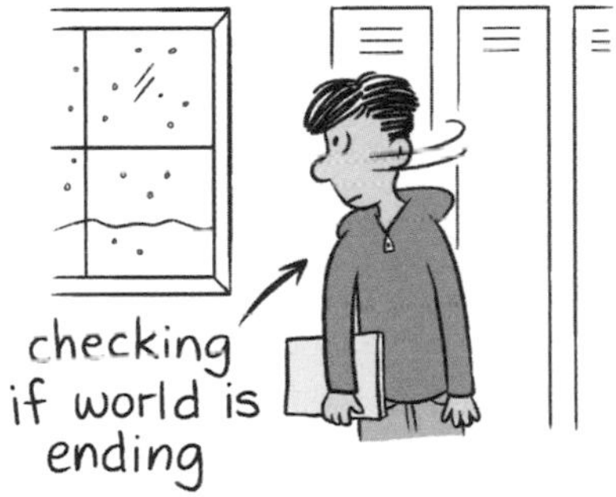
checking if world is ending

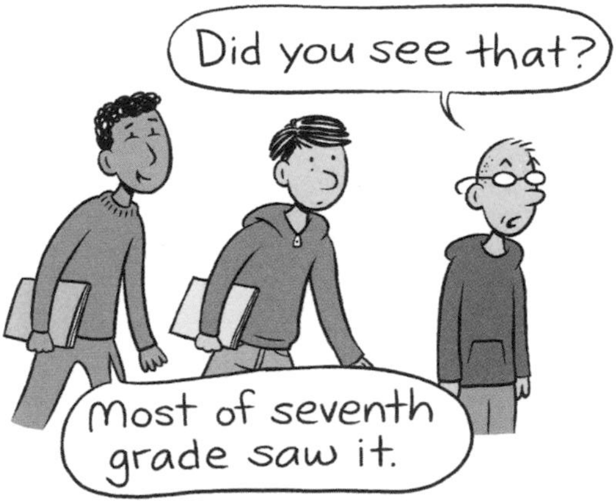
Did you see that?
Most of seventh grade saw it.

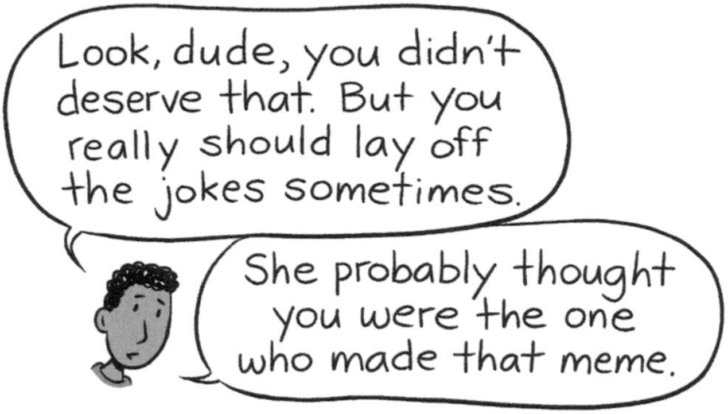
Look, dude, you didn't deserve that. But you really should lay off the jokes sometimes.
She probably thought you were the one who made that meme.

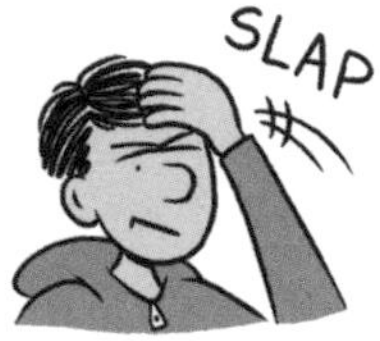
SLAP

Of course she thought that. Joe likes to tease her, probably 'cause she's quiet and he loves to get a reaction. He does the same thing with Sarah. She's not as quiet, but he's even worse with her. I've seen it.

The late bell rings. We hustle to get to homeroom.

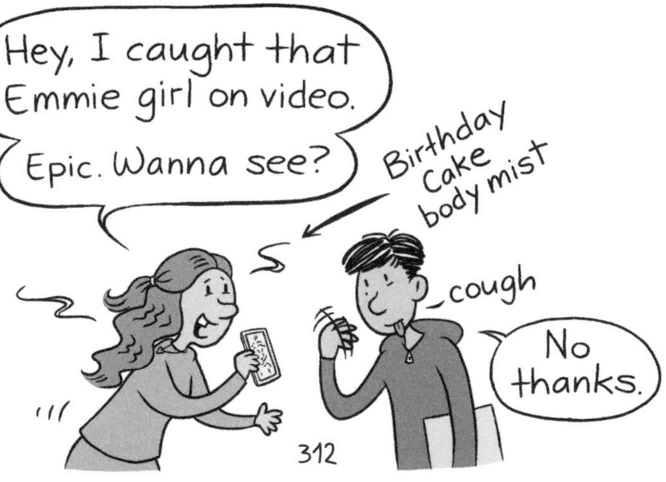
Hey, I caught that Emmie girl on video.
Epic. Wanna see?
Birthday cake body mist
cough
No thanks.

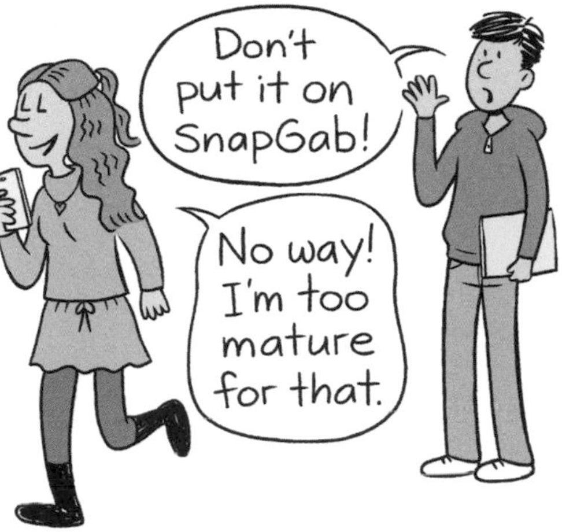
Don't put it on SnapGab!
No way! I'm too mature for that.

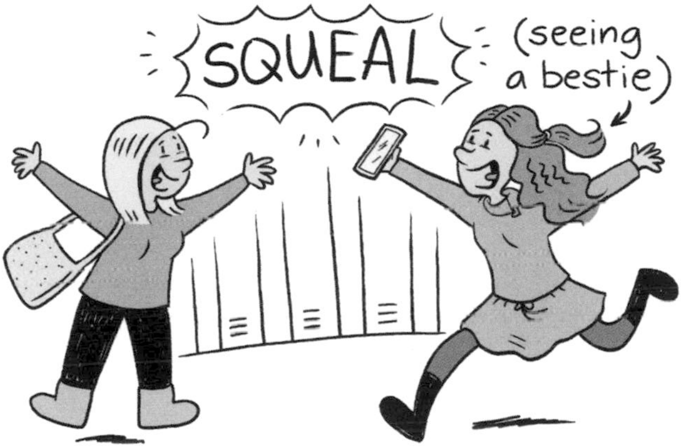
SQUEAL
(seeing a bestie)

As I walk into homeroom, something dawns on me.

Nah.

Emmie

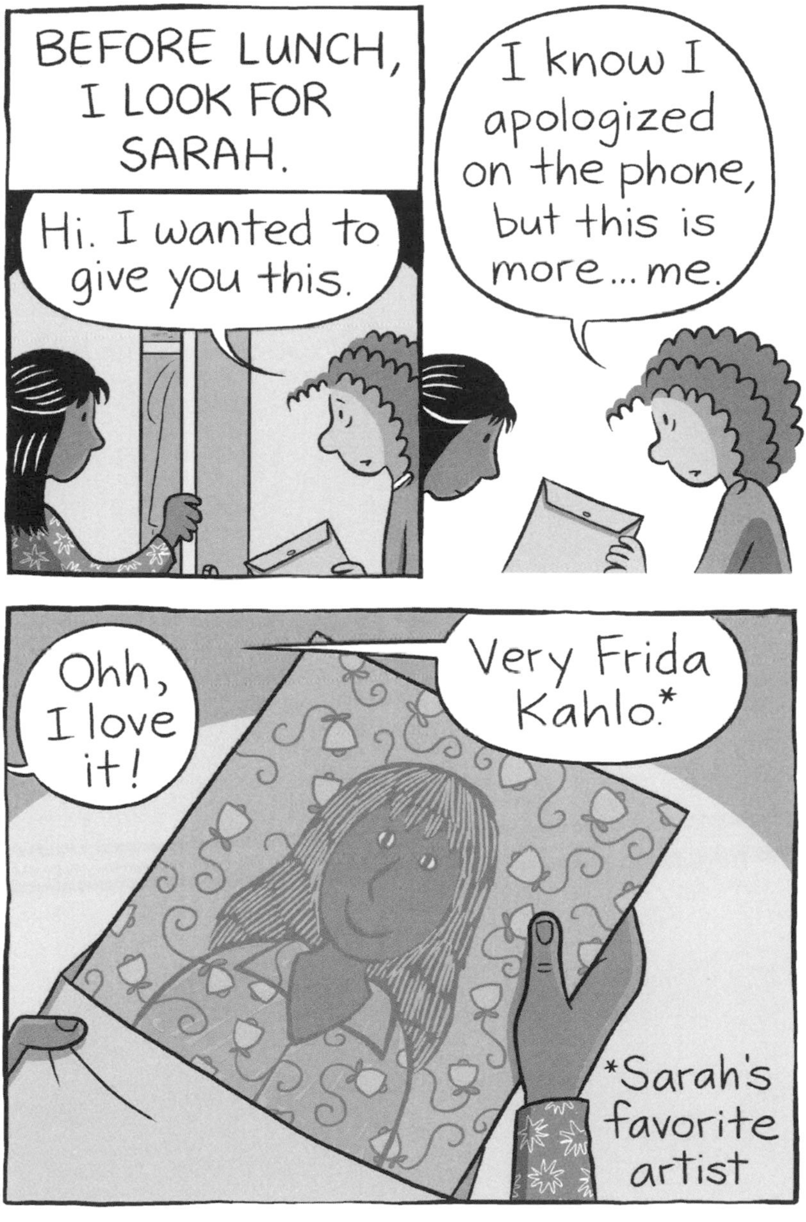
BEFORE LUNCH, I LOOK FOR SARAH.
Hi. I wanted to give you this.
I know I apologized on the phone, but this is more... me.
Ohh, I love it!
Very Frida Kahlo.*
*Sarah's favorite artist

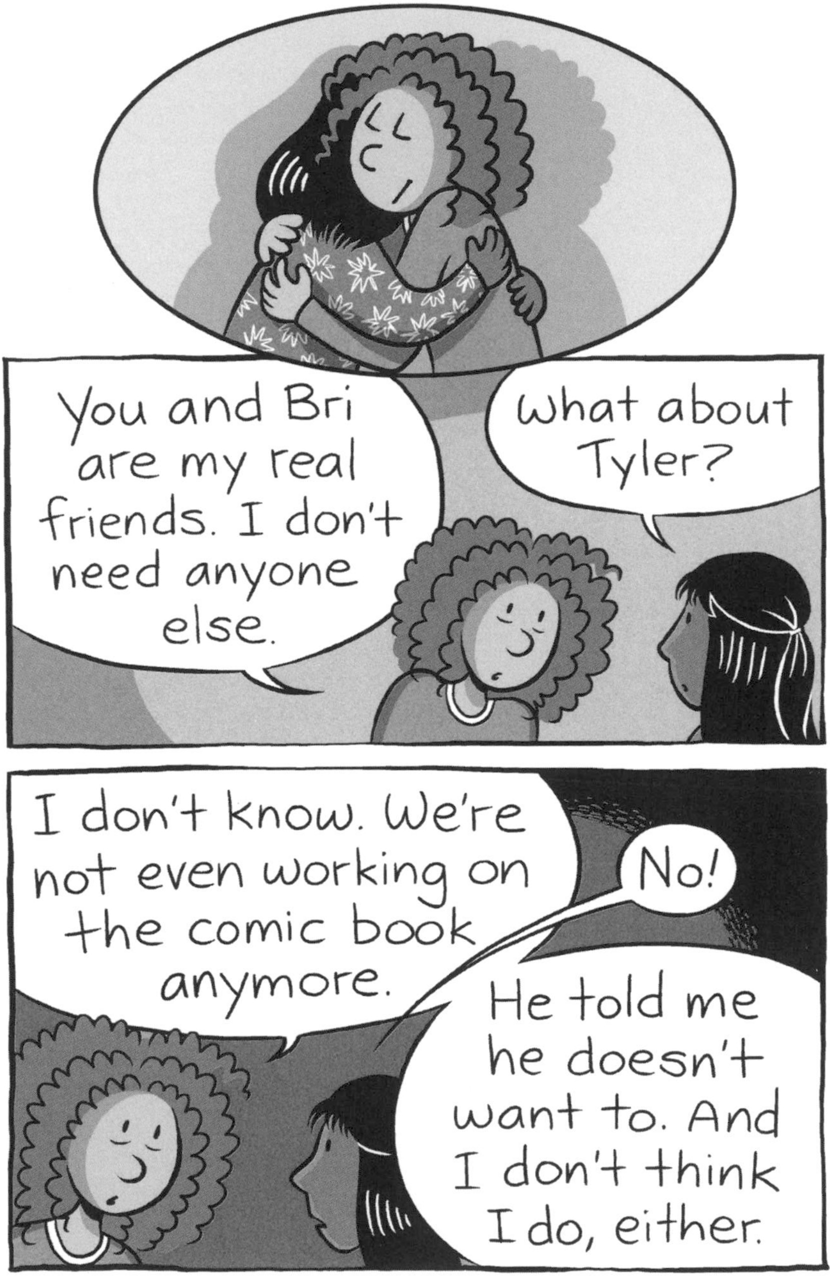
You and Bri are my real friends. I don't need anyone else.
What about Tyler?
I don't know. We're not even working on the comic book anymore.
No!
He told me he doesn't want to. And I don't think I do, either.

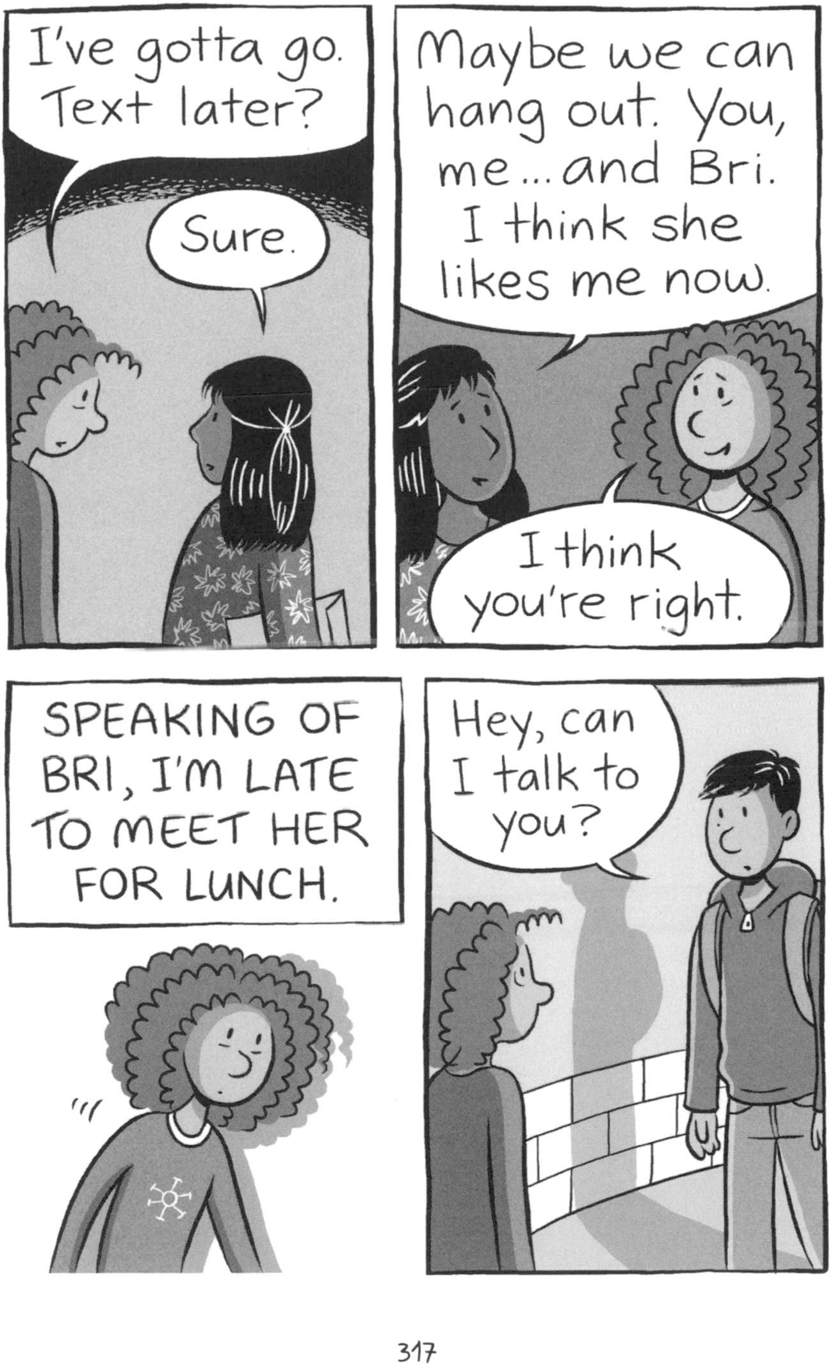
I've gotta go. Text later?
Sure.
Maybe we can hang out. You, me...and Bri. I think she likes me now.
I think you're right.
SPEAKING OF BRI, I'M LATE TO MEET HER FOR LUNCH.
Hey, can I talk to you?

TYLER

Emmie stands there, staring at me like I'm a cross between garbage and a slug.

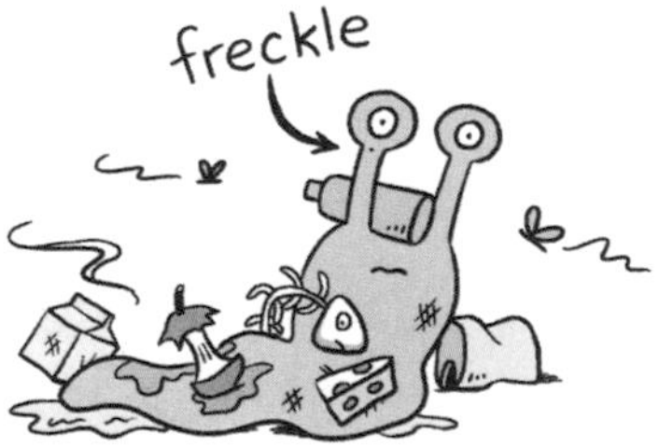
freckle

It's the first time she's looked at me this way. Usually, it's:

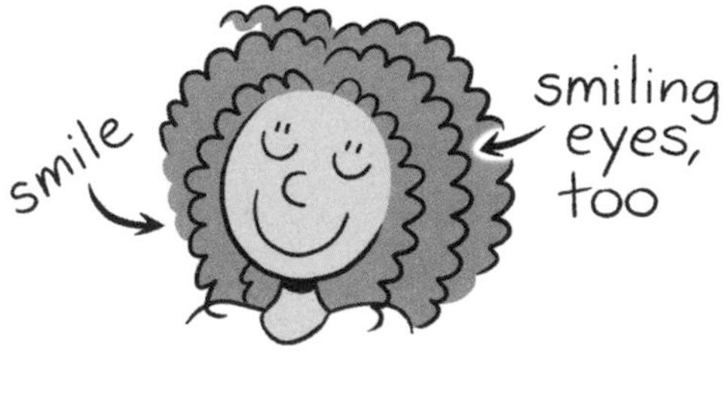
smile
smiling eyes, too

I reach in my backpack and pull out a thick folder.

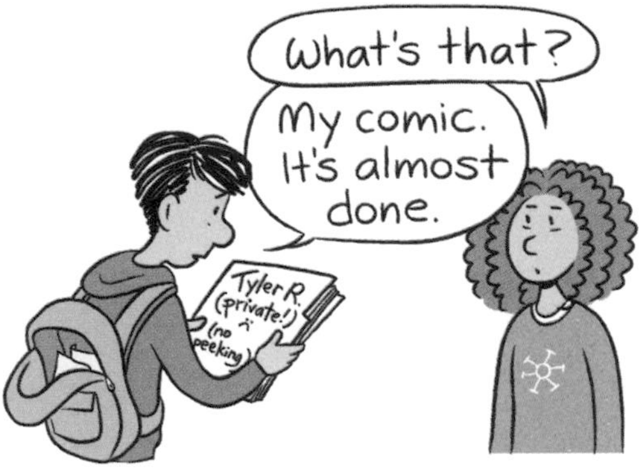
What's that?
My comic. It's almost done.
Tyler R. (private!) (no peeking)

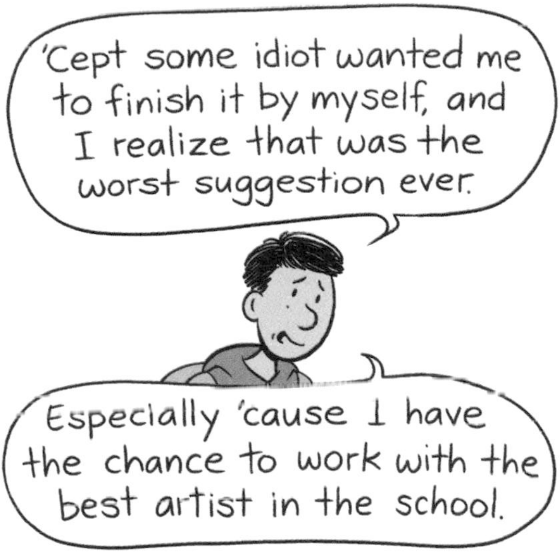
'Cept some idiot wanted me to finish it by myself, and I realize that was the worst suggestion ever.
Especially 'cause I have the chance to work with the best artist in the school.

I hand her the folder and she takes it silently.

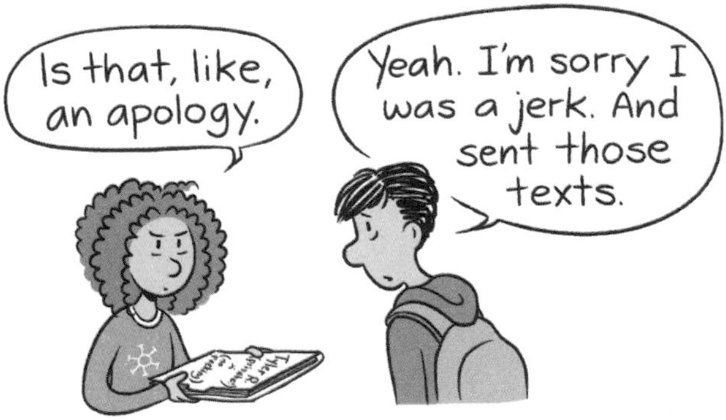
Is that, like, an apology.
Yeah. I'm sorry I was a jerk. And sent those texts.

Emmie still doesn't say anything, but she opens the folder and starts flipping through my drawings. I'm suddenly nervous, 'cause I worked really hard on the last batch. I spent all day Sunday finishing them.

I hold my breath.

For a long time.

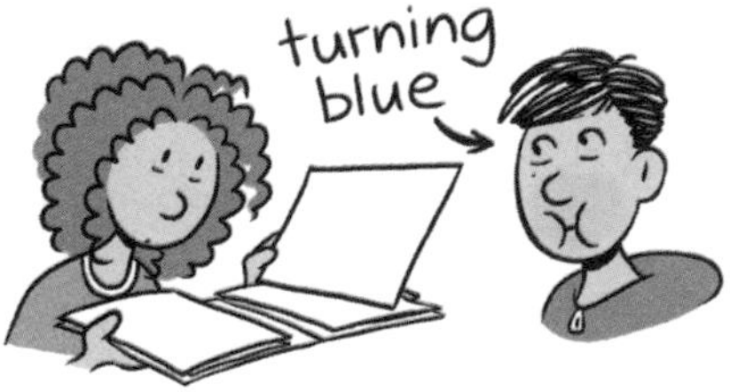
turning blue

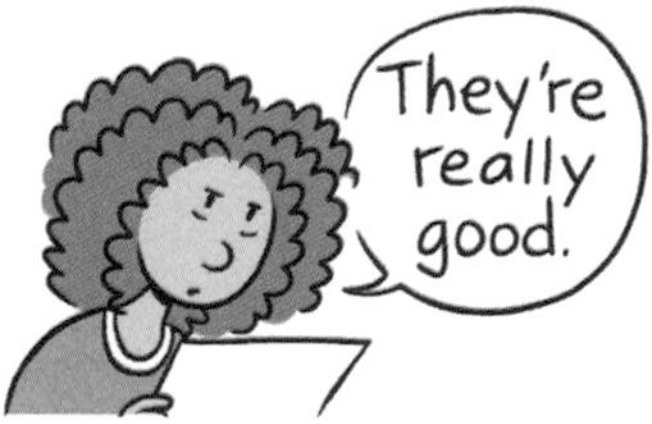
They're really good.

I release my breath.

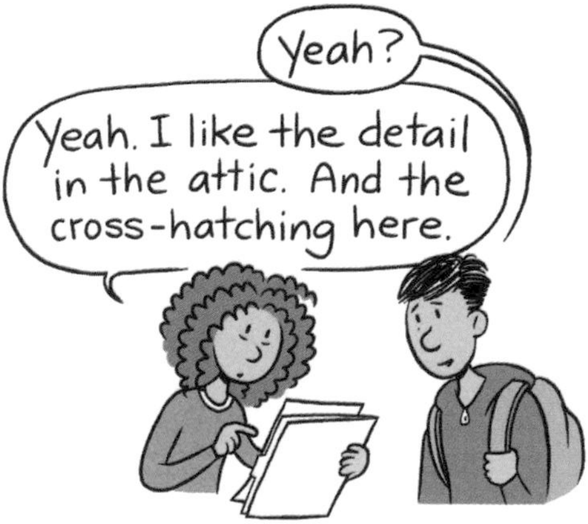
Yeah?
Yeah. I like the detail in the attic. And the cross-hatching here.

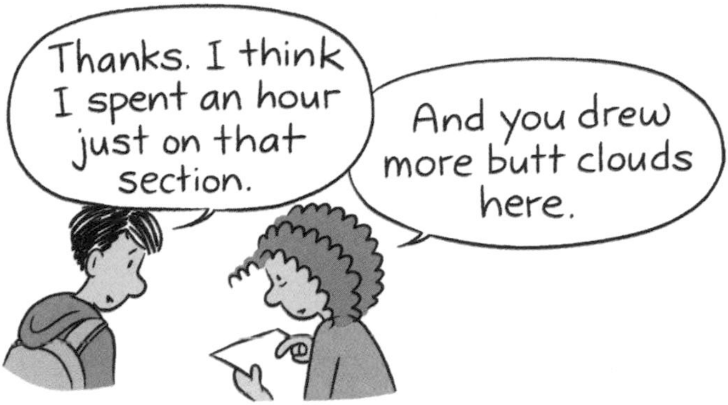

Thanks. I think I spent an hour just on that section.
And you drew more butt clouds here.

I laugh and she smiles . . . just a little.

I know we have to talk about something else. Something I really **don't** want to talk about.

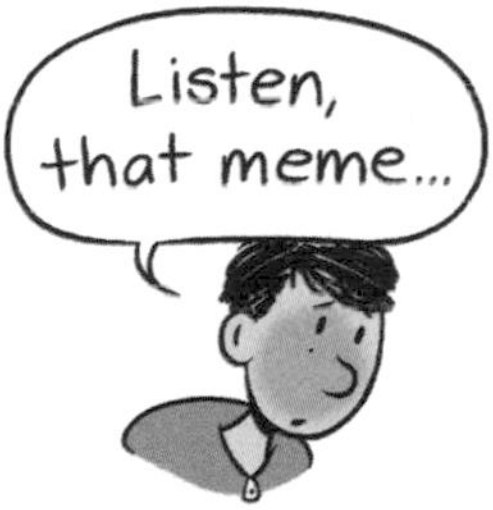

Listen, that meme...

She goes full-on Flamin' Cheetos. I think I do, too.

I say it quickly.

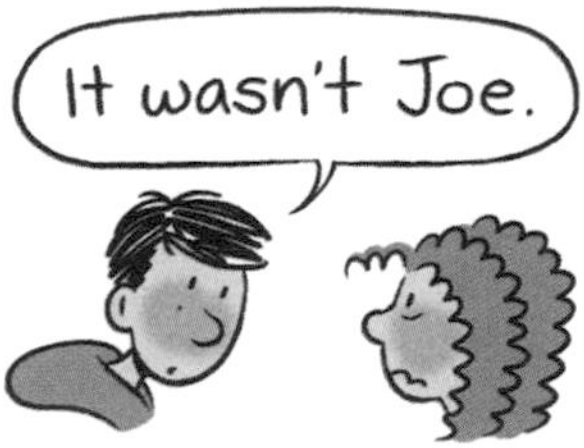

It wasn't Joe.

At first Emmie looks confused. Like she's trying to solve the world's hardest math problem.

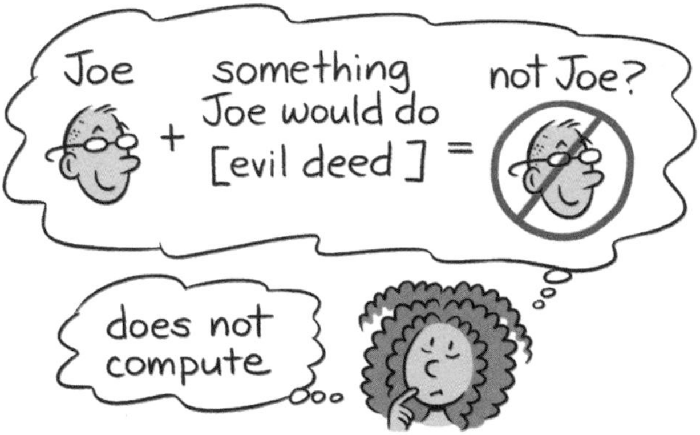
Joe
something Joe would do [evil deed]
not Joe?
+
=
does not compute

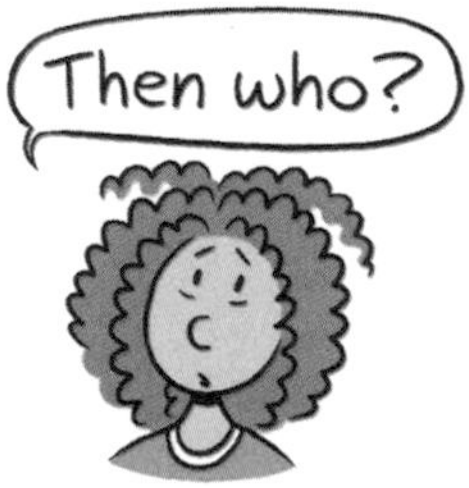
Then who?

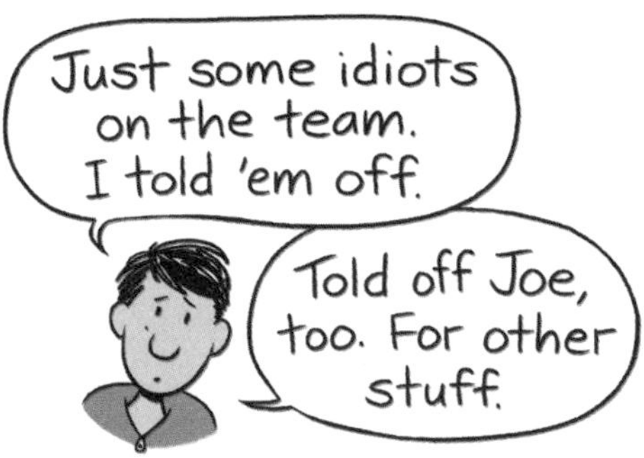
Just some idiots on the team. I told 'em off.
Told off Joe, too. For other stuff.

Emmie doesn't say anything.

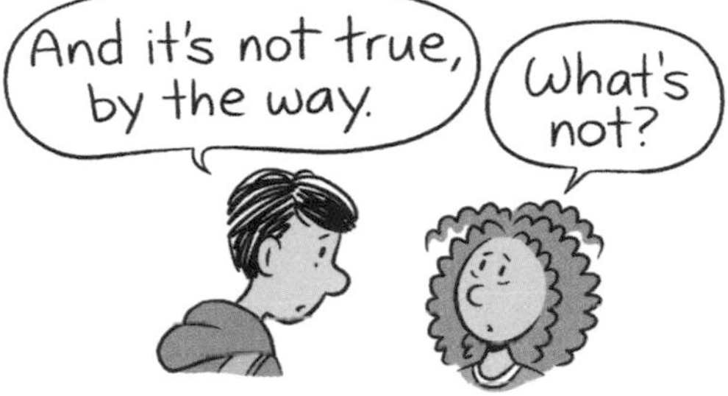
And it's not true, by the way.
What's not?

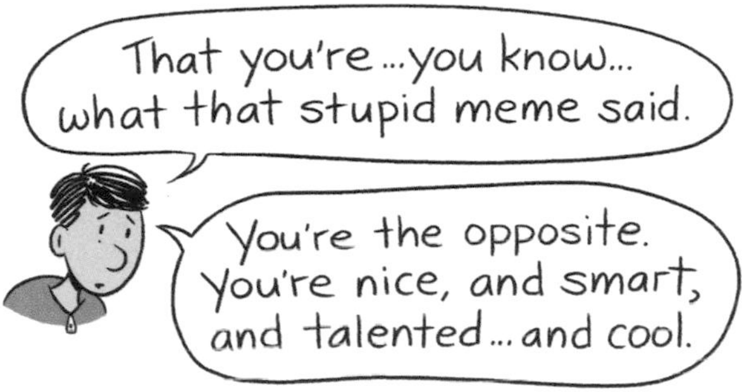
That you're ...you know... what that stupid meme said.
You're the opposite. You're nice, and smart, and talented...and cool.

Emmie looks at me, and I swear she's about to—

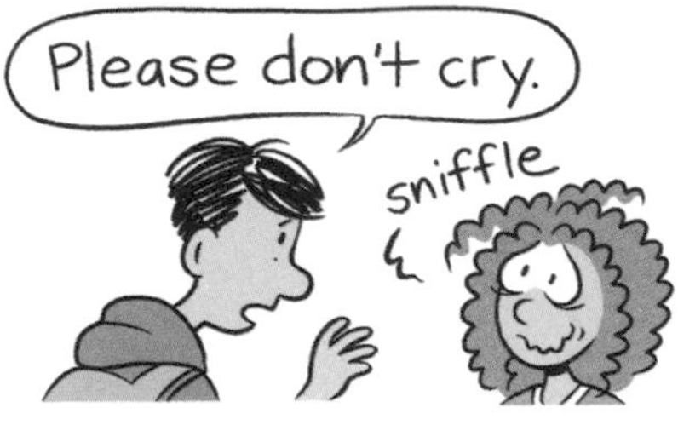
Please don't cry.
sniffle

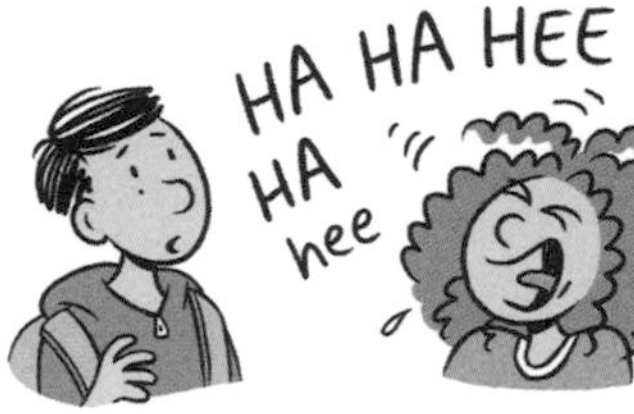
HA HA HEE
HA
hee

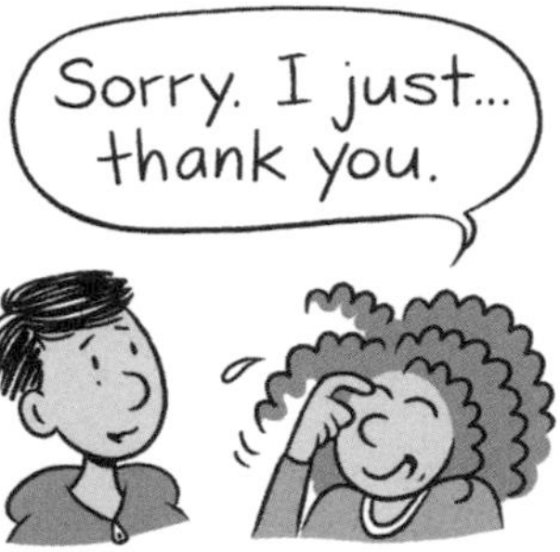
Sorry. I just... thank you.

We stare at each other awkwardly for a moment.

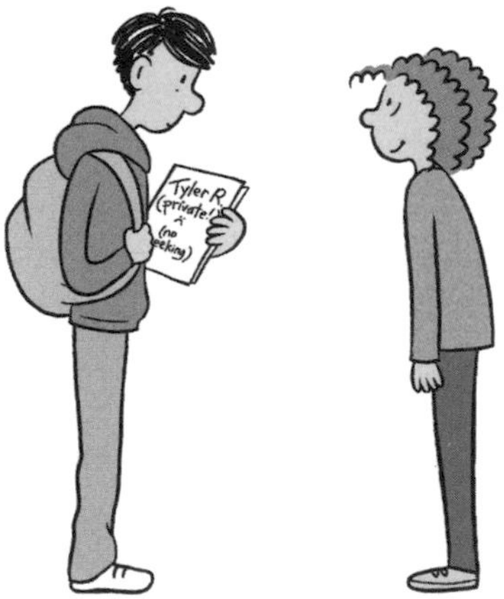
Tyler R
(private!

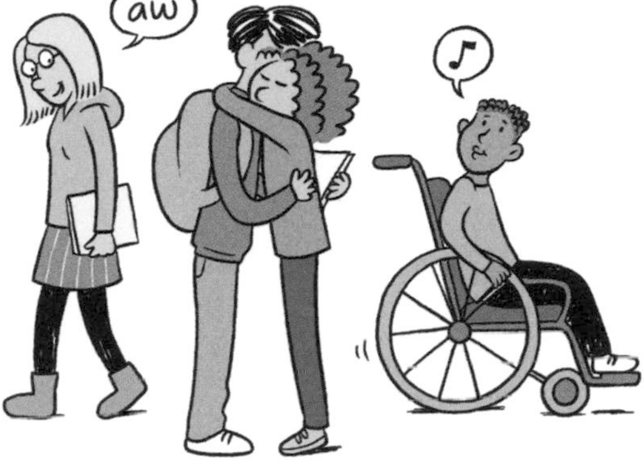
aw
♪

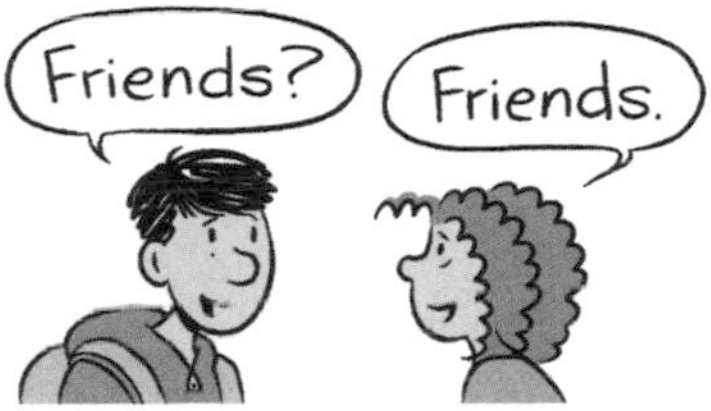
Friends?
Friends.

Emmie

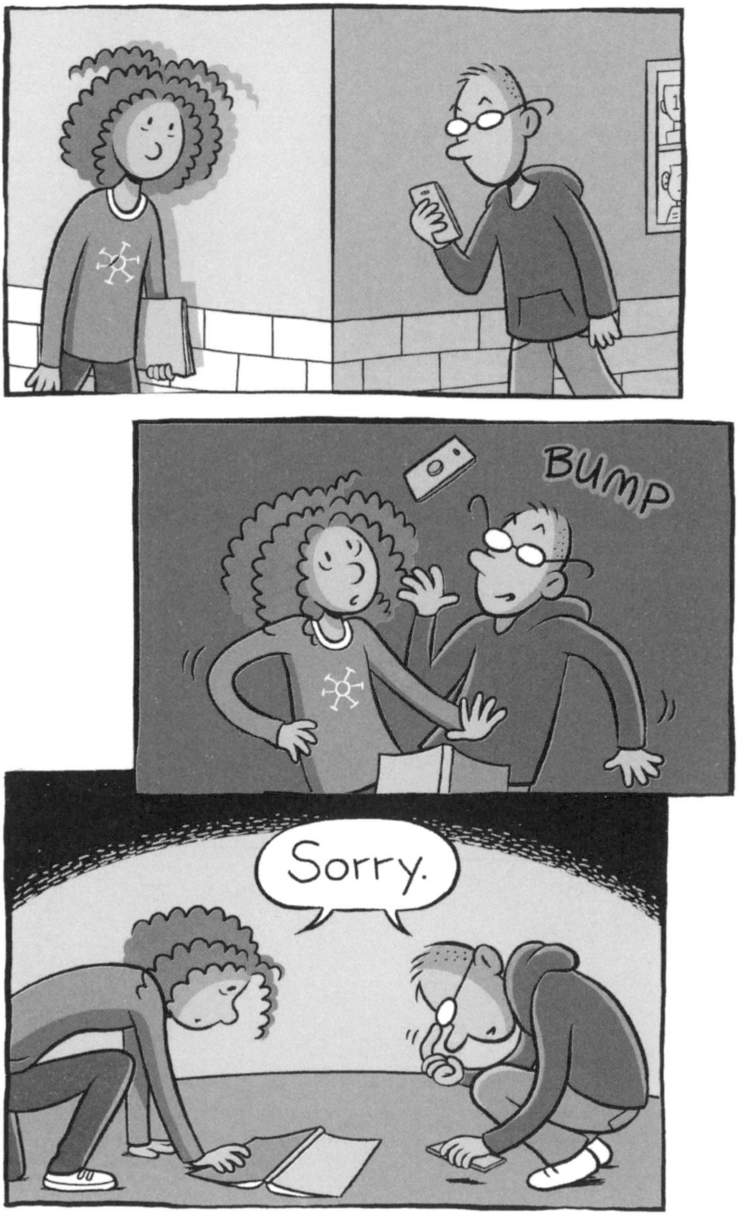
BUMP
Sorry.

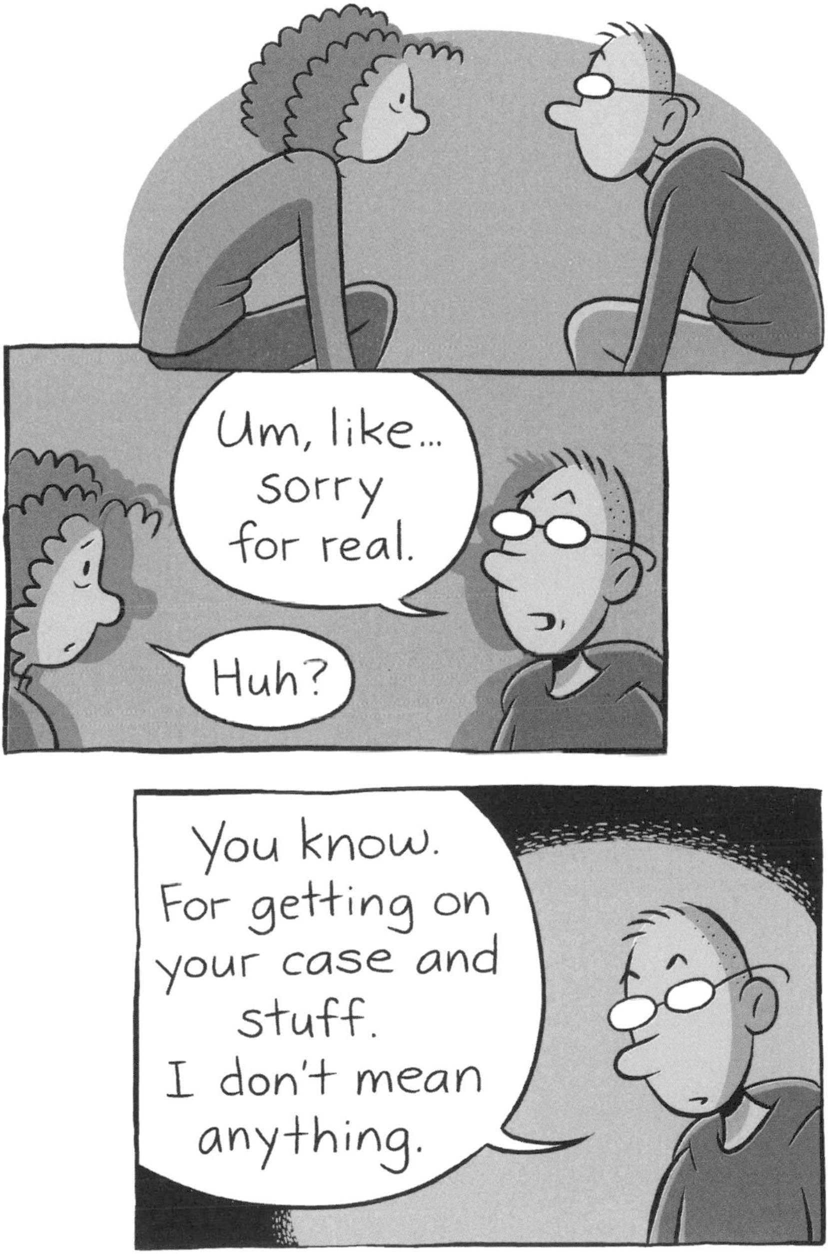
Um, like... sorry for real.
Huh?
You know. For getting on your case and stuff. I don't mean anything.

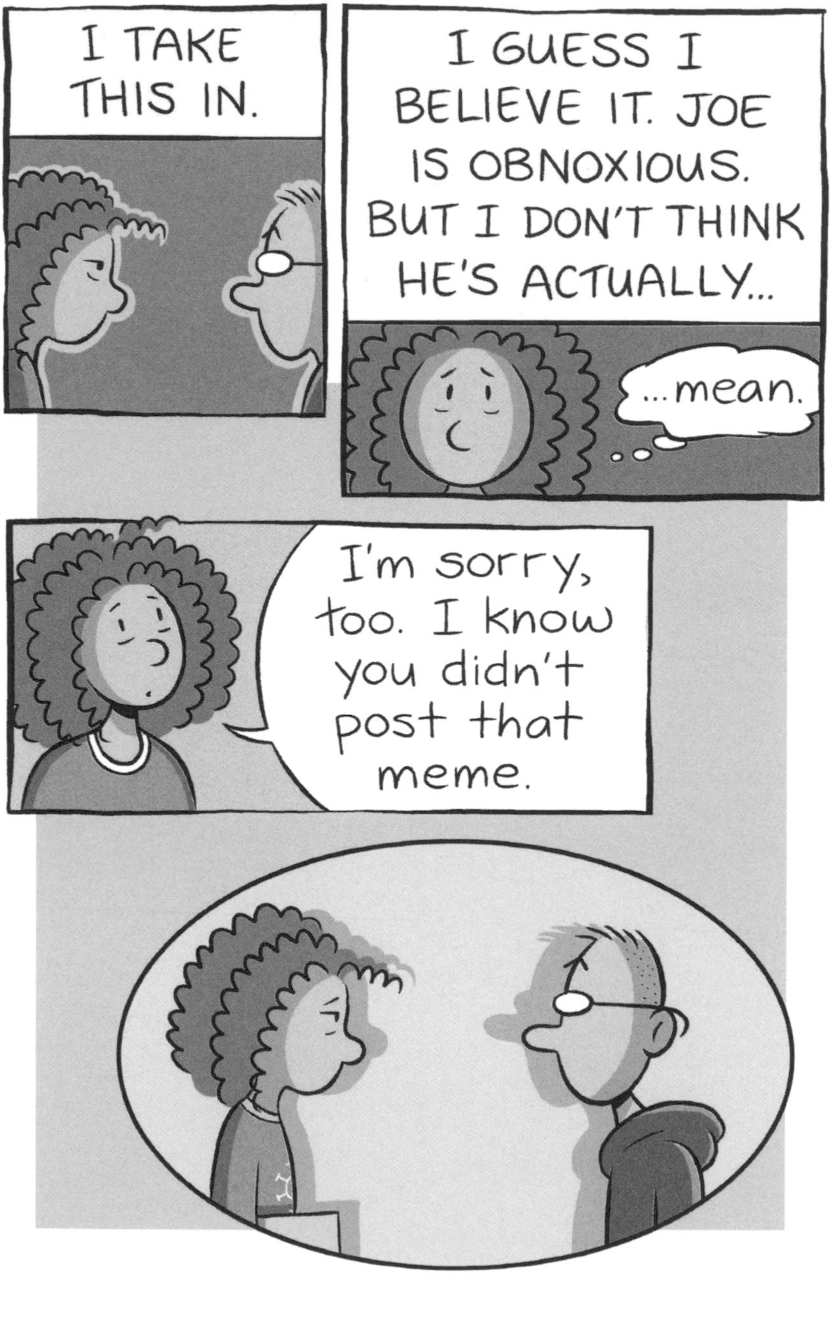
I TAKE THIS IN.
I GUESS I BELIEVE IT. JOE IS OBNOXIOUS. BUT I DON'T THINK HE'S ACTUALLY...
...mean.
I'm sorry, too. I know you didn't post that meme.

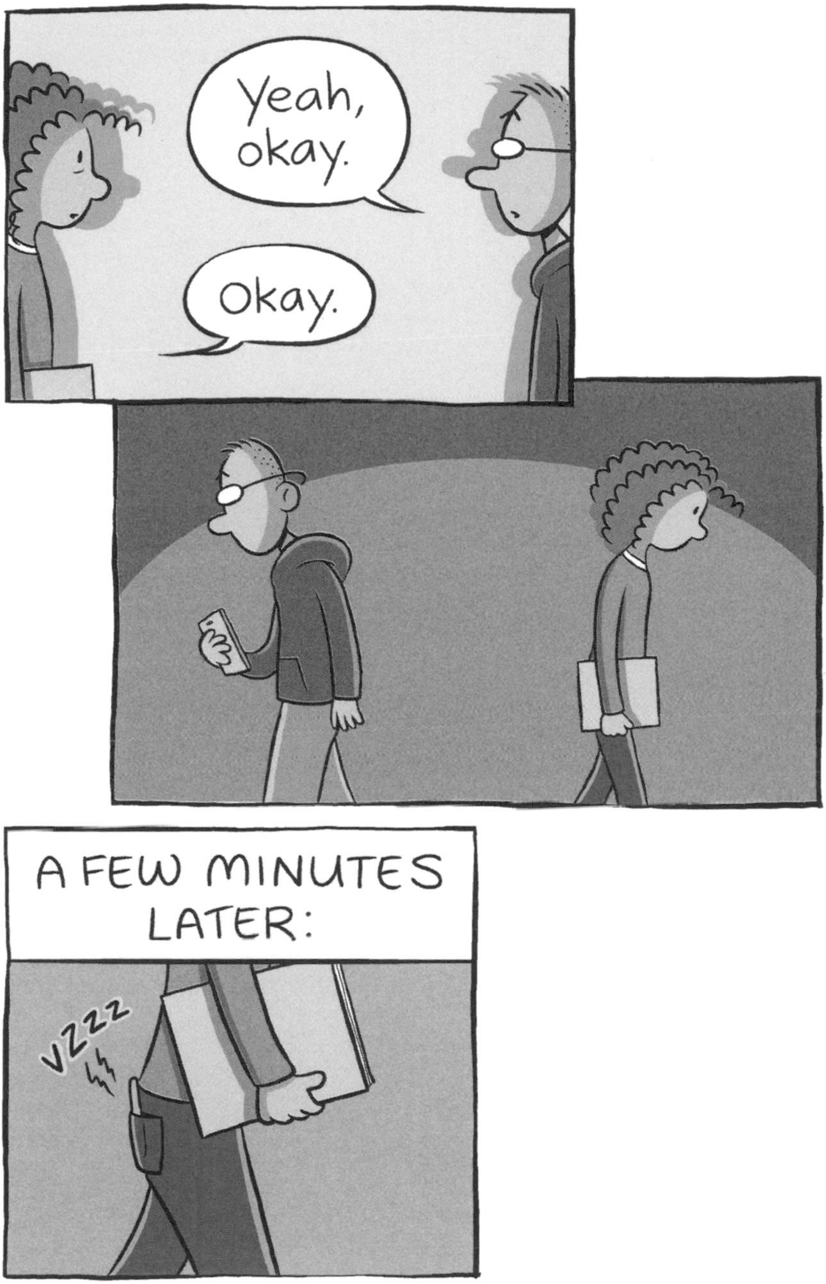
Yeah, okay.
Okay.
A FEW MINUTES LATER:
VZZZ

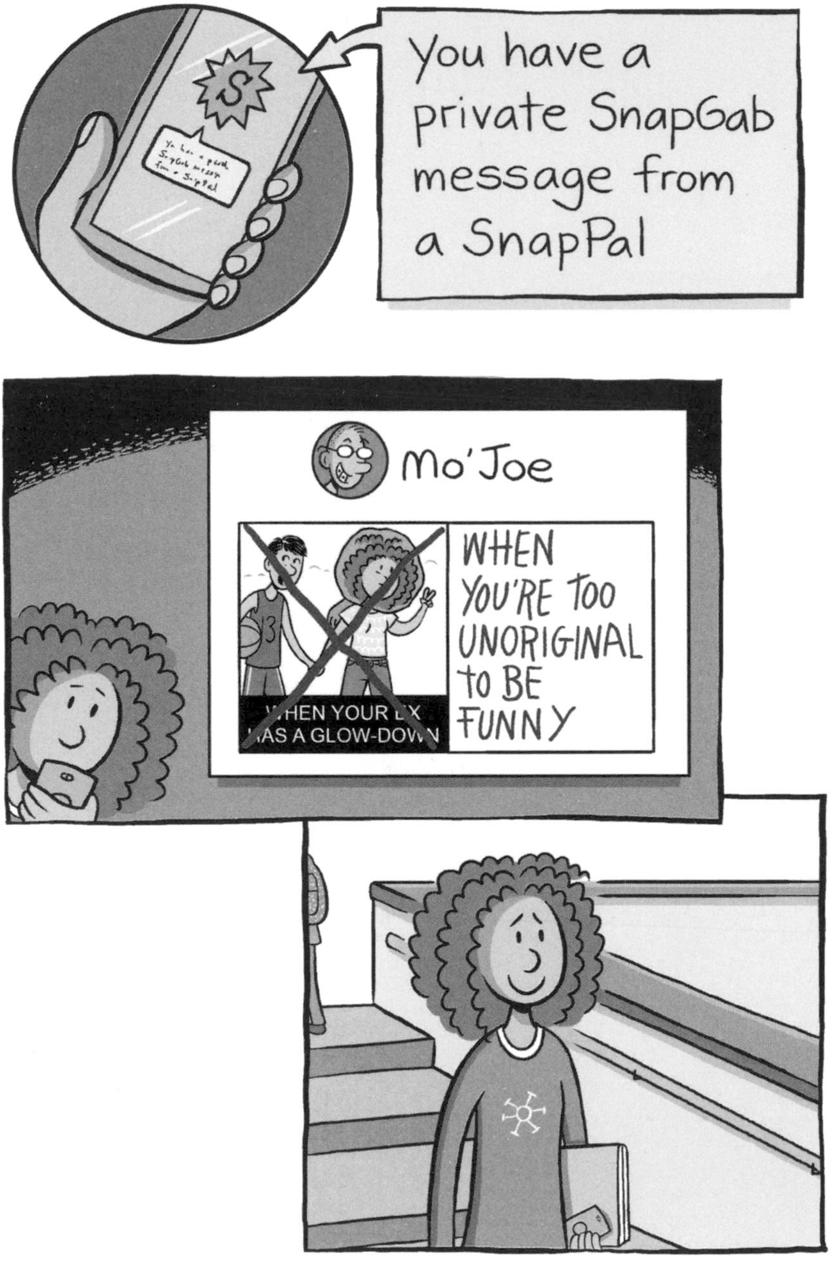
You have a private SnapGab message from a SnapPal
Mo'Joe
WHEN YOUR EX HAS A GLOW-DOWN
WHEN YOU'RE TOO UNORIGINAL TO BE FUNNY

TYLER

It's freezing out. Not looking forward to that bus ride home.

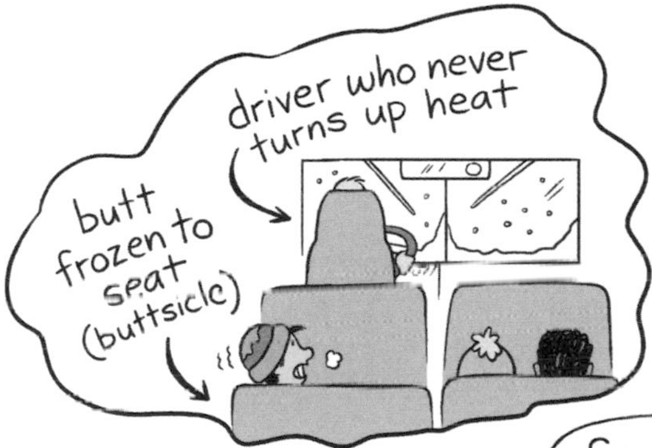
driver who never turns up heat
butt frozen to seat (buttsicle)

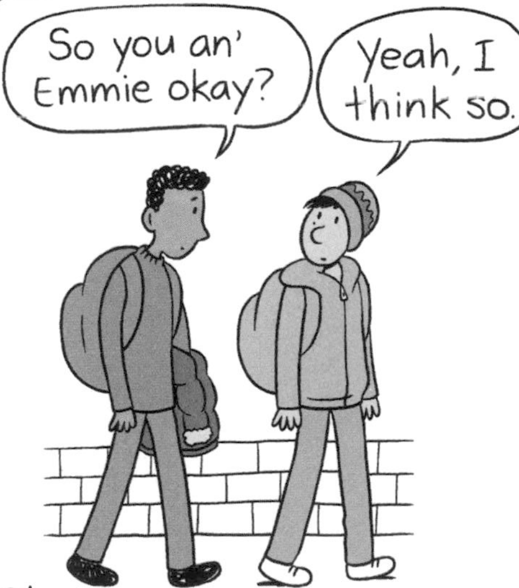
So you an' Emmie okay?
Yeah, I think so.

Anthony nods.

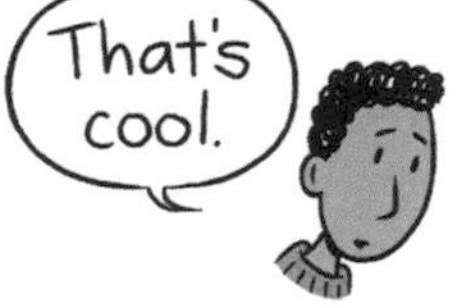
That's cool.

He starts to spit and stops. I think his ex, Nikki Lourde, has influenced him in her subtle way.

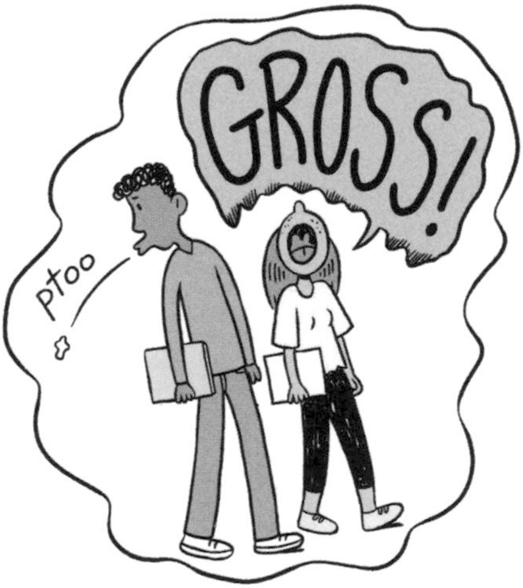
GROSS!
ptoo

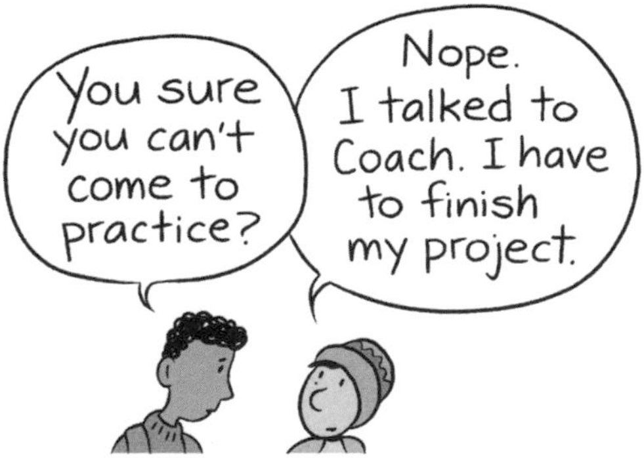
You sure you can't come to practice?
Nope. I talked to Coach. I have to finish my project.

He doesn't say anything.

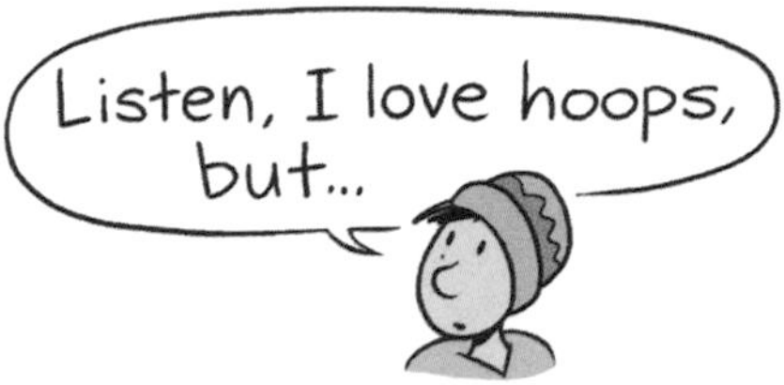
Listen, I love hoops, but...

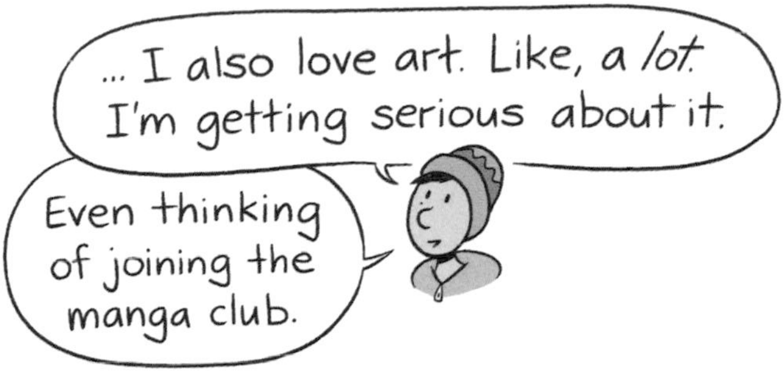
... I also love art. Like, a *lot.* I'm getting serious about it.
Even thinking of joining the manga club.

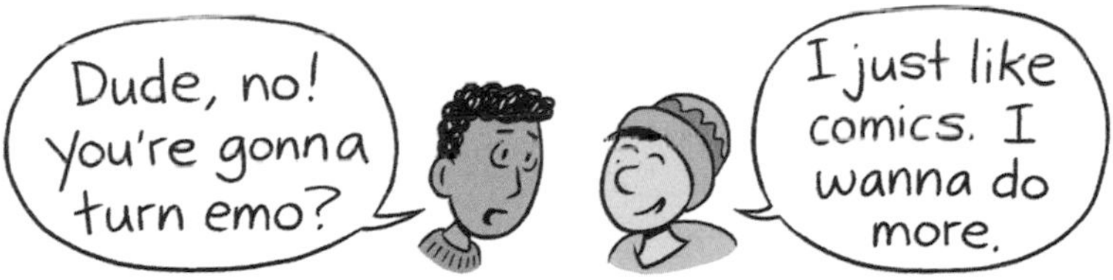
I just like comics. I wanna do more.
Dude, no! You're gonna turn emo?

I think about my dad and his (and everyone else's) expectations about b-ball and grades and stuff. And my own.

Maybe changing those expectations isn't the worst thing. Maybe even benching it for a game or two wouldn't be the worst, either.

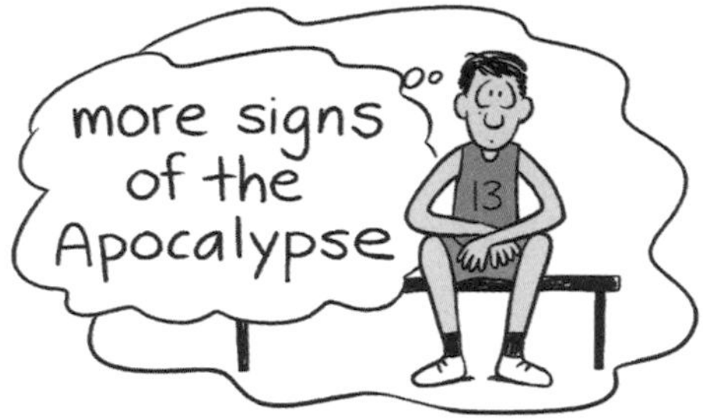
more signs of the Apocalypse
13

I just wanna stop all the pressure I'm putting on myself and go back to **enjoying** basketball . . . like art.

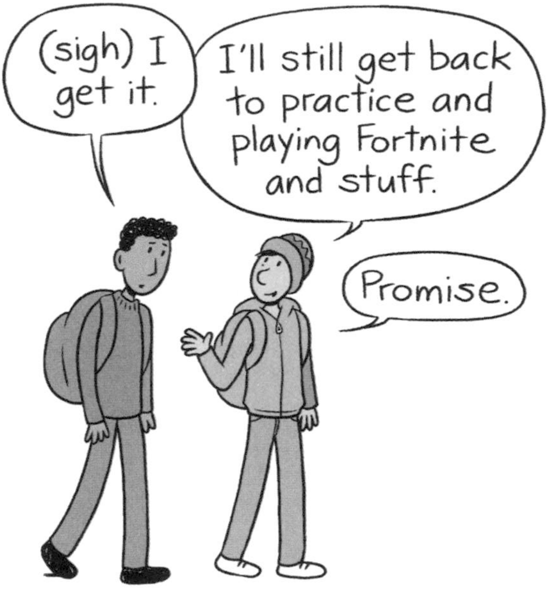
(sigh) I get it.
I'll still get back to practice and playing Fortnite and stuff.
Promise.

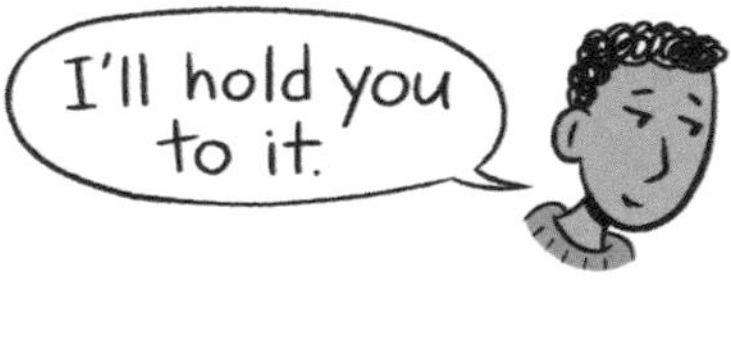
I'll hold you to it.

We split up. He heads down to the gym and I head out the door, when . . .

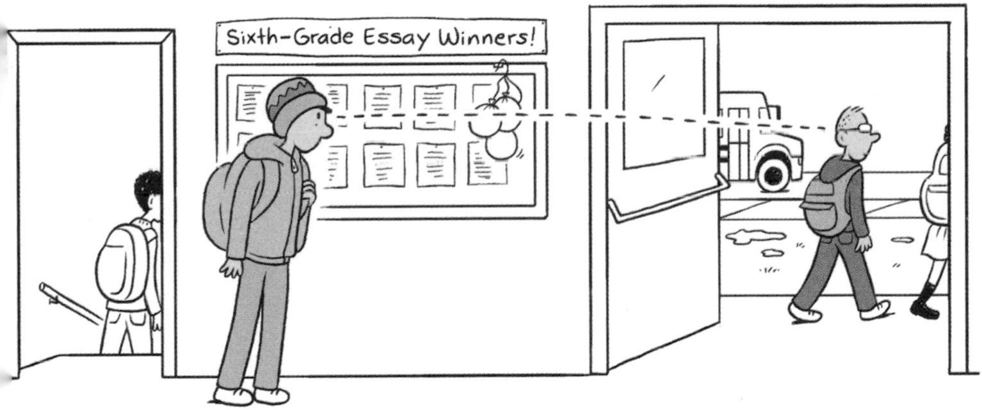
Sixth-Grade Essay Winners!

I hurry to catch up.

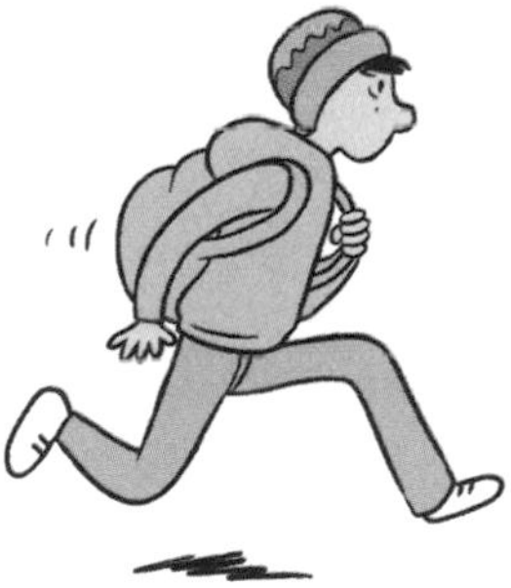

There's something I've gotta ask him.

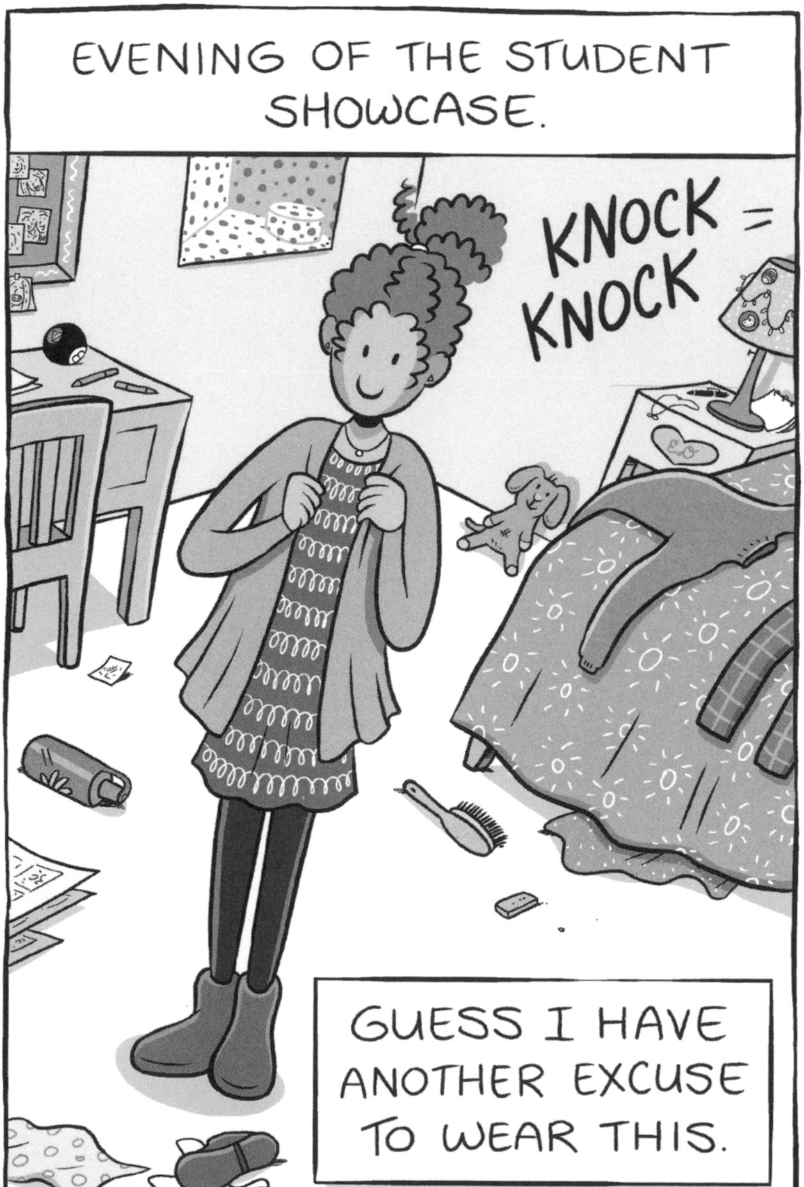
EVENING OF THE STUDENT SHOWCASE.
KNOCK KNOCK
GUESS I HAVE ANOTHER EXCUSE TO WEAR THIS.

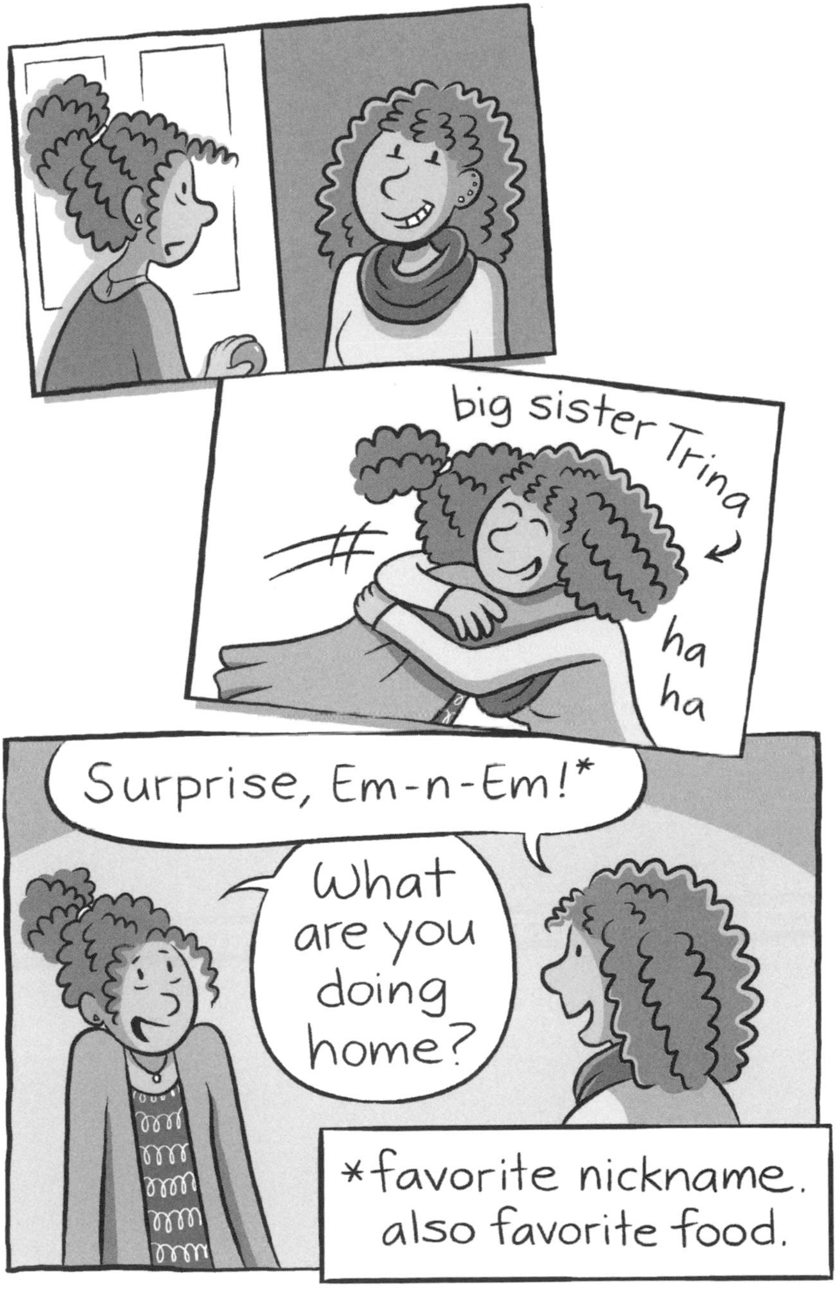
big sister Trina
ha
ha
Surprise, Em-n-Em!*
What are you doing home?
*favorite nickname. also favorite food.

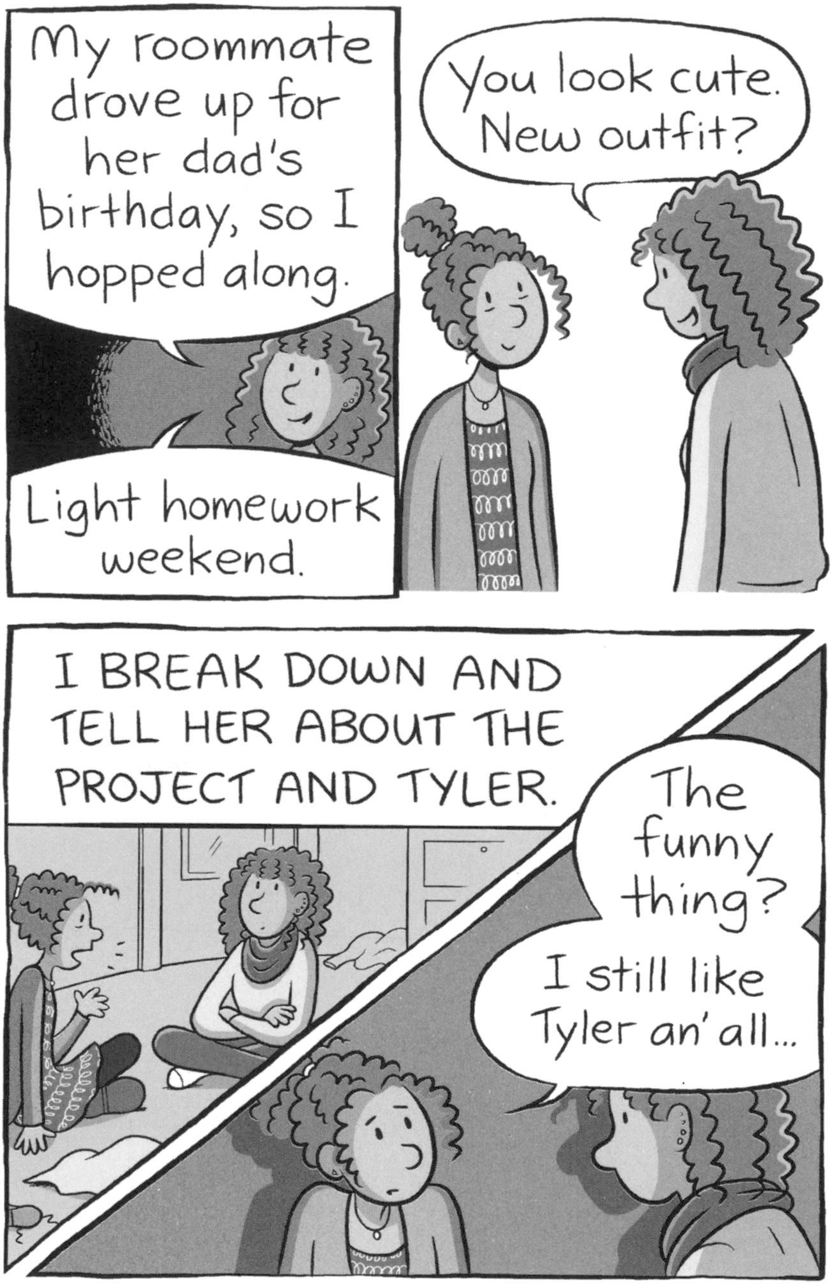
My roommate drove up for her dad's birthday, so I hopped along.
Light homework weekend.
You look cute. New outfit?
I BREAK DOWN AND TELL HER ABOUT THE PROJECT AND TYLER.
The funny thing?
I still like Tyler an' all...

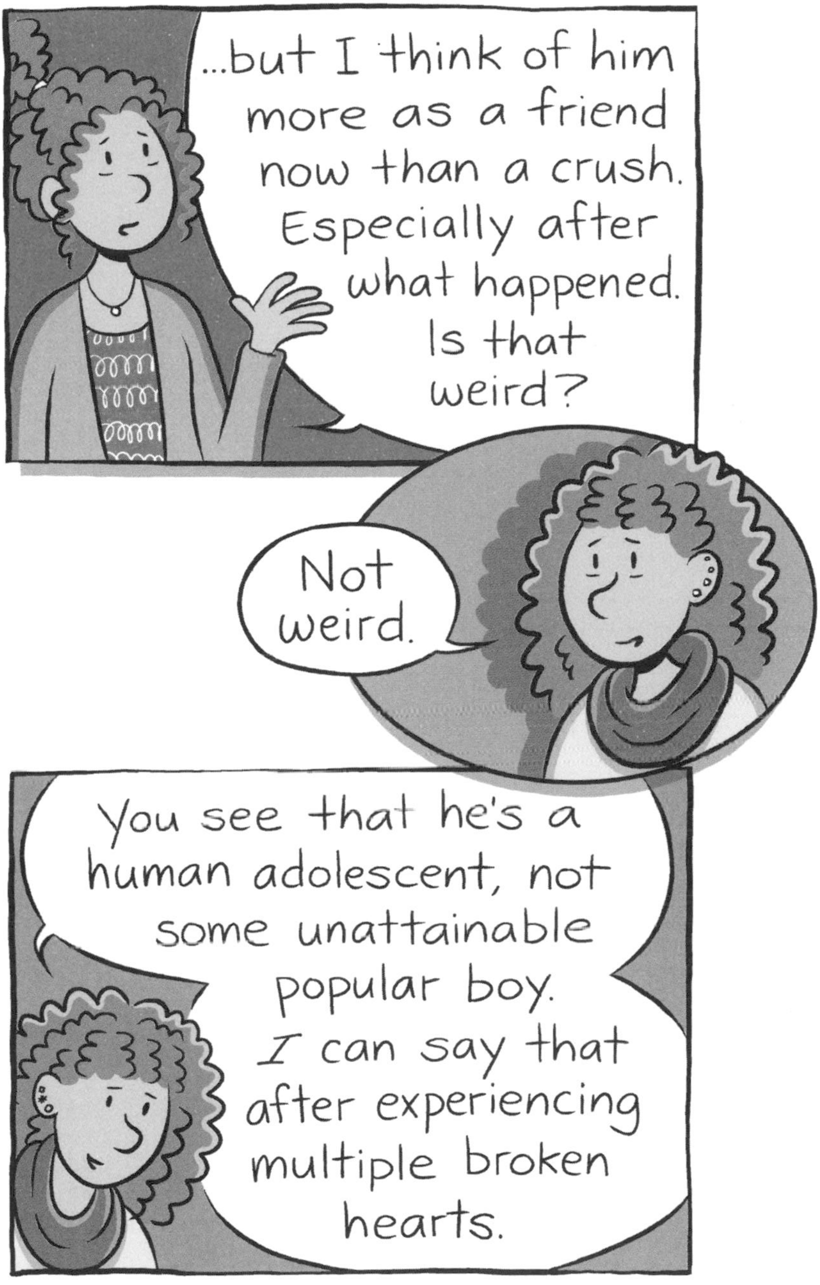

...but I think of him more as a friend now than a crush. Especially after what happened. Is that weird?
Not weird.
You see that he's a human adolescent, not some unattainable popular boy. *I* can say that after experiencing multiple broken hearts.

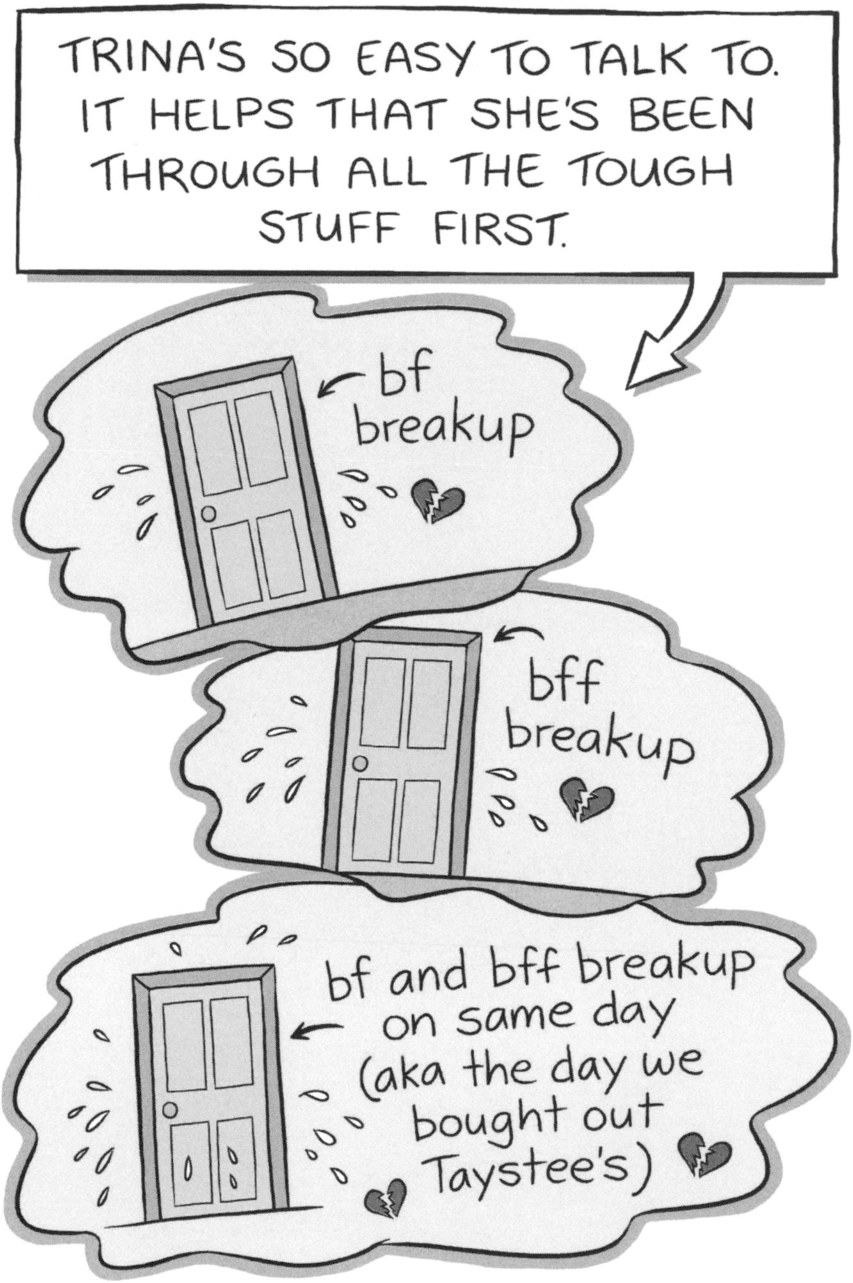
TRINA'S SO EASY TO TALK TO. IT HELPS THAT SHE'S BEEN THROUGH ALL THE TOUGH STUFF FIRST.
bf breakup
bff breakup
bf and bff breakup on same day (aka the day we bought out Taystee's)

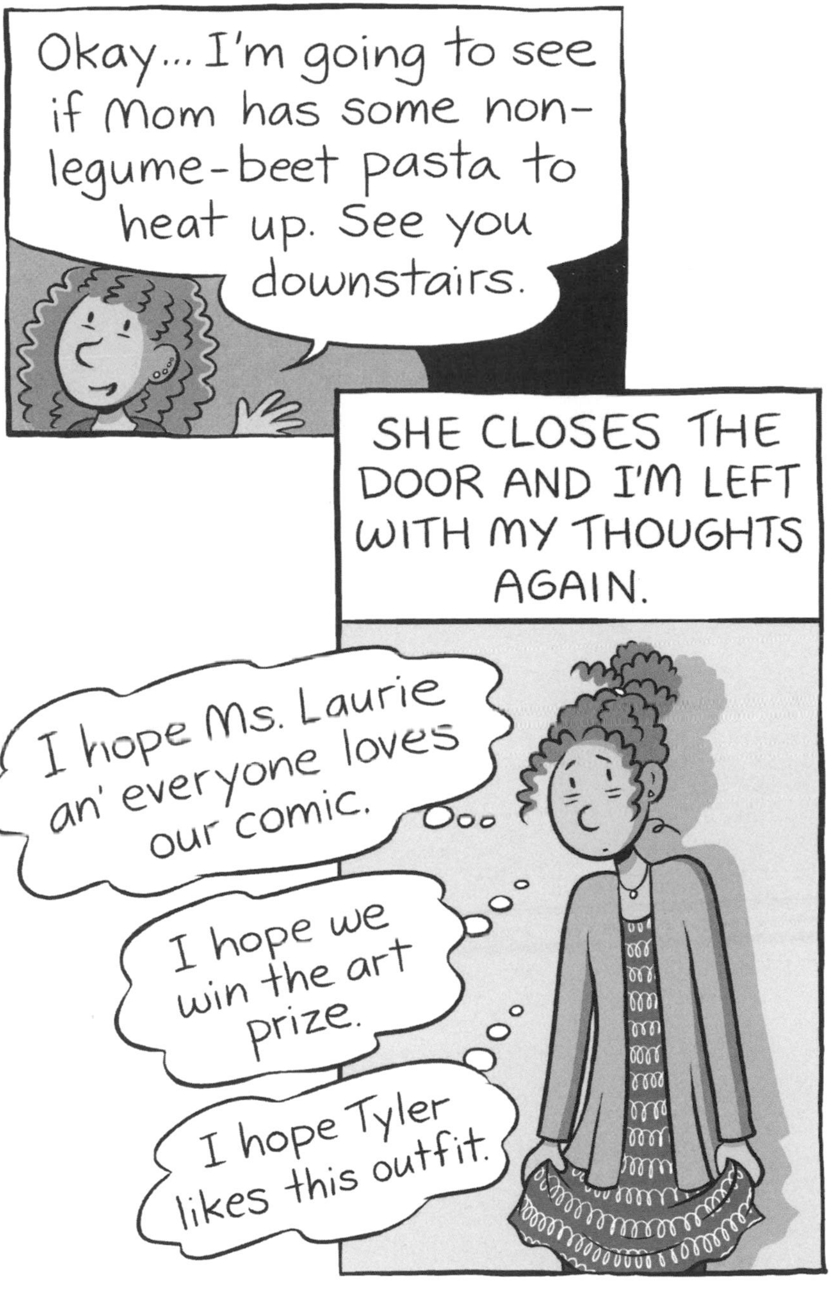
Okay... I'm going to see if Mom has some non-legume-beet pasta to heat up. See you downstairs.
SHE CLOSES THE DOOR AND I'M LEFT WITH MY THOUGHTS AGAIN.
I hope Ms. Laurie an' everyone loves our comic.
I hope we win the art prize.
I hope Tyler likes this outfit.

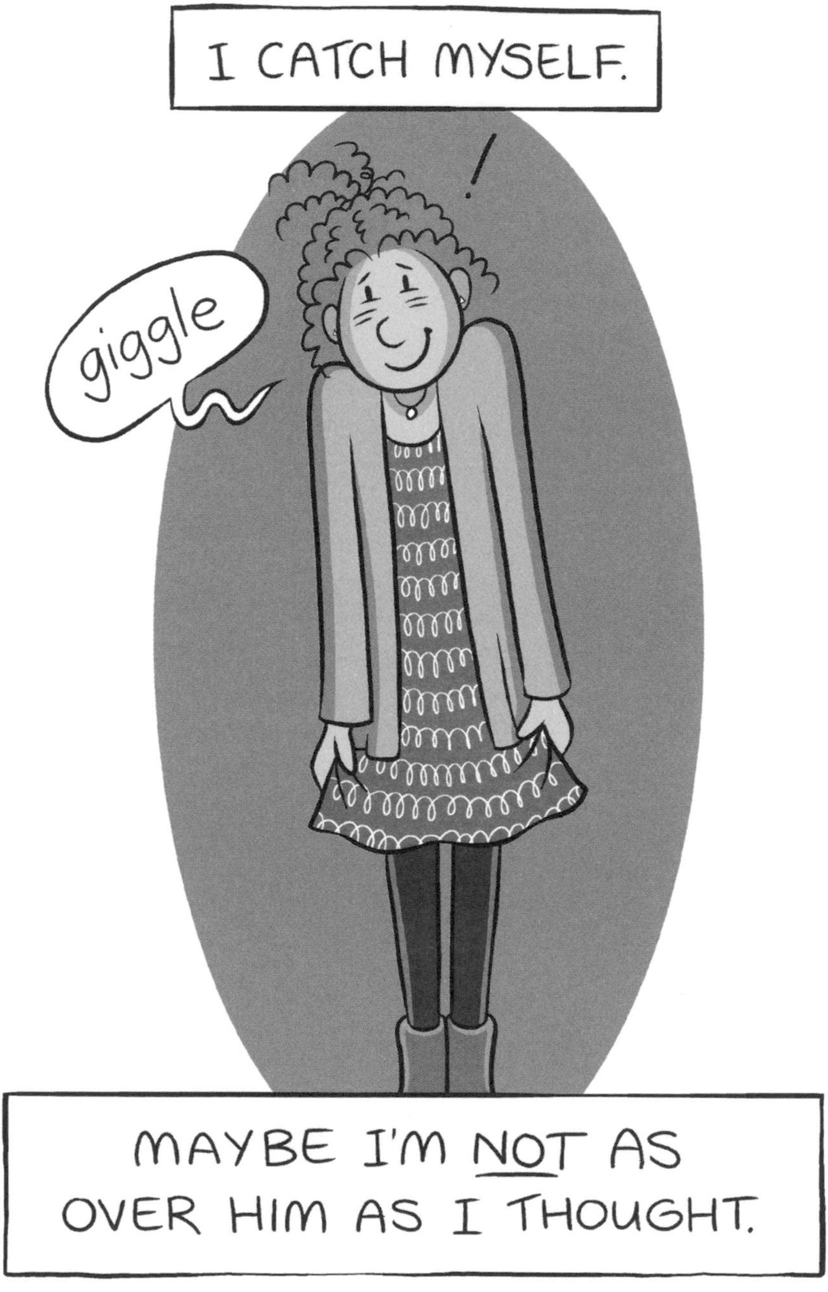
I CATCH MYSELF.
!
giggle
MAYBE I'M NOT AS OVER HIM AS I THOUGHT.

TYLER

Everyone and their brother are here at the Student Showcase. Even my **own** brother. I thought my mom forced him to come, but weirdly, he seems to want to be here. We just walked through all the other arts and academic showcases.

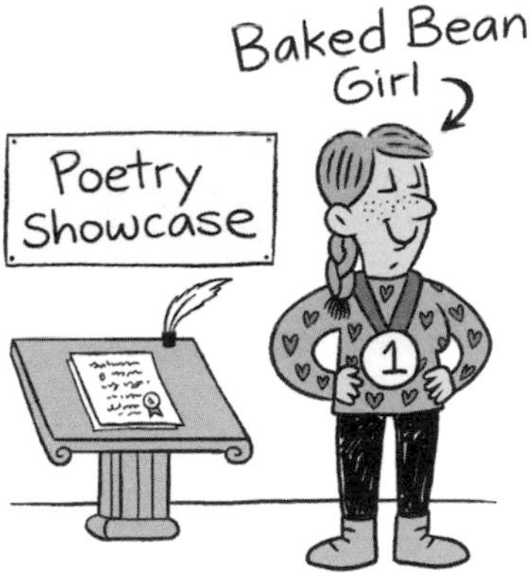
Baked Bean Girl
Poetry Showcase
1

I proudly lead my mom and Zach to our comic book, which sits on a long table with everyone else's. People are allowed to look through.

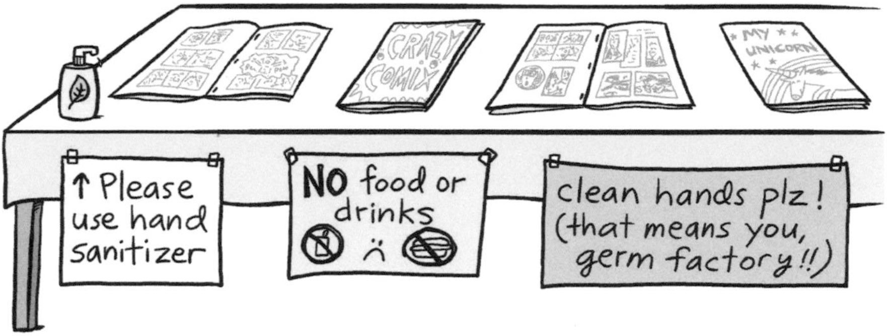
CRAZY COMIX
MY UNICORN
↑ Please use hand sanitizer
NO food or drinks
clean hands plz! (that means you, germ factory!!)

I think we have a good chance at the prize. I'm no longer wishing for that as much as **some** people, but still.

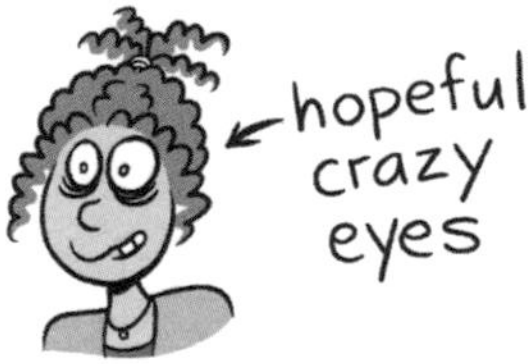
hopeful crazy eyes

Ms. Laurie will be here soon. She's going to announce the winners for best comic (by grade). Meanwhile, Anthony, Joe, Jaime, Maya, and a few other kids come to look at ours. Emmie's friend Brianna is here, too. Guess she won the science award.

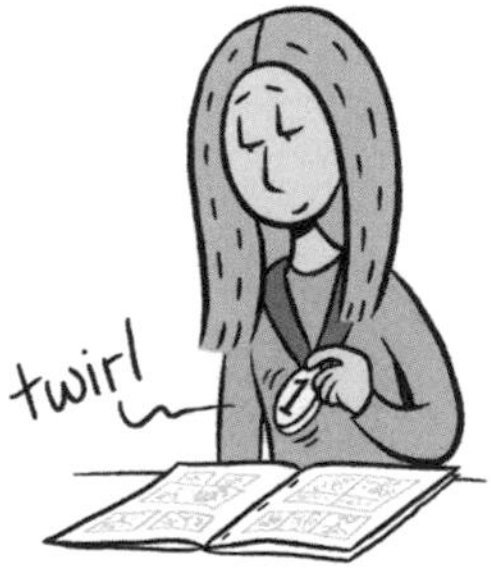
twirl

But everyone's waiting around awkwardly, 'cause Zach (to my shock) is leafing through our comic book, appearing to read every single word.

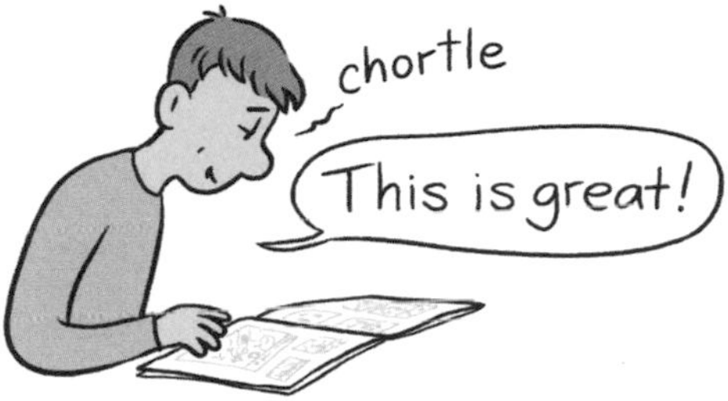
chortle
This is great!

Emmie looks like she might faint. She never met Zach, but she knows he's really popular and a basketball star. Also, he's not bad-looking.

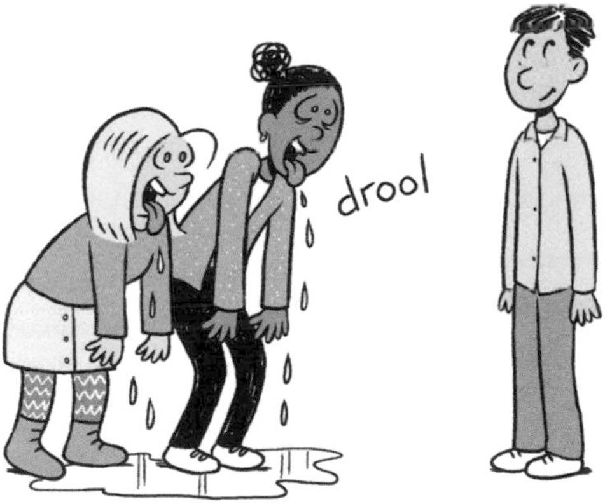
drool

Meanwhile, my mom—who doesn't get out much—is clearly enjoying being around other adults.

hat head

talking Anthony's parents' ears off

(may be asleep)

Emmie's parents and older sister are here. I don't know Trina, but Emmie's told me about both siblings. They're usually away at college, so she always feels like an only child. Makes me kinda glad Zach's still around, even if he's busy.

But here's the thing.

He's been different lately. He's still busy, but he takes more time to ask me about school and stuff and even promised to come to one of our practices next week.

WOO! YEAH! WOOT!

Hallway talk = breakthrough

Plus he's **here**, which is something. Or maybe he just likes the ego trip.

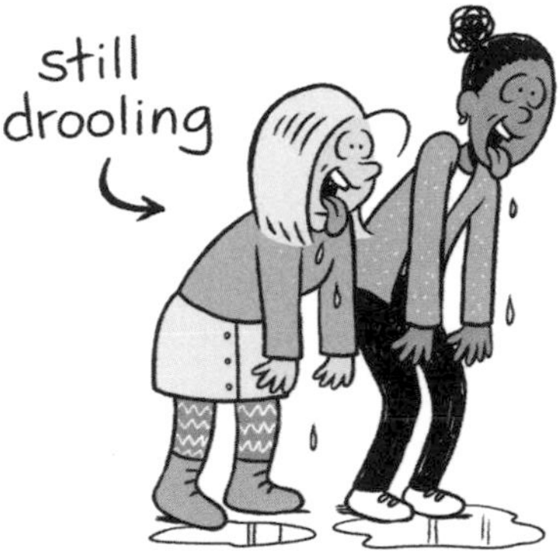
still
drooling

Ms. Laurie finally arrives to announce the winners. She's holding the mystery envelopes.

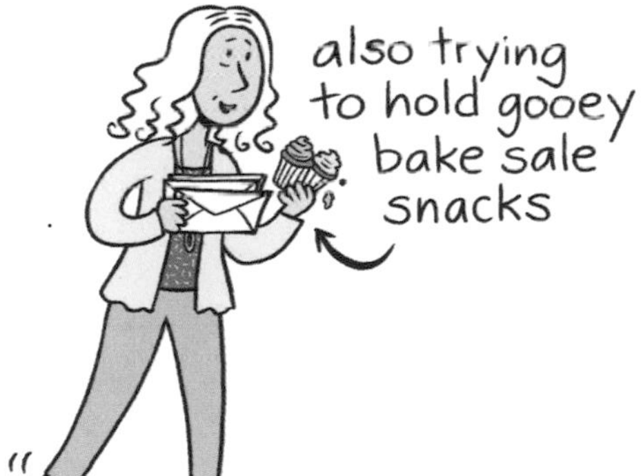
also trying
to hold gooey
bake sale
snacks

Suddenly, I'm kinda nervous.

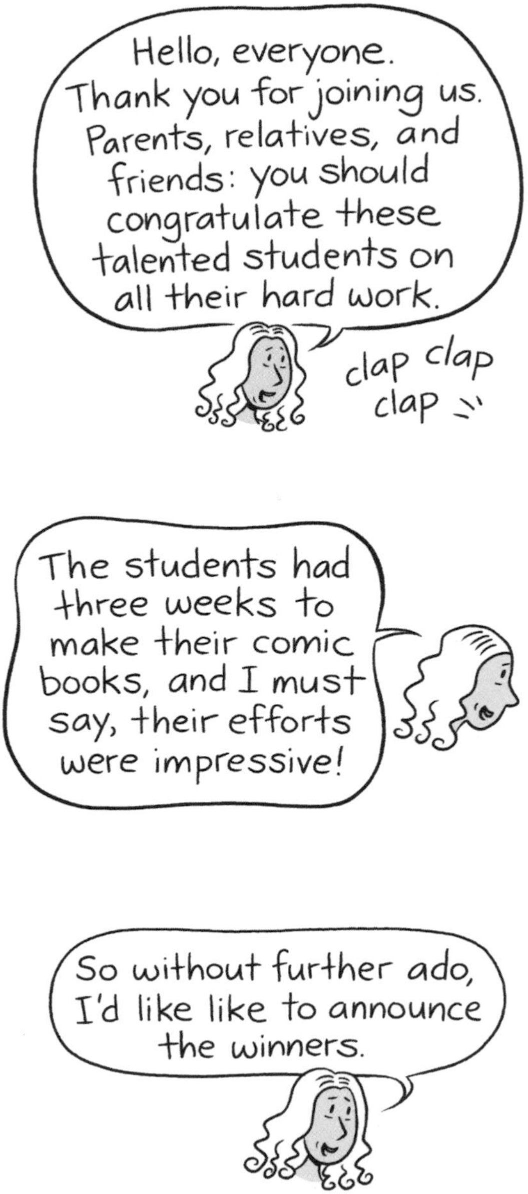
Hello, everyone. Thank you for joining us. Parents, relatives, and friends: you should congratulate these talented students on all their hard work.
clap clap clap
The students had three weeks to make their comic books, and I must say, their efforts were impressive!
So without further ado, I'd like like to announce the winners.

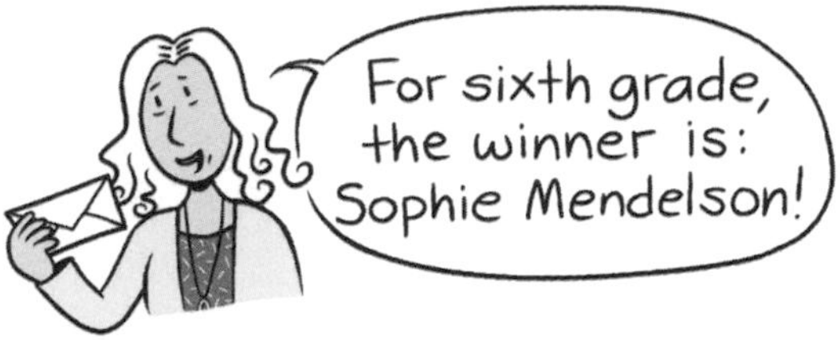
For sixth grade, the winner is: Sophie Mendelson!

A tiny sixth grader with a long braid excitedly takes the envelope and thanks Ms. Laurie. She tears it open before she even gets back to her parents.

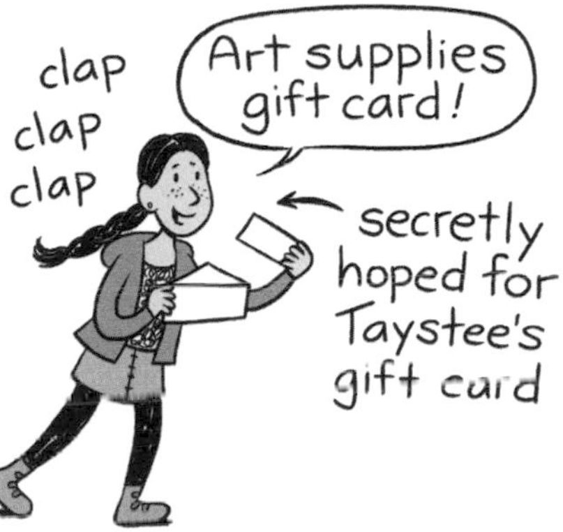
clap
clap
clap
Art supplies gift card!
secretly hoped for Taystee's gift card

I glance at Emmie, who looks like she's ready to tackle that girl for her prize.

Ms. Laurie clears her throat.

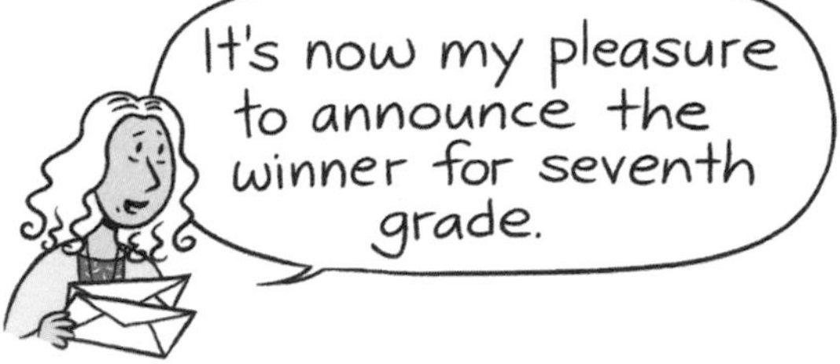
It's now my pleasure to announce the winner for seventh grade.

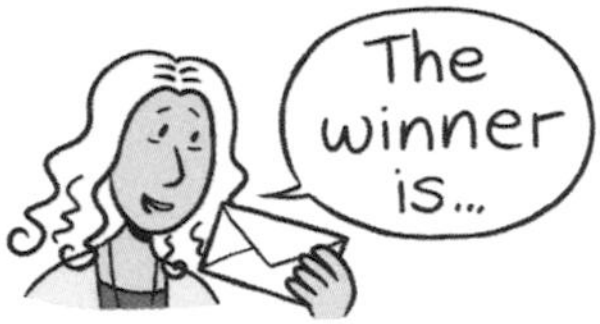
The winner is...

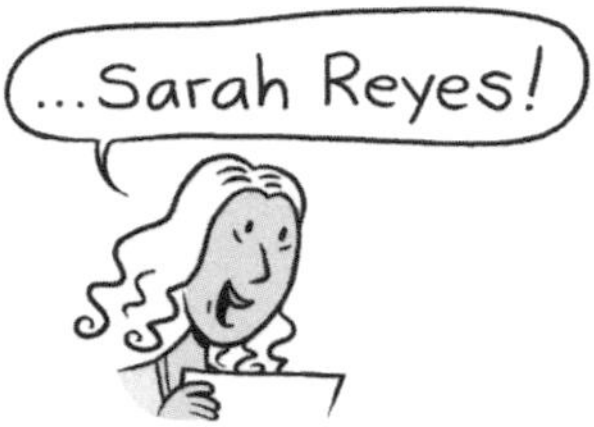
...Sarah Reyes!

My stomach drops with disappointment.

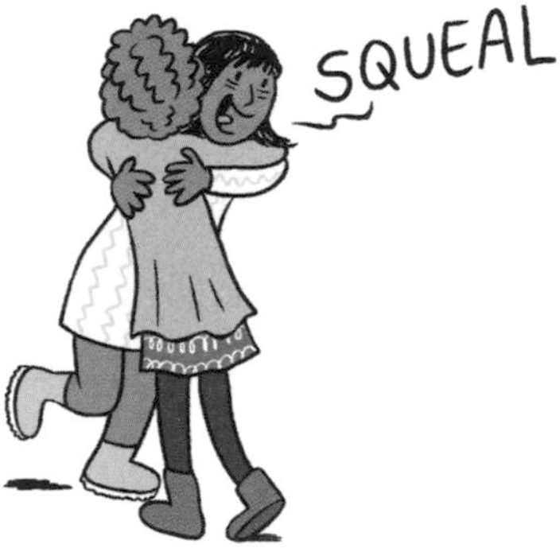
SQUEAL

Anthony gives me a consoling nudge.

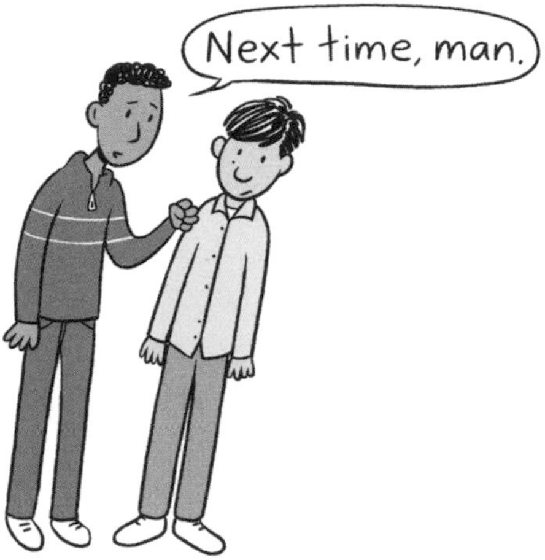
Next time, man.

My mom squeezes my shoulder and Zach says, "Tough break, Ty."

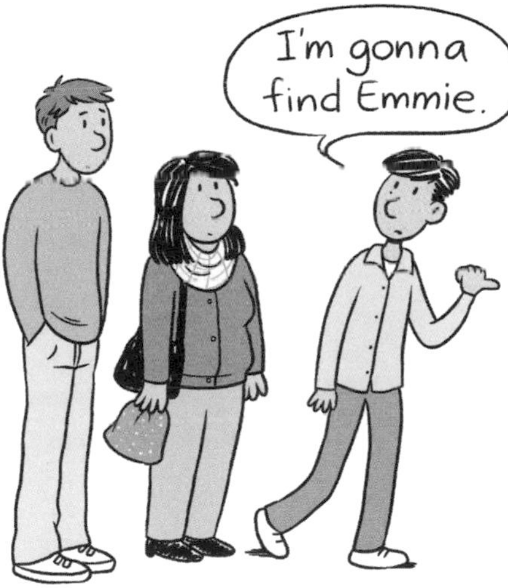
I'm gonna find Emmie.

While Ms. Laurie announces the eighth-grade prize, I cross the hall to Emmie. She's alone. Bri is at the water fountain and Emmie's family is checking out the art.

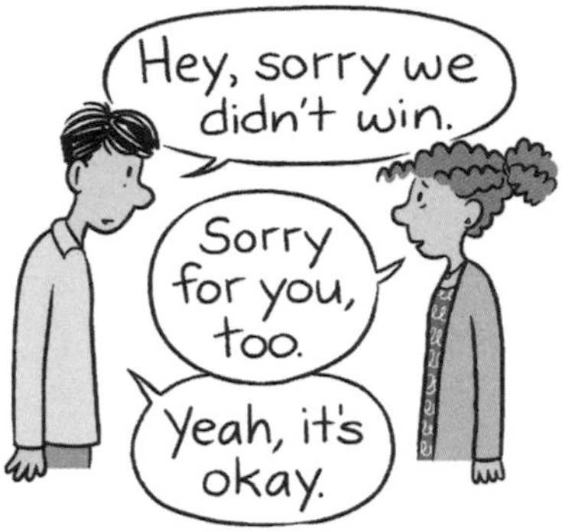
Hey, sorry we didn't win.
Sorry for you, too.
Yeah, it's okay.

And I mean it. For some reason, losing doesn't bother me that much.

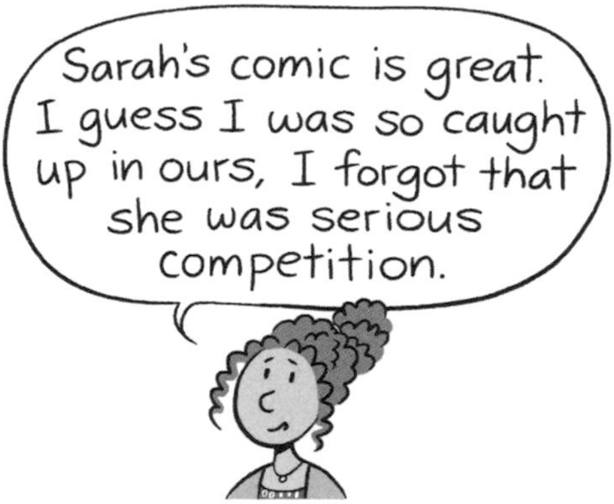
Sarah's comic is great. I guess I was so caught up in ours, I forgot that she was serious competition.

She smiles, and something unexpected happens.

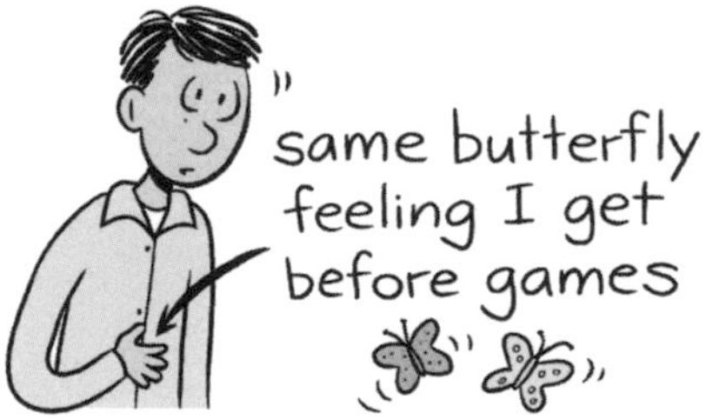
same butterfly feeling I get before games

Whoa. What was **that**?

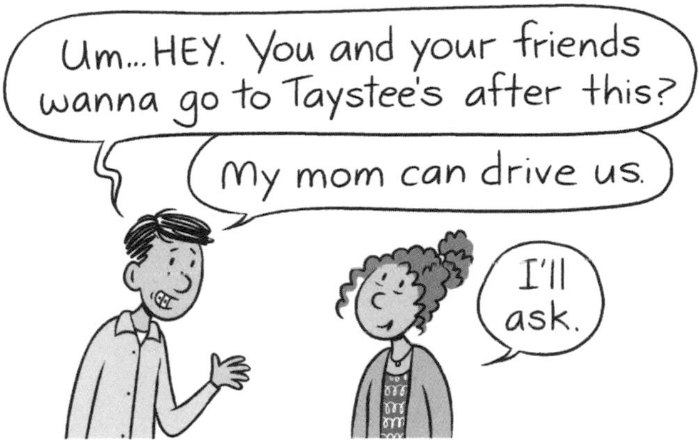
Um...HEY. You and your friends wanna go to Taystee's after this?
My mom can drive us.
I'll ask.

She goes to talk to her parents and Brianna.

Joe wanders over.

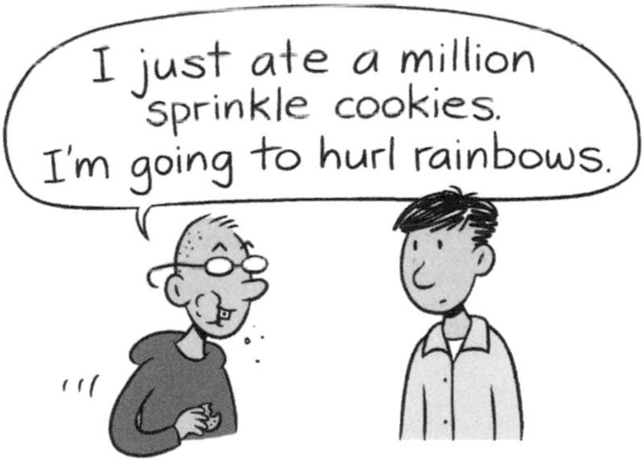
I just ate a million sprinkle cookies. I'm going to hurl rainbows.

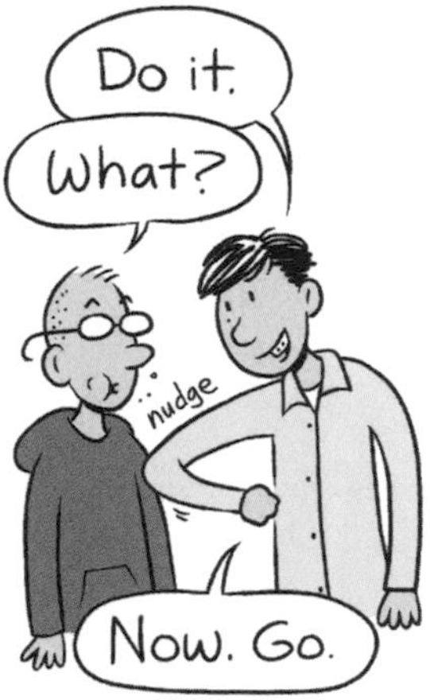
Do it.
What?
nudge
Now. Go.

I nod at someone across the hall.

It dawns on him. He looks like he'd rather get kicked in the head by a yeti. But he gulps once and crosses the hall.

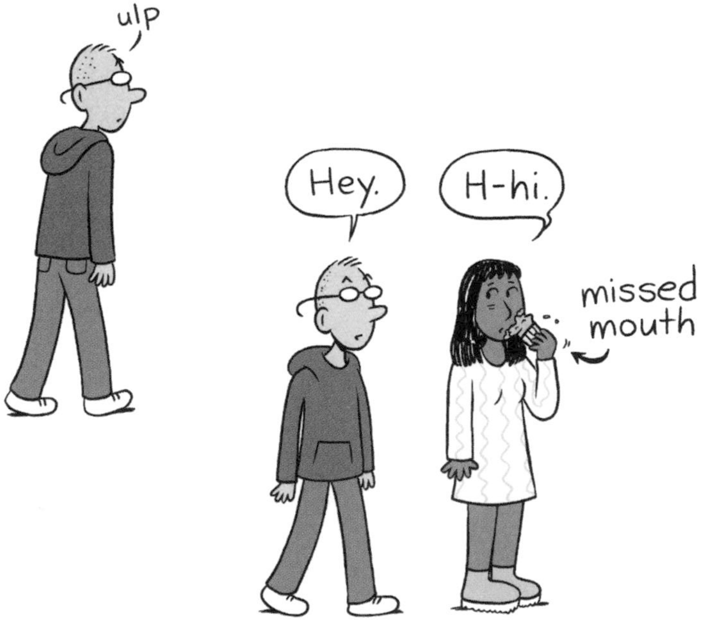
ulp
Hey.
H-hi.
missed mouth

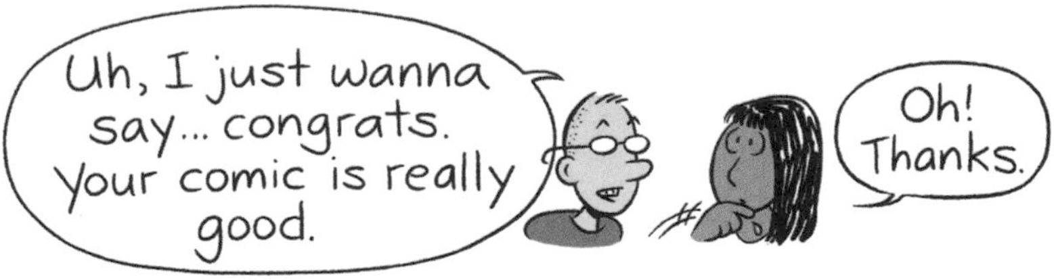
Uh, I just wanna say... congrats. Your comic is really good.
Oh! Thanks.

She stares at Joe, probably wondering what decent spirit took over his body.

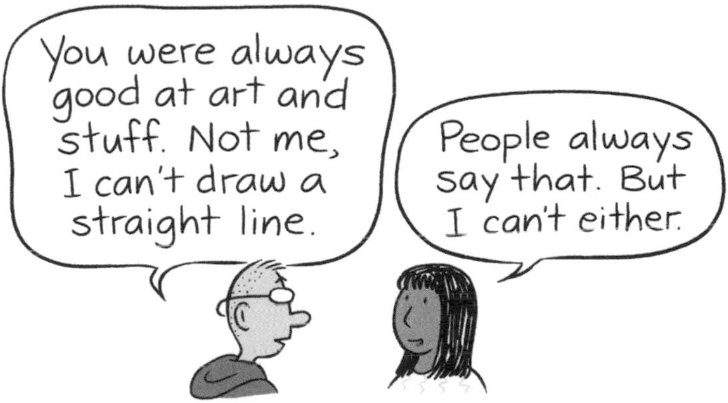
You were always good at art and stuff. Not me, I can't draw a straight line.
People always say that. But I can't either.

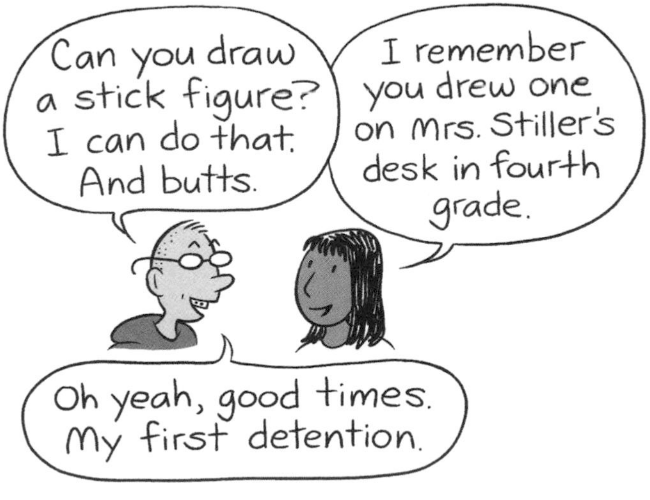
Can you draw a stick figure? I can do that. And butts.
I remember you drew one on Mrs. Stiller's desk in fourth grade.
Oh yeah, good times. My first detention.

They keep talking. I notice they're the exact same height.

I had thought about how Joe kept trying to get Sarah's attention. And how it was different from the way he usually acted. It was almost like he kept trying to . . . compliment her or something. In his twisted Joe way.

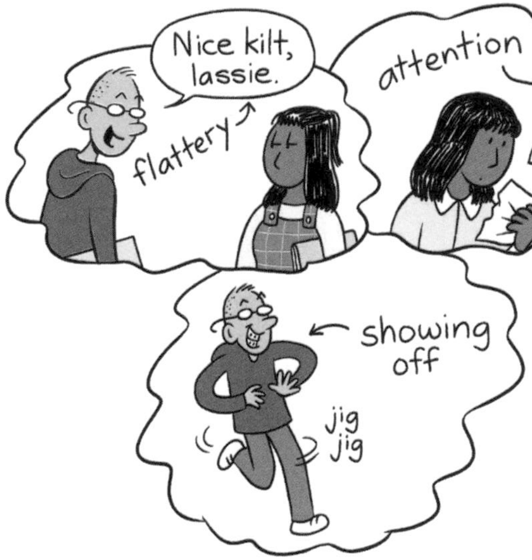
Nice kilt, lassie.
flattery
attention
Hi Lass!
jig
showing off
jig jig

I finally got it out of him.

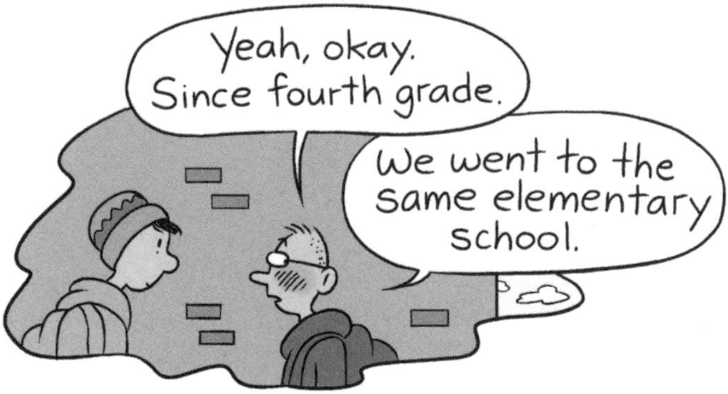
Yeah, okay. Since fourth grade.
We went to the same elementary school.

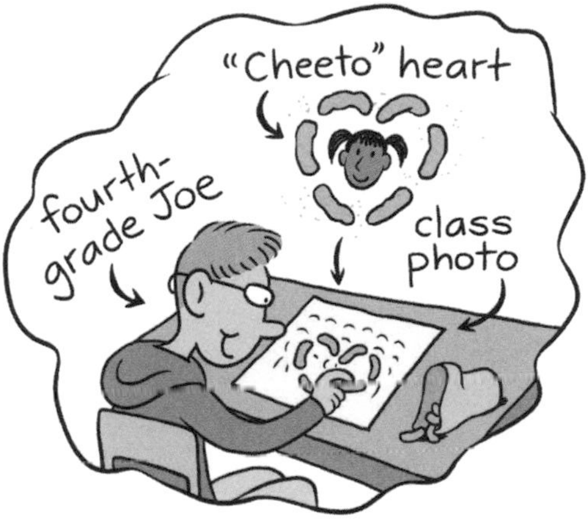
"Cheeto" heart
fourth-grade Joe
class photo

Surprising, since they seem so opposite. But crushes are unpredictable.

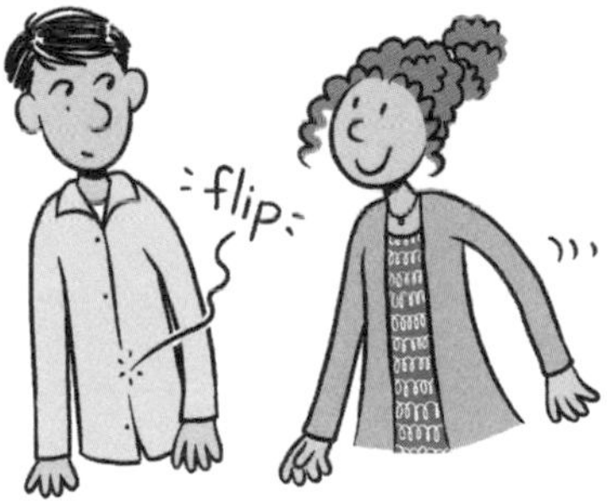
flip

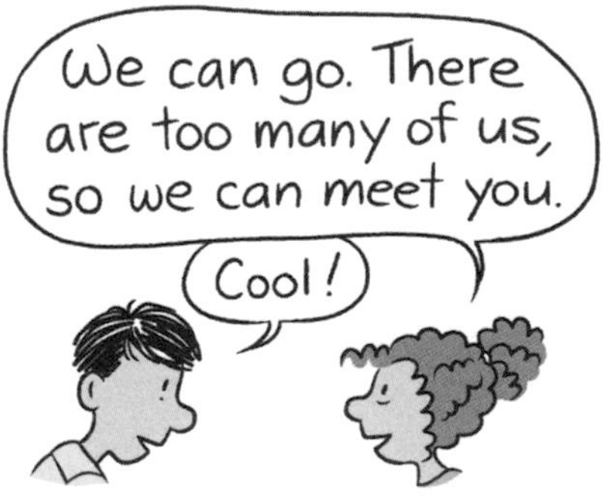
We can go. There are too many of us, so we can meet you.
Cool!

I hold up my hand. Emmie high-fives mine.

Ms. Laurie walks over, nibbling a brownie. I think that's her fourth one. The woman can really put 'em away.

Hi, guys. Well done! I wanted to let you know it was really close.

You should be pleased with your project. Good teamwork.

We tell her we are.

Consolation prize! I got these from the cupcake table. Shh, don't tell the others.

We laugh as she hands us a secret stash of mini cupcakes. Then she joins some parents.

I feel my phone buzz in my back pocket. I check. It's my dad on FaceTime. I'm kinda surprised and excited he remembered the Showcase.

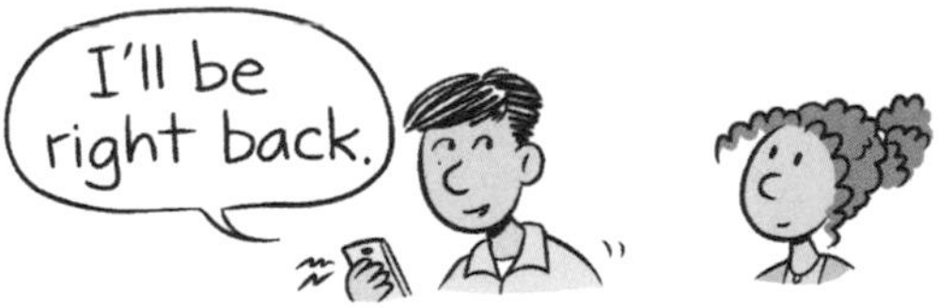
I'll be right back.

I walk around the corner to a quieter hall.

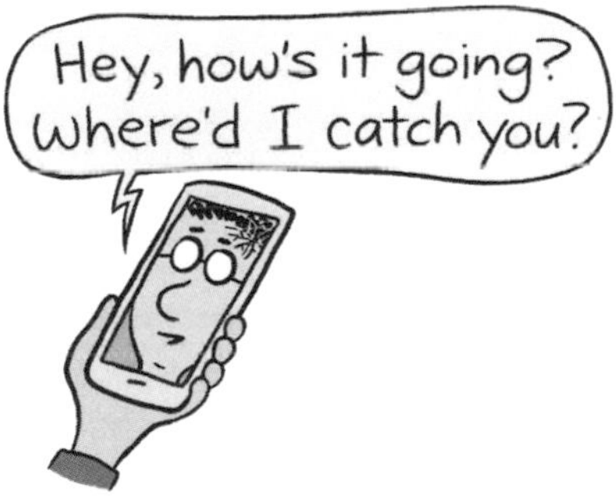
Hey, how's it going? Where'd I catch you?

My heart sinks. He forgot.

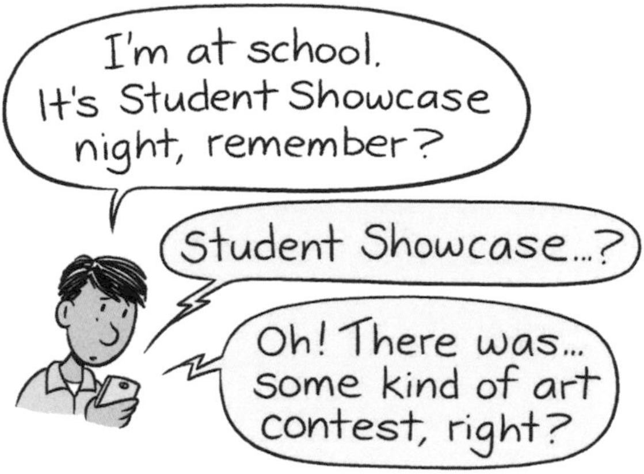
I'm at school. It's Student Showcase night, remember?
Student Showcase...?
Oh! There was... some kind of art contest, right?

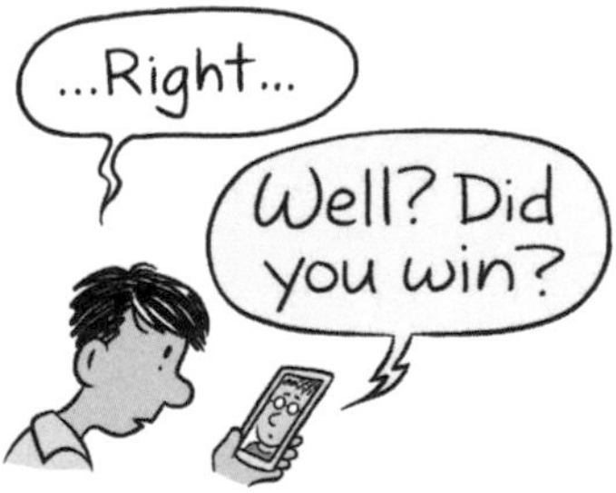
...Right...
Well? Did you win?

I groan to myself. I know it was just a question. And I no longer care that we didn't win. But he didn't even remember what it was that could win. That "it" was a comic book. And that I teamed up with Emmie. And that I worked my butt off for weeks.

But I try to let it slide.

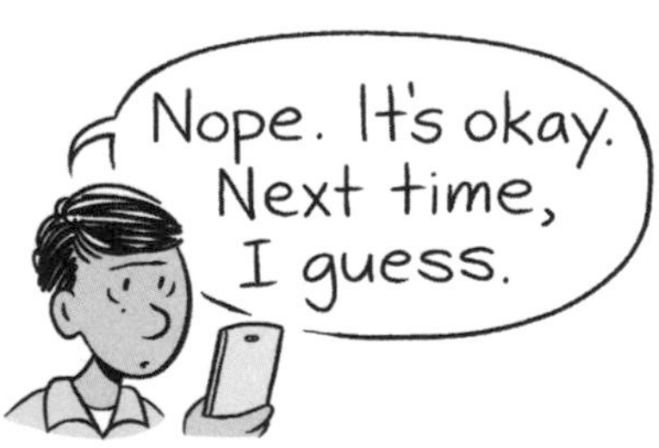
Nope. It's okay. Next time, I guess.

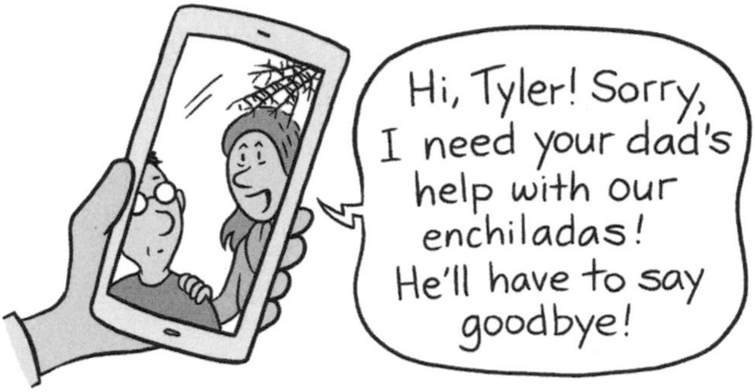
Hi, Tyler! Sorry, I need your dad's help with our enchiladas! He'll have to say goodbye!

Unbelievable.

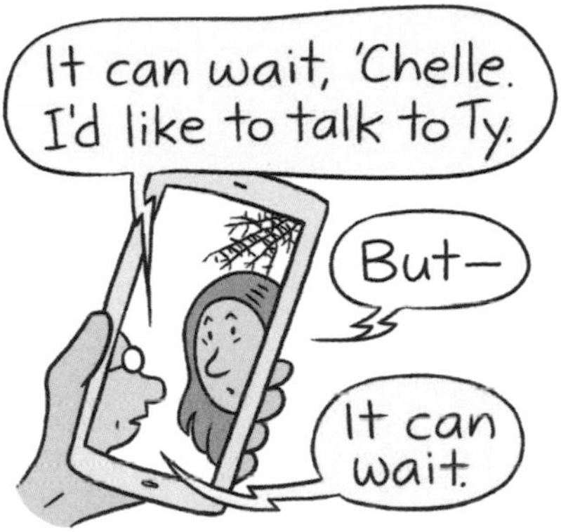
It can wait, 'Chelle. I'd like to talk to Ty.
But—
It can wait.

I can't believe he finally stood up to her.

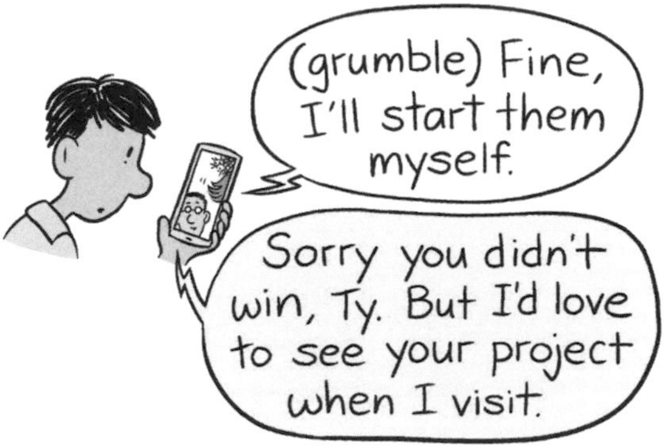
(grumble) Fine, I'll start them myself.
Sorry you didn't win, Ty. But I'd love to see your project when I visit.

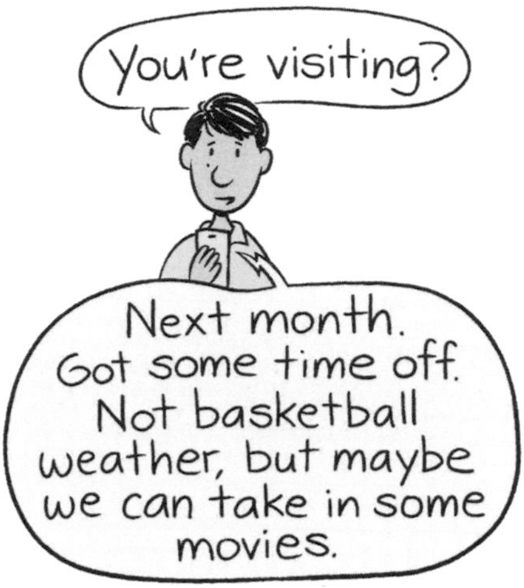
You're visiting?
Next month. Got some time off. Not basketball weather, but maybe we can take in some movies.

I cheer up instantly. That was not what I expected.

We talk a minute longer until I hear my name called. Mom.

I realize everyone is waiting.

(not so patiently)

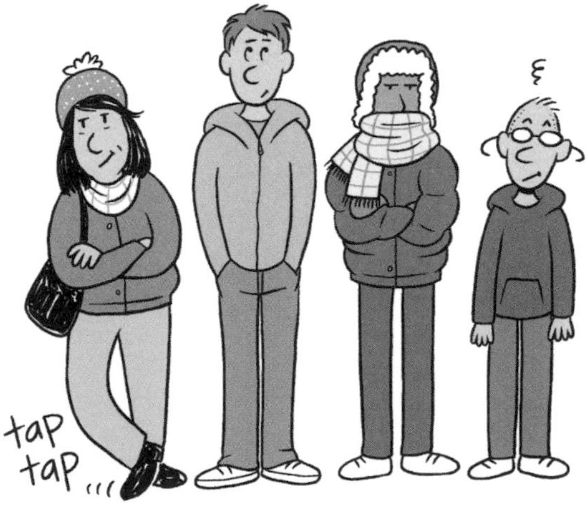
tap
tap...

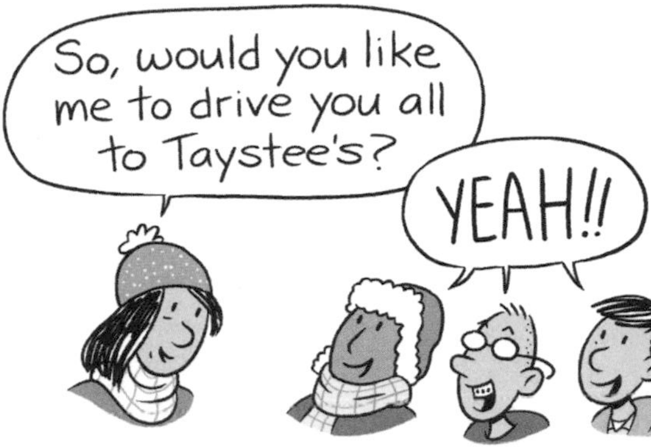
So, would you like me to drive you all to Taystee's?
YEAH!!

My drooling reflex kicks in at the thought of a double-fudge brownie sundae. Nice of Ms. Laurie, but those teeny cupcakes didn't cut it.

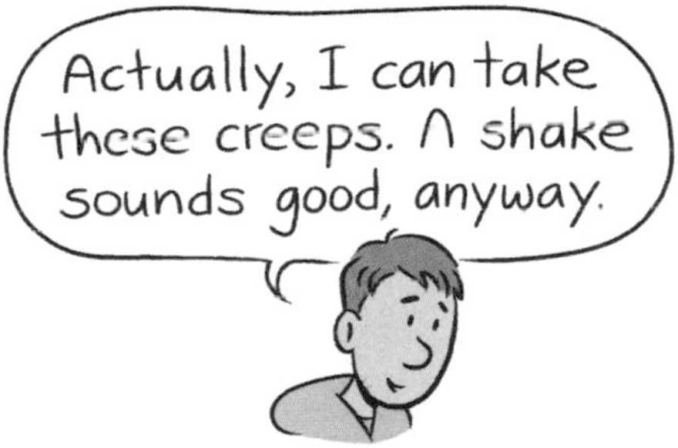
Actually, I can take these creeps. A shake sounds good, anyway.

Also not what I expected. I know there's an ulterior motive of shake and SUV privileges, but still.

We head through the front door. I look at everyone and think:

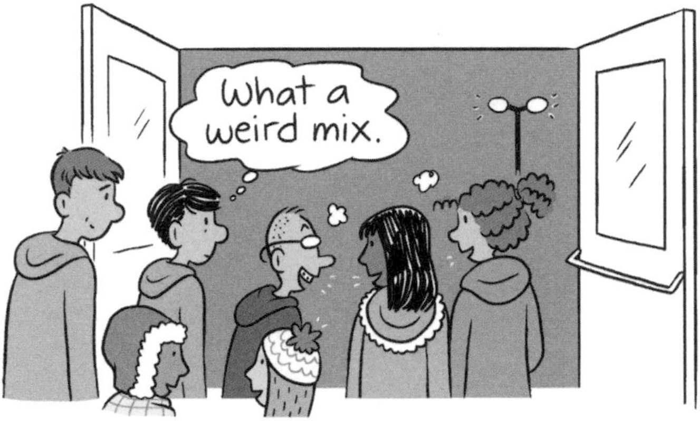
What a weird mix.

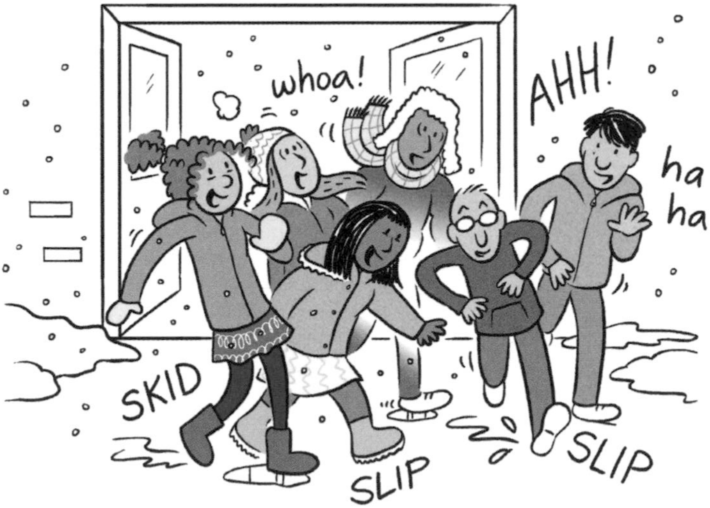
whoa!
AHH!
ha ha
SKID
SLIP
SLIP

But sometimes . . .

. . . weird feels just right.

EPILOGUE

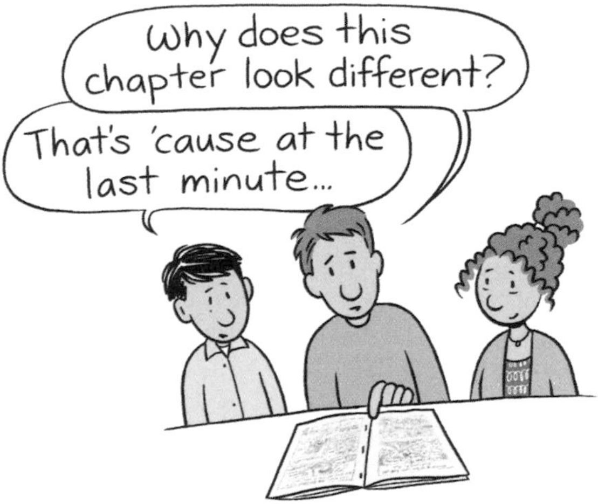
Why does this chapter look different?
That's 'cause at the last minute...

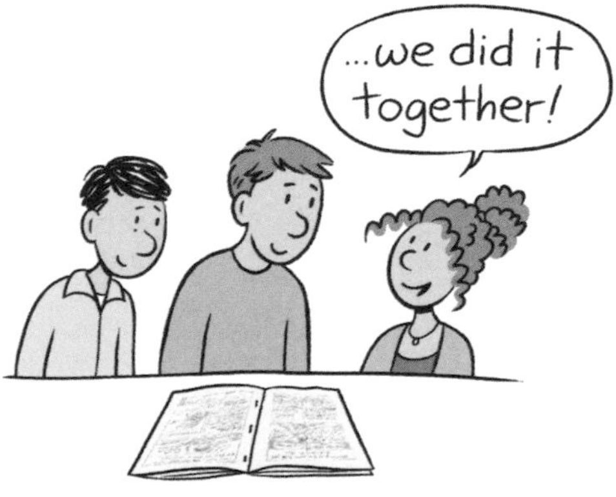
...we did it together!

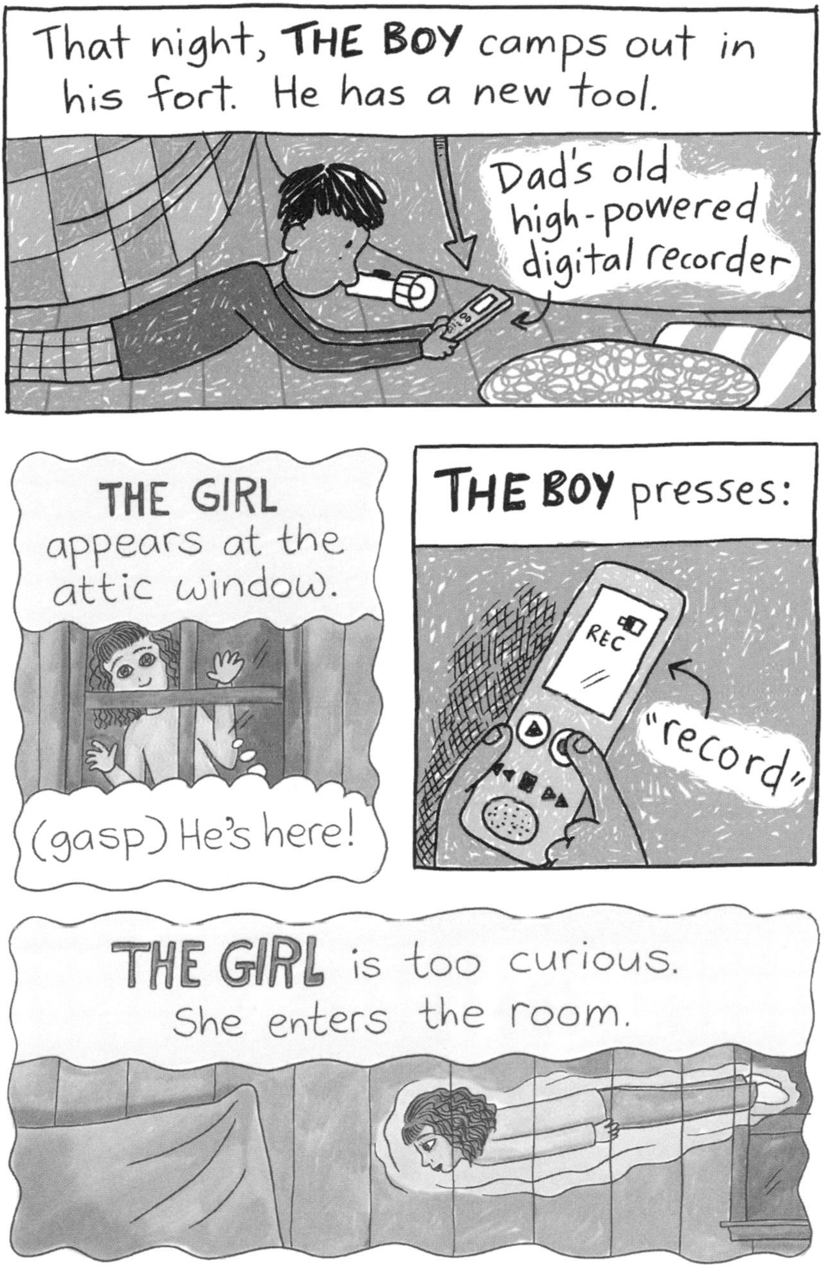

That night, THE BOY camps out in his fort. He has a new tool.
Dad's old high-powered digital recorder
THE GIRL appears at the attic window.
(gasp) He's here!
THE BOY presses:
REC
"record"
THE GIRL is too curious. She enters the room.

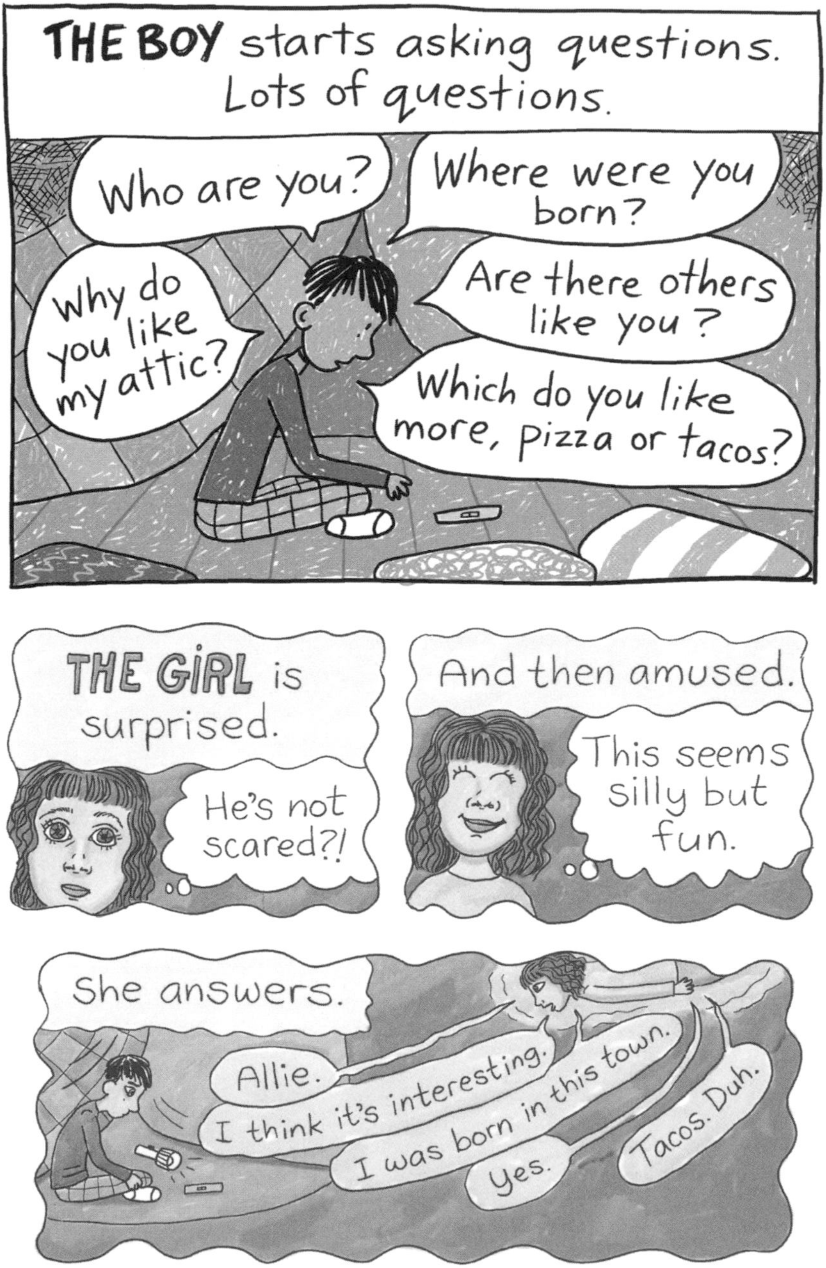
THE BOY starts asking questions. Lots of questions.
Who are you?
Where were you born?
Why do you like my attic?
Are there others like you?
Which do you like more, pizza or tacos?
THE GIRL is surprised.
He's not scared?!
And then amused.
This seems silly but fun.
She answers.
Allie.
I think it's interesting.
I was born in this town.
Yes.
Tacos. Duh.

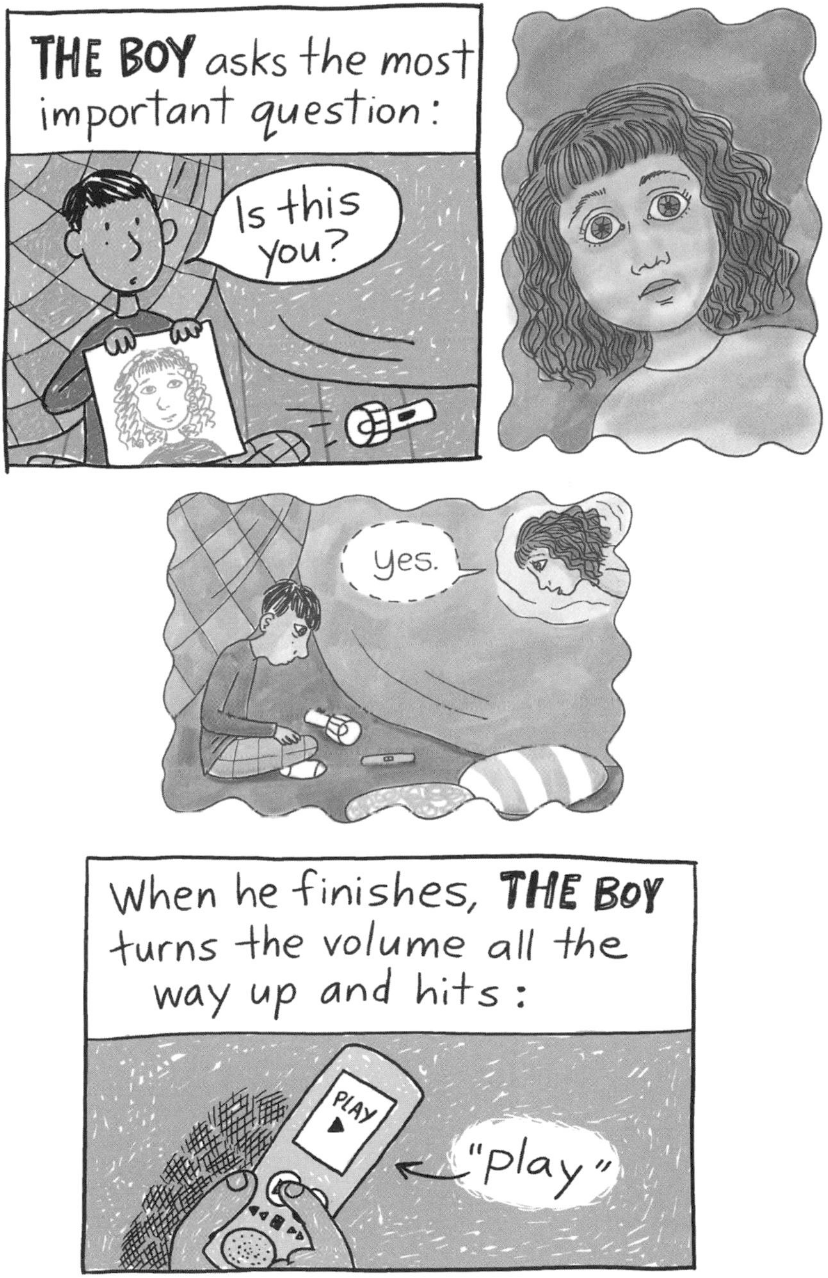
THE BOY asks the most important question:
Is this you?
yes.
When he finishes, THE BOY turns the volume all the way up and hits:
PLAY
"play"

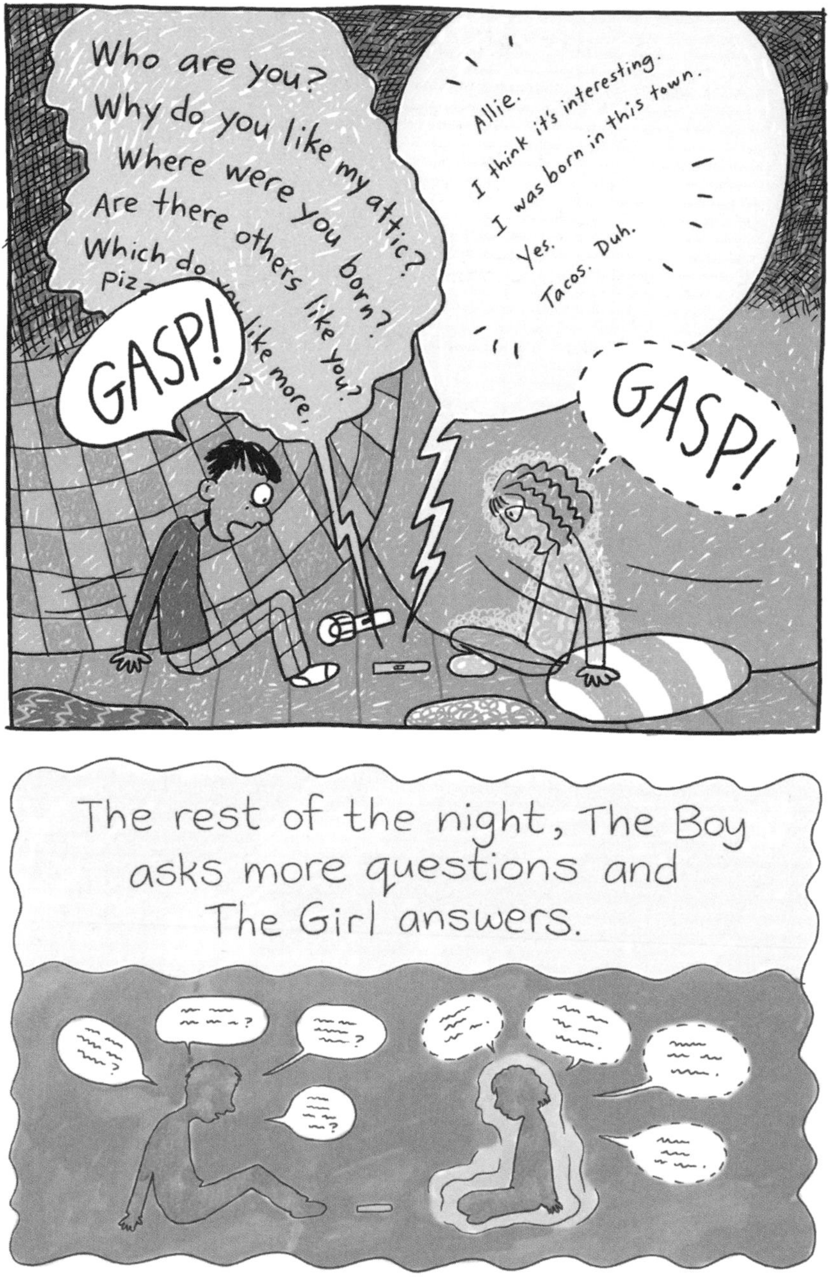

Who are you?
Why do you like my attic?
Where were you born?
Are there others like you?
Which do you like more,
piz
GASP!
Allie.
I think it's interesting.
I was born in this town.
Yes.
Tacos. Duh.
GASP!
The rest of the night, The Boy asks more questions and The Girl answers.

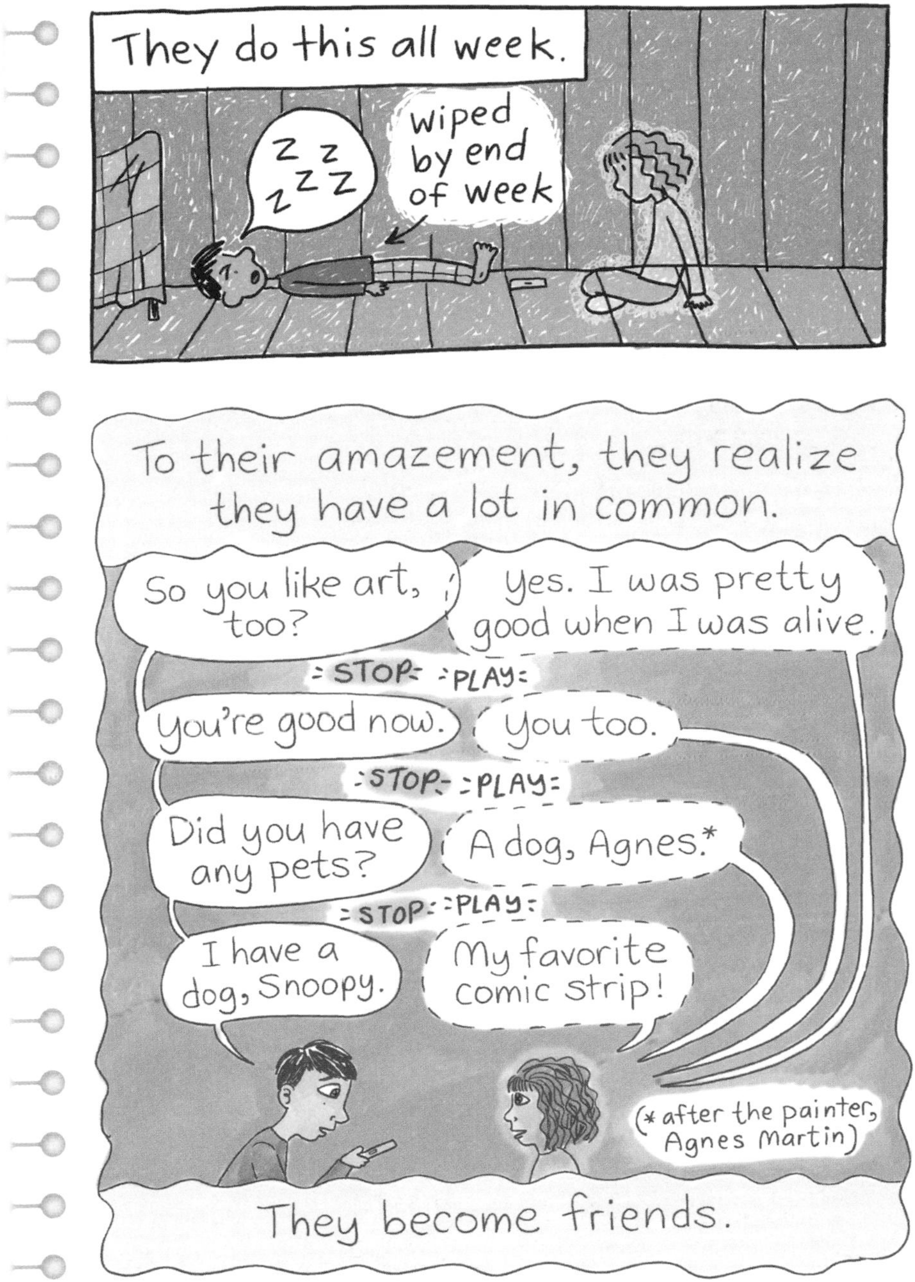
They do this all week.
z z z z z
wiped by end of week
To their amazement, they realize they have a lot in common.
So you like art, too?
Yes. I was pretty good when I was alive.
STOP PLAY
You're good now.
You too.
STOP PLAY
Did you have any pets?
A dog, Agnes.*
STOP PLAY
I have a dog, Snoopy.
My favorite comic strip!
(*after the painter, Agnes Martin)
They become friends.

One night, **THE BOY** invites his (human) friends to the attic to "meet" The Girl.

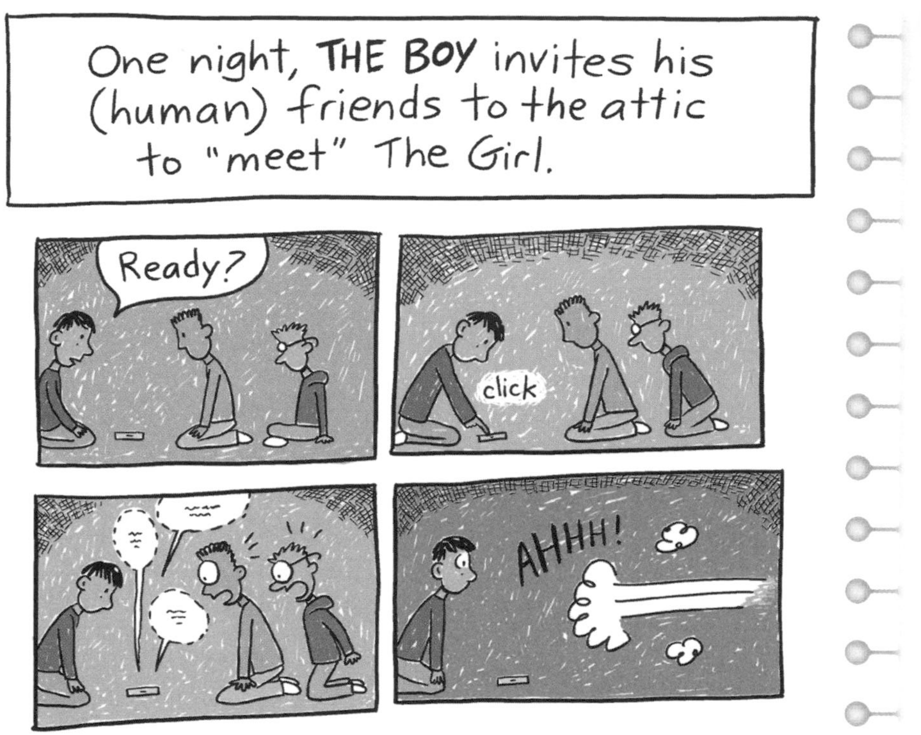
Ready?
click
AHHH!

It seems like no one approves.

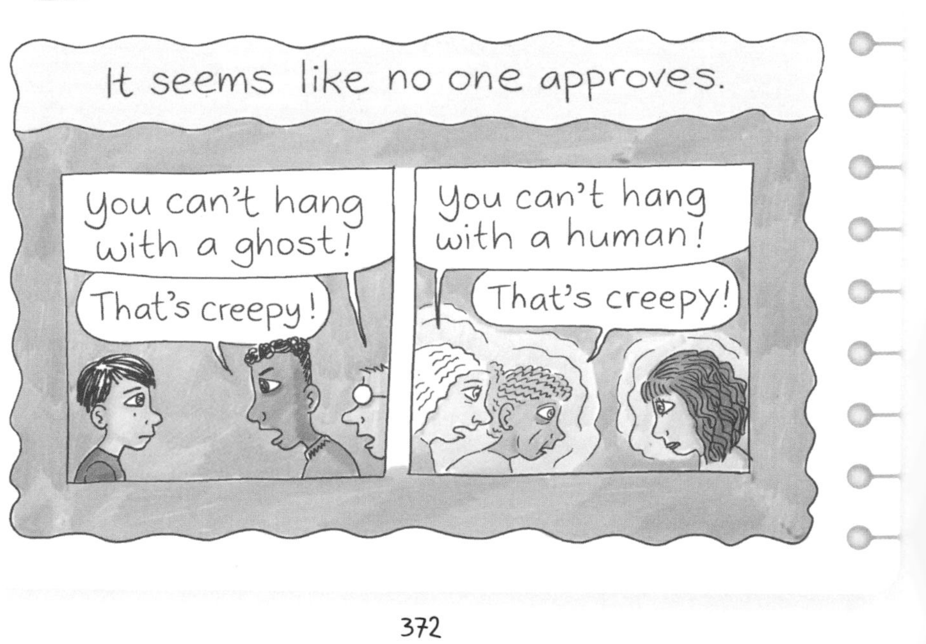
You can't hang with a ghost!
That's creepy!
You can't hang with a human!
That's creepy!

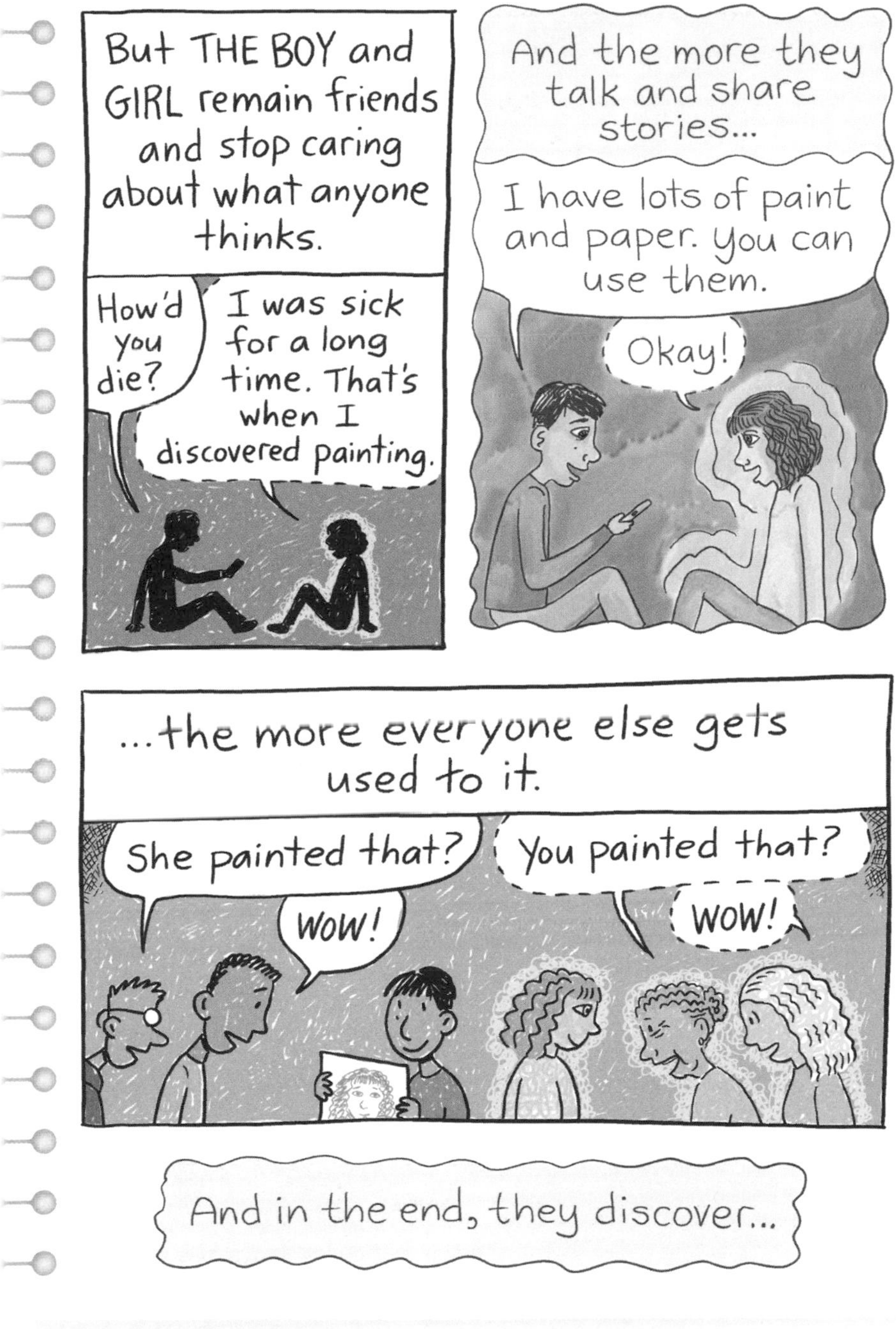
But THE BOY and GIRL remain friends and stop caring about what anyone thinks.
How'd you die?
I was sick for a long time. That's when I discovered painting.
And the more they talk and share stories...
I have lots of paint and paper. You can use them.
Okay!
...the more everyone else gets used to it.
She painted that?
WOW!
You painted that?
WOW!
And in the end, they discover...

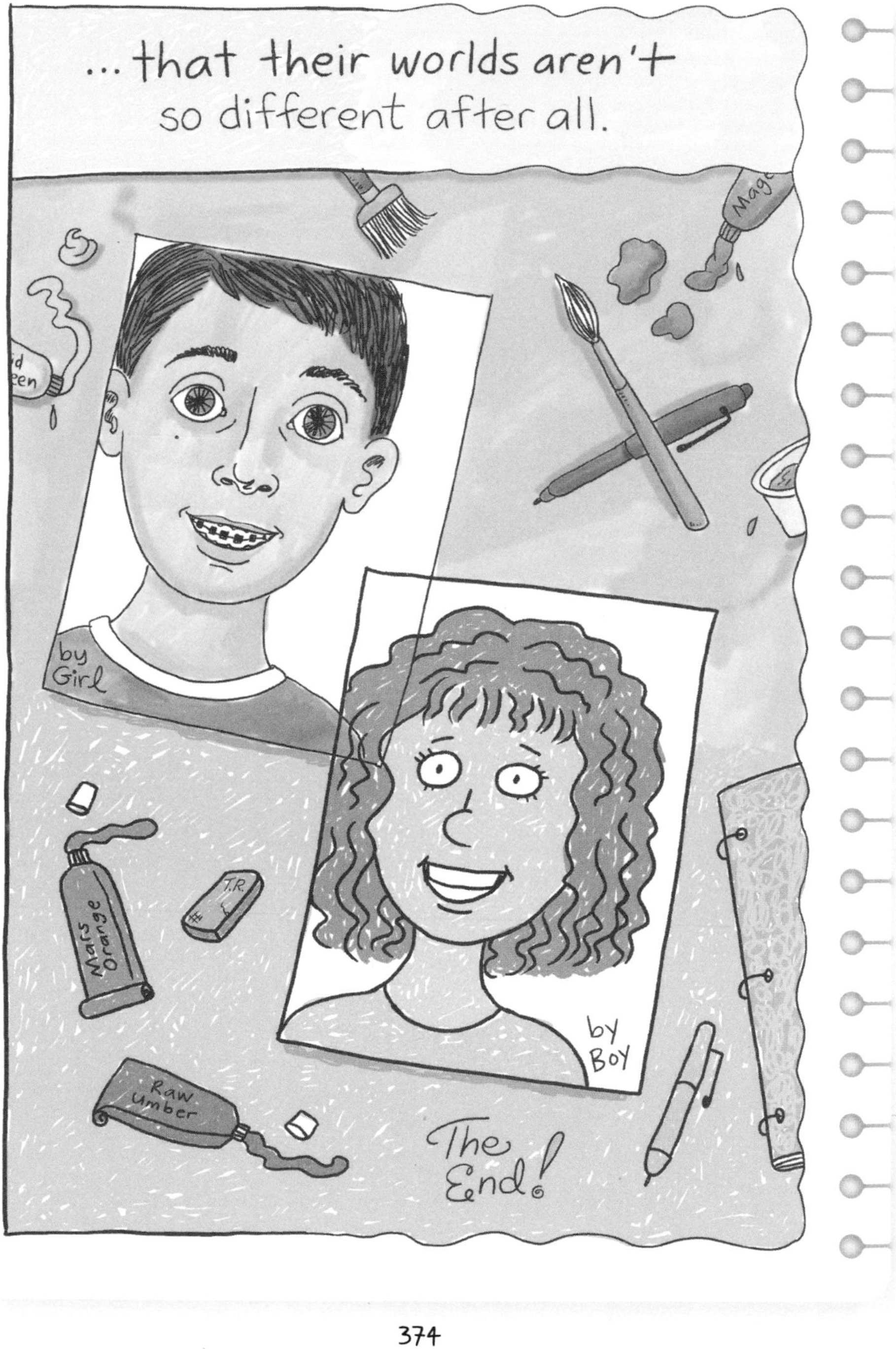

... that their worlds aren't so different after all.
by Girl
by Boy
Mars Orange
T.R.
Raw Umber
The End!

FROM THE CHILDHOOD ARCHIVES
OF TERRI LIBENSON

Kindergarten

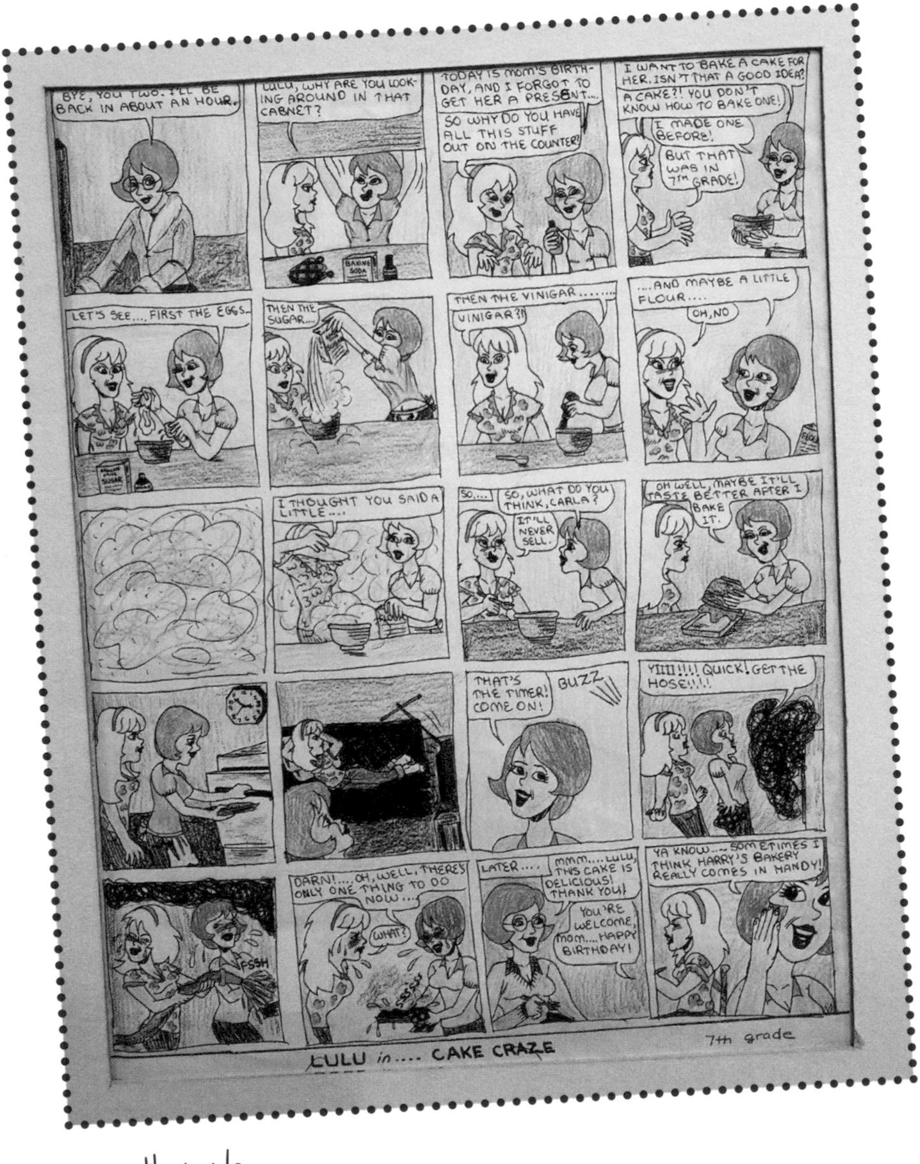
BYE, YOU TWO. I'LL BE BACK IN ABOUT AN HOUR.
LULU, WHY ARE YOU LOOKING AROUND IN THAT CABNET?
BAKING SODA
TODAY IS MOM'S BIRTHDAY, AND I FORGOT TO GET HER A PRESENT....
SO WHY DO YOU HAVE ALL THIS STUFF OUT ON THE COUNTER?
I WANT TO BAKE A CAKE FOR HER. ISN'T THAT A GOOD IDEA?
A CAKE?! YOU DON'T KNOW HOW TO BAKE ONE!
I MADE ONE BEFORE!
BUT THAT WAS IN 7TH GRADE!
LET'S SEE.... FIRST THE EGGS.
SUGAR
THEN THE SUGAR....
THEN THE VINIGAR........
VINIGAR?!
....AND MAYBE A LITTLE FLOUR....
OH, NO
I THOUGHT YOU SAID A LITTLE....
SO....
SO, WHAT DO YOU THINK, CARLA?
IT'LL NEVER SELL.
OH WELL, MAYBE IT'LL TASTE BETTER AFTER I BAKE IT.
THAT'S THE TIMER! COME ON!
BUZZ
YIIII!!!! QUICK! GET THE HOSE!!!!
FSSH
DARN!.... OH, WELL, THERE'S ONLY ONE THING TO DO NOW....
WHAT?
LATER....
MMM.... LULU, THIS CAKE IS DELICIOUS! THANK YOU!
YOU'RE WELCOME, MOM.... HAPPY BIRTHDAY!
YA KNOW.... SOMETIMES I THINK HARRY'S BAKERY REALLY COMES IN HANDY!
LULU in.... CAKE CRAZE
7th grade

seventh grade

ACKNOWLEDGMENTS

I wrote (and rewrote) Tyler during the Covid-19 pandemic of 2020. Admittedly, it was a struggle. Between having "quarantine (aka sluggish) brain," writing from a boy's viewpoint (gasp), and dealing with a rambunctious new puppy (see photo)—let's just say my recycling bin was overflowing. Ironically, I had retired my syndicated comic strip and its daily deadlines, yet for the first time I found myself stressed about getting this book finished on time!

Luckily, it all came together in the end, and it turned out better than I imagined. I was able to write authentically, eke out a story I loved, and even managed to create a book within a book. It couldn't have happened without the following people:

Donna Bray, my amazing and knowledgeable editor, whose phone conversations held me together.

Dan Lazar, my supersupportive agent, who also encouraged me like no other.

Laura Mock, Amy Ryan, Jon Howard, Vanessa Nuttry, Mitch Thorpe, Vaishali Nayak, Tiara Kittrell, and the rest of the team at HarperCollins, who are incredibly talented, kind, and tireless. You guys had a challenging year but made everything seamless.

Michael, my supportive and long-suffering husband, who has come to terms with the fact that I live in my office.

My kids, Mollie and Nikki—also long-suffering but wonderfully adaptable. Thank you for caring for the fur baby during these weird times.

Aaron, who I know is up there, still happily peddling my books to friends and strangers.

Amy and Mina, who kept me sane with our back-and-forth messages and memes. I needed that levity!

And of course, my readers, who send me the best letters, pictures, messages, and emails. I may not always be able to write back, but I **always** love hearing from you!

pandemic pup Rosie (summer, 2020)